The
Pregnancy
Surprise

These couples are facing up to
parenthood – fast!

Modern Romance™ – surrender to seduction
and passion in the most glamorous
locations in the world!

Medical Romance™ – brings you an
intensely emotional story packed full of
drama and desire…

Historical Romance™ – takes you back to
1813, where one night has dangerous
consequences…

*What happens when one night of passion
leads to an unexpected pregnancy?
Turn the pages to find out…*

The Pregnancy Surprise

HAVING LEO'S CHILD

by
Emma Darcy

AN UNEXPECTED BONUS

by
Caroline Anderson

THE HEART'S DESIRE

by
Gayle Wilson

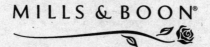

MILLS & BOON®

*First published in Great Britain 2003 by
Harlequin Mills & Boon Limited,
Eton House, 18-24 Paradise Road,
Richmond, Surrey, TW9 1SR*

THE PREGNANCY SURPRISE © Harlequin Enterprises II B.V. 2003

The publisher acknowledges the copyright holders of the
individual works as follows:

Having Leo's Child © Emma Darcy 1999
An Unexpected Bonus © Caroline Anderson 1999
The Heart's Desire © Mona Gay Thomas 1994

ISBN 0 263 83683 5

024-1003

*Printed and bound in Spain
by Litografia Rosés S.A., Barcelona*

CONTENTS

HAVING LEO'S CHILD

by
Emma Darcy

Initially a French/English teacher, **Emma Darcy** changed careers to computer programming before marriage, motherhood, and the very social life of her businessman husband, Frank, settled her into a community life. Very much a people person, and always interested in relationships, she finds the world of romance fiction a thrilling one and the challenge of creating her own cast of characters very addictive.

Look out for Emma Darcy's latest red-hot read:
THE BEDROOM SURRENDER
On sale in Modern Romance™ next month!

CHAPTER ONE

NEVER had Teri Adams known such all-consuming sexual excitement. It amazed her, thrilled her, and she didn't care that she barely knew Leo Kingston.

He *wanted* her—this incredible, dynamic, beautiful, sexy man—and she hadn't known what *wanting* really felt like until he'd evoked it in her the very first time he'd walked into her restaurant. Instantly. Shatteringly. It was as though her body just lit up with new fields of awareness, prompting reactions and responses she had no control over. None at all.

The same thing happened the second time.

And this…the third…

She had to know it all, wanted to feel everything he could make her feel. If it was only this once…

There was nothing to hold her back. Everyone was gone; the customers, the chef, the kitchenhand. No one left to bother about, except herself and the man who'd stayed on, wanting to be with her, wanting *this* as madly and urgently as she did. From the moment he'd come in, ostensibly to buy his dinner, she'd felt it. This was going to be the night. He was going to act, going to reach out and pursue what was sizzling between them. And he had.

Her mouth was throbbing from the wildly erotic passion of his kiss. Her head was throbbing from the sheer volume of sensation it was trying to encompass.

Her heart was pounding like some madly beaten primitive drum. Her legs were a quivery mess, so much so, in her rush to lead Leo to her bedroom above the restaurant, she tripped on stairs she had never tripped on before.

Leo, hard on her heels, saved her from falling, one strong arm swooping around her waist, holding her up, the other swiftly hooking her thighs, and she was hoisted against his chest with barely a pause in his forward momentum. On up the rest of the stairs he carried her, the pumping excitement increasing at this evidence of his power and strength.

With her arms flung over his shoulders and around his neck, her breasts squashed to the heaving wall of his chest, Teri dizzily absorbed the heat and the smell of him, a vibrant male earthiness that her fevered imagination attached to primitive instincts aroused and raging. Without even realising what she was doing she licked along the line of his jaw, compelled to taste, to saturate all her senses with him.

"Which door?" Leo growled.

"First one," she almost sang out of sheer exhilaration, revelling in the wildness of being carried off for mating by a caveman. Except Leo was clean-shaven and the taste of him was like champagne fizzing on her tongue and through her bloodstream. A modern caveman, wanting, reaching out and taking, and she loved it, loved being taken by *him*.

"Here?"

"Yes."

He kicked the door she'd left ajar, clearing their passageway, and whirled her into the bedroom. She expected him to crash onto the bed with her but he didn't, halting beside it and releasing her legs so they swung down to hang against his, and he caught her there while her arms were still wound around his neck, his hands clutching her bottom, squeezing her into a highly erotic knowledge of how powerfully excited he was.

He arched back, emitting an animal groan of pleasure as he revelled in the soft giving of her flesh. "You have the sexiest derrière I've ever seen on a woman, Teri," he declared. "And watching it twitch and sway under that snug little red skirt as you move around the tables in the restaurant..."

He dragged in a deep breath and it blew through her hair as his chin came down. Even in the semi-darkness his eyes had a mesmerising brilliance, cobalt-blue, glittering with the fully released fire of desire. "I tell you it's a diabolical tease," he went on, his voice furred with the lust she'd inspired. "My hands have been itching to hold you like this."

Her hands had been itching to touch any part of him, and if he had to talk about derrières, what his did to a pair of jeans was enough to make any woman start fantasising about taut and terrific flesh and muscle. Masculinity plus. And he was like that all over. But she contented herself with raking her hands through the lustrous black waves of his thick, springy hair as he kissed her again.

No one had ever kissed her like this. It wasn't a hard mash of his mouth against hers. It wasn't sloppy. It was a feast of sensation, his lips seductively shaping hers to be tantalised by little nips of his teeth and tingling caresses of his tongue, building excitement, then driving into an incredibly intimate sweep of her palate, electrifying every nerve-end, drawing her into a wild exchange of darting movements that brought such an intense rush of wanting, her whole body surged with need, demanding a carnal satisfaction that was shocking in its intensity.

"Phew! You've got me so steamed…" Leo gabbled gruffly as he lowered her onto her feet and eased back a bit. "…and I've barely started on all I've been aching to do."

Aching…yes…it felt as though every bone in her body was aching. She wasn't sure they were going to hold together.

He grinned a wild, wicked grin. "You know this smile printed on the red heart logo of your T-shirt? If you extend the curve upwards on either side…" He drew it with his two index fingers. "See? It goes directly to the peaks of your breasts. Beautiful geometry. Beautiful breasts…"

He circled her aureoles with his fingers, arousing acute excitement. "They're so perky and lush," he said huskily, his gaze dropping as he pulled her T-shirt from the waistband of her skirt and lifted it up…up…untangling her arms from his neck, tossing the garment aside, unfastening her bra, sliding the straps away. Then his hands were cupping her, his thumbs fanning her erect nipples and she could hardly breathe, so sharp was the pleasure of it.

The urge to touch him as he was touching her compelled her own hands to the buttons on his shirt, fingers travelling rapidly, parting the fabric, and his skin was as smooth as satin, hairless, tightly stretched over strongly delineated muscles. He felt wonderful, almost as though his skin was polished and her hands skimmed over him with sensual delight, amazed that a man could feel like this.

Wayne hadn't. But she instantly banished the memory of her ex-husband, long gone. There was no comparison to Leo. How could there be? This man was perfection.

In sheer fascination with him she rolled her thumbs over his nipples. He inhaled sharply, his chest expanding, seeming to pulse at the teasing touch, and a thrill of power zinged through Teri. The sure knowledge that she could and did affect him in the same way he affected her was intoxicating.

"Yessss," he hissed. "More…"

She slid the shirt from his shoulders and they were perfect, too, broad and strong and manly without being overly musclebound. While her hands revelled in gliding over the hard male curves of his upper arms, Leo freed himself of the constricting sleeves and hauled her close again, rubbing his bare chest against the soft mounds of her breasts, sensitising them further as he unbuttoned and unzipped her skirt.

It was so incredibly erotic…her flesh against his. She couldn't wait to feel the rest of him. Neither could he, scooping the rest of her clothes down, tearing his jeans apart, stepping out of them, shoes flicked off. Then there was nothing between them and they were free to embrace the totality of each other, skin against skin, exploring the differences with gloriously sensual and uninhibited fervor.

"You truly are…all woman," Leo said in a kind of awe that made Teri feel really special.

Though he was more so…everything she'd imagined he would be…complete and utter male power, sleek and strong and sure in his aggression, wanting her, revelling in her femininity, every taste and touch comprising a constant drive for more and more satisfaction in knowing her, all of her, and Teri could feel herself dissolving inside, like ice-cream subjected to heat, a thick flow of melting ice-cream, and he laid her on the bed and licked her as though he knew it and loved it and couldn't get enough of it, right down to every possible delicious drop.

Her mouth, her breasts, her stomach, and lower, parting her legs, moving to the most intimate folds of her and she was utterly helpless, her whole body focused on what he was doing to her, enthralled by the exquisite excitement of it…Wayne had never…but Leo…dear heaven! She closed her eyes and gave herself up to the pulsing ecstasy he was stoking with irresistible power.

And then his hand was touching her, too, cupping her, his thumb reaching into her, caressing, causing her to convulse with incredible pleasure, then sliding out to give way to his mouth…*his mouth!*…and she writhed to the terrible, wonderful madness of it, out of control, caught in the grip of sensations that simply rolled over any caring of what was done or how it was done as long as it kept going.

She cried out when it stopped, the need for continuance screaming through her. Her eyes flew open in urgent pleading. Her arms were limp, heavy, but she lifted them, compelled to hold, to urge more from him. But he was already coming to her, his knees between her legs, and he was hastily sheathing himself with protection.

Shock momentarily slammed through her mind. She hadn't thought…no matter…he had. It was all right. And seeing him readying himself for her, the brief cautionary cloud was instantly dispersed with a ringing chant of yes…yes…yes…all of him inside her…now, fast, hard, full-on, pounding as wildly as her heart.

He slid an arm underneath her, lifting, and her body instinctively arched to meet and welcome him, craving fulfilment of the promise, quivering with anticipation. She felt him slide into place, felt herself opening for him, wider and wider to accommodate his wonderfully solid fullness and she almost died of sheer delight as he pushed forward to the inner centre of her being.

If he'd stopped then, Teri would have been content, swimming in a sea of ecstasy. As it was, he paused long enough to gather her up and kiss her, heightening the sense of mutual possession, of melding with each other, arousing levels of awareness that exulted in the unifying force of this intense, physical mingling.

Stirred by the flow of his strength, Teri wound her arms and legs around him and he took her with him on a tumultuous ride that broke every barrier of experience she'd known until now. She was swamped with roll after roll of exquisitely sweet sensation as he immersed her in the beat of his mating, the powerful pacing of it pounding through her, consuming every bit of sexual knowledge from her marriage and imprinting a new encyclopaedia of sensory perceptions, all of them measuring far beyond the realities she'd accepted before this.

Not that Teri was actively recording anything. It was simply happening to her. Leo was making it happen… Leo Kingston…and never in a million years was she going to forget how it was with him. And even when he climaxed he didn't let her go, didn't let the pulse of excitement seep away. He cuddled her, stroked her, kissed her, murmured what he wanted from her, guiding, and she abandoned herself to following his lead, revelling in his encouragement, his fierce responses, the supreme sensuality he drew from her.

How many times they coupled, how many ways… Teri had no idea. Leo seemed to know endless paths of pleasure though no matter how aroused he was, there was always care for unwelcome consequences, always another sheath of protection against their wild excesses, allowing absolute freedom to indulge themselves wherever desire took them.

There was no ultimate time of satiation, though eventually exhaustion did drug them into languorous periods of sleep from which they stirred when the entanglement of their bodies inadvertently caused movement and another awakening. The hunger for what they gave each other never abated. Even when dawn came they found a new fascination in making love in the softly filtered light, seeing, watching, gloating over their visual discoveries.

Leo's vivid blue eyes caressed her with warm pleasure as he trailed his fingertips around her breasts in deliciously teasing circles. He was hitched onto his side, one hand propping up his head, and his face wore a relaxed, happy expression. Such a handsome face, Teri thought, though it was really more than handsome.

His black eyebrows had a wicked arch to them, making his eyes a riveting feature. His nose was strong and straight, with a slight flare to his nostrils that drew attention to a mouth any woman would envy, lips that were sharply defined, sensually curved, and perfectly balanced. These attractions were heightened by an innate stamp of authority, an aura of self-confidence that said his thirty-something years had not been wasted. This was a man who went after what he wanted and got it.

She didn't match him in looks. Her hair was dark but hardly spectacular, cropped short for convenience. She liked her eyes best. They were large, light grey, with reasonably long lashes to emphasise them. Her nose, slightly tilted at the end, was invariably labelled cute. Her mouth was a touch wide and her lower lip was too full for Teri's liking.

She was certainly not strikingly beautiful but she was passably attractive and there was nothing wrong with her figure. In actual fact, there was a lot right with her figure. Ever since her teens it had drawn attention from the opposite sex, but she'd been with Wayne most of her life, so such attention was irrelevant. She wasn't interested. She was even less interested after her marriage had failed. A body was simply functional. That was all. Until Leo.

He smiled at her, a slow, lazy, satisfied smile. "Feeling good?"

"Mmmh…" She felt like the proverbial cat who'd fed gluttonously on cream.

"So am I. Better than I've felt for a long, long time. You're a marvel to me, Teri."

She smiled, thinking all the marvels came from him. "The same for me, Leo."

"The thing is…" he started, then gave vent to a long sigh, withdrawing his touch which was a chillingly obvious sign of separation from her.

Teri instantly had the sense this was decision time. Morning had come. Where to next? Nerves that had been beautifully lulled, started twitching with apprehension. However physically intimate they'd been, Leo was virtually a stranger. He'd come prepared for sex. Did he make a practice of one-night stands?

His mouth tilted in apologetic irony. "I don't want to mislead you…"

She tensed, preparing herself for the worst-case scenario. Leo Kingston had given her something very special so she had nothing to complain about, even if it was to be only a one-off experience. Yet she couldn't help hoping this was the start of something more with him.

"…I love what we've been sharing…" he went on, his voice projecting strongly positive appreciation.

But… her mind supplied as her heart cramped. This was surely the carrot ahead of the stick. All along she had assessed him as too good for her, a high-flyer with class stamped all over him, which was why it was so amazing he'd wanted her, a working-class girl

in a service industry. Silly to have any expectations
of a deep and meaningful relationship.

"...but I'm not into marriage, Teri. I've been there,
done that, and it wasn't good."

Marriage! She hadn't given a thought to any such
future possibility. Now...with him...had completely
dominated her mind.

"You're divorced?" she asked. Although he had
declared himself *a guy on his own* the last time he
was here, Teri wanted to know if his wife was still
around.

"Very much so," he answered sardonically.

"So am I," she confessed. "No fun, is it?"

"None whatsoever."

"So what are you saying, Leo? You'd like an affair
with me as long as I understand wedding bells are
out?" she prompted, hoping she had the affair part
right.

That idea didn't upset her at all. *If* he was considering it. And she appreciated his honesty in warning
her off any marriage aspirations. It was best to know
where one stood. With Wayne, the sorting through
where both of them wanted to go had been long and
painful and the sense of failure a deep and scarring
torment.

"Are you okay with that, Teri?" Leo asked,
searching her eyes very seriously.

She wondered what scars he carried from his marriage. Needing some insight into where he was coming from, she asked, "Why don't you spell out what
you do want, Leo?"

His face lit with an irrepressible grin. "What we've

just had. Over and over again. As long as it's good for us.''

Her heart kicked with a wild surge of happy relief. She wanted that, too, as many times as he'd give it to her. Having lived twenty-nine years without experiencing half of what Leo had touched off in her, she'd be mad to pass up the opportunity to feel all this again. Nevertheless, he hadn't told her much. Only that their pleasure was mutual, which she already knew.

''So we're talking strictly sex, are we?'' she lightly probed, careful not to scare him off.

He frowned, clearly cogitating the equation he wanted. ''That sounds rather bald,'' he said slowly. ''I like you, Teri. Very much. And I don't want to offend you.''

''Honesty won't offend me, Leo,'' she assured him. ''I'd appreciate not being fooled in any way whatsoever.''

God knew she'd fooled herself with rosy expectations going into her marriage with Wayne. She'd sworn never to enter another relationship without pinning everything down. Having her eyes wide open and seeing straight left one a lot less susceptible to miserable disappointment.

It had also narrowed the field of possible men she'd accept in her life so drastically, Leo was the first who'd passed the barriers she'd put up. Though he hadn't precisely passed them. He'd burst through them. Which made her all the more fascinated by him. She studied his face—the self-knowing intelligence and determination so evident on it—as he answered her.

"I simply don't want the kind of relationship that hangs a whole lot of emotional blackmail on either of us, Teri. I don't have the time or the stomach for it." A flash of bitterness there, almost instantly softened by an appealing, whimsical smile. "I guess I want things free and easy between us. Which is probably completely selfish…" He shrugged, not caring that it was. It was how he wanted it.

"You mean no accountability. Just take it as it comes," she interpreted.

He nodded. "I travel quite a bit in my business. I can be away for weeks at a time, so don't expect some kind of regular arrangement. It won't happen…" His eyes hardened. "…and I won't be pressured into it."

It was clear their affair would proceed on his terms or he'd call it quits. Teri wasn't sure how she felt about that…the total disregard for whatever needs she might have. Though he certainly fulfilled one need. He was top of the pack on that score. Absolutely top.

Her gaze glided down his magnificent physique and the lust for more of him gripped the pit of her stomach. No love involved here. Once she would have thought herself…sluttish…for feeling as she did now, but love had only brought her disillusionment. Why not take what she could get from this man? At least it was something good. Better than good. Fantastic!

She'd been working hard, establishing her restaurant business, virtually to the exclusion of everything else except visiting her family now and then. She'd earned a bit of spice in her life. Hot spice! She couldn't help grinning at the thought and her eyes danced back up to his.

"Okay," she agreed. "No commitments. Just when it suits both of us."

Relief and sparkling delight shone from him. "Great! You're a woman in a million, Teri. Finding you is like winning the lottery."

She laughed. "Maybe I got a bottle of champagne in you, Leo."

"Then celebration is in order," he said with a purposeful gleam.

He kissed her and the champagne fizzed so beautifully, Teri had no regrets over the bargain it sealed with Leo Kingston.

Pure pleasure.

No harm in that.

As long as she didn't attach anything else to it.

CHAPTER TWO

Ten months on…

PREGNANT!

No doubt left.

She was having Leo's child.

In the time it took to walk out of the clinic where the doctor had handed her the definitive test results, Teri managed to get her mind, which had been temporarily shattered by the positive confirmation of her suspicions, into relative working order. It moved from baby to birth to the reminder that today was her thirtieth birthday.

When she'd married Wayne, she'd imagined having two children by the time she was thirty, their own little family. She certainly hadn't imagined having a baby on her own, by a man who had no desire whatsoever to become her husband. So here she was, presented with two big milestones in her life, and a very different kind of future in front of her.

There was no question about what she was going to do. Fate might have thrown her a curve with this accidental pregnancy, but it might very well be the best thing that could ever happen to her. She would get to be a mother, which she didn't want to miss out on. There was no guarantee about how long Leo would stay in her life. Or any other man, for that matter. A child was forever. Someone of her very own to love…without question…without limit.

Excitement at that thought welled and ebbed as she waited on the sidewalk for the traffic lights to change. Traffic roared up and down Oxford Street. Sydney was enjoying a brilliant summer and the late afternoon sunshine basked her in warmth. The fifteen-minute walk back to her restaurant in Paddington was an easy stroll and gave her time to recollect herself.

The red light changed to green and she pushed her legs into action, pushing her mind out of its fuzzy maternal wallow, as well. Single motherhood was not going to be easy. Maybe she was mad to take it on. But she couldn't bear not to. And one thing she could definitely say about Leo Kingston. He had fantastic genes.

If she'd actually been planning to have a baby without the support of a husband, and looking around for the best possible male specimen to supply the necessary, Leo would be a five-star choice…healthy, intelligent, good-looking, athletic, possessing the drive to get ahead in the world, and loaded with sex appeal.

How he'd react to being told he was going to be a father, Teri had no idea. Right at this moment, she didn't really care. She could do without spice…if she had to. A baby represented far more essential things to her.

Apart from finding her desirable, and companionable enough to enjoy chatting with her—occasionally—when it fitted into his business schedule—she didn't think Leo attached any importance to her role in his life. All his energy was poured into making his computer company more and more successful. Well, not quite all. When he focused his energy on bedding her, Teri still found it an irresistible force.

But he didn't even know it was her birthday today. Maybe over the past ten months she should have tried to make more of their relationship, though her experience with her ex-husband had taught her that pressing for anything would get her nowhere. Impossible to force what didn't come naturally. Leo had set the limits. *He* hadn't tried to change them, which surely meant he hadn't wanted to.

However, it was one thing to be free and easy lovers.

Parenthood was an even more permanent tie than marriage!

Having arrived back at her restaurant, Teri paused to view its street frontage, feeling a sense of pride in what she had achieved here. The idea of selling meals by weight had really taken off. Patrons could pile as much or as little as they liked on their plates and the price they paid for it was commensurate with how much they chose.

It was perceived as an exceptionally fair deal, the food was tasty, and Teri knew she had a lot of satisfied customers because they kept returning. In droves. Most lunches and dinners were sell-outs. It had become a nicely profitable little business. Nothing grand. But she could afford to employ a chef and a kitchenhand.

She didn't need financial support from Leo, should he choose to…not be around any more. She *was* capable of standing on her own two feet. Living in the apartment upstairs made the situation manageable. She would still be able to work and look after a baby.

As her gaze belatedly registered the name she'd given her restaurant, laughter gurgled up in her throat and spilled into a slightly hysterical peal. *Full Tummy—Happy Heart* was printed across the two front windows in a semicircular hump. A very pregnant hump, she thought in ironic amusement, and determined then and there, no matter how Leo reacted to her full tummy, she'd still have a happy heart about having his child.

She checked her watch as she pushed open the door. Four-thirty. The lull before the next onslaught of fast and furious activity. The tables were cleaned up and set for the evening meal.

Behind the weighing counter, Dylan, her chef, was busy cleaning up his open grill, ready for the dinner orders. Chunky, ginger-haired, freckle-faced, and invariably good-natured, he swung around as he heard her come in and shot her a cheerful grin.

"Leo called."

Teri's heart fluttered. Leo *never* called. Why today of all days? "What for?" she asked, hoping her voice sounded normal.

"Said he was flying in from New Zealand, and he'd be here about eight-thirty and if I was making that chicken mince stuff wrapped in spinach leaves, would I please keep him some?"

Food! Nothing personal. She heaved a sigh to get rid of the surge of absurd emotional hope for something different from Leo and aimed a smile at her chef. "Guess you made a hit with that dish, Dylan."

"Yeah."

He looked pleased. At twenty-two, he was still fresh from his long apprenticeship in a hotel and enjoying making his own little specialties.

"Mail came while you were out," he informed her, still grinning. "I put it in the kitchen."

"Thanks."

Probably birthday cards from her family, she thought, wondering how they were going to react to a new birth. Plenty of time before she'd have to tell them, but Leo...only four hours before he swept in, probably expecting two appetising meals. He'd get one. Then...

Well, it wouldn't be the end of the world if he dropped her flat. She'd coped fairly well after Wayne had walked out of their three-year marriage. She was used to being independent, working things out for herself, setting goals and reaching them for the most part.

At least this time, she wouldn't be left with nothing.

She was going to have a baby.

CHAPTER THREE

LEO KINGSTON was smiling as he strode out of the airport terminal and grabbed the first cab on the taxi rank. His business in New Zealand had been success-fully concluded, the flight had landed on schedule, he was bound to get the kind of food he really enjoyed eating at Teri's restaurant—tasty but not too fancy, and a proper plateful instead of the skimpy servings the classy restaurants charged a fortune for—then to top off everything, a night of sheer, uncomplicated joy with Teri.

"Where to?" the driver asked.

"Jersey Road, Woollahra."

Home first to drop off his bags, have a quick shower, change into more casual and cooler clothes than his suit, a three-block walk which was just about right to get rid of the claustrophic feeling of plane travel, and he'd be at the door of *Full Tummy—Happy Heart.*

He grinned over the great name Teri had chosen for her restaurant. It was spot-on. Delivered precisely what it said. No pretensions. Just like Teri herself. He was really looking forward to being with her again. Great woman. She didn't nag, didn't sulk, never called him to account over anything, had no unrea-sonable expectations of him, made no demands,

24

didn't keep a clock on him, always enjoyed their times together, and she had a fantastic body.

It stirred him just thinking about the way Teri was built. She was so curvy and *female*. No bones sticking into him, just soft rounded flesh a man could really sink into and revel in. A real woman.

He remembered when he first saw her. Must be almost a year ago now. It was soon after he'd bought the terrace house in Jersey Road, when he'd been scouting the area for restaurants that provided good meals. Teri's place had been a great find. No waiting forever to be served, either, though he hadn't minded sitting over his dinner because just watching Teri had been a real pleasure.

He'd liked everything about her—the way she smiled at customers and cared about them being satisfied with what they'd chosen. Beautiful eyes. Touchable hair. An efficient manner without being abrupt. And a body that most women—in Leo's experience—would have traded on. But there wasn't even a hint of *The Princess Syndrome* in Teri Adams. Which made her even more attractive. And desirable.

He hated the be-my-slave-because-I'm-beautiful attitude a lot of women gave out. He'd had a gutful of it from his ex-wife, expecting him to dance attendance on her, provide her with everything her greedy little heart desired, pouting and carrying on when he had to put business first.

It would be a long time before he shackled himself to another marriage. If ever. He'd been so deceived by Serena, how the hell could a man know when a woman was pulling the wool over his eyes? Besides, freedom was good. He'd had three years of it since the parting of the ways with his self-serving ex-wife and he liked it better all the time.

Teri obviously appreciated her freedom, too. Nothing like a failed marriage to get you thinking about what you really wanted to do with your life. She was a smart businesswoman. The way she'd tapped into a highly marketable idea was truly admirable. He had a lot of respect for Teri Adams. She could stand on her own two feet and meet him on equal ground.

The cabbie turned into Jersey Road and Leo directed him to the home he'd made his own, which was nothing like the status symbol house Serena had insisted upon, undoubtedly with an eye to taking half the proceeds of its sale as her divorce price. This place was all his.

It was ten past eight when he walked into his living room and glanced around, gleaning pleasure from the familiar, comfortable layout he'd chosen for himself and feeling a deep sense of satisfaction in his independence.

The cleaner had been in, leaving everything ship-shape. Didn't need a wife for that. There was his man-size leather chair and footstool with the coffee-table handy, placed directly in front of the maxi-screen television so he could watch his favourite sports in absolute comfort. No wife to complain about how much time he spent on it instead of sharing things with her—never mind her never trying to share things with him.

This was good. All it lacked was a woman in his bed. But the price of that was too damned high. And a wife didn't guarantee it, either. Sex was doled out at her convenience, not his, and only when he'd performed as he should in her eyes. Well, to hell with that!

Teri suited him just fine and he obviously suited her. Which reminded him to get moving. Shower, shave...full tummy, happy heart.

A very happy heart tonight!

CHAPTER FOUR

TERI checked her watch again—8:31. This *waiting* was dreadfully distracting, not to mention nerve-racking. So Leo was a minute late, she argued fiercely to herself. He might be half an hour late. He might not come at all. He hadn't *promised* anything. It was stupid to be working herself into a state with this constant clock-watching.

If Dylan had kept his mouth shut, she would have been sailing serenely through the evening, doing her job as she always did, without feeling as though she had a hive of buzzing bees inside her. In actual fact, she'd prefer it if Leo didn't turn up. Tomorrow night or any night in the future would be soon enough to tell him she was having his child. Then there'd be no possibility of feeling anything bad about going to bed alone on her thirtieth birthday.

Teri concentrated on counting notes out of the till. Most of her clientele were working people who didn't want to cook for themselves and they'd either been and gone home or were still eating. Nine-thirty was closing time. Which would fit nicely into giving a baby its night feed, she assured herself.

The doors whooshed open.

Teri's head jerked up.

Leo!

He came striding through the dining room, not

glancing at the buffet section where a tempting array of food was still laid out, paying no attention whatsoever to the people seated at the tables, what they were eating or doing or chatting about. The bright, red-check cotton tablecloths, the little bowls of daisies, the framed black-and-white cartoons of people feasting that she'd hung on the walls...none of them rated the slightest bit of notice.

Leo made straight for the weighing counter behind which Teri stood, exuding an energy that instantly had her heart zinging. His blue jeans and royal-blue sports shirt meant he was well and truly off work tonight and the twinkle in his blue eyes held an almost wicked glee in the freedom to do whatever he liked.

"Hi!" he said, leaning his arms on the top of the cash register and grinning at Teri, his handsome face radiating the strong power of a winning personality.

Teri tried to keep her feet on safe, sensible ground, despite her toes tingling. He had great teeth, she thought, white and straight, and somehow they combined with his eyes to deliver a charismatic impact that curled her insides and sent miniquakes down her legs. It would be good if their child inherited his teeth and eyes, Teri decided, trying valiantly to distance her mind from Leo's physical effect on her.

"Good trip?" she asked. Her mouth had a will of its own. It was smiling back at him. Or maybe Leo mesmerised her muscles into responding to the pleasure he was pouring out.

"Achieved what I wanted," he said with satisfaction. And he intended to do that here, too, his eyes said in no uncertain terms.

She was wearing the uniform she'd designed for the restaurant; a white T-shirt emblazoned with a red heart on which a simple white curve representing a smile had been painted, a neat little red skirt and comfortable white loafers on her feet. She could feel her breasts peaking into the soft fabric of the T-shirt and wished she had two red hearts positioned to disguise the fact.

"I can see success has put you in a good mood," she commented, intent on holding Leo's gaze on her face. If it drifted downwards the problem would surely worsen.

"Coming *here* puts me in a good mood," he replied, making the message very personal.

Maybe not after tonight, her mind clicked in, but her body didn't want to respond to that sobering piece of caution.

"Hey, Leo!" Dylan broke in, popping his head out of the kitchen. "I put four of the Changmai Surprise aside for you. I'll microwave them now if you like."

"Great!" Leo beamed at him. "And I'll follow them up with your lamb kebabs if they're on the menu."

"Will do," Dylan agreed cheerfully.

"That guy really knows what to do with food," Leo remarked as Dylan retreated into the kitchen. "You got a prize in him, Teri."

"Yes, I did. And every chef likes to have his creativity appreciated. It gave him a real buzz, your calling this afternoon."

He laughed. "Pure self-interest. The thought of

plane food did not appeal. Have you eaten yourself, yet?''

"Bits and pieces." Her stomach had been too screwed up to accept much.

His eyebrows slanted in charming appeal. "Join me at my table?''

She nodded. "When I've finished up."

He gave the remaining diners a quick scan. "Not too many left. Shouldn't take long." Another dazzling smile. "I've been looking forward to your company."

"You mean I rank up there with the food?" she lightly mocked, trying to quell the maverick rush of need to know how highly she did rank in his life.

His eyes danced, inviting her to be his partner in pleasure as he replied, "I have a hunger for many things."

"Mmmh…" she answered noncommittally.

"I'll do my best to tease your appetite," he promised.

And she'd probably rob him of his, Teri thought with savage irony. His black wavy hair was still damp from a shower. She could smell the tangy cologne he'd splashed on his newly shaven jaw. He was certainly primed for sexual action, and the mental picture formed of Leo stripped naked, his powerful masculinity all hers for the night…if she postponed telling him about her pregnancy.

The temptation to keep that vital piece of news to herself was suddenly very strong. Leo might value freedom above everything else but he was a great lover. Why deprive herself of one more sensational experience with him? She could look upon it as a birthday gift to herself.

"Teri?" Leo quizzed her silence.

Her mouth twitched. "Just thinking how good you look, Leo."

He grinned. "You, too, babe."

Babe!

She should be thinking of what was between his ears, not his legs. Even more pertinently what was in his heart! Would being a father *mean* anything to him?

"Here you go, Leo!" Dylan announced, sliding the plate with its steaming appetiser straight onto the weighing machine beside the cash register.

Leo sniffed appreciatively. "Love that sauce, Dylan."

"Combination of honey, sesame oil and soy sauce," Dylan confided proudly.

Teri took the printout of the weight, stapled on a customer number, gave the matching number to Leo, then spiked the bill for later payment. "Enjoy," she said with an encouraging smile.

"Back soon," he warned both of them and headed for his usual table against the wall from where he could watch all the action.

Dylan set to work grilling the lamb kebabs and Teri did the rounds of the tables, removing used plates while having a bit of chitchat with regulars. She was acutely conscious of Leo's eyes following her. It was almost like the caressing touch of his hands, shaping her body to his, or that was how it felt to her fevered imagination. His close presence made her so sexually aware, she escaped to the kitchen to sort herself out on some kind of sensible level.

"I'll do those." Mel Hudson, her kitchenhand, who was working his way through university, whipped the tray of dirty plates out of her hands. "You go and enjoy yourself with Leo." And the nineteen-year-old lanky boy winked at her!

Teri huffed and muttered, "He'll keep."

Mel proceeded to load the dishwasher, a knowing grin on his face. "The guy's on toast for you, Teri. You ought to put him out of his misery."

"When I want your advice, Mel,"—cheeky boy—"I'll ask for it."

"It's your birthday. Give yourself a break."

She frowned at him. "Who told you it was my birthday?"

"Dylan figured it had to be. The post came when you were out this afternoon and he said there was a whole stack of cards for you."

Which she'd taken upstairs to the apartment, out of sight, out of mind. Of course, her family meant well, but what woman wanted to be reminded of her thirtieth birthday? "Some people ought to mind their own business," she remarked darkly.

Mel shrugged. "So what's the big deal? Take the rest of the night off. Have fun. Dylan and I will finish up and shut up shop."

"I'm not ready," she muttered truculently.

"Ready for what?"

"Never you mind."

She banged some pots and pans around to indicate the conversation was over. Her mind chewed over her state of readiness. Was she ready to go to bed with Leo with him still in ignorance of his fatherhood? Ready to tell him she was pregnant? Ready to suffer his shock, dismay, rejection? This was extremely difficult to sort out.

She liked the man. She liked having him in her life, even if it was on a casual basis. In fact, if she was still a starry-eyed teenager she'd probably say she was in love with Leo Kingston, though from a more mature outlook, that was probably only chemistry. After all, she didn't know him through and through. Only that he was nice to people, nice to her, fun to be with, and great in bed.

Both Dylan and Mel liked him but that was a man-to-man thing. Leo, in their opinion, was a good guy. However, not one of them had any *claim* on him. Leo breezed in and out and he was much more out than in. Even so, was she really ready to say goodbye to him?

She'd been able to think much more clearly this afternoon. Somehow, Leo's being here, hitting her with so much vital attraction again, completely muddled her.

"Teri...customer leaving," Dylan called out.

She hastily pasted a smile on her face and went to handle the departing customer's payment for dinner. Leo was at the serving counter and Dylan was transferring the lamb kebabs from the grill to a plate that was already piled up with various salads chosen from the buffet table. Teri managed the money transaction smoothly, bade good-night to the family of four who appeared well satisfied, then went through the routine of weighing Leo's main meal.

"Join me now?" he pressed hopefully.

"Sure she can," Dylan popped in. "The grill's off for the night so I can handle the cash takings and Mel will do the rest."

A birthday conspiracy, Teri concluded, which was really nice, but not exactly timely when she wasn't ready for the outcome. "Something I've got to do upstairs first," she quickly excused. "Sure you don't mind filling in for me, Dylan?"

He grinned. "Piece of cake."

"You look perfect as you are," Leo remarked warmly, his eyes more than warm. The fire of desire was well and truly kindled.

She gave him a droll look. "If you think I'm going to titivate for you…"

He laughed. "That's what I love about you, Teri. Always *au naturel*."

"Hmmph," she said, and feeling a blush coming on, made a swift exit.

Love…she ruminated frenziedly over that as she headed upstairs. It was most probably a throwaway word, she argued, like Leo saying he *loved* Dylan's sauce. He couldn't mean he actually *loved* her.

Was real love ever held at the kind of distance Leo kept? Not in Teri's understanding of it. However, tagged on to the *au naturel* remark, it made sense. Oh yes! No doubt about how much he loved tangling with her naked.

And she loved tangling with him naked!

Which was what was making everything so difficult.

She reached her small and rather cluttered living room and raced over to the mantelpiece where she'd lined up her birthday cards. If…if she invited Leo upstairs tonight, she didn't want him to see them, didn't want him asking how old she was or bringing out the telling fact that neither of them knew each other's birthdays.

She bundled them up and was about to shove them into the drawer of her writing desk, when the one on top caused her to pause. It was the big pink flowery one from her parents with the gold inscription—*To Our Darling Daughter.*

A daughter…

She hadn't thought past…baby. Even a baby wasn't quite real to her yet, not enough to put either sex to it. A daughter…or a son…her heart turned over.

Slowly, she laid the cards in the drawer and slid it shut. Then she turned around and leaned back against the desk, her hands creeping up to spread across her flat stomach. As flat as it was, a baby was somewhere in there growing…a little girl or boy…her child…Leo's child.

She had to tell him.

And it had to be done tonight.

Impossible to make love with this huge secret swimming around in her mind, Leo touching her where their child was actually forming, not knowing about it.

The decision was very clear.

She was ready now…ready to tell Leo she was having his child.

CHAPTER FIVE

IT STARTLED Teri to see the dining room almost empty when she returned. There were only two couples left, eating their choice of sweets. Dylan was cleaning the grill and Mel was chatting with Leo who'd obviously finished his main course since Mel had cleared his table. A glance at her watch showed 9:15. Time had flown since Leo had arrived.

"Ah, here you are!" Mel said with satisfaction, and held out the chair opposite Leo's for her.

"Thanks," she said, her eyes quizzing this unanticipated gesture of gallantry from her teenage employee.

Mel grinned. "No problem. Leave you to it now."

Teri rolled her eyes to Leo who looked most amused at this little byplay. "Why do I feel I'm being pushed at you tonight? Are they up to no good behind my back?" she dryly remarked.

He laughed, his eyes twinkling like brilliant sunshine on blue water. "They like you, Teri. They like working for you. You make this a good place to be. They want to give you some time off. That's all."

She sighed. Leo really was a gorgeous man. "You know you've never told me how many people work for you."

He had explained his business as software conversions, but Teri hadn't probed much, not wanting Leo

37

to think she was interested in how big his income was. That didn't matter to her. However, she needed a safe, impersonal kind of conversation until they were absolutely alone together.

He shrugged. "Small team. Four crack computer programmers and one administrative assistant."

"Any females?"

"The assistant." He gave a crooked little smile. "Mavis is in her early fifties, frighteningly efficient while sort of mother-henning the rest of us."

She hadn't been checking out possible female competition, but it was interesting to know the kind of woman he'd hired. "Do you prefer your programmers to be men?" she asked, aware there were many women in computer fields these days.

Something negative flicked across his face. "It's easier," he said flatly.

"How so?" she asked curiously.

He sighed. "You'll probably accuse me of being some kind of male chauvinist, but the truth is most whiz-bang computer programmers are fairly young and a lot of young women trade off their sex appeal." An icy hardness flashed into his eyes. "They can bring tensions into a workplace I simply don't want. Guys start competing for their attention and an atmosphere of camaraderie is suddenly shot to pieces. It's just better avoided."

"You've seen this happen?" Teri asked, uneasy with his explanation which did smack of male bias.

He nodded. "Married women are usually okay but unmarried ones can play havoc with productivity and team spirit."

So it wasn't exactly a bias against women, more a pragmatic choice to guard against hormone battles. But he certainly didn't care for women who traded on their sex appeal. Teri couldn't help wondering what his ex-wife had been like. They'd never swapped marriage stories. Raking over that particular part of her past had not appealed to her. Still didn't. And she didn't have the right to poke into his.

Besides, even the mention of marriage might be misinterpreted when she had the highly sensitive subject of her pregnancy waiting in the wings.

She smiled. "I guess you consider Mavis safe."

He relaxed and returned her smile, pleased she wasn't critical of his employment policy. "Absolutely safe. Mavis is great. Reliable, responsible, has a place for everything and everything in its place."

Teri wondered if Leo applied some of those headings to herself…like *safe* and *in her place*. She certainly didn't constitute a distraction from his work. She suspected she was his break from it.

The big question was…how would he view a baby?

The shifting of chairs alerted her to the imminent departure of the remaining diners. She glanced around. Yes, all of them up, ready to go. Dylan was at the cash register, waiting to take their money. Mel had cleared the buffet table and was hurrying out of the kitchen to clean up the tables being vacated.

"Do you want dessert, Leo?" Teri asked, swinging her attention back to him. There'd still be leftovers in the kitchen.

He gave her a whimsical look. "It's being taken care of."

She raised her eyebrows. "More special service?"

"I think I've won special status by winning your favour."

"Leo, I suspect you'd win any woman's favour if you worked on it." And that was the plain truth, Teri thought.

"You miss the point," he argued, his eyes dancing at her again. "It's you who's special, Teri."

How special? Was he prepared to accept her as the mother of his child?

"Well, thanks," she said as graciously as she could manage when her nerves were getting strung out like piano wires. "It's nice to be appreciated."

"Oh, you are! Very much," Leo asserted, desire flowing from him in electric waves that instantly screwed the piano pegs up another notch or two and caused her stomach to go into spasms.

Fortunately Dylan provided distraction, escorting the last of tonight's customers to the door and locking up behind them. "You and Mel can go, too, Dylan," Teri instructed. "If there's anything left to do, I'll do it in the morning."

"Okay. We'll be off in a minute. Just got to hang up my apron," Dylan returned cheerfully.

One more minute and she could start unburdening herself of this dreadful suspense. A sixty-seconds countdown to desertion or togetherness or a continuation of their *sometime* relationship into *sometime* fatherhood. And the strange part was, Teri had no idea which outcome would be best in the long run.

"Is something wrong, Teri?" Leo asked.

It forced her to meet the quizzical concern in his

eyes. "Not really," she answered, wishing the boys would hurry up.

"You look a bit strained."

"Sorry." She tried a rueful smile. "There's nothing wrong." An innocent baby on the way could hardly be called *wrong*. "It's just…well, I have a lot on my mind."

"Anything I can do to help?"

The offer was genuine. She could see nothing but sincerity in his expression. Maybe…

"Happy birthday to you…"

Dylan's and Mel's voices raised raucously in song, instantly jerked her attention away. Her two young employees were marching out of the kitchen, Dylan carrying a cake with a single candle burning on it, Mel bearing a tray with two flute glasses and a bottle of champagne in an ice bucket.

"Happy birthday to you…"

Leo rose from his chair to join in.

"Happy Birthday, dear Teri-i-i…"

They were all grinning like Cheshire cats.

"Happy birthday to you!"

She almost burst into tears. She quickly propped her elbows on the table and covered her face with her hands. Let them think she was embarrassed. Let them think anything as long as she had a few seconds to fight back this awful flood of turbulent emotion.

She heard the plate with the cake being plonked on the table in front of her. "Come on, Teri. Got to blow the candle out," Dylan cajoled.

"Make a wish, too," Mel pressed.

A wish…

Please God, let Leo want our child!

And why that suddenly meant so much she didn't know!

She took a deep breath, dropped her hands, and blew out the candle. It wasn't difficult to blow out one candle. If there'd been thirty…but they didn't know about that milestone and she wasn't about to tell them.

Her effort was roundly applauded.

"Thank you," she managed huskily.

"It's an orange cake with lemon icing. Your favourite. Made it myself," Dylan said proudly.

"You shouldn't…" She stopped herself from shaking her head and aimed a wobbly smile at him. "It's very kind of you, Dylan."

"Pleasure. You have a good time, Teri. Everyone should celebrate their birthday."

"Yeah," Mel agreed. "We're nicking off now so you can have a great celebration. Good night, Teri…Leo…"

"I'll lock up after you," Leo offered, and they all set off for the door, leaving Teri staring at a cake she couldn't possibly eat and a bottle of champagne that was utterly wasted on this occasion.

They meant well.

Any other birthday she would have been delighted at being given such a sweet surprise. She must thank Dylan and Mel again tomorrow. Her eyes misted over again and she blinked furiously, clearing the moisture as best she could. Getting choked up was not going to help anything. She took several deep breaths and was more or less in control of herself by the time Leo returned to the table.

Her hands fluttered in a dismissive appeal. "I didn't realise they had anything like this planned. I didn't even tell them it was my birthday."

"I know." He leaned down and picked something off his chair. "This is from me," he said, handing her a slim, rectangular packet, wrapped in expensive silver paper. "Happy birthday, Teri."

His voice was a warm caress, stroking her heart into pumping with the wild hope that tonight might not be the parting of the ways she feared. She stared down at the packet as Leo slid back onto his chair. It raised a host of questions that clamoured to be answered.

"How did you know, Leo?"

"Dylan told me when I rang this afternoon."

"He had no right..." A painful flush burned into her cheeks as she imagined Dylan suggesting to Leo that he surprise her, too. Her eyes flashed an anguished apology. "I didn't expect you to..."

He reached across the table and stilled the agitated wave of her hand by capturing it and pressing reassurance. "I wanted to, Teri. In fact, it's because you don't expect anything that it's a very real pleasure to buy you a gift."

"But..."

"No buts. Open it," he commanded softly, releasing her hand so she could do so.

She wavered, wanting to, yet not feeling right about it, not in these circumstances. "I don't even know *your* birthday," she temporised.

"First of December," he tossed off carelessly.

Their baby would be born in October.

She barely caught herself back from saying it. Too bald a statement. Better to lead into it so at least he understood how it had happened.

"It won't bite," Leo dryly advised. "And you won't owe me anything, Teri. It's simply a birthday gift, no strings attached. Please...I enjoyed buying it."

A child was a big, big string, Teri thought, as she tore open the wrapping paper, hoping Leo had picked up something simple and relatively inexpensive. He'd probably ducked into one of the airport shops and bought the first thing that caught his eye...except the long flat box emerging from the silver paper was a white leather case on which was stamped in gold, the high-fashion designer name—Escada.

Her heart wobbled as she clicked open the lid. Sunglasses—streamlined class—the elegant black-and-silver frames suggesting a space age design.

"Put them on and let me see," Leo urged, eager to judge if his choice was right.

Teri had never owned or worn a designer label *anything!* The temptation—just to try—was too seductive to deny. Her hands trembled slightly as she lifted the beautiful and undoubtedly ruinously expensive glasses from their black suede nest and fitted them on her face.

"Yes!" Leo cried triumphantly. "I knew they were *you* the moment I saw them. Take a look in the mirror, Teri. They look fantastic on you!"

She couldn't resist, just to see. A mirror was positioned on the wall so most of the dining room could be watched from the kitchen. It only took a few moments to get up and view her reflection. The sunglasses were wonderful; chic, classy, perfect for her face and cropped hair, giving her an ultra modern, sophisticated look that instantly took away any angst over being thirty.

She couldn't help smiling at Leo for giving her this lovely gift, despite the deep reservations she held. "They are fantastic," she agreed wholeheartedly. "But they must have cost a fortune, Leo."

He shrugged, still grinning at her. "Worth every cent. All you need now are black leathers and a Harley-Davidson."

Laughter bubbled up from somewhere and spilled out. Teri tried to get a grip on herself as she resumed her seat at the table and returned the glasses to their plush case. She had to speak—*had to*—before she was drawn so far into Leo's charm-circle she'd want to forget the unforgettable.

"Time to open the champagne," he said happily.

"No...wait!" she blurted out, halting his movement to lift the bottle out of the ice bucket. She met his quizzical eyes anxiously. "There's something I've got to tell you, Leo."

"Okay," he invited good-humouredly.

Where to start? How to start? Why hadn't she given this more thought?

"Remember last month when you were here and I had a bit of a queezy stomach?" she plunged in, desperate to have him understand there'd been nothing planned about it.

He nodded. "The twenty-four-hour bug. I got it, too." He gave her a teasing smile. "Probably off you."

"Probably," she repeated. Her muscles had stiffened up. Impossible to return even a travesty of a smile. Get to the point, her mind screamed. Her voice obligingly recited, "Anyhow, I started vomiting after you left that night. And the doctor says that's why the pill didn't work."

Leo frowned as though he wasn't quite following her.

Teri took a deep breath. Obviously it had to be spelled out to him. Finding it too frightening to look him in the eye, Teri fastened her gaze on the snuffed-out candle on the cake and poured forth the truth.

"I'm pregnant, Leo. With your child. And I'm going to have it. Whether you like it not. So there you are. That's the situation." She heard herself babbling but couldn't stop. "I couldn't not tell you. Though I don't expect anything from you. I won't ask for anything, either. I want to have this baby. It's my decision. My responsibility. But I couldn't not let you know. It is your child."

The babble ran out.

Yet the words she'd said seemed to echo and echo in the long, long silence that followed, taunting her into finally looking up.

There was nothing coming from him.

Absolutely nothing.

Leo's face was frozen in shock.

CHAPTER SIX

PREGNANT…

Having his child…

Leo couldn't get it together in his mind. One level in his brain registered that the evening he'd planned with Teri was shot to pieces because this alien element had changed all the parameters. But the crux of everything revolved around…what was he supposed to do now?

He was floored. Knocked out for the count. And he seemed utterly incapable of picking himself up. He'd never got a woman pregnant before. He was careful about that. Responsible. He knew people were having babies when and as they liked these days, but he'd always thought if you were going to have kids, you did the right thing and got married first, set the process up properly.

And there was the sticking point.

He didn't want to get married.

He liked Teri. They had a good relationship going. At least, they had up until now. He didn't want it wrecked and there was nothing that wrecked a relationship faster than marriage. He'd already made one huge mistake with it and ended up paying one hell of a price for nothing.

But it wouldn't be nothing with Teri.

She was already pregnant with his child. A child

was definitely something. Though she hadn't meant it to happen. It was clearly an accident. In fact, she could have chosen to have an abortion, not telling him at all.

A savage recoil hit his stomach. He was glad Teri hadn't taken that path. Just the thought of her getting rid of his child stirred up a prickly nest of primitive instincts. He certainly had to hand it to her. She'd done the decent thing, letting him know, giving him the chance to...*be a father!*

His mind still boggled over being so unexpectedly presented with a done deal. It was wrong somehow that it should be an accident. Fatherhood was too important...a state to be approached with appropriate planning and a readiness to take it on.

This haphazard situation represented a big complication to his current lifestyle. Teri's, too. Big...*big!* They were looking at a responsibility that would spread over the rest of their lives. Pregnancy...baby...child...teenager...a lot of years involved here...and a kid deserved parents who were prepared to be parents and everything that meant.

He'd wanted a family before Serena had soured him on the whole deal. Here it was being handed to him. Well, not exactly a family. One child. A kid of his own to show things to, share things with.

He remembered the great times he'd had with his own Dad...camping, fishing, playing ball...the competition they'd had running for years, shooting balls into the basketball hoop they'd fixed above the garage door.

He was startled out of the pleasant memories by

Teri's pushing her chair back and standing up. Very abrupt it was, jarring, unexpected. They had serious business to discuss here and there couldn't be any running away from it.

He looked up to see her face was white and strained. Her grey eyes were oddly drained of colour, like a rain-washed sky, cold, dull and bleak.

"You don't have to worry about a thing, Leo. I leave you free and clear," she stated, a steely pride in her voice. "Don't forget to activate the lock on the door when you go."

With her head tossed high and a poker spine, she walked out on him, straight for the kitchen and undoubtedly heading for the privacy of her upstairs apartment.

Leo did nothing to stop her. If she'd slapped him in the face, he couldn't have been more stunned by the flat rejection she'd just handed him. He stared at the table, at the untouched cake, the uncorked champagne, the torn wrapping paper and the white leather case containing the *Escada* sunglasses. She hadn't even taken *them* with her...a gift he'd given in good faith.

Then he remembered how reluctant she'd been to join him at his table tonight, reluctant to open his gift. The words she'd spoken earlier came sliding back, gathering much more force...*I don't expect anything of you...I won't ask for anything...my decision...my responsibility.* It all added up to...Teri didn't want to share his child with him. She wanted to keep it to herself.

And damn it all! That wasn't right. He was the

father, wasn't he? It wasn't up to Teri to decide he could have no part of this. The kid was just as much a part of him as it was of her. That gave him a say in things, didn't it? He had a claim here, a flesh and blood claim, and he didn't want to be done out of it.

His mind moved into high gear, focusing strongly on the problem facing him. He could be on tricky legal ground with paternal rights. As a single Mum, Teri might be able to shut him out, or severely limit any fathering he might want to do.

Besides, going to a court of law rarely produced the best end result. A private settlement between the two parties was much better. In fact, his path was becoming very clear. He had to win Teri over to his way of thinking, show her he could be useful, supportive, worth having around when she needed help with the kid.

There had to be some way to sort things out. After all, the bottom line was Teri was having *his* child.

A child had the right to know its father.

That was a good line to take.

And what he had to do now was persuade Teri to accept it.

CHAPTER SEVEN

So, THAT was it, Teri told herself, staring numbly at the bed which she could have shared with Leo if she'd kept her mouth shut. She tried to banish the loneliness of the moment by sitting on it and ignoring the fact it was big enough for two. She'd need the extra room in it when she was heavily pregnant anyway.

She would have to go back downstairs soon, store the cake and champagne in the refrigerator, check that Leo had locked the door properly, and switch off the lights. No point in inviting a break-in. A thirty-year-old single mother had to be practical about the future.

She was on her own. No doubt about that now. She'd waited and waited for Leo to stop sitting on the fence and commit himself one way or another but he'd obviously found the situation too difficult to handle. After all, it was a bit crass to bluntly say, "I'm out of here," to a woman you've been bedding for a year, just because she'd fallen pregnant on a mischance.

And there really was nothing to gain by lying about how he felt being tied into fatherhood when she knew he didn't want permanent ties. Even if he'd manoeuvred for a few more nights of sex, the lie would be uncovered sooner or later and that would make him a sleazy rat.

At least she could take pride in letting him go with

51

grace and dignity on her part. Unfortunately pride didn't rate very highly at the moment. It didn't ease the ache in her heart. It didn't fill the awful emptiness of loss. It didn't stop her yearning for impossible things…like a man to love her, to stand by her regardless of what life threw at them, to be there for her when she really needed him.

Her long built-up defensive shield of self-sufficiency started cracking. She was only feeling these things because of the baby, Teri frantically reasoned, but tears began welling and it was hopeless trying to hold them back. Her eyelids couldn't contain them. They squeezed through her lashes and started trickling down her cheeks. She grabbed a handful of tissues from the box on the bedside table and did some mopping up, but the tightness in her chest needed some release and there was no one to care whether she wept or not.

The creaking of one of the old stair-treads jolted her into scooping in a deep breath. Had she imagined it? Her heart jumped as the creaking came again. It had to be the fourth and the ninth steps. Any weight on them and they…someone was coming up the staircase to her apartment!

"Teri?"

Leo!

He hadn't gone! He was still here…looking for her!

She held her breath and swiped wildly at the moisture on her cheeks as he moved down the hallway, past the open doorway to the blessedly dark bedroom, and on to the living room at the front of the house, overlooking the street. The light there was still on from her previous dash upstairs to put the birthday cards away.

He didn't call out again, despite finding the room empty of her presence. He probably figured she was in the bathroom. She wished she *was* there so she could wash her face. Though that wouldn't help the rest of her. Her mind was totally flummoxed, trying to find a motive for Leo's following her upstairs, and her heart was catapulting around her chest. He couldn't still expect—want—sex with her, could he?

She pushed up from the bed, sending a shot of fierce willpower to her legs when they threatened to give way. The shock had dried up her tears. She dropped the damp tissues that had balled in her hand. Whatever Leo's reasons for wanting to be with her, there was no escape from confronting them.

Dignity, dignity, dignity, she recited to herself as she left the bedroom and took the few steps down the hallway to the doorway into the living room. Several deep breaths helped restore composure, though her pulse was still going nineteen to the dozen. The sight of Leo calmly pouring champagne into one of the flute glasses stopped her dead.

She stood absolutely still, watching him, curiously mesmerised by the swift attack on her senses. He had so much impact—his strong male physicality, the aura of sublime confidence, the vital good looks—and this was the father of her child. She was always going to have a part of him.

Whatever else he could be labelled, Leo Kingston was, undoubtedly, a champagne man. He had definitely put some quality fizz in her life and it was possible he would keep on doing it. After all, he was still here, wasn't he? Or maybe the fizz was about to go flat.

Once he'd filled the flute glass to his satisfaction, he set it down on the tray he'd obviously collected from the kitchen, and picked up the second glass, proceeding to do the same again. The tray, which he'd placed on the small table between her two armchairs, not only carried the ice bucket for the bottle of champagne, but the cake Dylan had made for her, and the single candle had been relit!

"What are you doing?" The inane question spilled from her lips. It was perfectly obvious he was pouring out champagne. She should have asked *why* he was doing it. And why the cake with the lit candle?

Leo instantly flashed a happy grin at her. "There you are!" he said, which was also obvious.

Happy? Teri's confusion grew as she felt Leo pouring positive vibrations at her. "I thought you…" She stopped herself from uttering another inanity. When a man was standing in front of her, he certainly wasn't gone.

He put down the bottle, picked up the filled glass from the tray, and carried it over to her, his grin projecting a veritable flood of pleasure. "I thought we should celebrate." He handed her a glass and clicked it with his. "A toast to you on your birthday, and a toast to our child whom I figure is one month along, which is just as good as a birthday so I lit the candle for both of you."

He sipped his drink with every appearance of relishing the words he'd just rattled out and Teri followed suit, too dazed to question the turnaround from shock to celebration.

"When did you find out?" he burbled on. "About the baby I mean." His eyes expressed keen interest.

"Today," she answered.

"Only today?" There was a flicker of concern. "You're not going to change your mind about having it?"

"No, I'm not," she said decisively, inwardly tensing at the thought he hoped she might.

The concern cleared. "Right! Fine!"

His apparent relief and approval left her speechless. She just didn't understand what Leo was about. Was this an act to keep their relationship going for a while? Had he reasoned out she wasn't in-your-face pregnant yet, so he might as well ride along until convenience became inconvenience?

His expression changed to apologetic appeal. "I guess it took *you* some time to get used to the idea, too."

Was that all it had been downstairs? Time frozen as he groped towards getting used to the idea? Teri still couldn't dismiss the sense of disbelief stirred by his current behaviour.

"You don't mind about what's happened?" she queried, her eyes keenly searching his for any dubious signs.

"Do you?" he instantly countered, watching just as acutely for her reactions.

"Well, it wasn't exactly planned..."

"No, I know," he came in quickly. "Bit of a shock

being told you're going to be a father when you're not expecting it. Must have been a shock to you, as well, being told you're going to be a mother.''

''Yes, it was,'' she conceded.

''But it's okay. I mean you really do want it.''

He seemed quite anxious on that point.

''I would have preferred a more ideal situation,'' she said dryly. ''Being a single mother does have its drawbacks.''

''Yes, it does,'' he quickly agreed. ''In fact, I was thinking about that.'' He paused, and she had the sense of him steeling himself. ''Best course is for us to get married, Teri,'' he stated decisively.

The shock of hearing him suggest what she hadn't believed was a possibility rocked her for a moment, letting loose the host of clawing needs that had attacked her in the bedroom.

''But you don't want to get married,'' she blurted out before common sense could be eroded by foolish weakness.

He was visibly discomforted by the reminder. ''This is different,'' he claimed.

''You're prepared to settle into being a fulltime husband instead of a sometime lover?'' she shot at him, unable to believe such a miraculous turnaround.

He couldn't stop a grimace at that prospect. ''It'll take some adjustment,'' he conceded.

''You don't love me, Leo.''

He frowned, clearly not comfortable with the emotional word. ''We get on well, Teri,'' he argued manfully.

''When you're here. Which is not all that frequently. We're hardly talking day-in, day-out stuff, are we?''

"We're both reasonable people. Surely we could respect each other's differences. As we have this past year."

In limited doses, she thought, only too painfully aware how living together could colour everything differently. "Leo, you're not dying to have me as your wife and you're not my idea of a husband," she stated with brutal honesty.

"There is the child to consider, Teri," he came back strongly.

"I don't need you to do the honourable thing by me," she retorted, hating the idea he was screwing himself up to take her on for the sake of their child.

"It's not honour. Dammit, Teri! I want the child to have my name."

Male pride! Anger at his one-eyed view spurted off her tongue. "And what's wrong with *my* name? Is Adams too ordinary for your child?"

He rolled his head in exasperation. "It's not that! I just want…" His eyes blazed with determined possessiveness. "It's my kid, too."

"I'm not denying it." Her own stung pride urged her to add, "But I'm certainly not going to marry you just to give *my* child *your* name."

His jaw tightened. The strong tension flowing from him suddenly caught at Teri's nerves. This was not sexual tension. This was an entirely different energy force and it was daunting, giving her a jolting insight into the will of the man. Nothing wishy-washy about Leo Kingston. He was very, very different to Wayne.

She watched his eyes sharpen to laser intensity and quivered inside, realising they'd never argued before. This was a side of Leo she had sensed but never seen.

"Do you intend to cut me out, Teri?"

"Out of what?" she asked warily, unsure of her ground with him.

"When you walked away from me downstairs, I had the impression you were more than prepared to shovel me out of your life and the life of our child."

She shook her head at his interpretation of her actions which had been meant to free him of all responsibility. "I left it up to you. The choice was yours," she insisted.

"Then I'm in," he stated firmly.

"If you want to be."

The nerve-jangling tension eased. "I do. Very much," he said emphatically.

It surprised her. Though it shouldn't, she quickly reasoned, given his unexpected proposal of marriage. Yet this strong paternal streak didn't fit into his free-wheeling lifestyle at all. Would it waver once the idea of fatherhood was replaced with realities?

"Okay," she agreed. "I have nothing against our child knowing its father, but I won't marry you, Leo."

He looked relieved, then curious. "Marriage to me could be a good deal for you, you know."

"Only if we spent the rest of our lives in bed," she returned flippantly, offended he should think she'd be persuaded by status considerations. Belatedly remembering the glass in her hand, she lifted it with mocking intent. "I need more than champagne in a husband."

He laughed, his face lighting up with a dancing appreciation she didn't quite comprehend. But she felt his pleasure in her, a wave of warmth that muddled up all her straight thinking...Leo, the lover, eyes flirting wickedly with hers. Even now, when they were seriously discussing the future, he could set her heart pumping overtime and arouse little prickles of excitement in anticipation of what he promised.

"Oh, I don't know," he drawled, his mouth moving into a very sensual smile as he clicked his glass with hers. "I've always thought champagne a great starting point for wonderful things."

"Sex," she said flatly, determined on keeping a proper perspective with Leo.

"Uh-huh. We spend a third of our lives in bed," he said, totally unabashed by her attempted put-down. "And you'd have to admit I deliver on all fronts there." He grinned triumphantly. "We now have positive proof of my potency."

More male pride!

Teri eyed him with arch understanding. "So that's why you're suddenly cock-a-hoop about being a father. Now you know those little fellows of yours can make the grade."

She sashayed around him and headed for the table where the candle was now dripping wax onto the icing of the cake. Better that she keep some distance between them until she had Leo sorted out in her mind. He was lethal to any common sense when he turned on his sexual magnetism.

"Don't knock it!" he aimed after her, still with an exultant lilt in his voice. "Between us, I reckon we're going to make a great kid."

Which surely had to mean he liked the idea of her being the mother of his child. Teri felt a warm kick of pleasure, despite her disapproval of his other attitudes. In his heart, Leo did not feel she was wife material or he wouldn't have limited their relationship the way he had. She suspected he didn't see any woman taking up that role in his life again. But he must be seeing her as good mother material.

"Yes, I think we'll make a great kid, too," she agreed, then half turned to cock an eyebrow at him and ask the critical question. "Do you really intend sticking around to find out, Leo?"

"You bet I am," he answered without the slightest hesitation, his whole face lit with excited anticipation. He strode towards her, arms out expansively, the glass of champagne in his hand in danger of sloshing out its contents. "Any help you want, just ask me, Teri. You won't be on your own with our child. We'll be partners in parenthood. Okay?"

It was a far more generous stance than Teri could have imagined coming from him. She was stunned by it. Partners in parenthood encompassed a lifetime connection. Did he realise that? Had he given it serious consideration or was he riding on some wave of euphoria, revelling in the idea of having a child without really seeing the responsibilities that went with it?

He set his glass down on the tray and blew out the candle. Teri watched the smoke from it wisping upwards, curling, disintegrating, and wondered if Leo's interest in their child would be like that—a brightly lit candle tonight, insubstantial smoke in the future.

Then it seemed in one smooth fluid movement he was behind her, sliding his arms around her waist, snuggling her body back against his, hotly reminding her of what they'd shared most in coming to this critical night.

She closed her eyes, savouring the feel of him, the powerful masculinity that stirred such a deep uncontrollable response, like a fountain of sensation bursting into life, arrows of desire shooting through her, every nerve bridling with delight, skin tingling with excitement, and spasms of pleasurable anticipation pulsing inside her.

She'd wanted this contact with him from the moment he'd come striding into the restaurant tonight, wanted to forget the baby and simply luxuriate in what Leo could do to her. At least now she could let it happen. He still wanted her...even with child.

He planted a soft, sensual kiss on the curve of her neck and shoulder, and she instinctively stretched her head back to give him more access, loving the way he tasted her, slowly, seductively, spreading more and more delicious heat from his mouth. He trailed sweet, tantalising kisses up to her ear and gently, erotically teased her lobe with his teeth.

"I'm so hungry for you," he murmured.

"Mmmh..." she blissfully agreed, feeling like a cat who wanted her coat stroked as she rubbed her bottom across his thighs. He'd been away three weeks. She'd missed him. She needed more of him, more than he was ever likely to give. But her fuzzy mind quickly shied away from letting that thought break her concentration on the sheer physical thrill of having Leo holding her, kissing her, touching.

His hands slid up to cup her breasts. He squeezed lightly, a kind of gloating possessiveness she normally enjoyed, but a new tenderness there caused her to wince and she lifted her free hand to pluck at his in protest. "Softer," she instructed.

"I hurt you?" He sounded puzzled.

"They're tight, sensitive. The pregnancy, I guess."

"Making changes so soon?"

She sighed. "Must be. They've never felt like this before."

He released them, gliding his hands down to her stomach and lightly pressing in to the flatness there, making her acutely conscious of his state of arousal. "You feel the same to me," he said with satisfaction.

And would for a while, Teri thought, but what then? She was suddenly stricken by doubts again. Leo was hungry for her. Had he put on a paternal act just so he could pleasure himself with her? Torn between the desire to simply give in to his pleasuring and the need for honesty between them, Teri finally blurted out, "I'll probably have a thick waist by the time you drop in again."

"Will that worry you?" he asked, kissing her other shoulder while the caress on her stomach moved lower, causing an almost paralysing rise in sweet tension.

"You might find me less...less desirable," she babbled.

"What? With my son in there?" He gave a low, mellow laugh. "Making love will be twice as good."

His son?

Teri's mind made an abrupt leap into overdrive and a progression of fast and furious activity through her brain waves suppressed the palpitating buzz of sexual promise.

First his drive to give their child *his* name.

Then his pride in his potency.

Now their child had to be a boy.

And he was hungry for sex with her.

This was all macho male testosterone gone mad!

She jerked herself out of his embrace, slapped the glass of champagne she was still holding down on the tray, and swung around in fierce defence of her own gender.

"It might be a girl, Leo."

He looked startled. "A girl?"

"Yes! A girl like me. Not a boy like you. How do you feel about that?"

It was a challenge that was suddenly, vitally important to Teri. Somehow it involved all the shortcomings in their relationship that she tried to keep buried for the sake of having Leo in her life. If they had a daughter, would he care about knowing *her* birthday? Would he care about all the things that made up her day-to-day existence?

He was frowning heavily. "A girl..."

"People do have daughters as well as sons," she reminded him, her voice sharpening as a welling tide of hidden resentments started pushing forward.

He shook his head, still frowning. "I hadn't

thought of a girl. There aren't any girls in my family.'' He was clearly fumbling with this new view of her pregnancy.

"It's a fifty-fifty chance, Leo," Teri drilled. "You can't count on a son."

"Right," he said, but it was a very weak "right' this time, a token "right' that had no enthusiasm behind it.

The door buzzer for the restaurant sounded, startling both of them. Teri checked her watch—10:26—well past the closing time printed on the front door.

"Did you leave the lights on?" she asked tersely. For her, the celebration had turned sour. The sex had turned sour. Everything had turned sour.

Leo looked befuddled, trying to think. "Yes. I forgot about them."

She gave vent to an exasperated sigh and marched off to the staircase as the buzzer sounded again. In fact, she was glad of the interruption. She hated Leo for being so self-centred, hated herself for wanting a man who was never going to give her the kind of relationship that stood firm in all circumstances. She'd shortchanged herself, but no way was she going to let him shortchange their daughter, just because she wasn't a son.

"I'll come with you," Leo called, hastily striding after her.

"Fine!" she snapped, charging down the hall ahead of him. "And you can keep right on going, too."

"What?"

"You heard me." On down the staircase she went,

seething with the conclusions she'd come to. "I might be twice as good to you if I'm having a son, but I'm obviously only half as good if I have a daughter. If you think I'm going to bed with a man who has such a sexist attitude…"

"I didn't say that!" he protested, making the stairs creak loudly under his heavy feet.

"I should have known," she muttered, furious with her own weakness. "You only ever wanted me for sex. Blowing in when you felt the need for it, then farewell till the next time."

"Now hang on a minute," he argued as she swept through the kitchen. "Don't tell me we haven't had a mutual thing going between us."

"You set the limits to it. Food and sex. Satisfying your appetites." She shot straight into the dining room which was starkly empty of life now, and she emptied out the rest of her rage as she headed for the front door. "You didn't want to spend more time with me beyond that, Leo, and the thought of spending time with a daughter doesn't appeal, does it?"

"I don't know much about little girls. What they want and…"

"Not much about big girls, either," she fired at him.

"For God's sake, Teri! We've enjoyed a lot of times together."

"Food and sex," she repeated relentlessly.

"We talked, too. I like your company, damn it!"

"Not…enough!"

Having reached the door and uncaring of the shadowy figure on the other side of it, she deactivated the lock, and opened up.

"Wait!" Leo commanded, shoving past her to stand guard against any trouble with the person hovering outside. "The restaurant is closed," he stated, his tone terse and uncompromising.

"I know," came the mild reply, the male voice tantalisingly familiar to Teri. "I was hoping… Teri, is that you?"

Recognition burst through her brain and off her lips. "Wayne?"

He laughed at her surprise. "Yeah, it's me. Back home again. Thought I'd drop by and wish you a happy birthday. I brought you a box of your favourite Belgian chocolates."

Another one of his guilt visits!

"Who is this guy, Teri?" Leo demanded bruskly, measuring Wayne as though he were sizing him up for a fight. In actual fact, their height and build were similar, but Wayne's easy-going nature was no match for Leo's powerhouse of energy.

"If I'm intruding…" Wayne gestured his willingness to be off, probably intimidated by the waves of aggression coming at him.

"No," Teri hastened to assure him, realising this particular guilt visit was very timely. "Leo was just leaving, weren't you, Leo?"

Blazing blue eyes sliced to her. "Just who is this guy? And what's he doing, calling on you at this time of night?"

"He's a friend, Leo, an old friend. Some women do have male friends, you know. They even find out things about them, like their birthdays and what their favourite chocolates are.''

His mouth thinned. The acid little criticism was clearly not to his taste. Teri didn't care. Let him burn. He'd had everything his own way for too damned long!

''Yeah, you don't have to worry about me,'' Wayne chimed in cheerfully, intent on lowering the tension. ''Teri and I have known each other since we were kids.''

''Odd she's never mentioned you to me,'' came the bitingly suspicious remark.

He was like a dog protecting his territory, Teri thought, and he had absolutely no right to be possessive. ''Well, Leo, you've never spoken to me about your ex-wife,'' she pointedly reminded him, ''and you've never asked me about my ex-husband.''

He stared at her incredulously. ''Your ex?''

''Husband, yes. Do come in, Wayne.'' She stepped back from the doorway, making room for him to enter, then wriggled her fingers in a miniwave to her erstwhile lover. ''Good night, Leo.''

As she took in his glowering frustration, one part of Teri's mind warned she was probably going to regret giving Leo his marching orders, but the rest of it revelled in savage satisfaction.

However, Wayne didn't quite get past Leo. A hand clamped on his shoulder, halting him in midstride. Wayne jerked his head to Leo, alarm all over his face. He was subjected to a cutting blast from twin blue lasers.

''Just don't start getting any ideas about linking up

with Teri again, Wayne,'' came the blistering command. ''You might be her ex-husband but I'm the father of her child.'' The laser beams were transferred to Teri. ''And I intend *to be* the father of her child. No one's going to cheat me out of my own kid.''

Having delivered this fierce declaration, Leo released Wayne and walked off into the night, satisfied he'd torpedoed any reunion which could threaten his position.

CHAPTER EIGHT

HAVING spent most of the day, trying to focus his distracted mind on nailing all the paperwork on the New Zealand deal, Leo was finally able to pass over the tidy-up details to his ever-efficient assistant. With his office desk mercifully cleared, he relaxed back in his chair, and gave himself up to the same brooding that had consumed his weekend and looked like consuming his entire life.

Who could understand women?

The guy who wrote *Men Are From Mars, Women Are From Venus,* didn't get it right. He should have placed women from Pluto, a dark underworld planet. Venus was purely veneer, the trap to pull men in.

No doubt about that in Leo's mind. Women could be as sweet as honey when they were getting what they wanted, then turn on you like vultures intent on pecking out all your vital parts when you failed to play their game. And you weren't even told the rules!

"Leo?"

"What?" He glared at Mavis for cutting into his finely tuned train of killer thoughts.

She raised her eyebrows at him, disdaining to notice his temperamental mood. "Is there anything else you want filed on the New Zealand trip?"

He had to concede that Mavis Crosby was not from Pluto. Not from Venus, either. She was a nice, homely, middle-aged mother who belonged fairly and squarely on Earth. Neat brown-grey hair, bright brown eyes, green suit, well-cushioned figure, pleasantly lived-in face…very earthy, Mavis was.

Leo always felt comfortable with her. He could trust her to do the right thing all the time. She was reliable, predictable, sensible, the perfect assistant for his business life. Maybe women became normal people after they'd turned fifty.

"I need your advice, Mavis," he said, impulsively deciding to consult her on matters that could not be as foreign to her as they were to him. He waved her to the chair on the other side of his desk. "Stop hovering at that filing cabinet and sit down."

"Ah!" she said with knowing satisfaction, and wasted no time in settling herself to receive his confidence.

Leo grimaced, aware he'd been acting like a bear with a sore head all day. Not even work nor the sense of achievement he should have felt over the New Zealand deal had driven Teri from the forefront of his mind. Teri…having *his* kid, and showing him the door, preferring the company of her *ex-husband*. It burned him every time he thought about it.

"You're a woman, Mavis," he started, inadvertantly glowering at her.

"You can safely say that, yes," she returned dryly.

Not the brightest of starts, Leo thought, and leaned forward, resting his elbows on the desk to fix earnest eye contact. "Now I ask you…" he appealed man-to-man, ignoring the fact he'd established that Mavis was a woman. "For a guy like me…brought up mostly by my Dad because my mother died when I was eight…then sent to an all male boarding school when I was twelve…is it unreasonable for me to be thinking of my still-to-be-born child as a boy?''

Mavis cocked her head, giving him her serious consideration. ''Is this a theoretical question, Leo…or is someone expecting your child?''

Good old Mavis…straight to the point. No shilly-shallying around.

''Yes, she is,'' he affirmed. ''Told me on Friday night.'' He sat back and spread his hands, indicating his own open-mindedness about it all as he explained further. ''And there I was, offering her everything a parenting partner should, and what happens?'' He rolled his eyes at the sheer irrationality of Teri's behaviour. ''She goes off her brain because I didn't think of a girl.''

''Ah!'' It was the sound of slow and careful digestion of the facts.

Leo waited for some pearls of wisdom. When none was forthcoming, he grew impatient. ''Well?'' he demanded.

Mavis roused herself out of deep thought. ''Are you thinking of marrying this woman, Leo?'' she inquired, still not answering his initial question.

He waved a sharp dismissal. ''She doesn't want to marry me.''

''Ah!'' It was a longer *ah* this time, somehow gathering overtones and undertones that suggested Mavis was deeming it wiser to keep her mouth shut in this delicate area.

Which didn't serve Leo's purpose at all. He leaned

forward again, tapping his index finger on the desk to get her mind focused on the critical points.

"It's my kid, Mavis, and she has no right to shoot me out of her life. It's not as if this pregnancy resulted from some one-night stand. We've had a relationship for about a year and never an argument between us until this happened."

He rocked back and threw up his hands as frustration overtook him again. "Suddenly I'm not good enough for her. Not good enough for anything!"

"Uh-huh." Mavis nodded a few times, her shrewd eyes undoubtedly picking up all the body language signals being emitted. Cautiously she inquired, "Am I to understand you want the child, Leo, regardless of whether it's a boy or a girl?"

"Yes, I do," he declared emphatically. "I'm not some fly-by-night sort of guy. You know I've never shirked responsibilities, Mavis. Boy or girl, it's mine."

She nodded again, obviously agreeing with him since she had no reason not to agree. She'd been working with him long enough to know his character inside out. He could count on Mavis to understand what he was telling her.

"And you want my advice," she said, mulling over the situation.

"If you can throw some light…" He shook his head in vexed bewilderment. "It's beyond my understanding. She turned on me as though she'd never once been happy with me. And that's not true, Mavis. I swear it!"

"Pregnancy does make changes, Leo," Mavis advised slowly. "For a woman, nothing is the same as before. You should read up on it. Learn what you're dealing with."

He frowned. Teri had looked the same, felt the same. Nevertheless, Mavis might have a valid point here. Teri certainly hadn't behaved the same.

"I'll get some books," he said, relieved to have an answer he could grasp.

"They might be a bit on the technical side, Leo," Mavis warned. "Try women's magazines. They cover both the physical and the emotional side of pregnancy. There are lots of magazines about having babies available now."

"Right! Good thinking, Mavis. Anything else that might help?"

She hesitated, took a deep breath, eyed him warily, then offered, "Woo the woman."

"Woo? What do you mean...*woo?*"

Mavis sighed as though he were a hopeless case. "I mean give her things to show you care, to show you're thinking of her. Go out of your way to do what she wants. Find out what her needs are..."

The gentle flow of advice hit all the wrong places. "Are you telling me I'm not good enough for any woman unless I play that game?" He slammed his hands on the desk and rose to his feet in towering fury. "What about *my* needs? Is it always a one-way bloody street with women?"

He was too pumped up to wait for a reply. He stormed around his office, all the deeply held resentments from his marriage boiling over into a torrent of explosive energy.

"It's blackmail. A mean, malicious, power game. Grovel at my feet or you won't get what you want from me. Fall into line. Perform, or else. An endless testing of how much you'll do for them. And you're garbage if you don't deliver!"

He smashed a fist down on the desk. "What happened to simply liking each other? Respecting each other's differences? Can't a woman meet a man on mutual ground?"

"Leo, I don't know this woman," Mavis said quietly. "I was only suggesting…"

"It stinks, Mavis! It's the ultimate power grab. To hold a man's child over his head, to beat him into some kind of submission to her will…"

"I didn't say she was doing that, Leo."

"It adds up. It all adds up. Thank you, Mavis. You have made everything abundantly clear to me."

She stood up, taking his words as a dismissal. "Well, Leo, it's your life. Your decision," she granted graciously. "But I'd read up on pregnancy if I were you. That answers a lot, as well. And at the end of the day, there's still the child to be considered."

And giving him one of her wise looks, she sailed out of his office, leaving him to get his feet down to earth again.

CHAPTER NINE

ANOTHER weekend gone, five of them now, Teri despondently acknowledged as she ushered out the last Sunday brunch customer and put the Closed sign on the door. Leo was not coming back. It was stupid to keep fraying her nerves, checking who was entering the restaurant every time the door opened. It was never Leo. She might as well put a Closed sign on everything to do with him, too.

Outside it was fine and warm and sunny. Summer had lingered on into March and daylight saving gave her a long afternoon. She was free now until Tuesday, when another busy week would start, and brooding over the rights and wrongs of her hot-headed decision to cast Leo Kingston out of her future, and the future of their child, was not going to change anything. She had to get on with her life.

Since the weather was pleasant, Teri decided to spend an hour or two in her small backyard, potting her new plants. After all, she couldn't rely on feeling well tomorrow morning. Whoever said pregnancy was a happy state needed their thinking rearranged.

She finished locking up. Leaving Dylan in the kitchen, making up some special dish he wanted to take home to his mother, she headed upstairs to change out of her uniform, donning a pair of old stretch jeans and a comfortable baggy shirt. Her waist had thickened a bit. Not much. But enough for her to be relieved to get out of her snug skirt. She would have to design herself something looser to wear in the restaurant soon.

Her mind inexorably clicked back onto the night of the showdown with Leo. "What child?" Wayne had asked. "No one told me you'd had a child, Teri."

"That's because I haven't," she'd answered.

"Then what was that guy on about?"

She'd spilled it all out, needing a sympathetic ear and a shoulder to cry on, and Wayne, typically, had said not to worry. A guy who was set on killing a rival would definitely be back to fight another day.

Time had proven him wrong about that. Losing might not be in Leo Kingston's normal lexicon, but if winning meant putting up with a woman who dared to criticise his attitudes and who might deliver a daughter instead of a son, winning was clearly not such a great option.

As she sat on the bed to remove her loafers and strap on sandals, Teri told herself for the umpteenth time she was better off without Leo messing her around. She didn't have to worry about his reactions or any interference with her plans for their child. She could suit herself, what she did and how she did it. Being the sole decision-maker was definitely better. Definitely.

Feeling lonely would pass.

She took a deep breath, stood up straight, and with her mind determinedly set on living each day as it came—without Leo—she headed downstairs to get on with what she'd planned. An ironic smile came as she remembered a sign she'd read at some plant nursery—*When society wearies, there is always the garden.* Not that she had a real garden since her backyard was almost completely paved, but pot-plants served the same purpose.

She'd managed to buy a whole stack of small green pots with accompanying saucers very cheaply. By planting clumps of pansies and violas and polyanthus in them, Teri figured she could grow pretty little centrepieces for the tables in the restaurant. It was simply a matter of transferring the seedlings she'd chosen to the pots, and nurturing them along until they bloomed.

The balmy afternoon sunshine and the pleasant prospect of growing flowers lifted her spirits. It didn't take long to get everything she needed out of the storage shed and set it all on the trestle table in the open yard. She was happily scooping the potting mixture out of its bag and into the pots when a sharp, peremptory voice startled her out of her rhythm.

"What the hell do you think you're doing?"

The special mixture of soil and fertilisers in the gardening trowel went flying as she jerked around to find the man who was supposed to be out of her life, striding straight back into it, his face thunderously disapproving and his arms flailing around in vehement protest.

"Pregnant women can get bronchial infections from that stuff," he raved on. "Haven't you read up on things you should avoid?"

Before Teri could catch her breath or put two thoughts together, the trowel was whipped out of her hand and Leo was hauling her away from the trestle table, up to the end of the yard where she'd set a bench seat under the one tree she had. He sat her down and stepped back, obviously winding up to deliver a lecture.

Then he noticed he still had the offending trowel in his hand and tossed it back towards her work station. It knocked some of the pots off the trestle table, fortunately not the ones she'd already filled, but the sheer carelessness of the action snapped Teri out of shock and into fighting mode.

"Just who do you think you are, barging in on me and pushing me around?" she flung at him, her heart thumping, her stomach churning, her mind screaming that he had no right to appear at all after not appearing for so long.

"I thought you were sensible enough to take proper care, Teri," he shot at her, ignoring her question. "I come by to check on you and what do I find?"

"You find me minding my own business," she sliced in, incensed further at his thinking he had the right *to check on her*.

"And taking a stupid risk with your health," he declared with vehement conviction. "There's all sorts of unfriendly chemicals in fertilisers."

She was tempted to say they weren't unfriendly to flowers but in the face of Leo's fierce insistence they were harmful to her in her pregnant state, she wilted into muttering, "I just wanted to pot some plants."

Recognising it was a partial surrender to his will, Leo dropped his belligerent stance, glanced over his shoulder at the trestle table, heaved a sigh, then rolled his gaze back to her. "Tell me what you want done and I'll do it," he stated, determined purpose stamped on his face.

"You?" Incredulity billowed through her mind. "Have you ever potted a plant in your life, Leo?"

His eyes flared icy fire. "Do you get a kick out of cutting me down, Teri?"

She shrivelled inside. Guilt and shame mixed a brew of heat that burned up her neck and scorched her cheeks. Her lashes fluttered down, veiling the uncomfortable twinges of conscience that had plagued her this past month. She certainly hadn't been caring or courteous, not fair, either, the night she'd shut the door on him.

"I was surprised. That's all," she excused limply. "It's not the sort of work I associate with you."

"I don't imagine the task requires skilled labour and I am capable of following instructions," came the biting reply.

Teri took a deep breath and forced her gaze up again. "It's kind of you to offer."

His eyes locked onto hers in a fierce, tense challenge, and it didn't take any intuition to know she had wounded this man's pride very deeply. She had cut him down in front of her ex-husband, criticising him on the limits of their affair when she had happily complied with those limits all along. Her scathing indictment of him had not been deserved.

"It won't be good for the baby if you get an infection," he said tersely, dismissing any notion of kindness.

The baby...he was ramming it down her throat that

he did care about their child. She'd judged him meanly over that, too.

Taking it for granted she would stay where he'd parked her, out of the danger zone, he strode back towards the trestle table, bending to scoop up the spilled pots as he went. He examined those she'd already filled and remarked, ''I take it these contain the correct amount?''

''Yes. The mixture needs packing down a bit but that's the level I want,'' she answered matter-of-factly, trying to take her cue from him and silently resolving not to say anything contentious.

Dylan must have let him in, she reasoned. A nice surprise and one she'd welcome, her chef had undoubtedly thought, not knowing of the ruction between them. And seeing him again, Teri had to admit it *was* a welcome surprise.

Whatever it meant, she was glad he was here. Maybe something reasonable could be sorted out between them. In her heart of hearts, she had wished for another chance to discuss some possible future between them. After all, he was the father of her child. Not to mention the best lover she could ever imagine having.

He looked great—the black jeans and red cotton knit shirt clinging to his powerful physique. She found her own muscles clenching in need and yearning for the intimacy she had thrown away. Attraction had nothing to do with common sense, she reflected. It was so strong right now, it was difficult to cling to any rational thought at all.

She watched him dipping the trowel into the bag

of potting mixture and measuring out how much gave the right result. A natural bent for efficiency, she thought. No messing around. Get the job done. There was not the pleasure in it that she would have taken. Another difference between them.

So what? she argued. He was doing it for her and it didn't relate to either food or sex. Or maybe he was doing it for the baby, keeping *his* child safe. Either way, she couldn't call it a self-centred action. Hope for better things arising from this visit took a mega-leap.

It was a very real pleasure just to see him again. The afternoon sunshine gleamed on his hair, lustrous black waves, less tamed than usual and actually kicking into curls around the back of his shirt collar. He'd never worn it so long before. She wondered if he hadn't found the time to get it cut, or whether he couldn't be bothered. Her own hair needed a trim. She hadn't felt in the mood to visit her chatter-box hairdresser, but she must do it soon.

"How do you want these plants distributed?" Leo asked, frowning at the labels on the punnets of seedlings.

"Each polyanthus gets a pot of its own," she answered, eagerness creeping into her voice. It was really nice of him to help. "I thought I'd do three pansies and three violas in the others."

"All the same colour in the one pot?"

"No. A mix. The pansy seedlings are mixed already so you don't have to worry about choosing. With the violas, I planned to put one yellow, one apricot and one white in each pot."

"Right!"

"Leave a bit of space between them so the roots can spread out," she added anxiously.

He slanted her a sardonic look. "I may not be a gardener, but I'm not short on logic, Teri."

"Sorry. You did ask for instructions."

He worked on, without acknowledging her remark.

Teri sighed, wishing he wasn't thinking badly of her. They *had* enjoyed a lot of good times together. Her gaze followed the deft movements of his hands...hands that knew how to caress and excite and...she missed their touch, the comfort and pleasure they gave.

Had he missed her? Was that why he'd come, or was it simply to check on her...the mother of a child that might be the son he fancied...a boy in his own image?

Teri caught herself back from pursuing that grudge against him. She didn't know what was in Leo's mind. It was wrong to leap to possibly false assumptions. Sooner or later he would tell her what he wanted and then she would deal with it, maintaining due courtesy instead of reacting impetuously and meanly.

After all, he might have decided having a daughter wasn't so bad. She hadn't given him time to think about it when he'd fumbled the question, going off like a rocket and exploding into a destructive tirade.

Maybe she'd been suffering some hormonal imbalance from being pregnant. She certainly hadn't been well balanced at all. In fact, underneath her supposedly sensible reasoning that day, she'd been riding an emotional roller-coaster from the moment the doctor had given her the test results.

"How have you been, Teri?"

She jerked her gaze up from his hands, but if he had been looking at her, she'd missed it. "Oh, not too bad," she answered airily, determined on not being negative about anything.

He shot her a beetling frown. "No nausea?"

"Well, yes. A bit. Mostly in the mornings."

"Just whoozy or are you throwing up?"

She made an ironic grimace. "The whooziness tends to lead to throwing up."

"Are you doing anything about it?"

"I'm not taking drugs, if that's what you're asking." After his blast on chemicals, Teri figured it was his main concern. "I'm not entirely stupid, Leo," she added dryly. "I just hadn't heard anything bad about potting mixture."

"Heard?" Another beetling frown. "Haven't you been reading up on what you should and shouldn't be doing?"

Teri bit her lips and studied the dappled shade of the tree on the paving stones. The truth was she'd felt too down to read up on pregnancy. The truth was she'd been doing her best to ignore it as far as possible. It was easier not to make a big thing of it when there was no one to share it with.

The only person she'd told, apart from Leo, was Wayne, and she'd sworn him to secrecy. She saw no point in upsetting her family until she had to. They weren't going to like her being a single mother.

"Teri? Is something wrong?"

The anxious concern in his voice had to be answered. She looked up with a wry smile and a little shrug. "I thought having a baby was a fairly natural thing, Leo. It is what women are made for. I figured if I just took it as it came…"

"Don't you care about our child?"

Care? Now that was one step too far. *He* wasn't being fair to suggest any such thing. "Of course, I do," she retorted emphatically, her temperature rising at the implied criticism. "But I don't have time to obsess about it," she went on, heating up as she listed what she had to cope with. "I'm up early to go to the markets and I'm fighting morning sickness the whole time I'm buying food. Then it's back here to prepare lunch. By the time that crowd's gone, I'm so tired I have to take a nap before the evening rush starts. After I close up at night, I fall into bed."

She paused for breath, glaring belligerently at him. There he was, glowing with health and vitality, nothing different about *his* body, no side effects from having done the job of fertilising *her*. She was the one left carrying the baby and now he had the hide to suggest she wasn't doing it right.

"So, Mr. Know-it-all," she fired at him. "When do you suggest I read up on all the possible risk factors pertaining to my condition? I suppose you're going to say I should be doing it now instead of taking a break outside on a sunny afternoon, doing something I enjoy?"

"No," he said quietly. "It's perfectly reasonable you should need and want a break."

She should have been mollified. Yet somehow, seeing him looking so coolly in control struck her as even more unfair. "Well, thank you," she snapped. "If you were nine weeks pregnant with our child, you might not feel quite so efficient and on the ball yourself."

His face tightened. His mouth thinned. His eyes glittered so fiercely it hurt to look at him.

Teri closed her eyes and felt her heart sinking. She'd done it again. Despite all her good resolutions, she'd used Leo as a whipping boy because she'd had a miserable time by herself. He'd only been expressing concern for their child. How was he supposed to know she'd been aching for comfort and reassurance and help, wishing she hadn't sent him away, remembering how he'd promised whatever support she needed?

There was no satisfaction or pride in being independent when she was struggling with the downside of being pregnant. Though, to be absolutely honest, she really wanted someone to care about her, not the baby. She could hardly expect that from Leo after she'd flung a preference for her ex-husband in his face.

She heard water splashing and realised he'd turned on the outside tap. Washing his hands, cleaning off the dirt, getting ready to go, no doubt. No pleasure in staying with a shrewish woman who had nothing good to say to you.

Wearily, despondently, Teri opened her eyes to watch him leave. He turned off the tap and wiped his hands on the raggy old towel that hung from a nail on the wall of the shed. She didn't look at his face, didn't want to see the cold rejection there.

"Thank you for potting the plants for me, Leo," she said, aware her appreciation of his generosity was too little and too late.

"I'm not finished."

"I'm sure what you've done will be enough," she assured him, having lost interest in the project. She was never going to enjoy the pot plants now. Every bit of growth they had would be a reminder of having stunted any possible growth to a relationship with Leo.

"I meant I'm not finished with you, Teri, and I will not be dismissed this time."

The hard, purposeful words thumped into her heart, reviving hope. Her mind zinged with the heady anticipation of getting another chance. Or did he mean— her stomach cramped—he had some cutting down to do himself before walking out on her?

He covered the ground between them like a warrior pumped up to meet and demolish an enemy, striding with that arrogant carriage he had, emanating a total confidence in taking all before him. Teri was suddenly paralysed with confusion. All she could do was stare at him coming at her and wait for the hit.

"Now get this, Teri, and get it good!" he fired at point-blank range, his eyes blazing into hers, intent on burning off any opposition.

He grabbed her upper arms and lifted her up for a direct and close face-to-face confrontation, no quarter given. The full force of his energy hit her with mesmerising impact. When he started telling her what she had to get, she felt like a limp sponge being filled by a fire-hose on full power.

"*You* are going to marry me. *You* are going to do this because it's the *right* thing to do. It takes *two* people to make a child. It takes *two* people to do right by their child. And *we* are going to do that together, whether you like it or not. Have you got that?"

CHAPTER TEN

LEO WANTED to marry her?

Insisting that she marry him?

Despite all she'd said and done?

Teri's mouth fell open in sheer shock.

No words came. Her mind was thrown into utter chaos, all her previous thoughts smashed by this incredible stance from a man who...whose mouth was crashing onto hers.

There was no seductive pleading or persuasion in his kiss. It was hard and hot and urgent, passionately compelling, not seeking her surrender to his will but commanding it. Teri felt bombarded at first, still reeling from the verbal blast. Then the taste of him, the excitement Leo had always stirred, electrified her senses, triggering a greed that surged into a wild and wanton response.

Like a violent rainstorm after a long drought, the need for him beat through her, shooting rivulets of pleasure everywhere, filling the empty spaces that loneliness had dug, making her feel alive and very much a woman again. She moved instinctively, the desire to have his warmth and strength seeping into her so compelling, her arms broke Leo's hold in their eagerness to wind around his neck and pull him closer. Her body virtually sighed with contentment as she nestled it against his, revelling in feeling him as much as she could.

A wild exultation streamed through her as Leo clutched her buttocks, squeezing and lifting, fitting her into the cradle of his loins, letting her know and feel the excitement she aroused in him. Yes, her mind sang, loving the hard evidence of his arousal, anticipating the intimacy that would surely follow, the glorious togetherness they had enjoyed so many times in the past.

His tongue tangled erotically with hers, evoking the mating she yearned for, and she blissfully encouraged him, wanting all he was implicitly promising her. She'd lost track of everything that had parted them before. Only this was real, the sharing of themselves in a sexual heat that pulsed through both of them, building to an exhilarating fusion.

Except Leo didn't pursue it.

With bewildering abruptness, he broke the intimate contact with her, ending their kiss, easing himself back from her, his hands moving to her waist to stop her from closing the space he'd made between them.

Teri's nerves instantly jangled, screaming a silent protest at the loss of singing pleasure. Her mind, still clouded with brilliantly satisfying sensation, was slow to accept the fading of it. She opened her eyes, urgently searching for reason, and found him grim-faced, restraint and determination stamped on every feature.

''Don't you deny that was mutual, Teri, because you're a damned liar if you do,'' he bit out fiercely, his eyes searing hers with unshakable belief in what she'd just poured out to him.

Her hands had slid to his shoulders as he'd pulled away and she could feel the bunched muscles there, the tension of control mastering desire. He was *not* going to pursue it, regardless of how pumped up his body was with need.

A sense of loss cramped her stomach. Her heart, which had been pounding with wild elation, dropped a beat as it clogged with fear. The realisation sliced through the fog in her mind... Leo had not come to her as the lover he had been. She had wrecked that. Today he was an antagonist, fighting for his rights, seizing on a truth he had unmistakably demonstrated.

Food and sex, she'd thrown at him, as though she'd been insulted by his needs, while the truth was she'd been glad of both of them. And she was glad he was here now, giving her a chance to repair the damage she'd done, to overlay her harsh words with what she really felt about him.

"It was mutual, Leo," she acknowledged quietly.

"It was always mutual," he insisted.

"Yes," she agreed.

"You wanted me as much as I wanted you."

"Yes."

"And you still do."

"Yes."

"So that's something good we've got together if you're honest about it."

She saw the unrelenting challenge in his eyes and sensed a deep hurt and a bitter disillusionment that had been in place long before she'd ever met Leo. In a flash of sharp intuition, she knew her own reckless words had scraped old wounds raw again, and but for their child, he would not have revisited her.

"I'm sorry if I gave you the impression I didn't value what we'd shared," she said, determined now on being honest with him, her eyes eloquently begging his belief. "I did, Leo. Very much. It was just that when I found out about the baby, I guess I wanted…needed…more from you. And I didn't think I'd get it."

Anger kindled in his eyes. He reared back another step, effectively removing all physical contact between them. "I offered you support," he reminded her.

"I know you did. But after the marriage offer…you'd been so adamant against marriage…I knew you couldn't want it…then moving straight onto sex, which was what our affair was all about…the offer of support was…well, it wasn't real to me, Leo."

"I have never lied to you, Teri. Never made false promises. Never tried to mislead you or…"

"Please…I know you haven't. It was just…" She shook her head in anguished self-recrimination. Her hands fluttered in an agitated appeal as she desperately searched for an explanation he might understand. "I was reacting to things," she pleaded. "It was a…a big day for me, Leo. I prepared myself not to expect anything from you and then I felt…out of control. I'm sorry. You threw everything into chaos for me with almost all you said and did."

He frowned. ''You didn't think I was a decent enough man to shoulder my responsibilities?''

''Leo, how was I to know? I was scared you'd think I was trying to tie you to me. Having a child isn't a free and easy thing. You'd laid down your terms…''

''I said this was different.''

She gathered up one more effort to get through to him, her eyes wearily mocking the hard righteousness in his. ''We'd had almost a year of something else. You think that can be turned around in an instant?''

His mouth momentarily tightened. Then slowly he expelled a long, pent-up breath. The anger faded into a neutral expression. ''Fair enough. But I meant everything I said, Teri, and it's more than apparent it's no good your being on your own. The most sensible course of action is to let me fix the situation so you can take proper care.''

''How do you mean?'' she asked warily.

Intense resolution regathered and spoke. ''You said you wanted more from me. You've got it. Every bit of support you need. It's obvious you're running yourself ragged and not getting enough rest. You need more staff to help run the restaurant and take the load off you. I'll organise it. Pay for it. Anything you want.''

''That's very generous of you, Leo, but the restaurant is mine and…''

''Dammit, Teri! We're in this together. And I don't want you living alone here. Anything could happen to you. You'd better move in with me so I can keep an eye on you while we're waiting to get married.''

Married!...there it was again and nothing indecisive about it, either. Teri's heart hopped, skipped and jumped all over the place. He had meant it then...marriage for the sake of their child. And mutual sexual pleasure to help it stick.

Her head went dizzy, thinking about it. She stumbled back and sat down on the bench seat, trying to get her bearings on this extraordinary offer. It wasn't an empty commitment, as she'd thought last time. He was filing his stake in the future of his child. Their child.

"Are you okay?" In an instant Leo was down on his haunches in front of her scanning her face with urgent concern. "You've gone quite pale. Take some deep breaths and move your legs around, Teri."

"What?"

"It gets the blood flowing freely. Fainting is quite common during the first trimester of pregnancy. It's because increased progesterone causes the blood vessels to relax, and it takes longer for oxygen to reach the brain."

She shook her head in dazed bemusement at Leo being a font of information on her state. "I'm not about to faint," she assured him.

"You don't look good," he said worriedly.

The vivid blue eyes were still projecting caring...*caring for her.* Or was that mixed up with her having his child? With him crouched so near, her heart was pumping too madly for her to think straight.

"I just didn't expect you to make another marriage proposal," she blurted out. "I don't know how to take it."

"It's the logical step in the circumstances," he argued.

Logic had very little to do with feelings, Teri thought. "Are you sure you want this, Leo?" she probed.

"Yes. I see no other way to get things right," he said forcefully, eyes ablaze with intensity of purpose. "We've got to make this a real partnership, Teri, and I promise you I'll pull my weight. If you can bring yourself to meet me halfway, I'm sure we can make it work. For all three of us."

On the principle that where there's a will, there's a way, Teri thought, and the feverish hope pounding through her heart lost its wild momentum. A cold practicality swept the dizziness from her mind. She wondered if a rational commitment to a future together was a better basis for marriage than the rosy expectations that bloomed from a love-based relationship.

She had *believed* in a future with Wayne.

Leo was bluntly proposing they work at it.

Trying to see it from his point of view, Teri figured they had three things going for them—undeniably great sex, a similar taste in food, and a child they both wanted the best for.

The last consideration was by far the most important, obviously the driving force behind the proposal, and Teri was strongly swayed by it, though she couldn't help feeling…let down…by the starkness of Leo's logic. Couldn't he *feel* some personal gratification—apart from getting good sex—in having *her* as his wife?

She wanted to be at least special to the man she married. Did being the mother of his child make her special enough to Leo? It felt *second-hand* to Teri, yet regardless of any failings Leo might have, she did want to keep him in her life. She'd never felt so drawn to anyone else, not even Wayne. And the past month had stamped home that being alone and pregnant and thirty years old was not a happy state.

She took a deep breath and said, ''Maybe it's worth a try.''

''A try?'' Leo jerked up to his full height, anger unfurling, as well. '''A try'?'' he repeated contemptuously. ''What kind of wishy-washy approach is that? I hand you a full-on commitment and you're only prepared to put me on trial?''

Rigid with disgust, he stalked away from her.

Agitated by his negative reaction, Teri stood up to call him back. ''You haven't exactly led up to this proposition, Leo. We might not like living together. There are lots of things to consider.''

''No, there's not!'' He whirled around, jabbing a finger at her. ''There's only one consideration, Teri. Our child. And it's time you started thinking about it instead of pretending it doesn't need any of your attention.''

The criticism rankled. Her chin shot up and a flush of pride burned into her cheeks. ''I have a life, too, Leo.''

''So have I,'' he retorted. ''And I hope to God, you'll have the decency to respect it as I'll respect yours, because our lives have merged, Teri, and there's no going back to being selfishly single. Not if you care about the welfare of our child.''

"Fine!" she snapped, the accusation of selfishness hitting directly on her past experience of him having everything *his* way. Which he seemed to be setting up again. "Then how come I have to move in with you?" she shot at him. "Why don't you move in with me?"

He strode back aggressively as he answered, "Because *my* home is not connected to business premises where you're on call day and night. It has three bedrooms, one of which you can turn into a nursery." He stopped a metre away from her and gestured dismissively at the limited space around where they stood. "And the backyard is much bigger than this one, providing a reasonable playing area."

All cogent points, yet Teri couldn't help resenting his high-handed attitude, judging the issue instead of discussing it with her. "I'd want to see your place for myself before I agree to move into it," she argued.

"Then let's go and settle the question now," he retorted, seizing the initiative with glowering contempt for what he undoubtedly saw as petty arguments.

Furious with him for snatching the moral high ground and making her feel mean, she tersely reminded him, "You realise, of course, you've never invited me into your home before."

"With good reason." His eyes flashed hard suspicion. "Just remember I've never criticised how you've got yourself set up here. Everyone's entitled to their own sense of comfort."

Teri folded her arms and glared at him. "So I'm supposed to just fit in with you, am I? Don't touch anything? Don't change anything?" It was the same old scenario with Leo, and she wasn't about to continue it, not into a marriage. She raised her eyebrows in mocking challenge. "Precisely what was it you said about meeting halfway?"

His eyes narrowed on her belligerent stance. "We accommodate each other. Okay?"

"As long as we have that firm understanding," she agreed.

He heaved a deep sigh, expelling the explosive energy and settling himself into calm logic again. His eyes commanded the same from her as he stated, "I'm not an unreasonable man, Teri. I won't disregard your needs. I don't want mine disregarded, either. If that means compromise, I suggest we do it with as good a grace as we can muster."

"Fair enough," she accepted, her own temper cooling as she realised they had moved several steps forward in their involvement with each other.

Her curiosity was deeply piqued by his reservations in letting her into his home. She had the weird impression he was protecting a vulnerability he didn't want to lay open, and she wondered if he ever actually admitted anyone to his private life. He wasn't doing it for her, she realised. Most probably, he would never have done it for her. It was his child who had broken this barrier…a part of himself he couldn't shut out.

"Are you up to walking three blocks?" he asked bruskly. "I'll call a taxi if…"

"No. A walk will do me good."

"As you wish." He waved her forward to join him.

Teri held her ground. "Just one question first, Leo. How keen will you be on this marriage if our child turns out to be a daughter instead of a son?"

"I'll be giving either one a father who cares enough to provide a family unit for them. Can their mother say as much?"

She held his fierce challenge and threw it back at him. "Oh, their mother cares enough not to land her child in a *dysfunctional* family unit. Which is why we test the ground first, Leo."

His jaw tightened. His gaze raked down to her stomach and back again. "Well, you do hold all the cards, don't you, Teri?" he mocked savagely. "As long as I want my child, you can crack the whip and lay down the law because I have no legal rights. It's a nice little power game...holding off on marriage...seeing how far I'll dance to your tune."

It was like a hard, cold slap in the face, both shocking and highly sobering. She hadn't really stopped to think where he was coming from...a single father without any legal rights to his child...fighting for a foothold in a life she could deny him, simply by virtue of the fact she was the one who'd give birth.

"I wouldn't do that to you, Leo," she blurted out, her heart turning over at how blindly self-centred she had been in her arguments.

His eyes bored into hers, ruthlessly intent on probing her motives. "Then what are you doing, Teri? Why do you keep cutting down my plan for the future? Is your plan so much better, keeping our child to yourself?''

She flushed. ''I don't know. I just don't see it in the same clear-cut way you do. I'm sorry if that offends you. I'm asking you for time. That's all.''

''No. You're asking for more than that. But let me tell you, I'm not elastic you can keep stretching. Every person has a breaking point. You'd better start figuring out what you want because one day you'll have to answer to our child for your decisions.''

He stepped aside, pride and dignity underlining his scorn for her equivocations. ''Perhaps a walk will do us both good,'' he said with very dry irony. ''Ready?''

''Yes.''

She felt so shaken, she had to force her legs forward to fall into step beside him and go where he led. His home would reveal more about him, she thought, grasping at something concrete to hang on to. Leo had shattered her *one day at a time, take it as it comes* plan for dealing with her pregnancy. She couldn't go back to it. Though she couldn't feel comfortable about what he'd draw her into, either.

Would he be a good husband?

A good father?

There were worse things than being a single mother.

She had no real cause not to trust him, Teri reflected, glancing at the plants he'd potted as they passed the trestle table. He'd done that for her because she'd wanted it done. It was a measure of unselfish giving. And she couldn't say he wasn't taking the responsibility of parenthood to heart.

She suspected marriage was the ultimate sacrifice for him, an intrusion on his life he was struggling to tolerate for the sake of having his child. Maybe she should be more prepared to make sacrifices, too. Nothing was achieved without a cost. Certainly the willpower he was pouring into his decision impressed her. Very deeply.

The champagne man was not all fizz.

In fact, compared to Wayne, Leo might very well be a rock of stability. And that was worth having. It was something Teri really wanted in a man, especially in a life partner. It was hard, shouldering all the responsibilities. Another set of shoulders—strong, reliable ones—would make everything much easier. And there was a lot more of Leo she wanted, too, underneath all her fighting words.

She needed to have those critical items firmly imprinted on her mind before she opened her mouth again. Leo's warning felt very ominous. Stretch him too far…and snap! He wasn't made of elastic. No one was. And if inside his current stony exterior beat a good and caring heart, what a fool she'd be to drive him away!

CHAPTER ELEVEN

MARRIAGE!

Leo shook his head, barely able to believe he was fool enough to be fighting for it. Moreover, with a woman who looked like giving him as hard a time as Serena. Though, by God! he wasn't about to be taken for a ride in *this* marriage.

If Teri agreed to it.

Which she ought to, if she had any sense at all.

Having reached the back door to the restaurant kitchen, he paused to let her precede him inside. She flicked a glance at him and her eyes had such a poignant look of vulnerability, he was torn between the urge to wrap her in his arms and promise her she'd be safe in his keeping, and a more savage impulse to shake her into getting her priorities right.

It was perfectly obvious she needed him. But was she fair-minded enough to admit that? No! One look was all it had taken him to know he had to step in and get some appropriate management in place.

Her face was drawn with fatigue, her hair—which she'd always kept stylishly trim—was dull and almost shaggy, and her ignorance about the potting mixture…well, she'd explained that but the explanation itself was a clear manifesto for his intervention.

''Dylan's gone,'' she commented, frowning at the

clean and deserted kitchen. "He should have checked with me before he left."

"He was tidying up when I arrived. Probably didn't want to butt in to say goodbye," Leo excused.

She nodded, still frowning. "I hope he didn't overhear…" She sighed. "I guess they have to know I'm pregnant sooner or later."

The sooner, the better, in Leo's opinion. Then, at least, her staff could be watching out for her. He was sure she'd been on the verge of fainting earlier. He'd speak to Dylan himself about that. Speak to Dylan about more staff, too. The young chef might know someone who could fill in for Teri. Personal knowledge was better than advertising for help. In a small business like this, it was important for everyone to get on well with each other.

He watched Teri lift a key ring from a hook above the kitchen counter and proceed to lock the back door. Her baggy shirt somehow emphasised her fragility. She was losing weight instead of putting it on. When he'd held her close he'd felt the difference, though she'd still felt good. More than good.

As she checked that the lock was activated, his gaze dropped to her delectable backside, remembering the feel of her soft, sexy cheeks. The long shirt covered them, frustrating any visual pleasure, but he still stirred at the memory of how she'd responded to feeling him. At least his bed in this marriage shouldn't be a bargaining couch. No way would he allow it to become one, either!

"Done!" She swung around, and strode off into the dining room, leaving him to follow.

Leo strolled after her, suddenly reminded of the last time Teri had led him to the front door of the restaurant, shutting him out on the street and letting her ex-husband in. A host of highly basic and primitive instincts stirred.

Precisely *what* was Teri's relationship with her ex-husband?

Wayne she'd called him. Wayne with a box of her favourite Belgian chocolates. *Woo the woman,* Mavis had said. Had Wayne come wooing Teri that night? If so, how far had he got?

Teri was a very sexy woman. What's more, she enjoyed sex. She'd cut him off that night and he'd been in New Zealand for three weeks before that. It was nine weeks in all since they'd last gone to bed together. But surely she wouldn't...not with her *ex.*

She unlocked the front door and held it open for him to go out ahead of her. Leo swiftly noted there was no one lingering on the sidewalk this afternoon. All the same, he didn't move far, making sure Teri stepped out after her.

He watched her lock up again, brooding over the way she had welcomed Wayne. *Old friends.* If they were such good old friends, how come they weren't still married?

Which raised other prickly questions.

The pregnancy had been an accident. Teri wasn't keen on marrying him, despite his being the father of their child. Was she still hankering for her ex, wanting a second chance at marriage with him?

Leo didn't care for that thought at all.

Not one bit.

Having finished locking up, Teri pocketed the key ring and offered him a wry little smile. "So...lead me to your cave, Leo."

"Right!" he growled. "And you can tell me about Wayne on the way!"

CHAPTER TWELVE

TERI was wishing she'd taken the time to change her gardening clothes for something that matched up to Leo's smart casual attire. Having Wayne's name thrown at her wiped out the self-conscious feeling of looking frumpy. Her mind was jolted into a highly embarrassed recollection of shuttling Leo off in favour of her ex-husband's company, right here in this doorway.

"I'm sorry..." The words spilled out before she had time to formulate more.

Leo's eyebrows beetled down. "What for?"

"Using Wayne to...to..."

"To get rid of me?" he finished harshly.

"There's a...a comfort in old familiarity when you're in turmoil, Leo," she hastily explained.

"Uh-huh." His eyes grimly assessed her embarrassment. Then in a dry, sardonic tone, he commented, "I'd find no comfort whatsoever in my ex-wife's company. But perhaps your divorce was more amicable."

"Yes. I mean...I don't know about yours. Wayne and I...it was better for both of us to separate. But we still wish each other well."

"Very civilised."

The remark had a sour note to it that churned up Teri's stomach. She remembered Wayne's opinion that Leo had been lethally jealous. She hadn't believed it at the time, thinking a lacerated ego far more likely, not to mention sexual frustration. Jealousy implied more caring than Leo had ever shown her. Though he had bought her the Escada sunglasses. In fact, he'd always been nice to her, made her feel good about herself for the most part. And today...

"We go this way," he said, a flick of his hand indicating direction as he set off, turning up Elizabeth Street towards Oxford.

There was no taking her arm. No catching her hand. He assumed she'd accompany him since she'd agreed to it and Teri did so, but she was acutely conscious of his choice to walk apart. She would have liked some touching, a semblance of togetherness. The question of how much he cared kept tormenting her.

"Do you want to get back together with Wayne?"

The terse question startled her into glancing sharply at him, but he was looking straight ahead, his expression closed to her. *Was* he jealous?

"No. Not in any intimate sense," she assured him, hoping he wasn't imagining she'd had sex with her ex. "That's just not on, Leo," she stated emphatically.

"But you don't mind him visiting you."

That night was certainly sticking in Leo's craw. In all fairness, Teri couldn't blame him for thinking the worst. Playing one man off against another wasn't smart, and she'd really had no cause to do it to Leo. An explanation was due, particularly in these circumstances.

"Wayne usually drops in on me whenever he comes home from wherever he's been. It amounts to once or twice a year and is more or less a catch-up visit on where we are now. A guilt thing, as well, for walking out on our marriage. He checks to see I'm okay."

"He walked out?"

Leo halted, just as they were about to round the corner into Oxford Street. He turned to her and it was like being hit by a paralysing electric charge. Teri's feet stopped dead. Her heart contracted. She had always been aware of an energy force in Leo, a magnetism she'd been drawn to, despite knowing he wasn't seriously engaged with her.

The voltage was suddenly immeasurably stronger and harder-edged, and she had an instant memory flash of him coming towards her in the backyard, a warrior intent on blasting any opposition, very seriously engaged in achieving his purpose.

"Let me get this straight," he aimed directly at her, his eyes scouring hers for hidden traps. "Wayne walked out on your marriage and you still welcome him with open arms?"

Teri took a deep breath, needing to get some oxygen back in her brain. She tried to review what she'd said and belatedly realised it must have sounded inconsistent to Leo. To his mind, it didn't add up, which meant she was *lying* to him and he didn't like it.

He wanted honesty. He'd demanded it of her over the sexual issue and was pushing for it now over Wayne. It was a case of stand and deliver or else! No equivocation. He might want marriage for the sake of their child but he wasn't about to tolerate any two-timing from her.

Which meant he cared about what kind of relationship they'd have, too. Good sex wasn't enough for him. He wanted more. Respect and trust. Both of which were important to her, as well. Conscious of laying a foundation for their possible future together, Teri decided to hold nothing back, even though it meant revealing failures she preferred to forget.

"Wayne and I go back a long way, Leo. We lived in the same neighbourhood as kids. He was always in and out of our house with my brothers. They were best friends. We grew up together, went out together, eventually had sex together. It was the accepted thing that we'd get married. Which we did. Too young to know any better."

"But you must have known each other well," he said, frowning over the scenario she'd drawn.

"I guess there are always two sides of a coin," she answered ruefully. "Wayne has a winning, easy-going charm. It's almost impossible not to like him. But he's a natural born lily of the field. He believes something will always turn up for him instead of working hard at it."

"That didn't sit well with you?" he asked assessingly.

She shrugged. "I'm a natural born worrier. I try to manage things. Which was impossible with Wayne. Money slid through his fingers. Budgeting was an alien word to him. Trying to get him to take responsibility for anything was…well, it was easier to do it myself."

Leo grunted, his eyes flickering slightly as though he'd been plagued by the same experience. The force-field he'd generated eased and there was a less confrontational, more sympathetic air about him as he asked, "How long did you stay together?"

"Three years." Encouraged by the feeling he was really listening, Teri explained further. "Wayne was a guitarist in a band which he always reckoned would make the big time, given a lucky break, but the break never came and the band gradually drifted apart. I'd worked my way up from waitress to managing the kitchen in the local club and I wanted Wayne to get a regular job and settle down. When I talked about getting some security so we could eventually start a family, I think Wayne saw it as four walls closing in on him."

"So he opted for freedom."

"Yes. Basically, we wanted different things out of life. It hurt at the time. I'd invested so much of myself in trying to make things work between us, and then I had to face up to the fact it was hurting both of us, turning me into a nag filled up with frustration, making Wayne feel pressured beyond his capacity to deliver what I wanted of him."

Leo nodded, understanding evident in the softening of his eyes.

Teri flashed him a wry smile. "Which hardly recommends me as a wife, does it?"

His mouth twitched. "Pressure I can handle and security I can deliver. Which makes me an eminently suitable husband for you, wouldn't you say?"

Having neatly sidelined those possible arguments

against their marriage and jettisoned his suspicions about Wayne, Leo exuded the confidence of a conqueror as he tucked her arm around his and proceeded to escort her down Oxford Street.

The man in possession, Teri thought giddily, swamped by the sense that Leo Kingston was not to be shaken from any purpose he set his mind on. It was not surprising he had built himself a successful business. She had been wrong to name him the champagne man, though he could still inject an exciting fizz in her blood.

A lovely warm haze spread through her mind, seductively whispering she could lean on him, be carried along by him, and she'd be safe because he could be counted upon to support her and their child. He was strong and determined and he knew where he was going. Not like Wayne. Not like Wayne at all.

Ahead of them customers of the Kitty O'Shea Hotel had spilled out onto the pavement and it was evident from their raucous voices and unsteady behaviour they'd probably been drinking for hours. It was a popular pub on Sunday afternoons, featuring a live band playing Irish songs, and while the mood of these beer-swilling patrons was definitely merry, not aggressive, Leo smoothly changed position, sliding behind her to take her other arm and place himself between her and any unwelcome attention.

Nothing was said. Nothing untoward happened as they passed by. Yet Teri was intensely conscious of the protection Leo had instinctively given her. Once they were clear of the rowdy mob, he moved back to take the side closer to the street traffic again. It was nice to be looked after, Teri thought, and pride in her independence took another tumble.

Maybe it was general fatigue, or the extra responsibility of her pregnancy, or the loneliness of always having to look out for herself, but the appeal of having a strong capable man at her side struck deep. It wasn't until he led her into Jersey Road that it occurred to Teri she should question Leo about his marriage. Why hadn't *it* been given the full-on commitment he was promising her?

"What happened to your first marriage?" she bluntly asked, glancing at his face to watch his response.

There was a slight tightening of his jaw, a flash of derision from his eyes. "Your rolling stone ex-husband wasn't keen on gathering moss but my ex-wife was intent on gathering all the moss she could get before letting me know she had no intention of honouring her promises."

The acid comment clearly rose from a deep residue of bitterness. No one liked being used, Teri thought, or abused. She began to get a glimmering of why Leo had kept his distance, limiting their relationship to brief bouts of mutual enjoyment where nothing really was asked of either of them. No promises given. None to be honoured or not honoured. Which was precisely why his proposal of marriage had come as such a shock to her.

"Why did you marry her?" she asked.

"Oh, I was totally infatuated at the time," he answered self-mockingly. "And flattered, I suppose."

"Flattered?" Teri queried.

"Serena exuded class and style and winning her seemed like part of the success package. Which she pushed relentlessly after we were married. The right clothes, the right jewellery, the right house, the right vacations, the right social circle…''

The cynicism in his voice eased the little stab of inferiority Teri felt at his first words. The ''right' image had clearly lost any importance to Leo though the *Escada* sunglasses undoubtedly reflected his *training* in designer wear by the svelte and sophisticated Serena. Nevertheless, Teri couldn't help wondering if Leo's dalliance with herself was a backlash, considering she worked in the service industry and couldn't remotely be connected to *class*.

Wouldn't marriage to her be perceived as a comedown?

How would she be received by his friends and family?

Had Leo thought this through?

In increasing mental agitation, Teri thought of her own family who formed the core of what little social life she had. Her father was a builder and her two brothers had also gone into trade, one a plumber, the other an electrician. They all ran successful businesses and their wives helped with the office work. They were good, down-to-earth people, open to lending a hand to anyone, giving their time freely to help her set up her restaurant. But they were no more ''classy'' than she was.

Her stomach started curdling as she recalled Leo had never invited her out in public with him, never introduced her to anyone. *Food and sex…*her own refrain came back to haunt her. It took considerable willpower to force it aside, arguing fiercely to herself that Leo had asked her to marry him, and other things had to be more important to him than class, like honesty and integrity. Which reminded her...

"What promises didn't your ex-wife honour?" she blurted out, her inner battle so intense she couldn't look at him this time. She fastened her gaze on the line of trees they were walking under along the sidewalk of Jersey Road, well-clipped trees for a well-kept street in "classy" Woollahra.

Leo gave a harsh little laugh. "After stringing me along for three years and conning me into buying a luxury family home, she finally told me she didn't intend to have children. Not my child nor anyone else's."

His child!

Dear God! She'd got so hung up on her own insecurities, she'd forgotten the most critical point of all!

The importance of her pregnancy to him was suddenly heart-sickeningly clear. No wonder he'd been concerned about her carrying it through, wanting repeated assurances that she didn't have a termination in mind. *She* was having the child his wife had cheated him out of and if he had to marry her to ensure his paternal rights to his son or daughter, that was what he was going to do, come hell or high water!

The chicken had come first in his other marriage.

In this one, the egg had it, never mind the chicken who was going to bear it.

"Here we are," he said, steering her towards an ornate lace ironwork gate at the end of ornate lace ironwork fence which fronted a terrace house with pristine and correct period paintwork—a recently renovated state of the art terrace house in fashionable Woollahra with a much wider frontage than most.

It shouted *money.*

It shouted *class.*

Leo opened the gate for her.

Teri paused, wondering if she should go forward. Leo certainly wanted his child in his life but what about her? She'd only been good for food and sex until now. And company, she quickly tagged on, remembering Leo's words. Undemanding company. He had *liked* being with her. But she'd been something separate from his real life, not an integral part of it. Relaxation when he needed it.

"Teri…" he prompted.

It jerked her gaze to his and her fears and uncertainties rushed off her tongue. "Am I welcome in your home, Leo? Will you hate me being there?"

CHAPTER THIRTEEN

SHE was frightened.

Leo recoiled from this view of himself. Instinctively his hand lifted and touched her cheek to soothe, to impart reassurance.

"It's okay. Of course you're welcome. We've come to see if you like it, remember?" he pressed, his mind zipping through a fast replay, seeking reasons for her fear.

She bit her bottom lip and her lashes swept down, evading his probing gaze. Defensive.

He suddenly realised that all Teri's arguments against him and what he'd laid out were defensive. Maybe it wasn't him frightening her so much as the thought of being married again, thrust into a full involvement that demanded so much more than an affair.

He wasn't overly keen on that himself, but he wasn't *frightened!* He'd deal with whatever came, one way or another. Once a choice was made, he always followed through. But maybe she was feeling trapped, being pregnant with his child. One thing he was certain of, she hadn't tried to trap him. No deceit from her, either.

"Tell me what's troubling you," he urged, wanting to fix it if he could. He slid his hand to her chin, gently tilting it up, needing a response.

115

''I feel…like an intruder.'' She raised clouded eyes to him. ''This is your place. If you thought I'd fit, you'd have asked me before, Leo.''

His remarks about his home…judging her by Serena's attitudes…Damn! He shouldn't have done that. Teri was different. She'd never asked him for anything. Probably because her useless ex-husband had never come good with anything. She'd simply accepted what was readily given, and if he faced the truth squarely, she'd given more than he had, letting him into her private space, always hospitable.

''It wasn't that you didn't fit,'' he explained earnestly, moving both his hands to her shoulders to draw her into following his reasoning. ''In a way, I've been reclaiming my life after Serena got through with it, and part of that was arranging everything to suit myself. Now it's time to rearrange. And I'd rather do it with you than any other woman I've known.''

She focused sharply on him. ''Truly?''

He frowned at her insecurity on that point. Surely she realised…no, how could she? He'd held off too long, having had no understanding of where she'd been coming from. All the same, how he'd felt about her still held true.

''I did tell you at the beginning, finding you was like winning the lottery,'' he recalled, hoping to ease her concerns. ''That hasn't changed.''

She flushed. ''That was after sex, Leo.''

''No. The sex we had together affirmed it. What really got to me was…there you were, an absolute knockout, and not once did you use your body as a weapon.''

"A weapon?"

He couldn't help smiling at her incredulity. "Never a sign of it, and believe me, that's rare. It's what kept me coming back…the straight give and take. If we can keep that going, I'll count myself a very lucky man to have you as my wife."

And that was a fair statement, he thought, given that he'd committed himself to marrying her.

"Lucky," she repeated dazedly, as though she found it hard to believe.

"It's true. I wouldn't lie to you," he insisted.

"No," she agreed waveringly.

"And I promise you here and now, I'll give you much more of real substance than a sweetening up box of Belgian chocolates."

She heaved a big sigh and managed a shaky little smile.

Confident that he'd beaten off the spectre of her ex-husband's failings, and determined to make Teri feel welcome in his home, he slid an arm around her shoulders and drew her through the gateway, kicking the gate shut behind them.

"You might find my furnishings a bit sparse," he warned, remembering the homely clutter of her apartment above the restaurant. "You can add stuff of your own if you like."

As long as she didn't want to change what he had, Leo thought with a twinge of uneasiness. He kept that reservation to himself as he fished the key out of his pocket. There was no point in jumping fences until they came to them. Teri might like his taste in furniture.

He opened the door and took the next step, resolved on keeping an open mind. Changes would have to be made for the baby anyway. He smiled wryly to himself. When it came right down to it, a man would do anything for his child.

CHAPTER FOURTEEN

TERI did her best to hang on to the assurances Leo had given as he ushered her into his home, but she was instantly attuned to the uneasiness behind the cheerful note in his voice.

"This slate runs through the hall, the dining room, kitchen and laundry. It's a great colour. Hardly shows any dirt."

The floor actually looked spotless, the blue-green shades in the slate glowing from a charcoal background.

"Not that it's dirty," Leo hastily added. "I have a cleaner come through once a week to keep everything right."

Of course. A cleaner. A small cost compared to what had been spent on this place. "She does a good job," Teri murmured, concentrating hard on taking in her surroundings and trying not to feel nervous about the evidence of big money. Leo apparently took it for granted. He wasn't pushing it in her face.

The hall was wide enough to accommodate a staircase as well as easy passage past it. The light from the glass panes in the front door and the window above it prevented the area from being gloomy although all the colourings were on the dark side. The wooden banister had a black lacquered finish. The stairs were covered with a thickly woven burgundy carpet. A teal wallpaper with a silky sheen covered the lower third of the walls. This was topped by a border design in teal and burgundy and white, and above it a striped wallpaper in the same colours extended to a white ceiling.

"Last house I owned was decorated in cream and pastels," Leo remarked with a telling grimace. "Nightmare of a place to live in. It was shoes off at the door in case you might soil its pristine state. No problem with that here."

"Slate is serviceable," Teri agreed, having the weird feeling he wanted her approval, though why she couldn't imagine. The fantastic quality of colour in the slate had to put it out of the range of most people's pockets.

"I reckon this wallpaper won't show grubby little fingermarks, either," he said eagerly.

"It's very classy." The comment slipped out before she could catch it back, though it wasn't a criticism and it could hardly be called an offensive remark.

"But it's vinyl. Easy to wash," he pressed.

Teri's apprehension eased. Leo seemed more concerned with practicality than class. Still, she felt it important to find out how much stylish things meant to him. "Did you choose this wallpaper yourself?"

"No. The colour scheme came with the house. It did help sell it to me, though. Everything looked touchable. Even the carpet isn't the kind to show up wine stains or other accidental spillages."

Everyone is entitled to their own sense of comfort...that was what this house was about to Leo.

Nothing more, nothing less. Everything he was saying revealed a reaction against living with an obsessively house-proud wife who had maintained a cream-and-pastel showplace without any consideration to *his comfort*.

The realisation brought a huge wave of relief to Teri. She didn't want to be afraid of touching or damaging anything, either. "It all goes so well together," she said admiringly.

"You like it then?" he asked anxiously.

"Whoever made the choices did a wonderful job."

He smiled, pleased or relieved by her response. "Same carpet and wallpaper in the lounge room," he said opening a door to their right.

She stepped in and immediately noticed that most of the wall between the lounge room and the dining room beyond it had been knocked out, opening up the whole area. A combustion heater, set against the far wall, probably warmed up the entire lower floor in winter. Her father swore by combustion heaters, always trying to persuade people to build them into their homes, but the mess of feeding wood in deterred some. Leo clearly didn't mind a bit of mess. Comfort came first.

He also fancied black leather, probably for the same practical reasons. The dining-room chairs were upholstered in it and so were a big squishy sofa and two huge armchairs, one of which was set slightly askew with a deeply cushioned footstool in front of it. Following the direction in which it was pointed, Teri glanced over her shoulder and saw a huge black television set dominating one corner of the wall that faced onto the front porch. Its screen was at least four times the size of hers.

She shook her head in amazement as she turned to get the full effect. "That must be fantastic for watching sport."

"You watch sport?"

The sharp question was instantly intimidating. Was he terribly high-brow in his choice of programs? It brought home to Teri how little they knew about each other. However, there was no point in pretence. Best to sort out their differences right now. She took a deep breath and swung to face him.

"The lot," she confessed. "Football, cricket, tennis...there's very little other conversation in my family, I'm afraid. Both my older brothers and my Dad are sport fanatics and I was brought up with all of it. Besides," She shrugged. "I enjoy it."

His face broke into a happy grin. "Great! That's another thing we share." He took her hand, his fingers threading through hers in a possessive grip that shot electric tingles up her arm. "We're going to do fine together, Teri," he declared with ringing confidence, and the champagne fizzed into her blood again.

"Come and see my table," he invited, his eyes twinkling wickedly as he drew her with him into the dining room. "I saw it in a display window and it appealed to the animal in me."

"Panthers!" she gasped in amazement.

It was a glass table. Underneath it, supporting it, were two white rocks, one with a panther and its cub sitting on it, the other with a panther climbing up it.

"It's fantastic, Leo! I love it!"

"Yeah," he drawled happily. "Only piece of furniture I've ever felt I had to have.''' He rapped the glass top with his knuckles. "This is squash court strength. Won't break. Won't mark. You just wipe everything off and it's as good as new again."

The table and eight chairs sat on a rug that was abstractly patterned in burgundy and teal and grey and pink. "I love the rug, too," Teri said with sincere enthusiasm. "It's perfect."

"I was lucky there. It was part of the display. I just bought the lot."

Teri felt a stab of envy. To feel so free with money was simply not part of her experience. She'd had to budget all her working life and most of her furniture in both the restaurant and apartment was second-hand.

"Do you do much entertaining, Leo?" she asked, gesturing at the eight chairs, still feeling wary about the social aspects of his life.

"Quite a bit, business-wise, but not here. I can't cook well enough." His eyes flirted with hers. "I reckon you could help me out with that, Teri. If you'd like."

She couldn't help laughing at him. "Maybe," she answered, her confidence lifting with his easy acceptance of her being able to partner him.

"The way you work your customers at the restaurant…you're a natural hostess," he declared admiringly.

Now he was really making her feel good. "Thank you."

Leo virtually breezed through showing her the rest of the ground floor, relaxed, genial, charming, just as he'd always been with her during their affair, and Teri found herself almost dizzy with the pleasure of it. Besides, it was a great house. There was absolutely nothing she didn't like.

The kitchen was a dream, polished green granite on the benchtops, plenty of cupboard space, every modern facility, including a large, double-sided refrigerator. Beyond that was a well-equipped laundry, a small toilet, and built onto the original structure was an extra room which Leo used as an office.

The backyard was beautifully paved with brick tiles set in a herringbone pattern and fully grown gardens along the fence; fern trees, palms, ivies, and other exotic shrubs making it a lovely leafy haven. Two dark green aluminium chairs and a matching table provided an outdoor setting for breakfast in the morning sunshine.

"I've only furnished the one bedroom upstairs," Leo informed her, the male *animal* in him simmering in very bright blue eyes as he led her back inside. "You can do what you like with the others," he added, carelessly granting her carte blanche at this point.

He was assuming she *was* going to move in here and marry him and Teri didn't correct him. She couldn't even summon up some caution. All she could think of was the bed in the bedroom and how much she wanted to be in Leo's arms again, kissing, touching, drowning in the sexual chemistry that was alive and sizzling between them, now that other issues had lost their divisive force.

Her heart was galloping as he directed her to go

ahead of him down the hall to the staircase. She felt his gaze burning through her clothes. The wanting was very definitely mutual. It seemed to thicken the very air she was trying to breathe. A tremulous excitement ran down her legs as she reached the foot of the stairs and she grabbed the banister to steady herself on the upward climb.

The doorbell rang.

Teri almost jumped out of her skin. The sound was so harsh and discordant, breaking the fine tension running between them. Her gaze jerked to Leo who'd paused adjacent to her, on the other side of the banister. He frowned at the front door, vexed by the untimeliness of the visitor.

"Expecting anyone?" Teri asked.

"No."

The bell was activated again, suggesting urgency or impatience.

"I'd better see who it is," Leo growled. His eyes flashed her a look of hot command. "Wait here. I won't be a minute."

Teri took a deep breath as he strode to the door, very much in panther mode. Leo was primed to pounce, no doubt about it. And she couldn't deny her own eagerness to be pounced upon. It had been two months since they'd last shared a bed and her whole body was tingling with anticipation, yearning for the magic Leo could weave through it.

He opened the door.

A woman fell on him.

"Thank God you're here!" she sobbed, flinging her arms around his neck, and hanging on like a cling-

ing vine. ''I didn't know where to go, who to turn
to…''

''What the hell!'' Leo tried to pluck her off him,
then stopped, staring in shock at her face. ''You've
been assaulted?''

Teri couldn't see. From where she stood, a long
silky fall of gleaming ash-blonde hair hid any damage.

''He hit me and hit me,'' the woman moaned.
''And the cabbie wants to be paid. I have no money,
Leo.''

''Hey, mate!'' a loud aggressive voice called from
the street. ''Are you gonna pay like the lady said…or
what?''

''Be right there!'' Leo shouted, then turned sharply
to Teri. ''Will you take her into the lounge room and
sit her down while I pay the fare?''

''Sure!'' she answered, though the hostile look she
got from the woman whose notice was now drawn to
her didn't invite help, and the moment Leo removed
his support to go outside, her weak, shaken state made
a remarkable recovery.

What would normally be a strikingly beautiful face
was marred by an eye that was puffing up for a mon-
ster bruise and a lower lip that was split and swollen.
The injuries were quite shocking and if she'd continued to weep and wail, Teri's natural kindness might
have been tapped.

However, once Leo's back was turned, the woman
swung her silky blonde hair over her shoulder and
struck a model pose for Teri's benefit, and the rest of
her showed no damage whatsoever from being

mugged, apart from her mushroom pink silk blouse being unbuttoned enough and disarranged to show heaving cleavage. The figure-hugging crepe skirt in the same colour was astonishingly free of creases or smudges. The matching designer shoes were not the least bit scuffed and there didn't appear to be any runs in the smooth sheen of her stockings.

The damsel in distress, despite what pain she was feeling, eyed Teri's checked shirt and baggy jeans with distaste. "You must be the cleaner or gardener," she said snootily.

Teri fought down a flush of anger, stepping over to the lounge room door since the woman certainly didn't require *her* support in moving on her own two perfectly shod feet. "You can sit down in here," she said with an invitational wave. This was Leo's business, not hers, and she determined to stay right out of it until she learned what it was about.

But she didn't like this woman and she fiercely hated the thought that Leo was involved with her in any way. Despite the black eye in the making and the split lip, Teri's sympathy was not the least bit engaged as the woman swept past her and sailed into Leo's lounge room as though she had the right to intrude as she pleased.

Treating Teri's presence as irrelevant, she took one look at the television set and muttered, "Gross." Then her good eye fell on the heater. "Ugly." She huffed her disgust at these items and settled herself on the leather sofa, her legs gracefully disposed to show off the curve of hip and thigh, the blouse gaping seductively open.

Using her body as a weapon, Teri thought, and hoped Leo recognised it, too, since he was the one who'd given her the insight into this type of female manoeuvring. His initial reaction—to remove himself from her clutches—might have been because he was conscious of Teri witnessing it all. If he'd been alone, and not hot for sex with her...he certainly knew this woman. Which was a worry.

The drama queen tested the cushioning on the wide armrest of the sofa with her elbow, then cupped the bruised side of her face with her hand so that she looked appropriately doleful for the man she was targeting. Having set the scene to her satisfaction, she deigned to notice Teri again.

"I don't need you," she said in pettish dismissal.

"I'll just hold a watching brief," Teri said dryly.

Ignoring the baleful glare this comment evoked, she strolled past the sofa and sat down on Leo's footstool. Her gaze fell on a pile of magazines stacked on the glass-topped coffee-table beside her. *Having A Baby* was printed across the top one and underneath that caption, *Pregnancy Week By Week.* This had to be Leo's source of information.

"I said I don't need you. I want to be alone with Leo," her antagonist stated haughtily.

"He might not want to be alone with you," Teri retorted, fed up with the put-downs. She wasn't shifting until she knew what the situation was. After all, she was the invited one. Let Leo make his choice on whom he wanted with him.

"I won't discuss my private business in front of a stranger," came the next snipe.

"As far as I'm concerned, you're the stranger," Teri stated coolly.

"Which is all you know," the woman scoffed. "Leo and I go back a long way."

"I see. So you feel you can run to him for help when you get beaten up by another man."

A look of icy disdain was undoubtedly designed to freeze Teri off.

It didn't work.

She returned a look of blatant scepticism as she probed further. "Somehow I get the feeling you're not here for tea and sympathy. I take it the current boyfriend has struck out and Leo's your fallback."

"At least he's not a violent pig like Edward," she flashed out, before remembering Teri was not an appropriate person for such confidences. She immediately constructed another icy glare. "Would you please have the decency to make yourself scarce."

And leave the field free for her to climb all over Leo again? Not in a million years! The urge to torpedo this woman's act rose and fed off the snubs that had been handed out, gathering a momentum that couldn't be stopped.

"Actually," Teri drawled, "I was just about to go to bed with Leo when you interrupted. It would be much more pleasing to me if you made yourself scarce."

"In your dreams," the blonde jeered. "Leo wouldn't sink so low."

That stung. And the fact she was so sure of herself stung. "We've been lovers for the past year," Teri shot back at her, wanting to salvage her sense of superiority.

Her mouth compressed. As much as it could with a swollen lip. Her good eye glittered with malevolent fury. When she spoke it was with cutting contempt. "Do you imagine that means anything, you stupid little slut? You'll only make a fool of yourself if you do. You're completely out of his class."

"I don't think so," Teri said with more pride than belief.

"You might be a good lay but I'm the woman he married. Within three months of meeting, I might add. Now how do you measure up to that?"

For a moment, Teri's mind boggled.

This was the ex-wife?

"You're divorced!" she blurted out, recoiling from the thought that Leo had chosen this style of woman as his partner.

She smirked. "I know him so well I can correct that mistake."

Was it possible? Teri couldn't bear the thought. Yet if Serena worked on his protective instincts, made her body available, as was only too obvious...

But she wasn't pregnant with his child!

"You're too late!" Teri said in a burst of primitive satisfaction.

"Don't be absurd! I can make mincemeat of you."

"I'm having Leo's child."

"What?"

"You heard me. I'm the mother of his child. And nothing you say or do is going to change that!" She picked up the baby magazine and tossed it onto the sofa. "Read and weep, Serena."

She stared at the cover of the magazine, her smug composure cracking into ugly frustration.

"And what's more, Leo and I were planning our marriage when you so rudely interrupted," Teri stated, wanting to nail home her position in Leo's life.

Venom spat at her. "You calculating little bitch! You think you've got him. Well, let me tell you all you've got is a backlash from his marriage to me."

Footsteps in the hall.

"You're always going to live in my shadow," Serena hissed.

Leo strode into the lounge room, anger blazing from him. His vivid blue eyes lasered into Teri's. "Has she told you what this is about?"

"It's personal. Someone called Edward inflicted the damage."

"Leo, I can't go back to him," came the pitiful plea from the sofa.

He swung towards his ex-wife. "On your feet, Serena! The cab's waiting. The driver's been paid to take you wherever you want...hospital, police station, a friend's place, back to where he picked you up. I don't care. Just get out of my life and stay out!"

She rose from the sofa to a mocking provocative stance. "Such violent feelings, Leo! Nice to know you're not indifferent to me."

Having delivered her poisonous exit line she sashayed out of the lounge room, disdaining even a glance at Teri.

"I'll see that she goes," Leo said, emitting ruthless purpose as he followed her out.

A minute or two later, the front door was shut and Leo was more in control of himself when he returned. Teri hadn't moved. She felt displaced, and wondered if this was how Leo had felt when Wayne had turned up. It was not a good feeling.

"That was my ex...my very *ex*-wife," Leo informed her, grating out the words.

"Yes, I know," Teri replied quietly. "She told me."

He scanned her eyes in anxious concern. "Don't let anything she said upset you, Teri. She's a liar and a manipulator. God knows how she thought she was going to use me after all this time, but the cabbie told me she was as cool as a cucumber coming here. No tears at all."

Teri sighed to relieve the tightness in her chest. Whether Serena could have used him or not, some things she'd said had struck true. *The backlash*...this house...the opposite of a cream and pastel place, just as she was the opposite of the cream and pastel woman who'd so smugly represented a different class...and Leo tying himself to her for the sake of the child his wife wouldn't give him.

"Put her out of your mind, Teri," Leo urged, coming to take her hands and pull her off the footstool. "Let's get back to us."

The warmth he projected took some of the chill out of her mind. And there was caring in his eyes. Caring for her. She craved that from him, so much her heart was quivering from the touch of it.

"You were going to show me upstairs," she said. *The bedroom.*

The reminder brought instant ignition. Desire surged into his eyes and Teri didn't care if it was fueled by the need to wipe out Serena's disruptive visit. It was directed at her and she needed Leo to hold her, to warm her all over, to make her feel wanted for herself.

"Upstairs," he repeated. "As I said, you can have a free hand there, Teri. Come and tell me what you'd like."

Free... was there such a thing as real freedom, Teri wondered as she followed him. If she did tie herself to Leo, would she ever feel free of Serena's shadow? Could the child she was carrying make it go away?

CHAPTER FIFTEEN

IT FELT different. Right from the start it felt different. Leo, drawing her gently into his embrace, kissing her forehead, holding her close, just holding her as though he needed her warmth seeping into him, needed to feel the flesh and blood reality of her, his cheek rubbing over her hair, his mouth whispering in her ear.

"Is this okay with you, Teri?"

He'd never asked before, never shown any uncertainty over the strength of the desire coursing between them. It wasn't really a hesitation, more a caring about her feelings, beyond the physical readiness to respond.

"Yes," she answered, comforted by his embrace. It was nice just to rest her head on his broad shoulder, to breathe him in and wallow in the sense of Leo wanting to look after her.

"Just to get things straight," he murmured, "I am totally indifferent to Serena. I was angry that she came here. Angry that she even thought I could be used again. There's no way. No way at all, Teri. It's over. Like it is with you and Wayne."

"Mmmh..."

She sighed and turned her head to press her lips to the side of his neck. She didn't want to talk about his ex-wife. Nor her ex-husband. What Leo meant was it was impossible to go back. Whatever good had been there was irrecoverable. But it wasn't over. There *were* shadows, both on his side and hers. She wanted a man she could lean on, rely on. He wanted...not to be tricked.

His fingers threaded through her hair and gently tugged her head back. He kissed her, not hungrily, not passionately, more as though he was slowly relishing and deeply valuing every nuance of her openly given response. Then he tucked her head under his chin and heaved a big sigh.

"You're a great woman, Teri. And don't think I don't appreciate the person you are," he said fervently. "It's not just good sex. I've always liked being with you."

Because it had always been easy, she thought. But that time was gone, too, and it was up to them to take it from here. "I missed you," she confessed.

"Me, too. Thought of you every day. You and the baby."

His child...

"Am I holding you too tight?" He loosened his embrace. "Are your breasts still tender?"

Caring for her...

She smiled up at him. "It's okay. They're just a bit tight. I think they've got bigger."

He smiled back, bedroom mischief in his eyes. "Let me see."

With slow, teasing deliberation, he removed her shirt and bra and made his own assessment, measuring with soft circular caresses, exquisitely exciting, arousing urgent surges of need, a hot, heavy dragging feeling rushing to her loins.

"They're beautiful, Teri," he said in such a warm, loving tone, she couldn't hold back her desire for him.

"I want you, Leo. Now. Please?"

One look in her eyes and there were no more words to be said. A far more primitive communication held sway. It took only a few seconds to discard their clothes. They tumbled onto the bed, Teri wrapped her legs around him and Leo burst into her. She arched, her inner muscles gripping him possessively and into her mind came a wild pagan chant...*Mine, mine, mine...*

And the chant went on and on to the beat of his body reaching into hers. She stroked his legs with her feet, goading him into a faster, rougher rhythm. She clawed his back, digging into his skin, wanting him to belong to her so fiercely, it consumed every cell of her being. There was no room for doubts or fears about the future, no room for shadows from the past, only an overwhelming drive to seal a togetherness, a bonding that shut everything and everyone else out.

Whether Leo shared the same feeling she didn't know, but even after they'd both climaxed, he moved them into a position where he could still hold himself inside her, and when he stirred again, which happened faster than it had ever done before, he heaved her over on top of him, and his eyes glittered intense satisfaction as he watched her take her pleasure, helping her, drawing her into a wildly voluptuous indulgence of every possible sense of having him, feeling him, holding him, controlling everything until control was irretrievably lost and she collapsed onto him and there was only outside contact, heated skin against heated skin.

Still it felt wonderful with Leo clasping her close to him, kissing and fondling, and if it wasn't exactly *making love,* there was a lot to be said for this deep physical intimacy, the harmonious humming of bodies so completely sensitised to each other. The possessive pounding in her mind had stopped, but she marvelled at how strong it had been, strong and foolish. Impossible to own anyone. There was only sharing when both people wanted to. Like this.

The light from the window was fading. She smiled to herself over Leo's choice of furnishing the bedroom closest to the top of the stairs for himself rather than taking up the master suite at the front of the house. Convenience came first with him. Though he'd made it very comfortable, too, installing a queen-size bed with a lovely soft duvet and big pillows. She wouldn't mind sleeping in it. A bathroom was right next door. No problem getting to it in a hurry.

She was glad the burgundy carpet hadn't extended into the bedrooms. The light blue-grey colour in all three rooms was a nice change. And the walls were painted white. Which made it easy to furnish a nursery with pink or blue things...if she did end up marrying Leo. It would certainly give their child a lot of advantages, more than she could ever probably afford herself.

Rosy dreams, she told herself. It was all too easy to drift into them, being with Leo like this, contentedly intertwined, touching without any of the inhibitions that came into play outside the bedroom. Teri

was only too aware that what happened outside the
bedroom affected what happened inside it. Towards
the end of her marriage to Wayne, there'd been very
little desire left for any sex at all.

"Have you tried eating a dry biscuit before you get
up in the morning?" Leo suddenly asked.

"No."

He rolled her onto her back and propped himself
on his side. "It's supposed to help settle your stomach. Ginger and lemon are suggested, too," he said
seriously.

"Okay. I'll try it." A ginger snap was a dry biscuit,
one of her favourites, too, but sucking lemons was
definitely out.

Leo grinned at her and spread his hand over her
stomach. "I bet you don't even know how big he is
right now."

"He?"

"She...whatever. Our baby."

He said it so fatuously, Teri couldn't help grinning
back at him. "How big?"

"About the size of a strawberry."

"That small?" She was surprised.

"Uh-huh. But already he's got all his main organs
formed and his arms and legs are growing. His head
is becoming more erect and his neck more developed.
A tiny human being..."

His sigh was full of blissful happiness and Teri
couldn't bring herself to correct him on the gender
point again. Maybe it was just his way of talking.
After all, it didn't sound right to call their baby *it*. A

tiny human being...that image did make their child more real to her.

"There's stuff you should read up on for your own sake, Teri," Leo pressed earnestly. "Have you had a check-up with your dentist?"

"What for?"

"Well, your gums might have softened. Have they been bleeding when you clean your teeth?"

"No." She barely stifled a giggle. Leo was so unbelievably serious about all this, which was wonderful, but funny, too. Nevertheless, she didn't think he'd appreciate her amusement.

"You should make an appointment anyway." He frowned. "What about your diet? You shouldn't be touching coffee, alcohol, raw seafood or soft cheeses. No smoked salmon, either."

Teri grimaced. "I've gone off coffee. Actually I've gone off most things. I've been making do with an omelette or some soup and toast."

His frown deepened. "That won't do. You're getting thin."

"Leo, when you throw up half you eat, losing weight is a usual result."

"Which means we have to fix the throwing up," he said grimly. "I'm going to feed you dry biscuits and lemon and ginger every morning until this stage is over, Teri."

If he tried force-feeding her lemons, she'd throw up all over him. She arched an eyebrow, challenging his dictatorial stance. "Do you mean to keep me in this bed?"

"Best place for you," he asserted firmly.

Teri didn't really want to quarrel with that, especially if Leo was sharing the bed. Nevertheless, there were practical considerations, apart from the pleasure of having him as her lover.

"I do have a business to run," she reminded him.

He nodded. "We'll do something about that, too. Can't have you working such long hours. It's too much for you. I'll take tomorrow off work and get moving on finding someone to take some of the load off for you. Get the application forms filled out and lodged at the register office, as well."

"What application forms?"

"We'll need proof of who you are, your birth certificate, your divorce certificate…"

"Leo…" Her heart skittered at the way he was bulldozing ahead. "…I can't marry you."

He looked hard at her. "Why not? You need me to look after you, Teri."

She took a deep breath to quell the awful rise of temptation. As much as she'd like to have Leo as her husband, there was no escaping the truth or its consequences. "Because you only want to marry me for the baby," she stated baldly.

His eyebrows beetled down. "I'm sure we can make a go of it."

"Maybe," she conceded, hoping that would prove to be the case. "But it's too soon."

He thought she was quibbling and his impatience with it burst into voice. "Dammit, Teri! How can I look after you and our child properly if…"

"What if something happens, Leo?" she cut in earnestly. "Women do have miscarriages. I'm only nine weeks. If we got married and I lost your child, you'd feel tricked into a marriage you didn't really want.''

That gave him pause for thought. Nevertheless, he came back with, ''You're not tricking me, Teri. I was the one who proposed marriage.''

''I know. And I know you mean well.'' She had no doubts at all about his sincerity on that score. However, it made no difference to the crux of the matter. ''I wouldn't feel right about it, Leo. Not this early in the pregnancy.''

''Do you feel something is wrong?'' he asked anxiously.

''No. I just don't think it's a good thing to rush into marriage when there's a possibility, however remote, you won't get what you want out of it.''

''Hmmm...'' He chewed over this elemental factor. ''The danger period for a miscarriage is usually the first four months. Now I don't want any argument over this, Teri. You're moving in with me right now. We're not going to risk anything bad happening,'' he said sternly.

Her heart turned over. This child meant so much to him. She hadn't realised a man could be so wrapped up in having a child. All his reading up on it, and seeing marriage as the only way he could have full access...it would clearly be a dreadful blow if nothing came of it.

''Leo, sometimes that kind of thing is beyond anyone's control,'' she gently warned.

''That's no reason not to do our best by our kid.'' He determinedly shrugged off her fears and patted her stomach with an air of reassuring confidence. ''Don't you worry, Junior. Your Dad's taking charge. And your mother's going to do what I say because I'm the authority on your welfare.''

Despite her reservations, Teri had to smile. ''If you're going to turn into a dictatorial tyrant...''

He laughed at her. ''I'll reward you for good behaviour.''

''How?'' she demanded suspiciously.

''I'll let you choose the TV programs we watch.''

She rolled her eyes. ''Since we both like sport...''

''I won't complain about romantic movies,'' he grandly offered.

''I like action movies.''

''Great!'' He looked unbearably smug.

''You're just getting your own way,'' she accused.

His eyes twinkled wickedly as he leaned over and kissed her nose. ''Then I'll let you have your way with me. My body is yours. You can use me for your pleasure any time you like.''

Before she could come up with any smart retort, he covered her mouth with his and seduced her into thinking what more could she want?

Leo was intent on taking care of her and their baby and she didn't have to bear it all alone any more. He wanted her with him, in his home, in his life, in his bed. And he couldn't say she'd tricked him or tried to take him for anything. He could never say that.

She'd been absolutely fair.

As fair as she could be when she desperately wanted to keep him.

CHAPTER SIXTEEN

Two months on

DYLAN'S mother, busy cooking the bacon for the Caesar salad, looked up in surprise as Teri walked into the kitchen. "Didn't expect you to see you at the restaurant this morning," she remarked cheerily. "Aren't you having the ultrasound scan today?"

"Yes. But it's not until one-thirty. And the cleaner's at the house. And I can't stand being idle," Teri explained.

"Feeling a bit nervous about it, I expect," the older woman said knowingly.

Teri sighed. "Leo's so excited about it, Fay, I'll die if anything's wrong with this baby."

She smiled indulgently. "I'm sure there's no need to worry, dear. You've been looking so well since the morning sickness stopped. It's a good sign."

"I hope so." She'd suffered a lot of lemons to get rid of the dreaded morning sickness. In fact, she wasn't sure she could ever look another lemon in the face!

She flopped onto the stool Leo had insisted she sit on at the chopping bench and glanced down at her pot belly which wasn't so visible when she was standing. She'd replaced her red skirt with white bib and brace overalls, the red heart and smile emblazoned on the bib. The elastic at the back of the waist could be let out as she got bigger.

"At least he can't say I'm not gaining weight now," she mockingly remarked.

Fay laughed, highly amused by Leo's fussing. All of them—Dylan, Mel and Fay, who'd been only too happy to accept employment with her son, taking over much of Teri's work—had been constantly instructed by Leo about Teri's pregnancy, what she was allowed and not allowed to do, how she was to be watched over and looked after, what food was good for her, etc., etc., etc. *The Gestapo Father,* they'd christened him behind his back. With good humour, though. It gave them a kick to see how much he cared.

Teri swung from loving his caring, being scared by the all-encompassing nature of it, and finding it really exasperating when he stopped her doing things with insidious emotional blackmail. "We've got to think of the baby," he'd say, and then she'd feel guilty for even feeling the occasional urge to please herself.

"Here…" Fay passed her a bowl of boiled eggs, her eyes still sparkling with laughter. "You can shell these. That won't hurt."

Dylan's mother was a lovely person, a widow in her early fifties who'd been looking for employment. She was as good-natured and as easy to get along with as her son. A fine cook, as well, with a keen interest in food. Leo, of course, had discovered that.

Leo had taken charge with a vengeance. Teri certainly couldn't say he wasn't as good as his word. He'd even arranged for Dylan to take over the early morning food buying at the markets. Everything was working beautifully. The restaurant trade was as good as ever. Teri had never had life so easy. She had nothing to worry about.

Except having a healthy baby.

Dylan breezed in with the bread rolls from the bakery, filling the kitchen with their lovely freshly baked smell. "What are you doing here, Teri? Isn't it the scan today?"

"Yes, it is. I'm just filling in time, Dylan," she answered.

"Mel and I have bets on. I'm going for a boy and he reckons it'll be a girl."

"Dylan, Teri might not want to know which sex the baby is," Fay chided.

"How can she furnish the nursery right unless she finds out?" he argued. "That's why you're holding off doing it, isn't it, Teri?"

She shook her head. "It's too soon, Dylan. Basically I just want to know that the baby's okay."

"But you are going to see which sex it is," he pressed eagerly. "Then we can call it he or she."

"I'm sure Leo will want to know," Teri said dryly.

"Yeah." Dylan's grin was as wide as a house. "Leo won't want to miss out on knowing."

Teri was sure Dylan was right. Which was another reason she was on edge about the scan. Leo invariably called the baby *he*. Although he insisted he didn't care whether they had a boy or a girl, she suspected he would be disappointed if it was a girl and she didn't know how she was going to handle that.

It was that very question preying on her mind and playing havoc with her nervous system when she went to meet Leo at the medical centre at the appointed time. He was there before her, pacing up and down the sidewalk, exuding excitement and energy. When he spotted her coming, his face beamed such happiness at her, Teri almost fell apart. Her insides turned to mush and her legs only carried her forward because of the strong, magnetic field he threw out.

She loved this man. She really, truly did. It wasn't just fantastic sexual chemistry, though that certainly hadn't diminished. In fact, she'd never wanted nor enjoyed sex so much as she had lately. One of the plus effects of pregnancy, the magazines said, but Teri felt it was more driven by her wanting as much of Leo as she could have while everything was fine between them.

"That's such a cute outfit on you, Teri," he said as she reached him. "I was just thinking *Full Tummy—Happy Heart* applies to more than the restaurant right now." He grinned, throwing his arm around her shoulders and hugging her close. "Bet you never linked the two."

"I have actually." On the very first day she knew she was pregnant. And she'd vowed she'd have a happy heart about it no matter how Leo reacted. That wasn't quite so simple now. Her heart felt tied irrevocably to his reaction.

"Well…two great minds think alike," he said, his pleasure in the linking undimmed by her beating him to it.

He steered her up the steps leading into the medical centre, unperturbed by any doubts about the outcome of the ultrasound scan. "It'll be great having a photograph of our child," he enthused. "I mean really seeing him, not just knowing he's there. I think I'll get it framed. The first photograph."

"It may not be a he," Teri couldn't stop herself from cautioning.

"I know," Leo said blithely.

Teri tried to take comfort from this equable attitude, but once they'd been ushered into the room where the scan took place, and she was lying on the bed with her belly bare, she found it impossible to relax as the technician instructed. Leo sat on a chair beside her, holding her hand, full of happy anticipation, and that didn't help one bit.

"This gell I'll be spreading over your stomach will feel cold, but it's important for getting a good picture," the technician explained, her voice soothingly sympathetic.

Teri shivered as it was applied. Or maybe it was a shudder of apprehension.

"Now before we start, do you want to know the sex of the baby? I'll avoid that area if you prefer to keep it a surprise."

"What would you like, Teri?" Leo asked, dumbfounding her by handing her the decision.

Her immediate impulse was to put off knowing. Then everything could go on just as it had been without any sense of let-down. On the other hand, if Leo was bursting to know, he might regret giving her the choice and grow vexed with ignorance. Unsure which was the better course, Teri gave up on it.

"You decide, Leo."

"Hmmm...." He seemed in two minds, his head

cocking from side to side, obviously tempted yet...Teri could hardly believe her ears when he said, "Let's leave it as a surprise." His eyes danced at her. "I have this fantasy of the doctor handing me our baby and saying, 'Mr. Kingston, you have a...whatever.' It won't be such a big moment if I know already."

Teri laughed in sheer relief. It surely meant he really didn't mind if it was a son or a daughter. She turned to the technician, smiling her agreement. "That's it then. We don't want to know."

"Fine. I'm switching off the overhead light now so you get a better view on the monitor. Just watch the screen and I'll describe what I'm checking."

The monitor screen hung above the foot of the bed. Leo squeezed her hand as the room was plunged into darkness. Teri held her breath and fiercely prayed for everything to be normal. Then the screen lit up and there was her baby...recognisably a baby...head, neck, body, arms, legs, little feet tucked in. It was amazing, incredible, awesome.

The technician moved a dot around the screen, pointing out the heart, the spinal cord, and various other features that were simply a blur to Teri. What she saw was a tiny person with a nose and ears and chin and mouth, and unbelievably, as the technician clearly showed, he or she was sucking its thumb and the sucking motion was actually visible.

"The progression is precisely what it ought to be at eighteen weeks," the technician assured them.

Magic words to Teri.

Suddenly, the curled little hand attached to the sucked thumb opened up into a four-finger fan.

"Look, Teri! He's waving to us!" Leo cried excitedly. "He knows we're looking at him and he's waving to us."

True or not, it was so wonderful, tears welled into her eyes. Their baby...saying hello, telling them he was fine in his mummy's tummy and they weren't to worry about him.

"Isn't he great?" Leo said huskily, *his* fingers squeezing hers so hard they were almost pulped, but Teri didn't care. As a sharing moment, this had to be the most heart-moving in her whole life.

She was still treasuring it after the scan, while she redressed herself, and all the way out to the street where the afternoon sunshine added its sparkle to her glow of happiness.

And right there on the public sidewalk Leo turned her into his embrace and hugged her as though she was the most precious thing in the world to him.

"I can never thank you enough for giving me this, Teri," he said fervently. "It's so special..."

"Yes, it is," she whispered, her throat choked with emotion.

"I might have missed it, but for you." He heaved a deep sigh and eased back a bit, his eyes seeking hers, their irises a brighter blue than she'd ever seen them. "You have to marry me, Teri. It's the right thing to do. We made that baby. You and I, together. We're his Mum and Dad."

His voice was furred with deep feeling and she understood the emotions swirling through him. She was completely in tune with what he was saying. But it was their child...the image of a tiny hand waving to them...driving what he felt.

"This isn't the time, Leo," she said quietly.

"Yes, it is," he pressed with intense urgency. "I want to be married to you. We're a family, Teri...don't you see?"

"Not yet, Leo. When our baby's safely born. Then we'll be a family."

"But he's real now."

"Yes. But he couldn't survive by himself at this point. Let him be born, Leo, alive and yelling and kicking. When the doctor puts him in your arms and says, 'Mr. Kingston, you have a...whatever,' if you still want to marry me, ask me then."

"No." His eyebrows beetled down, lending a deep angst to his expression. "I want us to be married before he's born. He'll be illegitimate if we're not."

She shook her head. "That's not a social stigma anymore."

"You've been happy with me, haven't you?" he pressed, determined on persuasion. "It's been good, sharing our lives. I like coming home to you. It seems to me we've got it together better than most people, Teri."

"The baby gives us a common purpose," she gently reminded him.

"Exactly. So..."

Unable to bear any more, she reached up and placed her fingers on his lips. "Please...let it go for now, Leo. Please?"

He struggled with his own strong inclinations. "It's wrong," he said gruffly.

"No. It can wait," she corrected him as firmly as she could with her own emotions torn by caution. "I want to thank you, too, for giving me a wonderful memory today. I'll always hug it in my mind. Always." Tears pricked her eyes. "I'm going back to work now. Okay? I'll see you tonight."

She broke away from him before he could stop her and strode blindly along the sidewalk, her heart pumping madly. She half expected him to catch up with her and pursue his argument but he didn't. For which she was profoundly grateful. The tears would not be blinked away. They kept swimming into her eyes.

She'd wanted so much to say yes to his proposal this time.

But she couldn't.

It was wonderful that everything was fine with the baby. Even so, that was no guarantee she would carry it full-term without mishap. There were so many things that could go wrong. She'd read about them— awful lists of problems—in the magazines Leo had bought. And only a week ago, she'd watched a TV program where a healthy baby strangled itself on its cord when it turned around, just before it was due to be born.

If she lost Leo's child, the grief would be terrible. It would tear them apart. She knew it would. Only love could hold a couple together through such a terrible loss. And Leo didn't love her. Not for herself.

He only loved her because she was carrying his child. He would never have asked her to marry him otherwise. That was the truth of it and it was no use trying to fool herself otherwise.

CHAPTER SEVENTEEN

LEO could not get back into work. Useless trying, he decided. He'd been staring blankly at the monitor screen on his PC for the past hour, alternatively exulting over the fantastic image of his child in Teri's womb, and suffering considerable heartburn over her refusal to marry him. There was no reason to it that he could see. Which probably meant it was some female thing he didn't understand.

Disgruntled at not being able to figure out how to change Teri's mind, and not prepared to accept failure on this vital point, Leo did what he probably should have done in the first place instead of pummelling his male brain with questions that had no rational answers. He pressed the button on the intercom to summon assistance.

"Mavis, I need you in here."

He pushed away from his desk and stood up, lacking a sense of authority on this thorny subject and wanting to feel he was at least in charge of his office. Mavis came in and he waved her to the chair she usually occupied during work discussions. She settled herself and looked inquiringly at him.

He wandered around his desk and propped himself against it, determined to stay relaxed and reasonable, no matter what advice Mavis gave. After all, she had been right about the pregnancy causing Teri to get completely screwed up in her responses to him.

"This is a personal problem, Mavis," he stated to get her mind set in the right direction.

"Ah!" she said, the bright expectancy in her eyes wavering into wary reserve.

"You know I got Teri to move in with me."

She nodded.

"That was two months ago," he emphasised so his trusty assistant was clear on the time factor.

Another nod.

He proceeded to apprise her of the situation. "I've given Teri every consideration, listened to her needs and acted on them, eased her work situation so she gets plenty of rest, done everything I can to take care of her. In short, I've carried through precisely what you said to do."

Mavis apparently didn't see fit to comment on his thoroughness. Her eyes seemed to be weighing his words.

Leo couldn't think of anything he'd overlooked. He frowned over the sheer perversity of Teri's attitude. "She and I get along very well, Mavis. We don't have any of those picky arguments. We even like the same programs on TV. And there's certainly no problem with…uh…" He really didn't want to go into their sex life.

Mavis gave him an arch look. "I take it you mean you're happy together."

"Yes," Leo seized gratefully.

"And you love each other."

Leo felt an instant recoil to that power-laden word.

It held so many blackmail connotations from Serena's use of it, to attach it to any good relationship was tantamount to spoiling it. Teri evoked feelings in him that Serena never had. Never. From the very beginning it had been completely different with Teri. And now that he'd shown her he wasn't another Wayne…yes, this was the *real* thing. And the sharing was too good for the feelings not to be mutual.

"No problem there, Mavis," he firmly assured her. "And that's why this doesn't make sense. There we were at the ultrasound scan earlier this afternoon, both of us over the moon at seeing our baby. It was the perfect moment to ask Teri to marry me so I did. But she refused to consider it. Flatly refused. Now I ask you…" He spread his hands in appeal. "…why would she turn me down?"

"Did she say why?" Mavis asked cautiously.

Leo threw up his hands in perplexity. "Only that it's too soon. She said to ask her again after the baby's born, but that will be too late, Mavis."

"Too late for what?"

He grimaced. "Teri says it doesn't matter if our child is illegitimate, but I really don't like it. How will it be, Teri going into hospital under her own name and having our baby as though it has nothing to do with me. It's like she's cutting me out."

"But she hasn't really cut you out of anything so far, Leo," Mavis pointed out with her usual perspicacity.

It didn't settle his disgruntlement. "Why can't she marry me?" he demanded, wanting a direct reply.

"There could be many reasons," Mavis mused.

"Like what?"

"Some expressions of love count more than others, Leo," she said, her eyes gathering a distant look as though seeing much further than he could. "Have you met her family?" she asked speculatively.

"No." He frowned over the question. "Surely this is between me and Teri?"

"Has she met yours?"

He shrugged. "There's only Dad and he's tied up with his second family now. I don't see much of them myself since he moved down to the South Coast."

"So you've asked Teri to marry you, but neither of you have involved each other with your families," Mavis said, as though he'd missed something critically important.

"We're starting our own family," Leo argued.

"Is it your plan to leave them out of your wedding?"

"Oh, for God's sake, Mavis!" He rolled his eyes at such an irrelevant issue. "Teri and I are both divorced. We've been through the wedding rigmarole before. A register office ceremony will do fine. It's just a matter of getting married."

"You know this is how she feels?"

"We haven't got as far as talking about it," he said tersely.

"I see," she said, going into her wise nodding act. "Then you're telling me that what you want from Teri is a piece of legal paper to give you legal rights over your child. Have I got that right?"

"Well…yes. Though it's a commitment to our future together, too."

"If you mean to make a future together, I don't think you can ignore your families," she advised. "To my mind, that is elemental. They're part of you. Part of your life. There's more than a baby involved in a marriage, Leo. I think your Teri is very aware of that."

Leo mulled over this bigger picture. "So you think I should win approval from her family." It should be easy, he thought. He could talk sport to her father and brothers.

"I would imagine Teri would like to feel your family's approval, too," Mavis added pointedly.

Leo smiled, happily confident with this course of action. "No problem with Dad," he said with absolute assurance. "He'll think she's terrific after Serena."

"Then it could be a good move to set up meetings on both sides and start building a broader base for the future."

Leo could see the sense in forging some allies in the marriage stakes. "Thank you, Mavis," he said with satisfaction. "You reckon that will do the trick."

"Oh no!" she cried, shaking her head emphatically. "I very much doubt anything will do the trick."

That straightened him up with a jolt. "Then what's the use of what you've just told me?"

"It may give you a better chance of having your proposal accepted *after* the baby is born."

"Mavis." He eyed her sternly. "The whole purpose of this conversation is to change Teri's mind *before* the birth."

She didn't bat an eyelash, holding his gaze and

squarely returning it as she replied, "Well, Leo, if you want my opinion, you've got no chance of that happening and you may very well alienate Teri if you keep trying. She *said* after. And that was at the perfect moment. My advice is to work towards the next perfect moment, which may possibly be when you lay your child in her arms after the birth."

Leo's eyebrows beetled down in brooding frustration. It was uncanny her hitting precisely on what Teri had said. Women—even well-earthed Mavis—had a logic of their own that a man simply wasn't privy to. Except it wasn't *logic* at all.

"You can't suggest anything else?" he pleaded, hating having to accept defeat.

She stood up, preparing to go, having delivered her woman's wisdom. She paused a moment, cocked her head on one side, and said, "I really wouldn't press for your practical piece of legal paper. It has no soul."

"Soul?" he repeated, finding the word too nebulous to pin down.

"Soul," she affirmed, her eyes accusing him of being very thick as she turned to make her exit from his office.

No point in calling her back. Mavis had clearly had the last word. Leo brooded over it all for a long time. Eventually he came to two conclusions. He'd better follow his assistant's advice, and when he did ask Teri to marry him again, *after the birth,* he'd invite her to say how she'd like them to get married so he didn't get it wrong with the register office.

Maybe then he'd understand *soul.*

CHAPTER EIGHTEEN

TERI knew there was no hiding her pregnancy from her family any longer. The excuses she'd made not to visit over the past couple of months could not be extended forever, especially since they lived at Bateau Bay, only a two-hour drive away. Now that the scan had assured her a miscarriage was unlikely, she really did have to face up to the inquisition that was bound to follow breaking the news.

Nevertheless, she kept putting it off day after day, unsure if she should involve Leo or not. To her astonishment, he himself broached the subject one night over dinner.

"I called my dad today," he said, shooting her a dazzling smile. "Told him he was going to be a grandfather. He wants to meet you, Teri. He and his wife and my two half-brothers live down the South Coast at Kiama. We could go this Sunday if that's okay with you."

It was the first she'd heard of Leo's family. Apart from saying there were no girls in it, she knew nothing of his background. Having been handed the opportunity to probe a little, she did, finding out his mother had died when he was eight and his father, a professional accountant, had remarried when Leo was in his teens at boarding school.

"I usually visit them at Easter and Christmas," he

explained. ''The boys are still young enough to enjoy getting Easter eggs and presents from me.'' He lifted his eyebrows appealingly. ''I hope you don't mind my telling them about the baby.''

''No. I'd like to visit,'' she answered truthfully, curious to know more. ''It's nice that you get on with them. I mean your father's second family.''

''What about your family, Teri?'' He frowned. ''I don't know what you've told them, but I'd like the chance to assure them I mean to look after you and our child.''

She sighed in sheer relief. ''It would help.''

''Help?'' he picked up quizzically.

She winced. ''They live on the Central Coast and they don't know about the baby yet. I've been wimping out on it. I knew they'd want to meet you and I wasn't sure…''

He reached across the table and covered her hand with his, instantly causing her pulse to leap and her skin to heat. Her mind floundered momentarily, her thought patterns jammed by the intense flow of magnetic energy Leo poured forth.

''Teri, I'll back you up on anything,'' he said, his vivid blue eyes ablaze with promise. ''Just make a day for visiting and you can be absolutely sure of my support.''

''Oh!''

She was lost for words. Tears pricked her eyes. Her heart thumped so hard it hurt her chest. Surely this meant he cared about her, standing by her in front of her parents, ready to deflect any critical remarks and shoulder responsibility. She swallowed hard, trying to hold on to some composure.

"My parents are…well, rather old-fashioned," she warned. "And my brothers' marriages are solid. None of them ever really understood why Wayne and I broke up. It won't be easy, Leo."

There was not the slightest sign of faltering from him. "We'll take it as it comes, Teri." He squeezed her hand. "The sooner they see how good we are together, the better."

"You really don't mind?" she had to ask, hardly able to bring herself to believe he was willing to commit himself so far on her behalf. "They'll probably give you the third degree," she added apprehensively. "My father, in particular, is not known for his tact."

"Don't worry. I'll handle it. They're not about to turn their backs on our child, Teri."

Our child

It was like a douche of cold water on fevered hopes. Leo didn't love her. Everything he did to ease her life was really for their precious child. The core of their one-on-one relationship was what they shared in bed. Always had been and probably always would be.

Still, she had nothing to complain about. He was good to her. He took care of things with a generosity that invariably made her feel mean to even wish for more from him. She loved him. She just found it increasingly painful that he didn't love her and there was nothing she could do about it.

The following Sunday they drove down to Kiama with Leo assuring her of a warm welcome. Which proved to be true. Jim Kingston looked like an older version of Leo, and had the knack of giving kindly attention, putting her at ease. His wife, Donna, a vivacious redhead who clearly adored her older husband, talked so much herself she never allowed an awkward moment to develop. It turned out they were both highly relieved Teri was nothing like Serena.

"Such a cold, calculating woman," Donna confided. "It's obvious Leo is much happier with you, Teri. And it's such lovely news about the baby."

Her warm smile did a lot to diminish Serena's classy shadow. So did their home which was totally unpretentious—a large, sprawling weatherboard house with wide verandahs, set right on the edge of the beach. It was very much a family house, with Leo's two younger half-brothers having the run of it as they pleased, both of them bright, happy boys who constantly wanted Leo to play with them. Which he did.

"He'll make a good father," Jim Kingston assured her. "I'm glad he's got you and the baby in his life now. Leo got too caught up in making money. He needs to slow down. There's more to life than money and what it can buy. That first wife of his…" He grimaced and patted Teri's hand. "A pleasure to meet you, my dear. A real pleasure."

Leo hadn't slowed down much, Teri thought, but maybe he would after the baby was born. *If* all went well with the birth.

The visit could certainly be counted a success. Not only was it nice to have Jim's and Donna's approval, but Teri felt more comfortable about taking Leo into the midst of her family. He hadn't come from a snobby background. She thought—hoped—he would fit in with the same charming ease he invariably displayed wherever he was.

With the confidence of knowing Leo would stand by her, Teri finally screwed up her courage to confess her situation to her mother over the telephone, determined on answering all the tricky questions so that the shock factor, at least, was taken out of the face to face meeting when she and Leo turned up.

There were tears and recriminations and a great deal of talk of *"for the sake of the child,"* with Teri finally losing patience and shouting she didn't believe in shotgun marriages and no one was going to drive her into one and she certainly didn't need the stress of being made to feel guilty, or be put before a family jury telling her what she should do with *her* future. At which point she slammed the telephone down and dissolved into a flood of tears herself.

That night she told Leo he could forget about meeting her family, and proceeded to cry herself to sleep. The next morning, he told her he'd talked to her parents himself and had invited them to come down to Woollahra and have lunch with both of them at his home this coming Sunday, and if Teri was agreeable, she should call her mother and let her know.

Teri instantly flared with angry suspicion. "Leo, if you told them you're going to marry me…"

"You know I can't do that without your consent, Teri," he cut in, appealing to reason. "I merely said you were extremely distressed and were in a very delicate condition, being in the second trimester of pregnancy, and if they cared about you and the grandchild you're carrying, they'd give you every support instead of upsetting you.''

Of course. Nothing—absolutely nothing!—was to put at risk the safety of his child. Mr. Fix-it in action again. She almost hated him at that moment. Though when she did call her mother who was apologetic and anxious to smooth over everything, Teri had to acknowledge she was grateful for Leo's intervention, despite the awful jealousy she felt towards the baby he cared so much about. Her family meant a lot to her. She didn't want to feel at odds with them.

Her parents duly landed on the doorstep of Leo's home in Jersey Road. They were highly impressed by Leo and everything to do with Leo, even the panther table. They departed in the warm belief their daughter was *in good hands.* Which she was. Teri readily conceded it was so. Though it almost choked her.

It was the baby in good hands…the baby…the baby…the baby!

It was a struggle to keep herself on an even keel and not get neurotic about it. Leo was kind and considerate. He was very loving in bed, especially tender as she got bigger and bigger. He massaged her tight shoulders, rubbed her aching back, and worked oil into her skin, easing the itch of its stretching. When he insisted on going shopping with her for the baby, Teri knew it would be downright mean to put him off.

She selected basic nursery furniture and a few baby clothes, hoping she wasn't jinxing herself by this substantial assumption that nothing would go wrong with the baby.

He blithely bought a colourful array of wall hangings, falling in love with Pooh Bear and Piglet and Tigger. Teri had to drag him out of the soft toy department, but not without an armful of animals he fancied. Then he became entranced with mobiles of tropical fish and a moon with stars revolving around it.

To Teri, the whole nursery business was like a tempting Fate exercise. It represented expectations on a scale that kept growing and growing with every purchase Leo made. She wished he'd stop but she couldn't bring herself to spoil his pleasure.

She also nursed a gnawing wish he would buy her something, just especially for her, even if it was only because she was the mother of his child. He didn't think of it and it was undoubtedly unreasonable of her to want him to. After all, she hadn't bought him anything for being the father of her child.

Her fears about her pregnancy lessened as it stayed trouble-free through the last trimester. She bloomed. Everyone commented on it. And the baby moved around so much, Teri dubbed it "the ice-skater." It really was fascinating to see and feel a foot sweep across her stomach. Leo was enchanted by it.

Her mother called frequently to check on progress and give helpful advice. Leo met her brothers and their families. Despite their long friendship with Wayne, her brothers were favourably impressed by Teri's "new man." There was no sport Leo couldn't discuss with them and it was obvious he was devoted to Teri's welfare.

The waiting time grew shorter. Leo took her to the ante-natal classes at the hospital where he'd booked a private room for her. In one session they were shown a video of natural childbirth. Teri found it so scary, she didn't want to know any more. She went to the breathing lessons in the hope they might help her through what she'd seen, but flatly refused to go to the video of a Caesarian operation.

Leo went. He wanted to be prepared for all possibilities. Naturally. Anything that might affect *his child* had to be known, never mind what Teri had to go through to deliver it.

The due birth date finally came.

And went.

The waiting was dreadful. She stopped going to the restaurant, unable to bear the sympathy and continual inquiries, and the fussing. Each day Leo kept asking if she felt any symptom of labour, and Teri had to bite her tongue lest she snap his head off.

The doctor assured her the baby was in the right position, ready to come, but nothing was happening. She was as big as a whale. She couldn't see her feet. And all Leo could think of was the imminent birth of his child. The doctor promised that if she went five days overdue, he would induce the birth.

At eight o'clock on the night of the fifth day she went into hospital. A gell was applied to get things moving. Teri did as she was told and lay still for a couple of hours to give the gell every chance to do its work, but as far as she could tell, it was having no effect at all.

Leo had turned on the TV in the room and was

watching the Friday Night Football Match. She was supposed to be watching, too, to help pass the time. It was impossible for her to concentrate on the game and she had no idea who won. When it was over, Leo switched the set off and looked hopefully at her.

"Nothing," she replied dolefully. "I don't think this baby wants to be born."

"Just a matter of time, Teri," he assured her, excited anticipation in his eyes. "You're here in the delivery ward. It's going to happen."

The midwife they'd met in the ante-natal classes came in to check on her. "Any action?"

"Not a twinge," Teri said flatly.

"Then I suggest you settle down for the night and try to get some sleep. It's quite usual in these cases for labour not to start until morning and I wouldn't expect the baby to be born before late tomorrow afternoon."

A whole day of labour! Teri quailed at the thought.

The midwife turned to Leo. "You'd best go home to bed and try to sleep, too. You won't be any help to your partner if you're too fatigued to concentrate when it counts."

Leo frowned. "I don't like leaving Teri alone. What if it starts earlier?"

"We'll call you," the midwife assured him. "It is best that you go. Teri will be more likely to sleep without you here."

No, I won't, Teri thought, panic fluttering through her mind. She didn't want to be left alone. Tonight of all nights she needed Leo beside her. She was frightened of tomorrow.

"I guess it is the sensible thing to do," he said, reluctantly rising from the chair next to her bed.

No…no…stay! Teri screamed in her mind, fiercely willing him not to do the sensible thing this once! She wanted to tell him how she felt, plead…but she knew how he would reply. The birth would go better if she was properly rested. The baby would need her help tomorrow.

He leaned over and gave her a gentle good-night kiss. Her eyes ached with silent begging as he stroked her hair away from her face and smiled happy reassurance. "We'll be holding him this time tomorrow, Teri," he said. "Isn't that a sweet dream to have?"

She couldn't even imagine it. A long dark, lonely night loomed ahead of her. "Don't go," she croaked, fear choking her throat.

He hesitated, then grimaced appealingly. "The sooner I go, the sooner you'll get to sleep. Don't worry. I'll be here like a shot if I get a call."

"I know," she sighed, resigning herself to the inevitable. Though a spurt of rebellion made her mutter, "I don't feel like being sensible."

"Neither do I," he confessed, and kissed her again, causing her heart to flutter with hope. Then he murmured, "Try to have a good night's sleep, Teri."

After which he did the sensible thing.

He left.

And Teri didn't sleep a wink.

She decided she hated Leo, hated the baby, and hated herself for ever being such a fool as to think she would be happy to become a mother.

CHAPTER NINETEEN

LEO hated having to leave Teri. He forced himself to do it for her sake. She hadn't slept much last night, too uncomfortable to settle properly and fretful about the baby not coming. The labour would be more of an ordeal for her if she didn't get some good rest.

He knew she was frightened of what lay ahead. The video on natural childbirth had been too graphic. He wished she hadn't watched it. It was all right for him since he needed to know how best to help her, but he wasn't looking forward to seeing Teri in pain. He hoped it wouldn't be for too long.

The drive home from the hospital was only ten minutes. He parked the car in the street rather than garage it at the back of the house. A quick getaway was essential if he was called. Determined on being properly rested himself, Leo had a hot shower and went straight to bed. He applied every relaxation technique he knew and eventually dropped off to sleep.

The shrill ring of the telephone woke him. It was pitch dark. He fumbled for the receiver, bleary eyes targeting the digital clock next to the phone—2:47. So soon? Was something wrong? "Yes?" he barked at the caller, anxiety squeezing his heart.

"Mr. Kingston?"

"Yes!" he snapped impatiently.

"This is Nurse Williams calling to let you know Miss Adams is already in advanced labour."

"Advanced?" he shouted, appalled at having been left in ignorance. Teri, doing it alone...

"It's come on quickly," the nurse explained.

Leo slammed down the receiver and hurtled out of bed. He pulled on essential clothes at the speed of light, grabbed his keys and wallet and was off, savagely castigating himself as he raced down the stairs and out to his car. He shouldn't have left her. He should have sat by her every minute. He should have known the damned hospital staff couldn't be trusted to watch over her as he would have done, ready to be supportive and reassuring.

The streets were virtually deserted and he made it to the hospital in seven minutes. The elevator to the delivery ward was so slow he could barely control his frustration. Once it opened on the right floor, he sprinted down the corridor and burst into the room they'd put Teri in.

The bed was empty!

No-o-o-o, his mind screamed. Not yet. She couldn't have the baby without him.

He was about to yell for someone when his ears registered the ensuite shower running. The door was open. He looked in and there she was, slumped back on a white plastic chair, her eyes shut, one hand managing a manual shower spray which was shooting hot water over her stomach while she gingerly rubbed the tight mound.

For a moment, Leo was overwhelmed by the sheer beauty of her naked, the epitome of womanhood, large dark nipples and aureoles adorning her magnificent breasts, her smoothly distended abdomen full with child, lovely long legs in an ungainly sprawl that was somehow deeply endearing.

His heart swelled with his feeling for her. He wished he could photograph her just like this, keep this image of her forever, and the reminder of all she was to him...the woman who touched him in ways no other did, somehow fulfilling him as a man, giving him his child and so much more. So much...

Then her head tilted back and a tortured moan spilled from her throat.

"Teri..." Her name ripped from his. "I'm here, love. Tell me what you want."

Her eyes flew open, huge and hopelessly woebegone. "It's horrible, Leo," she wailed.

"I know, I know," he tried to soothe.

"You don't know," she cried. "It's not you suffering this...this...o-o-oh!" She bent forward, huddling over the pain of the contraction.

He crouched beside her. "Let me do the shower spray," he offered anxiously.

"I want pethidine," she sobbed. "Bad pain. Bad...bad pain."

"Nurse! Nurse!" Leo yelled, agitated by his own helplessness.

A woman came running in. "What is it?"

"Teri needs pethidine."

"Well, let's get her out of the shower and into the delivery room. Then I'll call the midwife."

It was a dreadful business, getting Teri dried and into a hospital gown. She kept doubling up and begging for pain relief. Leo assured her again and again it would be administered as soon as possible. But when they got her into the delivery room and the midwife examined her, it was too late for the pethidine. The baby was on its way and there wouldn't be time for it to work. It was better to concentrate on riding out the birth now.

"Riding!" Teri shrieked between panting for breath. "Are…you…crazy?"

"I'll go and call the doctor," the midwife said.

"Tell him…tell him not to…not to put a tie on. Hurry…"

"Roll onto your side, Teri," Leo urged. "I'll rub your back."

"You weren't here," she sobbed.

"I'm sorry, love. I'll try to make up for it now," he promised, easing her onto her side as gently as he could.

"Don't call me love," she moaned. "You don't love me. Oh God!…oh, God!…please let me die.…"

Leo got his hand working in circular caresses on her lower back and leaned over to kiss her ear. "I do love you, Teri. You know I do. And I'd hate it if you died on me. Now be a good girl and concentrate on breathing the way…"

"Only saying that to make me…oooh!" Her legs writhed up. "Never loved me," she sobbed. "Only the baby."

"That's not true."

"'Tis true."

It had to be the pain talking. She had to know in her heart how much she meant to him. "Teri, you're the best thing that ever happened to me," he declared fervently, disturbed by the flow of negative feelings.

"'Cause o' the baby," she cried accusingly.

"No!" She had it wrong. Wrong from the start. Damn Serena for screwing him up on the *love* word. If Teri needed to hear it...Damn, damn, damn! This was his fault and he had to correct it, had to make her understand. Here she was, having his child, and she didn't think he loved her?

"Before you say it was only ever sex," he blurted out, "it was always more than that, Teri. I just didn't realise how much you meant to me until you threw me out in favour of your ex-husband."

"You didn't...come back," she jeered through another agonised groan.

"So I had my nose out of joint," he readily confessed. "And I didn't want to admit you were important to me. I told myself I had to check on my child. But, Teri, it was *you* having my child that finally drove me back."

"Don't b'lieve you," she gasped.

"I swear to God! I love sharing my life with you."

"Never said." Her voice rose in a high-pitched scream, then choked into, "Never...never...said," as she burst into tears.

"I did say," he insisted anxiously. "After the scan I told you how I felt."

"Didn't love me," she sobbed.

"Dammit, Teri! I did. I do. Ask my father. Ask your parents. They know I love you. I went into battle for you and let both your mother and father know in no uncertain terms that they didn't know what love was if they let you down when you were feeling so frightened and unsure of everything. And I told 'em it was all that bastard, Wayne's fault.''

''Way-ayne?'' The name shuddered out of her.

''That's right. Him! Messing you up so you were scared of counting on anyone. That guy never loved anyone except himself. You'd better believe it,'' he said fiercely.

She curled up again, desperately panting. ''You… married S'rena…on'y three months…''

''Blind fool that I was.'' He rubbed her back frantically, uncaring that his own back was aching from leaning over to help her. ''I'm more married to you than I ever was to her,'' he asserted as the contraction eased. ''And we would have been married legally if you'd let me.''

''Give…child…your name,'' she cried in wretched misery.

''And you, Teri. You,'' he repeated emphatically, needing to get through to her, hating the fact that she had felt so insecure with him. ''But you wouldn't have me,'' he explained, ''and Mavis advised no pressure, to wait until after the baby.''

''Who…May…vis?'' Such awful laboured sounds.

''She works for me. Good woman. Knows I'm besotted with you. Can't work half the time for thinking of you.''

'''Sotted?'' It came out weak and quavery.

''I've tried to think of everything…everything…to keep you with me and make you see you can trust me, Teri. I'm here for you because I want to be here for you. If that's not love I don't know what love is,'' he cried in sheer desperation.

"Not…baby?"

The quivering uncertainty killed him. "The baby, too, because he's part of you, part of me, part of us,'' he pressed with passionate intensity. "But even if there was no baby, I love you, Teri. It's like…you've made a new world for me and it's good. It's so unbelievably good.''

"Yes…'' It was barely a hiss ahead of a long anguished moan. "I can't stand it, Leo. Make them stop it. Make them…oh, ple-e-è-ease!''

"We need help in here!'' he bellowed.

The midwife strode in accompanied by a nurse. "Doctor's on his way. We're going to administer gas, Teri. It will help the pain and regulate your breathing.''

"Thank God for that!'' Leo muttered.

"Deep breath in,'' the nurse instructed. "Now breathe out hard enough to make it rattle. Good girl. Breathe in again…''

"Head's engaged,'' the midwife informed them. "You'll feel like bearing down soon.''

Teri was sucking in gas so hard, Leo wasn't sure she'd heard. The nurse was getting her into a steady breathing rhthym. He'd been no use at all with the process they'd learnt together. He kept rubbing her back, hoping it helped, hoping what he'd said had helped, too. It appalled him that he'd left her lying in the dark, believing he didn't love her, thinking he only cared about the baby. What more could he have done to have shown her? Did she believe him now?

A groan of sheer anguish rattled his nerves. Teri rolled onto her back, the gas violently discarded. He grabbed her hand. Her fingers dug into his like talons as she lurched forward. He quickly slipped his arm around her shoulders, hugging her supportively. His heart was hammering.

"Go with the need to push, Teri," the midwife instructed, "but not too hard all at once."

The doctor made his entrance. "Ah...on its way," he said with satisfaction.

Suddenly it was all action. Leo remembered Teri wasn't supposed to give birth on her back but there was no time to change position. Nothing was going to plan. The hospital gown was drawn up out of the way. Instructions and encouragement were being called out. Teri was frantically trying to follow orders. Leo heard himself echoing what everyone else was saying, wildly anxious for it to be over for Teri's sake.

Then a tiny red and purple and white and black body seemed to rush into the doctor's hands and the distinctive cry of a newborn baby silenced all of them. Teri flopped back onto the pillow exhausted.

"It's okay," he murmured, stroking her damp hair away from her damp forehead. "It's born. It's over. And I love you more than I can ever say."

She smiled weakly at him. "What is it, Leo?"

He dragged himself away from her. The baby was being wiped and yelling its dislike of the outside world. "What have we got, Doctor?" Leo asked.

"Mr. Kingston, you have a fine, healthy daughter."

And the baby was placed in his arms.

"A daughter," Leo repeated in wonderment. He carried the baby back to Teri and carefully laid it across her bare tummy, just under her breasts. "We've got a little girl, Teri."

"Oh, Leo! Look at her hair! It's so black and so thick!" She touched the baby lovingly, then lifted big shiny eyes to him. "Do you mind that it's a girl?"

"Mind? I think it's marvellous. I could have done boy things with a boy, but a girl...she's going to show me a whole new world. Like you, Teri. Only this will be from the beginning and I'm going to love every minute of it."

Tears welled into her eyes. "I love you, too, Leo. I'm sorry I couldn't see past the baby."

He lifted one of her hands and kissed it. "Just say you'll marry me, Teri."

"I will. I'll be happy to, Leo. Very happy."

He sighed, his heart overflowing with relief and joy. The baby gave a funny, high-pitched little squeal, as though testing her voice again and they laughed, exhilarated by the new life they would share together. Then their eyes met and locked and the good feeling flowing between them went deep. Deeper than ever before. No barriers. No shadows. A pure shaft of glorious feeling.

It was a moment Leo would never forget.

The most perfect moment.

It had *soul*...open, loving, giving to each other.

And Leo's understanding of that word was complete.

CHAPTER TWENTY

TERI woke sluggishly, feeling muddled as to whether she wanted to open her eyes or not, yet there was something important swirling around the back of her mind, some sixth sense telling her it was good to wake up even though she was still tired.

Her hand automatically drifted to her tummy, a soft, spongy, deflated tummy, and the connection clicked. The baby! She'd had the baby! And it was a girl!

Her eyes opened in a flash. She was in the private room Leo had booked for her and broad daylight was streaming through the wall-long picture window. Along its ledge were baskets and bowls of lovely flowers, an abundance of pink roses and carnations. Who had sent them? And so soon?

Her gaze swung around the room, but there was no hospital bassinet. Then she remembered the nurse wheeling it away, saying they'd keep the baby in the nursery so Teri could get some good uninterrupted sleep. And Leo had said...

She jerked her head around to the other side of her bed. He was there, sprawled in a chair, his head dropped onto his chest, eyes closed, fast asleep. A smile burst across her face. He hadn't left her side. He'd stayed to make sure no one woke her up, either intentionally or accidentally. The hospital staff had steered him wrong last night and he wasn't about to be put off being right here for her today.

He was looking after her.

She relaxed onto her pillow and revelled in the pleasure of just looking at him. He was the loveliest man. His wavy black hair was mussed, lending an endearing, almost little-boy quality to his handsome face. Of course, his eyes changed that when they were open…such powerful, riveting, blue eyes. And his body was all man…the sexiest, most exciting body a woman could ever know and be pleasured by.

She was so lucky to have met him, even more lucky that he had come to love her. And it wasn't because he was gorgeous on the outside. What was inside was best of all…a caring, giving heart, lined up with a strength of character that didn't shy at anything that he considered had to be done. It was a wonderful feeling to have him at her side, ready to support and protect her.

There was a light tap on the door.

Leo snapped awake, his head instantly jerking up. He darted a sharp glance at the bed, caught her gaze on him, and his face relaxed into a sparkling grin. "Hi, new Mum!"

She grinned back. "Hi, new Dad!"

"You can come in," he called to the person at the door.

A nurse entered, smiling at Teri. "You've had a good sleep. Almost eight hours."

"Eight hours? Then it must be…"

"The 2:00 p.m. feed coming up and your little one needs to get started on it," the nurse said indulgently.

"But first, since you missed lunch, can I order something for you?"

"Tea and toast?" Teri asked, not really feeling hungry.

"Won't be long."

"Before you go, Nurse, could we have the baby in here?" she pressed hopefully. "I'd like to see her."

"I'll wheel her right in," the nurse promised and off she went.

Leo picked up a carrier bag from beside his chair and handed it to Teri, his eyes twinkling with happy anticipation. "Something I bought for you to wear in hospital."

"For *me?*"

She pulled out a lovely, soft, deep lavender-blue dressing gown in a light towelling fabric.

"I got Dylan's mother to sew the motifs on the pockets," Leo said eagerly. "She came by the hospital to give me the bag while you were asleep. Took a peep at our baby, too, and said to give you her congratulations."

It was her restaurant logo—the red heart with the white smile—sewn onto the pockets. A huge wave of emotion welled up and blurred her eyes with tears. She'd been so wrong about Leo not thinking of her, not buying her anything, not loving her. This lovely gift with the two happy hearts…he'd planned and arranged it especially for her, taking the time and effort to make it uniquely personal.

She took a deep breath and looked at him with her heart in her eyes. "I love it, Leo. Thank you so much. Not just for this. For everything you are to me."

She wished she had something to give him, to show him he was uniquely special to her, too, but all she could do was hold out her arms and hug him tight as they shared a kiss that encompassed a wealth of pleasure in their togetherness.

"Coming in…"

Their baby!

Leo broke away to grab the hospital bassinet from the nurse and roll it over to her bedside. He picked up the tidily wrapped white bundle from it and very carefully and gently transferred it to Teri's eagerly waiting arms. "She's still asleep," he whispered.

She looked down at a cute little feminine face framed by an unruly mass of black hair and her heart turned over. "She's so beautiful!" It was a sigh of sheer wonderment.

"She sure is," Leo warmly agreed, leaning over to drop a kiss on their daughter's head. "Absolutely perfect."

Teri glanced at the fatuous smile on his face and the word, *besotted,* came into her mind. "What will we call her, Leo?"

"You choose. You went through it all, giving birth to her."

His eyes eloquently retained the memory of her labour. Strangely enough, Teri could dismiss it now. It was over. Gone. And she had this beautiful baby girl…Leo's child.

"I want you to name her." It was something she could give him, the pleasure of his own choice.

"Well, I kind of like Lucy," he said slowly. He

shrugged and offered a whimsical smile. "Every time I look at her I think…Lucy."

"Then Lucy it is. Lucy Kingston sounds great. You could get the marriage forms on Monday, Leo," Teri rushed on, remembering how keen he'd been on their child having his name. "Lucy doesn't have to be registered for six weeks. We could get married before then."

His face lit up. "You mean it?"

"Yes, I do. There's no need to book anywhere. We could use a celebrant and have a wedding on the beach at Bateau Bay and a fun party at my parents' home afterwards. What do you think?" she cried eagerly.

Thank God for Mavis! he thought, making a swift mental note to bring his trusty advisor to the hospital to meet Teri and see their baby after he picked up the marriage application forms on Monday.

"A wedding on the beach?" *Definitely not a register office.* "Great idea!" he said with such enthusiasm, the baby's eyes flicked open and the newly named Lucy Kingston gazed wonderingly at her father.

Leo laughed. "Look at her, sizing me up."

Teri was absolutely certain Leo would always size up fine in their daughter's eyes. *My darling daughter,* she thought, remembering the card her parents had sent on her thirtieth birthday.

"Did Mum and Dad say if they were coming to visit when you phoned them?" she asked.

"They'll be here tonight. Dad and Donna, too." Leo grinned. "They can't wait to see the new addition

to the family. Your brothers and their wives wanted
to come, as well, but I told them tomorrow would be
better. I thought everyone at once might be too much
for you.'' His eyes flashed concern. ''Was I right?''

''Yes. It would be far too crowded and noisy with
all of them here together, though it's nice that they
want to come.''

''I got Dylan and Mel to stick a sign in the restaurant window for the customers, announcing It's A
Girl! They're both going to buzz in to visit us this
afternoon between the lunch and dinner shifts.''

She laughed. ''They're probably acting like new
dads themselves.'' A thought suddenly struck her and
she gazed with very clear eyes at the man who'd so
totally changed her life. ''You arranged everything,
didn't you?''

''What?'' He adopted an innocent look.

She smiled. ''It's the champagne.''

''Pardon?''

''The flowers, the visits, my happy heart dressing
gown...you always were the champagne man.''

His brow puckered. ''I don't know what you're
talking about, Teri.''

''You, Leo. I'm talking about you.''

She held out her hand, which he took, and a warm
fizz ran up her arm. She wondered if Lucy felt a warm
fizz, too, when her father cuddled her. The powerhouse of energy Leo stored in his heart probably ra-
diated all over her. As it did with Teri.

''Until I met you, all my life was like an ordinary
cup of tea,'' she explained. ''Sometimes it had sugar

in it. Sometimes…'' her mouth momentarily turned down ''…a slice of lemon.''

He nodded, listening with an intensity that encouraged her to go on.

''You were like champagne, Leo. My first taste of it. And I loved it. Loved you for giving it to me. And I think now, that falling pregnant with Lucy wasn't an accident. It was the champagne having its way, creating the magic that made all this possible. And you just keep giving it to me…the wonderful, happy, bubbly feeling that makes everything beautifully right. Does that make sense to you?''

''Yes,'' he answered huskily. ''It says it all. For me, too.''

In one accord they both turned their gaze to the baby in her arms, the baby they'd made together.

Lucy looked up at them with big trusting eyes.

The miracle, the magic of having Leo's child, Teri thought.

A circle of love.

Complete.

AN UNEXPECTED BONUS

by
Caroline Anderson

Caroline Anderson has the mind of a butterfly. She's been a nurse, a secretary, a teacher, run her own soft-furnishing business and now she's settled on writing. She says, 'I was looking for that elusive something. I finally realised it was variety, and now I have it in abundance. Every book brings new horizons and new friends, and in between books I have learned to be a juggler. My teacher husband John and I have two beautiful and talented daughters, Sarah and Hannah, umpteen pets and several acres of Suffolk that nature tries to reclaim every time we turn our backs!' Caroline writes for both the Medical Romance™ and Tender Romance™ series.

**Don't miss Caroline Anderson's brand-new book:
THE BABY BONDING
Out this month, in Medical Romance™!**

CHAPTER ONE

'He's gorgeous!'

Jo looked down at the baby girl in her arms and smiled. 'Mmm—but he's a she.'

Sue propped her arms on the edge of the crib and laughed softly. 'Not the baby, idiot. *Him*. Our Dr Latimer.'

'Oh, him. He's come in, has he? Such dedication to duty on New Year's Day.' Jo laid the baby down on her side, covered her up and straightened. 'I was just tucking up our first baby of the year. I nearly missed her arrival—in a bit of a hurry, weren't you, sweetheart?'

The baby ignored her, and so did Sue.

'You ought to see him—six foot something, dark hair, laughing grey-blue eyes...'

'Sounds like a cliché.'

Sue gave an exasperated sigh. 'Look, Jo, he's perfect. Just what you need—'

'Whoa there! Steady on.' Jo stopped what she was doing and met her friend's eyes. 'What I need,' she pointed out carefully, 'is calm, stability, security—'

'Fun, laughter, a social life—'

'A pension—'

'Pension!' Sue exploded. 'Why do you need a pension? You're twenty-nine!'

'Thirty—and because, as I've just proved, I'm getting older.'

Sue made a rude noise and bent over the baby. 'Hi, sweetheart. Welcome to the world of pensions and premature ageing. It'll be your birthday next week at this rate, you wait and see.'

Jo swatted her with the file and went out into the corridor, hiding her grin. 'You're impossible. I'm not interested in Dr Latimer. For all we know he could be married…'

'Uh-uh. Single—not even divorced.'

'So why's he taken a job in a quiet little seaside town in Suffolk? He's probably got totally unacceptable habits, or halitosis.'

Sue followed her down the corridor to the nursing station. 'No halitosis…'

'And of course you got close enough to find out.'

'Oh, yes. Matron introduced us. I swear, if I wasn't already married…' She paused. 'He's lovely, Jo, really.' Her eyes grew serious. 'He is. You wait till you meet him. He could be Mr Right.'

'I'm sure he is—for someone, but that someone isn't me, Sue. I don't believe in happy ever after.'

Sue propped herself against the wall and watched as Jo dropped the file back into the trolley. 'So have an affair.'

Jo laughed. 'In Yoxburgh? Got any more good ideas?'

'I mean it. It's time you got out and had a bit of fun. I think it's amazing that you're as normal as you are, the life you lead. You're closeted up like a nun—and what about Laura? Is she going to grow up thinking that men are a bad idea and living alone is the norm?'

Jo shook her head in disbelief and turned towards her friend.

'Leave it, Sue, please. Laura and I are fine. We don't need anyone else. I know you're only trying to help, but we're quite happy the way we are.'

Sue shrugged. 'Have it your own way.'

'I will. We're fine.' Jo sighed inwardly. It wasn't a

lie. They were happy, more or less. Sometimes they were happier than others, but most of the time they rubbed along all right, and if there were nights sometimes when the bed seemed cold and empty—well, they were few and far between, and she had plenty of friends to pass the time with.

She didn't admit to herself that passing the time was all she did, putting one foot in front of the other, taking the days one at a time, shuffling on towards retirement and the hereafter with little enthusiasm for anything but Laura and the mums and babies in her care—

Lord, how maudlin!

'Stop matchmaking, Sue,' she told her friend firmly. 'Anyway, haven't you got anything better to do?'

'Oh, tons—all my PNs. You can tell me what you think of him later. See you!'

Jo watched her go despairingly. She had a few postnatal checks to do herself, but first of all, since Dr Latimer was in the building, he could make himself useful.

She quickened her stride, bustling down the corridor towards the entrance, and as she rounded the corner she almost fell over a group of people standing clustered in Reception.

Matron, the receptionist, a nursing sister—and him. At least, she imagined it was him—and, yes, he was gorgeous, she supposed, if your taste ran to that sort of thing.

Tall, dark, handsome, clichéd—the stuff of fiction. As far as Jo was concerned, though, he was just a man like all the others.

Then he looked at her, those storm-grey eyes meeting hers and holding, and, like a display of baked beans in a supermarket, she felt as if someone had yanked out a tin from the bottom row and tumbled her into a heap at his feet.

'Ah, Jo—perfect timing.'

She blinked, breaking the spell, and looked away. To her astonishment she was still standing, rather puzzled by the strange hiccup in her heart rate and the fizzing in her veins.

Not because of him, surely? Men just didn't do that to her!

Matron smiled, holding out her arm to welcome her to the group. 'This is Jo Halliday—she's the senior community midwife. You'll be seeing a lot of her, of course, because she runs the antenatal clinics in your surgery as well as the classes here. Jo, come and meet Ed Latimer.'

Come and meet him? She might, if she tried really hard, be able to remember how to walk!

'Hi, there,' she said, thankful that her voice at least sounded normal. 'Pleased to meet you. Actually, I've got a job for you, if I could hijack you from the grand tour?'

'Oh, we've finished,' Matron said airily. 'He's all yours.'

He chuckled, a deep, rich sound that for some reason sent a shiver down her spine. 'At your service,' he said with a little bow of his head, and the grin that accompanied it made her heart do something crazy and stupid and not entirely normal. 'What did you want me for?'

She wasn't sure any longer. Her body seemed to have a hidden agenda all its own. She swallowed. 'New baby needs a check—I wonder if you'd do the honours.'

'Sure. Lead the way.'

She did, taking him back down the corridor towards the GP unit, aware with every step of his presence at her side.

'Here we are, female infant of Angela Grigson, born at eight-thirty this morning.'

'So, little baby Grigson is the first of the New Year?'

'Yes. It's a small unit, so it's amazing we've had one on New Year's Day. Sometimes it's days before we get a baby—last year it was the ninth of January.'

'Normal vaginal delivery, I take it? Was she booked for admission to the GP unit?'

'No. She was due to go to the hospital, it's only her first, but she didn't have time. I was hardly here myself! I've checked everything except the heartbeat, but I expect you'll want to check her again.'

She was running on like a steam train! She shut her mouth with a little snap and stepped back.

Ed Latimer gave her a quizzical little look, then turned his attention to the peaceful baby. 'OK. Sorry, little one, I'm going to wake you up.' He looked round. 'Where's Mum?'

'Gone to the loo. She's very relaxed about it all.'

'Not to mention hasty! What was the Apgar score?'

'Ten,' she replied promptly, glad to focus on the professional rather than the general. 'She was very alert and vocal at birth, bright pink and flailing furiously!'

'Excellent. No other problems, I take it, apart from the unseemly speed?'

'No, everything was perfectly normal, just fast. Mum had the shakes afterwards, but that's quite common with hasty deliveries.'

Jo watched him undress the tiny scrap, his big hands astonishingly gentle, his eyes scanning the baby for anything out of the ordinary. He checked the eyes, the ears, the mouth and nose, the fontanelles or soft spots on the head, both hands and feet, all the digits, then laid the baby face down over his palm and checked the spine with a big, blunt fingertip.

Then he checked her bottom to make sure that all necessary organs were present and correct, dropped her an inch onto the cot to test her Moro reflex and grunted in satisfaction as the baby flung her arms out and cried. She grasped his fingers and held on as he lifted her, and when he dangled her so her feet just touched the mattress she tried to walk.

'Good girl. Now the bit you'll hate. Sorry, poppet.' He folded her little legs up, bent them up against her sides and wiggled them to check her hip joints.

Predictably she wailed, and he scooped her up and hugged her. 'Sorry, little one,' he murmured, cradling her against his chest. Just to get her revenge, she emptied her bladder down his shirt.

'Well, that answers that question,' he said with a grimace. 'Her waterworks function.'

Jo laughed and, taking the baby from him, she put her into a nappy and laid her back into the cot so he could listen to her heart.

'That'll teach me to hug them when they're naked,' he said ruefully, blotting at his shirt with a paper towel.

'At least she isn't a boy. They always pee in your eye.'

He grinned at her, and once again her heart did that stupid thing.

Nuts.

She watched in silence as he checked the baby's heart for any unusual sounds, and then he folded the stethoscope and tucked it back into his pocket, before dressing the little one again.

'Can you manage?' Jo asked, which earned her a wry look.

'Why do you women think you're the only ones who get to play with the new babies?' he said softly, and turned his attention back to the little one in his hands. 'Can I manage?' he murmured. 'The nerve of the woman! Just so cheeky, isn't she? Yes!'

He was competent, she had to give him that. She wondered if there was a child in his life—or a partner not covered by the standard 'single/married/widowed/divorced' categories of the application form.

Very likely. He was the boy next door grown up, and if he was still single it was very odd.

Perhaps he had unspeakable habits after all?

Then he straightened and met her eyes, and there was something sad and lonely lurking in the depths of them—something that tugged at an echo in her heart. She wanted to reach out to him, to touch him, to ask what it was that made him sad, but before she could make a fool of herself there was a shuffling behind her, and a cheery voice said, 'Hello, there. Everything all right?'

She turned, dragging her eyes from his, and smiled at the young woman in the tatty dressing-gown who climbed up onto the bed and sat down cautiously.

'Hi, Angela. Fine—just a routine check on the baby. How are you feeling now?'

'Oh, fine. Bit sore.' She looked across at Ed and smiled. 'You must be the new doctor.'

'That's me—Ed Latimer. Pleased to meet you. Congratulations on a perfect little baby. I've checked her over and she's all present and correct—lovely. Well done.' He took her hand in a firm grasp, and Angela Grigson turned to putty. She smiled and dimpled and went all silly, and Jo rolled her eyes and looked away.

The woman was happily married and had been for the past five years, and yet one look at their new GP and she went gaga only hours after the birth of her first child.

Jo predicted a massive rush of minor ailments at the surgery in the next few days, checking out the new doctor. The grapevine would be humming like a guitar string and nobody would be able to talk about anything else!

'I told you he'd knock your socks off.'

'He's just a man.'

'Pooh. He's gorgeous.'

'We've done this conversation for the past three days. Can't anyone talk about anything else? I'm getting sick of hearing his name.'

'Whose name?'

They both jumped guiltily and turned towards the door of the surgery kitchen. 'Yours,' Jo said, not bothering to lie. 'Everyone in Yoxburgh is talking about you—and it's only Monday. You're the sole topic of conversation!'

He gave a short laugh. 'I hope it's good.'

'So far you don't seem to have irritated the dowagers or killed off their grandchildren so, yes, at the moment it's good. You might blow it yet, of course, once you start doing a few more surgeries.'

He laughed. 'Quite probably.' He propped his lean hips against the worktop and looked hopefully at the kettle. 'Any chance of a cup of tea?'

Sue scooted through the door. 'I'm off on my visits. Jo'll make you tea—she's the resident mummy.'

He quirked a brow. 'Resident mummy?'

Jo laughed a little awkwardly and flicked the button on the kettle. 'I make them look after themselves and eat properly, and I nag a bit.'

'You sound like an asset to the practice.'

She laughed again. 'They hate it, mostly—except when I'm dishing out tea and coffee. Then they usually form an orderly queue.'

He chuckled and reached for two mugs from the rack, handing them to her. 'Is it just us?'

'At the moment. Were you looking for me, or just the kettle?'

'You, actually.' He lounged against the worktop again, looking sexier than he had any right to. 'I wanted to go over the routine—you know I'm taking over all the obstetrics for the practice?'

'Yes, I did. Not a problem—we can sit down with our tea and go through it all. It's quite straightforward.'

'Have you got time?'

'Just about. I'm on call but it's quiet at the moment. How about you?'

He chuckled. 'I'm on half-timetable this week, just while I settle in. They wanted me to have a nice gentle introduction so I didn't get the screaming ab-dabs and run off into the sunset before I'd had time to get used to the place. It's quite a luxury, really, after doing locum work for six months and my GP training and obstetrics before that, but I must confess to being a bit bored.'

'It won't last,' she assured him drily. 'With this flu epidemic and the worst part of the winter lined up, you can be sure it'll deteriorate very soon.'

'I'm so glad. I was beginning to wonder if I'd have enough to do or if it was all a big mistake.'

Jo gave an astonished laugh. 'Just make the most of it,' she advised him with a grin. 'How do you take your tea?'

'White, no sugar—thanks.' His fingers brushed hers as he took the mug, and a shiver of something elemental and thoroughly silly ran up her arm and curdled her brain.

What *was* it about him? He was just an ordinary man—wasn't he? So he was good-looking—so were lots of men. She pulled out one of the chairs from under the table and sat down, giving her tea very much more attention than it really merited while she waited for her head to clear. He didn't help matters. He flipped the chair round, straddling it and resting his forearms on the back, the mug dangling from long, strong fingers.

Ridiculous. Even his fingers drove her crazy!

'So, tell me about how the obstetrics is arranged,' he said suddenly, dragging her back to earth. 'How many of our mums have their babies here and how many in the Audley?'

She latched onto the professional conversation like a lifeline and launched into a barrage of statistics. 'More and more are having them either here or at home—recently I've had one or two who've given birth at the Audley and gone into the GP unit for a postnatal period of two or three days, just to get a rest.'

'Yes, that's one of the problems of sending them all home so soon—I often wonder if they don't need more rest, but busy hospitals certainly don't seem to be the place to get it.'

She set her mug on the table, folding her arms to keep her fingers still. 'Most of the postnatal cases are mums with other children and just need a break, or their partners aren't able to take time off, but whatever their reasons we encourage them to use the unit, of course, because otherwise we can't justify its existence and it'll be closed.'

'Is that likely?'

She shrugged and pulled a face. 'Maybe. Several units in the Suffolk area have closed over the last ten to twenty years, and others are under threat. We use it for obs and gynae post-op as well as just a straightforward delivery unit to maximise the use of the beds, but it's certainly used to capacity most of the time one way and another and we try and keep it that way.'

He nodded thoughtfully, sipping his tea and gazing absently over the rim of his mug. 'So how many babies are delivered in the community every year?' he asked next, trapping her with his eyes.

Were they grey or blue? Hard to tell in this light...

'In our immediate area about eighty, either in the unit or at home. We refer whenever we feel it's necessary, and we never take chances. We've got fairly strict criteria for the GP unit, although if they don't comply with the criteria I might still let them have a home birth, but we watch them like hawks. We're too far from the specialist unit to be able to take risks.'

His eyes searched hers. 'Does that undermine your confidence?'

She smiled. 'It used to. Not any more. I think experience counts for a lot. I'm much more willing to let mums have a go now than I used to be.'

'Are you happy to rely on your professional judgement, or would you like tighter guidelines?'

'No. I like to be able to take each case on its merits. I rely on instinct as well.' She waited for the criticism, but to her surprise it wasn't forthcoming.

'So do I,' he admitted, 'although I'm not sure I always trust my instincts yet. Maybe when I've got more experience in general practice. In the meantime, I'd rather check with a colleague. I'm not afraid to admit I don't know all the answers.'

'So you won't mind when I keep you in order?' she said with a hesitant smile.

He chuckled. 'I'll be relying on it.'

She nodded, relieved that they agreed about something so important. Not that she'd meant to be so unsubtle about it, but there you go, she thought, not everyone's born to be a diplomat.

Her bleeper warbled, and she popped through to Reception, then came back. 'Got to fly,' she told him, 'one of my imminent mums. In fact, are you busy? I'll need an accomplice—this one's a home birth. You could gain a bit of that experience you were talking about.'

'Sure.' He drained his tea, flipped the chair back under the table and stood, ready and waiting. 'Your car or mine, or both?'

'I'll take mine because it's got my stuff in—you're welcome to hitch a ride or take yours, whatever, but I'll ring her first.'

She went into the office and rang through to Julie Brown, half her attention still on the man lounging on the wall behind her. 'Julie? Hi—Jo Halliday. How's things?'

'Oh, you know—I had a twinge so I finished feeding the sheep and came in, and once I stopped moving I realised things were getting on a bit. I don't think it'll be long.'

'Hang on, then. Is anyone with you?'

'No. Tim's down at the other farm and the kids are with Mum.'

'Right, unlock the back door, shut the dog up and go up to your room. Then lie down and *rest!*'

Julie chuckled. 'Yes, Sergeant-Major, sir!'

'Just do it. I'll be ten minutes.'

She cradled the phone. 'Farmer's wife,' she said to Ed. 'She says it won't be long. She's had two—I believe her. Are you ready? I'm going now.'

He nodded. 'Fine.'

'Are you going to follow? I'll have to stay two hours after the birth.'

'No problem. I've got nothing else to do and it might be useful. I'll come with you, if I may? I can ask you questions on the way.'

And distract me, she thought, but in fact he didn't. He sat very quietly and said not a lot until they'd arrived, and then as they got out she noticed he was a little pale.

'You don't take any prisoners, do you?' he said drily.

'I said we were in a hurry,' she said with a grin, and he managed a wan smile.

'Hmm. I'm not used to being driven. I find it a bit unnerving.'

She laughed, grabbed her bag out of the car and headed round the side of the house. A volley of barking heralded their arrival, and as she opened the back door the big black dog launched itself at her.

'Brogue, get down!'

The dog subsided, licking her hand, and with a frown she went into the kitchen and found Julie slumped over the table. She lifted her head and gazed at Jo.

'Couldn't make the stairs,' she said breathlessly. 'Think it's coming—'

'Good job you've got a decent-sized table in here, then, isn't it, since the floor's a bit doggy?' Jo said with a grin. 'Ed, give me a hand. Oh, Julie, this is Dr Ed Latimer, our new GP obstetrician.'

Julie peered up at him, and said weakly, 'Hi.' She dropped her head again. 'Oh, here we go again...'

'She's having a contraction—come on, let's clear the table and move her as soon as it's over so I can have a look.' Jo scooped papers and mugs off the table, and stacked cushions for Julie to lean against, then glanced at Ed over her shoulder. 'There's a big black box in the boot of my car. Could you get it?'

He went without argument, to her relief, and was back in seconds, by which time she'd shut Brogue in the utility room and was back with Julie.

'Thanks,' she murmured, lifting the lid off the box. Pulling out the delivery pack and a few inco pads, she spread them out on the top of the big old table and they lifted Julie onto it. Her dress was quickly hitched up, and as they dispensed with her underwear it was obvious the baby wasn't waiting for anyone.

'I'll just wash my hands,' Jo said, but there wasn't time to find gloves, because the baby was coming, and coming now. 'Just pant,' Jo told Julie, and the baby shot out into her hands in a slippery rush just moments later.

'Hello, little fellow,' she said with a smile. Lifting him, she put him down on Julie's abdomen and grinned at Ed. 'Three thirty-seven. Remember that. Didn't need us at all,' she added over the baby's indignant squall. Washing her hands again, she dried them on a clean towel from one of the kitchen drawers, put gloves on and checked for any problems.

It all looked very straightforward, and after the cord stopped pulsing she clamped and cut it. Wrapping the baby in another towel from the drawer, she handed him to Ed. 'Hold this,' she ordered.

'This,' he said softly. 'Is that any way to speak to you, son?' he murmured and, taking the corner of the towel, he gently wiped the baby's face.

Jo dragged her eyes away from him and tried to concentrate on the patient and her needs. She was propped on the pile of hastily assembled cushions, and she looked thoroughly uncomfortable on the hard tabletop.

'I'd like to move you to somewhere more comfy,' she was saying, when the back door burst open and Tim erupted into the room, his eyes wild.

'Ah, Julie, love, you could have waited for me!' he said with a laugh, and hugged his wife.

'It's a boy,' she told him, and he closed his eyes and hugged her again.

'Everything all right?'

'Think so,' Jo told him. 'We haven't really had time to check—he's only just been born a few minutes.'

'You check Mum, I'll check the baby,' Ed said, and

she was suddenly reminded that he was a fellow-professional and not just someone she'd dragged along for the ride. She wondered how badly she'd ordered him around, but couldn't remember.

Too bad. The baby was the first priority, and it was her delivery anyway. 'Do you want to wait for the placenta, or shall I give you an injection?' she asked Julie, knowing full well what the answer would be.

'I'll wait—I can feel a contraction now, I think.'

Jo laid a hand on Julie's soft abdomen and pressed down, and she could feel the uterus working. 'Yes, you're right. We'll wait. Are you OK there?'

'I'll manage.'

It didn't take long. She popped the afterbirth into one of the bowls and checked it quickly, filled the other with hot water to wash the mother down, examined Julie for any little nicks or tears and declared her to be fine.

'Baby, too. He's got good lungs,' Ed said ruefully, pulling the earpieces of the stethoscope out of his ears so the bellowing didn't damage his hearing permanently. 'I'll check his heart later when he's quiet but, judging by his colour, I can't imagine he's got a problem.'

'No. He's a lusty little chap,' Jo said, giving him her attention for the first time. She looked at the placenta more thoroughly, lifting up the membranes and checking for any abnormalities, then put it into a yellow clinical waste bag, sealed it and put it inside another one.

'Want to weigh him?' Ed asked.

'Not yet. I want to clear up a little first and then get Julie upstairs. You feeling strong, Tim?' she asked, bagging up the rest of the clinical waste and popping a pad between Julie's legs.

He grinned and scooped his wife up in his arms, carrying her up to their bedroom with the others trailing behind. 'Fancy having him in the kitchen,' Tim said affectionately as he set her down. 'You spend your life at that damn table—I might have known you'd have the baby on it!'

'It'll be something to tell the grandchildren when they come over for Sunday lunch,' Julie said with a chuckle.

'Hmm. Eating off the same table, I have no doubt.' Jo laughed. 'Right, we need to undress you and freshen you up, feed the baby, and then after your bath I think you'll need a rest—I should think you're exhausted after such a hard labour,' she said with a smile.

'Oh, yes—all of about an hour from the first twinge.'

'You should have rung me on the mobile,' Tim scolded.

'I did—you left it switched off,' Julie pointed out.

'Now, now, children, don't fight,' Jo said. She sent Tim off to clear up the devastation in the kitchen and make everyone a cup of tea while she helped Julie out of her clothes and into a dressing-gown.

Once Julie was undressed she was able to feed the baby, and Jo felt the usual surge of satisfaction as she watched the little baby suckle from his mother. He was the third of their children that she'd delivered or monitored in pregnancy, and it was gratifying to have been involved in the arrival of the whole family.

She looked up at Ed, wondering what he was making of all of this, and surprised a look of sadness and longing on his face again. How strange. He was so good with children—had he lost one? Was that it?

He looked up and caught her eye. His expression became immediately neutral, as if he'd carefully schooled his face to remove the traces of emotion.

'Teatime,' Tim said cheerfully, pushing the door open with his foot and carrying in a tray.

Ed stood up. 'Not for me, thanks. Things seem fine. I think I'll go for a wander—have a look round outside.

I'm still feeling a bit green after the white-knuckle ride—Jo doesn't exactly hang about. I'll be back in a while.'

His smile was a little strained. Jo sipped her tea and wondered what had put that look on his face and made him want to run away—because that was what he was doing, she was sure. She didn't believe he was still feeling queasy for a moment.

The baby dozed off, and Julie put her cup down and smiled wearily at Jo. 'I could murder that bath now.'

'Good idea. I'll run it, you stay there.'

It wasn't too hot because of the baby, but she made it nice and deep because there was nothing like a good wallow after delivery. Then she helped Julie into the bath, before unwrapping the baby that Tim was holding and lowering him carefully into the water between Julie's knees.

He woke up a little, blinking in the light and gazing up with those wonderful blue eyes of the newborn, and Julie helped her wash his soft, delicate skin with careful hands.

'He seems so tiny—you forget,' Julie said, her voice hushed and full of awe, and Jo looked at him and remembered Laura.

'You're right—you do forget. I can't believe Laura was ever this small.'

'No. She certainly doesn't look it now. She's so tall, isn't she? How old is she?'

'Twelve. She takes after me and my mother—we're both quite tall.'

Jo scooped the baby out of the water and wrapped him in a towel off the radiator, then sprinkled a few drops of lavender and tea-tree oil into the bath and topped up the hot water. Julie sank down for a good wallow and sighed with ecstasy.

'I can't believe she's twelve,' she said after a moment, sounding stunned. 'Almost a teenager. I can remember when she was born. I don't know how you cope alone.'

'I've got Mum. I couldn't work and look after her without my mother's help.'

Julie laughed. 'No, mums are wonderful. I'd be lost without mine during lambing and harvesting.'

Jo took the baby across the landing to the bedroom, leaving the doors open, and took the little spring balance out of the box Tim had brought upstairs. She hooked the nylon sling underneath it, popped the baby naked into the sling and held up the balance.

'Three point seven kilos—eight pounds three ounces,' she told the mother. 'How does that compare?'

'Heavier than Lucy, about the same as Robert.'

'What are you calling this one? Does he have a name?'

Tim came upstairs again and into the room. 'Michael, we'd thought.'

'Or Anna,' Julie said from the depths of her bath. 'I think Michael's more appropriate. I could kill another cup of tea.'

Tim went through to the bathroom, mug in hand. 'How did I guess?' he said, a smile in his voice, and for the millionth time Jo wondered what it would have been like to have a father for her daughter, a man who loved and cherished her and was committed to her, instead of—

She cut off the train of thought and concentrated on the baby. He was gorgeous, a lovely sturdy little chap with everything going for him. She put a nappy on him before he could catch her out, popped him into a vest and sleepsuit and tucked him up in the crib that was standing ready in the corner.

Then she helped Julie out of the bath, and while Tim

helped her into her nightclothes and down to the warm kitchen Jo went down ahead of them and tidied up her bag, settled herself at the cleaned-up table and wrote up her notes while they sat by the Aga and chatted about the delivery.

Jo lifted her head as Ed came back in, and Tim grinned at him.

'You must have heard the kettle boil. Fancy a cuppa now?'

Ed smiled, and the strain seemed to have left his face. 'Thanks. Don't mind if I do. Everything all right?'

'Yup. No problems.' Jo shut the notes, handed the file back to Julie and slipped her pen back into her pocket, before washing her hands again. 'Baby's upstairs in the bedroom if you want to check his heart now he's quiet.'

'Sure. Thanks.'

He came down a few minutes later, the baby in his arms, and handed him to Julie. 'He was chewing his fists and grizzling—I reckon you're going to have your work cut out feeding him. He's going to be a real trencherman.'

'Just like his father, then,' Julie said affectionately.

The couple exchanged a loving glance, and Jo looked away, staring down into her mug and wondering if Ed was all right now. He seemed fine, though, bright and perky, laughing with the Browns and seeming to enjoy himself while the baby tucked into his first proper meal.

Perhaps he really had been feeling queasy? She had driven rather fast.

Jo checked her watch, surprised to find that it was two hours since baby Michael had been born, and packed up her things. 'We'll be on our way now. Don't overdo it.'

'Would I?' Julie said with a smile.

Jo arched a brow, shrugged into her coat and loaded everything into the car with Ed's help.

'Take care, now, and ring me if you're worried. I'll check you again before ten, but call if you want anything.'

'We will, and thanks,' Tim said, and gave her a hug. He shook Ed's hand, and then they were off, bumping down the track towards the road.

'It's got colder,' she said, fiddling with the heater controls, and wished she'd got a pair of gloves. Laura had borrowed them, of course, like she borrowed everything these days. Goodness knows if she'd ever see them again.

They turned onto the main road and headed back towards the surgery. Out of deference to his nerves she drove much more slowly, and Ed commented on it.

'In case you hadn't noticed, we were none too early,' she reminded him with a laugh.

'Yes. I can see why you went fast—did you think she was that far on?'

Jo nodded. 'There was something in her voice—after a while you get an instinct for the little nuances. She just sounded—well, close, I suppose is the best way to describe it.'

'She was certainly that!'

He fell silent, and she drove back into Yoxburgh in the dark with her headlights gleaming on the frosty road. As she pulled up at the surgery she turned to him in the dark car.

'Ed—are you OK?'

He paused, his hand on the doorhandle, and looked at her warily. 'Fine. Why shouldn't I be?'

She shrugged. 'I don't know. I just thought—what happened back there? My driving isn't that bad, so what was it all about?'

He gave a wry smile. 'You noticed. Sometimes…' He

sighed. 'Sometimes I just get a bit choked. I wonder what it would be like—I expect you do the same.'

She relaxed, relieved that there was apparently no great tragedy hanging over him. 'I've got a daughter,' she told him. 'I know all about it—the pluses and the minuses.'

He looked surprised. 'I didn't realise you were married.'

'I'm not. I'm a single parent—always have been,' she added, so he understood her situation.

'Oh. I see. That can't be easy.'

'My mother helps. I couldn't manage without her.'

Her mobile phone rang, and she answered it, then turned to him with a sigh.

'Problems?' he said.

'I have to go out again—one of my mums might be in labour, and she wants to see me. I'll sort the car out, reload my box and go over there. You coming?'

'Do you need me?'

His voice was soft, and something funny happened in her chest—something she didn't understand, something that came out of nowhere and left her feeling empty and confused and a little breathless.

'No—no, I don't need you,' she told him hastily, and wondered if it was true...

CHAPTER TWO

'Mum?'

A door crashed in the distance, and Jo met her mother's eyes with a rueful grin. 'So much for our peaceful teabreak.'

'Mum?' Footsteps retreated, then returned, attached to a bright smile in a pretty heart-shaped face the image of Jo's. Long dark hair, again like her mother's, was scooped up into a band, and now at the end of the day strands escaped, drifting round her soft hazel eyes and giving her a dreamy look.

'Here you are. Hi, Grannie. Wow, a cake! Yum—can I have a bit?' She cut a chunk, hitched herself up onto a stool by the breakfast bar and sank her teeth into the cake, without waiting for a reply—or a plate.

Her grandmother slid a plate under the hovering hand and smiled. 'Good day, darling?'

'OK, I s'pose. Bit pointless at homework club because the staff hadn't got round to giving us any homework yet, but that was cool. We talked about Cara's new boyfriend.' Her eyes swivelled to her mother. 'Talking of which, I hear your new doctor's rather gorgeous.'

Jo nearly choked on her tea. 'I wouldn't have gone that far. He's all right, I suppose.'

'Cara's mum said he was really yummy. So's this cake—can I have another bit?'

'Will you eat your supper?'

Laura rolled her eyes. 'Mother, when do I ever not?'

It was true. She ate like a horse, thank God, in these days of eating disorders and unhappy children with ap-

26

palling self-images and huge expectations hanging over them. 'OK,' she agreed, and cut a rather more moderate slice. No point in going to the other extreme. 'So, let's hear about Love's Young Dream, then.'

'Cara's boyfriend?' Laura giggled. 'Oh, he's in year nine—the third-year seniors, a year above me, Grannie,' she explained patiently to her far-from-senile grand-mother, 'and he's tall and his hair's streaked blond and he's got an earring and a tattoo on his bum.'

'Bottom,' Jo corrected automatically. 'And how does Cara know that?' she added, dreading the answer.

Laura laughed. 'He had to do a moonie for a forfeit at a party she went to—she says it's a dragon and it's really cute.'

'Let's hope no one gets the urge to stick a sword in it,' Jo's mother said pragmatically, and cleared the breakfast bar while Jo tried not to choke.

'Can't I have any more?' Laura said in her best feel-sorry-for-me voice, watching the cake vanish into a tin, but her grandmother was unmoved.

'You'll just be sick. Go and wash your hands and come down for supper in half an hour.'

She disappeared, leaving her coat dropped over a chair and her shoes scattered on the kitchen floor where she'd kicked them off.

'A tattoo, eh?' Rebecca Halliday said with a murmur as the pounding footsteps faded up the stairs.

Jo rolled her eyes and picked up the shoes and the coat, tidying them away. 'Whatever next. I wish I could influence her choice of friends a bit more—she worries me.'

'She's fine. She's a sensible girl. She won't get into trouble.'

'You thought I was sensible,' Jo reminded her point-edly. 'So did I, come to that, and we were both wrong.'

'You *were* sensible. You were lied to. We all were.'

'You're very loyal, Mum.'

Her mother hugged her briefly. 'You've come through.' She dropped her arms and moved away, not given to overt displays of affection, and started scrubbing carrots like a woman possessed.

Jo helped her, and after a moment her mother looked up and met her eyes. 'So, tell me about this doctor, then. Gorgeous, eh?'

Jo could feel the tell-tale colour creeping up her neck, and busied herself with the casserole. 'Oh, he's just a man, Mum. Nothing special.'

'Married?'

Funny how one word could carry so very many little nuances. 'No, he's not married,' Jo said patiently. 'He's thirty-two, single, he started working in hospital obstetrics and decided he wanted to be a GP so he retrained. He's been doing locum for six months while he looked for a job.'

'And now he's ready to settle down.'

Jo put the lid back on the casserole with a little bang. 'How should I know? He's only been working since the first of January, we've had a weekend when he's been off and it's only the fifth now!'

Her mother slid the carrot pan onto the hob and flicked the switch. 'Don't get crabby, I was only asking. Anyway, you usually have them down pat in the first ten minutes.'

'No, that's Sue. I usually take fifteen.'

Rebecca laughed. 'Sorry. I stand corrected.' She deftly changed the subject. 'I gather Julie Brown had her baby yesterday.'

'Yes—another boy. Both well. I was so busy I didn't have time to tell you. It was a lovely delivery—on the kitchen table.'

Her mother smiled. 'So I gather. That'll make meal-times interesting for them. How about a glass of wine?'

'What a good idea.'

Jo took the proffered glass and followed her mother into the sitting room, dropping into the comfy sofa and resting her head back against the high cushion. It was more comfortable than her own little annexe at the other end of the house where she usually spent her time after work, but tonight her mother had cooked for them and obviously felt a little lonely.

So did Jo so that was fine. Since her father had died they'd found companionship and support in each other, and without her, as she'd told Ed, she wouldn't have been able to cope with bringing Laura up and keeping her career—

'It would have been your father's sixtieth birthday to-day,' her mother said quietly into the silence.

Jo's eyes flew open. 'Oh, Mum, I'm sorry, I forgot,' she said, filled with remorse.

'He was going to retire—funny how you make all these plans and the decisions get taken away from you and changed. I can't believe it's nearly four years since he died.'

'Or nearly thirteen since I had Laura. He really adored her.'

'Yes. They were great friends.'

Jo swirled her wine round and peered through it at the lights. 'You must miss him.'

'I do—every day, but life goes on.' She sat quietly for a moment, her teeth worrying the inside of her lip, then she met Jo's eyes. 'Maurice wants me to go to dinner at the weekend. I said I'd think about it.'

Jo thought of Maurice Parker, the senior partner who was due to retire soon and whose place Ed would fill, and wondered what her father would have thought.

They'd been colleagues and friends for years—would he have minded? Would Maurice's wife have minded, after all the suffering she'd gone through before she died? Would she even have known what was going on?

It was as if her mother read her mind. 'He had such a difficult time with Betty—Alzheimer's is such a cruel disease,' she said. 'She didn't know him, you know, not for the last three years. Your father used to say she'd be the death of him.'

'He aged, certainly. He looks much better now in the last couple of years without all the strain of her illness to weigh him down.'

'Awful, what love and loyalty can do to you. Must check the carrots and put the broccoli on.'

Jo let her go, sipped her wine and thought about her father. He'd always seemed so fit until the heart attack that killed him. There'd been no warning, no time to prepare. One minute he'd been there, the next he'd gone. Her mother had been devastated, and Laura too. Jo had been so busy propping them both up she'd hardly had time to grieve, and by the time she'd lifted her head above water again it had seemed too late, a little contrived.

She had grieved, though, in the privacy of her own room, shedding huge, silent tears for the man who'd been so fair and so kind to her all her life.

He'd been her best friend, a rock when Laura had been born, and without his support she wouldn't have been able to train. True, her mother had looked after the baby, but it had been her father who'd encouraged her and supported her financially, bought her a car and paid the running expenses and paid for everything Laura had needed.

They'd turned one end of the house into a separate annexe, giving Jo and her baby privacy but easy access for babysitting, and with their help she'd built herself a career of which she was proud.

Then suddenly, without warning, he'd gone, leaving Maurice, and James Kalbraier, to cope with the practice. Maurice had cut down his hours, taken on another doctor, Mary Brady, and concentrated on nursing Betty for the last few years of her life.

And now Jo's mother was talking about going out to dinner with Maurice.

Jo considered the idea, and decided it was a good one. They'd both loved their spouses, but they were gone and Maurice and Rebecca were still alive.

Yes. It would do them both good to get out. Who knows, they might—

'Supper!'

'Coming!'

She took her wine glass through into the kitchen and put it down by the sink. 'Mmm, smells good. Have you called Laura?'

'Well, I did yell, but she's got that music on so loud…'

'I'll get her,' Jo said with a grin, and ran upstairs. She banged on the door which was vibrating gently with the music her daughter was listening to, and opened it a crack. 'Supper, darling.'

'OK.' The noise vanished, and the silence was deafening.

'You really shouldn't have it on so loud,' she began, but Laura laughed and skipped past her, flitting down the stairs and running through to her grandmother's kitchen, ignoring the predictable lecture.

'Hi, Grannie, what's for supper—? Oh, yum! Can I help?'

Jo smiled and followed her through more slowly. She wasn't a bad kid—just a little loud, with questionable taste in friends. She supposed she could send Laura to the independent school her mother kept offering to pay for, but that would mean travelling to school, no convenient buses and after-school homework clubs, and her friends would be scattered far and wide.

This way, questionable though some of them might be, they were nearby, and when Jo was working that was very important.

'We've got a panto rehearsal tonight,' Laura reminded her as she joined them at the table. 'Will you test me on my lines?'

Jo laughed humourlessly. 'Just so long as you don't try and test me—I haven't had time to look at them since before Christmas.'

'Mother! Roz will skin you alive!'

'Don't I know it! I'll try and have a quick scan through after supper—perhaps Grannie will test you.'

'Of course I will, darling. How's it going?'

Jo laughed. 'It was awful before Christmas. We'll see if anyone has spent the last couple of weeks learning their lines or if they've all switched off and forgotten what little they did know. I suspect the latter.'

'Based on personal experience?' her mother said sagely, and Jo gave a rueful chuckle.

'You guessed. Oh, well, there's time.'

'Have they got anyone else for the chorus yet?' Laura asked, tucking into her casserole with huge enthusiasm.

'I don't know.'

'You ought to ask Dr What's-his-name—what *is* his name? The new guy?'

'Latimer—Ed Latimer. I doubt if he'd be interested.'

'You could ask,' she suggested round a forkful of carrots.

She could—but she didn't want to. She didn't want Ed Latimer any nearer her than he had to be, for any more time than was absolutely necessary. He was too disturbing, too masculine. Too male. Just—too much.

She finished her meal in silence, listening with half an ear to Laura and her mother chattering, then she loaded the dishwasher and excused herself for a quick shower before the rehearsal. The water was warm and silky and sensuous, sliding over her naked skin and making her aware of herself in a way she'd almost forgotten.

Her mind turned to Ed again, and she closed her eyes and moaned softly. Why? She'd spent years fending off flirts, and none of them had even so much as ruffled the surface of her peaceful existence.

And now Ed Latimer had come strolling into her life, his hands shoved casually into his pockets, all testosterone and laughing eyes, and her self-control was lying on the floor, belly-up and grinning like a submissive dog!

'This is awful! What on earth's the matter with all of you? Two weeks off and you've all keeled over and died!'

There was a chorus of feeble protest, and their hard-pressed producer threw down her script and stalked into the kitchen. Jo met Laura's eyes and smiled encouragingly, then went into the kitchen after Roz, closing the door quietly.

'Roz?'

'It's like this every year! I don't know why I do it! They screech through by the skin of their teeth, just about pulling the thing together by the final dress rehearsal—sometimes not even then! This is the thirteenth year, you realise that? I knew we ought to give it a rest, but they wouldn't listen. It'll be fine, they all said, and now look at them! Corpsed, the lot of them, the second you take their scripts away! Well, that's it. They're not having their scripts again, any of them, and they can just manage with the prompt!'

Jo soothed Roz's ruffled feathers and gave her time to settle down. 'Perhaps we ought to have our break early and let everyone calm down a bit—the urn's hot now. Why don't I make a big pot of tea and open the biscuits and we'll try again in a little while?'

Roz stabbed her hands through her hair and gave a stifled scream. 'They drive me nuts,' she confessed.

'You love it.'

'I know. I must be a masochist.'

They shared a smile, and Jo filled the teapot while Roz poured milk into the cups. 'We still need another man for the chorus—I don't suppose your new doctor wants to get involved?' Roz asked her.

She slopped the tea into a saucer and splashed her hand. 'Damn,' she muttered, and put down the pot. 'I don't know—why don't you ask him? I expect he'll be too busy.'

'Would you ask him for me, as you'll see him?'

And, just like that, she was forced into a corner from which there was no escape.

'Hi, there.'

Shivers ran up Jo's spine and made her hair tingle against her scalp. She turned, groping for a smile that wasn't completely idiotic, and forced herself to meet Ed's eyes. 'Hi, there, yourself,' she said, and was very proud of the fact that her voice only croaked the tiniest bit.

'How are things? Any imminent obstetrics for me?'

'Sorry.' She shook her head and smiled a more natural smile. 'They're all hanging on till their due dates.'

'Even your lady the other night?'

'Even her. Sorry. I've got an antenatal class at the

hospital in a minute—I'll ask them if they want to get a wriggle on for you, shall I?'

He chuckled and reached out to test the kettle, and the sun slanting through the window caught his hair, gleaming on the red lights in it and turning it a rich, deep chestnut. It was a lovely colour, much more interesting than plain dark brown, and she wanted to reach out and touch it…

'There should be enough in there for you,' she told him, dragging her attention back to the kettle. 'It's just boiled.'

'Tea for you?'

'I'm OK.' She held up her full mug to show him, and he nodded and snagged a mug off the draining-board.

'No doubt they'll all produce in the fullness of time,' he said, going back to their previous conversation. 'We've had two in the past week—I suppose that's my ration.'

'Absolutely. I've got something to ask you, by the way, talking of producing. The thirteenth annual Yoxburgh panto is short of a male chorus member—Roz asked me to ask you, but I told her you'd be too busy.'

He turned and met her eyes. 'Why?'

'Why are they short?'

'Why did you tell her I'd be too busy?'

She felt a little touch of colour brush her cheeks. 'I don't know—I just thought you would be,' she faltered. 'It's quite a punishing rehearsal schedule. It's up to you. Of course, if you want to do it you'd be more than welcome—I was just trying to give you a way out if you wanted one. It can be pretty tedious.'

She floundered to a halt and looked up at him again, to find him watching her with understanding.

'If you don't want me to do it, just say so, Jo,' he

murmured, and his voice was like raw silk, sliding over her nerve endings.

She laughed, a forced little hiccup of sound. 'Don't be daft. I just thought you wouldn't be interested. It's very amateur.'

'Are you in it?'

She nodded. 'Yes—for my sins, I've got the female lead. Heaven knows when I'll get time to learn the lines.'

'Is it fun?' he asked, and with a sudden flash of insight she realised he was lonely and would actually like to join in. Good grief, a willing volunteer. That was a first!

It was beyond her to exclude him just for her own selfish reasons.

'Yes, it is fun,' she told him, relenting. 'It would help your patients get to know you as a person as well. It could be good for your image—they're a bit slow to let you in round here.'

He shot her a quizzical look. 'I noticed.'

She coloured again, and looked down at her hands. 'I'm sorry. I just felt that if we had to work together all the time and ended up at the panto rehearsals, well, it might be a bit...'

'Much?'

She nodded.

'Does it unsettle you?' he asked softly. 'My proximity?'

She looked up into his eyes—those stunningly magnetic storm-grey eyes that seemed to see right to the heart of her—and nodded again, just slightly. 'A little,' she confessed.

His mouth tipped in a crooked and endearing grin. 'That makes two of us. I'm not exactly immune to you, either.'

She stood up, pushing her chair back and trying for a bit of authority. 'That doesn't mean we have to do anything about it. We have to work together, Ed. I don't think we can do that if we're...' She ran out of words, unusually for her, but he was there again.

'Involved?' he offered. A lazy smile lurked in his eyes.

'Exactly.'

He shrugged and grinned again. 'OK. If I promise to keep my distance, can I join the pantomime?'

'Of course you can.' She returned his smile. 'It is awful, though. Don't say you haven't been warned.'

He chuckled. 'OK. When's the next rehearsal?'

'Tonight. Quarter to eight, at the community hall. Wear something warm—it can be a bit chilly.'

He nodded, drained his tea and left her. She sat again, as if she were a puppet whose strings had been cut, and buried her face in her hands. So he felt it too—and she'd thought it was just her, being silly. Oh, Lord, this was so much more complicated. If she was the only one—

'You OK?'

Her head jerked up. 'Yes, just a bit tired. Did you forget something?'

'Where's the community hall?' Ed asked.

'Ah. Um—on the main street, nearly opposite the chip shop.'

'That black and white building?'

She nodded, avoiding those searching eyes. 'That's right.'

'OK. I'll see you then—unless you're back in the surgery after your antenatal class?'

'Antenatal class?' She gasped and leapt to her feet. 'I'd forgotten it!' she muttered, and, scooping up her pager from the table, she headed for the door.

'See you later,' he called. Jo ran out to her car, wondering if she'd been totally insane to suggest he should join the pantomime crew. Her brains were scrambled enough as it was!

She arrived at the hospital just about on time, and a couple of the mums were late. She decided to give them a minute or two because they were new. While they waited she ticked the names of those who were there on her register and encouraged them to mix and get to know each other while she set up her equipment.

She had a doll and a plastic pelvis so that they could see the way the baby would emerge through the birth canal, charts and diagrams to show the development of the baby, and lots of information about nutrition, exercise and so on.

The classes didn't have a beginning or an end, but ran on a continuous loop, with four sessions making up the whole set. In a way it made it harder, but it did mean that someone new to the area or only able to come intermittently didn't miss out. Each session included a lecture, a discussion and work on relaxation and pain control, and today was about the second stage of labour, the expulsive stage.

The latecomers arrived together, apologising for getting lost on the way, and Jo called all the patients to order, settled them down and started the class, by going round and asking the new members in turn to say a little about themselves, whether it was their first or subsequent child and what sort of delivery they were hoping for.

There were five women out of the ten there who wanted a home birth or who wanted to deliver in the GP unit. Of these five, only three were on Jo's mental list of possibles. One was a little too old, another had a previous history of stillbirth.

The other three couldn't deliver in the GP unit on the grounds that only second and third babies were permitted by their scheme, and these were all first-timers. Still, they could, if she thought they were suitable, opt for a home birth with consultant back-up, if necessary, at Jo's discretion. She still hadn't decided.

The older mother, however, was aware that Jo didn't want her to deliver at home, but it didn't stop her planning a home delivery, and Jo knew full well that when it came to the crunch she'd leave it too late to go to hospital, regardless of what they might say to convince her otherwise.

'I'd like to have the baby in the GP unit,' one of the new mums was saying, 'but I know I can't because it's my first, and my husband isn't happy about me having it at home. I'd like to come back to the GP unit straight afterwards, though.'

Jo nodded. 'That should be possible if everything goes well, or if you have support at home afterwards you wouldn't need to come in here at all.'

She looked doubtful. 'I don't know if I could cope alone. It's such a responsibility—what happens if you don't know why it's crying?'

Some of the others chorused their agreement, and Jo hastened to reassure them. 'You struggle on and try everything until you hit on something that works. Babies are remarkably tough and very good at getting their own way—I really wouldn't worry.'

'But what if I'm really clueless?' she persisted.

'You'll know what to do. I've only had one mum in all my years who genuinely didn't, and she gradually relaxed and started listening to the baby. You'll be fine—and, anyway, you wouldn't be alone. For the first ten days I'll come whenever you want, and once a day in any case, then the health visitor takes over so you won't be abandoned.'

She looked round. 'Right. A couple of you are second- or third-timers along for a refresher and the rest of you are having your first so I think we'll have input and comments from the old hands after the talk. I want to go through labour and delivery with you, just to make sure you all know or remember what all the stages are and what's happening at any point.'

They settled down and listened, and after Jo had done her demonstration with the elastic band and the plastic pelvis she invited questions and comments.

This was always a tricky one. Inevitably there would be at least one mother who would revel in going over the more traumatic and memorable moments of her labour, regardless of the dread she was inspiring in the first-time mums, so Jo was on the alert ready to cut off anyone who launched into a counter-productive monologue.

In fact, they were fine, and after a few minutes she got them all to lie down and relax.

'Think of every part of your body in turn. As you think of it, tense it hard, then hold it, then let it flop. Think about how you make it go floppy, and after a while you'll be able to home in on tight areas of your body and relax them. Right, start with your feet. Point your toes hard, but make sure you don't get cramp. Good. Hold—and relax. Totally floppy. Good. Now pull your feet up so your toes are pointing at your head. Tense—hold—and flop. Well done.'

She watched them, looking for the ones who found it difficult and the ones who had probably done yoga or had been to her classes before.

One new girl, thin and dressed in what Jo could only describe as 'hippy' clothes, was wonderfully relaxed. Her name was Mel, and Jo flicked through her notes and noticed her address—the travellers' site in the forest outside Yoxburgh, up on the heath by the edge of the trees.

It was a lovely spot, but Jo had a sneaky feeling, despite what she'd said, that Mel was going to go for a home delivery. The idea of delivering a baby in a converted coach or, worse still, a 'bender'—a shelter made of tree branches—filled Jo with horror.

What if anything went wrong? It was Mel's first—there was no reason why anything should go wrong, but what if it did? The baby was bound to be born at night—the more difficult the location the more likely it seemed to be, and there was no power out there, no light, no running water. How would she deliver her safely under those conditions? Jo vowed to have a word to make sure Mel understood the risks. Mel had a few weeks left to go so she'd use them to try and talk sense into her.

Jo led them through the relaxation, then the breathing, and finally she got them to grip each other's forearms with both hands and twist firmly in opposite directions to pull the skin. Called 'Chinese burns', they were a thing schoolchildren did to each other to see who was bravest—harmless but painful, Jo found they were a useful tool to help women practise breathing through the 'contractions' and remaining relaxed. When they'd all had a rest for a moment and she'd done the question-and-answer session and they'd put the mats away, she sent them all off.

Still thinking about Mel, she packed up all her stuff, cleared away the cups and made sure the mats had all been stacked properly in the cupboard. They used the maternity day-room for their classes, and she didn't want to leave the place untidy.

One of the staff midwives stuck her head round the door and grinned. 'Got time for a cuppa?'

'I'd love one. Did you see my traveller?'

'Yes—is she going to be a problem?'

Jo laughed. 'I hope not, but I suspect so. I think she's just unconventional, not stupid, but I've got a suspicion

I won't be able to persuade her to go to the Audley. I just have a feeling.'

'Birth in a bender, eh? That'll be a first, won't it?'

'Don't.' Jo sipped her tea and sighed with relief. 'Perhaps I'll get Ed Latimer to talk to her—see what he's made of.'

'I don't know, but if you can get the recipe, I'd like one the same, please!'

Jo laughed, but inside her stomach the butterflies were working themselves up to a frenzy. The remark had reminded her about Ed, and about the rehearsal. It was panto time in three hours, and she'd have no professional guise to hide behind, no protocol—just herself, and Laura.

That was it! She'd be Laura's mother. It would make her seem middle-aged and boring—with any luck!

CHAPTER THREE

ED PAUSED outside the black and white mock-timbered building that was the Yoxburgh and District Community Hall, and wondered if he was out of his mind.

Jo had made it pretty clear that she found his presence disturbing, and that the sensation wasn't welcome. In a way he felt the same, and yet there was something about her that drew him so forcefully that he just didn't seem to be able to ignore it.

He didn't want to be a nuisance, and he was being very careful not to crowd her at work or flirt with her, but every cell in his body was screaming for more contact—and the pantomime seemed like a gift from the gods.

Anyway, Jo aside, he had to get to know people and make some friends. He couldn't be GP to all of them—surely there'd be lots of people who'd be happy to be social without fear of compromising their relationship.

His father was a country GP and they'd always had a fairly hectic social life, but Jo had warned him about the locals, not letting newcomers in.

Well, he'd find out, wouldn't he? He put his hand against the door and pushed, and found himself sucked into a fantasy world. Little bees ran about the floor, giggling and shrieking, a young girl was complaining that her dragon didn't do up down the back and could the hooks be moved, costumes were piled in heaps on every surface, and in the middle of it all stood Jo in a wedding dress, her hair pinned up and a tiara perched in the dark,

43

gleaming curls, laughing with a tall man in a blue satin suit with floppy lace cuffs.

He bent and said something and Jo laughed, her eyes sparkling at the joke they shared—and Ed wanted to kill him.

She turned just as the murderous thought was being put aside, and he wasn't sure if he imagined it or if a flicker of panic brushed her eyes. Then she excused herself and came over to him, weaving her way through the crowd.

'I thought you'd bottled out—you're late.'

'I couldn't get away from the surgery—someone collapsed in the waiting room with a tummy bug and I admitted her to the hospital for fluids and supervision. It took ages. Anyway, I'm here now. Who do I need to see?'

'Roz—she's going through a scene. Come with me.'

He followed her, wondering how she could look so radiantly beautiful in what on close inspection seemed to be a set of net curtains skilfully flung together into a wedding dress. 'Roz, this is Ed Latimer,' Jo was saying, and he smiled automatically and shook her hand.

'Oh, you look very useful,' Roz was saying, eyeing him up with a grin. 'Can you sing?'

He chuckled. 'Well enough, I expect. Why?'

'Because the other male chorus can't. Go and see Anne for a costume, and we'll get you kitted up as a villager to start with. It might be tricky—you're quite big, aren't you? Then you need to see Mr Music over there—Andrew, we've got a new victim for the chorus. Can you give him a music sheet? Here's a script—you're a love. Thanks.'

And Roz vanished into a crowd of villagers and the back end of the pantomime horse, leaving him with Jo.

He looked down at the script. '*Beauty and the Beast*, eh?'

'Yes.'

'And you're the Beauty?'

She nodded. 'Belle.'

'How appropriate,' he murmured, and she tutted and gave him a look. 'You want me to lie?' he asked, but it didn't help. She sighed and stepped away from him, looking back over her shoulder.

'Come on, I'll take you to Anne,' she said shortly, and he reminded himself he'd promised to keep his distance. Damn. Why couldn't he keep his mouth shut?

They were crossing the room towards the back when a girl of about twelve skidded up to them and slithered to a halt. 'Hi—I'm Laura. Are you the new GP?'

He eyed her with interest. She was unmistakably Jo's daughter, from the tip of her pert little nose to the soles of her stocking-clad feet, and she was eyeing him very, very frankly.

'Yes, I am,' he replied, wondering why she was so interested.

'This is my mum,' she told him unnecessarily.

'I guessed. Pleased to meet you, Laura.'

'So, are you going to be in the panto?' she asked, her head on one side in a gesture so reminiscent of her mother it was almost comical.

'Looks like it,' he told her.

'Good—Mum thought you wouldn't want to, but I think you'll like it. It's a laugh.'

'Laura! They need you for song practice!' Jo said.

'Oops—have to fly. See you.'

She shot off across the room to the man at the keyboard, and without any further incident Ed was introduced to Anne, measured and sized up and offered an armful of musty clothes to try at home later.

Breeches, a full-sleeved white shirt, a waistcoat, long socks—he was going to look a peach! Ah, well, it was all in a good cause...

Jo tried to concentrate, but every time she looked across at Ed the air seemed to crackle between them and she forgot her lines.

Predictably Roz got cross and scolded her, and she got through the rest of the rehearsal by not looking at him. Blow Roz and her invitation! It would have been so much easier if he hadn't been there—and much less fun, she had to admit as they were practising the winter medley.

Ed had a lovely voice, deep and rich and full, and he was instantly seconded to sing a solo for the Beast, who had no voice at all. As the Beast would have a huge mask on at the time, it didn't matter that the voice would come from behind the scenes.

He was taken off to practise it, and Laura came up to Jo and tugged her sleeve. 'He's gorgeous! I think you should marry him,' she whispered.

Jo coloured and shushed her daughter. 'Laura, don't be silly. I hardly know him,' she whispered back.

'So get to know him.'

'No—look, I'm not talking about this here. Just hush.'

The rehearsal was wrapped up at about ten, and Jo scooped up her costumes and rounded up Laura. Ed was standing by the door chatting to a group of men, and they were stopped on the way out by the groom, the back end of the horse and the Beast. 'We're going up to the Dog and Fox—want to join us? Ed's coming.'

She met his eyes, reading nothing from them for a change, and shook her head. 'No—I'd love to but I mustn't. I'm on call tomorrow night, and this young lady's got school tomorrow. Perhaps another time.'

Was that a flicker of disappointment, or relief?

Hard to tell—his face hadn't really moved a muscle. They snuggled down into their coats for the short walk back to the house, and as they cut through the little side streets Laura was clearly fizzling.

'What is it?' Jo asked her, resigned to a lecture.

'Him—Ed Latimer. I just think he's perfect for you.'

Jo sighed. 'He's just a man, Laura!'

'So—what do you want, a woman?'

'Of course not—'

'So stop saying he's just a man. It's the right starting point, at least! And, anyway, he's not just a man, he's gorgeous, and he's a doctor, so you've got medicine in common, and he's the right age—I can't see the problem!'

No. At the age of twelve, Jo doubted if she would have seen the problem, either. It was only as she'd grown older and wiser that the pitfalls had become obvious.

Like the fact, for example, that he was thirty-two and still single.

There had to be a reason for that. Most men of that age were married, divorced, living with someone in a settled relationship or just not fit to live with. She knew he wasn't married or divorced, she knew he was living with Dr Parker for now until he found somewhere, and there didn't seem to be a woman on the scene. That left unfit to live with.

Wow! What an option!

Something else was worrying her, too. She slung an arm around Laura and gave her a little hug. 'Why are you trying to marry me off, anyway?' she asked lightly. 'Aren't we OK as we are?'

Laura's steps hesitated slightly. 'I suppose—it's just that sometimes you look sort of lonely, and there are things we can't manage to do—lifting things and stuff

like that. It would be useful to have a man around sometimes.'

Jo chuckled and hugged Laura hard. 'Darling, I can't
just marry someone because it would be useful to have
a man around to lift things!'

'No, I s'pose not. Still, if he was the right man...'

'He's not,' she said emphatically, and changed the
subject fast.

'Ah, Jo—could we have a word?'

She paused in the corridor. 'Sure. What can I do for
you, Dr Parker?'

'Um—I wondered if you're busy on Saturday night?'

'Me?' She looked up into Maurice Parker's kindly
eyes and wondered what he was up to. 'No, not that I'm
aware of. Why?'

'Because I've invited your mother round for dinner,
and Ed will be there, of course, as he's staying with me,
and—ah—well, I thought if there were some other people there too—well, it might make it a little less, well,
intimate, really,' he concluded, and his neck went an
interesting shade of brick.

Realisation dawned. After all the years of his marriage
to Betty, Maurice Parker was shy about dating her
mother—and her mother was probably shy about dating
him.

How lovely.

She smiled, suppressing the little flutter of nerves because she was going to be spending the evening with Ed
as well, coincidentally, and agreed without hesitation.
'That would be lovely, Dr Parker. Thank you, I'll look
forward to it. What time would you like us?'

'Eight?'

'Right. How formal are we being?'

He laughed. 'Well, I can't cook for nuts so don't dress

up too much or you'll put me to shame. I tell you what, let's call it supper, shall we?'

She shared a smile. 'Let's. We'll see you at eight.'

And I get to spend the evening with Ed, she thought again, and wondered how she'd cope.

Not that she could have got out of it, of course. There was no way she could let Maurice down, and dating again after all that time must be awful.

She tried to imagine how she'd feel, hardly having dated at all since before Laura's birth, and a shiver of nervous anticipation ran through her veins. She'd been out, of course, but mainly with people from work or the pantomime, and always in a group.

She hadn't been out alone with a man since Laura had appeared on the scene, and the very thought made her mouth dry and her heart pound. How would it feel, to be alone with Ed, for instance? What would he do? Would he try and kiss her goodnight?

And would she let him?

She thought about the firm, chiselled lips that were so ready to quirk into a smile, and wondered how they'd feel against her own.

A tiny moan escaped her, and her eyes fluttered shut. Exquisite—

'Jo?'

Her eyes flew open, hot colour flooding her cheeks, and with a muttered excuse she pushed past Ed and went into the kitchen.

He followed her, letting the door close behind them, and she could feel his eyes on her. 'Are you all right?'

'Fine—just a bit hot,' she told him, and wished she had a better grip on her emotions. She didn't want to react to him—she wanted to be professional and impartial and neutral—

No, she didn't. She wanted to be kissed until her

bones melted and her lungs were bursting and her heart sang.

'Idiot,' she muttered.

'What?'

'Nothing. I've forgotten to order something,' she lied. 'Did you want to see me, Dr Latimer?'

'Ed—and, no, not really. You looked a little shocked in the corridor. I wondered if everything was all right.'

'Fine,' she said in what she hoped was a breezy voice, and flashed him a brilliant smile. 'I gather we're both going to be playing gooseberry on Saturday night so my mother and Maurice Parker don't feel too threatened by their date.'

He looked surprised. 'Is it a date?'

'I think so. Sounds like it.'

His mouth softened into a smile. 'How delightful. I shall look forward to gooseberrying with you—it'll make a change from learning the panto songs.' And he clicked his heels together, tipped his head in a little bow and left her.

'I feel as if I'm sixteen again,' Rebecca said crossly. 'It's ridiculous, at my age!' She stood back from the mirror and patted her stomach, frowning at the little bulge which was all but hidden by the flowing lines of her dress. 'I'm getting fat—are you sure this dress looks all right?'

Jo sighed. 'Mum, you look wonderful. Stop worrying. Maurice Parker didn't invite you for dinner so he could measure your waist!'

'Why *did* he invite me?' she asked softly, sitting on the end of the bed beside her daughter.

'Because he likes you? Because he respects you, and cares about you? Maybe even because he finds you attractive?'

Rebecca blushed. 'Don't be silly! I'm nearly sixty!'

'So's he. What's wrong with that?'

'Well—nothing, I suppose. If he was thirty I'd have something to worry about.'

'Exactly. Now, are you ready?'

Rebecca ran a critical eye over her daughter. 'I am, but I don't think you are. What are you wearing?'

Jo blinked. 'Well—this.'

'No. Go and put something pretty on, not that plain dress that makes you look like a secretary.'

'It's the only suitable thing I've got—unless you want me to wear the trousers I use for work?'

Her mother tutted and stood, going to her wardrobe and rummaging through the rails of clothes. 'What about this? Your father always used to say I looked wonderful in it, and we're about the same size except for the tummy.'

'You haven't got a tummy.'

'Nor have you, so it should be fine. Try it.'

Jo took the dress her mother thrust at her, holding it up against her. It was a lovely muted charcoal blue, almost navy, a softly draping knitted dress with long sleeves. It came down almost to her ankles, and had a wonderfully flattering deep cowl neck.

'It'll look lovely with those navy boots of yours. Put it on, and it needs a belt—here.'

Jo shrugged, unzipped the formal dress she was wearing and slipped the new one over her head, then belted it with the broad navy leather belt her mother handed her.

'Much better,' her mother said approvingly. 'Oh, yes, darling, you look fabulous in it! Have it. I'll never wear it again—not now, without your father, and it seems a shame to have it hanging in the cupboard when it looks so pretty on you.' Her mother's eyes filled, and Jo hugged her.

'Are you sure? It was Dad's favourite.'

'He'd approve,' she said firmly. 'Now, get the boots, let your hair down, brush it out and let's go.'

There wasn't time to argue and, anyway, it was her mother's evening out, not hers. She pulled on her big thick coat with the snuggly collar, and they walked the two hundred yards down the road to Maurice's house. The wind was blowing off the sea, but they were used to it and Jo loved it.

She couldn't imagine living anywhere else, and she took a great deep breath of salty air and sighed with contentment. 'What a lovely night—I expect we'll have a frost. The moon's up.'

'Mmm, I expect it'll get my camellia—it does without fail. Do you think Laura will be all right with Cara?'

'Yes—her mother's pretty firm. They'll be watching videos half the night, I expect.'

'She'll be ghastly tomorrow.'

Jo laughed. 'Of course—that's half the fun of a sleepover. Still, at least she's got a day to get over it. I wonder what's for supper? I'm starving.'

They walked up the path of Maurice Parker's big Victorian seafront house and rang the bell. He opened the door almost instantly, ushering them in and taking their coats, and Jo thought he seemed a little flustered.

He smiled distractedly at Jo, then bent and kissed her mother on the cheek. 'You look enchanting, my dear. It's lovely to see you again.'

Jo felt a lump in her throat. He really did seem genuinely fond of her mother, and it was wonderful to see the smile blossom on her face.

'You don't look so bad yourself these days,' Rebecca

was saying, and patted him on the cheek affectionately. 'It's been a long time, Maurice.'

'Too long,' he murmured, and then seemed to collect himself before leading them into the drawing room. A fire crackled cheerfully in the grate, and Ed unfolded himself from one of the chairs and smiled a greeting.

Maurice cupped her mother's elbow and led her forward, and Jo noticed he seemed nervous. How diverting. He'd never looked even slightly flustered in all the time she'd known him until tonight. She suppressed a smile.

'Rebecca, I'd like you to meet my young lodger, Ed Latimer,' he was saying. 'Ed, this is Rebecca Halliday—and Jo, of course, you know.'

Ed took Rebecca's hand. 'Delighted to meet you, Mrs Halliday.'

'And you—you're the talk of the town. I've heard a lot about you.'

'Not from me,' Jo put in hastily, and Ed laughed.

'I didn't think so for a moment.' He released her mother's hand and turned to Jo. His eyes skimmed over her and came back to her face, approval clear in his eyes. 'You look lovely,' he said softly. 'That colour suits you.'

'Doesn't it?' her mother chipped in. 'She ought to wear things like that more often, but she never goes out.'

'What a waste.'

'I'm busy,' Jo said firmly, and, taking the glass of sherry Maurice held out to her, she retreated to the corner of the settee.

'Fancy a nibble?' Ed asked, settling himself into the settee beside her and leaning towards her with a bowl of peanuts. A teasing smile played around his lips and—whether it was the warmth of the fire, or their bracing walk along the seafront, or just plain Ed, leaning over her with that laughing look in his eyes—she felt her cheeks heating.

'Are you going to behave?' she murmured under her breath, and he laughed and leaned back.

'I only offered you a peanut,' he said softly.

'Really?'

She took a few, nibbling them and trying to ignore his proximity. The rat, he knew he stirred her up!

'So, how's the pantomime going?' Maurice asked her, breaking the silence.

'Oh, well, chaotic as ever. Ed's been sucked in.'

'So I gather—he seems to have enjoyed it. Good way to break into the community. They can be a bit closed at first to strangers, but I suppose that's true of any rural community.'

'Forget rural,' Ed said drily. 'I worked in a city and it was just the same. If you weren't born there, they didn't trust you.'

'I was born here,' Jo told him. 'In a little house just down the road, backing onto ours. We've got it as a holiday cottage now and we let it out, but I can remember growing up there for the first few years until we moved. I was just saying to Mum, I can't imagine living anywhere else now but Yoxburgh.'

'Talking of letting things,' Maurice chipped in, 'Ed's looking for a place to rent—there isn't anything suitable on the market at the moment and he seems to have some fool idea about buying something decrepit and doing it up in his spare time.'

'I just need to wait for the right thing to come on the market, but in the meantime I need a house—I'm driving Maurice crazy being permanently underfoot.'

'How about the cottage?' Rebecca suggested, and Jo felt a flutter of panic. It was too close to their house, much too close!

'Isn't it let?' she said hastily, hoping her mother would pick up her hint, but, no, she ignored it.

'Not till Easter,' she said cheerfully. 'Would that give you long enough? It's sitting idle at the moment, and it would probably do it good to have a tenant. I imagine you're house-trained?'

'Marginally.'

Maurice laughed. 'Oh, he's marvellous. He can cook, too. I confess he's done the meal tonight, but I didn't think a set of TV dinners would impress you.'

Rebecca chuckled, and Jo turned to Ed and arched a brow. 'You cooked? Are we safe?'

'Oh, I should think so. I dropped the meat on the kitchen floor a couple of times, but I gave it a wipe.'

'Right.'

His eyes twinkled, and she let a slow smile touch her lips. 'What are we having?'

'Baked peppers as a starter, *porc aux pruneaux* for the main course and cheese and a fruit fool for pud.'

She blinked in surprise. 'Amazing. Hidden talents.'

'Oh, I've got all sorts of hidden talents,' he murmured, and she felt the embarrassing colour climb her cheeks again.

'Warm in here, isn't it?' he added softly. 'I have to put the veg on—want to give me a hand?'

'Can't you cope?'

'Sure—I just get lonely.'

'Shame,' she teased, but she went with him anyway, carried by legs with a mind of their own. The kitchen was a scene of organised chaos, and she tidied some of the pans away into the sink to soak.

'Leave that. I wanted to talk to you about Maurice and your mother. They seem to be getting on well,' Ed said quietly.

'They always did,' she said, remembering the times they'd all been gathered in this kitchen before Betty's illness and her father's death. 'The four of them were great friends. I've wondered if they'll get together, but they didn't seem to show any sign of it.'

'Giving themselves time?' he suggested. 'I think after something so traumatic you need time to rebuild yourself as a single person. If you've been half of a couple for years and years, it's a hell of a shock.'

'He's sweet with her.'

'He's a gentleman. She'll be safe, Jo. He won't hurt her.'

'I didn't imagine he would,' she replied, then took a deep breath. How odd, to think about her mother in a relationship with anyone but her father. 'Can I do something?' she asked.

'No. Just keep me company. It's nearly done.'

She propped up the worktop and watched him scald the broccoli, mash the potatoes with a huge dollop of *crème fraîche* and put it back into the oven to keep hot, next to the pork steaks.

Then he drained the sprouting broccoli and turned to her with a grin. 'OK, we're done. Shall we get them?'

'That was wonderful!' Rebecca said, setting down her spoon with a sigh. 'Ed, you're very clever.'

'Superb. Excellent meal, thank you,' Maurice added. 'Far better than anything I could have produced.'

'Or me,' Jo said with a laugh. 'I'm spoiled—I've never really had to cook.'

'Ah, well, you have my mother to thank. She gave me a cookery book when I left home, and to my amazement I discovered I enjoyed it—well, this sort of cooking, anyway. Weekday meals are a bit of a drag.'

'You don't say,' Rebecca said with a chuckle. 'You wait till you're sixty and still trying to think up something different!'

'I'll put the coffee on—I can do that,' Maurice offered. 'Ed, why don't you take the girls through to the drawing room—I'll clear this lot.'

'No—we'll clear up. You take Jo,' Rebecca said, and got to her feet and started gathering plates.

Thus dismissed, Jo and Ed went through to the drawing room. Jo sank onto the settee, far too full and very grateful for the expandable nature of the dress, and rested her head against the back cushions.

'That really was a super meal, Ed, thanks,' she said.

She felt the settee dip beside her. 'You're welcome,' he murmured. 'I thought I ought to rescue you—Maurice isn't joking about his cooking.'

She chuckled. 'Oh, dear—that bad, is it?'

'Absolutely. He's a dear, but he can't boil water. I hate to think what the coffee will be like.'

'My mother will help him,' she said lazily from the depths of the cushions. 'It'll be fine.'

'Good.' There was a pause, then she felt him shift in his seat. 'Jo, about this cottage—is it really empty?'

She opened her eyes, wondering if she could put him off, but her generous nature got the better of her. 'Yes—as Mum said, the next let is at Easter.'

'Is it furnished?'

'Oh, yes—fully equipped. It's a holiday cottage, it's got everything.'

'I don't suppose I could look at it?'

'Sure,' she agreed, giving in to the inevitable. 'When?'

He shrugged. 'Whenever—tomorrow?'

'OK.' She glanced at her watch, looking for a diversion. 'I wonder how they're doing? Do you think we ought to go and give them a hand?'

A deep, masculine laugh rippled down the hall towards them, and Ed shook his head. 'I think they sound just fine.'

Pity. She felt altogether too alone with Ed, but it wasn't for many seconds. The others arrived moments later, Maurice bearing a tray of steaming coffee and Rebecca armed with mint thins. They sat on the settee opposite, poured the coffee out and handed round the chocolates, then turned back to each other, totally absorbed.

Jo sipped her coffee and watched them, and she would have had to have been blind not to see the rapport between them. Maurice said something and her mother blushed and dimpled, and beside her Jo could feel Ed chuckle.

She turned her head and met his eyes, and he jerked his head towards the door, one brow arched in enquiry.

She nodded, and they rose and left the room, without the other two even noticing they were gone. Ed pushed the door to and grinned. 'Walk by the sea?' he suggested.

She nodded. 'Good idea. Blow the cobwebs away and work off some of that wonderful food.'

He took Jo's coat off the hook, holding it out for her and snuggling it round her shoulders as she settled into it. Then he shrugged into his own thick quilted jacket, opened the door and ushered her out into the moonlight.

They walked down the path to the sea wall, and the wind tugged at them, reminding them that it was only January.

'Where shall we go?' he asked. They were facing the sea, and she shrugged.

'Want to see the cottage?'

'What, now?'

'Why not?'

'OK.'

They strolled side by side along the sea wall, listening to the crash of the waves on the shingle, and far out to sea they could make out the lights of ships like tiny glow-worms on the horizon. The noise of the town was drowned out by the rush of the sea and the bluster of the wind, and they could have been alone in the world.

It was wonderfully romantic, even though the wind was cold, and she felt herself moving closer to Ed. He stopped, looking out across the sparkling water towards the ships in the distance, and then he turned to her. 'Are you warm enough?'

'Fine—you make a good windbreak,' she said with a smile.

He moved closer. A strand of hair had blown across her face and caught in her mouth, and he lifted a blunt fingertip and brushed it away. His knuckles grazed her cheek, and then his thumb caught on her lip and dragged the soft skin tenderly.

Her lips parted, her eyes searching his in the half-darkness and seeing nothing. She lifted a hand and touched his face, forgetting the distance they were supposed to be keeping—forgetting everything but the man standing between her and the wind. His jaw was rough, the stubble scratchy against her palm. The texture fascinated her.

'Jo?' he murmured. His hands cupped her cold cheeks, and they were warm and firm and gentle. His thumbs grazed her cheekbones, and then he lowered his head and those firm, chiselled lips of her fantasy settled against her mouth like the kiss of an angel.

Sensation exploded in her, making her weak with longing, but it didn't matter. He had hold of her and she wasn't going anywhere. She found her arms under his coat, wrapped around his waist so that her hands were snuggled against the warmth of his back, and his arms enfolded her, supporting her against the broad expanse of his chest while his lips teased and tormented her.

She felt the velvet sweep of his tongue and her lips parted for him. With a ragged groan he cupped her head in one hand to steady her.

The kiss grew deeper, hotter, more urgent, until with a ragged groan he broke it and tucked her head in the hollow under his chin. Her ear was against his throat, and she could hear the thundering of his heart and the uneven rasp of his breath.

'Are you OK?' he murmured after an age.

'I think so. I don't know. Maybe.'

He gave a gruff chuckle and eased away from her. 'Can you stand up?'

'I don't know—can you?'

'Maybe.'

They laughed together, and he reached for her hand, enfolding it in his and leading her back down to the road. 'This cottage,' he said after a moment.

'Hmm?'

'Does it have a bed?'

She stopped dead. 'Yes,' she said warily.

'In which case, I think it might be a very good idea if your mother showed it to me tomorrow, don't you? Because just now, after kissing you like that, I really don't think it would be too smart to be alone with you in a private place—unless you want to?'

She did, possibly more than she'd ever wanted anything, but she knew it was just the knee-jerk reaction of a healthy woman who'd been on her own too long.

'No,' she managed to say, despite the howls of protest from her body. 'In fact, I think I might go home. We're almost there. Do you suppose Maurice will mind walking Mum home?'

'I don't suppose so. It's a beautiful evening.'

She stopped at the front door of their house and turned to him.

'Thank you for the walk—and the meal.'

'My pleasure. We must do it again.'

Do what? she wanted to ask. The walk? The meal?
The kiss…?

CHAPTER FOUR

'Darling, I hate to be a nuisance but I'm expecting a phone call—you couldn't pop over to the cottage with Ed, could you?'

Rebecca dangled the key in front of Jo and, with him standing there watching, there was no choice. He wondered if Rebecca was on his side, and decided it was quite possible. In fact, he wondered if she'd engineered her daughter's invitation the night before.

Jo took the key. 'Sure. We'll have to go in the back way.'

She led him down the garden, across the narrow alleyway at the back and through the gate into the other garden. Ed looked round at the evergreen plants making a show of colour even then, in January. There was a little porch at the back, with honeysuckle growing over it, and in the summer he imagined it would smell wonderful.

'It's pretty,' he said, studying it as they walked up the path.

'It's just a little Georgian artisan's cottage—nothing special. It's quite sweet, though.' She opened the door in the porch and went in, crossing to the window at the front to pull back the curtains. The winter light flooded in, revealing the clean, simple lines of the furniture and the delicate summery colours.

'It's a little bit musty, I'm afraid, but it's been closed up since October, except for Christmas.'

'It's fine.' Ed looked round the simply furnished sitting room and imagined it with his things there—the hi-fi system, the books, the general clutter that would make it his home—and he felt a smile tug at his lips. 'I like it.'

'You haven't seen the rest—it's not huge,' Jo cautioned.

'There's only me—how huge does it need to be?'

'Oh, well, there's plenty of room for one. We lived here when I was tiny—we used to look over the fence at the one we're in now and say, "That's a nice house. It would be wonderful to live there."'

She laughed. 'Of course we couldn't afford it then, but it came on the market later and we just had to buy it. Then by coincidence a few years later this came up for sale again. My father thought it would be ideal for a holiday cottage, and it's done quite well, really. People seem to like it, anyway.'

'I'm not surprised.'

She was rabbiting, he thought, running on as if she had to fill the silence. Was she so uneasy with him? Perhaps it was because of his remark about the bed last night.

Oh, hell. Surely she realised he wasn't about to jump her bones? 'This is the kitchen,' she said unnecessarily, standing as far away from him as possible in the tiny room.

Although it was small it was fully equipped and spotless, with a view out into the garden. He wondered if she'd come if he invited her to dinner. He would enjoy cooking for her here.

'Is that your house?' he asked, looking across the gardens.

She nodded. 'Yes. Laura and I have this end.'

He looked at the windows and wondered which room was hers. Would he see her light from here? Or maybe her shadow on the curtains?

He stifled a groan and dragged his eyes away from the window before she could smell a rat.

'What's upstairs?' he asked her, which was nearly as bad.

'Two bedrooms. You can see the sea from the main bedroom,' she told him, and led the way, keeping out of reach. Through a gap in the houses he could see the grey swell of the North Sea, the gulls wheeling low over the surface, the thin winter sun gleaming on their wings.

'It's gorgeous. I love the sea.'

'It's only a glimpse.'

'Even so.' He turned towards her, and she backed away, heading for the door. He stopped her with a hand. 'Jo?'

'Come and see the other bedroom and the bathroom—'

'Jo, come here.'

She stayed where she was, and he dropped his hand. 'Jo, it's OK. I'm not going to jump on you.'

She regarded him warily. 'Last night,' she began, and fizzled out.

'Last night we were intoxicated by the wine and the sea and the night air. Jo, you're safe. Trust me, please. We need to talk about this.'

'About what?' she asked guardedly.

'This—whatever it is—between us. I don't know what it is, or where it came from, but I know you feel it too.' He sat on the edge of the bed and patted the mattress beside him. 'Sit down. Talk to me.'

She sat, but she hardly relaxed. Still, he supposed it was a start.

He sighed inwardly. 'I've got a suggestion. We're both free, there's no reason why we shouldn't get to know each other—'

'We work together—'

'That's how most couples meet. As I was saying, there's no reason why we shouldn't get to know each other—go out together, spend some time together, just see where this thing leads us.'

Jo met his eyes, and there was clear determination in the hazel depths. 'I'm not going to have an affair with you, Ed. I have to live in this town, and bring up my daughter. I have a reputation to preserve—'

'And I don't? Anyway, I'm not suggesting we should make love in broad daylight in the middle of the beach!'

A smile tugged at her mouth, and he almost sighed with relief. Thank God! He'd thought for a moment she'd lost her sense of humour.

'So what are you suggesting? A few drinks, a meal, and then after a decent interval bring me back here and seduce me? My daughter's bedroom overlooks this house.'

'We could always make love in the dark,' he said rashly, but she caught the twinkle in his eye and smiled.

'Ed, I'm serious, I'm not looking for a relationship. I like you, and, yes, I find you attractive, but I've been on my own for years. I'd find any presentable man attractive.'

'Would you?'

'Yes.'

'So attractive that you'd kiss him in the moonlight until your legs turned to jelly and your brain turned to mush?'

'Don't be silly.' She looked down at her hands. Her fingers were twisted together, knotted up. She unravelled them. 'Ed, it won't work.'

'Give it a try—please? I like you, Jo. I'm wary, too. You aren't the only one who's ever been hurt, but sometimes we just have to take a risk.' He reached for her hands, covering them with one of his, squeezing the mangled fingers gently. 'Please?'

She looked up again and in her eyes he could see a sort of yearning, as if she longed to take that risk. 'I don't want to be rushed,' she told him, and the tension seeped out of him like air out of a punctured balloon.

'I won't rush you.' He stood and drew her to her feet. 'Thanks.' He bent, unable to stop himself, and brushed her lips with his. Then he let her go, despite the nagging of his instincts that told him to grab her and hang on tight, and she showed him the bathroom and the other bedroom.

He didn't take any of it in. He wasn't interested, not really. It was clean, pretty, functional—that was all he asked. And, as an unexpected bonus, it was near Jo. Very near. So near she could pop in for coffee or a drink, or—

He yanked his mind up short. No. He'd promised to give her time, and if he started thinking like that he wouldn't give her ten minutes.

He followed her out of the little door and back across the gardens. They found Rebecca in the kitchen surrounded by the delicious aroma of fresh coffee.

'Well? What did you think?' she asked, looking from one to the other.

'I think I sold it to him. Excuse me, I just want to see what Laura's up to. She's got homework to do.'

They watched her go, then Rebecca looked at Ed searchingly for a moment, before smiling. 'So, is it any good?'

'Perfect. I love it,' Ed told her. 'I don't know what rent you want, but if it isn't too outrageous I'm sure I can manage—'

'I don't want anything!' Rebecca said, looking appalled. 'It's empty—have it, dear. I'm going to have to chuck you out before Easter, anyway. No. You have it for nothing, please. It will do it good. You can pay the running expenses.'

'Well, of course I will. Are you sure? That seems absurdly generous...'

She tutted and brushed him aside. 'Don't be silly. It'll be nice to think of someone living in it. I don't think being empty does houses any favours at all. No, you enjoy it. There's a phone, but for incoming calls only, I'm afraid. I expect you could get it connected if you wanted.'

'It would be useful. When can I move in?'

'Oh—well, today, I suppose, if you want. I'll sort out the linen—'

'I've got sheets and towels. I'll use my own, then I won't feel so guilty!'

'Idiot,' she said affectionately. 'I've made coffee— can you stay?'

'That would be lovely. Was that your coffee last night?'

She gave a musical little laugh. 'You guessed. Poor Maurice, his coffee's dreadful. By the way, that was a delicious meal you cooked for us. He was very grateful.'

'My pleasure. It was a very pleasant evening, wasn't it?' he added, fishing for her reactions.

They were everything Maurice would have wanted. 'Lovely,' Rebecca replied, and her eyes seemed to lose focus. 'Really lovely. I felt quite spoilt.'

Ed smiled gently. 'It must be hard, being on your own.'

'Oh, but I'm not. I've got Jo and Laura.'

He said nothing, and she gave a rueful smile. 'You're right, of course. It isn't quite the same. I do miss having a man around—a different perspective. I wish...' She trailed off and gave him a searching look.

'You wish?'

'Nothing. Let's go through to the sitting room—Jo'll probably join us in a minute.'

He doubted it, but it didn't matter. There'd be plenty of other opportunities. He stopped the smile before it took over his face...

'Hi. What brings you here?'

Jo shut the car door, schooling her face into impassivity. She wasn't going to smile, just because he was here—well, only a bit. 'Oh, just a meeting. What about you?'

'Casualty—a query fracture.'

'Ah, well, you'll be lucky. The radiographer's here so you can have pictures.'

'So I gather.' Ed fell into step beside her and her traitorous body seemed to come alive at his nearness. 'How long do you expect to be here?' he asked.

'About an hour. Why?'

He shrugged. 'Just wondered what you were doing about lunch.'

She paused at the door and met his eyes, forcing herself to be sensible. 'Nothing. I don't tend to have lunch.'

'You should. It's bad for you not to eat regularly.'

'I eat regularly. I eat breakfast and supper.' She changed the subject. 'How's the cottage?'

'Fine—lovely. I'm really delighted. I like Maurice a great deal, but it's wonderful to have my own space.'

'I suppose you're used to living alone,' she said.

'Are you fishing for information?'

She coloured. She had been, but she didn't like being caught out so blatantly! 'Not really,' she lied. 'Just passing comment.'

He laughed without humour. 'You're right, of course. I have been alone for a long while—about four years?

My partner at the time decided she didn't want to relocate when I did. She opted for her career.'

Hence his remark yesterday about not being the only one who'd been hurt.

'I'm sorry,' she said softly.

He shrugged. 'That's life. Anyway, there hasn't been anyone significant since. How about you? How long have you been alone?'

'Why are we suddenly talking about me?' she asked, feeling as if he'd pulled the rug out from under her. She had no intention of talking about herself!

'Fair's fair. I told you about me.'

'There's nothing to tell. It's just me and Laura.'

His eyes were searching, touched with curiosity and compassion. 'That's sad,' he said after a pause.

'No, it's tidy. I told you I wasn't looking for a relationship, and I wasn't just saying it. I'm not. We're happy, Ed.' She looked at her watch and pushed the door open. 'I must get on, I'm going to be late. I'll see you round.'

Ed watched her go, wondering what was wrong with all the men in Yoxburgh that a beautiful woman like Jo with a warm personality and a lively sense of humour could still be alone after all this time.

He knew she was, of course. Maurice had been more than happy to talk about Rebecca's family, and yesterday Rebecca had been fairly forthcoming while Ed had sat there like a sponge and blotted it all up. There'd been no man in Jo's life, by all accounts, since she was eighteen and pregnant and had been abandoned by her lover.

And now she was thirty.

Had Laura's father hurt her that much?

He felt a boiling rage towards the unknown deserter who had left her so carelessly. Without her parents her life would have been much harder, and Laura's too. And he thought he'd had problems!

He went into the casualty department and found his patient, a young lad with a slightly bent-looking arm. He smiled reassuringly at the woman beside the boy, and dropped to his haunches in front of them.

'Hello, there,' he said, eyeing the distorted limb. 'I'm Dr Latimer. So, what happened to you?'

'I fell off my bike—are you going to take an X-ray?'

'That's right. Mind if I feel it?'

'It hurts,' the boy said warily.

'I'm sure. Can you wiggle your fingers for me?' Ed asked, and watched carefully as the boy moved them very slightly. They were pink, and when he touched them the boy could feel it all right, so he was confident there was no serious disruption to the nerves or blood supply, despite the slightly strange angle.

'I think we'll need a picture of that before we do any more,' he said. He straightened and smiled at the woman again. 'Are you his mother?'

'That's right—Mona Davies. His name's Richard.'

'OK. Right, well, we need to ask the radiographer to take some pictures of Richard. If it's a fairly simple break we can set it here and plaster it, otherwise he'll have to go to the Audley, I'm afraid.'

'Oh, I do hope you can do it. We haven't got a car at the moment and it's such a long way on the bus.'

'I'll do my best. Right, let's get these X-rays.'

He found the nurse, filled in the X-ray request form and went into the office while he waited.

'Anything else for me while I'm here?'

'A child with a bead up her nose. We can't get hold of it, and she can't blow it out.'

'I'll get it out. Got any superglue and a match?'

'Somewhere. Do you want to do it now?'

'Better, in case she sniffs it up and it goes down into her lungs.'

He was taken over to the little girl, who was sitting on her mother's lap, looking sorrowful.

'This is Mrs Barham—and this is Emily,' the nurse said.

'Hello, there, Emily,' Ed said with a smile. She buried her face in her mother's neck and he switched the smile to the mother. 'Hi. I'm Ed Latimer. I gather she's got a bead up her nose.'

'Yes—it's all my fault. I let her play with a broken necklace. I never thought she'd be silly enough to stick it up her nose.'

'Not silly,' the little one mumbled through her mother's jumper.

'Of course not. It was just an accident, wasn't it? Are you going to let me see it?'

The blotchy little face appeared slowly from the hollow of her mother's shoulder. 'It's up there,' she said, shoving her finger up her left nostril.

'Don't push it,' he cautioned, catching her hand. 'Can you turn round so I can see?'

She swivelled, and he took a pen torch from his pocket and shone it up her snub of a nose. 'Oh, yes—it's a pretty pink one. Right, well, I think I can probably get that out without too much difficulty, but you'll have to lie very still for me. Can you do that?'

She nodded solemnly, and he ruffled her hair and stood. 'I'll just get the gear. Can you come into the treatment room?'

He laid her down, made her promise not to move and put a drop of superglue on the end of a matchstick. Very carefully, he held the end of the matchstick against the bead until it had stuck, then pulled it carefully out.

'There you go! One bead.'

'Can I have it?' she asked.

'So long as you promise not to stick it back up,' he warned, and he handed her the matchstick and bead. 'Now, young lady, remember, you must never stick anything up your nose.'

'Not even my finger?'

He stifled the smile. 'Not even your finger,' he agreed. 'OK.'

'Thank you, Dr Latimer,' Mrs Barham said with a heartfelt smile. 'I'll go and put the rest of the necklace in the bin.'

'Sounds like a good idea, although I think she might have learned her lesson.'

'I hope so!'

He watched them go, then turned back to the nurse. 'How's the X-ray coming on?'

'It's ready.'

'Right, let's go and have a look and see if it's within my scope.'

It was, just about. Given the distance, the discomfort of joggling on the bus and the likelihood of them not doing it any differently in a bigger hospital, Ed decided to have a go.

'I want to pull it out a little straighter so I'll give you an anaesthetic into your arm to make it numb, and then we'll do it.' He turned to the nurse. 'I'll need a compression bandage and lignocaine to numb the arm,' he told her, and then explained to the boy and his mother what he intended to do.

'I'm going to squeeze all the blood out of your hand and wrist, and put some local anaesthetic into the blood vessels. That numbs the area very successfully, better than any other way. Then I can pull the arm straighter, without hurting you, and put the plaster on.'

'It sounds very complicated,' Mona said cautiously.

'It's not. It's fine, really. It's quite time-consuming, but it works. The good thing is there's no nerve damage and the blood vessels are OK, otherwise he would have to go to the Audley.'

They raised his arm, bandaged the hand from the fingertips down to cut off the circulation, put a strap round his arm to prevent any new blood from coming in, then removed the bandage and injected the local anaesthetic.

'Better?' he asked after a few minutes, and Richard nodded.

'It doesn't hurt now.'

'Good. Right, I just want to see if I can straighten it a little.' Ed took hold of his hand, gripped it and the top of the forearm firmly and eased them apart. There was a crunch, and the bones realigned satisfyingly.

'OK?' he checked, and the boy nodded. He looked a little pale, but he wasn't screaming the place down so the anaesthetic must be working.

The arm seemed quite stable so Ed asked for another X-ray to check the alignment. It was as good as he felt he could get it so he took off the strap, let the circulation back into the arm and, once the hand had recovered, he checked the colour and warmth of the fingers.

'Can you feel anything?'

'Yes—it's odd, but I can still feel things a bit.'

'Just not pain.'

'That's right.'

'Good. OK, we'll plaster it.'

It took another half-hour before Ed was happy with Richard's arm, and then he had visits to do. What a good job he hadn't talked Jo into lunch!

The afternoon passed quickly—too quickly. He was back at the practice for evening surgery, and finally he was able to go home at seven.

He was starving—too hungry to cook—and there was

a chippy down the road. He pulled up outside it, bought good old cod and chips, parked the car by the cottage and walked down to the seafront to eat his meal.

He leaned on the sea wall, looking out over the dark water and listening to the low roar of the surf on the shingle. The wind, always present, tugged his hair, and he turned his face to it and closed his eyes. He loved the smell of the sea—the strange mixture of salt and tar and seaweed on the high-water mark.

The food was good—hot and freshly cooked and delicious. He wondered what his patients would think if they could see him eating something so high in fat, but he didn't care. He was hungry, it filled the hole and the fish was highly nutritious.

He screwed up the paper, scrubbing his hands on it, and turned his back to the sea wall. Jo's house was in front of him and slightly to the left, and as he looked he saw a light come on upstairs.

Her room? She'd said Laura's room looked out over the back. Did Jo have a sea view? Probably.

He thought of their kiss, and ached. Was she thinking of him?

A car swept onto the drive of her house, and he recognised it as the evil machine that had nearly given him heart failure. Unable to stay away, he strolled over and stood on the other side of the garden wall, waiting for her to get out.

She smiled and slammed the door. 'Hi. What are you doing?'

'Just finished supper,' he said, holding up the paper so she could see it in the streetlight. 'How about you? Have you eaten?'

'Yes—I've just come back from a visit.'

He leaned on the wall and met her eyes in the strange yellow light. 'Fancy a coffee?'

'Is your coffee as good as your cooking?'

'Better,' he promised.

A smile brushed her lips. 'OK. I'll just tell Mum. Go and put it on. I'll come via the garden.'

He went back and ran an eye over the sitting room. There were still a couple of boxes scattered about, but he'd only been there two days—less. He put the kettle on, warmed the cafetière and made the coffee, lit the gas fire and went to the back door, switching on the outside light.

He was impatient. Excitement thrummed in his veins, a curious buzz of anticipation that he couldn't remember having felt in years. He stood at the door, waiting, and then he heard the creak of the gate and his heart jerked against his ribs.

Jo.

Ed was standing in the garden, by the slightly open door, waiting for her. Her footsteps faltered, but she told herself not to be a fool. He might be attractive, he might be a flirt, he might be all sorts of things, but he was also a gentleman.

It was funny how she knew that. Even knowing him as slightly as she did, she knew she could trust him to keep his word.

And he'd promised not to rush her.

She found herself hurrying down the path towards him, and he reached out with his arm and gathered her in against him for a quick hug before pushing the door open and ushering her into the sitting room.

The gas coal fire was lit, flickering a welcome, and the enticing smell of fresh coffee drifted from the kitchen. 'Have a seat,' he said, and went into the kitchen, emerging a moment later with a tray.

'Smells wonderful. I've been so busy today I've hardly had time to turn round.'

He laughed. 'Tell me about it. That fracture took hours—it's a good job we didn't arrange to meet for lunch.'

'There you go, then. I was right.'

'For the wrong reasons,' he pointed out, and handed her a mug of coffee. 'Shortbread?'

'Home-made?'

He chuckled. 'In which spare minute? No, it's not home-made.'

She had a finger of it anyway. It was her Achilles' heel, and she wondered if he'd known that. She decided as she bit into it that she didn't care.

He stretched out in the chair, and she watched him out of the corner of her eye and wondered what it was about him in particular that made her pulse do silly things.

'Tell me about your day,' he said quietly.

'My day? Oh. Busy. Postnatal checks, a meeting, a couple of antenatal checks, booking someone in. The usual.'

'How's Julie Brown?'

'Fine. The baby's growing like a weed.'

Ed grinned lazily. 'Thought he might. He's got a good appetite. Have another bit of shortbread.'

'You're bad for me,' she told him, reaching out to take another finger. He took one too, and she watched his clean, even white teeth bite into it and had to stop the little sound that tried to erupt from her throat.

For heaven's sake, how could eating a piece of shortbread be so erotic?

She kicked off her shoes and curled her feet under her, cradling her mug and staring into the coffee so she wasn't looking at him. Clearly, watching him wasn't going to do her any good at all so she might as well not do it!

Instead she looked around the room—at the music system he'd got set up in the corner, the books on the shelves, the little touches that made it his.

'It seems really homely,' she said in surprise. 'I mean, we try to make it welcoming but without personal touches it's very difficult.'

'It's lovely. I'm thrilled with it. The bed's brilliant as well. It's big enough, and it's firm enough. I hate saggy beds.'

'So do I,' she said, and wondered how they'd got onto the subject of beds.

Ed unwound himself from the chair, went over to the hi-fi and fiddled through a collection of CDs which was threatening to take over, finally selecting one and putting it on.

Soft, romantic music flowed round Jo, and he topped up her coffee and sat down again, watching her over the rim of his mug. 'How's your mother?'

'She's fine.'

'Maurice can't talk about anything else. I think he's suddenly opened his eyes and seen her for the first time.'

'I know. She's the same.'

'How do you feel about it?'

She shrugged and stared into the fire. 'I don't know. It's odd. She's my mother—it seems really strange to see her flirting with him.'

'It must be.'

'I don't mind,' she added hastily. 'Don't think that. I'm glad for her, it's just…'

'Odd.'

'Yes.'

She set down her coffee-mug and wriggled her feet back into her shoes. 'I have to go. Laura won't do her homework unless I nag, and I don't want her getting to bed too late. You won't forget the panto rehearsal tomorrow night, will you?'

'No, I won't forget.'

'You didn't come yesterday.'

'I was moving. I won't miss any more—not unless I'm on call and I have to go.'

'Get the others to change their rotas for the panto week. You can't slide off during a performance.'

'Yes, miss,' he said dutifully, and she laughed and shook her head.

'I'll see you tomorrow. Thanks for the coffee.'

'My pleasure.' He walked her to the door, and she wondered with a tremor of anticipation whether he'd kiss her goodnight.

For a moment she thought he wouldn't, but as they reached the door he drew her into his arms. 'One last thing,' he murmured, and then his lips touched hers and she was lost.

His mouth was gentle, coaxing, and despite her resolve she parted her lips and kissed him back.

He groaned deep in his throat and his arms tightened, easing her closer. She could feel the pounding of his heart against hers and the slight tremor in his limbs. His chest was heaving under her hands, and then he lifted his head, trailing his lips down the curve of her jaw and taking tiny little bites from the tender skin of her throat.

A helpless moan escaped from her lips, and he returned to them, his mouth gentle, sipping, tasting, driving her wild. She leaned into him and his hands came up and steadied her, easing her away.

'You'd better go,' he said gruffly, and she could see the raw need etched on his face.

She nearly didn't leave. She so, so, nearly stayed, but out of the corner of her eye she caught sight of Laura's bedroom window, and remembered all the reasons this was such a bad idea.

Without a word she turned and opened the door and walked away.

She didn't look back until she was safely inside her own house. Then she went into Laura's empty room, turned off the light and crossed to the window.

He was still standing there, looking up at her, and she closed her eyes and pressed her lips together against the little sound of need. She didn't need him. It was only physical. She'd been fooled like that before, and look what had happened.

She turned away from the window and nearly fell over a heap of discarded clothes dropped in the middle of Laura's floor.

No, there were plenty of reminders of what could happen if she let her heart rule her head. She'd better not let it happen again.

CHAPTER FIVE

JO DIDN'T know how she'd feel with Ed after that kiss but, apart from a quick smile and a wave as he dived into his consulting room, she didn't see him the next day until the afternoon antenatal clinic, and then they were working in tandem anyway so she didn't really see him to speak to until afterwards.

He found her in the kitchen, boiling the kettle and rinsing out the mugs.

'Tea?' she offered brightly.

'Please. Anything interesting to report?'

'No, not really. Everybody's chugging along nicely. Actually, that's not quite true. I've got one baby small for dates—I'm sending her for a scan, but her other two were on the small side so I think it's just the way she does it.'

'Maybe she doesn't have very good placentas. Some women just don't.'

'Maybe. We'll see.' She poured the water into the mugs, mashed the teabags and fished them out. 'Here,' she said, sliding the mugs across the worktop. 'Milk's in the fridge behind you.'

He did the honours and put the milk away, then dropped onto a chair and propped his feet on another. 'What time does the rehearsal start?'

'Seven forty-five—always.'

He nodded. 'I've got a full surgery. Apologise to Roz for me if I'm a bit on the drag, would you? I don't even know if I'm going to be able to stay awake that long.'

He closed his eyes, and she couldn't resist the opportunity to study his face.

It fascinated her. His lashes lay like dark crescents against his cheeks, and she could see the shadow of his beard on his jaw. Her palm remembered the rough scrape of stubble, and she had to stop herself reaching out to touch him—to run her hand over that angular jaw, to trail her fingers over the soft fullness of his lips or trace the laughter lines that bracketed his mouth—

His lids flicked open and their eyes met and held.

'I couldn't sleep last night after you left,' he said quietly. 'The house just seemed—very empty.'

'That's silly,' she told him. 'I'd only been there a few minutes.'

'You underestimate the force of your personality. Believe me, I missed you.'

She felt absurdly pleased. 'You're daft,' she said, and, dipping her finger in the tea, doodled on the table top.

'Just very attracted to you and wondering how to deal with it,' he replied, leaning forward and catching her hand, stilling it. 'I kept thinking about that kiss—about the feel of your lips, and the softness of your mouth, and the intoxicating fragrance of your skin.'

Heat suffused her, and with a little sound of protest she pulled her hand away and stood, going to the sink and rinsing her mug. 'Ed, stop it,' she pleaded quietly. 'Don't do this to us. It isn't fair.'

'Why not?' His voice was right behind her, his breath brushing her ear, teasing her skin. 'You're a beautiful woman, Jo. How can it be wrong to tell you that?'

She spun, ready to tell him off for harrassing her, but the look in his eyes was totally sincere and honest, and the protest died on her lips. 'I'm not beautiful,' she said instead, and could have kicked herself for falling for his charm.

He smiled, a knowing, gentle smile. 'We'll have to agree to differ,' he said, and, putting his mug in the sink, he left her alone with what was left of her brain. She washed out his mug, put it on the draining-board and wiped her hands.

Why was she such a sucker for a pretty line? Surely she'd have learned her lesson by now!

'Right, can I have you all here, please? I want to run through the end of the first half, with Belle meeting the Beast for the first time.'

Ed watched Jo playing the innocent virginal Belle, and as the Beast gathered her into his arms and trod on her toes for the third time he found himself growing more and more frustrated.

'Is there a man here who can dance?' Roz called out. 'I just want someone to show Peter how it's supposed to look.'

There were catcalls and jokes and stupid suggestions, but nobody actually got to their feet.

Ed gave a resigned sigh and moved forward. He could dance, but he wasn't sure if he could hold Jo in his arms and whirl her around, without disgracing himself.

'Ah, Ed,' Roz said with relief. 'Are you volunteering?'

'I don't know if I can do it any better, but I'll have a go. My mother insisted I should learn when I was a child, but I think I've forgotten more than I ever knew.'

'I never knew it,' Peter confessed with a chuckle, 'and if I go on like this Belle will be in a plaster cast on the night.'

'Right—over here. You ask her to dance, you have the little bit of repartee, then she says, "I would be honoured," and you take her in your arms and sweep her off around the stage. OK? Can we have the music, please?'

Ed bowed, Jo curtseyed, he held out his arms, she drifted into them, and then, as if they'd done it for years, they circled the stage, perfectly in tune. When they got back to the front and he bowed, a cheer went up and Peter shook his head.

'Don't suppose you'd like my part, would you? I can't sing, I can't dance—the only reason I got it is because I'm the only one who's taller than her.'

'You just want to get out of learning your lines,' someone called, and everyone laughed.

'Don't involve me in this,' Ed said, throwing up his hands. 'Anyway, you're fine. I was watching you. You're holding her in front of you, instead of slightly to the side. If you hold her like this, her feet are around yours and not under them. Try it.'

He did, and it seemed to work a little better. Ed retreated to the back of the hall and watched, then winced as Peter trod on Jo again.

'Sorry, Belle,' he said heavily. 'I just can't seem to get it.'

'Keep trying,' Roz said cheerfully. 'You aren't going to get out of learning the lines, Peter. Right, everyone, let's have the village scene and Belle and the Beast can go off and practise.'

They met again in the teabreak, and Jo took him on one side. 'Thanks for your help,' she said softly. 'He was getting desperate. He really hasn't ever danced. I'm sure he'll be fine now.'

'How about your toes?' Ed asked her with a grin. 'Will they survive?'

'Just be ready with the aspirin,' she said with a laugh, and then went off to practise some more.

He watched her go, wishing he had been able to be

the Beast. There was a huge part of him that wanted to do it because he wanted to be the one to dance with Belle, he wanted to be the one to hold her, and kiss her, and marry her in the finale.

And maybe not just in the finale.

What a sobering thought.

Anyway, he wasn't an option, in any shape or form. 'Ed?'

He looked up and smiled distractedly. 'Hi, Roz.'

'Thanks for your help just now. You really are turning into an asset. Have you done panto before?'

'Yes, loads of times when I was a child. I just hope I can fit it all in. I really do have a lot of commitments and I don't want to let anybody down because I haven't been able to give it the time it needs.'

'You'll be fine. Having done it before helps, of course. You know how to fit in.'

'Yes, you just heckle the producer, isn't that right?'

Roz laughed and disappeared into the throng, and Laura materialised at his side, hitching herself up onto a table. 'I think you should have been the Beast,' she said without preamble.

He looked down at the mini-Jo, and gave a lopsided smile. 'Why's that?'

'You're much better. You look the part. You need to be good-looking when the mask comes off, and Peter's sweet but he's just not—well, he's no prince, is he? Not enough machismo.'

Ed gave a startled laugh. 'Laura, if you keep on like this my head will get so big I wouldn't get in the mask anyway,' he said with a grin. 'Besides, what does a prince look like?'

'I dunno, but in the absence of a real one I guess you'll do,' she said with a cheeky wink and, slipping off the table, she left him.

'What did she want?'

He looked at Jo and chuckled. 'Me to be the Beast. She says Peter doesn't look like a prince when he takes his mask off.'

'And you do?'

He couldn't stop the smile. 'So your daughter says. I can take a lot of her flattery.'

'You're so susceptible.'

'No, I just know how to take a compliment,' he said, tongue-in-cheek.

Her mouth twitched. 'You'll get swollen-headed.'

'That's what I told her.'

'I'll have to have a word.'

'Spoilsport,' he said.

He looked down at Jo and wondered how in such a short time she could have come to dominate his life to such an extent. Two weeks ago he hadn't even met her, and now for two pins he'd take on a major part in the pantomime just to stop her toes getting crushed!

Jo had a phone call at lunchtime, summoning her to the house of Liz Bateman, the woman whose baby was small for dates. She arrived at two, and the woman opened the door to her in tears.

'It hasn't moved since last night,' she told Jo, and scrubbed at the tears on her cheeks. 'I keep telling myself it's nothing, that I'm just imagining it, but…it seemed to move quite violently for a while, and since then there's been nothing.'

'Oh, dear,' Jo said gently. 'Well, let's not get ahead of ourselves. It might have just worn itself out yesterday and be having a rest. Did you have your scan this morning?'

She shook her head. 'No. Roger wasn't here to drive me, and I was too upset to drive myself.'

'OK.' She looked around the living room, and moved a couple of toys off the settee. 'Just lie here and I'll have a listen.'

She lifted Liz's jumper up and pulled down the front of her trousers to expose the firm curve of her pregnancy. She felt gently for the lie of the baby, and it was quite normal—head down and with the baby's spine pressed against the right side of Liz's abdomen. 'How many weeks are you? Thirty-four?'

'Yes.'

She wasn't big enough, Jo thought again, rummaging for the equipment. 'OK.' Kneeling beside the settee, she spread a little gel on the skin above the baby's back. She turned on her Sonicaid, and ran it over the skin slowly, searching for the heartbeat. After what seemed like an age, she sank back onto her heels and turned it off.

'Liz, I'm sorry, I can't find anything. The battery might be flat. Let me try with the old-fashioned trumpet.'

She took out her wooden Pinard stethoscope, wiped Liz's abdomen dry and pressed one end of the trumpet to where she thought the baby was, putting her ear to the other end.

Nothing. She tried again, felt the lie of the baby once more and made a further attempt, but it was no use.

'It's dead, isn't it?' Liz said quietly.

'I don't know. I can't tell you without a scan, but I am concerned. I think we ought to go in, don't you?'

'But I can't get there.'

'I'll take you. I'll just ring the hospital, if I may?'

'Sure. The phone's in the kitchen. Help yourself.'

Jo stood and went into the kitchen at the back, closing the door behind her before dialling the antenatal unit. 'Hi, it's Jo Halliday here. I've got a query intra-uterine death for scan—I want to bring her in now. Elizabeth Bateman.'

'OK. About half an hour?'

'Something like that. Thirty-four weeks' duration, third baby, first two normal but a bit small. It's small for dates—she was booked for a scan this morning anyway but her husband couldn't bring her.'

'Fine. We'll see you in a bit.'

She hung up the phone and went back into the room. Liz was lying there still, tears coursing down her cheeks.

'I know it's dead,' she said softly.

'You can't be sure. Come on, let's go and have the scan, and we can talk about it when we've got the result.'

Liz nodded and stood, rearranging her clothes absently. 'What about the others? I'd better ring my friend and ask her if she can hang on, and I probably ought to ring Roger.'

'I'll pack up and wait in the car. I've got a couple of phone calls to make anyway. Bring your notes.'

Jo put her things away, went back to the car and rang the surgery. 'I'm taking Mrs Bateman to the Audley for a scan—any calls for me?'

'No. You're the only one, though—the place has gone mad.'

'OK. I'll take the mobile, but if you can get someone else to cover if possible it would be good. I don't want to have to leave her.'

Liz came out at that moment and got into the car, giving Jo a wan smile. 'Come on, then, let's go and get this over with.'

She was silent all the way there, although Jo could practically feel the thoughts coming off her in waves, and when they arrived they were seen almost immediately.

The person who did the scan was very good, patient

and careful to explain what they all already knew in their hearts.

Liz's baby had died because the placenta had failed. 'See, it's quite small. The placenta usually covers a larger area than that, and the baby is very small for its age.'

'I knew it was dead,' Liz said heavily. 'I knew last night. You knew, too, didn't you?' she said to Jo.

'I was fairly sure. It's unusual not to find a heartbeat at this stage. Earlier, maybe, but by now the baby's heartbeat is quite strong and unmistakable. I would have been able to detect it if it was there—and I heard it yesterday.'

'So what happens now?' Liz asked after a pause.

'Now you see the consultant, and he'll arrange for you to come in and have the baby here.'

'Can't I have it at home?'

'We'll talk to him.'

They did, and he explained that it was unlikely that she'd go into labour spontaneously and would probably need to be induced.

'If you do go into labour, I'd still recommend that you come in because obviously it will be quite sad and you'll need a lot of support. Sometimes mothers need quite a lot of pain relief because it can be a fairly negative experience, and we don't want it to be any worse for you that it has to be.'

Liz nodded. 'OK,' she said.

And that was that. She didn't say another word until they were back at her house, and then she turned into Jo's arms and sobbed her heart out. 'Oh, Liz, I'm sorry,' Jo murmured, and rocked her gently until she stopped crying. Then she led her into the kitchen and made them a cup of tea.

'I don't want to go to hospital,' Liz said tearfully over

her tea. 'I want to have it here. It just feels wrong to change everything just because the baby's dead.'

'I can't induce you here, though,' Jo explained.

'Can I wait till Friday? Maybe by then I will have gone into labour.'

It was Wednesday. 'Sure,' Jo said gently. 'It will give you time to get used to the idea, but I'm not sure that you'll start without help so do be prepared for that.'

'But if I did—would you let me have it here?'

Jo nodded slowly. 'If it's what you really want, yes, of course, I'll be with you. Talk to your husband, see what he feels.'

She nodded. 'Will I be able to see it and hold it?'

'Of course—either here or in the hospital. You can spend as long as you want with it.'

'Will it look—funny?'

'Probably not. I expect it will be quite thin, but otherwise it will look quite normal, I would imagine.'

She nodded. 'I think I'll lie down for a while. Thanks for taking me.'

Jo hugged her. 'You're welcome. Will you be all right alone? Can I call Roger for you?'

Liz shook her head. 'I'll ring him—he'll be home soon anyway, I expect. I'll be fine. I'm not going to do anything stupid. I've got two lovely children and a husband who adores me. I'm very lucky. I'm just sad. I'll be all right.'

'OK.' Jo left her sitting in the kitchen with a second cup of tea, and drove slowly back to the surgery. Liz needed time to come to terms with the situation, and Jo was pretty sure she'd be sensible.

'Any messages?' she asked the receptionist.

'No. You've got away with it. How was the mum?'

'Not good,' Jo told her. She didn't want to talk about

it any more. No, that wasn't true—she did, but only to
Ed. 'Is Dr Latimer about?'

'You've just missed him—he's gone out on a call. Dr
Brady's on call but she was out already and it was urgent
so he said he'd cover it. I don't expect him back now
until tomorrow.'

'Right.'

Jo went home, ran a bath and sat in it, staring at the
wall, until Laura came and banged on the door. 'Grannie
says supper's ready and don't forget the panto.'

'I haven't,' she replied, and slid under the water. She
wanted to wash away the day, rinse all the sadness off
her skin and start again. She needed to talk to Ed. Was
he back?

She lifted the corner of the blind and looked out over
the garden, but there were no lights on in his cottage.
He must still be out on the call.

Oh, well. She'd see him later. She'd just have to hang
on...

There was something wrong with Jo. Ed watched her
over the script as he tried to learn his lines, and when
she looked across and caught his eye he could almost
feel her pain.

What on earth had happened? He hadn't been back to
the surgery. He'd been involved with a car accident and
he'd stayed with the trapped victims until they'd been
able to free them, acting as back-up for the paramedics.
It had been pretty hectic, not entirely successful and, in
the manner of these things, time-consuming.

He'd dived home for a quick shower and he'd only
just got to the rehearsal on time. He still hadn't eaten.
He'd found a pile of biscuits in the hall kitchen and was
munching through them steadily while he watched Jo
and stared at his script.

Laura came and found him. 'Hi,' she said with a grin. 'How's it going?'

'Slowly. Is your mum all right?'

Laura looked up at the stage and shrugged. 'Dunno. She's been very quiet since she got in from work. I expect something happened—sometimes it does and then she goes funny for a bit.'

He nodded. 'I wondered. I'll talk to her later.'

'Thanks. I don't suppose you want to test me on my words? I still don't know the songs.'

'Nor do I. I was trying to learn mine.'

'That's easy. Nobody interrupts you. Barry's got the worst part—or the Ugly Sisters. That's difficult.'

'They're funny—they do it very well, don't they?'

'Brilliant. They ad-lib the whole time and put everybody off, but they're fantastic. I love them. You've only got a boring part, really.'

'Hmm. Let's just hope I don't make a complete ass of myself.'

'Oh, go on! It would make it really funny!'

'Thanks.' He swatted Laura round the head with the script, and she laughed and ran off with some of his biscuits.

Then Roz was waving and calling him, and he had to go and put his money where his mouth was and start acting. He felt silly at first, but everyone was so good-natured about it that he soon relaxed into the part.

It was hardly unfamiliar after all his experience in the village panto as a child and, as he got into it, it all came flooding back. If it hadn't been for Jo, he would have enjoyed it.

'That was marvellous!' Roz said to him as he left the stage for their break.

He smiled distractedly and thanked her, then followed Jo out into the entrance.

'Are you OK?'

She looked at him, her arms hugging her waist, and shook her head. 'Not really. Can I talk to you later?'

'Sure. Your place or mine?'

'Yours. It's a patient—I don't want to talk about it with Laura around.'

'OK. I'll go back and put the kettle on. You take Laura home and then join me when you're ready.'

She nodded, but she looked on the verge of tears so he took her back inside, gave her a cup of tea and jollied and joked and talked about the pantomimes he'd done as a child to distract her.

Finally it was over, and he went back and waited for her.

She wasn't long. She walked through the door into his outstretched arms and howled her eyes out. Then she hiccuped to a halt, scrubbed her cheeks on her sleeve and sniffed. 'Got a tissue?'

'Kitchen roll?'

She sniffed again, and he followed her into the kitchen and opened a bottle of wine. 'Here,' he said, and handed her a glass. 'Now, come and sit down and tell Uncle Ed all about it.'

She trailed after him, sat beside him on the settee and told him the sorry tale of Liz Bateman's baby.

'She wants to have it at home. I really want to let her, but only if you'll support it and be there too, and she does know the chances are she won't be able to.'

He pursed his lips and stared at the fire. 'Is it wise? They can often give up pushing, get disheartened. What were her other deliveries like?'

'First was normal, in the Audley, the second she had here in the GP unit. This one was planned for home.'

He shrugged. 'I'll be guided by you. As you say, it

may not happen. Now, drink up. You need another glass of that.'

She shook her head. 'No, I'm only having one. I've told her to call me at any time if she wants to, and I don't want to let her down.'

She put the glass down and looked at him. 'Ed?'

'What is it?'

'Will you hold me?'

He let his breath out on a sigh and reached for her, drawing her into his arms. 'Poor baby. Have you had an awful day?'

'Not as bad as Liz Bateman.'

'No. Oh, well, at least you were there for her.'

'I keep wondering if I'd picked it up earlier, if the baby would have been all right...'

He hugged her shaking shoulders and wished there was something he could do to take away the pain. 'How could you have picked it up earlier? These things are often quite sudden—the placenta just packs up and that's that. You can only pick it up when the baby fails to grow enough, and it takes time to see that. You can't scan everyone all the time—it just isn't practical.'

'I know that,' she sniffed, and scrubbed her nose again. 'Oh, I'm being silly. It was just a horrible day.'

'They happen. Mine wasn't brilliant. I sat by the side of the road and held someone's hand while he died. Sometimes that's all you can do.' The man's face swam in front of him, and he squeezed his eyes shut.

'I'm sorry,' she said softly. 'I'm going on about my patient and you've had a grim day as well.'

'Still, it isn't all bad. Peter didn't tread on your toes tonight.'

'No.' She gave a half-hearted little laugh. 'No, he didn't, thanks to you. He's very grateful—and so am I!'

'Good. At least someone's happy.'

He hugged her closer, snuggling down into the corner and pulling her over so she sprawled against his side. 'I ought to go home,' she mumbled sleepily.

'Stay for a while. We both need a hug.'

'Mmm.' She cuddled against him, her head on his chest, and within moments she was asleep. He left her there and sat, sifting her hair through his fingers and remembering the details of his day, until in the end he drifted off as well.

They were woken by the sound of her mobile phone. Jo struggled to her feet, grabbed it from her bag and answered it.

'Right. OK. I'll come now. That's OK.'

She switched it off and looked at him. 'Liz Bateman's in labour. I'd better go and tell Mum.'

'I'll come with you,' Ed said, and, pulling on his coat, he flicked off the lights, locked the door behind them and followed her down the path.

It was a solemn but beautiful birth. The baby was a girl, very small, very thin, but quite perfect, and Liz held her and cried. Jo finished the delivery and shook her head over the size of the placenta. One half of it was shrivelled and withered, the other half very small to support a growing baby.

The vicar came and baptised the baby and they all cried, even Ed. Jo was glad to see him cry. Nobody she would want to know could have been unmoved by it.

She drew him aside and left the couple with their baby and the vicar.

'I need a cup of tea,' she told him, taking him downstairs.

'Me, too. Thank God it was an easy labour.'

'I thought it would be. I'm so glad I let her stay.'

'What happens now?'

She shrugged. 'When they're ready the baby and the placenta need to go to the hospital for examination to find out why she died, but it's obvious, really. Then they'll have a funeral, and start all over again, I expect.'

He nodded. 'Yes. Probably. I don't know where women find their strength. She's been marvellous.'

'She's a mother. That's what it means.'

Ed swallowed. 'Yes, I suppose you're right.' He gave her a hug, then patted her shoulder. 'Shall we take the tea up?'

'Good idea. We could be here for hours. Do you want to go?'

He shook his head, to her relief. 'I'll stay with you, if you want me to.'

'Don't you mind?'

'No. No, Jo, I don't mind.'

'Thanks.'

She gave a half-hearted smile, and he reached out for her hand and squeezed it. 'That's what friends are for.'

It was dawn before they went home. They turned into the drive as the sun crawled over the horizon, and by tacit consent they stood on the sea wall and thought about the night. Ed's arm was firm around Jo, and she leaned her head against his shoulder and gazed sightlessly out to sea.

'You OK?' he asked softly.

'I'll live. Thanks for being with me.'

'Any time.'

He turned her into his arms, cupped her face in his hands and placed a feathery kiss on her lips.

'Why don't you go to bed?'

'It's time to get up—I have to get Laura off to school.'

'Do you have a clinic?'

She shook her head. 'Just some baby visits.'

'Try and get your head down—that's an order.'

She dredged up a smile. 'Yes, sir.'

'That's it. Chin up, you're doing a grand job,' he said softly, and, kissing her again, he left her there and walked swiftly down the little alley and round the corner out of sight.

A moment later her mother joined her.

'Are you all right?'

She turned to her and smiled tiredly. 'I will be.'

'Kettle's on. Come on,' she said gently. She put her arm round her daughter's shoulders, and led her into the house.

CHAPTER SIX

'Jo? IT'S Moira Clarke. I'm sorry to ring you so early but I've been feeling ill all night. Hal's away, and the kids are playing up, and I just can't cope…' She paused, and Jo could hear her fighting tears at the other end.

'Don't worry, Moira, I'm on my way. You just lie down and rest, and I'll be with you.'

She tugged on her clothes, grabbed her mobile phone, changed the battery and ran downstairs. There was no time for a hot drink so she filled a glass from the tap and took a swig, scribbled a note to her mother and Laura and ran out.

Moira lived up the coast a little way, in a house almost on the beach. It was isolated, beautiful and in almost permanent danger of flooding, but the Clarkes loved it. Jo loved it too, but she wouldn't live there, especially not with three boisterous boys and another baby on the way.

Please, God, don't let it be another tragedy, she prayed. The Batemans' baby was still in her thoughts every waking moment, and the prospect of another such disaster filled her with dread.

It also made her drive even faster, but at six o'clock on a Saturday morning that probably didn't matter. There weren't a lot of cars about, but she gave the odd rabbit a fright.

She slithered to a halt in the drive of Driftwood Cottage, grabbed her bag and phone and ran to the door.

It was opened by a six-year-old ragamuffin, with spiky blond hair and gappy teeth and a runny nose. 'Mum's in bed,' he told her, without taking his eyes off the Gameboy in his hand. 'She's been chucking up.'

'Thanks, Oliver.' She ran up, forcing herself to go slowly into the room and be calm. Moira was lying on the bed, her eyes closed, a bowl clutched to her chest.

'You look a bit peaky.'

Her eyes opened and she looked at Jo and groaned. 'I feel dreadful. I can't understand it. I just feel—I don't know, off colour somehow. Oliver, turn that thing off!'

The sound of the Gameboy faded into the distance, and Moira dropped her head back and sighed.

Jo put her bag down and frowned. This wasn't a tragedy—this was, unless she was very much mistaken, a woman in labour! 'Have you had any contractions?' she asked, dropping her coat on the chair and rolling up her sleeves.

'No—well, only the practice ones.'

'I'll just wash my hands—I want to have a look at you. Can you slip your things off?'

She went into the bathroom and washed her hands, found a clean towel in the airing cupboard and dried them, then took another towel back with her. Seconds later she was glad she had because there was a gush of fluid and Moira's waters broke.

Jo smiled in relief and mopped with the towels. 'I thought so. You're in labour, my love.'

'But I can't be! It's not due for two weeks, and Hal's away in Germany!'

'Sorry—I think this baby's coming now. And I'll tell you something else—I don't think I've got time to get my box out of the car. Let's have a look.'

She pulled some gloves on with a snap, felt Moira's cervix and rolled her eyes.

'Do you know why you're feeling so horrible? You're in transition. Any moment now you'll be throwing a paddy and then we'll be in business. Mind if I use your phone?'

'Go ahead,' Moira said, sounding and looking shocked. 'It's not due yet! I can't be in labour!'

'Ed?'

'Jo? What is it?' he mumbled, fighting sleep. She had a pang of guilt about waking him when he wasn't on call, but he wanted experience.

'Can you come? I've got a home delivery for you— head north out of town on the coast road, and after about two miles there's a white cottage nearly on the beach— Driftwood Cottage. That's it. Can you come quickly? This one's in a hurry.'

'Aren't they all? Hasn't anyone in Suffolk heard of a nice, steady labour?' he grumbled gently.

'Thanks.'

She cradled the phone, a silly smile on her lips, and turned back to Moira. 'Dr Latimer's coming, too. Have you met him?'

'I've got an appointment with him for Tuesday.'

'Well, you won't need it. Right, let's get the bed stripped. Have you got a sheet of plastic?'

'It's on the bed, under a layer of towels. My labours always start with my waters so I've learned my lesson!'

'In which case, let's just leave you there and put some pads under you to make it more comfy for now. Do you want to walk round?'

'The only thing I really want is a drink, I'm so thirsty— Oh, golly, I can feel a contraction now. Jo, do you think I ought to go to hospital? Perhaps I'd better pack—can you give me a hand?'

Moira flailed her arms, trying to get to her feet, and Jo smiled to herself and helped her up. 'Just walk round for a moment to let it ease. That's it, lean on me—lovely, well done.'

'Jo, I want to go to hospital,' she said, sounding fretful. 'Please, call an ambulance. I need to go. I can't do this here without Hal.'

'Sorry, my love, you've got no choice. Come on, keep going, you'll be fine.'

'Dammit, listen to me! I'm not staying here!' she shouted, and burst into tears. The next moment she was reaching for the sick bowl, and Jo held her and walked her round and soothed her.

Then she handed back the bowl to Jo, smiled weakly and apologised.

'Sorry—transition,' she said. 'I'll be good now.'

Jo laughed. 'I thought you were going to walk to the hospital,' she said.

'So did I. Oh, here we go…Oh, Jo, I want to push.'

'OK. Let me check your cervix is fully dilated—'

'No. I have to push, I *have* to…'

She knelt and leaned over the bed, then with a groan she pushed down and Jo saw the baby's head crowning.

'We're there, Moira. Just pant—that's a good girl. Lovely. Nice and steady… Oh, yes, little one, hello. Welcome to the world.'

Moira turned and sank to the floor, and Jo whisked a towel under her, laid the squalling baby over her leg and glanced up.

'Oh, look, it's the cavalry,' she said, and smiled at Ed.

'Thanks for coming.'

He leant on his car door. 'My pleasure. Sorry I was too late to help. Lovely baby.'

'And a girl, to boot. They will be pleased. They've got three boys, and they're monsters.'

'Little boys always are—and little girls get worse as they get older.'

She chuckled. 'Sounds about right. Oh, it's the most gorgeous day.' She looked around at the sea and the sky and the heathland behind, and wondered what she had done to deserve it all. 'I love it here.'

'It is beautiful, isn't it? We ought to go for a walk— take advantage of it. It'll probably snow next week.'

'Good idea. I tell you what, I have an antenatal check to do on someone in the forest—do you want to come? They're travellers, and I want to try and talk sense into her because she wants a home delivery and they've got no power, no water, no nothing.'

'Brilliant. Sounds like the perfect scenario,' he said drily. 'I suppose you want me to come in and play the heavy uncle?'

She chuckled. 'Sort of. Perhaps a word in her ear? It's a lovely spot,' she added. 'We could go for that walk.'

'Mmm,' he said, but he didn't sound convinced.

Jo had a pang of conscience about hijacking his Saturday morning off, and said so.

Ed gave a wry grin. 'I wasn't doing anything—well, I was asleep when you phoned, but let's just say I had no plans to do anything. I could do with breakfast, though, before we go out. How about coming round for coffee and croissants? The bakery should be open.'

'Good idea, but why don't you come to me? I ought to see Laura and Mum before I go off out for the day— perhaps Laura could come for the walk too?' she suggested, and then wondered if that would put him off. Apparently not. He nodded his agreement without hesitation.

'Sure. Will she be happy to hang around while we talk to your traveller?'

'I don't know. We'll ask her. I'll see you at home.'

'I'll get the croissants.'

She smiled. 'I'll make the coffee.'

They set off down the coast road at a much more reasonable speed, and Jo found herself singing.

She was happy. Moira's baby was fine, her sister was with her now and would stay until Hal got back from Germany, the sun was shining, Ed was coming round for breakfast—the world was looking brighter than it had for ages.

And Ed was going with her to talk sense into Mel.

What more could she want?

'There it is, up ahead there by the edge of the trees, I think,' Jo said. 'We could park here and walk.'

Ed pulled off onto the side of the road, cut the engine and looked at Jo. 'Tell me what you know about her.'

'She's twenty-eight, lives on income support with her partner, no fixed abode unless you count this—and seems quite contented.'

'Health?'

Jo shrugged. 'She seems very well. She's a vegetarian, but I think she eats sensibly. She certainly looks in good condition—hair, skin, that sort of thing.'

'It must be all the fresh air,' Ed said drily. 'OK. Let's go and meet Mel and her other half and find out what's in store for us.'

They left the car and strolled along the sandy track through the heather. It was a lovely morning for a walk, but Laura had declined to come. She had a better offer from Cara, and they'd gone off on the bus to the cinema. How she could shut herself up on such a lovely day Jo didn't know, but kids would be kids.

'This lot look a bit unfriendly,' Ed murmured, drawing her attention to the encampment up ahead. A group of four coaches, lorries and old caravans were clustered together around a central area. A fire smouldered in the middle, an old mattress hanging half out of it, charred

and blackened, and a few mangy dogs detached themselves from the shelter of the vehicles and ran towards
them.

Moments later they were surrounded by the barking
dogs, their fangs bared, their welcome none too friendly.
Grubby curtains twitched, and Jo felt the hair rise on the
back of her neck.

A man appeared in the doorway of one of the battered
old coaches, dressed in combat trousers, boots and a tat-
tered sweater. He swore at the dogs and they subsided,
growling instead from a distance.

'Hello,' Jo called, dredging up a smile. 'I'm looking
for Mel Jenkins. Is she here?'

'Who wants her?'

'I'm the midwife.'

The man looked searchingly at her, then stepped down
from the coach and stood, facing them, his arms folded
and his legs slightly apart. It was meant to be intimidating, and it worked.

He jerked his head at Ed. 'Who's he?'

'Dr Latimer—my colleague.'

His eyes flicked over Ed and came back to rest on Jo.
They were the coldest, hardest eyes she'd ever seen, and
she instinctively moved closer to Ed.

'They don't live here,' the man said.

A woman pushed past him and came out, a baby dangling on her hip. She had a black eye and a yellow bruise
on her lip. 'She's up the track about half a mile. They've
got an old caravan parked at the edge of the trees. She's
all right, isn't she?'

'As far as I know,' Jo confirmed. 'I was just coming
to do a routine home visit—I always do when I get a
new patient.'

The woman nodded. 'Just go up here and fork left at
the pit. You can't miss them.'

'Thanks.'

She disappeared back inside, but the man stayed, watching them with those cold, hard eyes as they walked away.

'Nice man,' Ed said softly. 'I wouldn't want to meet him on a dark night.'

'No. Let's hope we can talk sense into Mel so we don't have to! Did you see her bruises?'

'Yes—and the baby's. I think we ought to report them.'

'I'll contact the liaison officer—I know him,' Jo said. 'He'll keep an eye out.'

They followed the track, and suddenly came to a little clearing. An old caravan with questionable suspension stood at the back of the clearing, and there was a lean-to built at one end of it. A battered pick-up was parked beside it, with a dog in the back. It jumped down and barked but, unlike the others, it wagged its tail and seemed friendly.

Ed bent and held out his hand, and the dog ran up, wiggling its rear end and sniffing him.

'Mel?' Jo called. 'Mel, are you here?'

The door of the caravan opened and a man appeared. Here we go again, Jo, thought, but he stepped down and came over to them with a smile.

'Gizmo, come here,' he said, and the dog ran to his side, tongue lolling. 'Can I help you?' the man asked, and Jo was surprised at how well spoken he was.

'I'm looking for Mel. I'm the midwife—Jo Halliday. I just wanted to come and say hi and find out where she is, in case she needs me urgently, so I can find her in a hurry.'

He smiled and held out his hand. 'I'm Andy Roarke— her partner.' Jo shook his hand, and his grip was firm and straightforward. She felt happier—marginally.

'This is my colleague, Ed Latimer. He's the GP in charge of obstetrics in our practice.'

Andy Roarke shook his hand, too. 'Hi, Ed. She's inside. Come on in.' He opened the door and led them in, and Jo was surprised to find it clean and tidy and organised.

'Visitors, Mel,' Andy said. 'The midwife and the doctor.'

'Oh, hi, Jo. Come in. There's tea in the pot—Andy, could you?'

Mel was sitting with her feet up on a caravan-type bench seat, a steaming cup of tea on the table beside her, and she tried to struggle up.

'Stay there,' Jo told her. 'We're fine.'

She subsided again, and Andy cleared some papers off the other end of the bench so they could sit down. 'Have a pew. How do you take your tea? Milk and sugar?'

Jo could see Ed eyeing the sink and weighing up the possibility of catching something, but she was used to far worse than this. 'Just white, both of us, thanks. I hope you don't mind us popping in—it's just a routine visit so we know where you are in case you have a problem in the middle of the night.'

Mel's face lost some of its tension. 'I wondered,' she confessed. 'I thought maybe you'd come because the social services liaison officer had been on to you—they keep telling me I ought to go into a council flat or something. They just don't seem to be able to accept that we've chosen this lifestyle quite deliberately, and our baby's going to be safe.'

Andy sat beside her, sliding the mugs of tea across the table. 'We used to live in London,' he told them. 'I was an interior designer, Mel had a soft-furnishing business—that was how we met. Things just got too tight, and we were chasing smaller and smaller margins, and then one day we sat back and said, ''What the hell are we doing this for?'' We were miserable.'

'So we stopped, sold everything we had and bought the van and the pick-up, and here we are,' Mel said, smiling affectionately at him. 'Andy does odd jobs and a bit of drawing for a local firm just to keep us ticking over, and I make tie-dye cushions and shawls and things for a craft market, and we get by. I know it's a cop-out, but we're happy.'

Jo laughed softly. 'I can see the pull. Sometimes things just get on top of you, don't they? Most people don't have the guts to get out.'

'We had to. We were talking about a suicide pact—only jokingly, but it brought it home to us.'

Jo nodded. 'So, what are your plans for the baby?'

They looked at each other, then back to Jo. Mel's eyes seemed a little shifty suddenly. 'Well, I have to go to hospital, don't I?'

'No. Not necessarily.'

Her eyes lit up. 'I don't?'

Jo shook her head. 'No. I'd like you to because out here you've got no electricity, no running water, no proper heating—it must get damp with the gas heaters. I can remember caravanning with my parents as a child, and the windows used to stream when we cooked. Your baby's due—when? March?'

'Yes. It'll be warmer then, and we can have the windows open.' She looked down at her hands. 'Jo, I really want to have it here. It's so beautiful in the forest—if the weather's nice I'd like to have it outside, just surrounded by nature. I think that would be so beautiful, don't you?'

Jo sighed inwardly. 'Yes, I do—in theory. But what if it's raining? What if it's cold? What if it's night-time?'

'Lots of babies are born by candlelight. I'd hate harsh electric lights and my feet up in stirrups and men poking me around—'

'Hey, hey, hang on!' Jo said with a laugh. 'It's not like that! My deliveries are all very calm and low-key and beautiful. There's no harsh light or stirrups or anything awful.'

Mel's eyes flicked to Ed, who had remained silent, and he smiled ruefully. 'I'm just there for insurance. She's the midwife, she does the delivery. I have yet to attend a labour where there was time for me to do more than take my coat off before it was all over! I just get handed the baby and told to hold it.'

'What a shame,' Jo teased. 'You see, we really don't aim for high-tech labour. Women were designed to give birth. I'm here just to make sure it's as safe as possible for them to do it.'

'Look, I've been reading about it,' Mel said. 'I'm young, it's my first pregnancy, I haven't had any problems, my mother didn't have any problems—there shouldn't be any reason why I can't give birth at home.'

Jo nodded. 'I agree. I have reservations, though, about you giving birth here. The lack of running water, particularly, worries me. How do you get water?'

'There's a standpipe down at the other settlement,' Andy told them. 'I carry it. African women have done it for centuries, I'm sure I can manage with the help of the pick-up.'

'And electricity?'

'We've got a light that runs off a battery. It's not brilliant, but it works. We use it for emergencies—it's a car inspection lamp.'

'I know the sort of thing,' Ed said. 'I've got one. They're quite effective, but not ideal.'

Mel twisted her fingers, then looked up at Jo challengingly. 'If we can't agree, and I go into labour and won't go to hospital, does that mean you won't come and help me?'

Jo shook her head slowly. 'No, of course not. You're still my patient. Of course I'll come and help—but you have to understand that if, when I get here, I think there's the slightest danger that things are going wrong, I'll want to transfer you to the consultant unit immediately. You've got to agree to that.'

'Just because we're out here?'

'No. It's the same for any home birth. If it starts to go pear-shaped, we give up. I won't let you compromise your baby's life, and I'm sure you wouldn't want me to. I want things to go well for you, and I don't want to interfere unnecessarily, but you've got to trust my judgement.'

Mel nodded. 'So you'll let me try?'

'I want to know the moment you're in labour. I want to check you, check the baby, see if I feel I can work with you under these conditions—there's always the option of the GP unit.'

'But that hasn't got any special facilities, has it?'

'No—just light and heat and running water.'

Mel smiled. 'We can make it warm and light, and Andy can run with the water!'

Ed chuckled, then his face sobered. 'You're really determined, aren't you?'

'It's what we want,' Andy said. 'It's the way we want our baby to start its life. Everybody thinks we're crazy, but it's our life and this is how we want to lead it.'

Ed nodded slowly. 'I don't think you're crazy,' he said. 'I think you're doing what's right for you, but I have to endorse what Jo's saying. If at any time either of us feel that things are getting out of hand, you must agree to be guided by us.'

'And if we don't?'

'Then there's a good chance your baby will suffer,' Jo said calmly. 'I don't panic. If I can deal with a problem, I will. I just know when things aren't right and I need more help. If you choose to ignore that, you'll have to choose to accept the consequences.'

Andy nodded. 'OK. Thanks.'

Jo and Ed stood. 'Just one last thing,' Jo said with a smile. 'If you've got to have it here, can you try and have it in daylight, please?'

Mel chuckled. 'I'll do my best. Thanks, Jo.'

Andy saw them out, and paused at the foot of the steps. 'Mind that lot down there. There's a strange bloke—hard-looking. He's not very friendly.'

'We've met,' Jo said drily, remembering the man with a shiver.

'Ah. Well, steer clear of him. He's a bit dangerous. We're going to move on once the baby's born—get away from him. He makes Mel nervous.'

'I can understand that,' Jo agreed. 'He's got odd eyes.'

'Dead eyes. He gives me the creeps, but he hasn't done anything to us, and so long as he's left alone he's OK, they say.' He lifted his hand. 'Cheers, now. Thanks for coming by. We'll keep in touch.'

They walked back down the track, steering well clear of the other group of travellers.

'Well?' Ed said as they got back to the car.

Jo sighed, rehashing the conversation in her mind. 'I think there's no point in trying to persuade them. They're clearly highly intelligent, educated people. They're just a bit off the wall. If it's what they want, we can't do anything about it. We can hardly section them under the Mental Health Act and lock them up till it's over, can we?'

Ed laughed. 'Probably not. She looks well, though, as

you say. I don't anticipate problems. Have you done a pelvic assessment?'

'Not yet. I think it'll be fine, though. I'll do it when she's nearer. There's no point yet—the baby's still going to grow.'

Ed started the car, and Jo dropped her head back against the headrest and sighed.

'Tired?'

'A bit. I'm glad Laura wasn't here in the end. It made it easier to talk to them.'

'Not that it did a lot of good.'

'Oh, I don't know.' She rolled her head towards him and smiled. 'Thanks for coming with me.'

'My pleasure. As you said, it's a good idea to know where they are in case of problems. I don't like the look of their neighbours.'

'No. I'll talk to the liaison guy.'

'Right, where are we going for this walk?'

'Walk?' Jo said, surprised.

'Yes, walk. You don't call that feeble little stroll a walk, do you?'

Jo groaned and wondered why she'd suggested it. He was obviously a fitness fanatic.

'Seascape or landscape?'

'Can we have both?'

She nodded. 'We'll go up the coast to Dunwich. It'll be windy,' she warned him.

'I can cope. And you'll be all right—you'll just walk in front of me!'

She felt the grin, but couldn't stop it.

'Which way?'

'Left.'

They left the car in a car park, and walked along the top of the shingle bank for miles. There was hardly a soul about, and the wind tugged their hair and froze their ears and cheeks. She found Ed's arm round her shoulder, her hip against his, and his head bent close to hers.

They strolled along in silence for a while, enjoying the sun and the wind and the sea, and then suddenly Ed spoke.

'Tell me about Laura,' he said softly.

She stumbled. 'Laura? What about her?'

'Oh, all sorts of things. How you came to have her, for instance. How you coped alone. Why you're so wary.'

Jo swallowed and caught her lip in her teeth. She hated talking about it, but she supposed he had a right to know if they were getting this close.

'I was seventeen,' she told him. 'I was just about to do my A levels. Richard was twenty-five, mature, witty, rich—at least, he seemed rich to me, compared to the other boys I'd been out with. He smoked French cigarettes, he drank gin and tonic, not beer, he flattered me— told me I was beautiful and that he loved me.'

'And you fell for it.'

'Oh, yes,' she said with a bitter laugh, remembering the impressionable girl she'd been. 'Hook, line and sinker. He told me he was divorced, that his wife hadn't understood him and she'd lied to him. She had two children from another relationship, and she didn't love him any more—you know the sort of thing.'

She could feel Ed stiffening. 'Yes, I know,' he said quietly. 'So what happened?'

'I became pregnant, and I told him. I was sure he'd be delighted because he'd said he'd wished his wife's children had been his own.'

'And they were, of course.'

'Of course. They weren't divorced at all. She lived in London, and was waiting for him to find them a house up here. He went back to her. I never saw him again.'

Ed was silent for a while, just the tension in his arm around her shoulder indicating to her he was angry.

'Bastard,' he said softly, after an age. Then he brought her to a halt, and turned her into his arms. 'I am not married,' he told her very clearly, 'and I never have been. I have no children. I am not a liar.'

She smiled at his vehemence, and reached out to touch his cheek to reassure him. 'No. I know.'

He hugged her gently. 'I'm sorry.'

'I'm not,' she told him honestly. 'I've got Laura and I can't imagine life without her. She is, without exception, the best thing that's ever happened to me, and I can't bring myself to regret her.'

Ed smiled. 'I like her, too. She's got lots of character.'

Jo rolled her eyes. 'Too much. Still, I'd rather have it that way.'

She shivered, and he pulled her back into the shelter of his arm. 'Come on, let's go back,' he said softly, and she felt cherished and cared-for and protected. It was scary how good it felt...

CHAPTER SEVEN

Jo's simple story of her betrayal and abandonment stayed with Ed vividly. He was busy at work, coping with the rash of new cases of flu, going out on visits and driving around hopelessly lost trying to find the patients' houses or dealing with minor casualties at the hospital, and all the time her words rang in his head.

The most significant thing she'd said had been that she wasn't sorry she'd had Laura. To have a child at eighteen must have played havoc with her plans for the future, and yet here she was, twelve years down the line, saying her daughter was the best thing that had ever happened to her.

Ed found that immensely heartwarming, but it didn't really surprise him. He'd seen enough of Jo to know that no baby could be anything but a joy to her, and her obvious grief at the loss of Liz Bateman's baby had been just another part of the woman that she was.

Of course she didn't regret her daughter's birth. How could she? It wasn't in her. No, she would selflessly deny her own wants and needs to give her child the life she felt she should have—it was probably why she was still alone.

That, and a natural wariness about men, which Ed couldn't blame her for. A man like that would put most women off for ever.

It was a crying shame, he thought, watching her at one of the panto rehearsals. She was such a warm and giving person, she'd make a wonderful wife and mother. She was naturally very friendly and open, and she brought a smile to so many faces with her cheerful greetings.

She knew everyone, of course, and everyone knew her. It reminded him of the village he'd grown up in, and he felt suddenly homesick for that warmth and welcome—and for the warmth of Jo's arms.

Then she looked up and caught his eye, and her smile extended to him, drawing him into the group and warming him.

Jo was irresistible.

And Ed was perilously close to falling for her.

A shadow seemed to hover over him. Would she want him? When the chips were down would she still be there, or would she, too, turn away?

'Right, village scene again,' Roz called, 'and can we have a little more enthusiasm, please? We've only got three more rehearsals before the final dress rehearsal, you know!'

He put thoughts of Jo and the future away. There would be time for that later. Just now he had to go back a hundred years or so in time and be jolly.

He gave a quiet snort, shrugged himself away from the wall and joined the others on stage.

Ed seemed preoccupied, Jo thought. He was very busy. Maurice and the others had obviously decided he could cope, and any gentle introduction was now well and truly over. He'd been chucked in at the deep end, and she'd hardly seen him since the day they'd visited Mel and she'd told him about Richard.

That had been three weeks ago, and their duty rotas, Laura's commitments and the rehearsals for the panto seemed to have contrived to keep them apart.

He came up to her at the end of the rehearsal and gave a diffident smile. 'Are you busy now?'

She glanced at her watch. It was ten-thirty already, and they weren't home yet. 'What did you have in mind?'

'Coffee, listening to some music, relaxing.'

She smiled. 'I was going to relax in bed,' she said, and his mouth quirked.

'Sounds good.'

'Alone,' she said repressively, squashing her smile, and he grinned.

'Shame. Can I talk you into being a dirty stop-out for half an hour? I can't remember when we last spent any time alone together. It seems like ages.'

'I know.' She looked round at Laura, who was chatting to friends. As she watched, Laura yawned hugely, and Jo had a pang of conscience. 'I ought to get her home to bed. She's shattered, and I think she's getting a cold.'

'Come round later.'

She nearly said no. She thought of all the good reasons why it was stupid, but then she met his eyes and her resistance disintegrated.

'OK,' she said softly. 'I won't stay long, though.'

'That's all right. I'll light the fire and make the coffee and wait for you.'

'Hi, guys!' Laura ambled up to them, stifling another yawn, and leaned on her mother's shoulder. 'I'm tired,' she said. 'Can we go home?'

'Yes.' Jo didn't mention going round to Ed's. It didn't seem necessary or sensible. She met his eyes over Laura's head and read the promise in them, and wondered if she was totally mad.

Laura went straight to bed and crashed out, but it was still after eleven o'clock before Jo left. She went to tell her mother she was going out, and she eyed her daughter's coat curiously.

'I didn't think you were on call tonight.'

'I'm not. Ed asked me for coffee.'

Her mother's eyes searched her face, and she smiled understandingly. 'OK. I'm off to bed. I'll see you in the morning. Don't be too late.'

Jo thought it was probably already too late, but too late for what? She let herself out, slipping across the gardens and in through Ed's back door. He was there, waiting, with a hug, and she sank into the warmth of his arms with a sigh of relief.

'I've missed you,' he murmured. 'It's been ages since I've held you. I haven't seen you alone for weeks.'

'I know.' She snuggled into his shoulder and sighed again. 'I've missed you, too,' she confessed, letting down her guard a little. His arms tightened, hugging her closer, then he released her and led her over to the settee in front of the fire.

A fresh pot of coffee sat on a tray, with shortbread and cheese and biscuits and other titbits, and she noticed there was soft, romantic music playing in the background.

A scene set for seduction, she asked herself, or just a friend entertaining in a welcoming manner?

Or both? She decided it didn't matter. She was tired, and it was very pleasant, sitting there with Ed. She sipped her coffee and stopped trying to analyse his motives.

'You OK?' he asked softly.

'Mmm. Tired. Don't be surprised if I doze off on you.'

He chuckled. 'Be my guest.'

Ed's fingers trailed over her shoulder, tormenting her with the delicate touch. He was turned half-sideways on the settee, one knee hitched up, his foot tucked under the other thigh. His arms were spread along the side and back, and he looked masculine and a little dangerous. His eyes regarded her steadily.

'I wish we could find more time to be together,' he said in a low voice, his fingers circling slowly. 'Time alone, without the rest of the cast or the other members of the practice or a clinic full of patients.'

'Quality time,' Jo murmured. His touch was like a drug, almost hypnotic in its effect.

'Just quiet time. We're always so busy—there's never time just to sit and be together. No time to talk.'

She turned her head towards him. 'What do you want to talk about?'

A shadow seemed to cross his face. 'Us? There's still so much we don't know about each other.'

It was true. She knew hardly anything about him, but it didn't seem to matter. He'd told her what she needed to know, and the rest was just the icing on the cake. She could do without the icing. Richard had been all icing, and under it the cake had been rotten to the core.

'I know all I need to know about you,' she said softly.

'No, you don't.'

'I do. I know you won't lie to me.'

His fingers drifted up the side of her neck to her jaw, and traced its outline from her ear to the point of her chin. 'No, I won't lie to you,' he agreed. She turned her head and pressed her lips to his fingers, and with a little sound of satisfaction he leaned forward and took her mug before she dropped it.

He was going to kiss her again. She swallowed, and her eyes fluttered shut. The suspense was unbearable…

He shifted his weight, and she felt the hard length of his thigh against hers. One hand cupped her shoulder, the other curved around her cheek, cradling her head as his lips descended and brushed hers just lightly.

She whimpered and moved closer, reaching up to him,

and his arms slid round her, lifting her against him. 'You feel so good,' he murmured gruffly. He kissed her eyes, her cheeks, her chin, the tip of her nose—light, feathery kisses that teased and tormented and drove her crazy so that when his lips finally closed over hers she gave a little cry of relief and returned his kiss with feverish intensity.

One hand slid round and closed possessively over her hip, shifting her nearer him, and she squirmed closer. It wasn't enough. She needed to be closer still, much closer. Her fingers threaded through his hair, sifting the texture, loving the soft, silky feel of it against her fingertips.

His lips moved down her throat, pushing the soft fabric of her blouse aside, and he dispensed with the buttons and slid his hand round to cup her breast. Her bra was in the way. He muttered something and it was gone, unclipped and disposed of, pushed aside to give him access to his prize.

He didn't take it straight away, though. His tongue moved over the nipple, teasing it, and he blew softly across it so it pebbled even harder in the cool air. She arched, crying out his name, and his lips closed over it, drawing it in, suckling deeply.

How could it be so different? The last touch she had felt there had been her baby's, the soft, hungry rosebud mouth suckling greedily as Laura had lain in the curve of her mother's arm. This man's touch, with his rough stubble and skilful tongue that wrapped her nipple and drew it deep into his mouth, was light-years from the innocent suckling of a child. This was fierce and elemental and made her cry out, sobbing with the strength of emotion he aroused in her.

His touch gentled, his tongue soothing now, his lips soft against her delicate skin where his beard had scraped. He lifted his head and met her eyes, and she saw the question in the storm-grey depths.

'I want you,' he said softly. 'I'm not trying to rush you, but I want you to know how I feel.'

She closed her eyes. He was giving her a way out. Did she want to take it?

The phone rang, sounding far away, and with a muffled curse he rose and went over to it, his face taut.

'Latimer...Oh, hi, Rebecca. Yes, she's here. I'll get her.'

He held out the phone to Jo. 'Your mother.'

She stood, tugging her blouse closed across her aching breasts, and took the phone from him. 'Mum? What is it?'

'I'm sorry to interrupt, darling, but Laura's not very well. I think she might have flu. She's been sick, and she's got a temperature and a sore throat.'

'I'll be right home,' Jo promised, and hung up. Turning to Ed, she said, 'Laura's got flu. I have to go.'

He nodded. 'Perhaps it's just as well.' He nudged her hands aside and refastened her bra, then buttoned her blouse, before kissing her again softly on the mouth.

'The offer's open, remember. I'm not going anywhere, and I won't turn you away—any time, day or night. You're always welcome, whatever you come for. Don't feel if you come back we have to make love. We don't. Only if you want to.'

She did want to, that was the trouble. She wanted to so badly she could hardly force herself to walk out on him, but Laura was sick and Laura had to come first.

Perhaps it was just as well to remember it.

Laura's flu lasted three days, and left her with a hacking cough and no appetite. Jo, fortunately, didn't catch it, but she felt guilty, going to work and leaving Laura with her mother. She'd done it before, but for some reason—maybe because of Maurice—she was beginning to worry that she took her mother's help for granted.

She also felt guilty about being with Ed and fooling around while Laura needed her, and so she kept away from him.

Not that it was difficult. She was so busy it was ridiculous. She saw Mel at one of her antenatal clinics, although she'd finished the course of parentcraft and relaxation classes. Mel still had five weeks to go before the baby was due, and Jo was relieved to see that she was healthy and that everything was proceeding normally.

She didn't fancy trying to convince Mel that things were not straightforward enough to allow a home delivery. She had a feeling the woman would simply think that it was a ruse to get her to deliver in hospital, but fortunately it wasn't an issue.

The baby was the right size, the scan dates were spot on, the presentation was textbook perfect. Jo found the baby's heartbeat with the Sonicaid, and they listened to the steady, rapid rhythm as it was amplified by the little device.

'Oh, wow,' Mel said with a grin. 'It's so nice to hear it. It wriggles about all the time, but just to hear its heart—it makes it seem more alive—more real.'

Jo laughed. 'Oh, it's real. You wait a few weeks and you'll fine out just how real!'

'I know. Sioux—that's the girl down the track, you met her that time you came over—she's brought her baby up sometimes if Mick's been out, and she's cute but she's very, well, there! You can't forget her!'

'How are your neighbours?' she asked as Mel straightened her clothes.

'Well, Sioux's all right, but Mick's a bit scary. He's

got form, I think—not a nice man. Andy says we'll move on once the baby's come.'

Jo nodded. She'd spoken to the social services liaison officer, and yes, Mick did have a prison record, having caused grievous bodily harm to some poor innocent householder from whom he'd been trying to thieve. He'd also been convicted of dealing drugs. Not the sort of neighbours you would want in such isolated surroundings, particularly not with a baby around.

Jo knew it was none of her business, really, but Sioux's baby worried her. 'Mel,' she said carefully, 'does he hit her?'

Mel looked worried. 'I don't like to interfere. It's nothing to do with me.'

'No. I can understand that. I just thought I saw bruises on her face, and the baby's hand looked a little yellow, as if it might have been bruised at some time.'

Mel's eyes were downcast. 'I couldn't say,' she told Jo a little nervously. 'I try not to notice—it's none of my business. I just want to stay out of his way.'

Jo nodded. 'Yes. It sounds like a good idea. I expect the liaison officer knows.'

'Probably. He's been around a few times, but if Sioux won't say anything he can't do anything about it, can he? I think she's scared. I would be. I think she'd like to leave him, really, but he won't let her out of his sight.'

She stood and edged towards the door. 'I have to go—Andy's waiting. Look, you won't say anything, will you? If it got back to Mick that I'd said anything about it—'

'Anything about what? Didn't you know I'm deaf?'

Mel smiled gratefully. 'Cheers, Jo.'

'Take care. See you next week.'

She watched the woman go, and sighed, then picked up the phone. She needed to speak to Joe Saunders, the liaison officer, about Sioux and Mick and the baby. She'd spoken to him once, but she was more worried than ever about the baby now.

He was busy so she passed the case on to the health visitor as the baby was technically in her care. Hopefully something would be done before it was too late.

She looked at her watch. It was Tuesday afternoon, and she had calls to make after she'd finished her clinic. The final dress rehearsal for the pantomime was tonight, and then tomorrow they had a night off before the first performance on Thursday evening.

There were to be four performances—Thursday, Friday and Saturday evenings and a matinée on Saturday afternoon. The tickets were already sold out, and she just hoped everything would come together in time. Roz was getting a little panicky, but she usually did at this stage.

Still, tonight would be the acid test. If they got through it without a hitch it would be a miracle!

Ed stood backstage and watched Barry, the groom, flirting with Belle. His Belle. Once again, he'd hardly seen her for a week, and now here she was standing there while Barry made sheep's eyes at her.

Which would have been fine if they hadn't had such cameraderie off-stage as well!

Ed recognised his jealousy for the feeble thing it was, but it didn't stop him feeling it. The Beast was no better, smiling and teasing Jo and then getting to hold her in his arms on the stage and dance with her.

Ed wanted to dance with her, but not here, like this, in front of an audience. He wanted to dance with her somewhere private, where he could hold her close and be alone with her.

The audience seemed to be loving it, though. They laughed and clapped and cheered and roared and stamped and took part in all the usual 'Oh, no, he isn't' and 'Oh, yes, he is' banter that made pantomime what it was, and to everyone's amazement they fumbled their way through with only a few prompts.

It was the second night, and they were halfway through the run. Only two more performances, two more gatherings of this diverse collection of people, and it would all be over.

Ed knew from experience that there would be a flat spot afterwards, a strange emptiness on Wednesday nights at a quarter to eight. Before that, of course, there would be the adrenaline high of the final performance. There was a party planned for after they'd cleared the hall and packed up, and everyone was bringing something to eat and drink.

Knowing this lot, he thought as he prepared to go on for the finale, there would be a hell of a party.

He and the other villagers went on to the usual applause, and he took his place at the back of the stage and sang the penultimate number as the rest of the cast came on in pairs for the walkdown.

As Belle and the Beast were due to come on, there was a thud behind him and a sound like a pistol shot. He looked round, and Peter, the Beast, was standing on one leg, gasping with pain.

'Are you all right?' Jo was asking worriedly across the back of the stage.

'I'll be fine,' he whispered loudly. He limped on, and came down the stage, leaning heavily on Belle.

The final scene was mercifully short, and how Peter got through it Ed would never know, but as the curtain closed he sank down to the floor and grasped his ankle.

Ed was beside him in a moment. 'What happened?' he asked.

'I fell off the stage.'

'I heard.'

'I think the damn thing's broken.'

'I would say so. Let's move you.'

The groom, the back of the pantomime horse and Ed lifted Peter and carried him through to the dressing room, then set him down on top of the carpet bowls chest.

'What's happened?' Roz asked, squeezing through the crowd.

'He's broken his ankle. He needs to go to A and E. We can strap him up in Casualty at the hospital first, before the journey, but we can't do anything more with it here because the radiographer's not in till Monday.'

'Broken?' Roz said, horrified. 'Are you sure?'

'Certain,' Ed said. He'd got the shoe off by then and was looking at the ankle, and it wasn't good. Unless he was mistaken it would need plating.

'Will I be able to do tomorrow's performances?' Peter asked worriedly.

'No.'

'But I have to!'

'The show must go on? Certainly, but not with you, my friend. You'll still be in hospital. You've broken your fibula.'

Jo appeared at his side. 'I hate to add to the stress,' she said quietly, 'but whoever plays the Beast tomorrow will need those breeches, and if they go to A and E with him they'll cut them off.'

'They can't cut them off, they're hired!' Anne said, panic-stricken.

'Take them off,' Peter said. 'Quick, before the feeling comes back too much.'

So they did, there in the dressing room, carefully wiggling the trousers off his uninjured leg first before supporting the bad one and easing the second trouser leg down and over the foot.

By the time they'd finished Peter was grey and sweating, but the breeches were intact.

'Brilliant. Well done. Now all we have to do is work out who's going to be wearing them tomorrow,' Roz said, looking round. 'It needs to be someone with a minor part, but who knows the play well enough to learn Peter's lines and moves by two-thirty tomorrow—someone of about the same size.'

Ed was bending over Peter's foot, winding a scarf around it as a makeshift support so they could take him to the hospital. He heard the room go quiet and, glancing over his shoulder, he saw they were all looking at him.

'What?' he said. 'What is it?'

'Can you roar?'

His eyes widened. 'Oh, no. Oh, no, Roz, I can't! You can't do this to me! No! Absolutely not! I refuse!'

Laura was right, Jo thought, Ed made a wonderful Beast. He could sing, he could dance, he had stage presence—and he didn't tread on her toes once.

He'd fluffed his lines in the afternoon performance, but not so badly that anyone had noticed, and the rest of them had all picked up and carried on regardless. The Saturday night performance was the one to worry about, she thought, because he was likely to be put off by all the audience participation and last-night mayhem.

She just hoped nobody did anything nasty to him to make him corpse.

Ed's first scene was when Belle's father picked the rose, and he entered with a mighty roar that brought a howl of laughter from the audience.

Oh, dear, it's going to be like that, she thought, but he waited, gave them time to laugh and continued like a pro. He'd done it before, of course, but not for years. He must just be a natural, she thought, and wondered if he realised he'd be in it for life now.

The audience were quieter for the first meeting between Belle and the Beast, and as they stood close together she could feel the tension in him.

He's got stage fright, Jo thought, and wondered if he'd get through it, but there was no trace of nerves in his voice.

'Are you frightened of me, Belle?' he said.

'No, I'm not frightened.'

'And do you like my magnificent castle?'

He gestured at the amateur stage flats, the hand-painted interior of the 'castle', and somehow she stopped the smile that always rose to her lips at that point. 'Yes, it's very—magnificent,' she said, deadpan.

'Good. Then you will stay for ever!' He held out his hand, grey-gloved, with cardboard talons taped on the ends of his fingers. 'Dance with me,' he ordered.

She stepped back a fraction. 'Haven't you forgotten something?'

'Dance with me *now!*'

'No,' she said firmly. 'A gentleman should be good mannered towards a lady. Will you dance with me, *please*?'

He held out his hand again and paused, as if chastened. 'Will you dance with me—*please*?' he said humbly.

A shiver of awareness ran down her spine. 'I should be honoured,' she replied, and curtseyed deeply.

The audience aahed, the music of *Beauty and the Beast* started, and she moved into his arms. Immediately the audience receded, and it was just the two of them, alone, moving in harmony as they circled the stage in a slow waltz.

His hand lay lightly over the small of her back, guiding her, and she could feel the imprint of it against her skin long after the scene was over.

It wasn't only his touch, either. In the next scene, after the interval, there was something in his voice. She couldn't see his face because the mask came down too low, but when the Beast asked Belle if there was someone in her former life, someone she might have married, there was more than just the script involved.

'Oh, no,' she replied, 'I shall have to fall in love before I marry.'

'And how will you know when you've fallen in love?' he asked, and she could have sworn he was asking her, not Belle.

She wished she could see his eyes. 'I don't know, it hasn't happened yet,' she replied, and he hung his head in a gesture that made her want to comfort him. The audience felt it too, and sighed softly. 'But I'm sure I'll know when it does,' she added, and it was for him, not the Beast, that she said the words.

The next time they were on stage together was the last scene, and it was one Jo hated doing. That afternoon Ed had been struggling with his lines, but now he seemed word perfect, and because she didn't have to worry about him her concentration was on the scene itself.

In the scene she arrived back at the Beast's castle just as he was dying, and had to throw herself, weeping, beside him. In fact, it was Peter's wife, dressed as the Beast in the mask and lying behind some bushes, but it was Ed she spoke to, and Ed's voice that told her he loved her.

'Oh, Beast,' she sobbed, 'don't die! I love you too. Can you hear me, Beast? *I love you!*'

The lights dimmed and the scene changed to spring.

As the lights came up, Ed, dressed now as a handsome prince, walked downstage towards her.

His eyes locked with hers, and she didn't dare believe the look in them. Had those words of love really been for her?

The audience was laughing and catcalling the so-called 'Prince', the girls were wolf-whistling at him, but she ignored them, transfixed by the look in his eyes.

'Don't you know me, Belle?' he ad-libbed at last, and she realised she'd fluffed her lines.

'Who are you?' she said hastily. 'Where is my Beast?'

His mouth quirked, his eyes gleamed with approval and he went on, 'I am a Prince. You see me as I once was, before an evil spell transformed me into the Beast. Now the spell has been broken, thanks to you, Belle.'

'But how?' she asked.

'By loving me,' he replied, and the look in his eyes intensified.

The scene moved on to the end, carrying her in a daze, and then the Prince held out his hand. 'Marry me, Belle,' he commanded.

She smiled, her heart thumping in her chest, and groped for her lines. 'Haven't you forgotten something?'

'Marry me *now*?' His face quirked in a smile, and then it faded. 'Will you marry me…please?' he asked sincerely.

'I should be honoured,' she replied. At least, she would have done, but her voice stuck and she lost the words. Tears filled her eyes, and she felt absurd, but the rest of the cast then became involved in a bit of silliness, and she had a moment to compose herself before the end of the scene. The curtains closed for the ten-second change into her wedding dress, and she was all fingers and thumbs.

Was it true? Did Ed love her, or was he just acting? Had he really just proposed?

He appeared behind her when she was standing in her underwear, and leaned forward, his mouth by her ear. 'Do you have any idea how fetching you are in those net curtains?' he murmured, and she spluttered and tugged the wedding dress on.

'Just zip me up and don't be cheeky,' she said, and someone elbowed him out of the way, scooped her hair up into a bun and jammed the tiara on her head.

Then came the walkdown to the finale, and in the tumult of the applause a huge bouquet of flowers appeared in her arms, just as they launched into the final chorus. She nudged Barry. 'What do I do with these?' she said through a smile that wouldn't be controlled.

'Pass them back,' he said, and she handed them behind her and joined in.

The audience wouldn't let them go, calling them back again and again, and in the end they just closed the curtain and went off. The applause continued even after the house lights came on, and backstage it was a scene of utter chaos and delirium.

Everyone was clapping Ed on the back and telling him he was fantastic, but Jo just wanted to get changed and get out of there. Something had happened between them tonight, something magical, and she wanted to be alone with him and talk about it.

'Mum, you were brilliant,' Laura said, hugging her, and then she turned to Ed, standing there in his breeches with his shirt hanging open, and hugged him too. 'Told you you'd do the Beast well,' she said smugly, and vanished to change.

Jo was trying not to look at him. He was altogether too enticing dressed like that, and she didn't want to embarrass either of them by staring at him. She went behind the costume rail that doubled as a screen, peeled off the dreaded net curtains and tugged on her jeans and sweatshirt, then assembled her costumes and took them out to Anne.

'Here,' she said. 'Do you want me to do anything with them?'

'No, that's fine. Thanks. You were marvellous—and isn't Ed a find?'

Jo smiled. 'Isn't he?' She left Anne and went to help clear up. The quicker it was done the quicker they could be alone—and the quicker she would have her answers.

The party was a riot, but Jo's heart wasn't in it. There was food, and music, and they were all congratulating Ed and thanking him for stepping in. Then he managed to escape from them all and grabbed Jo, towing her into a space.

'Dance with me,' he said.

She laughed. 'Haven't you forgotten something?'

'Dance with me *now*?'

She laughed again. 'Some people never learn,' she said, and went into his arms. This time he held her close, and the heat flared between them in seconds.

'Come to me tonight,' he murmured. 'Please?'

She met his eyes and her heart jerked against her ribs.

'Yes,' she said simply.

CHAPTER EIGHT

ED WAS waiting for her. The door opened as Jo went down the path, and he drew her into his arms and kissed her gently.

'I thought you'd changed your mind.'

'No—I had a shower. I was all greasepaint and hot lights.'

He smiled briefly. 'Ditto.'

She touched his hair, and it was still damp, roughly towelled. A tiny rivulet ran down into his collar, and she followed its path with her fingertip. 'You're dripping,' she told him.

'I was in a hurry.' He looked away, then looked back, his eyes alight with a strange intensity. 'Dance with me?' he said with a little smile. The music was soft and romantic, a compilation love album that went from one slow and dreamy number to another.

She'd thought their loving would be hurried, but Ed seemed in no hurry at all. He held her close against his chest, one hand on her back, the other holding her hand folded against his shoulder, and he swayed slowly in time to the music, letting it wash over them, letting the mood carry them.

Finally, his control seemed to snap, and he stopped and looked down into her eyes. 'Make love with me, Jo,' he said, and his voice was gruff and low and unsteady.

A tremor ran through her. She reached up on tiptoe and kissed him in answer, and he scooped her up into his arms and carried her up to the bedroom. The lights

131

were low, the quilt turned back in readiness, and he undressed her without preamble, stripping off his own clothes before turning back to her.

She felt almost sick with anticipation. It had been so long, and she had crushed any feelings so ruthlessly that she wasn't sure what to expect. She just knew there was no going back.

Ed held out his hand and drew her to the bed, then lay beside her, propping himself on one elbow so he was facing her. Jo lay on her back, her eyes fixed on his, wishing it was over, wishing he would do something—

'I love you,' he said softly.

Her eyes filled with tears. 'Oh, Ed,' she whispered, and reached for him.

He was tender and generous. He didn't hurry her, despite the fact that he was shaking with the effort of holding himself back, and when she splintered in his arms, only then did he let himself go, crying out her name as his body stiffened in her arms.

His chest heaved, his breathing harsh and ragged, and he shifted his weight so that he lay half beside her, his head on her shoulder, one hand lying possessively over her breast while he waited for his heart to slow.

The air was cool, and after a while he moved, pulling the quilt over them. 'Are you OK?'

She laughed a little unsteadily. 'I think so. I'm not sure—I don't feel as if I've quite come back down to earth yet.'

He chuckled. 'I know the feeling.' He kissed her lightly, brushing the hair from her eyes. 'You're so beautiful,' he murmured, and for the first time she dared to believe him.

She tunnelled her fingers through his hair. 'So are you.' She ran her hand over the smooth skin of his shoulder, feeling the hard muscle of his arm under her palm. 'I just want to touch you—you feel so good.'

He groaned softly as she slid her hand down and over his hip. 'I want you again,' he murmured.

His mouth brushed hers, and unbelievably she felt the renewed stirrings of desire. This time he was more relaxed, lazier and even less hurried, and by the time they drifted back to earth the second time she was almost asleep.

'I have to go home,' she mumbled sleepily. 'Laura doesn't know where I am.'

'Isn't that just as well?'

She felt her responsibilities pulling at her. 'Probably.' There were other responsibilities preying on her mind as well—or perhaps, more accurately, irresponsibilities.

'Ed, I don't want to put a damper on things,' she said, 'but do you think it would be an idea if you wrote me out a prescription for the morning-after pill? I don't recall us doing anything about it, and I've already had one unplanned pregnancy.'

His eyes were shadowed. 'Don't worry,' he said quietly. 'I can't get you pregnant, Jo. I'm sterile.'

'Sterile?'

The shock froze her for a moment, then compassion rose in her and she reached for him.

'Oh, Ed—I'm sorry.' No wonder he'd looked sad when all the babies were born!

'It's all right, Jo,' he murmured, hugging her. 'I'm fine. I knew it was going to happen so I had time to do something about it. I can have children, just not like this.'

She looked at him, then wriggled out of his arms and sat up against the pillows, hugging her arms around her. 'What do you mean?' she asked. 'How did you know?'

He shifted so that he was beside her, and pulled up

the quilt. 'I had testicular cancer when I was twenty,' he told her in a matter-of-fact voice. 'I found it early, they removed the affected testicle and gave me chemotherapy which knocked out the sperm-producing cells in the other one, but not until I'd had the chance to have some frozen, just in case.'

'And are you OK?' she asked, far more worried about the threat to his life than the fact that he couldn't have children. 'Are you clear?'

'Oh, yes, I've been clear for years,' he assured her, and the tension left her.

'I didn't notice,' she said with a strained laugh. 'Just shows how much attention I was paying.'

'You wouldn't be able to tell. They put in an implant so, as far as anyone's concerned, I'm no different. I just—fire blanks.' He gave a wry grin, and she took his hand and squeezed it.

'Oh, Ed, I'm sorry. Why didn't you tell me?'

He looked away. 'I just—I don't know. Selfish reasons, really. In the past it's put people off. They—um—they don't seem to think they want to get involved. I don't know if they feel there's still a threat, or if they feel they could catch cancer from me, or if they feel I'm less of a man—'

'But that's nonsense!' she protested.

'I know,' he said heavily, 'but it's the way it is. I just didn't want you walking away from me too. Somehow I knew that would hurt far more than anything else had ever done, and I didn't dare risk it.' He squeezed her hand. 'I'm sorry. I should have told you.'

'Oh, Ed. I wouldn't walk away from you!' she whispered unsteadily. 'I don't think I could!'

His arm came round her and he hugged her close. 'Oh, Jo...' His voice was choked, and she slid her arms round him and hugged him tight.

Words seemed unnecessary. Instead they merely lay there, wrapped in each other's arms, just enjoying being close. The CD player had come to a halt, and the house was quiet. Outside a gate creaked, and then running footsteps sounded in the garden.

'Who's that?' Ed said, lifting his head, a frown creasing his brow.

'I don't know—have a look.'

He turned out the light and went to the window, just as there was a knock on the back door.

'I can't see. I'll go down. Stay here.'

He pulled on his clothes and ran down the stairs, and Jo dressed herself more carefully and crept to the top of the stairs. Then she froze. There was no way she could go downstairs because their visitor was Laura!

'Laura? What's wrong?'

'Can I come in?'

He opened the door to the tearful girl. 'Of course you can come in. What's the matter?'

'I just need to talk to someone, and Mum's out. I saw your lights on—I hope you don't mind?'

'No, of course not. Come and sit down—do you want a cup of tea?'

She shook her head. 'No. I just wanted to talk to you...' Without warning, she threw herself into his arms and sobbed her heart out.

'Laura,' he said gently, and led her to the settee. Where's Jo? he thought. She ought to be here. God alone knows what's wrong.

He let Laura cry for a while, then handed her a clump of tissues and waited while she mopped herself up. 'OK, let's have it. What's upset you? You seemed OK earlier. Has something happened?'

'Grannie...'

'What about Grannie?' he asked, concerned. 'Is she ill?'

Laura shook her head. 'No. She's fine. Dr Parker came round—they were at the panto and they came back to the house afterwards. I came back with Mum after the party and went to bed, but I couldn't sleep. I got up and went down to get a drink, and we didn't have anything much in our fridge so I went into Grannie's kitchen— well, I *was* going into Grannie's kitchen.'

'And?' he prompted.

'Grannie was there with Dr Parker. I was going to go in, but then he said something…'

'What did he say?' Ed asked when it was obvious she wasn't going to go on.

She sniffed. 'He said…she was very beautiful, and he loved her. He said he wanted to marry her. He told her to think about it.' She twisted her hands together. 'Then he kissed her goodbye—properly, you know. Not just a peck on the cheek, but a real kiss.'

'I see.'

'He shouldn't have done,' Laura said emphatically. 'She's Grandad's wife. It didn't seem right.'

'But they're both alone now, Laura. Maybe they're lonely.'

'They still shouldn't do *that*!'

Ed sighed inwardly. 'People do, you know. I know it can be hard to accept, but when you're in love there usually is a strong physical element—'

'But not *Grannie*!' she said, and burst into tears again. 'She's going to marry him, and then what will happen? She'll move out, and Mummy will be out at night, like she is tonight, and I'll be all on my own.'

'Does it frighten you,' being on your own?'

'No. I just hate it, and I hate change, and everything's going to change, and I like it like it is…'

She curled up in the corner, sobbing into the tissues. Ed looked up and saw Jo, hovering in the doorway at the bottom of the stairs. He shook his head, and she moved back out of sight, her face tormented.

'Let's go in the kitchen and fix a drink,' he said clearly, and put his arm round Laura's shoulder. 'I think I've got some cola—do you fancy a glass? I might have some chocolate biscuits as well.'

She sniffed and nodded, and he led her out of the sitting room. Please, God, Jo, use your common sense, he prayed, and out of the corner of his eye he saw her slip across the room. Then there was a knocking on the door, and it opened and Jo called out.

'Ed? I don't suppose you know where Laura is, do you? She's not at home.'

Thank you, God, he mouthed, and stuck his head round the door and winked at her. 'She's here. She was a bit upset, so she came for a chat.'

Jo walked into the kitchen, took one look at her daughter and held out her arms. 'Oh, sweetheart, what's the matter?'

'I missed you, you weren't there,' Laura mumbled from the depths of her mother's sweatshirt. 'And Grannie's going to marry Dr Parker.'

Jo patted her shoulder and met Ed's eyes over Laura's head. Her eyes were drenched with misery, and she bit her lip. 'Is she?' she said finally. 'I didn't know.'

'He asked her tonight.'

'And did she say yes?'

Laura shook her head. 'She didn't say anything, but I know she will.' She lifted her head. 'He kissed her, Mum. It was really tacky.'

'Tacky?' she said gently. 'Or just a bit unexpected? Did they know you were there?'

She shook her head. 'No, of course not, but I couldn't

get away without them seeing me. I had to sneak off when he was kissing her. I think I could have danced round them and they wouldn't have noticed. It was gross.'

'But they wouldn't have done it if they'd known you were there.'

'And that's better?'

Jo closed her eyes and hugged Laura again. 'I don't know. Come on, it's late. Time for bed.'

'Where were you?' she asked, and Laura met Ed's eyes in desperation.

'I had to visit someone,' she said, and he could tell from her eyes that she hated deceiving Laura. Now, though, was obviously not the time to tell the child the truth. 'Come on. Ed, thanks.'

He gave her a reassuring smile. 'My pleasure,' he said softly, and her eyes filled a little. He laid a hand on her shoulder and squeezed gently. 'I'll see you both in the morning.'

Jo nodded and took Laura out. He watched them go up the path in the moonlight, then locked the door with a heavy sigh.

Poor Laura, coming face to face with reality. It was a hard lesson to learn. Still, Jo would talk to her.

Ed went up to bed, and the sheets held the lingering traces of Jo's perfume, mixed with the warm, musky scent of their loving.

He lay down in the tangled sheets and breathed in her scent and wished that she was there.

'How is she?'

'Oh, mixed up. She's gone out with Cara—they're meeting some friends. She's hardly seen them, she's been so busy with the pantomime.'

They strolled along the seafront, their arms brushing.

Ed didn't hold her hand or put his arm round Jo, although he wanted to, but she seemed withdrawn. He shoved his hands in his pockets instead.

'Have you spoken to your mother?'

'Yes. She told me all about Maurice. She's worried about Laura. I didn't tell her what happened—I didn't want her to feel distressed, and I know she would. She's still thinking about his proposal, but she's got her sparkle back. It's odd, I never thought she would, but they seem to have given each other a new lease of life. They're both acting like spring chickens. I just wish Laura could be happy for them.'

'Mmm. I know what you mean. Maurice seems endlessly cheerful, and your mother certainly seems bright.'

'She's worried about Laura, though. She seems to think that if she marries Maurice and he retires, they'll be spending a lot of time away. That's what he's talking about, going on the holidays he'd planned to take when he retired, doing all the things he's always wanted to do. And that means, of course, that if she goes with him she won't be here for Laura.'

'That might not be such a problem,' he said carefully.

'Why?'

They reached a breakwater, and he drew her down to sit on it, looking out over the sea. He caught sight of a striped pebble, and he picked it up and turned it over in his hands, inspecting it while he cast about for words.

'Last night—being with you, loving you—was the best thing that's ever happened to me,' he told her quietly. 'I meant it when I said that I love you. I do, probably more than I can ever tell you. I want to spend my life with you, Jo. I want to marry you, and be with you for the rest of my life. If we can, I want us to have children, but if not it doesn't matter. You've got Laura, and I'd do everything I could to be a good father to her.'

He searched her eyes, and saw misery there in their lovely hazel depths. 'Oh, Ed, we can't,' she said heavily. 'Not now, anyway. Not with my mother getting married.'

'But it's ideal! We could work our nights off so that there was always someone there for Laura—'

'And be permanently exhausted because we had broken nights every night? Ed, it wouldn't work. It's not that I don't love you. I do. Last night proved that to me if nothing else could. You were wonderful with Laura.'

'So what's the problem?' he said. 'We can work it out, Jo.'

She shook her head. 'I just feel…it would be too much for her, with my mother as well. She's really very shocked about it. She wouldn't look at her this morning.'

He tried another tack. 'What will you do when your mother marries Maurice? Who will look after her when you're on call?'

She shrugged. 'I don't know, I haven't worked it out. I'll have to do something—get a lodger? Find an au pair? I don't know, I haven't had time to think. I just know this isn't right for her, not now.' She turned to him, and he could see the sadness in her eyes. 'I'm sorry, Ed. I can't—not now. Maybe later.'

He searched her face, then nodded. 'OK. You know her better than I do. We'll give her time to get used to the idea—but I'm not giving up, Jo. There's too much at stake, for both of us. I love you. I'm not going to stop loving you just because it isn't easy.'

She slipped her hand into his and squeezed it, and he returned the pressure reassuringly. 'Thanks,' she said softly. 'I knew you'd understand.'

He looked out across the waves, his heart impatient. He wanted to be with her now, to have the right to walk hand in hand with her, without anyone looking and commenting. He wanted to hold her at night, to make love to her, to have children with her.

He wanted it all and, because she was the woman she was, it wasn't possible.

Not yet, anyway.

Hopefully, Laura would come round in time.

'Have you ever said anything to Laura about us?' he asked curiously.

'No. Why?'

He shrugged. 'I just wondered. She might not react like you think.'

Jo shook her head. 'Ed, I can't risk it, not now. She's so shaken up about Mum I just daren't rock her boat any more.'

'So where do we go from here?' he asked, dreading her answer. 'Is that it? Do we stop seeing each other?'

Their eyes locked. 'I don't know,' she said miserably. 'I would just feel so awful if she caught us—last night could have been dreadful.'

'Maybe we need to go somewhere else. Perhaps I need to move.'

'That would just make it harder.'

'What do you suggest? We drive out into the forest and make love in the car? Jo, we're too old for that sort of thing. Knowing our luck, we'd get caught by the police.'

She gave a little laugh. 'Yes, very likely. Ed, I don't know the answer. Perhaps we just need to spend time together in front of her—come round for a meal, have coffee, play cards with her, watch a video—just be part of the family.'

'You don't think she'll feel she's in the way then? She must have friends with single parents who are having relationships—how do they cope? This happens all the time, Jo. It's not just us that has this problem.'

'I don't know.' She stood up. 'I need to go back. I've got things to do I've been putting off because of the panto—washing and tedious things like that.'

'Me, too. I'll come with you.'

They turned and headed back. The beach was almost deserted, just a few fishermen and someone walking a dog. It was peaceful and beautiful, and Ed wished things were different. He'd just proposed to Jo, and it should have been the happiest day of their lives.

Instead it was filled with uncertainty and confusion.

Damn.

He kicked a pebble, frustrated and disappointed and yet understanding, and Jo sighed.

'I'm sorry, Ed.'

'Don't be. You're doing what you have to do. I'll still be around. Maybe Laura needs to go out for sleep-overs occasionally.'

She laughed. 'I can't send her off to friends every night—she'd smell a rat!'

'Just every now and again. You've got rights as well, Jo. Don't forget that.'

He hugged her briefly, then released her and looked up. A fisherman up ahead was casting his line, and a young couple had wandered onto the beach behind him.

'That line's very close,' Ed said, just as there was a scream and the woman threw her hands up to her face. 'Whoops. I think he's hooked her. So much for my day off.' He headed across the beach at a run, with Jo after him, and arrived at the woman just as the fisherman did.

'Sorry, love, I didn't see you—are you all right?' he was saying.

'It hurts!' she wailed, and the man with her was hugging her and yelling at the fisherman.

'I'm a doctor,' Ed said, cutting through the pandemonium. 'Can I have a look?'

'It's my eyebrow,' she wailed. 'He's stuck it in my eyebrow!'

'Let me see,' Ed said firmly. Taking her hands, he lifted them away to reveal the hook firmly embedded in her left eyebrow, about two-thirds of the way along.

'Oh, hell, Tammy,' the man said, and turned away, gagging.

'Pull it out,' she said frantically, but the fisherman intervened.

'No, you can't, it's barbed. You'll have to take it—through—you need to cut the end off. Here.' He pulled some scissors out of his pocket and lifted them towards her face.

'Oh, no,' the man groaned. Running down to the water's edge, he lost his breakfast.

'Wimp,' the girl said scornfully as the fisherman snipped through the line, leaving the hook where it was. 'Bloody hell, it hurts worse than having my nose pierced. How are we going to get it out, then?'

'We'll have to do what he says,' Ed told her, 'but I'll take you down to Casualty and do it there. I'll give you a local anaesthetic first, and then we'll worry about it.'

'I'll come,' the fisherman said. 'I'll pack my gear up and follow you.'

'What about your friend?' Jo said to her.

She looked down the beach and shrugged. 'What about him? He'll come. Hey, Paddy, come on. We're going to the hospital.'

He walked reluctantly back to them, dragging his feet. Ed noticed he had rings and studs in his ears and nose and one eyebrow, anyway, so why the fish-hook should upset him so much he couldn't imagine.

'Do you want a lift, or have you got a car?' he asked.

'We'll come on the bike,' he said.

'Not like this, I'm not!' the girl protested. 'Can I come with you?'

Ed nodded. 'You coming?' he asked Jo. 'I might need a hand.'

She hesitated, then seemed to catch on and, to his relief, agreed. The last thing he wanted was to be alone in his car with a girl who later accused him of anything suspicious. With Jo there, it wouldn't happen.

They arrived at the hospital in convoy. Paddy followed them in at a distance and sat on the other side of the waiting room, shielding his eyes. 'Turns me right up,' he confessed, and picked up a magazine.

'Lot of use you are,' Tammy grumbled, and went through with them to a cubicle, leaving the fisherman to keep Paddy company.

Ed asked her to lie down, then injected the area with local anaesthetic. Once it had taken effect he asked Jo to hold the hook steady while he snipped off the end with some cutters and pushed it through.

The end of the barb came out through the top of her eyebrow, and Ed showed it to her. He washed the area well and, using a syringe, he squirted saline through the puncture wound to flush it. 'You'll need antibiotics,' he told her. 'I'll give you a prescription, but you must take them, otherwise you could get a nasty infection.'

'OK.'

He stood back. 'There you go, then. All done.'

She stood up, grinned and thanked them, then disappeared into the Ladies. A few moments later she reappeared and called Paddy.

'Hey, cool!' he said with a laugh.

Ed and Jo looked up, and Ed blinked. 'Am I seeing things?' he asked.

Jo chuckled. 'I don't think so.'

Tammy met their eyes and grinned. 'Seemed a shame

to waste it,' she said. As she turned to go out the sun glinted on the sleeper that was now threaded through her eyebrow.

'Cheers, mate,' she said to the fisherman, and followed Paddy through the door.

The fisherman turned to them and shrugged. 'Takes all sorts,' he said with a grin. 'Think I might go home now. Wait till I tell the missis what I caught for dinner!'

Ed laughed and waved, and turned to Jo. 'Back to our chores?'

'We should.'

'Thanks for coming down with me. I didn't fancy getting stuck with a sexual harassment claim if she'd decided to get rich quick. It's been done.'

'I don't think she would have done, but she might have propositioned you.'

He laughed. 'In which case, even more thanks. I've seen some strange things in my time, but that just takes the biscuit. Anyone who can do that to themselves is too kinky for me.'

He drove Jo home, parking outside the front of his house. 'I don't suppose I can entice you in?'

She smiled. 'Better not. Laura might come back.'

'OK.' He leaned on the car roof, and looked into her eyes. 'I love you,' he murmured.

'I love you too, Ed. I'm sorry.'

'Don't be sorry. We'll work things out.'

He watched her go, and wondered if he was just being a dreamer or if there really was a chance for them.

So near, and yet so far...

CHAPTER NINE

'MUM, can I stay with Lucy? Her brother's going away for the weekend and she's allowed a friend. Can I go?'

'Sure,' Jo said with a smile, and wondered if her daughter could read the guilty delight in her eyes. A whole weekend? And, furthermore, they weren't on call!

She had to stop herself running down the path to tell Ed. The last ten days had been hell, trying to snatch moments alone, worrying about Laura, trying to convince her mother to take the happiness Maurice was offering and not feel guilty about it—and now here was the weekend on a plate!

She told Ed the next morning instead, and he smiled for the rest of the day. Jo did, too, wandering round humming and chatting to everyone, and it made her realise how dismal she'd been feeling.

Then, as luck would have it, Lucy's mother became ill with tonsillitis, and the whole plan was cancelled.

'Can she come here?' Laura asked on Friday night, miserable at the thought of her spoilt weekend.

Jo, whose weekend had been ruined anyway, agreed, and rang Ed. 'I'm sorry, we're going to have to cancel,' she told him in a hushed voice. 'Lucy's mother's ill so Lucy's coming here.'

'Ah. Well, why don't we do what you suggested some time ago, and I'll come to you? I've bought food—why don't I come round and cook it for you there, and they can make pizza or whatever and watch telly, and we can sit in the kitchen and chat.'

'It's not the same,' she said, disappointment in her voice.

'No, but I'd rather be with you and the girls than without you.'

'Really?'

'Of course really. I'm well aware of what being the parent of a teenager involves—my older sister's got three. I'll come round soon—six-thirty? Then you can chat to me while I cook.'

'Thanks,' she said softly. 'You are kind. I'm sorry.'

'I just love you. See you soon.'

She cradled the phone thoughtfully. He did love her, she realised, quite genuinely. He'd been very patient. Perhaps he was right—they ought to start getting Laura used to his presence in her life.

She went out of the kitchen and found Laura sprawled on her stomach in front of the television, eating crisps. 'Ring Lucy. She can come here. I'll fetch her as soon as she's ready.'

'Really? Thanks, Mum, that's magic!'

She leapt to her feet, gave Jo a flying hug and ran to the phone.

'That was wonderful. You are the best cook.'

He chuckled. 'You can wash up.'

'No problem. I'll stick it in the sink now to soak. I don't suppose you want to make the coffee while I do that?'

'Some people will use any excuse to get out of a chore,' he teased, but he made the coffee anyway while she cleared up the kitchen. Then, like a magician pulling a rabbit out of a hat, he produced a box of chocolates and put them on the table. '*Voilà*,' he said with a grin.

'Oh, wow, chocs!' Laura said, wandering into the kitchen. 'Are they for us?'

'Us, you and Lucy, or us, all of us?' Ed asked, smiling.

'Oh. Are they yours?'

'No, they're ours,' he told her. 'Open them and help yourselves—if you're allowed?'

'Mum?'

Jo nodded. 'Don't eat them all. You can have two each.'

'Bags the hazelnut whirl,' Lucy said, and they dived into the box.

Ed met Jo's eyes across their heads, and he winked. The girls went off with brimming glasses of fizzy drinks and their hoard of chocolates, and disappeared back into the sitting room.

'I bet they've taken my favourites,' Ed grumbled good-naturedly, fishing through the chocolates.

'Serve you right for being so generous. I would have told them to take a hike,' she said with a chuckle. 'I'll be all right, I like the coconut ones.'

They drank their coffee at the kitchen table, and after a while Ed leant back in his chair and said, 'Would they mind if you came back with me for a bit? Half an hour or so? They seem happy enough, your mother's in—how about it? No strings, just another cup of coffee and a hug?'

'Sounds wonderful,' Jo said, and wished she dared to make it longer. She stuck her head round the door. 'I'm going to help Ed take the dishes and things back to the cottage, and have a coffee. I'll be about half an hour, OK? Grannie's here if you want her.'

'OK,' Laura said, not bothering to turn her head, and Jo wondered if Laura actually minded or if she herself was being too fussy.

'All right?' Ed said as she went back to the kitchen.

'Fine.'

They picked up all the dishes and the rest of the chocolates, and went across the gardens to Ed's. It was so close it was silly to worry, especially as they could see the house from the cottage, but Jo still felt a little pang of guilt.

Ed, predictably, noticed. 'Stop it,' he said gently. 'You're allowed a life.'

'Am I?'

'Yes,' he said firmly. Taking the dishes from her, he put them down in the kitchen, put the kettle on and lit the fire. It wasn't cold as the central heating was on still, but it made the place cheery. He found a CD—classical this time, moody but not seductive—put it on and dropped into the corner of the settee beside her with a grin.

'Alone at last,' he said in a theatrical tone, and she laughed.

'Yes, but not for long,' she told him. 'A quick cup of coffee, that's all.'

'And a hug,' he reminded her. 'Don't forget the hug.'

She smiled and wriggled over into his arms. 'One hug coming up,' she said, and his arms wrapped round her and drew her closer. They sat in silence for a while, listening to the music and just being together, then he tipped his head and looked at her. 'OK?'

'Mmm. You're very comfy to rest on. I wish I could stay here for ever.'

'So do I.' He sighed and buried his lips in her hair. 'I miss you so much,' he told her. 'I know it's silly— we see each other all the time, but it's not the same as being alone.'

'You just want to have your evil way with me,' she teased.

'I do, you're quite right, but there's much more to it

than that and you know it,' he said quietly. 'Still, I'll wait. Our time will come.'

'It'll go as well,' she said regretfully, easing out of his arms. 'I have to go.'

'Already? We haven't had coffee.'

'No time. I don't want to cause problems—you know how Laura's feeling.'

Ed stood up and pulled Jo to her feet, then drew her into his arms. 'I know. How about a goodnight kiss— are you allowed that?'

'Ooh, a little one,' she said with a smile, and he chuckled, then lowered his mouth to hers.

It was meant to be short and sweet. In the end it was white-hot, passionate and stopped only because they needed to breathe. Ed sagged against the door, pulling her with him, and laughed weakly. 'You'll be the death of me,' he muttered into her hair, and hugged her. 'Go on, go home while I'll still let you, or you won't be back before midnight.'

She went up on tiptoe, dropped a kiss on his cheek and moved him away from the door. He followed her, standing on the step and watching her. It made her feel safe somehow, knowing he was looking out for her as she went home. Not that it was dangerous, exactly, in Yoxburgh. It was the fact that he cared enough to do it.

She turned at the gate and waved, and he lifted a hand. She was very tempted to go back, but she didn't. She turned away, closed the gate and went back to the girls. As she let herself in through the back door, she heard them talking in the kitchen.

They hadn't heard her come in, and Lucy was talking about Ed.

'It was nice of him to bring the chocolates—did you see that meal he cooked your mum? He must really fancy her.'

'Don't be daft,' Laura replied. 'They just work together.'

Lucy giggled. 'Don't be daft yourself. Didn't you see the way he looked at her? I reckon they're having an affair.'

'What?' Laura sounded shocked, and Jo rolled her eyes and inched back against the door, out of sight. 'Of course they're not!'

'Why not? My mum's having an affair with her boyfriend—they think I don't know, but I do. It's quite sweet, really. He's nuts about her. He looks at her like Ed looks at your mum, and she's potty about him. I think they'll get married soon, but I expect Mum wants to be sure first. She doesn't want another messy divorce.'

Jo decided she'd heard enough. She opened the door noisily, banged it shut and called out, 'Hi, girls, I'm back— Oh, there you are. Everything OK?'

Laura looked searchingly at her. 'Yeah, fine. You weren't very long.'

'I said I wouldn't be,' she reminded Laura, and could have kicked herself for not staying longer, although on second thoughts that might not have been such a good idea. The way their conversation had been going, the girls would have had them married off.

Oh, what a wonderful thought. Perhaps she should have been longer—given Lucy time to work on Laura.

'Right, girls, bedtime,' she said firmly, and chivvied them up the stairs.

On Tuesday night Jo was on call, and after she'd returned from a visit she parked the car in the alleyway beside the house instead of on the drive, and went in to see Ed. It was ten-thirty. He was in the shower and he answered the door in a towel, gave her a slightly damp kiss and told her to put the kettle on.

'I'd rather join you in the shower,' she said, and after a second a grin broke out on his face.

'Last one in's a chicken,' he said, and ran upstairs, with Jo in hot pursuit.

After their shower, and the inevitable sequel, they lay in his bed, wrapped in each other's arms and enjoying just being together.

'I wish we could do this more often,' he murmured, and she wondered if Laura would be as accepting as Lucy seemed to be, or if she would find it all too much. Were they making a mountain out of a molehill?

'Mum, I've got a call—I'll have the mobile if you need me, but could you keep an eye on Laura? It's likely to be a long delivery.'

'Sure. Have fun.'

Jo laughed. 'I doubt it somehow. It's in the forest, in a caravan—a traveller. I just hope nothing goes wrong. It's night-time, there's no power, no water, their neighbour's been done for GBH—it sounds brilliant.'

'Sounds as though she should be in hospital,' Rebecca said doubtfully.

'Tell me about it. She won't listen, and I can't withhold care on the strength of my opinion. Anyway, I'm off. See you later.'

'Have you got anyone with you?'

Jo laughed. 'Too right—I'm taking Ed. Nice and big and strong—he can carry water and keep the neighbours under control.'

She went out to her car and found Ed waiting, his bag at his side.

'Bringing your gear?'

'My obstetrics kit. You never know when you might need it. Jo?'

She met his eyes across the car. 'Yes?'

'Drive slowly—please?'

She laughed. 'You're safe, there's no rush. Get in.'

'Hmm.' He slid in beside her, folding up his long legs, and settled back against the seat. Bracing himself? Probably.

She drove carefully anyway because the roads were dark and a little slippery. It was quite mild, and it had rained earlier. A thin fog hung about the woods as they drove in, and she parked her car as far up the track as possible. Then they set off on foot.

Mel was walking around when they arrived, chanting a mantra with her eyes closed, and Andy was lying on the seat with the dog on his lap, watching her.

The dog growled, and Andy shushed him. 'Have a seat. She's doing her own thing at the moment. Want a cup of tea?'

'Yes, please. Hi, Mel,' she added, greeting the woman who had paused beside them and opened her eyes again.

'Hi. I'm trying to meditate through my contractions—it really seems to help.'

'How are you? What are they like—how often, how severe?'

'Oh, you know—one minute it's OK, and the next you think your legs are going to collapse. They're quite often now—Andy's timekeeping.'

'About every four minutes? They seem to last about a minute or so,' Andy offered.

Jo nodded. 'Right, can I have a look at you?'

'Sure.' She lay down on the bunk in the corner, and Jo felt around to check the presentation. 'Have your waters broken?'

'No—don't think so.'

'I think you'd know. Sometimes you can't tell, but usually it's pretty obvious. I'm going to examine you, see how far on you've got. Are you happy for Andy to be here?'

'Sure—and Ed. That's fine.'

Jo washed her hands, pulled on gloves and had a quick check to see how Mel's cervix was progressing.

'About six centimetres,' she said. 'That's good. You've got a while to go, but you're well under way. It's certainly not a false alarm.'

It was predictably slow, but with the conditions they were working under Jo was happier about that. It gave her time to feel her way through the labour, see if a pattern was emerging, check the contractions and make sure Mel was coping.

It was nearly four-thirty in the morning before Mel started to get too distressed, and then she stood up and headed for the door.

'I want to go outside, Andy,' she said.

'OK,' he agreed, and scooped up blankets, hurricane lights and a pillow.

'What?' Jo asked, stopping him with a hand on his arm. 'What's going on?'

'She wants to do this outside, in the forest. It's OK, I've built her a shelter. It's beautiful.'

Jo and Ed exchanged despairing glances, but there was no sense in arguing. Outside was as good as in so long as the presentation remained normal and Mel could cope. Her pelvic assessment had shown no evidence of disproportion, her baby was coming right on time, and they really had no justification for spoiling her delivery.

'I'll blow the whistle if necessary,' Jo said, and Ed nodded.

'OK. We'll go with it for now. She must be nuts, though, it's freezing.'

They followed the strange procession round to the other side of the caravan and inside what looked at first like a heap of branches. On closer inspection it was a three-sided shelter, with the open side facing east across a little clearing. There was a heap of bracken and heather piled up, and Andy laid blankets and quilts down over the bed to soften it for Mel.

She crawled in and lay on her side, panting and listening to the sounds of the night, the rustlings of the little animals, the hoot of an owl. It was beautiful, but perhaps not entirely practical.

Jo exchanged glances with Ed, and he shrugged. Go with it, he seemed to say. She checked Mel again, crawling into the shelter with her, and found that she was almost there.

'You're doing really well,' she told her. 'Just breathe through the last few contractions, and then you'll be in transition—can you remember about transition?'

Mel gave a wry grin. 'That's when I get crabby and tell you all to go to hell, isn't it?'

Jo laughed. 'Probably.'

'I want to get up,' Mel said suddenly. 'I want to walk round.'

'Andy, Ed, could you support her?' Jo asked, and they helped Mel out and walked her slowly round. She was doing fine until she came to push, and then she hung around Andy's neck. Jo spread a sheet of polythene over the forest floor under her, and she strained, and cried out, and panted, and strained again.

And nothing happened.

Ed looked at Jo. 'How's she doing?' he asked, crouching down beside her.

'Nearly crowning, but not progressing. Her pelvic floor's very strong.'

'Just push for me, Mel, one more time,' Jo coaxed.

'I can't,' Mel sobbed. 'I'm too tired. It hurts. I want my mum.'

'Oh, love,' Andy groaned. Shifting his grip, he hugged her, holding her up and supporting her. His muscles must be screaming, Jo thought, but he didn't for a moment suggest Mel should lie down.

Jo was struggling with the light of the hurricane lamp, and she wasn't happy. 'I need more light,' she said. 'Mel, I think you're going to have to lie down for a moment. Andy, can you lay her in the shelter? I want that inspection light you were talking about.'

It helped a little, but only to show her what she already knew. The baby was almost there, but stuck somehow.

'I wonder if it's a shoulder dystocia?' Ed murmured.

'I don't know. Her pelvic floor's so tight I can't tell, but that in itself shouldn't hold it up.'

'I'm not going to hospital,' Mel said desperately. 'I can't. Please, help me.'

'I just want to get something from my bag,' Ed said. 'Jo?'

She followed him round the other side of the caravan. The sky was lightening. At least, Jo thought, the ambulance won't have to find us in the dark.

'You want to take her in, don't you?'

Ed shrugged. 'It would be sensible, but I don't think she'll go and I'd like to try for her if I can. Episiotomy and another check?'

'If you like. Do you want to do it? At this point I'd probably call for help. She's been in the second stage for over an hour and got nowhere. What would you do in hospital?'

'For query dystocia? Episiotomy and ventouse, I think—more room and a little bit of suction probably. That's irrelevant. We haven't got the ventouse, and she needs help now. I don't want to hang about. I don't like the colour of that baby's head. I think it's getting distressed.'

'I'm happy to hand over to you,' Jo said, relieved that he was there and had so much obstetric experience. Up to now he'd been little more than back-up and an interested observer. Now, finally, she was able to lean on him—and he was there, with answers. 'Do whatever you want—I'll assist.'

Ed nodded. 'Right. I want to do a small cut, as much as anything so I can feel what's happening. Then I'll decide, but I've got forceps here if necessary. I don't suppose there's the slightest chance we can get her inside?'

Jo snorted. 'She's getting more stubborn by the minute. Let's just get the baby out. We can tidy her up anywhere later.'

'OK.'

They went back with Ed's bag, and explained what they were hoping to do.

'Oh, no! I want it naturally,' Mel sobbed. 'I knew it would be all instruments!'

'Mel, love, hush,' Andy pleaded. 'Listen to them.'

He calmed her while Ed gave her a local and then snipped carefully. The baby didn't advance at all and, putting one hand on her abdomen to press the baby down, he felt around its head with his other hand.

Mel gasped, and he apologised, but he kept on feeling, searching for that elusive something that was holding up the delivery.

'It's the anterior shoulder—it's hitched on the pubis symphysis—I'm going to try and push it back.'

'You're not lambing,' Jo said in his ear, and he chuckled drily.

'I noticed. Sheep are a damn sight easier. OK, Mel, just try and relax. That's it… No, I can't shift it. I want you on your hands and knees, and you're going to have to push like hell when I say so—all right?'

'I can't,' Mel sobbed. 'I want to die!'

'Rubbish. Come on, you can do it! Think of your baby,' Jo urged encouragingly, and they helped her onto her hands and knees.

Ed eased his hand in over the baby's head, lifting Mel's spine up away from the baby to expand her pelvis. He felt it give, felt the tiny shift in the baby's position, and then the surge of a contraction. 'OK, Mel, push!' he ordered, and lifted against her spine.

She did, dredging up a huge effort, and to his relief the baby slid forward. 'OK, stop pushing and pant— that's it, little breaths, good girl.' He eased his hand away, she pushed gently again, and the baby slithered into the world.

With a sob Mel collapsed against Andy and Ed scooped up the baby, flipped it over and checked it. He swept its mouth with his little finger, but it still didn't cry, and he didn't like its colour at all.

'It's flat—suction, please.'

Jo slipped a catheter into the infant's mouth and nose, sucking out the mucus in its airways. Then Ed clamped and cut the cord without ceremony, picked up the baby by its feet and swung it around.

'You should have been a vet,' Jo said in an undertone as the baby started to cry.

Ed grinned, checked it again and placed it on Mel's now-soft abdomen. 'Your baby,' he said gently, and she reached out and laid her hand over the baby's back.

'Hello, little one,' she murmured in wonder, and the first rays of the morning sun spilled over the horizon and turned her tears to gold...

'I'm sorry, but you can't stay here. You got your wish, and had the baby here, but you need several layers of sutures in that tear if you want to have a decent pelvic floor, and I can't do it with an inspection light. Ideally I'd want to do it with a general anaesthetic, but I'll compromise with you. You come to the GP unit and let me do it, and you won't have to go to the Audley and have a general. That's the choice.'

'Bully,' Mel said, but she was smiling at her baby. 'Can she come too?'

'Of course. I wouldn't dream of separating you. I'll get the ambulance to come for you now, and you can have some breakfast in there together and then we'll do it.'

Jo tidied up, packaging the clinical waste and sorting out the instruments, and wrote up notes. It had been nearly an hour since the baby was born, and they were back in the caravan in the warmth.

'I'll call the ambulance,' Ed said, and stepped outside into the lovely morning. A sound from his right caught his attention. Breaking glass? Something smashing?

'Sounds like Mick's having another trashing session,' Andy said, peering across the forest. 'He has a bad trip every now and again and goes berserk.'

They heard the sound of running footsteps, stumbling through the heather, and then Sioux burst into the clearing with blood streaming from her face, her baby clutched against her breast.

'Help me! He's going to kill me! Help me!'

Ed lobbed the phone at Jo. 'Call the police and an ambulance. Get them here now—fast. Tell them he's armed and dangerous.'

'Is he?'

'I don't know, but I wouldn't be surprised. And stay inside.'

He shoved Sioux through the door of the caravan, told

Andy to stay and guard them and, dropping down, zig-zagged through the forest. It had been years since his army training, but some things you never forgot.

Like bullies, and cruelty, and how to stay alive.

The smashing noise was coming from up ahead by Jo's car, and he slowed and peered round a tree. Mick was laying about the car with an iron bar, shattering the windows, smashing up the body panels—destroying it.

'Lying bitch!' he was yelling. 'I'll teach her to grass me up!' The headlights went, one after the other, and Ed waited. The car was wrecked. There was little more he could do to it but set light to it, and as long as he was here he wasn't near the women and children.

Ed wondered where the other men were, the ones from the other old coaches parked with his. Why didn't they do something to stop him? Were they all afraid, or didn't they think it was any of their business?

A groan from beside him attracted his attention, and he turned his head slightly. A man was lying in the heather, his face battered, his arm lying at a strange angle. Another victim?

Ed dropped onto his front and crawled across to the man. 'It's OK, I'm a doctor. Lie still, he's over there. Don't move.' He ran his eye over the man, noticing that although his clothes were casual, he wasn't dressed like the travellers.

'He'll kill Sioux,' the man whispered, grabbing Ed's arm in a surprisingly powerful grip. 'Stop him. He's dangerous.'

'It's OK, the police are coming. I can hear them.'

So could Mick. He threw down the iron bar, and ran towards one of the battered cars that lay around the fringes of the site.

Anger surged in Ed. There was no way he was going to get away. He ran after him, his legs pumping furiously, and tackled him just as he reached the car. They fell together into the dirt and rolled round, punching and kicking and struggling, until at last Ed found a purchase—the little tail of hair at the back of Mick's head.

He yanked it round, twisted him face-down into the sand and straddled him, kneeling on his arms.

'Don't move a bloody muscle,' he said viciously, 'or I'll beat you to a pulp.' He yanked the hair, just for good measure, and Mick gave a feeble scream and lay still. The sirens wailed to silence, and doors slammed.

'Over here,' Ed yelled. There was the sound of running footsteps and the police took over, handcuffing Mick and dragging him to his feet before leading him to one of the patrol cars.

The ambulance arrived—and then another one, for good measure.

'Excellent,' Ed said, dusting himself off and smiling grimly. 'Right, there's a man here with head injuries, a broken arm and possible internals, and a woman up the track with facial injuries and a baby that might have been chucked around a bit. I didn't have time to look. I suggest you take them both in one ambulance to the Audley, and then in the caravan up the way there's another woman with a new baby to go to the GP unit at Yoxburgh for postnatal care.'

'Busy night,' the ambulance driver said with a grin.

'Just a tad.'

He went with the ambulance to Mel's and Andy's caravan, and found Sioux still shaking uncontrollably.

'She's in shock. What's happened?' Jo asked.

'Police have got him.'

She looked at his filthy clothes in disbelief. 'What happened to you?'

'I was playing commandos,' he said with a grin.

'Action man, eh?'

He chuckled and hugged her. 'Something like that. Right, let's get this lot sorted out and have some breakfast—I'm starving.'

The police had to wait to interview Ed until Mel was stitched and comfortable. It turned out that the man he'd found by the car was Joe Saunders, the social services liaison officer who'd been trying to help Sioux.

'They've got a thing going between them, apparently,' Ed told Jo later that day at the surgery. 'Been going on for a few weeks.'

'Since I reported it to him. I hope he's all right.'

'I gather they are, all of them, and Mel had her dawn delivery.'

'You make it sound like the milkman,' Jo said with a laugh, then she sobered. 'You were wonderful. I don't know how you got that baby out.'

'Enormous skill—and brute force.'

Jo chuckled. 'Whatever, well done. And I gather you tackled Mick like something out of the SAS.'

'I was an army doctor,' he pointed out. 'That's where I did my obstetrics—on a military base in Germany. I learned a few sneaky tricks on the way.'

'Evidently.' She yawned hugely. 'I'm shattered. I'm going home to bed.'

'Lucky you. I've got an evening surgery. I'll see you tomorrow.'

'OK.' She hugged him. 'Thanks for your support. I couldn't have given Mel what she wanted without you.'

'Any sane person would have sent her to hospital, but maybe it's just as well we didn't or we wouldn't have been there to help the others.'

'And I might have had a car,' Jo said wryly.

'Look on the bright side—you get to choose a new one.'

'I liked it,' she said firmly. 'It was fun to drive.'

He groaned. 'Buy a milk float, for my sake.'

Jo snorted, and went home in the car she'd borrowed from her mother. She'd have to sort out a hire car tomorrow, but for now she was too tired to worry about it.

She went home, waved at everyone and went to bed, going out like a light. She woke the following morning, feeling heavy-eyed and sick.

Too much excitement, she thought, and sat on the edge of the bath, waiting for it to fill. The smell of burnt toast drifted up the stairs, and without any warning she felt a huge wave of nausea wash over her. She only just got her head over the loo in time.

Shaken, she washed her face and sat on the bathroom floor. Why was she feeling so sick? What had she eaten?

Nothing much. That might be the trouble. Perhaps she needed to eat something. The very idea turned her stomach, and she gulped in some air and stared at the ceiling. The last time she'd felt like this she'd been eighteen years old...

And pregnant.

CHAPTER TEN

JO WAS stunned. She couldn't be pregnant! Ed was sterile, he'd told her so—unless the effects of the chemotherapy had worn off and the sperm-producing cells had recovered.

Was that likely? Or, if not, was it at least possible? She consulted her books on infertility, and found nothing of any help or consequence. She carried the secret with her for the rest of the day until she could get into the surgery and do a pregnancy test. If she was right, and she was pregnant, she was sure Ed would be delighted.

Richard had been furious, but Ed loved children and had told her he'd like to have them with her. How wonderful it would be if they could have them naturally and not have to rely on technology to help them.

The test, when she found time to do it, was positive. She waited until Ed had finished his antenatal clinic, then slipped through the door.

'Have you got time to do one more quick antenatal check?' she asked him, bubbling over inside.

He glanced at his watch. 'Possibly. Who is it? Have you got the notes?'

She shook her head. 'No notes yet.' She drew a steadying breath. 'It's me.'

His head jerked up and he stared at her, then he gave a grunt of laughter. 'For a second there I thought you said it was you.'

'I did. It is.' She went over to him and stood by his chair. 'I'm pregnant, Ed,' she said, her happiness flowing over. 'We're going to have a baby.'

He stared at her for an age, hope warring with disbelief, then he stood up and slammed his chair back against the wall, making her jump.

'How could you do that, Jo?' he said, his voice strangled.

'Do what?' she asked, stunned at his apparent anger. 'Don't you want a baby? I thought you wanted children. You said—'

'I know what I said.' He was staring out of the window, his eyes wide and sightless, his voice ragged. 'Dear God, of all the ways to hurt me, why did you have to choose this one?'

She hurried to his side. 'Ed, no, listen! I really am pregnant. I'm having our baby—honestly! Ed, it's real. I've done a test. I'm about five and a half weeks—almost six.'

He turned and stared at her, but his eyes were icy cold and empty. 'So you might be, but not with my child, Jo. I'm sorry, you've picked the wrong man to try and fool. I know it isn't possible, and however desperate I might be to have children I'm not so desperate that I'll believe that.'

She gazed at him in disbelief. 'But, Ed—of course it's yours! Who else's could it be?'

'I don't know, you tell me,' he said harshly. 'How about Barry? Was it Barry? The groom in the panto? He fancies you—how do I know it's not him?'

'Of course it isn't! Don't be daft, he's a pillar of the local church! His wife did the costumes—his children were in the chorus! He is very definitely married!'

'So? So was Laura's father, and it didn't stop you last time—'

There was a sharp crack, and Jo felt the sting in her palm before she realised what she'd done.

'Bastard,' she whispered. 'You absolute bastard! How dare you?'

He stood motionless, not flickering so much as a muscle, and the perfect imprint of her hand slowly appeared on his cheek.

'You can deny it all you like,' he said distinctly, 'but if you're pregnant somebody else has got you that way. It isn't me and, OK, it may not be the guy in the panto, but you've been having an affair with someone, of that I'm sure.'

'In this community?' she raged. 'Do you really suppose, if I were having an affair with anyone else, that you wouldn't have heard about it?'

'Why should I?' he asked indifferently. 'No one knows about us.'

'Of course they do! Everyone knows! You can't do a damn thing in this town without a running commentary.' She rubbed her hand against her hip. Her palm was still stinging. God knows what his face felt like. She wasn't sure she cared at the moment.

'I'm going home. When you've calmed down and had time to think about it, perhaps you'd like to come and talk to me about how you suggest we tell Laura.'

'Tell her what you like,' he said coldly. 'It's nothing to do with me after all.'

'Ed, please, listen—'

'Just go, Jo. Get out of here, please, before I do something I'll regret.'

She searched his face and found no comfort, no compassion, no inkling of the love they'd shared. With a sob, she turned on her heel and ran...

Ed sat on the beach, miles along the coast from Dunwich, dropping pebbles in a little pile between his feet. His hands hung between his knees, his head was bowed and he felt sick.

He was gutted. After all she'd said, all the love they'd shared, the tenderness of their love-making...

A sob tore at his throat, and he clamped his jaws together and held it back. He wouldn't cry for her. She wasn't worth it. She was a liar, through and through.

He wondered how much of the story about Laura's father had been fabrication. All of it, probably. She'd probably had an affair with some spotty youth and got herself into trouble. Maybe she thought a married man sounded more grown-up, more interesting.

Oh, hell.

Well, she'd certainly had him fooled! He could have sworn she loved him, that she would have stood by him, but maybe all the talk about not pushing Laura was just an excuse to cool it? Maybe she'd got this other lover lined up, and Ed was just a convenient stop-gap if the other man was too busy...

He hurled a pebble out to sea, and then another, and another, until his little pile had vanished. Then he stood, dusted off the seat of his jeans and tramped back to the car. He had things to do—a house to find, for instance. He went into town, picked up a copy of the local rag and scanned it for property.

It was in the classified ads at the back—a property for renovation in an isolated setting on the edge of the forest.

Not everybody's cup of tea, but it would suit him down to the ground. He had money sitting waiting, he only had two weeks to find somewhere—this might just be the answer.

It was a private number, and the man offered to show him round that evening. He went, even though it was getting dark, and found the cottage on the road to the travellers' site, about half a mile this side of it. It was pretty, or could be, a little place with red brick and flint walls and a red pantiled roof set in a delightful little cottage garden, and he agreed a sale on the spot.

It took four days to do the deal—four days in which he kept the curtains closed at the back so he didn't have to look out over Jo's house, and harangued the solicitor mercilessly.

That evening he moved into his damp and chilly purchase, with its rotten window-frames and antiquated plumbing, the leaking roof and primitive kitchen. At last, in its peaceful surroundings, he found a place to lick his wounds.

'It seems strange without Ed in the cottage,' Rebecca said one evening as they were all sitting together in the drawing room.

Maurice was there, and Jo felt his eyes keenly on her.

'Yes, it is odd,' she said expressionlessly. 'Maurice, more coffee?'

'Thank you, my dear.' He passed his cup, watching her closely. 'I went and saw him at his new place over the weekend. It's very charming, I suppose, but it's rather tumbledown—needs a lot of work. Personally I wouldn't have thought it was fit to live in at the moment. It's near those travellers.'

'He should have stayed a little longer, and found himself a flat to move into, or a caravan to live in for a while. Heavens, Maurice, he could have moved back with you, or stayed here even! The cottage is free again after the Easter holidays. There was no need for him to rush into it. Most odd, if you ask me. Did he say anything to you, Jo?'

She shook her head. 'No, nothing. I think he just wanted to be independent.'

She sipped her glass of mineral water and tried not to notice the smell of the coffee, but all the time she could feel Maurice's eyes on her.

'Excuse me, I think I'll go and get on. I've got some notes to write up.'

'Before you go, dear, Maurice and I have got something to tell you both.' Rebecca reached out and took his hand, looking at him lovingly. 'He's asked me to marry him, and I've said yes.'

'That's wonderful,' Jo said with as much enthusiasm as she could muster. 'I'm really pleased for you both. I hope you'll be very happy together.'

'Laura?' Rebecca said, looking at her granddaughter in gentle reproach. 'Aren't you going to wish us well?'

'No—I don't want you to get married again! I want you here, with us! You're Grandad's wife, you can't marry him!'

And she leapt to her feet and ran out, sobbing.

Jo got up to follow. 'Mummy, I'm sorry, I'll talk to her—'

'No, I'll talk to her,' Rebecca said firmly. 'You stay here. I can deal with this better than you.'

She left the room, following the sound of Laura's running footsteps, and Maurice turned to Jo.

'When's it due?' he asked quietly.

'What?' She felt the colour drain from her face and sat again abruptly. 'I didn't hear you.'

'Yes, you did. It's Ed's, isn't it?'

She closed her eyes and nodded miserably. 'Yes. Yes, it is, but he doesn't believe it can be. He had testicular cancer twelve years ago, and the chemotherapy left him sterile, supposedly.'

'Only it hasn't.'

She gave a short laugh. 'You try telling him that. He thinks I've been having an affair with someone else.'

'Which, of course, you haven't. Oh, dear, what a shame. Do you love him very much?'

She nodded, fighting back the tears. 'Yes, I do. I thought he loved me too. He said he did, he even asked me to marry him, but Laura was so upset about you and Mum that we didn't like to spring anything else on her so we kept it quiet.'

'Upset? When was this?'

'A few weeks ago—the night you asked her to marry you. Laura saw you kiss her.'

A shadow crossed his face. 'Oh, dear,' he said heavily. 'I know how she adores her grandmother. Oh, blast, I wouldn't have hurt her for the world. And this happened at the same time?'

'Yes. Then I found out I was pregnant.'

'And that foolish boy doesn't believe it's his.' He shook his head. 'What a coil. I'll talk to him—'

'No. Don't bother. If he can't trust me and believe in me, he's not worth having. I just wish for his sake that he could believe it, because this child will grow up without him knowing he's the father, and that's so sad…'

She felt the warm, heavy comfort of Maurice's arm around her, and turned her head into his shoulder, allowing herself to cry at last. Then he mopped her up, fetched her another glass of water and sat down again.

'We were thinking… My house isn't in such good repair as this, so we wondered how you would feel about us living here. Then we'd be there for Laura—and we could help with the baby, too. I imagine you'll want to go on working?'

She shrugged helplessly. 'I don't know. I haven't got that far. I'm just getting through the days at the moment.'

'Well, think about it. Laura will come round. She just needs to accept that Graham's gone, then she'll be happier about Rebecca marrying me. It's a shock, too, discovering that your aged relatives have feelings and needs of their own. She needs time to come to terms with it.'

'And how will she feel about my needs and feelings when she finds I'm having a baby? I haven't even got a loving stepfather to present her with! What do I tell her—the stork brought it?' Jo shredded the tissue in her lap. 'She really adored Ed. They got on so well, he seemed really fond of her. Why won't he believe me?'

'Because it means too much? He's been told he could die. Then he's been told he won't die, but he won't have children. It's a sort of trade. He's clung to it all these years—presumably he's had other relationships and no one else has ever become pregnant. It would make it hard to believe you.'

'And, of course, it's easier to believe I'm a liar and a cheat.'

'Probably not. He looks like hell. If it's any consolation, I think he's desolate. He daren't believe you because there's too much at stake.'

She dropped her head into her hands. 'What am I going to do, Maurice? How can I convince him?'

'I could always persuade him to have a test. That would prove it.'

She lifted her head. 'Of course! That would show his sperm count had picked up—why didn't I think of that? Maurice, would you? Please?'

He reached out and patted her hand. 'I'll try. It may not work, but I'll do my best.'

Jo went to see Mel to check on her stitches and the progress of the baby, and passed Ed's car in the drive of a little cottage just off the road. So that was where he was living, she thought, and her heart ached. She drove right down the track this time, past the other set-

tlement to Mel's caravan, and found Ed outside with
Andy and the baby.

She got out, her heart pounding, and went over to
them. 'Hi. Anything wrong?'

'No, just having a neighbourly chat,' Ed said distantly.
'I have to go. I've got a surgery in half an hour.'

He turned without a word to her and walked off across
the heath in the direction of his cottage. Jo stifled a pang
of grief and held her hands out to the baby. 'How is she
today?' she asked, cuddling the little bundle.

'Fine. Mel's resting, she's been up at night a lot. The
feeding's going really well.'

'Good.' She scraped up a smile and climbed up into
the caravan. 'Hi, there. How are you feeling?'

'Tired, but OK. My tail's a bit sore. I've been sitting
in a washing up bowl of salty water umpteen times a
day, but it's still tender.'

'It will be. You ended up with a nasty tear, but at
least the baby's all right. She's beautiful, you know.'

'I know. I'm so glad she was all right.'

Jo put her down. 'Can I feel how your tummy's going
down?' she asked, and checked her patient quickly. She
was recovering well, despite the unconventional surroundings, and Jo was pleased. The stitches had nearly
all dissolved now, and the last couple she would take
out the following day. She filled in her notes and
propped the file back up behind the pan rack.

'Right, I'm off. I'll see you again tomorrow,' she said
with a smile.

She went back to her car and drove down the track,
and Ed was just pulling out of his cottage as she went
past. He followed her all the way back to the surgery,
haunting her rear-view mirror, and yet when they arrived
he got out of his car, locked it and went in through the
door without a word.

She might as well not have existed, she thought, and a great lump came up in her throat.

'Damn you, then,' she said quietly, and slammed the car door hard.

'Mr and Mrs Reynolds? What can I do for you?'

They were a couple in their late thirties, and they both looked drawn and worried, although it was Mrs Reynolds's notes Ed had in front of him.

'It's my wife,' Mr Reynolds said. 'She's been feeling off colour, and recently she's been having trouble with her waterworks—getting up and down all night, going every hour or so in the day, and, well, we can feel this lump over her bladder.'

Ed looked at the woman. 'Lump?' he said.

'Yes, a hard swelling. It doesn't hurt, but it presses.'

'Have you brought a urine sample?'

'Yes.' She fished a little pill-bottle out of her bag and handed it to him. It was impossible to see through the brown bottle so he put it down. He'd come back to it in a minute.

'I think I need to have a look at you. Could you slip your things off for me? I might need to examine you internally.'

He drew the curtains round the couch, and gave her a minute to undress while he asked the husband a few more questions about the onset of the problem and checked the urine in a clear bottle over the sink. It was normal in appearance, not cloudy or full of sediment, no streaks of blood or pus. He capped the bottle and washed his hands, then went behind the screen.

She was lying under the blanket, naked from the waist down, and he turned the blanket back and checked her abdomen. There was, indeed, a swelling just behind the pubic bone, but unless he was very much mistaken...

He pulled on a glove, squeezed a strip of lubricant on his fingers and gently inserted them, feeling for her uterus.

Idiot! If he'd been thinking clearly he'd have asked the question before, but he hadn't been. 'How are your periods?' he asked now.

'That's the other thing. I haven't had one for a while—not since before all this started.' She swallowed and summoned up her courage. 'Do you think I've got cancer of the uterus or bladder?' she asked with exaggerated calm.

He smiled wryly and stripped off the glove. 'No, I don't. I think, Mrs Reynolds, that you're going to have a baby—in about six months, at a guess. A scan will confirm the exact dates.'

'A baby?' she said incredulously, and sat up, swinging her legs over the side. 'But I can't be! We can't! Rob's sperm count's too low—we've been trying for fifteen years!'

And she burst into tears in her husband's arms.

Ed sat down with a bump. How ironic. Another faithless woman, cheating on her husband—but he, poor fool, was swallowing it hook, line and sinker.

'Well, I'm pretty sure,' he told them, summoning his professional calm. 'A test will confirm it, and then you'll need to make an appointment with one of the midwives—'

'Jo Halliday,' she said instantly. 'I've heard she's wonderful. Oh, I can't wait to tell my mother—she'll be thrilled for us! Oh, Rob, love!'

They hugged again, and Ed quickly dealt with the notes and sent them off with a test request. 'Just hand this in at Reception with your urine sample, and call back tomorrow for the result. Jo will see you as soon as it's confirmed and make arrangements to take over your care.'

Not that she'll be here at the end, he could have added, but it was up to Jo to sort that out. He couldn't be sure when her baby was due. All he could be sure of was that it wasn't his.

'We've been hoping for so long now we'd forgotten about it. Every month I used to wait for my period, and every month it used to come without fail, but after the tests we stopped worrying about it. I can't believe I didn't even think of it, but they were so negative when they did Rob's test we gave up hope then really. That was years ago.'

Jo couldn't believe what she was hearing.

'What did Dr Latimer say?' she asked.

'He just told me to get the result of the pregnancy test and then come and see you. He seemed pretty sure I was pregnant.'

Jo nodded. She'd been sure from her first look at the woman, but she wondered what Ed had made of the business of the low sperm count. Maybe this will convince him it's possible, she thought.

After her clinic Jo went to see if Ed was there, but he'd gone for the day. She went home, did some washing, helped Laura with her homework and then told her mother she had to go out on a visit.

It wasn't, strictly speaking, a lie. She was going to visit someone—just not a patient.

She headed slowly out into the forest and turned into Ed's drive, her heart in her mouth. His car was there, but there was no sign of him. She banged on the door, and light spilled down the hall from a room at the back. His firm tread approached, and the door swung inwards.

'What are you doing here?' he asked flatly.

'I wanted to talk to you.'

'I've got nothing to say.'

'But I have.'

He started to close the door but she blocked it and pushed her way in. She knew he wouldn't hurt her, no matter how hurt and angry he might be. 'Ed, please.'

He let go of the door and walked away, back down the hall to the light. She followed him, closing the door behind her, and found herself in a gloomy little kitchen. The plaster had been ripped off the walls, the wires dangled here and there, and the sink was propped up on a broom handle. 'What do you want?' he asked abruptly. 'I'm busy.'

She sighed, swept the plaster dust off a chair and sat down. 'Mrs Reynolds came to see me today.'

'Ah, yes—the immaculate conception. There's a lot of that about.'

She stared at him. 'What are you getting at?'

'Tell me,' he said with a humourless smile, 'do all the women in Yoxburgh cheat on their partners?'

'You don't have any trust in anyone, do you?' she said sadly. 'Not me, not Mrs Reynolds, not the rest of the pantomime cast—why can't you believe, Ed?'

He hit a section of plaster with a hammer and bolster, and it fell to the floor in a choking cloud of dust. 'Why should I? I know you're lying.'

'Why don't you have a test?' she suggested cautiously.

There was a crash, and the hammer fell to the floor on the other side of the room. 'Rather a pointless waste of resources, don't you think?'

'Absolutely, but since you won't believe me you obviously need proof.'

He picked up the hammer and attacked the wall again.

She tried another angle. 'All right, then, if you won't

have a sperm count, will you agree to a DNA test once the baby's born? That will prove paternity.'

He hit his thumb and swore viciously.

'Why don't you get the hell out of here and find some other sucker to bring up your baby, Jo? I'm not interested. Just give it up, for God's sake...'

His voice broke, and he dropped his head against the wall and dragged in a huge, unsteady breath.

'Oh, Ed,' she murmured, and stumbled through the rubble to his side.

'Don't touch me,' he bit out. 'Just go, Jo. Leave me alone. Stop torturing me.'

She stepped back. 'You're torturing yourself. If you'd only listen you'd be able to find out the truth, but you're too pig-headed to take anyone's word but your own. You want to be left alone? Fine! Well, I hope you rot in your miserable isolation. You deserve to!'

She turned and stumbled across the room. She tripped, going out into the hall, and banged her knee, but she scrambled up again and ran out, leaving the door open behind her. She could hardly see the road, and when she turned on the windscreen wipers it was no better.

With a broken sob she pulled over to the side of the road, rested her head on her arms and wept.

'I'm glad you could find time to come and see me. I've been talking to Jo,' Maurice said without preamble.

Ed's heart sank. Not him as well. He wondered why he'd been called into Maurice's consulting room after surgery.

'Maurice, it's between us. Leave it, please.'

'No, I won't leave it. This needs saying, and perhaps I'm the best person to say it. I've known Jo all her life. I've known her parents since before she was born, and I was the first person to know that she was expected.

I've also been her GP for the past thirty years, and I feel I have a knowledge of her that puts me in a unique position.'

Ed stared at his hands, his jaw set. 'What is your point, Maurice?'

'She's a dear girl—she's friendly, and jolly, and she makes friends easily—but she's nobody's fool. She was badly hurt twelve years ago—very badly hurt. She was devastated when she realised she was pregnant and the father wasn't interested. It's taken every one of those twelve years to screw up the courage to try again—and now that she has, because of your arrogant assumption that you couldn't possibly be wrong, she's going to have to bring up another child alone.'

Ed felt the tears threatening again. 'Maurice, it isn't arrogance,' he said roughly. 'I know it can't be mine—'

'Do you? When were you last tested? Twelve years ago, when you were twenty-odd? Smoking, drinking, sleeping with any woman that would have you, wearing tight jeans and snug little underpants? We've all been there, Ed. Isn't it possible that all of that might have affected your fertility?'

It was true, of course, every word. And it was possible that, over the years, his cells had recuperated a little.

Unlikely—but possible.

'Go and have a test, son. Don't do this to yourselves. I know that child's yours, just as I know the sun's going to rise tomorrow. You need to know it too.'

Maurice laid a heavy hand on Ed's shoulder and squeezed, then left him alone.

You need to know it too.

Ed reached for the phone, dialling automatically.

'So, this patient of yours is believed to have a low sperm count?'

Ed nodded, crushing his guilt for distorting the facts to his friend and one-time colleague.

'And they're having difficulty conceiving?'

'Um—well, not exactly. Apparently they have conceived—at least, she has. He doesn't believe it's his.'

Max straightened from the microscope he was peering into and shot back the seat. 'Well, he should. It could well be. Have a look.'

Ed stood slowly and went across to the microscope, bending to look into it. A handful of little tadpoles thrashed around in the light, wriggling furiously.

'So, are there enough there to do the business?' he asked a little unsteadily.

'Sure. It's a low count, true, but they're pretty fit little chaps.'

'So, given the right conditions...'

'Downhill with a following wind, yeah, why not? I wouldn't guarantee it, but people do the lottery every week for far worse odds. If I had that much chance of winning the lottery, I'd sell everything I owned to buy the tickets—and I'm not a gambling man.'

Ed watched the sperm for another minute, then straightened and met Max's altogether too perceptive eye.

'Thanks,' he muttered.

'Who is she?' Max asked gently.

There was no point in lying. 'Her name's Jo,' he said, and his voice sounded shaky.

'You love her, don't you?'

Ed nodded. His eyes were prickling again, and he looked down at his hands. 'Yes, I love her. I might have burnt my boats, though.'

Max's hand landed on his shoulder. 'You'd better go and find out, then, hadn't you?'

*   *   *

The door of the cottage opened quietly, and Jo came to the top of the stairs. 'Mum?' she called.

There was no reply. She started down, just as Ed appeared at the foot of the stairs. He looked defeated.

'Can I talk to you, please?' he said quietly.

'Now? I'm busy. We've got guests tomorrow—'

'It won't wait.'

She came down the stairs a little. 'OK. We'll go to the house—'

'No, here. There's no one here, is there?'

'No.' She sat down on the step, and he climbed the stairs and sat beside her, his leg resting against hers, his shoulder beside hers. He looked awful.

'I've been to see a friend who's got a lab,' he began.

'And?'

'I owe you an apology. You were right. My sperm count's picked up. It's not good, but it's good enough— just.'

Jo felt a huge pain in the region of her heart, and she lashed out. 'So, because this friend says it's OK, you're going to believe me now, are you?'

'I always wanted to believe you,' Ed said, his voice low and ragged. 'For a moment, when you told me, I almost let myself, but I've known for so long that it wasn't possible—if it had been, it would have happened before now. Victoria didn't become pregnant, and we weren't taking any steps to prevent it. We were together for two years. If it had been possible, it would have happened then.'

'Maybe we were just very lucky, if that's the word,' Jo suggested bitterly. 'I'd just ovulated—I know that because I get a little pain sometimes. Perhaps we just hit it right.'

'Downhill with a following wind,' he said softly.

She looked at him in surprise. 'Something like that.

Anyway, that's beside the point. The real issue here is that you didn't trust me. You couldn't believe in me. Do you have any idea how much that hurts?'

Her voice broke, and she felt Ed's arm hover uncertainly around her shoulder for a moment. Then, with a ragged groan, he drew her into his arms. 'Don't,' he said unevenly. 'Jo, don't. I never meant to hurt you. I'd die before I could willingly hurt you—'

'You were so cruel—'

'I know. I knew it couldn't be mine, and there was only one other way. The thought of some other man touching you, loving you the way I had—it hurt so much I lashed out. I can't tell you how sorry I am. I wanted to trust you, but I don't believe in miracles. It meant so much to me, and it seemed like such a cruel twist of fate.' He bowed his head. 'Forgive me, Jo—please? Let's start again.'

She felt the pain in her heart disintegrate. So he'd hurt her, but only because he'd been so hurt in the past. She stood up and held out her hand to him, drawing him to his feet.

'Can we?' she whispered. 'I've missed you so much.'

His eyes searched her face incredulously, and then with a cry he swept her up into his arms and hugged her tight. 'Oh, Jo, I've missed you, too. I thought I'd die without you. The thought of the rest of my life without you was unbearable.'

His lips found hers, and he kissed her tenderly, almost reverently. 'I love you,' he whispered against her hair. 'Marry me.'

She leaned back in his arms and smiled. 'Haven't you forgotten something?' she teased.

He smiled back. 'Marry me *now*?' he asked, and then his voice cracked. 'Marry me—please?'

'I should be honoured,' she said gently, and lifted her face to his kiss…

EPILOGUE

'HE'S gorgeous.'

Jo looked down at the baby in her arms and smiled. 'Mmm—just like his father.'

Sue propped her arms on the edge of the crib and laughed softly. 'You're biased.'

'Of course.' Little Thomas was asleep now, his rosebud mouth soft around her nipple. She eased him away and handed him to Sue while she fastened her clothes, but he started to grizzle so she took him back again as soon as she was done. 'Let's go back down to the others. We can't abandon them.'

'It's been a lovely christening—what a good idea to combine it with the house-warming.'

Jo laughed mirthlessly. 'It's been hell—what are you talking about? The place was in chaos until yesterday.'

Sue looked around the hall as they joined the others. 'Well, it looks wonderful now.'

'Doesn't it, just?' Maurice said, glancing around the sitting room of his old home. 'I hardly recognise it. I must say I think you've done wonders—it was a very old-fashioned sort of house when I lived here.'

Ed laughed. 'It was a lovely home—but anything we've done we have Andy to thank for. He's been fantastic.'

'And Mel—the curtains are all hers. She's done a wonderful job.'

'Don't, we'll get swollen-headed,' Mel said with a chuckle. 'I think I'm going to have a holiday now—

perhaps we'll have time to get back to work on our house.'

Ed gave a rueful grin. 'Sorry—it was a bit much to sell it to you in that state and then ask you to help with this straight away.'

'No problem. Just put our name about, that's all,' Andy said with a smile. He shifted his little daughter to the other arm, and she reached out to touch Thomas's head.

'He's cute,' Mel said.

'He's my baby brother,' Laura said proudly. 'D'y'know, I really wanted a sister, but he's so nice I love him to death. Anyway, we'll be able to play football, won't we, sport?'

'Maybe next time,' Jo said, exchanging glances with her mother.

Rebecca gave a secretive smile and turned away. 'Come on, Maurice, I want to show you what they've done out here in the kitchen. We might try something similar in our new house.'

Ed and Jo wandered through their guests, laughing and chatting, and then by a miracle found themselves alone in the conservatory at the back. Early geraniums bloomed in pots, and it was leafy and cosy and private.

'Are you all right?' he asked her softly. 'Not too tired?'

'I'm fine. You?'

He smiled tenderly at her. 'Just counting my blessings. I can't believe how everything's worked out in the last year. You know, when I met you, I thought how wonderful it would be if I could persuade you to marry me. You'd already had a baby so I didn't feel I'd be cheating you if things didn't work out—and then Thomas appeared on the scene.'

'It was a bit early—I've often wondered if you would have liked more time before starting our family.'

He shook his head. 'No. There's only one thing I'd change, and you know what that is.'

'I've forgiven you for that,' she told him softly.

'I haven't. I'll never forgive myself for doubting you—and the more I know you, the more I realise how much it must have hurt.'

'Forget it. It's over, Ed. I love you.'

'I love you too. I loved you anyway. Spending my life with you would have been more than reward enough. To have Laura and Thomas as well—it's just an unexpected bonus.'

She smiled and handed him his son. 'You think he's such a bonus—you change his nappy.'

Ed grimaced. 'Thanks.'

'My pleasure. You'd better get used to it. I'll need your help more than ever when the next one comes along.'

'If it does. Let's not count our chickens before they're hatched.'

'I'm not. I'm counting our blessings—and at the last count there was one more on the horizon. You're getting another bonus, Dr Latimer.'

He stared at her, not quite able to believe his ears. 'What?' he said weakly.

She smiled. 'Downhill, with a following wind...'

He closed his eyes and reached for her. 'Wow,' he said softly. 'It's a good job we bought this big house off Maurice. Looks like we're going to need lots of room.'

'Mmm. We'll be supplying the whole of the junior chorus in the panto at this rate. *Babes in the Wood* might be appropriate.'

'Just so long as we don't do *Ali Baba and the Forty Thieves*!'

THE HEART'S DESIRE

by
Gayle Wilson

Gayle Wilson taught English and world history before turning to writing full time. A winner of a number of prestigious writing awards, she is also the author of over ten contemporary romantic suspense novels. Gayle Wilson is married, with one son, and lives in Alabama, USA.

Watch out for Gayle's next book:
HER DEAREST SIN
On sale November, in Historical Romance™

Prologue

Spain, 1813

The interior of the small adobe house was not noticeably cooler than the sun-drenched plaza, but the shade at least gave an illusion of relief from the unremitting heat. Lady Emily Harland shaded her eyes with her sunburned hand and watched her maid carry the heavy wooden bucket across the small square. As Aimee walked, the water sloshed gently over the edges of the pail and fell in steaming puddles onto the flagstones.

Emily brushed back a few red-gold tendrils that curled against the perspiration on her neck and loosened the third button at the throat of her gown. She had long ago given in to the dictates of the climate rather than obeying the rigid code that governed the dress of women of her class, though no one but her maid knew how little she wore under the simple muslin dress that comprised one half of her remaining wardrobe. She sometimes wondered what had become of all the baggage she had lost to swollen rivers, French raids and other disasters in the past five years.

She took one last look down the narrow street leading to

the docks for any sign of her father before she moved out of the narrow doorway to permit Aimee to enter with her burden. The maid set the bucket down and used her sleeve to wipe the sweat that beaded her brow and upper lip.

"How is he?" she whispered, glancing into the dark interior.

"I think he's sleeping. I hope. His fever's up," Emily answered, the concern for her brother clear in her voice.

"That happens in the afternoon heat. He ate better today. That's a good sign," the maid said comfortingly as she bent to lift the brimming bucket.

"Let me," Lady Harland said, taking the handle. "You've carried it far enough."

The years they had spent together in this war-ravaged country had blurred the lines between friendship and service, and on more than one occasion the mistress had cared for her maid, tending to her needs in sickness, brushing and braiding her hair or even washing her clothing with her own.

She carried the water toward the bed that had been pushed against the back wall of the room, as far from the broiling sun and the driving rains as they could manage, and found that the fever-bright blue eyes of the man lying there were taking in her every move.

"You're awake," she said with a smile, and watched the answering smile cross his cracked lips.

"I haven't slept," Devon answered, and she saw his eyes turn to the water.

"Are you thirsty?" She found the gourd that served as a ladle and filled it with water, which was still cool from the well. She put her hand behind his neck and carefully eased his head high enough to allow him to sip it.

"Enough," he whispered finally, and she gently lowered his head to the straw mattress. His eyes closed against that small effort and she watched his hands tense with the pain.

"Let me get the laudanum," she said, knowing before she asked that he would refuse.

"Later. When it's cooler and I can sleep. Is Father back?"

"No, and maybe that's good news. The villagers say that the transports are held up by storms at sea. I don't know how they can know that."

She watched the smile move again across his face, but he didn't open his eyes, fearing perhaps that she would see more of the pain than he intended.

She used the gourd to fill the cracked basin on the table beside his bed and dipped a soft cloth she had made from one of her remaining cotton petticoats into it. She began to gently bathe his face and neck, as much to give him relief from the heat as to fight the fever. She turned the coarse sheet down and exposed his bare chest and carefully washed his arms and upper body. He was so thin, the fever wasting away the hard muscles that only a few short weeks ago had urged his spirited horse to carry Lord Wellington's orders to every corner of the battlefield.

The charger was dead, a victim of the same shrapnel that had torn into the once-strong body she now cared for. The field surgeons had removed what they could, but much remained, and the most dangerous souvenir lodged too close to the spine to be tampered with.

The doctors had warned them not to move him, but Emily and her father had watched him slowly dying despite their care and had determined on this last desperate gamble.

"It will be on your head," the chief surgeon had told her father as he wiped his instruments on his stained apron. "You're sure to kill him."

"My God, man," her father had exploded, "he's dying already. I've lost two sons to you butchers, to these slaughter pens you call hospitals. I'm taking him to the coast and then to England.''

''If that metal moves against his spine, he'll be paralyzed as he was immediately after he was hit. Inflammation of the organs is the inevitable result of a cessation of body functions. You'll never get him to the coast.''

''I'll get him there,'' the general had answered grimly. ''I'll get him there if I have to carry him in my arms all the way. And I'll get him to England. I am not going to lose this son.''

Emily had recognized the determination in the eyes of her father and she knew that when General William Burke made that kind of promise, he carried it out.

And he had. Devon had been carefully placed on thick straw mattresses in the bed of the wagon, and the pace had been kept necessarily slow. And he had survived. Survived, Emily suspected, by sheer force of will. And a promise.

''Devon,'' she said softly, thinking again of that promise, as she moved the sheet to wash his legs and feet. They had long ago discarded the nightshirts, recognizing that trying to keep them clean or to change them was impossible given the climate and his condition. And he was cooler without them.

She watched the blue eyes open and find her face and wait.

''Let me write to Elizabeth. We'll be in England soon. Home among doctors who know what to do. It isn't fair to her to let her believe—''

''And I suppose it would be fair to let her care for me as you have these weeks,'' he said. ''Fair to burden her with someone who may never regain the full use of his body. Is that what you feel Elizabeth deserves? To spend her life caring for an invalid husband?''

''I think she deserves a chance to make that decision,''

she argued, knowing how she herself would feel. "You've decided for her, and in the most hurtful way you could devise."

"But it was my decision. Have I kept my part of our bargain, Em? Have I done what I promised?" His voice was stronger now in his anger, as he used a weapon she could not fight.

"Yes," she acknowledged. He had begged her to write as soon as he had realized the extent of his injuries. Begged her to write the letter he was physically unable to pen. And in spite of what she had felt, she had written it, blackmailed into putting on paper all the painful lies he had concocted to hide the reality of his condition. She had written to her friend, a woman she had long thought of as already a sister, agonizingly explaining that her brother had met and fallen passionately in love with a Spanish noblewoman, whom he had quickly married.

The pain Emily had expressed in the letter had been real, but she had set down the untruths he had demanded. For in exchange, she had his promise that he would not give up. That he would live in spite of the despair she had watched grow daily in his eyes. And he had kept that promise through all the long days, all the despairing nights. He had eaten when the thought of food sickened him and drunk water when his stomach rebelled even at that. She had seen the force of his will keep him alive because she had done what he had demanded. And she was suddenly ashamed that she had attempted to renege on the bargain he had so faithfully kept.

"Yes, my dear," she said, pulling the sheet over his body again, "you have kept your promise. I won't mention it again."

"Don't be angry with me, Em," he said with a smile, the low voice coaxing now, "my most beloved of sisters."

"Your only sister," she whispered, kissing his forehead, then pushing back the dark brown curls to gauge the afternoon's fever. It was an old joke, but the love between the two was strong, and she knew that whatever choices he had made, he truly felt that they were the only ones he could live with.

The afternoon's heat built in the room and she bathed him again to cool his suffering body. They waited and hoped that when the general returned he would bring news that the ships had arrived and that they could soon sail for home.

"What will you do in England?" Devon asked as twilight at last broke the heat and the glare.

"I can't imagine!" She laughed, and they both recognized the truth of the statement. "Can you see me doing needlework or watercolors or pouring over the latest fashions in *La Belle Assemblée?*"

"I don't know about the watercolors, but as for needlework, you've had plenty of practice darning shirts and socks for the last five years. And, my dear, I don't pretend to know the latest Parisian style, but I don't think that's it." He nodded carefully at her faded dress. She stood and performed a graceful curtsy, spreading the narrow skirts so that the scuffed riding boots she wore were revealed. "I think you have some catching up to do," he said with a laugh.

"Oh, Dev, sometimes it all seems so remote. I don't know that I can ever fit in again. I don't know that I want to. When I think of all the things I once thought were important…" She shook her head.

"I suppose we'll all find it difficult to adjust."

"What do you look forward to most?" she asked, a new version of an old game.

"Steak-and-kidney pie. Roast beef and Yorkshire pudding. Plum pudding and hard sauce." As he talked, she thought of the gallant effort he made to get down the simple rough fare that the villagers shared so willingly. She pulled her mind away from the endless time it took to feed him, to make sure he had enough, even if the rest of them did without. "Afternoon tea and real coffee in the mornings," he was saying. "And the coolness. Fog. Summer rain. The smell of the Thames and the sound of the traffic. Even the things I used to complain about. They all mean England."

"I know." She smiled, allowing herself for the first time to think about every aspect of home. "Soon, my dear, soon. I think if the ships aren't here tomorrow, Father will begin to row you home himself."

"Well, you needn't worry about that." Her father's voice spoke from the doorway. "The ships docked this afternoon and I've already made arrangements for our passage. We sail as soon as they've loaded the other wounded and the provisions."

Emily could hear the relief in his cheerful voice. Another hurdle overcome, another step closer to survival for Devon. Closer to London and home. She turned back to her brother and watched him swallow to control the emotions that the thought of home evoked.

"Only a little while longer, Dev," she promised. "I'll race you in Hyde Park. We'll frighten the sedate procession on Rotten Row out of their wits. It will be the scandal of the season."

"A nine-day wonder," her brother replied. "There are always too many things going on for anyone to take much notice of what we do. But I'll beat you," he said softly. "I promise you, Em."

"I'll count on it. Another promise to keep."

She watched his eyes lock on hers as he nodded, and she knew that if he could—if it were possible—he would keep that promise as well.

"The laudanum tonight, I think, Dev. You need a good

night's rest for tomorrow. The move to the ship will tire you."

"Tonight. But after that…"

"We'll see," she hedged, knowing that it was the only thing that allowed him to sleep, and that he hated and feared the drug. It might be fashionable in London even among the ladies, but here, where it was used to alleviate the agony of shattered limbs and amputations, all were aware of the darker side of addiction. Emily mixed the drops carefully with water and gave him the dose, then left the small room to allow her father to tend to Devon's private needs before he slept.

The night heat was oppressive, but at least the merciless sun was gone and there was a breeze from the ocean. Emily leaned against the outside wall of the building and waited for her father to join her.

When he did, she moved against his bulk and he squeezed her tightly.

"He'll do it, girl. I know he will. We're going to make it home to England and Devon is going to live."

She hugged him and prayed that he was right. It seemed the hard part was over. She wanted so much to believe her father spoke the truth. She wondered how much had changed in the five years she had spent on the Peninsula. And she wondered why she was even thinking about it. Whatever was going on in London no longer mattered to her at all. As long as Devon got well, the rest of London and its artificial society she had once so longed to storm could go hang.

Chapter One

London—Four months later

The Duke of Avon allowed his valet to ease the coat of gray superfine off his broad shoulders. As Moss hung the garment carefully in the vast closet of his Mayfair mansion, he removed the sapphire stickpin and threw it onto the dressing table, then began to loosen the heavily starched cravat. His mind was already ranging ahead to the mission he must undertake tonight. The most important of the couriers was to arrive from the Continent this very evening, and every effort had been made to ensure the safety and secrecy of the dispatches he carried from Paris. This time there must be no mistake. Only Avon and General Burke's office in Whitehall were privy to the arrangements.

And that is the problem, the duke thought regretfully. He had begun to trust no one. The information that passed through his network to the battlefields of Spain and from his operatives all over Europe to the War Office was too important to trust to mischance. And he had now begun to believe that the suddenly increased dangers those couriers faced were no longer simply a matter of bad luck.

"Your grace." Moss's discreet voice pulled him from his painful reverie, and he allowed the valet to remove the silver-and-white striped waistcoat and then the linen shirt. He stood clad only in the straight black trousers he favored even for evening wear. The glow from the wax candles liberally lighted the massive chamber that was the duke's bedroom, casting flickering shadows over the broad chest and the muscles that moved like those of a finely conditioned thoroughbred under the brown skin of his back. The strongly muscled upper body narrowed to slim hips, but Avon never wore the stylish, skintight pantaloons that the young bucks of the ton favored so highly. Avon set fashion, but he did not necessarily follow it. Nor had he ever been concerned with either endeavor.

The black shirt Moss slipped over his employer's body was certainly not the mode in any part of London that Avon might be expected to frequent. Certainly not in his clubs, the most exclusive in the capital, nor in the town houses of his acquaintances. But the duke was tonight seeking concealment, and in the environs of London he would visit, neither his face nor his name was familiar. A few of the inhabitants might shiver and clutch their rags closer about their throats at his title, but only a few.

"You'll want the Mantons," Moss offered, already checking one of the pair of heavily chased dueling pistols that had belonged to Avon's father. The duke turned and watched the valet's preparation consideringly.

"You may take them if you wish. To remain with you in the coach. I think the sword cane tonight, Moss. There are still some advantages in silently dispatching one's enemies. Especially in this business." Avon shook out the heavy lace that graced the wide cuffs of the shirt supposedly chosen to be inconspicuous for this clandestine meeting. "Lace, Moss?" he questioned in amusement. The valet simply shrugged, but Avon knew how jealously his dignity was guarded by those who served him, and so he hid his smile.

"Advantage to whom, your grace? I hope you don't intend to get close enough to any enemy to be able to use that concealed blade," Moss said as he reluctantly replaced the pistols and closed the case.

"I expect to meet the courier, send him on his way and return here with his papers. I am engaged for supper at one, and I'll need time to change. I don't think this costume is particularly appropriate for a romantic interlude," the duke said as he glanced almost unseeingly into the cheval glass. He fastened the long black cloak Moss handed him at his throat, and it swirled to fall in soft folds around the tall body. He then took from his valet's hand the heavy cane with its hidden blade and checked the mechanism for releasing its wicked length. The sword hissed smoothly from its hiding place. The candlelight briefly caressed the softly gleaming Toledo steel, and then Avon pushed it home again with a snap.

"She wouldn't care how you were dressed," Moss said, clearly overstepping the bounds of even the most trusted servant. Avon's dark brows rose over the remarkable silver eyes to regard him questioningly. "She knows which side her bread's buttered on," the valet finished. It was a long-running battle.

"And I assure you," Avon said deliberately, his amusement clear to the man who knew him so well, "I take care to see that it's buttered on all sides. She is, Moss, a most satisfactory mistress. I should hate to annoy her."

"You don't give a damn whether you annoy her or not. You never did. She's a convenience." Moss spat his contempt for the woman they were discussing.

"But a charming one, you must admit." The duke laughed as he thought of the graceful woman who would wait patiently for his visit tonight. If he were late, she would never express whatever annoyance she might feel in the interim. She was far too wise for that and understood him far too well. He found that the anticipation of possible danger gave an added spice to the thoughts of a visit tonight to his mistress. However, he tried, as he had all day, to convince himself that nothing would go wrong this evening. He was meeting this agent himself simply because of his failure lately to protect the dispatches that were so vital to the war effort. And Avon did not like to fail.

He wore no hat, the darkness of his hair its own disguise, matching the depths of the night. Of necessity he followed Moss slowly down the narrow and twisting back stairs and finally into the coach that waited in the darkness.

Moss gave the directions to the coachman, then watched the man he had served so long from the shadows of the opposite seat. The pure profile was limned against the passing lights that alternately illuminated and then shadowed the interior.

"Do you have any reason, your grace, to believe that there's some danger to this courier?"

Moss's voice interrupted Avon's thoughts and he turned to the man who was far more than his servant. "There's always danger. But I have to admit...I have a feeling that something's not right—a premonition so strong I can almost taste it. Something important's going to happen tonight. These dispatches are too vital to leave to chance, and so I'm giving in to my superstitious forebodings," he said, and Moss heard the self-derision. "Considering all that's happened lately, I've finally learned to pay attention to my instincts."

"Then you'll let me come with you?" Moss asked, trusting his master's presentiment. He shivered suddenly at the surety in the dark voice.

"And frighten away whatever prey we might flush? I think not. This is a hand I intend to play alone. It's by far the safest way."

"Safest for whom, your grace? Certainly not for you."

"Surely that's not anxiety I hear? Have you begun to doubt my ability at this late date? I must be getting old."

"You're *getting* too damned arrogant. You think you're bloody invincible. Well, you're not. You're flesh and blood like the rest of us—your reputation notwithstanding," he said bitterly, and heard Avon's quick laugh.

"I don't think I want to know what that reputation entails. Don't worry, Moss. I don't intend to let anything happen to me tonight. I told you—I have a rendezvous at one. And I must admit, I'm looking forward to it with more than the usual anticipation."

"You've not fallen in love with her, have you, boy?" Moss asked, his concern making him forget the carefully formal facade they always maintained.

He was relieved to hear the genuine amusement in the rich laughter. "In love?" Avon questioned unbelievingly. "God, I must be getting old if you can ask that." But the voice had darkened when he spoke again. "You know better than that, Moss."

The valet watched the handsome visage turn back, to be silhouetted again against the passing lights.

"Well, you're not invincible to that either, your grace. It happens eventually to us all. Your time will come," he said, and again heard the quick, disbelieving laugh. And I should give a great deal to be there to watch when it does, Moss thought, but he wisely kept that conclusion to himself.

Finally they were out of the city and into countryside so thinly populated as to allow the courier to arrive and conduct his business without witnesses. Of course, neither could know of the watcher who was already in place, already eagerly awaiting the arrival of the man whose downfall he had planned for so long. Whose downfall he was now, finally, about to achieve.

At the meeting place there was no sound but the brush of the river against the wooden pilings and the rustle of the weeds in the breeze that was just beginning to lift the mist over the surface of the water. The stench from this stretch of the Thames was one of garbage, of raw sewage and of human misery. The sea was too far away for even a hint of ocean salt. There was only a slice of moon frequently obscured by the shifting clouds. The courier had come, but his messages would never be delivered. He lay in a rapidly congealing circle of blood, with the assassin's knife still in his back. And now all the watcher in the darkness had to do was to wait.

He checked again the pistol he held, one of the pair he had primed and loaded earlier this evening. It was all well and good to catch the courier unaware and to depend on the element of surprise to take him. But not Avon. No, Avon was too clever by far to chance anything going wrong. He was going to put a bullet into that bastard's black heart, and he was marksman enough to know that he could. And then it would all be over and everything would go back as it had been before.

In the distance he finally heard the noise of a coach, the rising breeze deadening the sound of the horses' hooves. The listener concentrated now, blocking out the soft lap of the water, waiting for the footsteps that would identify his quarry as surely as the crest on his coach. And finally he heard them, first on the path and then on the open banks of the river. Footsteps as distinctive as a signature.

Come closer, you bastard. Here's your courier, just where you told him to be. Come on. Come on.

As if compelled by the watcher's thoughts, the cloaked figure came, perfectly aligned with the waiting pistol. The moon briefly glided from behind the clouds, and the watcher could see the sheen made by droplets of mist that had condensed on the broad shoulders of the man he stalked. The moonlight glinted quickly off the silver-headed cane he carried in his right hand and then outlined the figure, a perfect target for the assassin.

But the moon must have been reflected by something on the ground also—perhaps the open, unseeing eyes of the courier, who performed then the last service for his master. For in the same split second the assassin squeezed the trigger, the cloaked figure turned to his right and began to stoop to see what had attracted that gleam of moonlight. In spite of the movement, the watcher's bullet slammed home and the figure fell, to lie as soundless and motionless as the corpse.

The attacker waited breathlessly for movement, for some outcry. When there was none, he approached silently, the mate to the deadly dueling pistol he had just fired held lightly and very professionally in his hand. He pointed the weapon at the back of the undefended neck and prepared to pull the trigger, but it was a motion those steady fingers never completed. The body on the ground exploded into action, and the heavy, silver-headed cane whipped the pistol from the assassin's hand. It flew harmlessly, to land with a muffled splash in the murky depths of the river.

The fallen man instantly swept an arm around his surprised assailant's ankles and threw him hard to the ground. Avon's straining arms locked around the slighter man's struggling body and he attempted to hold him on to the packed earth of the clearing, for they both knew that there lay his only chance at success. Without losing the grip of his right arm, he tried to raise his damaged left to reach the black domino half mask that hid the murderer's features, an added precaution even in the darkness of a nearly moonless night. Avon gasped as a well-directed fist exploded against his midsection, but he knew he couldn't weaken, couldn't allow his hands and aching muscles to react to that pain.

He exerted pressure against the point in the neck that he knew would mean instant agony and surrender, but the assassin pushed the heel of his hand into Avon's injured shoulder, and in spite of his determination, the duke reacted to the pain, losing his hold enough for the man to pull his neck from the grasping fingers. Avon hit him then, his left knee brought up hard into the gut, and heard with satisfaction the grunt of air leave the man's lungs. The assassin clung suddenly, able for a moment only to hold Avon's arms at his side and away from his own heaving body.

As they grappled, both men became aware at the same instant of running footsteps and voices raised in questioning response to the sound of the gunfire. Recognizing that he was only seconds away from capture, the assassin desperately drove his own knee hard into the duke's right hip, a procedure he hoped would cause enough pain that he could escape. He felt with gratification the sudden loosening of those muscles he had never expected to be so well developed. He almost laughed at the whistling, agonized breath his opponent drew and, as Avon fought to remain conscious against the darkness that gathered over his senses, the murderer used the opportunity he had created to break away and run for the woods along the river's bank, to the point where he had tied up the skiff.

He hoped the servants would be too concerned with their master's wound to give more than a halfhearted chase, and if he were very lucky, the single bullet might be enough to bring down his enemy after all. If not, he could always try again.

For I have the advantage this time, your grace, he thought as the skiff glided quietly into the darkness of the middle of the river, leaving behind the shouts and demanding voices of Avon's servants. "I know who you are and you don't know me. I can take you at any time. At any time I choose."

Moss was the first to reach the clearing, where he found Avon struggling to raise his body from where he had fallen. The valet caught the swaying figure, the rejected Manton primed and held ready in his hand. His only concern was for his master, whose heavy weight leaned gratefully into the valet's solid chest. But because he knew so well the man whose injured body he held, he gave the necessary orders to those who followed.

"Toward the river," he shouted, thrusting the pistol into the hands of the coachman. "Stop him however you can. Kill him if you must, but don't let him get away. He probably has the dispatches."

Moss felt Avon's body jerk and then straighten at those words, and saw the effort he made to hold himself upright. Avon had clamped his right hand over his left shoulder, and dark blood welled through his fingers. The duke's lips tightened against the pain as he moved his hand to grip Moss's shoulder. He had somehow lost the sword cane in the battle with the assailant, and before he could stop to find it, he had to know if his valet was right. With his help, Avon moved awkwardly to the courier's body, knelt down and turned it so that the glazed eyes of the corpse stared unseeing up into the moonlight. Moss's prophesy proved to be correct. There was no pouch, no papers.

"Damn him to hell. The bloody damned turncoat. That traitorous bastard." Avon's voice was harsh in the darkness, the profanities heartfelt. "There's no way he could have known the importance of this information. No one but General Burke and I knew what that pouch contained."

"Perhaps the papers weren't his primary target," Moss suggested carefully. "I think he wanted you, your grace, and somehow he knew where you'd be."

He helped his master rise and watched his face in the dimness, and when the gray eyes closed and the tall form swayed again, it was Moss's arm that supported him.

"Let's get you home so I can look to this shoulder. I don't like the way it's bleeding."

"Tie it up," Avon ordered. "And tie it tight enough to stop the damn blood. I have a call to make, Moss. One that can't wait."

"Your grace, you can barely stand. You're in no condition—"

"Pad it and tie it, Moss. Nothing's broken. I can move the arm. It's all right. But I have something to do before we go home. By God, someone's going to pay for tonight's work. Someone is going to pay for the leak our network has suddenly sprung after all these years, and I have a good idea where to start."

"Your grace—" Moss began, and was cut off.

"Bind the damn arm," Avon said slowly and deliberately, in a tone the servant knew better than to argue against. "You may come with me or stay here. I really don't give a damn which you choose, but I have a call to make and I intend to do it tonight."

"You're going to be making a call on the undertaker if you aren't careful," Moss muttered, but he knew better than anyone the uselessness of trying to change this man's mind when it was set. And so, instead, he found the cane where it had fallen and placed it in his master's hand and saw him lean gratefully against its support.

He folded the duke's handkerchief and pressed the pad tightly against the hole that continued to well blood darkly in spite of the time that had elapsed. He tied his own cravat tightly around the shoulder and then tried to use the ends to fashion a rough sling to support the weight of the arm.

"No," Avon said bitterly, "no sling. Judging by events so far tonight, I may need this arm. And I don't want to attract attention to the fact that I've allowed that bastard to put a ball in me."

Because he knew what was expected, Moss draped the cloak loosely over the left side of the duke's form and stepped back to survey his handiwork.

"You'll do," he said gruffly as he watched the damaged body straighten under his scrutiny. "You'll do, unless you're planning on dancing at Almack's or visiting Carlton House," he said sarcastically.

"A rout," Avon said, and smiled at the disbelief in the eyes of the man who watched him with concern, in spite of his attempt at ridicule. "I don't believe I was invited, but I think I shall attend. As you know, I was never one to abide by the social niceties."

The duke began the short but painful journey to the waiting carriage, while Moss stood in shock over the body of the dead courier. Avon finally turned and smiled at him again, with a smile that had frightened braver men than the valet knew himself to be.

"Are you coming, Moss?" he said gently. "We're very late. I would imagine the dancing has already begun." The tall form moved through the dim light of the clearing and into the shadows of the woods, and Moss finally closed his mouth and hurried to follow.

Chapter Two

Lady Harland suddenly realized that her father had, quite literally, disappeared. Since their town house was full of members of London society who had come to welcome back and honor the very man who had now gone missing, Emily was becoming concerned.

General Sir William Burke had recently been knighted by a grateful government for his services to king and country during the Peninsular Campaign, and although the town was supposedly almost empty for the summer of those who composed the world of the ton, she had been gratified to find the rout she had planned a decided crush. She had complimented him earlier as they had together welcomed their guests.

"They've come to honor you, sir. The hero of the hour," she'd said with a smile as she kissed his cheek.

"Bosh," had been his gruff answer. "They're here for free food and the latest gossip, to see and be seen. You and I, at least, have no illusions about the motives of this mob."

And indeed, he was right. After the five years she had spent with Wellington's forces, Emily found that she no longer cared a snap of her slim, elegant fingers for the opinions of the elite. Ironically, or perhaps because she no longer cared, she was now one of the toasts of the very crowd who had so humiliated her in her first season.

She had been too tall and thin, her hair titian and not the blond that had been de rigueur that season. And having been raised by three older brothers and a father in a world of military derring-do, she had had none of the gifts these people deemed important.

Used to the easy cameraderie of the young friends of her brothers, she had not known what to make of the lazy, drawling fops with their quizzing glasses, their watch fobs and their impossibly high starched collars. And their conversation might as well have been in Greek. It had seemed to her an endless stream of gossip and meaningless drivel.

She had not changed, but the ton had apparently decided she was an original and now, years after it had ceased to matter a fig to her, they admired her intelligence, her candor, her unusual coloring and her decision to wear colors and styles that best complemented her tall, slim body, rather than those slavishly copied from *La Belle Assemblée*.

Life and death mattered to Lady Harland. Her family and friends mattered, but certainly not what some dandy in knee breeches, sporting a ring on every perfumed finger, might think. As for the hostesses and patronesses who dictated the rules of the ton, she would have been more impressed if she thought they could bandage a wound with skill and compassion, ford a river in full flood on horseback, make stew for ten from a half-starved rabbit or shoot a French marauder who threatened the baggage train. Those were skills Emily admired, but the thought of the probable reactions of these pampered darlings to any of those situations brought a genuine smile to her lovely oval face.

The sight of that smile caused more than one masculine heart in the salon to beat a little irregularly. Not only was Lady Emily Harland more beautiful than any woman had a right to be, she was also, they had found, not easily flattered or influenced. In short, she was a lady of mystery, rumored to be devoted to her invalid brother, and not very interested in a flirtation at all. The widow was not, unhappily, merry or willful. She had proven to be elusive and far too clear-eyed when it came to spotting the genuine, and especially the less-than-sterling, characters among them.

But since hope does spring eternal, Emily's smile was enough to cause at least three gallants to beg the pleasure of the next set. However, they certainly could not tell her what she wished to know, so she laughingly excused herself with the plea of duties to attend to and set off to find Ashton, her father's butler. He had run this household since her grandfather's day, and he was the one man who knew everything that occurred in the house, which he quite properly considered his domain.

When she found him, he was supervising the opening of another case of wine, but he turned to her immediately, prepared to handle whatever emergency had sent his charming mistress to the kitchens in the middle of her carefully planned party.

"Ashton, my father seems to have disappeared. Although I don't really blame him..." Emily saw the impact her statement made in the way his hand trembled as he dabbed at the perspiration dotting his forehead.

"Oh, my lady, he's with that man. I didn't want to do what he asked, but I swear, the state he was in, I didn't dare refuse." The butler's voice trembled in his agitation.

"My father with what man?" she asked in bewilderment. "What has happened to distress him?"

"Oh, no, my lady. It was him that was in a state. Avon," the old servant answered, as if the name explained the entire situation.

"Avon? But I don't understand. There was no Avon on the guest list."

"The Duke of Avon," the butler insisted. "He came in the back entrance. I swear he had murder in those eyes. I've never seen a man in such a rage. Never raised his voice, but ready to kill someone. And pale as death. It fair took my breath, it did. I told him we were entertaining, but he said to tell the general to come to the library or, by God, he'd go get him himself. I didn't know what else to do, so I took your father to him." The old man shook his head. "I should have come to you, my lady. I knew it the minute I walked away. You don't suppose he means to harm your father, do you? They say he's cold-bloodedly killed his man at dueling any number of times, but until tonight I wasn't sure of the truth of those tales."

Almost before the old man was through with his impassioned explanation, Emily was hurrying down the servants' hallway that would lead her to the rear of the structure and to the back of the library. This was far faster than to fight her way through the throng that still danced in the front of the house.

The logical conclusion that the visitor's entering at the back might have been occasioned by a desire to avoid the curiosity of the ton or to have this late-night meeting with her father unknown, rather than by any plan to harm her father, flashed through her head. But the old man had seen the anger and she had not. All she could do was trust his instincts that this guest had indeed intended violence.

Emily halted outside the heavy doors. The general might never forgive her if she interrupted a confidential meeting. She knew that his new job dealt, to some degree, with the covert operations that had become a part of the war effort. Was it possible that the man Ashton had brought here was from Whitehall, officially sanctioned to demand her father's attendance even in the middle of a rout held in his honor?

She pressed her ear against the heavy oak. She could hear the murmur of masculine voices, but no sounds to suggest violence of any kind. There was really only one way to find out, and lifting the skirt of her emerald silk gown, Emily turned the handle and walked into the room.

A deep voice that was definitely not her father's was saying, "...Only since you've come. I hold you personally responsible for his death and I warn you—"

The speaker became aware of her presence and the threat was cut off immediately. The eyes of both men turned to Emily. In her concern, she first sought the figure of her father and was relieved to see that he looked perfectly at ease, leaning against the mantel of the huge fireplace with a glass of brandy in his hand.

Comforted by his apparent well-being, she turned to the other occupant of the room, who was seated in one of the tall wing chairs flanking the hearth.

She encountered a pair of cold gray eyes, the pale irises rimmed with charcoal, and for the first time believed that the butler's agitation might be well-founded. Her startled senses gradually began to recover from the shock of their icy displeasure and to register the rest of the visitor's features.

If one desired a model for the face of Lucifer, that so charismatic and tragically fallen angel, one need look no further. It was breathtaking in its classic beauty. The eyes themselves were surrounded by a sweep of long, black lashes that had now fallen to veil his expression. The forehead was high and broad. The lips and nose were as beautifully chiseled as a da Vinci statue. And yet the face wasn't unmarred: the lines there were not of age, but of pain or grief, for Emily had encountered both of those often enough not to mistake them.

The light from the single branch of candles on the table beside his chair glinted in his hair as if it were still damp from the night mist. The only relief from its blue-blackness was the sliver of silver that swept back from each temple. He was dressed completely in black and the cloak he had not bothered to remove covered his left side. His long-fingered right hand was adorned by a single, crested ring, and the paleness of his skin contrasted sharply with the unrelieved black he wore.

The visitor's eyes moved to his host, as if waiting for him to handle the unexpected and awkward arrival of his daughter. Knowing Emily as he did, the general acknowledged the necessity of treating this meeting as an ordinary social occasion, which of course necessitated an introduction—one that he would certainly rather not make.

"Your grace, may I introduce my daughter, Lady Harland. Emily, my dear, I'd like you to meet an old friend, the Duke of Avon."

Since Emily had never heard her father mention this friend, and, indeed, had never even heard the title before tonight, she didn't doubt that her usually truthful father was creating this old friendship out of whole cloth. Nevertheless, she curtsied gracefully, and holding out one slim hand, greeted him easily in her low, musical voice.

"I am delighted to welcome so old a friend of my father's to our home. I hope you'll feel free to call more frequently in the future, your grace, so that I, too, may name you friend."

The duke neither rose nor acknowledged her outstretched hand, leaving Emily in the awkward position of having to withdraw it rather hurriedly.

"Madam." He nodded coldly, raking her tall figure with

those silver eyes. Emily saw quite clearly the brief flaring of nostrils of his aristocratically elegant nose.

Stung by his rejection, she rode rein on her temper and smiled charmingly at him. Although the same smile had worked wonders with the men in the ballroom this very evening, it had no effect on this man. If possible, the gray eyes became a degree or two colder, and his obvious impatience for her departure goaded Emily into doing something she had never intended. She smoothly turned and took the other wing chair, calmly arranged her skirt and then looked smilingly at the rather startled expression on her father's face.

"Now don't let me interrupt. Please carry on as if I weren't here," she said breathlessly.

God, she thought with disgust, I sound like an idiot.

Aloud, she managed to ask, in what she hoped was the realistic simper of a girl who would have no more sense than to interrupt what was obviously a very private conversation, "Were you discussing what seems to have been the major topic of conversation tonight, the scandal concerning the Earl of Kent and his lovely young bride or—" and here she turned her green eyes fully on the visitor, giving him the opportunity to establish his mission as being a legitimate intrusion on her father's evening "—perhaps the latest news from the Continent?"

The general couldn't imagine what had gotten into his daughter, who was giving a very passable imitation of being a fool, which he certainly knew she was not. Nor could he decide how best to answer her question. He couldn't fathom Emily's believing he and Avon were discussing anything of a trivial nature. The caliber of the man who was seated opposite her was so obvious to the general that he thought he might as well try to explain why he had introduced a cobra into his parlor or brought a leopard into church. He could think of no lie Emily would believe that would explain Avon's midnight visit to his library.

While her father sought a way out of his dilemma, Avon quickly decided that the general was losing control of the situation and so, using what he knew about Lady Emily Harland, he decided to get rid of the redhead as quickly as possible. He considered the fact that she had followed the drum for years and that she had lost not only a husband, but also two brothers with the forces in Spain. He wagered mentally that he could have her out of the library in a matter of minutes, and by her own choice.

He knew now that Moss had been correct, and that his presence here had been a mistake, precipitated by his losing his infamous temper for the first time in several years. He recognized his increasing need to be gone, and he certainly did not intend Emily to be around to witness his departure.

Assuming the guise of a London fop, a role he had played before, he answered her question himself.

"I assure you we weren't discussing anything now going on in Europe. Since Wellesley and his crew made perfect cakes of themselves by allowing the French to chase them all over the Peninsula, I've determined to concern myself with nothing coming out of Europe except possibly a fine old brandy," Avon drawled in a smooth baritone, its tone exactly matching the lazy inflections of the blades whom Emily had earlier overheard regretting the increasing difficulty in acquiring Belgian lace for their cravats.

"'Making cakes of themselves'?" Emily echoed, with only a hint of the ridicule she wished to express allowed to creep into her voice. "As they did at Salamanca and at Vitoria recently, I suppose?"

She smiled again into the gray eyes and waited for him to negate Wellington's last stunning victory.

Avon flicked an imaginary speck of dirt from his knee

and wished he had a lorgnette. "Oh, one must allow he brings off the occasional triumph. But the cost, my dear, the cost."

"The men who died in those battles were well aware of the importance of their sacrifice, your grace," Emily said quietly, thinking of her brothers, "and more than willing to make it."

"Lives were lost, of course. The ultimate price of any victory, you know," the duke drawled, as if that were an argument not worthy of consideration. "No, I was speaking of the costs here at home, the sacrifices those of us here have been forced to make through the years. The things we have given up, my dear, you can't imagine."

At this point he held his brandy up to the candlelight, as if evaluating its age and quality by the golden color. "Now if you or your father knows a reliable smuggler who might be willing to bring in a cargo from the Continent for the right price—"

"I assure you that my father and I know no smugglers, sir, and that particular French brandy you're enjoying was put down in my grandfather's day, long before the naval blockade was begun," Emily ground out, holding on to her temper with a rare effort. How dare he complain about the inconveniences of the blockade or imply that her father would sanction its avoidance?

"I just don't understand why everyone gets so upset by Napoleon's posturing. All this military running around interferes with a civilized existence." The duke's voice had taken on a plaintive quality that Emily found especially grating.

"Compared to conditions in Spain and, indeed, on much of the Continent, sir, your existence seems to be remarkably civilized," she commented, slanting a look at the shadowed face.

She was surprised to catch an unholy gleam, much like that in Devon's eyes when he used to tease her unmercifully—just to see the "fireworks," as he had called her ready temper. Although the amusement had been quickly hidden by those ridiculously long lashes, the eyes were certainly several degrees warmer than they had been when she first entered the room, and he seemed almost to be enjoying himself.

Realizing that his relish in his own performance had nearly given him away, Avon designed his next statement to drive any logical thought process from the young woman's head.

Indeed, Emily felt her temperature rise as he turned to her father and said with what was very definitely a whine, "I really never understood all that save-the-world business you military types persist in spouting. After all, Napoleon wasn't bothering us. Give him the Continent and let's get back to the way things used to be. It seems eventually even you glory hounds should get tired of all the fighting. Of course, all that business never interested me." Here the duke lifted his right hand gracefully to cover a yawn.

Emily watched the gesture with the same fascination she would afford a snail crawling through a bouquet of roses.

"No, I'm certain," she said, finally allowing the disgust she felt to fully color her voice, "that your grace would have no interest in combat at all."

He smiled charmingly at her and then lazily allowed his eyes to focus again on her father. "Very fatiguing, I'm sure. And far too dirty and dangerous to be appealing. I really don't understand how you've managed to stick it all these years."

The general was at a complete loss. He was in a room with two people he thought he knew well, and they both seemed to have run mad. Neither had acted in any way that might remotely be considered normal.

Emily, however, found her tongue ready to answer not only this man, but all the slights on the military effort that she had so far managed to ignore in London.

"How can you question the necessity for Napoleon's defeat? Don't you realize that Wellesley and that crew, as you call them, are all that stand between your so-called civilized existence and the sort of horrors that occurred in France?" She paused briefly to catch her breath, so that she could renew the attack on this—this *thing* who dared sit in judgment on men like her father.

"And as for the inconveniences imposed on your life by the blockade, have you never realized that those ships are all that have allowed you to sleep soundly for the last ten years, without fear of invasion?"

"Invasion," scoffed Avon, waving a wrist in her direction. "An old threat, I think. Merely an excuse now to keep all those naval chaps gainfully employed."

For Emily it was the final straw. "I'm sick to death of hearing you cowards mock and degrade men whose boots you aren't worthy to lick. Perhaps you should join a front-line regiment or one of the blockaders for just one week, and then you'd appreciate the price that men like my brothers have paid for your useless existence."

At some point in her tirade Emily had risen to stand in front of her hated opponent. Luckily, he made no reply. Indeed, he had the grace not to meet her blazing eyes. Even in her rage, she knew that she couldn't strike a guest in her home. There seemed nothing left to do, and no one prevented her hurried departure from the library.

As the door closed behind her, silence fell on the two men who remained. Avon was the first to speak, and his voice held none of the plaintive quality that had so irritated

Emily. It was instead utterly deadly. "You have a problem, and if you don't handle it soon, I shall be forced to."

The general's only reply was to drain his brandy, as if he had a real need of the fortifying liquid.

Chapter Three

Emily left the library and crossed the back foyer. She hurried up the three shallow steps that led through a French door and out into the rear garden. The coolness of the night air soothed her heated face and she breathed deeply, trying to restore calmness in place of her rage.

The voices of her guests were a low murmur, and an occasional burst of laughter drifted to her, as did the soft strains of music. She glanced toward the window of her brother's darkened bedroom and hoped that the sounds wouldn't disturb him.

As soon as he had realized the extent of Devon's wounds, the general had decided to leave the field and had requested a position at Whitehall in hopes that the London doctors could save his youngest and only remaining son. So far the sacrifice had appeared to have been more than worthwhile. Devon no longer hovered near death. His strength grew every day, but the scrap of shrapnel that had lodged near his spine resisted all efforts to remove it. As a result he was confined to a wheeled chair and looked to be a permanent invalid. The contrast between his quiet gallantry and the self-centered indifference of that creature in her father's study almost refueled Emily's fury, but she knew she mustn't allow herself to dwell on the contempt she felt for him and his kind.

In spite of the fact that she had been absent from her guests for only a short time, she must calm herself and return now, while she could still easily explain her absence with the excuse of some domestic crisis. She turned resolutely back, but as she entered the house and stepped down towards the foyer, the handle of the library door began to turn. Knowing she couldn't face her father's visitor again and maintain her composure, she opted for the better part of valor and turned from the steps, slipping quickly behind one of the urns that, with their huge flower arrangements, flanked the library's double doors. She watched the edge of the duke's cloak move past her hiding place and could only pray that he had not seen her.

As Avon crossed the short space of the back foyer, the silver-headed cane, which Emily had not noticed leaning against the wing chair, now performed its accustomed duty, and what had not been revealed in her first encounter with him was now painfully obvious. He leaned heavily on the cane and his right leg dragged awkwardly. His uneven gait was as ungainly as his face was beautiful, and the contrast distressed Emily as she watched his limping progress toward the steps.

As always, the suffering of others touched her deeply. She watched the play of muscles in those broad shoulders, necessitated by his use of the stick, and recalled the accusations she had shouted at this man such a short time ago. No wonder he avoided the discussion of military matters. Even his rudeness in not rising at her father's introduction was explained. All her reasons for disliking the Duke of Avon were swept away in the simple explanation of his disability.

He paused at the foot of the shallow steps, as if preparing

to climb some impossibly high mountain, and then, tightening his grip on the heavy cane and placing his left hand on the banister, he began to pull himself up. Each level seemed such a struggle that Emily was paralyzed by what she was sure he wanted no one to witness. She stood, not breathing, but mentally making the painful effort with him.

When he finally reached the top, he leaned back gratefully against the French doors. The cost of his success was obvious in the pallor of his face, in the set lips and closed eyes.

Emily would never know if she involuntarily made some sound or movement that revealed her presence, but suddenly those ice gray eyes were open and looking down into her staring green ones.

"Shall we add eavesdropping and spying to your many talents?" the duke asked bitingly, in a voice far different from the one he had used before. "Tell me, do you submit all of your father's guests to this, or am I being singled out for special attention?"

She recognized his anger and instinctively knew it was because she had seen his vulnerability, had seen the man behind whatever role he had played in the library.

"I wasn't spying, I assure you, your grace. I went into the garden to recover my poise and when I came in, you were leaving. Feeling that I had already sufficiently made a fool of myself, I simply sought to avoid another encounter with you," Emily was forced to explain, with only her pride holding her eyes on the face above her.

"For shame, madam," Avon taunted. "After all your brave talk of cowards, you hid from the enemy. What would those gallant heroes you so ably defended tonight think of you now?"

Two spots of color appeared on Emily's high cheekbones.

Otherwise her face was as pale as the face of the man looking down on her.

She had called him a coward, had accused him of allowing others to fight and die to maintain his way of life. Since it was now obvious that the simplest activities engaged in by every young blade of the ton—fencing, boxing, dancing, perhaps even riding—were forever denied this man, it seemed an unspeakable cruelty to chide him for his lack of participation or even interest in combat.

When she remembered Devon's hatred of his own restrictions, she bitterly regretted the accusations she had hurled at the duke. Her first instinct was simply to turn and flee again, but Emily knew that because she had allowed her ready temper to control her tongue, she must now make amends.

"I must apologize for what I said earlier—"

"Really?" he interrupted, one dark brow slanting upward in disbelief. "I'm amazed. And I had thought you quite enjoyed what you said earlier. What parts do you wish to retract? An admission that surely by now Napoleon has given up any notion of invasion?" he asked sarcastically.

Since Emily had known very well that particular danger had long since passed, she felt as foolish as he could have wished when he pointed out the flaw in her argument.

"I do realize it, your grace. I know the fleet is now simply countering the French blockade—"

"Which, even at its height, was highly ineffective," he said. "About the only thing it successfully kept out was legal French brandy. It certainly hasn't hindered the illegal from entering the country. Half the peerage is drinking the stuff and pretending it was 'put down in grandfather's day.' Your father has a lot of company."

Emily's temper had already begun to flare at his continued insults of her father, and at the same mockery of the war effort she had heard out of the mouths of countless Londoners in these last months. She might have launched another unthinking attack like that in the library had she not noticed the careful shifting of weight off his right leg, even as he baited her. He leaned back gracefully, his broad shoulders resting against the door as if relaxing for an enjoyable interlude, but she knew now, having watched that struggle on the stairs, that he was deliberately distracting her attention.

"I'm sorry, your grace, but I won't be baited again. I apologize for losing my temper with a guest. And I'm sorry for my suggestion about your joining a military unit. I didn't realize then that you are..." Here her voice faltered, for there was no graceful euphemism for what she had seen. At a loss, she simply stopped.

There was a flash of something in his eyes, and then they dropped to the heavy stick he gripped. "This?" He laughed suddenly, showing a flash of white, even teeth against that beautiful visage, and raised the cane easily in a brief salute. "Merely an affectation, my dear, so wipe the guilt off your face." There was an infinitesimal pause. "I find that I much preferred you spitting fire."

"An affectation?" Emily echoed, not understanding.

"Are you so provincial that you don't know that Byron has made limps all the mode? I find that if I limp, the ladies consider me tragic and irresistably romantic. If one is wise enough not to pursue a military career, which as your family has ample cause to know can be very dangerous, then one must do something to attract the attention of the ladies," he mocked. "You have only to consider the complete reversal of your feelings as you watched my pitifully affecting performance in climbing the stairs to realize how effective this is."

"Performance? Do you mean…are you saying that it was all an act?"

"Little girls who hide behind flower pots shouldn't be too indignant if what they spy isn't exactly what it seems."

"You knew I was there," Emily accused bitterly.

"Well, my dear, if you desire to blend in with the furnishings, that gown will clearly have to go. Far too flamboyant. But even so, we would still be left with the problem of your hair. Most distressing." He shook his head as his eyes dwelled on her gleaming copper curls, and then offered helpfully, "Tell me, have you ever considered—"

Emily was suddenly so angry she couldn't breathe. He had known she was there, had seen her dash for the urn and had taken his revenge. He had played on her ready and well-known sympathies with a fake limp and had pulled her in like the gasping fish she knew she resembled at this moment. She felt her fingers curl into claws, and she knew that if she moved, she would fly at him and scratch at his eyes like the fishwife he had twice reduced her to.

"How dare you!" she hissed. "You cowardly fop! I've known too many good and brave men maimed and crippled to watch you fake a limp to elicit sympathy. You don't deserve to breathe the same air as men like my brother. The thought of your being under the same roof with him sickens and disgusts me. If you don't get out immediately, I shall call a footman to remove you."

Avon's eyes glinted with genuine amusement under the quirk of his dark brow. "But surely," he began, and she could hear the laughter lurking in the deep voice, "surely you don't need help. I feel certain you could handle more than one—what was the phrase?—cowardly fop. And I promise I won't fight back. You may do with me as you wish. I am entirely at your mercy."

Even Emily was aware of the sexual implication in the

last of his speech, and his laughing eyes only reinforced what she knew he was suggesting. She stalked to the bottom of the steps and allowed her voice to reveal all the contempt she felt for his entire performance.

"Get out of this house before I have you thrown out bodily. And be very sure, your grace, that I shall do it. You're right in that I could probably manage it myself, but I would hate to waste my efforts on such an unworthy opponent."

She wondered suddenly what she would do if he didn't leave. In spite of her threats, one did not throw a duke of the realm out the door, no matter what the provocation.

But Avon merely laughed and sketched her another salute with the cane. Turning, he opened the door with his left hand and limped out. The awkwardness of his movements seemed even more obvious than before.

I wish to God I had something to throw at you, Emily thought. She turned back toward the library, and by the faint music was once again made aware of her responsibilities to her guests. Unmindful of her gown, she dropped to sit on the bottom step. For a moment she buried her face in her hands and fought to control her emotions. She was exhausted, wrung out with her anger and with her bitterness over the fact that he had so completely made a fool of her. Yet she must now return and continue to smile and talk for hours.

She raised her head with resolution, and from that level became aware for the first time of the crimson blotches marring the shining perfection of the white stair railing. It looked as if someone had bled on the banister. Emily slowly stood up and moved closer to examine the stains. They proved to be exactly what they had appeared—bright bloodstains, very red and very fresh. And the only possible person who could have left them there was the infuriating man who had just departed.

After the Duke of Avon closed the door that led out to General Burke's garden, he moved quietly along the back wall of the house. When he had gone as far as he was able, he leaned his head against the building to ease the ringing in his ears and to prepare himself for the journey to where his coach awaited. But even as he steeled himself for the last phase of what was becoming an increasingly difficult night's work, he felt a strong hand grasp and support his right elbow.

"Are we ready to go home now, your grace, and get the ball out of your arm, or do you have any more little side trips on your agenda? A call on the Regent? A leisurely visit to White's?" Had Avon not been so grateful to hear that particular voice whispering in his ear, he might have taken time to censure Moss's wit. As it was, he simply leaned against that strong support for a moment and then straightened.

"There is one small matter, Moss, that I believe you must attend to…"

"Christ!" said Moss, exasperated. "What now?"

"Well, if you'd only tied this thing tightly enough, it wouldn't have happened. As it is, I seem to be bleeding like a stuck pig. And I just bled all over the general's pristine white banister."

"Oh, God." The valet began to examine the cravat he'd tied over the wound, which was indeed seeping heavily. The sleeve of the duke's shirt was wet with blood, which by now was dripping rather frighteningly from his fingers. Moss tightened and retied the makeshift bandage, then took out a large white handkerchief and prepared to enter the back hall from which the duke had lately emerged.

"Watch yourself," Avon said with a laugh that turned into a gasp when he jarred his arm. "There's a red-haired virago in there who was almost ready to finish what our assassin started."

The fact that he could have been subjected to the injury and disappointment he had sustained tonight and still laugh was typical, and the valet recognized that in spite of what he had said about the woman, the duke had enjoyed whatever had passed between them.

"Just see you don't move. I don't want to have to crawl around this bloody dark garden looking for your body while you're bleeding to death 'cause you're too stubborn to do the sensible thing. Never heard of anybody going visiting with a hole in his arm." The valet's complaints faded as he crept to the back door and then peered inside.

The duke closed his eyes and leaned against the cool stones of the wall. Moss was back, it seemed, before he could have done the job Avon had given him.

"No need to trouble, your grace," Moss said grimly. "Your redhead took care of it. Right efficiently, too."

"Damn," said Avon feelingly. "Are you sure?"

"Of course, I'm sure. I watched her do it. However, if she interests you, I have to confess I can't say much for her housekeeping skills. She balled her bloody handkerchief up and stuffed it in a vase."

Here Moss revealed the gory object on his outstretched palm. The duke took the handkerchief in his right hand and then held it almost wrapped around the head of the cane.

"To be fair," Avon said with a laugh, "I suppose it would be difficult to explain a bloodstained cloth at a party. Let's just hope she can keep her mouth closed." He paused reflectively and went on with that same trace of humor, "Of course, from what I heard tonight, that is probably far too much to ask."

The two figures made slow, halting progress across the lawn to the waiting carriage. As he helped the duke into the vehicle, Moss could see the faint smile that still hovered around Avon's lips.

Well, let him enjoy whatever joke he's found. He'll have little enough to smile about if I have to dig to get that ball, he thought, wondering about the woman who had provided a few minutes of amusement for the duke. He deserves whatever enjoyment he can get, and that's the truth. Whatever he can get.

When they reached Avon's town house, they entered through the back, and Hawkins, the duke's trusted and efficient butler, helped without questions as they made the difficult climb to the duke's chamber.

"What happened?" he finally asked Moss as they eased their master onto his high bed and began to undress him.

The duke himself answered, although it was through clenched teeth. "The bastard was waiting for us. The courier was dead, stabbed in the back, and the dispatches missing." He took a long drink of the brandy Moss had handed him, and then another, welcoming the burning warmth. "God," he said with disgust, "he seems to have better information than I do."

"Well, that's certainly true now, since he's got the latest dispatches," said Moss calmly as he began to examine the wound. "You're just lucky he didn't kill you in the bargain."

"I moved. Something glinted on the ground—maybe his own knife. Whatever, it was enough to throw off his aim. I damn well wish I'd moved a little quicker." He gasped as Moss probed the wound.

"The ball's still in. Undercharged, I suppose. Or his powder got damp," Moss said laconically.

"You sound almost disappointed by his inefficiency," the duke said through gritted teeth.

"Well, if he'd been more careful with his equipment, the ball might have gone through, and then we wouldn't be looking at what's going to be a very painful few minutes for you, I'm afraid."

"Then more brandy, I think, Hawkins, if Moss is going to start digging through my shoulder. It hurts like hell as it is."

"Oh, I'll get it. Never you fear, your grace. But it ain't going to be so pleasant as if it'd just whizzed through on its own."

For the next few minutes there was no conversation at all, and the only sound in the room was the harsh breathing of the duke as Moss dug for the ball.

It was with gratitude that Avon finally heard his valet's triumphant, "Now then!" and the sound of the object landing in the small and priceless early Ming dish the butler held. Moss cleaned the hole with salted water for, as he explained to his fascinated audience, his father had walked horses with cut knees in the surf at Sandemer and they had healed up right and tight.

"If I am ever cut up in my forelegs, I shall remember that," said the duke with tight-lipped courtesy. "For now, however, I believe I've endured enough of your gentle ministrations. Bind it up."

When the wound was padded and bound, the two servants turned back to the ball that had been extracted. Together they examined the object with a blood-thirsty interest, until the duke interrupted their discussion in a cold voice. "If you could possibly analyze that elsewhere, I'd like to try to get some sleep."

"Of course, your grace," said Moss in his best imitation

of what he believed a gentleman's gentleman should sound like. "I'll get a nightshirt and be right back."

Avon closed his eyes, exhausted by the pain and loss of blood, and must have drifted, for it seemed only a second before he felt Moss carefully slipping the left sleeve over his hand and up his arm. When the valet reached for the duke's right arm, he found his hand folded into a fist. Glancing up, he saw that his master's eyes were still closed. He carefully uncurled the clenched fingers and discovered the bloodstained lady's handkerchief he had handed him earlier. He removed it and laid it on the counterpane. He finished putting the duke into the nightshirt and turned to put out the lamp.

"Moss," the man in the bed said quietly, "give it back."

The valet knew immediately what he wanted, and placed the handkerchief in his master's hand, watching the strong fingers close around it once again. Then he turned down the lamp and left the Duke of Avon alone in the darkened room.

Chapter Four

After spending a practically sleepless night, Emily was determined to escape the inevitable household uproar that was involved in cleaning up the remains of a party for over a hundred people. She also wanted to put off as long as possible the well-deserved lecture she was sure her father was anxious to administer. Not only had she interrupted a private meeting, she had been rude to his guest. She could only be glad that he had not been a witness to the second, more-disastrous meeting between the Duke of Avon and his daughter.

Her father had been tight-lipped and grim faced enough last night as they had finally said good-night to the last of their guests. He had not suggested a father-daughter session, and she had hurriedly left the salon as the servants began the preliminaries for the cleanup that would go on today. She had reached the harbor of her room and had tossed and turned through the remaining few hours of darkness, reliving each of her encounters with the man who had disturbed her emotions more in one night than any other had in her entire life.

She had found that as darkness gave way to dawn, she was no closer to a conclusion concerning her very mixed feelings about the Duke of Avon than she had been when she'd lain down. Was he the murderous villain Ashton had painted, the whining fop of the library or the cold and angry mocker on the stairs? And why had he come, bleeding and in pain, to interrupt her father's evening?

She donned her riding habit without ringing for her maid and sneaked down the back stairs and ordered her mare brought around. A boringly sedate ride in Hyde Park was not Emily's usual solution to problems, but since coming to London she had decided that if this were the best she could do, she would deprive neither herself nor her mare of the exercise. The gallop did seem to brighten her spirits, and she returned after less than an hour, determined to investigate the mystery of her father's ''friend,'' Avon.

The household was already stirring, and as Emily entered the breakfast room, she was delighted to see her brother at the table, enjoying a selection from the sideboard. She studied him briefly and was pleased to note that the too-thin face had better color today and that the shine was returning to his dark brown hair.

She had entered the room slapping her riding gloves against her palm in a fashion not in keeping with her hard-learned tranquility, and Devon inquired calmly, ''And did the horse survive?''

''Survive what?'' she asked in surprise.

''Whatever managed to overset your equilibrium this morning?''

She bent to place a kiss on his cheek, gripping his shoulder. Devon's hand came up to cover hers and he squeezed it slightly. She and Devon had always been close, and the tragedies they had weathered together had created an unspoken bond.

''You know I'd never abuse good horseflesh, whatever the provocation,'' she retorted with a laugh, helping herself to a breakfast she found she was surprisingly hungry for—surprising until she remembered how little she had eaten the day before. As she sat across the table from her brother, she looked up to catch him watching her with his head cocked to the side and a speculative gleam in his dark blue eyes.

"Obviously you feel there's been provocation. Don't tell me someone dared to snub the reigning belle of the ball last night. I won't believe it after the glowing reports of my little sister's unqualified success at storming the ton."

"Of course not. They wouldn't dare." She answered, laughing. "I'm far too much the latest celebrity."

She played with a bit of toast and decided that Dev might be the very one to confide in. He would never betray her interest, and he had a wider acquaintance in the world of the ton than she.

She looked up to find his shrewd eyes still watching the play of color in her lovely face.

"Do you know the Duke of Avon?" she asked casually.

His reaction was all that she might have hoped for. He banged his cup into its saucer, unmindful of the hot tea that spilled over onto his hand. "Where the hell did you meet Avon?" he asked in amazement.

"In the library last night. Father introduced us," she answered, demurely sipping her own tea. She purposely left out the details of that introduction and her unwanted interruption of their meeting.

"Bloody hell!" Devon said again. "I don't believe it. Father wouldn't let Avon run tame in the library with you around."

"Why are you so surprised?" She watched him shake his head in disbelief. "Obviously there are elements of the gentleman's character that Father failed to warn me of. Would you like to play big brother and tell me just what Avon has done to provoke that reaction? I'm not of such tender years that I can't be introduced to a rake...." Here Emily's lovely, carefully shaped brows rose in question, but all Devon seemed capable of was shaking his head. "A libertine? A murderer?" she went on. "Well, what, then? A traitor? Oh, Devon, surely not that!"

At the sound of the terror in his sister's voice, Devon knew that it was too late. The damnable, beautiful face that had attracted so many through the years had moved Emily. He could not believe that his usually logical sister had been caught in that flame like a doomed moth. He pushed the wheels of his chair backwards and half turned.

"You stay away from him, Emily. He's not for you. He's not for anyone whose emotions are as easily touched as yours. He'll break your heart and never look back."

Emily was aghast at the outburst. Since his injury, Devon had guarded his inner feelings with lighthearted gallantry. The distress obvious now in his posture was so foreign to the usual picture he presented that Emily rushed to his side and, dropping to her knees beside his chair, took both his hands in hers.

"Dev, I promise you my heart's untouched. But he's such an unusual man and I really couldn't imagine what he was doing here in father's library last night. Why would the thought of my meeting him distress you so?"

And smiling at the brother she loved so well, she wheedled, "If you want me to forget Avon, you'd better tell me all you know. Remove the mystery, Dev. You know it's by far the best way to handle me."

Her laughing challenge, in which he recognized a very accurate assessment of her character, drew an answering smile. "You're right, of course, and I overreacted. But Avon's dangerous, and you've had enough to bear in the last few years. For a moment the thought of his particular kind of poison touching you unnerved me." He paused and then said, "As a matter of fact, I knew him quite well, from school, and in spite of my reaction just now, I always liked him. Dominic Maitland," he said reflectively, "who is now the Duke of Avon."

The story Devon unfolded began years before, when he had been sent to the same preparatory school his older brothers had attended.

"Dominic had been there for several years, although of all the schools his father might have chosen, with its emphasis on military training, it was the least suited for someone like him." Devon paused as if to think how to make her feel something she had never experienced.

"Dominic wasn't really part of that controlled little world. He was by far the richest and noblest born of any boy there. We all knew that at his father's death he would inherit one of the oldest titles and one of the largest fortunes in England. We also knew he had become his father's heir when his mother and two older brothers drowned in a boating accident. It was rumored that their deaths had driven the old duke to the point of insanity, and he had immediately sent his remaining son to the harshest, most restrictive school available." Devon shook his head at the travesty of that choice and then went on.

"Perhaps he sent his son away so that he could drink himself to death in privacy, a feat he accomplished in less than a decade. Whatever the old man's reasons, Dominic was there and would remain there for ten years. He never left, even when the school closed."

"But surely, even if his father didn't send for him, someone, even one of the other boys, took him home for Christmas, for end-of-term holidays?" Emily questioned. Remembering the joy in having her brothers home, she could not imagine the existence of the boy Devon was describing.

He shook his head. "I wish now, of course, that I had,

but at the time I couldn't imagine inviting him to my home. And I don't imagine anyone else had the nerve, either. His self-possession was daunting, even then. And I think he had rather deliberately alienated himself from the rest of us.''

''But why? If he had no one else…''

''By the time I arrived, Dominic had ceased to participate in classes and had embarked on a course of private study, guided by the more gifted of the teachers. He was admired, I suppose. Looked up to, certainly. And feared,'' Devon added quietly. ''Had he chosen, he could have become a leader, a major influence among the boys. He had the gifts.''

''But he didn't choose?'' Emily prompted softly.

''Only once, the time he chose to rescue me. Although that's not a word he would have used, that's exactly what he did.''

''What happened?'' Emily asked quietly. She had not realized that the story she had asked for would affect Devon so, but he smiled at her and continued.

''The recognized leader at the time was a boy…'' Here Devon paused, as if again searching for words that would make her understand. ''He was a bully, but a bully whose unusual cruelty marked him even in an environment where cruelty was too often considered an acceptable substitute for strength.''

Devon took a deep breath. ''I ran afoul of him from almost the first day. Will and Ben had paved the way. They were popular and reckless—you know what they were like. They had been older and apparently he had resented their popularity with the masters and the other boys. And then they went on to university. They were out of his reach, but I showed up, just as he was at the peak of his own powers. Clearly, he hated me. With the help of his followers, he began a campaign of harassment, of pranks, terror. Maybe he saw me as a threat. I'll never know his real motives. And it doesn't matter, but it was painful enough at the time.''

Emily saw his involuntarily shudder at the memories. He suddenly looked down and smiled at her, sitting like a child at his feet, and his blue eyes dismissed the ghosts he had created in this sunny room.

''And then Dominic took a hand. Maybe because he had known Will or Ben or had, at least, admired them. Or maybe he was just bored. I never asked. I was too grateful at the time to consider why he bothered.

''He fought my tormentors with his intellect and his tongue. He seemed to know instinctively each chink in their mental armor and he exploited them unmercifully. They were forced to endure the public exposure of their deepest fears, of their cowardice, of hidden depravities. Dominic was ruthless, and although I was more than relieved that the harassment had ceased, I was eventually sorry for some of the boys. No one needs his soul stripped bare in public.

''I tried to thank Avon, but, of course, he saw through me. 'You hate me now almost as much as you hated him,' he said. And at the time, I guess he was right. I couldn't condone what he had done, even if it had been on my behalf.''

''And now,'' Emily asked quietly, ''from the perspective of all these years?''

''I still don't know.'' Devon shook his head. ''He told me something then that I never forgot. I used it in Spain and I know he was right about this. He said that if one intends to win, one discovers his opponent's weakness and attacks there again and again until victory is assured. 'If your cause is worth winning, it's worth using whatever weapons the enemy offers you.' I did that time after time in the Peninsula and won engagements I had no right to win.

"I guess, though, I'm not a very apt pupil after all. In spite of the successes, there was always in the back of my mind the idea that there was something a little unworthy about a victory achieved in that way."

When at last his voice faded, she asked the question that had troubled her since the scene on the foyer steps. There had been something about Avon's final taunt that had not rung true.

"Did Avon use a cane when he was at school?"

Devon's startled eyes came back from his memories and he couldn't seem to focus on an answer to her question.

"Did Avon have a limp then, Dev?" she repeated, remembering the cruel contrast between the seeming perfection of the seated man and the struggle on the stairs.

"I thought you told me you met Avon," Devon said incredulously.

"I did, Dev, last night, but you haven't answered me."

Devon paused and looked down at his own legs and then into Emily's eyes. "We called him Cripplegate. Behind his back, of course. After Barrymore. But always behind his back. It was, I suppose, another reason for the distance between us all. He could never participate in the physical activities that occupied so much of the day for the rest of us. But no one dared to taunt Avon openly about that twisted leg. They said that's why the old duke sent him away. They said he couldn't bear to see that ancient and noble title given to a cripple."

The silence stretched between them at the brutal word, and Emily's eyes reflected the pain she felt for the boy who had been cruelly rejected so long ago.

"Oh, God, Em," Devon said with a laugh, "don't begin feeling sorry for Avon. I promise you he's more than capable of fighting his own battles. We may have called him Cripplegate, but no one ever got the better of that coldhearted bastard. He was the deadliest shot and still is, if only half the stories are true. He regularly beat us out of our allowances in any kind of card game, in spite of the fact that he must have needed the money less than any of us. And as for his leg, it has certainly not made him any less appealing to the fairer sex—both of the ton and their less-noble sisters.''

He hesitated and then decided this, too, was something she needed to know. "It was rumored that Stevenson's youngest daughter killed herself because he refused to marry her. It's a fact that he keeps a very beautiful and charming mistress. To his credit, he seems to have confined his amours to that class in the last few years. He was a prime target for the marriage mart for a decade, but he's virtually removed himself from society and even the most match-making mama has probably written him off as a dead loss. That appears to be one title that will die off with the current bearer and, knowing the man, it's probably just as well.''

For some reason Devon's cold assessment of Avon didn't have the effect he desired. At the most ridiculous moments Emily found herself thinking of those dark-lashed silver eyes and that incredibly beautiful face. He was, by far, the most exciting man she had met in London. Nothing Devon had said, not even the story of Charlotte Stevenson's death, could make her forget the man who had played with her like a cat with a mouse and then thrown in her face the emotions she had kindheartedly felt for his disability.

In the next few days her emotional balance teetered between anger at his manipulation of her feelings and something that she failed to recognize as sexual tension. She knew she was attracted to Avon, but in spite of the nine weeks she had been married to the Viscount Harland, she was virtually unawakened sexually.

Her marriage had been a result of the disastrous first season she had spent in London. Feeling constantly like a fish out of water, she had become more desperate by the day. She had danced the requisite number of dances and was always partnered in to dinner, but she was well aware that her brothers saw to that. In truth, the kindest thing that was said of her during that interminable season was that "she just didn't seem to take."

"And I won't ever take," Emily had raged at her family after a particularly humiliating musicale at which she seemed to be the butt of more than one snickered remark and the target of several uncomfortable silences. "I'm too tall and too different. No one will ever want to marry me."

When her father's answer had hinged on how much better he expected her to go on the next season, she'd had a sudden vision of herself left in London while they went haring off to Spain, where the partisans were offering the first solid native resistance to Napoleon's domination of the Continent. And so she had begged to go with them. Dozens of other ladies, highly respected wives of officers, followed their husbands in the train of the army. She couldn't understand why her father, who had seldom refused her anything, now balked.

"If you think I'm going to drag a gently reared young girl in the tail of an invading army—" his lecture had begun, only to be interrupted by the laughter of her brothers at the description of Emily, who had been raised on army postings from Ireland to India, as gently reared. He had ignored them and continued grimly "—you've another thought coming. And the difference in the wives you've mentioned is just that—they're wives, not unmarried girls. It's just not done." And beg as she would, he would not be budged.

As always, Emily had appealed in her need to her brothers

who, perhaps from habit as much as anything, set about giving Emily what she wanted. How they had persuaded Mark to offer for her, she never found out. If Emily wanted to come to Iberia and if his cooperation were needed to make it possible, he could see no reason to refuse. So the offer had been made and gratefully accepted by both Emily and her relieved father, who believed he might now, finally, have some peace.

The wedding had been small and quiet as befitting the imminent departure on military status of so many of the participants. Emily's honeymoon was equally brief, and she had endured Mark's unpracticed and rather brutal taking of her virginity as a small price to pay for her inclusion on an adventure she had had no intention of missing.

She had, therefore, no experience with men whose aloofness aroused a very different response. And she certainly had no armor to protect her against her fascination with Avon.

It was nearly a week after she had met him that a package appeared on the hall table with her name scrawled across the front. She didn't recognize the hand, nor was the crest with which the package was sealed familiar. But the contents certainly were. It contained the spotlessly laundered handkerchief, her initials embroidered in one corner, with which she had cleaned the blood from the stair railing. There was no note, but she was sure that if she traced the crest on the seal, it would be his.

She couldn't remember how she had disposed of the handkerchief that night, but she remembered looking down on the stained cloth and knowing that she couldn't take it back into the ballroom. How and when Avon had retrieved it were beyond her comprehension. That shouldn't surprise her, for nothing about the man since she had met him had been comprehensible.

Suddenly it seemed to her that he shouldn't have everything his way. Why should he be in control of the entire relationship, teasing her into anger just to get rid of her? For by now she had recognized that that was the meaning behind the mocking light in his eyes as he'd systematically attacked, that night in the library, all that she held dear of family, comrades and country. He had skillfully used her own weakness, her damnable temper, to get her out of that room. And before she could go all maudlin and apologetic later on for remarks he had goaded her into making, he had touched on her well-known devotion to her crippled brother by pretending his own disability to be faked, faked to arouse the very sympathy he so obviously never wanted.

Devon was right about one thing—he was a coldhearted bastard and he'd never again be pitied by her. He neither wanted it nor deserved it, but there was no sense in letting him have all the fun. And she wanted to see him again. Until she had met him, she hadn't realized how bored she had been. She supposed that like a soldier, she had become addicted to the excitement that danger brought, and Avon was certainly dangerous.

Ashton believed her trumped-up story of having a servant return the duke's gloves, which he had supposedly left that night. Although the butler had offered to handle the matter for her and the task should have fallen within his province, she assured him that it was all arranged with her father's man. When she left that afternoon for the lending library, Avon's address—which had been provided by Ashton—was carefully hidden in her glove.

Chapter Five

Blissfully unaware of what fate and Lady Harland had in store for him, the Duke of Avon was spending a boring afternoon going over his neglected personal affairs with his extremely able secretary. Avon had long ago been forced to acknowledge privately that his secretary didn't approve of him or his mode of living. Since Francis was more than capable of handling this business, the duke had already suggested that he simply do so. His suggestion had met with what he had come to call "the look," and he had resignedly turned himself to the affairs his secretary considered to be the most pressing.

It was the first full day Avon had spent out of bed since his multitalented valet had dug the ball out of his arm, and he was feeling less sanguine about his ability to remain up and dressed than he had when he had refused the suggestion that he was "pushing it." He was dressed in a fine white lawn shirt and a pale blue waistcoat. His fawn trousers topped gleaming boots, but he had agreed with Moss that they would never get one of Creed's coats over the bulky bandage that covered the wound. His left arm still rested in a black silk sling, but the loss of blood that had drained the color from his face was less noticeable. He'd looked remarkably like himself that morning, which was the only reason the valet had given in to his insistence on dressing.

He would have welcomed almost any interruption of what was becoming a most tedious exercise in tact except the one that unexpectedly and immediately stopped all activity in the library.

When Hawkins entered, Avon was aware of the air of careful dignity he carried about him like a cloak.

"What is it, Hawkins?" the duke asked gratefully. Perhaps escape was possible after all.

"I beg your grace's pardon," Hawkins began and then discreetly cleared his throat.

"Go on," Avon encouraged.

When the butler continued to hesitate, Avon finally brought his full attention to his servant's face, to become aware of the concern in the perfectly correct features. At the question in his master's eyes, Hawkins announced, sotto voce, "There's a young lady, your grace, who desires a private audience."

All three men were, of course, aware that no young lady might properly be admitted to a bachelor household, even in the middle of the afternoon. And especially not to this household.

Avon's mind quickly reviewed who among his female acquaintances might be gauche enough to believe he would welcome an afternoon call.

"Is she alone, Hawkins?" he questioned softly.

"I believe so, your grace," the straight-faced butler announced truthfully, but a tinge of red was creeping into his closely shaven cheeks.

"A lady, Hawkins?" the duke asked, suggesting his doubts with one dark, expressively raised eyebrow. He wondered why Hawkins had not simply gotten rid of her with his usual skill.

"Yes, your grace, most definitely a lady," Hawkins insisted. And he would certainly know.

"Did she give you her name, man?"

"Yes, your grace." Hawkins glanced at the secretary, hesitated, and then, at the look in the duke's suddenly cold eyes, continued, "A Lady Harland, your grace."

There was a moment of silence as the two listeners absorbed the information, each with a certain degree of shock.

Damn, the duke thought sincerely, but since he had questioned at the time his motives in returning her handkerchief, he supposed he was only reaping the inevitable results of what he had sown. He knew he had secretly hoped to provoke some response, but he hadn't dreamed of this.

"Francis, I'm afraid that we must again postpone the resolution of these matters," Avon said with what he hoped was the proper degree of regret in his voice.

"Of course, your grace," his secretary replied as he gathered up his scattered papers.

"I rely totally on your discretion," Avon reminded him, a definite touch of steel in the quiet command.

"Of course, your grace." By this time the papers were stacked and carefully tucked under Francis's arm.

"I'm sure that I don't deserve you, Francis," said that same soft voice.

"No, your grace, I'm sure you don't," was the parting comment as the secretary glided quietly out the door opposite the one the butler approached.

Avon laughed softly and found that in spite of the impropriety, he was looking forward to his visitor with an unaccustomed anticipation. He carefully removed the black silk from around his neck, placed it in the drawer of his desk and nodded. The butler turned to open the door to the hall.

"Lady Harland, your grace," Hawkins intoned as he ushered Emily into the duke's study.

Emily smiled at Hawkins as he took her cloak, and as the butler left the room, she briefly met the calm eyes of the man behind the huge desk. Feeling the quick lurch of her stomach, she stopped at the gilt mirror by the entry to allow herself time to control the sense of excitement that the beautiful dark face had aroused. She lifted her arms to remove the smart bonnet whose sarcenet ribbons exactly matched the russet of her low-cut walking gown.

Avon watched the thin fabric stretch across her high breasts as she smoothed her hair and wondered exactly what mischief she had in mind with this very improper afternoon call. She placed the bonnet and her gloves on the table under the mirror and moved to stand in front of Avon with the expanse of his highly polished desk between them. She did not, as she had done before, offer him her hand.

"Good afternoon, your grace." She smiled into the gray eyes that had haunted her last few days and nights.

Avon made no answer except to reach across the desk and capture her slim fingers in his strong right hand and bring them to his lips. She watched as he lowered his head, the afternoon light from the window behind him glinting off his midnight hair. Ignoring convention, he didn't halt his lips in the air above her hand, but gently kissed the smooth skin above the knuckles. She felt the flash of heat burn deep in her body and wondered if anyone had ever fainted on the duke's desk before.

When he turned her hand over, she was powerless to do anything but let it rest trustingly in his larger one. He looked up to watch her reaction as he now placed his lips on the sensitive skin of her inner wrist. Instead of kissing, he suckled the milk white, blue-veined area, and then she felt his teeth trail down the pad of her thumb. Her fingers had curled into her palm, and as she looked down into that beautiful face, her thumb involuntarily moved to caress the line that ran from his chiseled lips to his nose.

She wanted to smooth away the mark that she had recognized on their first meeting as one caused by pain or bitterness. She could see by the surprise in the gray eyes that her reaction was not one he had expected, and he slowly released her hand. She allowed it to fall to her side and sat down in the chair that his secretary had so recently vacated. She hoped he was unaware that her knees had been threatening to give way from the first moment he had touched her.

He studied her a moment, fully aware of the emotional havoc he had wrought, and then turned to the bell. When Hawkins answered the summons, the duke's eyes never left the slightly flushed face of his guest and he said, "Tea, Hawkins."

"Tea, your grace?" The question hovered in the air.

"Tea, Hawkins."

"Of course, your grace," the butler agreed, somehow relieved that his assessment of the visitor had apparently been correct, and moved quietly from the room.

Having ascertained that seduction was not the purpose of his guest's visit, although based on his knowledge of Lady Harland, he had doubted the possibility from the start, the duke now sat back to watch the unfolding of whatever plan she was about to put into motion. He was surprised to find himself intrigued and wondered that he was so bored with his present existence that the visit of an apparently inexperienced young widow could cause such anticipation.

He had felt a tightening in his groin when he'd held her hand and was honest enough to admit that he was attracted to her. He knew he had dispatched that handkerchief like a boy outside a sweet shop pounding on the glass to attract attention, and in doing so, he had broken his own rigid rules of self-conduct.

He had concluded several years ago that there were women enough who wanted the same things out of a relationship that he did. He didn't need an involvement that came trailing a doting father and brother, an excellent family name and too little experience with the games he played. The only things women like Lady Harland were suited for were marriage and babies, and neither of those had ever been part of his future. He doubted that she could be attracted to him anyway, after the impression he had made on her the night they had met. She probably envisioned him as a candidate for an invalid chair or for Bedlam.

Neither of them spoke. The duke had learned long ago that he obtained more information through his rather intimidating silences than by questioning. He simply sat totally at ease and watched the young woman in the chair before him. His contemplation had reduced strong men to terror, and he was again surprised that she seemed perfectly willing to return his look with a calm half smile on her lips.

Her hair was still streaked with the gold the Spanish sun had burned into it, so that it looked like burnished copper. He enjoyed studying the cool oval of her face with its high cheekbones and slightly tilted emerald eyes, but she seemed equally content to let her own eyes wander over the planes of his face, down the strong column of his throat and across his broad shoulders. He was aware by the widening of those eyes of the exact instant she perceived the thick bandage under the fine lawn, and then her eyes fell to the scrap of lace she held in her hands.

"I wanted to thank you for the return of my handkerchief," she said in her low, pleasant voice.

"In this instance it seems that the indebtedness weighs more heavily on my side of the scales." He watched her eyes come up to meet his. "I am particularly grateful because my valet assures me that those bloodstains were not the topic of conversation in any of the clubs about town. I appreciate your discretion."

"In that case, do I get an explanation?" she asked with a smile.

"No," he said, returning it.

She was intrigued at what the smile did to his face and knew instinctively that this was one expression that was not carefully thought out. He had simply answered her emotion, and she began to have hopes that the ogre her brother had tried to create in her mind didn't really exist.

Avon couldn't imagine why he had allowed himself to smile back at her. He knew that in doing so he had relinquished a fraction of his control of the situation and had encouraged her belief that whatever she had planned was going to come off.

Hawkins returned with a laden tea tray, which he set on the desk to Emily's right, assuming she would pour. He quietly left them alone again.

The ritual of tea preparation took several minutes. "Cream and sugar, your grace?" she questioned softly, and he became aware that he had watched the movement of her fingers over the items on the tray.

"Nothing, thank you," he said quietly and watched her pour her own cup.

Emily was not surprised when the duke refused tea and ignored the delicacies on the tray, but she was relieved at how fortified she felt as she began to sip hers.

Avon watched the movement of her long, slim throat as she drank and decided to visit the small, elegant house he maintained in Russell Square this evening, even in his less than perfectly fit condition. He had a mental vision of the bed in the Russell Square house, but the hair that he imagined spilling over the pillow in the lamplight was red-gold, not blond, and the long, elegant limbs he saw in his mind's eye intertwined with his own belonged to the woman who was calmly sipping her tea on the other side of his desk.

His irritation that his usually controlled body and even his disciplined mind persisted in betraying him drove him to his feet. Taking the cane that he had propped against the desk, he moved to the tall window behind him and looked out unseeingly on the traffic below.

The duke's abrupt movement startled Emily, and she again watched that uneven gait with a queer twisting in her chest. But for some reason the awkwardness was no longer so appalling to her, simply part of this man who continued to fascinate and titillate her.

Avon didn't look at her again until he heard the cup being replaced in her saucer, and then he turned and asked as bluntly as possible, "Why are you here? You must know what damage a visit to this house would do to your reputation."

"I'm not exactly a debutante whose behavior must be governed solely by a fear of gossip. But since I've kept your secret, neither did I expect my visit here to become the subject of conversation at your clubs. Or am I wrong about that?"

The gray eyes glittered dangerously at the question. "You know, I think, that I am no gossip," he said softly.

"And I also know that you are, or were, a friend of my brother's." She watched the memories move across the harsh planes of his face.

"How is Devon?" he asked finally.

"Confined to his bed or chair. In constant pain." She took a deep breath to control what she felt and then continued more strongly. "And the same as when you knew him. Determined that no one will ever know that he hates and

dreads every day of his existence. I wonder sometimes..."
She stopped that thought, because it was unbearable and
because she was betraying Devon's courageous facade to
this cold stranger. But the look in the gray eyes when she
again forced herself to meet them was anything but cold.
The long lashes quickly veiled whatever emotion she had
surprised there, and when he spoke again, his voice was
mocking.

"And of course, Devon knows that you're here," he
taunted and watched the betraying color move again under
the ivory skin. "Even someone who has spent the last several years removed from this society must know that a
young and attractive woman, even a widow, should not be
in my home."

"And why not?" she said softly. "Or are all the stories
true?" She watched the quickly controlled intake of breath,
and then he shook his head and turned back to the window
and the street below.

"Enough of them," he said simply, and she couldn't read
the emotion that laced the dark voice.

"Why are you here?" he asked again when the silence
stretched painfully between them.

"Because I want an explanation of your presence in my
father's library and of why you threatened him."

Avon realized suddenly that she must have listened at the
door and was amused because it was exactly what he would
have done.

"Why don't you ask your father for an explanation?" he
asked simply, and his question disturbed her more than anything he might have said. It implied that in some way it was
her father's place to explain, as if whatever wrong had been
done was to be laid at his door rather than at Avon's.

Emily's unease pushed her out of her chair. She came to

stand in front of him, where she suddenly realized she had wanted to be all along.

He watched her eyes trace his features.

The strong afternoon light from the window revealed evidence of his recent injury still clearly etched in his face. She knew that the faint flush across his cheekbones suggested the afternoon fever a convalescent usually suffered. She stood closely enough to feel the heat emanating from his body and to smell the mingled masculine scents of fine tobacco, the leather of his handmade boots, the starch from his cravat and the tang of the soap his valet had used to shave him that morning.

"Because I'm asking you, and if I don't get a satisfactory answer, I intend to go to the authorities," she said quietly.

Avon laughed suddenly and his eyes mocked her seriousness. "But, my dear," he said gently, "your father *is* the authority."

Emily swallowed convulsively at the obvious ridiculousness of her threat. Nothing had gone as she had planned and she realized that she had never had the least control over the situation. And she knew now that no one would ever make this man do anything other than what he wanted. He would answer none of her questions.

"Get it over," Avon commanded himself, watching the emotions move across her face. He knew, and had known almost from the beginning, her real reason for being here, although he doubted she was fully aware of her own motives. He had seen the same look in too many eyes through the years. He had recognized her attraction to him for what it was and knew he owed it to her father to destroy that attraction before his own interest in her could hurt her, hurt her even more than he knew he would today.

"I suggest, Lady Harland, that you remove yourself from this game. You are not a player and it is very possible that your interference may result in someone getting hurt. I also sincerely doubt that you want me to treat you as your unaccompanied visit here suggests that you desire.''

He watched the color rush into her cheeks as anger and then humiliation chased across her features.

''Your grace—'' she began, but he interrupted harshly.

''I don't know what you think you're playing at, but surely to God you're cleverer than this. You can cause nothing but harm. They may have let you play at soldiering in Spain, but not here, not now.''

If possible his voice became even colder, its mockery cutting her confidence to shreds. ''Go home, little girl, and choose new ribbons for all your bonnets or sew a fine seam or redecorate the morning room, but for your father's sake, stay out of his business.'' His voice softened dangerously. ''And for your own sake, stay out of mine.''

Emily looked as if she'd been slapped, and the need for his deliberate humiliation of her angered him as her interference in his affairs could never have done. He found he desperately wanted something to remember, something for himself, before he drove her away.

Suddenly he leaned his hip back against the window ledge and, using his cane, pulled Emily against him. He turned the stick so that it slanted across her waist and he caught the tip in his left hand. Emily was held prisoner between it and his broad chest. Then, locking his eyes on hers, he lowered the cane until it rested below her hips.

He lifted and Emily found her lower body pulled against his obviously growing arousal. He had moved so quickly that her arms were caught at her sides, and she found she was helpless as a child, with her body pressed tightly along the entire hard length of his.

He lowered his head and his tongue trailed slowly from the soft tendrils of hair at her temple to the shell of her ear.

He explored every ivory crevice, tracing the inner hollows until Emily forgot to breathe, to think, to do anything but feel the sensations that his probing tongue and his strong body were causing in her in response to his practiced lovemaking.

His tongue left her ear just as she thought she could stand no more. A lifting of the cane moved her body upward so that the hollow of her throat felt the demanding caress of his mouth. The air cooled the damp trail his tongue left on her skin, and as his lips finally found the deep cleavage between her breasts, Emily felt as if her lower body were a melting stream of slowing coiling honey. She knew he must feel her heart's pounding. His tongue ran teasingly along the low neckline of her gown and her lips lowered to move against the fragrance of his softly curling hair.

That unconscious response and the involuntary moan she made deep in her throat let him know that he had achieved his purpose. He lowered her body and stepped away from her so suddenly that she sagged and might have fallen had he not gripped her chin hard with his left hand.

"God, madam, did your husband teach you nothing of this?" he mocked, his voice rich with disgust. "Go home, little girl. And don't come near me again unless you're ready to complete what we started here today. I'm not interested in a flirtation. I outgrew that years ago. Go try your teasing on someone who plays by the rules. Those are something else I forgot a long time ago."

He released her chin and watched while tears of anger and humiliation swam into her emerald eyes and spilled over onto her cheeks. She rubbed at them with the heels of her hands like the child he had made her feel, and then suddenly she scrubbed at her throat and breasts with her palms, as if to remove all trace of his mouth on her skin.

"How dare you?" she demanded, her voice quivering with fury and shame.

"I dare because of the position you placed yourself in when you came to my home. Or am I wrong?" he jeered. "Perhaps you intend to tell your father about this visit. And of what just occurred between us. Or Devon, maybe? What do you suppose Devon will feel?"

They both were aware of the probable reaction of those two men, and especially cruel was the thought of Devon's frustration at his inability to protect his sister's reputation. Avon's lips quirked as he saw the realization of what her father would do reflected in her suddenly colorless face, and the remembrance of the duke's reputation with dueling pistols held Emily speechless, as he had know it would.

"Exactly," he said softly, his voice full of derision.

He reached behind her and rang the bell. He waited with his body between hers and the door, and when he heard Hawkins's entrance, he never looked at the butler, but kept his eyes locked on Emily's, which continued to spill tears that streaked the delicate powder on her cheeks.

"Lady Harland is leaving, Hawkins. Will you bring her cloak and arrange for her to be conveyed to her desired destination?"

"Of course, your grace."

When Hawkins had left, Avon gripped Emily's arm above the elbow and dragged her to the table under the tall mirror.

"Put it on," he said in that same emotionless voice he had just used to flay whatever pride she had left. She couldn't think what he wanted her to do and she stood like a beaten dog, shivering before him. Her trembling was almost his undoing and he steeled himself to finish what he had begun.

"By God, put it on or I'll do it for you." And he handed her the bonnet. He watched her hands begin to shake as she put it on and tied the ribbon beside her ear. As she did, she felt the hair at her temple, still damp from his mouth, and the tears started again. He watched her in the mirror and she could feel his eyes, but she never raised her own to meet them.

When Hawkins opened the door to bring her cloak, the duke limped to him and took it before the butler could enter the room. "Get the carriage," he said, closing the door in Hawkins's slightly stunned face. He limped back to Emily and, propping his cane against the table, placed the cloak over her shoulders and reached around her to tie the cord. He could feel the deep shudder of what he supposed was revulsion rack her body as he did so. Then, retrieving his cane, he stepped back, still watching her face in the mirror.

She never looked at him as she turned and made her way to the library door. And he wondered at the emotion he felt as he watched her raise her chin before she opened it and stepped out.

He waited until he heard Hawkins's polite murmur and the closing of the outer door. He waited unmoving until the sound of the carriage wheels faded in the distance. Finally, his eyes flicked back to the mirror, and seeing his own reflection there, he raised the silver head of his cane and smashed it into the glass, shattering it into a thousand pieces.

Chapter Six

Emily gave Avon's coachman the address of her father's town house. It was all that came to her mind. Her only concern was to hide herself as quickly as possible in the safety of her bedroom and attempt to forget the events of the afternoon.

She had gone to his home to tantalize him with her celebrated charms, she supposed. How he must now be enjoying that joke. She had been put in her place with a vengeance. She was so unappealing that he had mocked her inexperience and belittled her ridiculous questions about his relationship with her father.

She was a fool. Avon had known that her concern, while legitimate, had only been an excuse to see him again. No mere woman could tempt that cold, emotionless bastard. The ice in his eyes extended into his soul. Why had she gone there? Why had she given him the opportunity to humiliate her so thoroughly? Her troubled thoughts raced in a circle and the journey home seemed to take only a moment.

It was only as the carriage stopped and the coachman climbed down to assist her that she realized she had no explanation for arriving home in the middle of the afternoon in the Duke of Avon's carriage, having left earlier with the avowed intent of visiting the lending library. When she entered the house, her relief that Ashton was not at his post was so great she could have wept, until she realized that fate had not done her a kindness.

Devon's man opened the door to her brother's rooms and said courteously, "The colonel would like to speak to you, my lady. He asks if you'll join him in his sitting room."

Emily's first impulse was to refuse, to run away. But because he couldn't come to her, she took a deep breath and quickly rubbed her cheeks to remove any traces of her tears, then went to face her brother.

Devon had been concerned when he had seen, from his accustomed place by the front window, his sister alight from Avon's carriage, and now his worst fears were confirmed by the sight of her face. He held out his hand and said only, "Come in and talk to me."

Once they were alone in the quietness of his room and away from the prying eyes of the household, he pulled her down beside his chair and, taking both her hands in his, asked, "Can you tell me what happened?"

The kindness of his smile and his lack of recrimination undid whatever composure Emily had found on her journey home. She buried her head on her brother's knees and wept again. It was doubtful that Devon understood half of the incoherent explanation, but he knew well enough that Avon had hurt her pride bitterly. At one point he pulled her head up, and holding her chin as Avon had done earlier, made her look directly into his eyes.

"Did he touch you?" he said. "Did he hurt you?"

She didn't verbally respond, but the color that washed through her face and the look in her eyes, a look that cut him to the heart, were the answers he believed rather than the quick shake of her head.

"I made a fool of myself. I dared question his activities

and he warned me off. He showed me what a silly, vain idiot I really am. He simply gave me a lesson I deserved, Devon." Her voice faltered, then strengthened as she added, "But I'll hate him all my life."

"Good." Devon smiled. "I'm sorry you were hurt, but I can think of no emotion I'd rather you feel toward Avon than hatred."

He wouldn't let her retreat to her room, but kept her with him, eventually even teasing her into entertaining him with her wickedly accurate portrayals of the more-eccentric members of the ton. Devon always enjoyed her company, and her silliness in mocking the elite lightened the tedium of his long hours of inactivity. But today he kept her there to minister to her with his love and acceptance.

When her father arrived that evening, she was able to greet him with composure. When she was finally allowed to seek the privacy of her room, with the intention of freshening up for a rare family dinner at home, Devon gave his father an abbreviated version of the afternoon. To do him credit, he was as fair in his assessment of Avon's motives as Emily had been. He didn't mention his suspicion that the duke had taken liberties with his sister. He intended to deal with that in his own way.

The general was obviously disturbed when Devon had finished his story, and after dinner he asked his children to join him in the library. Knowing his daughter as he did, he should have given her an explanation at the beginning, but his innate good sense had been unbalanced by the recent events surrounding his department at the Horse Guards. It was time to try to put to rights some of the damage his reticence about Avon had caused.

"The Duke of Avon is one of the more valuable resources England has been blessed with in this damnable war," he began with a trace of reluctance in his voice, knowing the secrets he was about to reveal were not his alone. "He virtually controls intelligence gathering for the government. And has for years. I don't know what motivated him, a man of his wealth and position, to become involved in espionage—"

Devon interrupted his father. "I should imagine the same feelings that motivated us all. Avon was raised in the same tradition of love of country." He caught Emily's eye and then continued, "He knew he would never be able to lead a cavalry charge or command a battery, so he obviously looked for a way in which he, too, could serve."

The general nodded at Devon's assessment. "You're right, of course, and he has done that. Through his network he supplies intelligence to both Whitehall and Wellington, often having his French sources send information straight to Spain. It was Canning who first discovered Avon's abilities, when the duke offered the foreign office his expertise in decoding. He's also been in charge of those efforts for years."

"In short," said Emily bitingly, "a jack-of-all-trades. I'm sure we can't win the war without him." She didn't want to hear anything good of Avon. She far preferred that he remain the villain she had that afternoon decided him to be. But it had been this way since she had met him. She had been forced to constantly revise and reevaluate her impressions of the man whose fascination had lured her into making a fool of herself.

Her father recognized that it was the hurt she had suffered speaking and he continued as if she hadn't interrupted. "Once Avon was given complete charge of intelligence activities, the tide in Spain finally began to turn. And, Emily, Avon has been as important to those victories as any commander who fought on the battlefield."

Devon asked quietly, "Can we assume that his role is

secret? I've never heard his name associated with any of the activities you've mentioned.''

"His identity is known to only a few in Whitehall. My predecessor was one of those, so I inherited Avon with the position,'' the general said, smiling in remembrance of his first meetings with the duke.

Emily had not looked at her father since her bitter comment earlier. Devon, who had known for years the quality of the man they were discussing, wasn't surprised by the general's story. He had suspected some legitimate connection between Avon and his father since he had heard of the scene in the library.

"Shortly after my appointment, things began to go sour, especially, but not exclusively, in Avon's network. Couriers died or disappeared. Plans were leaked to the enemy. It became obvious that we had a traitor, a spy in our system. Shortly before Vitoria, our forces suffered a minor defeat that we believe was the result of the enemy's prior knowledge of troop deployment. I can only estimate how many good men have died as a result of the traitor we can't uncover.

"Avon and I have spent the last two months going over every hiring, assignment, replacement. We've checked credentials, financial situations—in short, everything known about the people in the department. There is nothing there. No one new...good men with good records, most of them with military experience in line regiments.... I began to believe the leak must be among Avon's contacts, but he has checked exhaustively and we can find nothing.''

Having reached the point of his explanation, the general again paused and looked at Emily, who still refused to meet his eyes.

"On Saturday night a courier with valuable information concerning Soult's intentions was murdered, his information stolen, and an attempt was made on Avon's life. It seems that since the duke's identity is surely known to our enemy, it can't hurt to entrust it to the two people I love most in the world. I should have done so that night.'' He paused, thinking how best to phrase what he wanted to tell them, and then continued softly, ''I also want you to know that should anything happen to me, you must trust Avon to protect you.''

Emily's eyes were now fastened on her father's face and he realized he had frightened her.

''I truly don't believe I'm in danger. So far the duke has been the assassin's target, for I think he knows that Avon won't stop until he's tracked him down and destroyed him. At least two of the duels Avon fought in the past were to rid the world of those who profited by selling their country's secrets to the highest bidder, but whose guilt could not be proved. In so many ways, the duke has been an irreplaceable asset to this country, and I personally value his friendship.'' He spoke directly to his daughter now. ''I hope you can forgive me, my dear, for not explaining to you immediately.''

Emily rose and kissed his cheek and then hugged her father tightly. ''There is nothing to forgive. Whatever folly I've committed was well and truly on my own head.'' She looked down for a moment. She had tried to be fair, but she couldn't resist adding, ''But please don't ask me to consider Avon as a friend or protector. It is not a role I will ever assign him.''

Emily left her father and brother in the library and spent the night staring at the windows of her room, watching the moonlight play on the curtain. She was still awake when dawn broke and she rose, determined never again to think about the Duke of Avon.

* * *

As Avon was at his breakfast the following morning, his secretary carried in the duke's social correspondence, as he had done every morning of the two years he had been in his employ. The duke's answer to his question as to which invitations he should accept and which politely refuse was the same as it had been every morning of those two years. "Decline them all, of course."

Instead of his usual polite response before taking himself off to carry out that task with his well-paid-for tact, the duke's secretary stood there with a rather hesitant expectancy. He cleared his throat with the first trace of nervousness Avon ever remembered him displaying and held out a single missive for his inspection.

"I believe you may be interested in personally responding to this one, your grace."

The duke looked at his secretary and the note he held out.

"It's from Colonel Devon Burke." There was the faintest trace of satisfaction in the secretary's perfectly correct tone and Avon didn't care for the interested gleam in his eye. Apparently his secretary was aware that Colonel Burke was Lady Harland's brother.

"Thank you, Francis. You may leave it."

The duke returned to the apparent enjoyment of his interrupted breakfast, and when the secretary remained an instant longer, the duke lifted his gaze again from his plate and raised an eyebrow.

"Is there something else, Francis?" he inquired with the deadly softness that the man recognized as displeasure.

"No, your grace," he said, hating the blush he felt sweeping into his cheeks. "I thought you might wish me to compose your reply."

"No, thank you, Francis. That will be all, I think."

When the disappointed secretary had left the room, the duke wiped his mouth and threw his napkin down into his plate. Breakfast had become suddenly tasteless. He rose, and taking Devon's note to the window, read that Colonel Burke requested the Duke of Avon call on him at his earliest convenience, this afternoon if at all possible.

Promptly at two o'clock that afternoon, Devon heard the arrival of his expected guest. He had dressed with care and at the last moment had thrown the rug off his legs. He'd be damned if he'd look any more like an old woman than he had to.

"His Grace, the Duke of Avon," Ashton intoned as he solemnly ushered Avon into the colonel's sitting room. Devon had instructed Ashton to bring his guest here rather than to the larger, more formal drawing room across the hall. This refuge was more private.

Devon didn't ask Avon to sit, and the duke moved only far enough into the room to allow the door to close behind the retreating butler. He was broader of shoulder and, of course, older than Devon remembered. Although his face was still of classic perfection, the lines that bracketed his mouth were deeper and his features were harder than they had been so many years ago. The handicap of the twisted leg was barely noticeable, especially when he stood perfectly still as he did now. It was something he had learned to do early in life so that his father's attention would not be attracted.

As he waited for his host to speak, Avon completed his own assessment. He knew of Devon's injuries, down to the last medical detail, but the compiled information had not mentioned the frailness and the lines of pain carved in the colonel's own face.

"Devon," he said in greeting and waited for what he knew was to come.

"I'll be very brief because I know that you're an extremely busy man.'' There was no trace of sarcasm in the comment. It appeared to be Devon's real evaluation of his guest's status, and the duke was slightly surprised.

''I simply wanted to tell you that if you ever put your hands on my sister again, I shall kill you.''

Devon had expected to see amusement, perhaps even to hear Avon laugh at the thought of him managing to do the duke any harm. His face was impassive, however, and he continued to meet Devon's eyes.

''I mean that. If I have to crawl, I will hunt you down and shoot you.''

The duke nodded and said simply, ''I understand.''

Devon lowered his eyes. He felt he had nothing else to say, and emotion alone having carried him this far, he wasn't sure what to do next. Surely one didn't threaten to kill a man and then ask him to sit down for a drink.

He hoped that the duke would simply turn and go, but instead Avon limped to the sideboard, picked up the decanter and brought it to the table behind Devon's chair. He returned to the buffet, picked up two glasses in his left hand and came back to the table where he had placed the decanter. He poured a splash of brandy into one glass and held it over the back of Devon's chair, lightly resting his hand and the half-filled glass on Devon's shoulder.

Compelled by an emotion he didn't completely understand, Devon reached up and took the tumbler. Avon filled his own glass and then limped to sit in the chair facing Devon. He took a long drink of brandy, then, reaching down, lifted his right leg and stretched it out carefully on the low stool at his feet.

He met Devon's eyes for the first time since answering his threat, and Devon saw nothing there but the friendship they had once shared.

''I understand from your father that you were wounded

at Salamanca. What do your doctors tell you?'' Avon adjusted his own leg into a more comfortable position on the stool and awaited Devon's answer.

''That if I am a very good boy and sit very quietly in this chair, the fragment of metal that's resting against my spine may not shift again.'' No trace of bitterness was allowed into that controlled voice, but his listener was used to reading men and their voices.

''And if that happens?'' the duke asked quietly.

''Then a return of the paralysis I suffered immediately after I was hit.'' Devon carefully kept his voice emotionless. ''A loss of control of bodily functions, the use of my hands. I decided several months ago that I could endure this, to prevent that,'' he answered truthfully.

He had never discussed his feelings about the situation with anyone, but it felt remarkably right to talk about it to this man who had his own hard-won understanding of physical limitations.

''There is no paralysis now?'' the duke asked, dropping his eyes for the first time to Devon's legs.

''The feeling's gradually returned. I can move my legs to some degree, and I believe that if I dared try, I could eventually walk again.'' Devon paused and a slight shudder, quickly controlled, moved through his thin body.

''But then I think of being unable to perform the simplest tasks for myself, of being cared for again like an infant, and I try not to think about what I can't do, but be grateful for what I can.''

He raised his blue eyes to Avon's face for the first time in his painful recital, as if assessing the effect of his remarks. ''I suppose that makes me a coward, but I've made my choice. And I know that it's the only one I can live with.''

Avon made no comment and offered no opinion on the rightness or wrongness of the decisions Devon had been forced to make. The silence between the two men lasted for some minutes, until the duke broke it.

"And how do you occupy your time?" he asked as he studied the contents of his glass.

Devon's only response was a short, bitter laugh.

"Your father told me that he confided to his family my relationship with Whitehall. You know, of course, of our problem with security." Avon stopped and considered Devon's carefully polite face, and then extended an invitation he had not intended to make when he came here today. "I have work you can do, valuable work that you are eminently suited for," the duke said quietly.

"Oh, God," Devon ground out, "did my father put you up to this? Give the poor cripple something to keep him busy, some charity job to make him feel useful. Well, no, thank you, Dominic. You and he can keep your trumped-up work. I'm not interested."

The duke said nothing for a long moment.

"I'm sorry," he said finally. "It's a job that's kept *this* 'poor cripple' quite busy for the last ten years. I'm sure there were people in the government who thought they were accepting my offer out of charity, to make *me* feel useful." He paused and his mouth slanted quickly into a half smile. "And they turned out to be right. I have felt remarkably useful."

He drained his glass and, using his cane and the arm of his chair, pushed himself to his feet. "Let me know if you change your mind."

As the duke began to limp to the door, Devon knew a moment of shame. Avon had been invaluable to the war effort—his father had certainly verified that. And he had done it with his brain, his intellect, and not his body. Was it possible that he himself could really be of use? The possibility of once again feeling that he had something worthwhile to contribute came like the rush of adrenaline during a charge.

"What could I do? I mean, what use could I be to you?" The eagerness in the question was apparent to both men.

"Do you mean you're interested?" Avon turned back, smiling slightly.

"Damn you, you know I am. You look like a cat that's been into the cream, and I find I don't care if my father did twist your arm. But I still don't know what I can do."

"You know me well enough, I believe, to know that arm twisting is remarkably ineffective in convincing me of the rightness of any course of action. Your father knows nothing of my offer." Avon hesitated. "As for what you can do? You can provide me with information—about terrain, the commanders, their personalities, their strengths and weaknesses. You're fresh from the battlefield and you've known most of these men, friend and foe, for years. You can read and then evaluate reports, using your background, your intuition. And you can help me put it all together until it makes sense, makes a pattern that we can understand and use." Avon spoke with conviction and none of the lazy drawl he sometimes used. For the first time, Devon caught a glimpse of the man his father valued so much. "And perhaps you'll be able to help us with your father's more immediate problem," he added bitterly.

"Wait—I don't know that I'm capable of doing that."

"Then start with what you can do. Tomorrow I'll bring you the latest dispatches that we have questions about. You may see something in them we've missed. You have the kind of mind we need and the perfect cover." He smiled in sudden real amusement. "You can tell everyone you're writing your memoirs."

Devon watched the duke limp to the door, pause and then turn back.

"Devon, I am sorry about your sister. I'd ask you to convey my apologies, but for reasons you wouldn't understand, I believe that the situation between us is better left as it is." He then turned, opened the door and was gone.

And Devon found suddenly that for the first time in months, he was looking forward to tomorrow.

Emily was returning from another of the hard gallops she used to relieve her useless self-anger. The ride in the moist London air had loosened tendrils from the tight knot into which Aimee had secured her hair, and they curled damply around her face and neck. She was tapping her crop unthinkingly against the heavy skirt of her habit as she walked, head lowered in thought, up the path that led to the back of the town house. She became aware suddenly, almost subliminally, of the figure blocking the path before her and looked up into the eyes of the last person she could wish to encounter.

"What are you doing here?" she asked as bluntly as he had the day she had come to his home.

The gray eyes studied her features, flushed from her ride, and read the fear revealed there.

"I came to see Devon, who is, as you reminded me, my friend."

"And?" she demanded, dreading whatever he might have revealed about what had passed between them.

"And you were right. He is the same," Avon said softly. "In every way that matters."

"What did you tell my brother?" she asked, hating the tremor in her voice.

"About you? I told him nothing. And he didn't ask." He finished with the truth and watched the gradual relaxation of the tension that had held her.

"I don't want you here," Emily said forcefully, gathering

her courage now that she knew he hadn't betrayed all that had happened between them to her brother. "You've made your duty call on Devon, and I don't ever want you to come here again. Do you understand?"

As those silver eyes calmly studied her face, she remembered the responses he had aroused so easily and felt the return of the sick humiliation that had just begun to fade.

His answer was nothing she had anticipated.

"I've offered Devon a job."

"A job? Don't be absurd. How could he possibly work for you?" she ridiculed unthinkingly, and missed the brief flare of anger in his eyes.

"I failed to notice any impairment of your brother's mental abilities. But, of course, you would know better than I the reality of that," he said politely, raising one dark brow in question.

"Impairment? But there's no…you talked to Devon. How could you suggest that?"

Avon smiled slightly. "But I didn't suggest it, Lady Harland. I thought you did. And if your brother's mind hasn't been affected by his wounds, I see no problem in his working for me in intelligence. As a matter of fact, he seemed to be looking forward to having something to occupy his time." The duke paused and then went on smoothly, "However, if you prefer that I rescind my offer…"

Avon thought of the reports about Lady Harland that he had read and now reread countless times: the stories of her courage in Spain, her endurance of conditions that would have sent most of her countrywomen mad, her ready compassion for the victims of the war's devastation. The portrait that information had painted only heightened the startling impact she had had on his emotions. Because of his title, he was accustomed to toadying sycophants who agreed with his every word. She had, instead, launched a spirited defense of all she valued against his mocking condemnation, and then had had the courage to apologize for her remarks doubting his courage as soon as she realized his limitations, an apology few would have been brave enough or generous enough to offer in light of their heated exchange.

Her generosity of spirit did not disappoint him now, in spite of all he had done to her. "No," she said softly, "I don't want you to do that." If Devon desired this, then she couldn't let her tangled feelings about Avon stand in his way.

"You realize, of course," the duke's deep voice continued, "the only way Devon and I can work together is if I come here. For security reasons I shall only come at night, and hopefully you won't even be aware that I'm in your brother's rooms." He paused and there was a subtle change in his tone. "And if our own accidental encounters are too frequent, you can always have your butler throw me out."

The thought of Ashton, old and fragile as he was, attempting to toss Avon into the street was ridiculous, and she looked up to find her own sudden amusement mirrored in his face.

"I'm sorry," he said softly, and again he had caught her off guard. "I don't often commit errors of that magnitude in dealing with people. Too many lives depend on my judgment to allow me to make the kind of mistake I made in my treatment of you. I think, for Devon's sake, you must put what happened between us behind you. I won't ask for your forgiveness, not yet, but perhaps we might make an honorable truce. For Devon's sake," he offered, an argument she could never deny. The calm silver eyes waited for her decision.

He had taken the blame for a situation that had been of her making, and he required nothing of her in return, nothing but a chance for Devon. He had made it possible for her to relinquish her anger and keep what pride she had left. She recognized, but could not acknowledge, the skill of the negotiation. Finally she nodded, not trusting her voice, and moved around him and into the safety of her father's house.

Chapter Seven

Emily's solution to her feelings about the Duke of Avon was to throw herself into the social scene of London with renewed determination. During the next two months she danced, dined, rode, promenaded and visited the theater with a succession of the most eligible men her world had produced. If Avon found her gauche and uninteresting, these men certainly did not.

Although she was aware that her brother was by far the better for the renewal of his friendship with the man who had so humiliated her, she also knew a sense of betrayal deep within. She was torn between ignoring a relationship that was so obviously to her brother's benefit and spoiling it by giving him an uncensored version of that afternoon's events.

Avon had become a frequent late visitor to her brother's rooms. She had even seen him there once when, returning from a rather dull dinner party at Lady Holland's, she had slipped in to share with Devon a particularly delicious *on-dit* that had circulated that evening.

What she had found were two men totally absorbed in the papers spread out on the low table before them. Avon, whose back was to the hall, had his leg resting on a low stool, and he was absently massaging the muscles of his thigh. Her brother was speaking in a low tone, but with more animation than she had seen in the months since their return to England. When he glanced up and noticed her in the doorway, Emily hurriedly put her finger to her lips, and turning quickly, made her way up the stairs to her own chamber.

That had been another night she spent watching the play of moonlight across the floor of her room. Although she listened intently, she never heard any sounds to signal Avon's departure, and it disturbed her that even the thought of his presence under the same roof could rob her of sleep. She obviously had not been successful in erasing him from her mind or from her senses.

It was shortly after this incident that Emily encountered an old friend of her own. She had been trying to catch her father in his office in hopes that she might persuade him to join her that evening at a performance of the new Philharmonic. She was mounting the steps to his office when a cheerful voice hailed her from above.

"Well, if it isn't the popular Lady Harland. It's remarkable that the hoyden some of us remember from the past has managed to become the darling of both the dandies and the old cats. However did you pull off that trick, my love?"

She looked up into the laughing blue eyes of the Honorable Freddy Arrington, late lieutenant of His Majesty's forces, and ran up the steps to present both her hands to his eager grasp. He made a show of kissing them in the elaborate French manner and then turned her around in a graceful circle to admire the teal walking dress she was wearing.

"Quite a change from that infernal black you insisted on trailing all over the Peninsula. What the Viscount Harland ever did to deserve such devotion is beyond me. Except maybe getting himself killed in the first charge at Rolica.

Hadn't even been in the country long enough to get a sunburn when, bang, he's dead and you're the merry widow. Enormous favor to us all, I must say. Come on, confess, you donned all that black because you felt guilty to be so relieved the pompous blockhead was dead.''

Freddy had always been, and apparently still was, the most outrageous and irreverent person she knew. Nothing was sacred and he would probably have been less well accepted by his army friends had his courage in battle not been just as outrageous as his tongue. Although he had been quite flattering in his attentions to her long before she had attained any other fashionable gentleman's notice, she had not thought about him in years. He had been forced to sell out when his father died and had returned to the family estate in Kent to care for his invalid mother. It had been rumored at the time that his father had run up enormous debts and the family was ruined.

Emily tried to look offended, but recognized the truth in the accusation that she had been relieved when Mark had ceased to exist and she was excused from the occasional fumblings he had submitted her to. She had supposed that she was one of those women who could not find pleasure in the coarser relations between men and women, but she knew now that the fault didn't lie in her body's inability to respond to lovemaking. Indeed, she had learned from Avon that her body was fully capable of sexual arousal. However, her marriage was something she certainly didn't discuss, so she simply shook her head at his comments.

"Freddy," she said with a laugh, "you are, as ever, incorrigible. And as for me, why, look at you! You're as fine as a new sixpence." She subjected him to the same pointed scrutiny he had just given her attire, and in the back of her mind decided that the stories of imminent poverty were highly exaggerated.

"What are you doing here?" she suddenly asked, realizing that Whitehall was an unusual place to find someone of Freddy's bent.

"I went to work here for my uncle shortly after I sold out. I moved my mother into town and decided to do my part for king and country with a pen rather than a sword. Rather boring, actually, but it puts champagne in my mistress's slipper."

The whole time he was talking, he was sweeping her down the steps and away from her destination. Emily found it hard to imagine that Freddy's mother had agreed to pull up roots at her age and come to London, especially as she remembered some of the more amusing anecdotes Freddy used to tell about her terrorizing the local gentry. She must miss being such a big fish in her little pond.

Finally Emily dug in her heels and stopped dead on the bottom of the steps. "Freddy, I'm going to see my father and you've pulled me down a half-conquered flight of stairs already. Where are we going?" she laughingly protested.

"To lunch with my mama. She'd love to meet you, you know. She'll ferret out all your little secrets and criticize your gown and your manners. Oh, it will keep her occupied for quite a fortnight—and delightfully out of the nefarious activities of her only, too-well-beloved son. Say you'll come and my heart is yours." Suddenly the cornflower blue eyes became serious. "Not that it hasn't always been. You cut your teeth on it, didn't you, my sweet?"

Emily laughed and realized that Freddy had indeed always seemed to be partial to her charms. She couldn't think why she hadn't responded to his flirting. He was a tall, blond Adonis who looked almost as handsome in his town attire as he always had in his uniform. Under the dark coat, his shoulders were fashionably broad. His athletic and strongly shaped legs were shown to perfection in the skintight doeskin pantaloons and shining Hessians. And he still seemed to be quite flatteringly bowled over by her own charms.

Deciding that Freddy Arrington was just the kind of distraction she needed, she placed her gloved hand on his arm. She laughingly agreed that she would love to have lunch with his mother if he were sure the inclusion of an unexpected guest wouldn't disrupt the smooth running of his household.

"Oh, I expect they'll flutter around in the kitchen a bit and water the soup, but no one will mind. You know there's always more than enough." He smiled down into her eyes.

"There's just one small favor you could do me in return," she begged charmingly.

"Name it and it's yours, my darling. My family fortune sold to buy you a perch phaeton and a matched pair of white steppers? My heart chopped into small pieces and fed to the birds in Hyde Park? A wedding ring?"

Emily laughed as he had intended and said, "No, nothing so demanding. Only an escort to the Philharmonic's performance tonight."

"Oh, God, music!" Freddy threw his hand dramatically to his brow. "You know, I'd far rather it be the birds in Hyde."

Laughing, they walked arm in arm out to the street, where Emily looked up into the face of the Duke of Avon, who was driving his famous grays down Whitehall.

His eyes held hers as he wheeled by, and he briefly saluted her and then her companion with his whip raised to the brim of his tall beaver hat. She involuntarily shivered and glanced at Freddy to see if he had noticed her agitation. He was looking at her strangely and in some concern.

"Emily, my love, don't tell me you know the iceman himself." He shook his head and said unbelievingly, "There are depths to you, my love, that I can only imagine." He pulled the hand resting on his arm closer to his side and patted it tenderly.

Freddy's mother was as welcoming as he'd promised, but spent most of the luncheon complaining about the high price of everything nowadays and blaming the military for not being able to put an end to that ridiculous little man and his silly blockades.

"When my husband was alive," she assured her guest when Freddy had deserted them to find a fine old sherry he wanted Emily to try, "I was never subjected to such cheese-paring ways as I am forced to adopt today. But Freddy, you know, just doesn't seem to be able to manage as well as his father always did. If only my older son had lived...so tragically lost to cholera several years ago." She delicately wiped her eyes, careful not to disturb the cosmetics that were still favored by her generation.

"Of course, Freddy tries so hard, but, well, my dear, he really doesn't have the discipline for estate management, and everything has gone downhill since he took charge."

Lady Arrington played with the lobster *en casserole* that she had barely tasted. "I'm sure I don't know how we shall go on." She smiled tremblingly and reached to pat Emily's hand. "You will visit me one day in the poor house if my indifferent health doesn't carry me away before Freddy manages to lose everything his father worked so hard to amass."

Since the price of the elegant day gown Lady Arrington was wearing would have housed and fed a family in many sections of London for a year, Emily was hard-pressed to sympathize, but she was polite without agreeing with his mother's assessment of her son's character.

"It seems that Freddy's taking very good care of you in this lovely new home. You're a lucky woman to have such a devoted son," Emily chided gently. Their quiet tête-à-tête was interrupted by Freddy's return.

"Hear, hear," he laughed when he overheard Emily's comment. "Please don't let me interrupt. Continue, by all means, to praise my character. Shall I return to the cellars to give you greater opportunity to convince my mother of my worth?"

"There's no need to go to the trouble," Emily assured him tartly. "I really can't think of another complimentary remark to make about you."

They laughed at her refusal to feed Freddy's vanity, but she was relieved when she could legitimately take her leave. She almost regretted having invited Freddy to accompany her that evening. But perhaps he deserved to enjoy himself with an evening out, and he certainly seemed eager to see her again. If Emily were forced to live with the constant carping that Freddy laughingly shrugged off, she knew that she would soon lose her temper and treat the old harridan to a lecture on the realities of the world today.

Her estimation of Freddy Arrington rose several notches when he tenderly kissed his mother's wrinkled cheek and promised to bring her the latest novel from the lending library on his way home.

Her mood lightened further with Freddy's nonsense on their walk back, and when they parted, Emily discovered that she was looking forward to the evening with more anticipation than she had felt for any activity in the last several weeks.

As Arrington became her almost-constant companion during the remaining weeks of the summer, she found a mind whose quickness matched her own. He never talked to her as if she were incapable of understanding the complexities of the events of the world, but rather kept her informed of the news from the Peninsula and even of friends who were still there. He was charming and attentive, but undemanding of more than her companionship. In short, she delighted in his friendship and basked in the real admiration in his beautiful eyes. She only wished that the picture of those laughing blue eyes would intrude more successfully on the memory of the cold gray ones that belonged to the Duke of Avon.

As summer gave way to the welcome coolness of early September, the social opportunities in London began to grow in preparation of the return of the *haut ton* and the beginnings of the so-called Little Season. Emily had just spent a pleasant evening at the newly rebuilt Drury Lane Theatre. She had gone with the Lady Simonson, but to no one's surprise, Freddy had shown up at the interval. His laughing comments had added to their enjoyment of the comedy on stage, which Emily had been finding slow going. With Freddy's wit the evening progressed into hilarity, and Emily and her party found themselves in good spirits at the end of the play, with no thanks due the playwright.

Freddy was invited to ride with them to accompany Emily to her door, and it was he who jumped out of the carriage and handed her down on her front step.

He smiled into her eyes, which still held the echo of her earlier amusement, and she thought, What a dear friend he has become.

"What are you thinking, my sweet?" he teased her when she unconsciously traced his handsome features with her now-serious eyes.

"About how much I enjoy your company," she answered honestly.

The amusement faded from those blue eyes, to be replaced by a look from whose intensity Emily shrank. Instantly Freddy felt her retreat and smiled again as if in reassurance. He knew that she was not ready to hear the feelings he longed to pour into her ears. He was wise enough to know that if he wanted to continue to see Lady Harland, and only he knew how much he did, he must remain within the boundaries she had established for their relationship, at least for a while longer. And so Freddy simply kissed her hands and wished her good-night.

Emily entered the town house quietly, hoping that her brother was already asleep. She knew that there were nights when he was unable to block out the pain and suspected that more often than she could know he sat or lay without sleeping in his darkened room until morning.

Emily was never sure what she heard that made her aware that things were not as usual. Somewhere a door closed, and she heard vaguely the sound of low voices. Her first concern, as always, was that something had happened to her brother. She quickly ran to his door, thinking that perhaps Devon's valet had roused her father and had brought him back to Devon's rooms.

As she approached, she again heard the sounds of muffled voices, and she opened the door, expecting to see the nightmare she had lived with so long played out before her—Devon in crisis, occasioned by some movement of that deadly sliver of shrapnel that haunted his life, with her father in attendance.

The scene that greeted her could not have been more unexpected. Her father and Devon were there, all right, but their postures were not of crisis. They had obviously been about to propose a toast or to drink to one that had been made, for their glasses were filled and held high.

Her father looked up at the opening of the door and said only, "Emily?"

She had not been expected, and when she became aware of the third person in the room, she knew that she had again blundered, imposing herself where she was neither welcomed nor wanted.

The Duke of Avon stood much closer to Emily and the door, leaning against the sideboard that held the decanters. He, too, held a glass. She hurriedly began to excuse her presence so that she could leave with some poise intact.

"I heard voices," she explained, "and I was afraid that something had happened to Devon."

She knew that she was embarrassing her brother, who avoided any reference to his condition, especially before strangers. But her explanation was true, and she wanted to make it and be out of the room, without taking time to fabricate excuses.

She had already turned to the door when Avon's long fingers touched her wrist. He waited a heartbeat and, when she made no move to avoid his hand, he pulled her gently into the room and closed the door.

"Wait," he said, and he smiled at her as he had once before. "You have a right to join this celebration tonight. San Sebastian has fallen."

The implications of that simple statement were obvious to Emily as he had known they would be, obvious and important.

"Then the frontier's open to Wellington."

"The castle was taken on the fifth and the French retreated across the border. We're drinking to the beginning of the end." He paused and smiled down into her emerald eyes. "Join us. You're more than welcome." He turned to the sideboard and splashed another glass with a swallow of brandy and put it into her hand.

"To Wellington and the army," he said.

As they repeated it, emotions were heightened by the thought of comrades in arms, some still there, but more often thoughts intruded of those who had not lived to see this moment and would not celebrate Napoleon's ultimate defeat, which now finally seemed to be possible. Emily could not imagine a world whose whole impetus was not the defeat of the French.

When she looked at the three men gathered there, she knew that, like so many others, their lives had forever been changed by the machinations of that power-hungry man who had dominated the affairs of Europe for so many years.

She raised her glass again. "And to you all."

She saluted each man in turn and then finished her toast, "Your work here in London has made what has happened possible, but I know where you each would rather be tonight."

She found her eyes drawn to the face of the enigmatic Avon, and she saw that her words had touched a chord. She had included him in that circle of men of action she admired and loved.

"Thank you," he said softly, but she saw the emotion as he held her eyes a long moment, and then, as always, hid what he felt behind the fall of dark lashes. He turned to limp to the chair beside Devon.

But Emily was unwilling to leave and wanted, beyond all reason, to be here with this man who had attracted her from the beginning, and who in this mood of joy and friendship was even more compelling than before.

"Can you give us details?" she asked, seeking to prolong the episode.

Devon answered her question. "Dominic's sources had supplied Wellington with very good intelligence several weeks ago that Soult was moving to attack at some point along the coast. We postulated that it would be San Sebastian and it was."

"And our losses?" Emily asked that hardest question of all.

"Almost 4000 Allied casualties," the duke himself answered. "I haven't yet received any lists or breakdowns, so I can't give you specifics."

"Will Wellington follow the French immediately?" she asked, moving to stand behind Devon's chair and slipping her arms around his neck. Her brother pulled her head down and kissed her cheek.

Avon answered her question, but his thoughts had strayed from the discussion of tactics to the memory of Emily in his own arms.

"Probably not. The Spanish government is proving to be less than cooperative."

"As always," her father commented.

"Mañana. Perhaps tomorrow," Emily said in imitation of the words they had heard so often on the Peninsula, and they all laughed.

"But the news is also good from the northern front. Napoleon is definitely on the ropes, and it won't be long until the Allies march triumphant into Paris," Devon said. "I refuse to have my good mood shattered by the Spanish refusal to act."

"I agree," said Avon. "The news is, on the whole, too encouraging to quibble over trifles." He paused, and they all knew what he was thinking. "If only we could succeed as well here."

There was silence as they realized that their time to find and convict their traitor was limited. It would be almost impossible to prove his guilt once the need for secret dispatches and traffic in the spy network had lessened.

The three men talked quietly and with the ease of old friends. Emily sat and listened, sometimes offering a comment or thought, but mostly just watching the strong hands of the duke as they held and occasionally raised his glass. He laughed once at something Devon said, and her heart stopped and then resumed its steady beat, but nothing in her world would ever be the same. Perhaps feeling the intensity of her gaze, he raised his eyes to lock with hers and, recognizing what was revealed there—the self-discovery she had not had time to hide—the gray ones fell.

Avon rose shortly after that and moved to take the general's hand. "I apologize for disturbing your household. I confess I not only wanted to bring you the news, I wanted someone to share my elation with."

The general replied sincerely, "You are always welcome here, your grace."

"I'll see the duke out while you help Devon," Emily offered, and wondered at her own foolishness. Playing with fire, she thought honestly and then blocked her apprehensions and escorted Avon into the hall.

When the door to Devon's room had closed behind them, she asked the question that had risen unbidden from the camaraderie of that small room.

"Why?" she said softly, and his eyes didn't avoid hers now.

"Why?" he repeated, smiling slightly, questioning her meaning.

"Why aren't you always that man? The man you were tonight. The man you are with my brother."

"Because that room isn't my world," he said simply.

"But it could be," she whispered, bothered by the conviction in the dark voice. She couldn't know that she was offering him the key to a door that had been locked against him all his life. And despite his knowledge of its impossibility, he wanted to allow her to unlock what had always been barred.

"No," he said simply, limping forward to find where Ashton had hung his cloak.

''But why?'' she persisted. ''How can you deny that side of your nature? You can't prefer the loneliness.''

He met her troubled eyes, knowing that he was about to hurt her again.

''And you believe I'm lonely?'' She saw his amusement at her naïveté.

''You wanted someone to share your feelings with. I took that to imply…''

''Loneliness?'' He smiled, gently mocking her concern. ''Not everyone in London is as involved in what's happening in Spain as the four of us. I think you reminded me of that the night we met,'' he said, revealing, had she only thought, how well he remembered their conversation. ''And tonight I wanted company who understood what this news means. But that doesn't mean that I don't have other friends—'' he paused and then continued, watching her face ''—to answer other needs.'' There was nothing sexually suggestive in his calm voice, but she had no doubt about the needs he referred to. And knew that he had told her deliberately.

Avon watched as she absorbed the import of what he had said, and then she lifted her chin at his denial of the friendship they both were aware she had offered.

''Of course,'' she said, color washing under the clear, transparent skin. ''How foolish of me to think we might have anything the Duke of Avon could need. Or that you might share our very human desire for friendship.''

He wanted to touch her then, to kiss away the embarrassed tremble of her lips that his second rejection had caused, and he recognized that his control when he was around her was melting as rapidly as fog exposed to the summer sun.

She's not for you, he reminded himself bitterly. And wondered how many times he had thought those words since he had met her. For someone else. For Arrington, perhaps, he thought with sudden, painful jealousy, but not for you.

But he stood before her and felt his hands tighten as he denied the need to take her into his arms. And he was to wonder later what he might have done had she not turned at his silence and retreated into her brother's rooms.

Avon stood a long moment in the hall and then let himself out.

In Devon's room Emily listened to the distinctive footsteps fade, then began to gather up the glasses they had used and return them to the sideboard for the servants tomorrow.

"Don't be fooled by the fact that he seemed human tonight, Em," her brother said quietly. "He's still the same man."

Emily was glad her back was turned and he couldn't see what she knew would be in her face, but she made no comment, for she recognized the validity of, and the necessity for, her brother's warning. She turned from the sideboard and walked across the room with every evidence of composure. She kissed him gently and then climbed the stairs to her own room. His words were still echoing in her mind when she finally fell asleep.

Chapter Eight

The beginning of October brought nothing but endless rain, the sky constantly overcast and the wind presaging the severity of the winter that would follow. The damp chill penetrated the damaged nerves and muscles of Devon's back, and the whole household talked softly and worked on tiptoe on the chance that the colonel might have found peace long enough to slip into a restless sleep.

Emily sat with her brother through the long, dark afternoons, racking her brain for anything that might entertain him, recounting anecdotes and stories from their days in Spain, reliving the freedoms of their childhood. Although he always responded with laughter, she saw the suddenly clenched hands when he was moved into the chair and the exhaustion in his eyes when he was once again lifted back into his bed, a refuge he sought earlier and earlier as the days shortened and twilight finally signaled permission to accept that longed-for retreat.

Emily's heart jumped with fear when Devon's valet announced one gloomy morning that the colonel had decided to lie abed today.

''Not that anything's wrong, my lady,'' he lied reassuringly, seeing the question in her eyes. ''Just going to relax with the new dispatches the duke brought. He'll be wanting a report soon, and the colonel can spread them out on the coverlet far better than trying to hold them in his lap.'' He backed hurriedly out the door with the small breakfast he hoped he could persuade his master to taste.

Emily stared unseeing at the suddenly unappetizing selections on her plate. Devon had sometimes chosen to have supper on a tray in bed, but never breakfast. Mornings were always better, freer from pain after his long hours of rest. She carefully folded her napkin and laid it beside the plate. She walked to the windows and looked out at the garden through the rain-streaked panes. She longed for a hard ride through open country, hatless, her long hair released to blow in the wind, perhaps even whipped by the rain.

She suddenly remembered Devon's long-ago promise to race her through Hyde Park and she closed her eyes. It seemed now that that would never happen, and she wondered if they had been wrong. Would it have been better to let him die quickly in Spain, where he had been so alive, so much larger than life, so strong? Or better to release him from his promise to cling to life in order to allow him to chance the surgery that each physician had deemed sure death? Devon had never asked for that release. But she had seen his eyes rest on hers, waiting for permission to break that promise, as each doctor gave his verdict. A promise extracted under blackmail. One she was beginning to bitterly regret. Was this what she had condemned him to?

''We weren't wrong.'' Her father's voice broke through her despair, and she wondered how he could read her mind so clearly. In her abstraction she had not even heard him enter the room.

''How can you be sure?'' she asked, fighting the tears, her eyes held resolutely on one drop sliding gracefully down the tallest pane of the mullioned window. "How can we ever be sure that this is what he would have chosen?"

"Because he is Devon," he answered simply, and she felt his hands close strongly around her upper arms. He squeezed tightly, then released her and walked to the sideboard. She turned to watch as he helped himself liberally to the array of dishes still piping hot under their silver covers.

"Surely you haven't forgotten that?" he said, glancing up at her suddenly from under thick, gray brows.

"No," she said softly and smiled at him. "I haven't forgotten that."

And she was able to sail into her brother's room only a few minutes later to drop a quick and seemingly casual kiss on his forehead.

Devon caught her hand and held it a moment. "And where are you off to in such a hurry?" he asked with a laugh.

She allowed her eyes to briefly study the dark shadows under his smiling blue ones and knew that her father was right. He was still, in spite of it all, Devon.

"Aimee and I are determined to get to the bottom of Grandmother Saulke's linen press. Probably most of it will end up fit only for rags, but Aimee believes that some of the sheets simply need the lace repaired or bleaching in the sun. Wish us luck," she said cheerfully.

"Of course," he said, "but it sounds a perfect fright of a day to me. I can't imagine—"

"I know. I'm sure all those lists and numbers are far more interesting than bed linens."

"Actually…" he began, and she laughingly held up her hand.

"No, I don't want to hear. I hope you find your informer, but I can't stand another explanation of your endless charts.

Don't work too long," she said, and heard the concern slip into her voice.

"No, I won't," Devon said automatically, his attention already returning to the papers spread across his bed. "But Avon's coming tonight and I want these ready to show him."

"Then I'll come back this afternoon and you can practice explaining them all to me," she offered.

Devon looked up suddenly and laughingly shook his head, and she said it for him: "Do you mean that Avon understands this more quickly than I? Is that what you're trying to say?"

"I would never be so ungallant," her brother lied, and she blew him a smiling kiss, leaving him alone with the only thing he seemed able to enjoy.

When she returned that evening, it was to find her brother's head back against the stacked pillows and his thick lashes lying like fans over the bruised-looking skin below. She'd begun to back quietly out of the room when he spoke.

"Don't run away. I'm not asleep. How goes the battle of the bed sheets?"

"Devon," she said softly, and at her tone, his eyes finally opened, to focus on her face. "What's wrong?" she whispered.

"Nothing." He smiled. "I'm just working up the energy to dress."

"To dress? But why? I don't understand. It's after eight," she said, reaffirming her guess by a quick glance at the mantel clock.

"I told you Avon's coming," he said, as if that explained it all.

"But surely—" she began.

"No, Em." His tone was the old Devon of the battlefields. She had forgotten the cold determination that quiet voice could contain. It was not a tone he often employed with her.

"Devon," she said again, trying to think of some argument to change his mind.

"Would you ask Timmons to come in? I think we'd better start now if I'm to greet my guest with any degree of composure," he said, smiling at her. At her continued hesitation, he said softly, "Now, Emily, if you will."

She knew nothing she could say would change his mind. But since she was his sister, she began anyway. "Do you honestly believe Avon has never seen a man in his nightshirt before? Or that it will matter to him how you are dressed?"

"Of course not," he answered simply. "But it will matter a great deal to me."

She waited a moment longer and then nodded.

She knew her father would never condone her duplicity, knowing that he would feel she had somehow diminished Devon by her lie, but Ashton, as ever, was her willing ally.

He pounded the front knocker himself, carried on a remarkably believable conversation with the imaginary caller and delivered the fake message with the skill of any Covent Garden actor.

"His Grace, the Duke of Avon, regrets that he will be unable to keep his appointment tonight, Colonel Burke. Some urgent business that's come up unexpectedly."

"Did the messenger give you any idea…" Devon began, and then realized Avon was too careful for that. He hid his disappointment and smiled at the old man. "Thank you, Ashton. I'm sure you said everything that was correct."

"I hope so, sir. Will that be all?"

"Yes, thanks." Devon turned his head on his pillows to

look out into the darkness, and Ashton wondered if his mistress had been wrong. But it was too late now to question that decision.

She thought about asking Ashton to meet Avon and send him away, but she knew that was the coward's way out. Whatever her faults, no one had ever accused Emily of being a coward. Besides, the thought of the old man shivering in the cold dampness of the dark back alley drove that tempting escape from her mind. So at a quarter of ten she slipped furtively down the back stairs, snagged the downstairs maid's cloak off the rack and let herself quietly out the kitchen door.

The grass was wet and she knew she was ruining her slippers, but she hurried across the lawn, dodging the lights from the windows of the town house and darting like a poacher from shadow to shadow.

She had finally reached her destination and settled into the deepest pocket of the alley's darkness when a massive figure loomed suddenly out of the fog.

Emily's scream was automatic, and her reward was a callused hand clasped unceremoniously over her mouth and a muscular arm slipped quickly around her upper body. He smelled of fish, and she gagged against the palm and then kicked out viciously with her right foot. Had she been wearing riding boots, she might have had some effect, but the soft slippers seemed to only amuse him, and he stepped nimbly out of the way, never losing his quite professional and highly effective hold.

"Whoa, me pet," he said, and bent closer to her face. She could smell the ripe odor of beer and rotting teeth, and realized with horror that he intended to put that foul mouth on her own. She struggled fiercely against his hold, and then the body was miraculously drifting back and away from hers, and she wondered dazedly how she had managed to accomplish that.

It was not until the attacker landed with a whooshing thump against the opposite wall that she realized she had, of course, not accomplished any part of the maneuver. The tall man who now stood between her and the cringing figure had apparently managed it without even disturbing the soft folds of the cloak that draped unmistakably against the heavy cane he gripped in his right hand. His left held a dully gleaming pistol unfalteringly trained on the crouching assailant.

"What the hell do you think you're doing?" he demanded harshly, and for a startled second Emily thought he must be talking to her.

"A mistake, governor. I swear," the man against the wall wailed out. "I thought she was the maid come alooking for her sweetheart."

Avon waited a long moment, and then the line of that rigid left arm relaxed infinitesimally and Emily took a breath for the first time in a very great while.

"Emily?" he questioned softly, and she knew he wouldn't want to turn from the man he held pinned with the dark eye of the pistol.

She moved on trembling legs to stand behind him, then put her hands on the broad shoulders and leaned gratefully against that hard strength. The pleasant aromas of his body transported her briefly back to his library, and she felt his quick inhalation and then the smooth shifting of his weight to the sound left leg. His right arm, still holding the cane, came around to pull her hard against his solid warmth and behind the safety of his body.

"If I thought," he said, his tone utterly deadly in spite of its whispered softness, "that you dared—"

"I swear, milord," the man whined coaxingly, "a mistake. I swear...you know I would never—"

"Shoot him," Emily said suddenly, wondering why Avon was hesitating. She watched unbelievingly as the gray eyes turned, wide with shock, over his shoulder to find her face.

"What?" he asked, incredulous, and so she repeated it.

"Shoot him. What are you waiting for?"

She felt the laughter begin to shake his back, and at the first rich sound that escaped his suddenly relaxed body, the man was off and running toward the light at the end of the dark passage.

"Of all the..." Emily began in exasperation as she broke from the circle of that hard arm and moved to confront him.

"If you're not going to shoot him, let me," she said, grasping the barrel of his pocket pistol as she narrowed her eyes to estimate the runner's speed and the distance to the end of the alley. If she hurried, she believed she might down him before he could turn the corner and disappear into the darkness. It would all depend on how accurate the small pistol proved to be at that distance.

Iron fingers gripping her wrist put an end to her calculation.

"Release the pistol," he said softly, but the command was as unmistakable as that he had given the man who was now disappearing into the dark London night.

"My God, why didn't you shoot him?" she demanded again, but she released the pistol and watched him tuck it into a hidden pocket of the cloak. "You've let him get away to attack some other unsuspecting woman."

His eyes studied her too-white face, and he touched her chin and turned her head to force her eyes to meet his. "Emily," he said softly, ignoring her complaint, "are you hurt? Did he hurt you?"

"No, of course not," she denied strongly, and at the look

of sudden tenderness in the depths of those silver eyes, she found it hard to breathe. "No," she repeated, and then, for something to break the spell his concern had woven, she asked rather plaintively, "but why didn't you shoot him?"

He smiled at her and suddenly bent to kiss her lips, which parted in response. It was what she wanted, and all that had passed between them before was forgotten in the gentle movement of his mouth against her own. It was over almost before she could realize what had happened. Or what it meant. She had shared kisses before, of course, but she thought there had never been one as surprisingly moving as the soft touch of his lips.

Avon moved back from her body and, finding control again, answered what she had asked. "Because I find it very difficult to get rid of a corpse in the heart of London," he said reasonably, denying any significance to what had just occurred.

"And have you had to do that before?" she asked, curious in spite of the turmoil he had created in her emotions.

He laughed and said, "On occasion," and she knew he was telling the truth.

"What are you doing out here?" he questioned, taking another step back, away from the dangerous closeness he had just allowed between them. In his fear for her, he had been unable to deny his need to touch her, to know that she was really unharmed.

"I came to meet you," she said bluntly, and watched his eyes narrow.

"Not that I'm not flattered, you understand, but I am somewhat surprised." And he smiled at her again.

"You don't understand," she denied, pulling the maid's cloak more tightly about her shivering body.

"Then why don't you explain," he invited softly. "Are you in trouble?"

''It's Devon,'' she whispered, knowing that she was about to betray her brother, and how he would hate what she was doing if he knew.

''What's wrong?''

''He's in pain. He was unable to dress today. Or get out of bed. And then tonight, because you were coming, he was…'' Her voice faltered.

''Are you telling me that Devon sent you here to ask me not to come?'' She could hear the disbelief.

''Of course not. I think you know my brother better than that. I told him you couldn't come. He was determined to dress and greet you as he normally does, and I knew what that would cost him. So I came to stop you, so he wouldn't know I'd lied to him,'' she explained, finishing the painful confession.

''And you think you are doing your brother a service by treating him like this? Protecting him like a child who's unable to make his own decisions?'' he asked coldly.

''You don't understand—'' she began.

Avon's voice ruthlessly overrode her protest. ''There is so much, so *much*,'' he emphasized, ''that he can't control, can't manage anymore, and now you deny his ability to decide what he can bear and what's worth his pain. And it is *his* pain. You can't bear it for him and you shouldn't be allowed to decide how much that pain will limit his ability to function.'' He stopped suddenly.

''Whatever he can bear, whatever he can stand, you must let him do,'' he continued softly. ''And now you've included me in your lies.'' He went on more strongly, ''I would never break my word to Devon. I told him I would call tonight and I intend to do just that.''

Emily swallowed against the realization that he was right, and she had been wrong, so blindly wrong. But she couldn't bear it if he told Devon of her treachery. At the silence that seemed to be her only answer to what he had said, Avon began to limp toward the walk that would lead to the back door he always used.

"Please don't tell him," she begged, and watched him pause and then turn back to face her.

He hesitated and asked finally, "What excuse did you give him?"

"Only that something urgent had come up. The very vaguest of explanations. I couldn't think of anything else."

He nodded and turned to move again over the rough walk. Suddenly feeling deserted, Emily followed the limping figure through the broken pattern of light and shadow of the back lawn.

He was admitted by Devon's man, and when he saw the surprise and then the sudden gladness in the man's eyes, knew he had been right to come.

But he understood Emily's concern when he moved quietly into the dimly lit bedroom. The papers had now been stacked carefully on the cluttered table beside the bed and the lamp trimmed low. The thin face of the man who lay there turned at the sound of the limping footsteps, and Avon saw the sudden flare of emotion, felt an unaccustomed thickening in his own throat.

"Dominic?" Devon said questioningly and watched as the valet moved a chair close to the bed and the duke limped forward gratefully. He, too, knew the cost of cold and rain.

"The footstool, Timmons," Devon instructed, but Avon negated the command with a lifted hand and the servant left them alone.

"Your message said you'd been called away. Something urgent?" Devon questioned.

"A false alarm. I'm sorry I'm late."

"It doesn't matter. I decided to simply lie here and think

about all the information we have. Hoping that if I relax enough and stop trying so hard to make it fit, something will suddenly leap out at me. Something we've missed.''

''And has it?'' Avon asked softly.

The sudden laugh was reassuring. ''Not a thing. I'm as hopelessly confused as ever. And I find that tonight my mind won't even stay on the problem.''

''Maybe there are other problems that compel your attention.''

''Is it that obvious?'' Devon asked, understanding the gentle probing.

''Perhaps,'' Avon agreed, ''but then I've had a great deal of experience. Is there anything I can do?''

''I don't know. You can tell me, out of your experience, what works.''

''There are always drugs,'' Avon suggested carefully, gauging the reaction of the taut mouth that he watched move quickly into a smile.

''And do you use them?'' The blue eyes demanded the truth.

''No,'' he said, ''but I won't deny having thought of it.''

''Then why not?''

''Because I value control too much, I suppose,'' the duke admitted, and watched the slow nod in response.

''There is release for this,'' Devon said, and Avon felt the cold finger of fear touch his heart. But before he could react, the soft voice continued. ''But I balance the pain carefully before I seek it. Another piece of metal is working its way to the surface. I'll ask my father to call in the surgeon tomorrow and I'll go under the knife again. They'll cut this one out and we'll fight the inflammation and then perhaps I'll have some weeks of peace.''

''You haven't told your family?'' Avon asked, thinking

of the white-faced woman who had begged for his complicity in her attempt to protect.

"Tomorrow. I think they dread the surgeries more than I. Emily especially. It's easier to bear your own pain than to watch someone you love…"

Devon's voice stopped at the sharp movement of the man sitting beside his bed. The face was perfectly controlled now, but there was some underlying emotion Devon couldn't read. He gave up and closed his eyes again against the onslaught of the pain. He could never have said what force compelled him, but he lifted his thin hand from the sheet and held it in the quiet darkness of the room until he felt the strong, warm fingers close tightly around his.

"I'll send my doctor," Avon said finally. "And I'll be here."

Devon didn't open his eyes, but his thin fingers tightened slightly and he said only, "Thank you. I'd like you here."

It was a long time before Avon finally placed the relaxed hand against the whiteness of the sheet again. He stood carefully and watched the composed features for a long moment, then turned down the lamp and made his way out of the room by the light from the adjoining one.

The valet was nowhere in sight, so Avon found his own cloak and moved across Devon's sitting room, opening the door to the hall. He began to limp heavily down the narrow passage to the back of the house and found her standing quietly at the end, where the shadows began.

At the look on his face, she took a deep breath and whispered, "Thank you."

"Don't ever doubt his strength again," he said softly, and against his will his thumb moved to wipe the single tear that had escaped to glimmer briefly on her cheek in the dim light. He watched her lips lift slowly into a smile.

"I know. And Dominic," she whispered, using his name

for the first time, so that he waited, caught by its sound on her lips, "for what you've given him...I'm grateful. We all are."

He shook his head and didn't attempt to explain the unfairness of that exchange. He moved past her into the dark hallway, knowing that he had been granted more tonight than he had ever hoped for. And that it was at an end. He had long ago stopped questioning why this was the woman, and had simply acknowledged that it had, as Moss had warned him, finally and irrevocably happened. But this bud could not be cherished into flower. It must be crushed underfoot, never allowed to grow.

Not for you, his heart whispered again. He didn't look back to see her still standing, watching as he disappeared into the shadows.

"I have a message." The now-subdued voice spoke from the depths of the alley.

Avon fought to pull his mind from the personal and back to the professional.

"I assumed you would," he answered the hulking shape in the darkness. "Why else should someone like you be lurking in General Burke's garden? I doubted you'd come to admire the roses."

"They said it was urgent," the voice whined.

The man watched in fear as the limping figure moved from the faint light into his darkness. This was not someone it was wise to anger, and he had debated whether it would be better to come back to deliver the message he had been given or to thank his luck for the narrow escape earlier tonight and simply disappear into the riverfront again. But he knew that if the Duke of Avon wanted to find someone, he would. And so he had come to give the message, hoping to make amends for the near-fatal mistake of a few hours ago. He could still feel the ice of the eyes that had pinned him against the wall.

"It was a near thing tonight." The soft voice spoke directly in front of him now. He could feel the faint tremor in his knees and hoped that in the dimness, Avon was unaware of his fear. "A very near thing," the voice whispered.

"I swear, your grace—"

The whiteness of the raised palm was clear even in the darkness and its message plain. The man stopped his quavering voice with a convulsive movement of his throat muscles.

The palm moved suddenly, to lie flat and as steady as a rock before him. Realizing its intent, the man drew the folded paper from its hiding place in his filthy coat and laid it carefully on the outstretched hand. He watched the long fingers close over the note and imagined them squeezing the trigger just that smoothly.

"I don't ever want to see you again," Avon said with that same deadly softness. "I suggest you might wish to leave the city. Perhaps one of the colonial holdings…" he mused gently.

The messenger made no verbal response to the suggestion he had just been given, but he found himself running down the dark passage again, just as quickly as when he had imagined the pistol trained on his retreating back.

When the man had disappeared once more into the darkness, Avon took a deep breath. He could still smell the pungent odor of fish and sour beer that had emanated from the trembling body, and he thought briefly about those hands touching Emily. Then, knowing the futility of those thoughts, he turned and limped in the opposite direction to the coach that he knew would be waiting patiently in the dark street.

Chapter Nine

The slender, dapper man who called on Colonel Burke the following morning was no one Ashton recognized, but the elegance of his apparel and the quality of the leather case he carried were obvious to the well-trained eye. The butler ushered him into the hall and began to divest him of the exquisitely tailored greatcoat that he wore against the early morning chill.

"Tell the colonel that Avon sent me," the visitor said to the hall mirror, straightening the fashionable cravat and adjusting the gold fob that dangled smartly across his waistcoat.

"I—I beg pardon, sir," Ashton stammered in surprise.

"Avon, man. The Duke of Avon. Don't worry, the colonel will know." He glanced at the butler and turned back to the mirror to check again the correctness of his attire.

Ashton entered the colonel's rooms, hoping that he would find him still asleep, but the blue eyes turned from their contemplation of the dismal panorama of the rain-soaked garden to meet his.

"A visitor, Colonel. He didn't give his name, but he said to tell you that Avon sent him," Ashton said doubtfully.

Comprehension broke across the face of the man in the bed. "Of course, Ashton. Please send him in."

The visitor entered to find the white face turned bravely in his direction. He had seen that particular look too often not to recognize the dread at the back of the smiling blue eyes.

"I'm Pritchett. Avon said to tell you that the anticipation is sometimes more painful than the actual procedure. He thought as soon as possible."

"Now?" Devon questioned softly. "Do you mean now?"

"Why not?" The visitor smiled suddenly, appearing quite different from the pompous peacock Ashton had pegged him for. "Do you have some reason to wish to prolong your suffering?"

Devon laughed, and the professional eyes watched the pain that even that small movement now caused, but the invalid answered as Avon had known he would.

"No reason at all. I assure you I have nothing else scheduled this morning," he agreed.

"Good," the surgeon said briskly and turned to the hovering Timmons. "I shall need you to boil water in that fireplace. There is a hook, I presume?"

At the fascinated nod, he continued with his list of instructions and gestured impatiently for help in removing the well-cut frock coat. He then began to turn back his sleeves.

His long-fingered hands were white and very clean and well-cared for—dainty even. But in spite of their marked difference to the blood-encrusted nails and grimy fingers of most of the doctors who had worked on his back through the long months, Devon felt the familiar tightening of his stomach muscles. He lay and watched the careful preparations, the setting out of instruments that had been removed from clean flannel rolls in the deep leather bag, the careful washing of hands and knives, their edges shining as they emerged from the boiling water Timmons had prepared.

Devon finally closed his eyes and began to breathe deeply in an attempt to prepare his mind and body for the ordeal. He asked, only because he thought he knew what the Duke of Avon's word was worth, "I thought Avon—"

He was interrupted by the precise voice. "Of course. He said to tell you that he'd be here before we begin. I believe I hear him now." The carefully shaven face turned consideringly, and they both listened to the limping footsteps and the murmur of voices in the hall.

"A bad night," the doctor said suddenly and smiled at Devon's unspoken question. "He doesn't take care of himself, you know. He will never admit…" But whatever confidence he had been about to share was cut off by the opening of the door and the arrival of the duke.

The demeanor of the doctor altered subtly. Apparently he was willing to relax his dignity before Devon, but his air now that the duke had arrived was seriously businesslike and properly respectful. He might be privy to secrets that Avon would allow no one else, but he knew better than to infringe on their professional relationship.

"An examination first, I believe, Colonel." And he bent to help Timmons with the painful turning of the thin body. From his stance by the window where he watched the slow drizzle begin again, Avon could hear the gasps and shuddering breaths, but he did not offer to help and did not even glance at the bed until Devon lay prone and painfully revealed to the three pair of eyes. The doctor's were detached and professionally interested; the valet's long inured to the sight; but Avon felt again last night's unfamiliar thickening in his throat at sight of the brutally scarred skin stretched too tightly over the long bones.

One delicately shaped finger reached and touched a small

mound that even Avon could see. Devon's gasp was quite clear in the quiet room and as quickly cut off by teeth sunk in suddenly colorless lips.

"Here, of course," the doctor said softly.

"Yes," Devon forced himself to answer.

"You should have called me earlier. You've made my task too simple. It has almost worked its way through the muscle. A small cut and lift and it's gone. The work of five minutes," the calm voice said reassuringly.

His hands gently explored the scars and muscles, finally touching tenderly the lump that lay along the spine. Devon's inarticulate sound had no effect on the probing fingers that continued to examine that most wicked souvenir of the battle.

When he had finished, he finally met the watching gray eyes of the man at the window and slowly shook his head. The duke returned to his contemplation of the scene that lay beyond the glass.

It was not until Devon had been dosed with laudanum, and the doctor began to take from his bag the leather straps that would be used to fasten Devon's wrists to the posts of the bed that Avon spoke again.

"No," he said quietly, and instead moved Devon's left hand to grip the wooden post. Devon listened as the limping footsteps circled the bed and then Avon was seated, as he had been last night, beside him. The duke took into his own the right hand, and felt the thin fingers tighten gratefully around his before he nodded at the waiting surgeon. At the first downward pressure of the knife, he felt the fingers grind painfully into his bones and heard the rasping breath. Avon lifted his eyes again to the window and was thankful many long minutes later when he felt the pressure ease. The colonel had finally fainted.

* * *

Avon and the doctor emerged together and found Emily standing as patiently as she had last night. The doctor smiled reassuringly and let Ashton ease the greatcoat over his shoulders as he gave his instructions.

"Let him rest today. Liquids, but nothing else. I doubt he will feel like eating. You may poultice tomorrow with cloths dipped in boiled water to which salt has been liberally added."

At Avon's quick laugh, the doctor smiled and said, "I never question the source of a procedure that works."

"Is he all right?" Emily asked, needing to hear this elegant figure's confirmation.

"For now he's fine. And in a day or two he'll feel better than he has in weeks." The doctor considered the rest of what his examination had revealed. "However, the removal of that fragment near the spine is beyond my skill. It would almost certainly kill him—if not immediately, within a matter of days. It's too near the nerves that control the body's central functionings. I'm sure you've been told that before." He waited for Emily's nod. "I wish there were something I could do. You may feel feel free to call upon my services at any point in the future."

By this time he had placed the gleaming beaver on the stylish Brutus cut, picked up the bag and was moving past the startled Ashton toward the door.

He turned back to say, "And as for you, your grace…"

But at the warning in those quickly raised gray eyes, he thought better of whatever advice he had been about to offer and simply shook his head, departing with an air of hurried efficiency.

"Thank you, Ashton," Emily said softly. "That will be all." She waited until the old man had gone.

When she turned to meet Avon's eyes, there was nothing in them of the tenderness she had seen last night. They were as cold as they had been in her father's library. And as distant.

"For Devon's sake," he said levelly, "I think it might be better if I don't come for a while. You were obviously right to try to protect him. It seems that what I've asked of him is beyond his strength. Of course, his courage will never allow him to admit that. And so I have to make that decision for him, as you tried to do last night."

"But I was wrong last night. And you know that. You know what this work means to him, what your relationship means. He needs your friendship. Even if you don't need anyone, don't deny Devon's needs," she said, and he heard the echo of his rejection.

She hoped he might reconsider his decision, but his voice was still as composed and as decisive when he said, "I think it's better that we allow Devon time to recover. Perhaps later we might resume our work. If he's stronger."

"Dominic, please," she begged, putting her hand on his forearm. The rigidity of the muscle under her fingers should have warned her, but she was too concerned with what he was doing to Devon to notice. "I don't know why, after all you said last night, that you've decided..." She became aware suddenly, by the very quality of his stillness, that she was touching him. And that he didn't want her to.

She removed her hand, frightened by the look in his eyes.

"My God," she said softly. "Devon's not the reason you don't want to come here again. I am. You're using his condition as your excuse, but I'm the reason for this sudden change of heart."

Because he feared he was losing the ability to dissemble, to hide what he felt for her, Avon had waited for her accusation. But when she spoke, he realized that she still didn't know. And he wondered how she could not be aware of his feelings, feelings he had fought against since the night they'd met.

"Because I came to your house. And last night," she went on. "You think I'm so infatuated with you that you have to avoid me. It's not Devon you're trying to protect. It's yourself." She waited, but when he didn't deny what she had suggested, she took his silence as confirmation.

And he accepted the escape she offered him.

"No," he said softly, "not myself."

For a moment Emily didn't know what he meant. "Me? You're protecting me? From my feelings for you?" She was furious with his opinion of her control. "I'm not a child," she challenged. "And I've made my own decisions for a long time. I don't need your protection of my emotions. I assure you I'm more than capable of managing my own life and conducting my own affairs of the heart."

She had given Avon the means then to destroy forever what he had watched develop in their few meetings. He couldn't explain what had happened between them; mutual and elemental, it had struck uninvited and unsought. And would remain, in his case, forever unchanged, he knew. But he could destroy what she felt for him. She had just invited its destruction.

"I told you I've moved beyond flirtations. And I'm experienced enough, perhaps, to recognize the responses. A look. A touch." He stopped the catalogue of all she supposed he had read in her reactions and smiled in what appeared to be polite boredom. "Forgive me if I confess more than a passing familiarity with the signs of infatuation."

Emily wondered how many women through the years had made those unspoken offers. And how many he had accepted.

He interrupted her painful reflection. "So if you're suggesting a furthering of our relationship into other, less conventional directions, I am, of course, delighted. You are a very beautiful woman. And given your nature, one who will be, I believe, remarkably passionate. You have only to say if that's your intent, my dear.'' The silken voice was softly caressing now, and he raised the fingers he had just rejected to his lips and lingeringly kissed them.

What he was offering her, in place of what he wanted to offer, sickened him. But there was nothing that didn't sicken him about the situation—what he was doing to her. And to Devon. He waited for her refusal, which, given all he knew of her, he had never doubted.

''No,'' she said softly, but her eyes had the look of a trapped animal, and she didn't remove her hand from his. ''You know…'' she began, and her voice faltered at what he now allowed to be revealed in his face.

''Yes,'' he whispered, smiling at her, and she wanted him then. Any way. Anything he was willing to give her. She recognized the pit that loomed at her feet, but she couldn't move back from the edge. Like the sheltering warmth of her father's house against the bitter rawness of a winter's wind, what he was offering drew her.

''No,'' she said again, but when his lips lowered to find and move against her own, they opened under his. And then his mouth found the silken texture of her throat, igniting again the passion against which she had no defense. She whispered his name and he pulled her within the protection of his arms and she felt the length of his tall body pressed along her softness. She was aware then of how much he wanted her, and the evidence of his hard passion reminded her that desire was the sum of what he offered. Weighed and balanced against all she wanted to give him, it was not enough.

She stepped away from the encircling arms and he let her go.

"No?" he said, watching her eyes. "Then I was mistaken?" he suggested, almost questioning. "This isn't what you want? Or do you know what you want? It is always your decision, you know."

She had no answer, nothing to fight his sardonic assurance. And so she bargained not for her soul, which was already lost, but for Devon's.

"What must I do, Dominic? Promise to be gone when you're here? Promise not to talk to you? Not to touch you again? I can't help what I feel. And I'm sorry that the signs are so obvious," she whispered bitterly. "Tell me what I have to promise, Dominic. Whatever you want—for Devon's sake. Don't punish Devon to punish me."

"I think it would be better for everyone," he began, the reasoned tone emotionless, "if I didn't come here again."

"Don't deny Devon what you've given him these last weeks. Whatever else you have to do, don't do that." She found the courage to meet his eyes, but at the denial in his features, she thought she had failed. Her eyes fell and she shook her head. Her fault. He had told her from the beginning that he couldn't want her in any other way. She had always known he was out of her reach.

She looked up again only when he spoke, compelled by her pain, against his will and judgment.

"If you would, Lady Harland, tell your brother that he may expect me the day after tomorrow. We have unfinished business."

"Dominic…" she began, but the cold voice interrupted before she could formulate whatever words she might have found to thank him.

"Good day, Lady Harland." She watched him leave, unaware that she lifted her chin as she had once before against his mockery.

* * *

The Duke of Avon rested both hands on the fine Adam's mantel in the small jewel-box house on Russell Square and stared unseeing into the dying fire, the only light in the darkened bedroom. His thoughts were not on the events that had taken place tonight in this room or on the exquisite woman whose blue eyes watched him by the flickering firelight.

The woman had always known that this moment would inevitably come, but now that it was happening, she found she was far less prepared to deal with it than her sophistication would ever allow her to admit. Especially to him. A little dignity, she reminded herself gently as she slipped from between the sheets and pulled on the silk negligee his generosity had paid for. And he had been generous. She had never had any complaint about that. "Or about anything else," she thought, feeling an unaccustomed stirring in a heart she had thought long dead to emotions she would have belittled as ridiculously romantic. She would miss him, she thought and, unbelieving, felt the tears burn behind lids that had not known their flow in more than a decade.

She blinked to control them and moved as gracefully as ever to place her long, pale fingers on the wide shoulders, feeling them shift under her hands. The withdrawal was slight and quickly controlled. She removed her fingers and simply waited.

Finally he spoke. "I think you know..." he began.

"Of course," she said softly. "I have known for some time that something's changed."

"I'll arrange for the deed to this house to be made over to you."

"Thank you, your grace." And still she waited.

"And you won't find me, I believe, ungenerous until such time—"

"You have never been ungenerous," she said quietly.

For a long time there were only the soft sounds of the dying fire and his breathing in the dark room.

"I'm sorry," he said finally, and at last he turned to meet her waiting eyes.

"Oh, my dear," she said softly at what she saw in his gaze. He met her look questioningly and she reached to touch the corner of the mouth that had given her so much pleasure. This time he controlled the urge to move away from her fingers, but she removed them suddenly and stepped back.

"I'm sorry, too," she said gently, and was amazed to find that she was.

He waited, searching her face, thinking that there was surely more, after all this time, that they should say to one another.

"Don't you know? My darling Avon," she laughed gently, "don't you know, even now?"

His eyes held hers for a moment, and at the pity he read quite clearly there, he finally took her hand and raised it to his lips. They were both aware that he barely touched the fine skin on the back of that slender, youthful hand, and she wondered briefly if he knew how hard she worked to keep it so young.

"I know," he said finally. "But I didn't realize it was so obvious."

"Perhaps only to someone who knows you well, who has known you for so long," she said gently.

She helped him to dress in the fading light, a task she had performed so many nights, and then he stood before her and smiled, genuine and without artifice and even, she believed, with affection. The smile gave her courage to straighten the darkly gleaming ruby nestled in his cravat.

"And shall I wish you happy?" she asked with a smile.

"I think you know better than that." Bitterness ran darkly under the calm voice.

"My dear," she said again, and at his look, she controlled her tone. "Then why—"

"Because I'm cheating us both. And because I can't do that any longer."

He waited a long time, and when she finally raised her eyes again he was surprised to see the glint of tears.

"And if I tell you that I find I'm willing to be cheated?" she whispered.

"Then I should be forced to tell you that I have found I'm not," he replied softly, sorry for the pain he watched move across the delicately painted face.

And then her smile was as composed and lovely as always, and she reached on tiptoe to kiss his lips, and then watched him open the door and disappear into the darkness of the hall.

The bending figure ran his finger down the list on the desk in the deserted office and tried to think what might be valuable here. He had only a few minutes to decide what he could use. It was becoming more difficult every day to acquire information that he could sell. And he knew very well who was responsible for the drying up of this profitable wellspring he had drunk from these long months. One man. One man between him and success. Between him and safety.

The tension of constantly covering his tracks and of knowing that, no matter how carefully he proceeded, that soulless devil was only one step behind him was becoming more than he could bear. It was a personal hatred now, a deadly game of nerves that he was determined to win.

So long as Avon couldn't identify the source of his problems, he still had a chance to pull it off, to get out of this with his skin intact. But it was only a matter of time. It had been more than a month since San Sebastian had fallen, and Wellington was even now ready to cross the frontier into France.

He was intelligent enough and well informed enough, as he should be with access to the finest intelligence network in the world, to know that things were winding down and that Napoleon's star was rapidly descending. Only a few more months and he would have achieved what he wanted. Only one man really stood in his way. No one else would find him out, but he recognized the quality of this particular opponent. Oh, yes, it was very definitely time to try again. But this time he would be rather more careful to distance himself from the scene and rather more sure of obtaining the results he wanted.

On an October night almost three weeks later, the Duke of Avon found himself tiring rather quickly of the smoke-filled atmosphere of White's. The play had been deep and, as usual, he had been a winner. His ability with cards was legendary and he was sure no one knew that it had been honed through necessity. His father had made him no allowance at all in the long years he had denied his son the refuge of his family's country estate, which he so loved.

The decision to send the boy to school had been undertaken with no concern for his new grief over the deaths of his mother and his older brothers. And the prospect of having his physical inadequacies exposed to a group of cruelly taunting boys had been almost more than Avon had thought he could bear. He had survived those early days at school by calling on the inbred arrogance of several hundred years and on every ounce of intelligence and ingenuity he possessed.

He had quickly learned that money changed hands even in that schoolboy environment and he had mastered the art of keeping up with each card that had been played and estimating the odds mentally of what was still to fall. Now, as then, he was unrivalled at whist, basset or faro and usually enjoyed a challenging game.

Tonight, however, he found his mind returning to Devon's most recent discovery that information had almost certainly been leaking from the Horse Guards for well over a year, and from other sources than the department presided over by General Burke. Someone had been dribbling scraps of intelligence to the enemy for far longer than Avon had previously suspected.

Damned bloody traitor, he thought, throwing down his cards with a violence quite foreign to his usual languid air. "Excuse me, gentlemen, but I believe I shall make it an early night." Since it was well after one in the morning, no one was overly surprised.

He only seldom frequented his club, but he still found that an occasional overheard bit of conversation could provide a link to some half-understood rumor, and he had made the effort in the past several weeks to utilize all channels of information in hopes that he could find the key to his unsolved puzzle.

He dispatched a message for his carriage, feeling in his hip and in the muscles of his right thigh the price he would pay for sitting so long at table. As he made his way to the front entrance, he was stopped innumerable times by acquaintances and by those who hoped for an acquaintance with someone who was literally a legend in the ton. His duels, his wealth and quiet elegance of dress, his affairs, had combined to give him the reputation of being a rake of the first order, and more than one gentleman called a question or comment about his luck or his horses in hopes that they would be seen talking to Avon and considered to have acquired some town bronze by their association with him, however slight.

One of the young bucks in attendance tonight, Freddy Arrington, was just returning to his table of friends as Avon made his halting way out of the card room. He knew that Freddy had become Emily's constant escort and companion, and he felt a knot of anger in his stomach as he watched the young man stroll gracefully between tables until they were eye-to-eye. Avon fought the urge to wipe the charming smile off that handsome countenance with his fist. He found the thought of this athletic ex-soldier putting his hands on Emily as repulsive as the remembrance of the man in the alley touching her.

Intellectually he knew that if not Arrington, she would be spending her time dancing and riding with someone else, but this actual face-to-face encounter caused a look of such malevolence to cross Avon's features that Freddy actually felt a cold chill move up his spine. He moved quickly back to allow Avon's passage, and as the duke limped by, effected a low and sweeping bow, as if royalty had just passed. A gasp of startled laughter from the gentlemen around the table was quickly smothered. Young they might be and foolish, but one did not annoy the Duke of Avon. They knew that his reputation for getting his own back was too well deserved.

Avon heard the sniggers and was well aware that Arrington had done something to evoke that quickly suppressed reaction. Hot, black rage rushed through his body. But he chose to ignore the scene, recognizing that if he turned back to face Arrington, he was perfectly capable of provoking a challenge. How Lady Harland would interpret his meeting her latest love interest on the field of honor he could imagine.

He accepted his beaver and cloak from the doorman, who

informed him that his carriage had just arrived. Avon thanked him and stepped out into the damp night in time to see his carriage disappearing around the corner. He knew that Hawkins had recently engaged a new coachman, but he couldn't believe he had found one imbecilic enough to think that the Duke of Avon exited White's from the side.

"Incompetent bastard," Avon muttered under his breath. He began to limp along the deserted street and around the corner, only to see his coach roll slowly past the side entrance as well. Feeling his temper beginning to slip out of control, first at the slight offered him by Arrington and then at the stupidity of this idiot whom he would certainly direct Hawkins to dismiss tomorrow, Avon quickened his steps as much as he was able.

It was not until he was passing the dark alley that backed the fashionable club that his instincts came into play, instincts that had been displaced by the thought of Arrington's hands on Emily's body. He suddenly felt the short hair on the back of his neck begin to rise, but by then it was far too late.

The rough hands that grasped his right arm from the rear knew all too well what they were about. The strength with which his arm was pulled backward at the same time a heavy foot was placed in the center of his back dislocated his right shoulder, and his cane fell with a clatter from his suddenly nerveless fingers. The kick propelled him against the railing on the brick steps of the building on the other side of the alley, and with desperation he clung with his left hand to the rail in an attempt to keep from going down before the three attackers. He knew that if he fell, he would never be able to get himself to his feet again without his cane or the use of his right arm.

Two swift kicks with heavy boots to his right hip and thigh produced such agony that all thought of remaining upright was banished from his mind, and he fell heavily in the corner made by the steps projecting from the wall of the building. Avon could feel the pistol he carried in the concealed inner pocket of his cloak grinding into his back, and he struggled to turn his agonized and unresponsive body so that he could reach it. As he fought to reach the gun, he kicked out with his left leg and heard a satisfying grunt of pain. Unable to find the small pistol in the folds of his cloak, he attempted to land a blow with his left fist, hoping to hold them off until he could grasp the elusive gun, but his nearest opponent stepped out of his reach, laughed softly and again kicked his leg. He felt ribs crack with the next blow, and then he fought to stay conscious as a foot struck his temple.

I'm going to be kicked to death in the heart of the most cosmopolitan city in the world, and no one will even notice until they stumble over my body tomorrow.

That was almost the last conscious thought he had as the blows continued to fall on his undefended body and head. He felt his life beginning to slip away and it was several minutes before he realized that he could hear voices and that other people were now in the alley. Only one of the Mohocks seemed to be still kicking him, and with detachment he heard a shot and watched through the blood that was veiling his eyes as the man's body fell heavily to lie beside his own battered one.

He knew he must be delirious when he recognized the figure holding the still-smoking pistol with calm surety. She was outlined against the light from the lamp on the main street, and he could see Lady Harland's face quite clearly as he sank into oblivion.

Chapter Ten

For Emily and her father, the evening had begun at Carlton House. Emily had worn a gown of heavy ivory-colored taffeta made with a new-style overtunic the color of café au lait and had been pleased with the result. The gleam in several pairs of masculine eyes as she danced a series of waltzes made the effort she had put into her toilette well worth her time.

She missed Freddy, who had not been invited. She had come to depend on his tart and witty comments to endure the endless round of musicales, routs and dinner parties at which she listened to the same gossip night after night. Despite herself, she too often found her eyes searching the crowded rooms for a glimpse of gray eyes or broad shoulders, and even once or twice believed that she might have seen him across a ballroom, only to discover later that it was, after all, some other tall, dark-haired man.

It was very late as they waited for their carriage. Once they were away from the crowds who had thronged the Mall, her father directed the coachman to take a less-direct route home in hopes of avoiding the main part of the crush. Soon the streets they traveled were free of traffic and the quiet of early morning London seemed as peaceful as the drifting fog.

"Did you enjoy yourself, my dear?" her father inquired as he settled his solid figure in the corner of the coach.

"I suppose," Emily answered tiredly.

"I noticed that you were busy entertaining a series of young gentlemen. Anyone interesting enough to relieve your boredom?" he asked, knowing her too well.

When she smilingly made no answer and looked out pensively on to the night streets, her father decided to press a point he had been forced to think about lately.

"Missing young Arrington?" he asked.

It was a moment before Emily replied. "I enjoy his company. He's amusing and he flatters me outrageously." There was a reminiscent light in her eyes. "What woman wouldn't enjoy the attentions of such a charming and handsome young man?"

"He's in love with you, you know. Has been for years," her father offered. "He haunts my office in hopes of seeing you or to check on your plans for the evening. You didn't think that it was an accident that he manages to turn up at every entertainment to which you've accepted an invitation, did you? Can't imagine how many of them he's crashed. If he weren't so handsome, he wouldn't get away with it at all."

"No hostess would be averse to admitting another eligible young gentleman with such pretty manners and style as Freddy. I can't imagine anyone showing him the door," Emily said, laughing.

"Shall I give my permission if he asks to 'pay his addresses with the object of matrimony'?" Her father asked, smiling at her. "I feel that he's working up to it. Yesterday he came into my office and stood around for no reason I could ascertain except to talk about you. Kept casting me speculative looks from under his brows as if weighing his chances of catching me in a good mood. I finally had to throw him out to get some work done.''

"Knowing Freddy, I'll have plenty of warning before he approaches you. He's apt to get his cart before the horse and ask me first.'' She looked at the gloves she had removed and was twisting in her hands. "It's flattering that he enjoys my company so well, but I haven't moved past thinking of him as a flirtation,'' she said, knowing very well the reason Freddy had no effect on her emotions. "I hope we'll be able to maintain that status for a while longer.''

Emily again looked out the window of the carriage as the quiet buildings drifted by, shrouded in the ever-increasing mist. A carriage was standing, half blocking their passage, and their coachman was forced to slow to guide his team carefully around it.

"Some young fool, probably drunk as a tinker and sleeping it off in the seat,'' Sir William grumbled as he peered into the fog for any evidence of the occupant of the seemingly deserted coach. But instead, as they passed, he saw the familiar markings and then the reins that trailed over the necks of the finely conditioned bays, which stood patiently waiting until someone should once again direct them.

"What the hell…'' Her father turned to look out the back of their vehicle at the coach they had just passed. Suddenly he was pounding with his stick on the partition between them and the driver, and before the coach had stopped, he had opened the door and was attempting to dismount.

"Something's very wrong here, girl. Don't leave the coach, no matter what.'' With that command, he turned and, calling over his shoulder for the coachman to follow, ran for the corner they had just passed and disappeared into the fog.

Emily sat for a moment and then, dropping her gloves,

pulled the loaded traveling pistol from the side pocket of
the coach. Her father had begun carrying it several weeks
ago, but had had no occasion to use it. Tonight in his agitation he hadn't thought to take it. Emily hitched up her
skirt with one hand and, holding the pistol in the other,
stepped out of the coach and followed her father and Tom
the coachman down the street. Unsure of their direction, it
was not until she heard the unmistakable sound of blows
that she turned toward the dark alley that twisted behind the
elegantly fronted buildings.

As she rounded the corner, she could hear her father curs-
ing quietly as he struggled with one of the three men who
had been in the alley. Tom's opponent was giving as good
as he got from the burly coachman, but it was to the figure
of the remaining man that Emily's eyes were drawn. He was
kicking at a bundle of some kind that sprawled in the darkness formed by the jutting brick steps of the building. As
Emily stepped into the alley, she realized that the bundle
was, or had been, a man. Her anger was so great at this
casual taking of a human life that she had no compunction
in raising the pistol and carefully drawing a bead on the
man's back.

The shot that dropped her target put a quick end to all
activity in the darkness. The thugs turned tail and ran. Tom
gave chase, while her father quickly realized he had more
important things to attend to.

Emily walked slowly to the side of the man she had
felled. She had no doubt that he was dead, since she knew
that her shot had been true, but she had also a great deal of
common sense. Just as she was deciding to her satisfaction
that the man was no longer a threat, her father knelt beside
the body in the corner.

He felt for a pulse in the neck and Emily heard him whisper, like a prayer, "Thank God, thank God," as he began to carefully survey the damage.

Emily could see only long legs in black trousers and gleaming boots sprawled on the filthy cobblestones. As she bent over her father's shoulder, she watched as he attempted to straighten the right arm, which was twisted at an awkward angle. Her eyes finally sought the face of the man who had been so violated. The pistol dropped from her hand and she knelt in her ball gown in the bloodstained water that covered the stones beside his body. The face was battered and beginning to swell, and covered with blood that continued to seep from a laceration over the right eye, but it was still quite recognizable as the face of the Duke of Avon.

"We've got to get him out of here, and without anyone seeing us." General Burke took charge of the situation, immediately realizing not only the danger to their lives if the attackers returned, but also of the speculation that would be the inevitable result of the Duke of Avon being attacked so near the center of fashionable London.

"Dominic," the general whispered and then louder, "Dominic, wake up." He knew from his years on the battlefields of Europe that injured men responded not to titles, but to the names their mothers and nurses had called them.

From a distance the duke heard his name, and he tried to respond, to at least lift his eyelids. After a great effort, it seemed to him that he could see the cloudy features of the man who bent above him.

"Thank God," Sir William whispered again and said hurriedly, "We have to move you. I'm afraid it's going to be painful."

The duke attempted to nod to indicate he understood, but he found that his success in opening his eyes was all the response his body would make to his demands. He felt Sir

William shift him upward against the wall at his back and he gasped at the resulting agony.

"You can't move him. You'll kill him. He probably has internal injuries. Get a doctor," Emily begged.

Avon heard the second voice plead in agitation and remembered his earlier vision of Emily standing in the entrance of the alley where he had been sure he was about to die. God, I don't want her here, he thought bitterly, and wondered what she would think if he cried out when they moved him again. He was determined not to make another sound and tried to lock his teeth in his bottom lip. It tasted of blood.

"Get Tom to bring the coach. If they come back, they'll bring reinforcements and they'll kill us all. Go, now," the general ordered his daughter in a tone he knew she would obey. He watched as she finally began to run to the main street in response to his command.

He knew he was playing a very dangerous game with Avon's life. He could get help, quite near at hand at White's, but instead found himself hoping that if any in those elegant rooms had heard the shot, they would ignore it and go on with their play. Discovery of the situation in this alley would perhaps put an end to Avon's usefulness and reveal his relationship with himself and his office, which had so far remained a secret. It seemed by far the best plan to hide the duke in some safe location and tend to his wounds there. At that point, he could send for a physician and attempt to swear him to secrecy, although he had little hope of being successful in that endeavor.

"Dominic, I'm going to hurt you again, but soon we'll be home and we'll see what we can do to ease some of this. Hold on now." The general lifted the half-raised body into position over his shoulder, as he had, when younger, carried men from the field. The duke was heavy, but desperation gave the older man strength, and he adjusted his burden and staggered out of the alley. The duke had made no sound at the general's manipulations due to the simple expediency of having fainted dead away.

Avon awoke some time later to the murmur of low voices, and was aware by the movement that he was in a well-sprung carriage going at a good speed. He felt his face resting against the softness of silk-covered breasts that smelled faintly of attar of roses. The slight sweetness of the perfume and the motion of the coach nauseated him, and he tried desperately not to retch. He turned his head and the pain that throbbed through his skull was blinding in its intensity. He forgot his nausea in the new sensation and again heard himself groan. He seemed unable to keep a tight rein on his reactions, and he hated the loss of his iron control.

"Shh, my darling," she said as she found his left hand and caressed it with her own slim fingers. "I'm afraid to touch you anywhere else." She brought his hand to her lips and kissed it, then turned her cheek so that it rubbed against the back of his knuckles.

He wanted to say her name, to let her know that he had heard her, but he could not think how to form the words. He put all of his feelings into the look he gave her as he held her eyes. But the darkness drifted in again, and he was not aware when they arrived at their destination.

"Where are you going to put him? We'll never get him up the stairs without arousing the whole household," Emily said. She was already dreading the thought of the agony they would cause in unfolding that long body from the coach and could not think what carrying him upstairs would do, at least without a great deal of help.

"There's the room behind, in the carriage house, my lady.

Since I married, I don't use it anymore. Don't nobody come there," the coachman suggested.

"Tom, you're a genius," her father said with relief, motioning for him to take Avon's booted feet and help get him out of the coach. Emily didn't want to watch, nor did she want to leave, but at the first tug, she turned and ran toward the house for scissors and bandages and anything else she could think of that might help.

When she returned, her father and Tom had deposited Avon on the unmade, narrow bed in the dark room. Its only other furnishings were a chair by the window and a washstand, basin and pitcher. She set the lamp she had taken from the kitchen on the chair and sent Tom to fill the basin with water; then she approached the still figure on the bed.

In the lamplight the injuries looked infinitely worse than they had in the alley. His face was terribly battered, and there was quite a bit of blood on his coat and down the long length of his right leg. Gray smudges of dirt showed clearly on his black evening dress where the attackers had kicked him again and again, and Emily felt her panic grow as she wondered how he could sustain such a beating and live. She put her hand on his right knee and moved to sit beside him on the bed. She looked down and realized she was touching his crippled leg. Without conscious volition, her hand caressed this thigh and then, as her father had done earlier, she bent down and whispered his name.

"Dominic," she said, brushing the sweat-soaked, bloody hair off his forehead.

Her father was cutting up the sleeve of his coat and then across the shoulder seam. Avon opened his eyes and watched the destruction for a moment and then said with a trace of his old arrogance, "My valet will be very annoyed."

Relieved to hear him speak, Emily smiled and answered

the familiar, self-mocking tone. "Yes, but think how well pleased your tailor will be."

Avon's eyes drifted to her face, then closed, as if he wanted to shut out her presence. Unwilling to allow him that luxury, she spoke again. "What's the worst? Can you tell us where to begin?" she asked, just to keep him conscious and talking.

Avon tried to marshal his senses enough to give an analysis of where the pain was most concentrated, but it seemed that his whole body was one great pain and he simply shook his head.

By this time, Tom had returned with the basin full of water. Emily dipped one of the cloths she had brought into the water and gently began to clean the dirt and blood from his face and head. At the first touch of the cloth, Avon's eyes opened and he flinched away, but then he made no movement to avoid her efforts and simply watched her face as she worked.

Her father had moved to the other side of the bed and had almost succeeded in cutting the front of the coat and shirt away from his body. He worked as Emily cleaned, and soon he lifted the entire section from Avon's chest and shoulders, tugging the shirttail out of the front of his trousers.

The duke's chest and sides were marked with abrasions and splotches that were rapidly taking on the purple of new bruises. She knew that broken ribs were highly likely and watched her father's hands as he examined as gently as possible the distorted right shoulder and then the rib cage.

"Dislocated only, I believe, but the ribs are cracked and will have to be bound," he said finally.

The general was certainly no doctor, but he had been around sporting and military activities all his life and had raised three sons. Emily had full confidence in his diagnosis.

She knew, however, that the more serious injuries might not be apparent for several days, not until the bodily systems began to fail.

"The quicker it's put back, the better," the older man warned, waiting until the import of what he intended to do sank into the duke's pain-fogged brain. Avon merely nodded, mentally preparing himself.

"Emily," her father said, and knowing what was expected of her, she put down the basin and moved to the left side of the bed. She wanted it to be done as quickly as possible and hoped that she and her father had the skill and the strength to do it the first time. She saw the same determination in her father's eyes as they met hers across the body of the injured man. They both knew he couldn't stand much more.

Emily knelt and slipped her right arm under Avon's shoulders. He tried to help by raising them slightly from the pillow. She put her head on his good shoulder and laid her left arm across his chest. She interlocked the fingers of her hands under his right armpit and prepared to exert force to lift the arm upward and back into place. Her father bent Avon's elbow and aligned the upper arm at what he hoped was the exact angle he must find to reset the shoulder. She prayed this would work.

She could feel the duke's breath stirring her hair and felt him inhale in an effort to prepare himself for what was to come.

The general said, "Now," in a strained voice and Emily lifted, forcing herself not to think of how they were hurting him, but of how she would care for him when this unpleasant business was over. She would have license then to touch his body, to care for him, whenever she wished.

Lost in her self-devised escape, she heard and felt the

shoulder slip back into place and echoed in her mind her father's softly spoken, "Thank God."

If possible, Avon's face had grown grayer, and the general wanted to get the worst past now and to then let him rest.

"Tear that into strips, Emily, so we can bind his ribs," he instructed as he held out his hand to Avon. "You have to sit up, your grace, so that we can wrap your chest. Tom, lift his legs off the bed so he can sit on the edge." He turned back to the duke, who placed his left hand in the general's outstretched palm. As the general heaved, Tom moved Avon's legs off the bed. As the right one was lifted, the patient's hand tightened convulsively and then his head fell forward on his chest. The general struggled to hold him upright.

Almost immediately, Avon came to and helped to straighten his own sagging body. "I'm all right," he whispered, but they found no reassurance in that claim.

Emily brought the strips of cloth and helped Tom support Avon's body as the general wrapped the bandages tightly around his ribs and then bound his right arm against his side, with the elbow bent and the right hand resting against his chest. They finally eased him back against the pillow she had brought as the general himself lifted Avon's legs up onto the bed.

This time Emily could see Dominic's face twist in an effort to avoid making any sound against that agony, and she met her father's eyes again.

"Go get some blankets and brandy, girl, while I take a look at the leg. And bring me something to cut away this boot," he instructed.

She turned and hurried from the room, shutting the door behind her. She leaned against it and breathed in great gulps of cool night air. "God," she whispered, "please let him be all right, please, dear God." But as she had prayed that same prayer many times over Devon's wounded body, she was not a great believer that all such requests would be granted.

Back in the room, the general was efficiently cutting down the right leg of Avon's trousers. As the leg itself was exposed, for the first time in twenty-five years the eyes of someone other than his valet and his doctor were allowed to examine that twisted limb. The general didn't hesitate, and using his same gentle touch, felt for the telltale signs that would denote fracture. The deformity was such that he couldn't be sure, but when he was finished, he felt relieved in his own mind that there was no greater damage than what nature had already inflicted.

"Leave it," the duke finally grated. "It can't be any worse." The general pulled the two sides of the cut trouser leg together and waited for Emily's return.

"You can come back in half an hour," her father said to her as she returned with the decanter, a glass, a blanket and his razor. "Go change your dress and clean up before you wake someone and we have to answer unwanted questions."

Since their servants were by far too well trained to ask inconvenient questions, Emily recognized the ploy to get her out of the way until the general had used the razor to cut the boot away and had finished undressing Avon. When she slipped back, in somewhat less than the alloted half hour, Avon's lower body was covered by the blanket and her father was raising his head slightly off the pillow to let him sip brandy.

Sir William and Tom left shortly after that to handle the details of getting Avon's coach out of the street. She had heard Avon's response to her father's quiet question, "My man, or Hawkins. No one else,'' and knew that the duke's disappearance would be handled with the help of his most trusted servants.

And then they were alone.

She touched the cut above his eyebrow and gently traced down to the abrasion on his cheekbone. She watched his eyes open and focus on her face.

''Don't cry,'' he said hoarsely. He had never wanted her tears; feared them, perhaps, above anything he had ever feared, but he was too tired now to explain to her.

''I always seem to be awash with tears when I'm with you. Do you suppose there's a moral in that?'' she said and smiled at him.

''Yes,'' he whispered. The bindings they had put around the broken ribs made it hard to breathe. ''But I'm not sure anymore what it is.''

''That I should avoid you? That you'll only bring me unhappiness?'' she whispered tenderly.

''You know that,'' he said, but it was a warning he was reluctant to give.

''Then do you want me to go away?'' she offered and saw the answer in his eyes before his faint voice responded.

''No. But I know that you should.'' His left hand lifted and his knuckles skimmed weakly along her chin. ''We both know that you should.''

''I don't know that at all.'' Emily smiled again and bent her head, and as gently as his lips had found hers in the alley that night, she touched her own to that broken mouth.

When she raised her eyes to look at him, he smiled at her again and whispered, ''I've wanted you so long...and when you're finally here...''

''Did I hurt you?'' she asked, tracing with one finger the cut that slashed across his lips.

''You shouldn't be here,'' he said.

"Now you've decided you want me to leave?" she asked, certain of his answer.

"No," he said again, "I don't want you to leave."

"What do you want, Dominic? Or do you even know?" she mocked his earlier questions to her, reading clearly the confusion in his responses. He was no longer in command. And the emotions she read in his eyes were balm to the agony he had caused before.

"I want you to kiss me," he whispered truthfully, wondering why he no longer had any control. When her lips caressed his again, he met her kiss with his tongue.

It was Emily who finally broke away, regretfully lifting her mouth from that beautiful ruined one.

"Tonight," he said, and his voice faded with the massive effort it took to think, the effort to tell her what he wanted.

"Tonight?"

"Stay with me tonight. Don't go," he begged softly. Then he closed his eyes, the only way he could hide what she would read there. Closed them so that she wouldn't know that what he felt for her went far beyond the sexual desire he had admitted.

And because she thought that the Duke of Avon had probably never begged anyone for anything in his entire life, Emily smiled and moved the chair beside his bed.

During the rest of the long, dark night, Avon was forced by his pain again and again to try to find a more comfortable position for his aching body. Each time he opened his eyes she was there, and finally he stretched out his good arm and she placed her hand in his. She gently caressed his fingers until, finally, he slept.

Chapter Eleven

The duke awoke to the sight of his valet bending over his bed. For an instant it seemed like any other morning—until he tried to move, and then the events of the night came rushing back. He realized he was certainly not in the high-ceilinged bedchamber of his home, but rather in a small, sparsely furnished room. He looked for the chair beside his bed where the quiet figure had kept vigil, and was disappointed to find that it had been moved to a position by the window.

"All right, your grace, let's see what damage you've done to yourself," said Moss cheerfully.

"I can assure you that none of the damage was self-inflicted." The duke found the strength to answer with his old sarcasm and began to relate the events of the previous night while he submitted to Moss's examination, which was rather more extensive and less gentle than the general's had been. Avon was reduced to gritting his teeth against the slightest manipulation of the crippled leg.

When Moss realized the extent of the pain he was causing, he turned his attention without comment to the other injuries. The valet said nothing until after he had also helped his master deal with one of the more humiliating aspects of being bedridden.

But Moss was secretly relieved as he stepped back after several long and painful minutes and said, "Well, you'll piss blood for a week, I've no doubt, but you'll mend, you'll mend." He slanted a quick look at Avon's perspiring features. "Unless you want me to call in that fancy doctor of yours," he offered.

"For a few bruises? I think not," the duke said, trying to dismiss, as always, his health as a topic of conversation.

"More than bruises. As you have cause to know better than anyone. But we both ken well enough what he'll tell you. And since that shoulder's going to be strapped for a week or more, you'll not have a choice. Simply staying off that leg will do more good than all his probing and prodding."

"As you say, I don't have a choice," Avon agreed, and Moss's eyes narrowed at the bitterness of his tone.

"It seems to me you've nobody to blame. I don't understand what you were doing chasing your own coach down the street and not realizing that it was havey-cavey. Must have had your mind on something else, and that's the truth, your grace. Not at all in your usual style. Unless you think they were common footpads. A random attack on someone who appeared an easy target."

Moss regretted the words as soon as they were uttered, but Avon ignored the unthinking reference to his limp. "As I certainly proved to be," he said bitterly. "But this was no chance encounter. They knew too well what they were about. Their first action was to dislocate the shoulder, effectively leaving me on my back and at their mercy. The next blows were all directed at my right hip. Too well informed to be accidental," he said carefully.

"Then it was another nearly successful attempt to put an

end to your meddling in our traitor's affairs. And you walked right into it. I still don't know what you were thinking of. Not protecting your own neck, it seems.''

Moss continued to mutter observations about Avon's recklessness as he carefully shaved the duke's swollen face and put the linens he had brought on the narrow bed.

Finally tired of hearing himself castigated as the fool he knew he had been, and in more pain from Moss's activities than he would admit, Avon broke in on the monologue.

''What have you given out to explain my absence? I suppose it will be several days before I can return home.''

''I'd say more like weeks if you're planning on getting there upright and under your own power,'' Moss answered calmly. ''You won't want to be pushing yourself, for you'll just slow down the healing.''

Knowing his master as he did, however, he doubted he'd be able to keep him abed more than a few days. After that, much would depend on the duke's determination. Moss had seen him push his body to extremes in the past.

''After all,'' he said as he finished patting the pillow into place under the duke's head, ''you're not as young as you once were, your grace.''

Since Avon had just reached his thirty-fifth year, he was justifiably disturbed that Moss thought him past his prime.

A little ice crept into his tone. ''And where am I supposedly spending these weeks while my decrepit body heals?''

''You're in the country, your grace, checking on the progress of your plan to drain the marsh behind Sandemer. Tired of the social scene of London, no doubt.'' Moss grinned as he removed a napkin from the tray that he had brought from the general's kitchen. He knew full well how little Avon mixed with the ton.

''Who else knows what happened last night?'' Avon asked.

"Hawkins, of course, and we had to tell Francis. Otherwise he'd be getting letters from your agent at Sandemer asking questions that you were supposed to be right there to answer. We couldn't think how to get around telling him, since he handles all your correspondence."

"I wish that had been unnecessary," the duke mused aloud. "The fewer who know the story, the better."

"What's done can't be undone," said Moss philosophically as he laid the napkin over the duke's chest and began to crack the shell of a boiled egg. He looked up at his master. "The staff here think you're the coachman's nephew recovering from injuries received when you fell off the roof you were repairing." He carefully spooned egg into the duke's mouth as he talked, and gave him an occasional sip of tea, although that operation was more difficult.

Moss wiped the duke's mouth gently to avoid the split lip and tried to feed him a bit of toast soaked in the soft yolk of the egg. "They don't seem all that interested anyway. To them you're just one more mouth to feed. I doubt Cook will save you any of the fine scraps from the family table, but she won't let you starve to death, either. Keeps calling you 'that poor boy.'"

The duke turned his head from the last few bites and Moss left him alone, feeling he had done well to get that much food past the hurt mouth.

The day was interminable. There was no comfortable position to be found, and in the afternoon the pain built enough to cause Avon to wish he didn't feel so strongly about the dangers of opiates. His mind went back again and again to the scene in the alley and he berated himself for his stupidity. He knew that the delay his injuries would cause in finding his quarry would no doubt cost lives.

Moss tended to Avon's personal needs with quiet efficiency, and the duke finally dozed through the late afternoon. During the period when he was awake, he tried to remember all that he'd said to Emily last night. He knew he had revealed too much, and he wondered if he could ever make her believe the denials he intended to make. He didn't want to face her, was not prepared to face her, but he had watched the door and waited for her to come all day. Irrationally, he wondered how she could stay away when she must know now how much he cared.

It was finally evening. Moss had just finished spooning the contents of a cup of broth into the duke and was cleaning his mouth and gathering up the napkin and utensils to take back to the kitchen when the door opened and Emily looked in.

It was dark enough that the valet had lit the lamp, and she saw that Avon was awake and propped up slightly on his pillows. Emily had briefly met Avon's highly unusual valet when he had arrived near dawn, and although not accustomed to servants who suggested that she'd be better off in bed, she had liked him for his genuine concern for his master and for his pains to reassure her that Avon would survive. "He's got a remarkably hard head," he had gently teased her, reading correctly the loving worry in her green eyes, "even for a nobleman."

Emily smiled at Moss and asked if she might come in.

"He's been fair itching for something to do. You keep him company while I take these to the kitchen and flatter Cook for my own dinner." Moss winked at his master as he picked up the tray and left them alone.

It was obvious Emily was dressed for an evening out. Her gown was white tissue crepe and the silver ribbon threaded in her curls matched the wider one that circled the dress's high waistline. Her red hair was gathered in a soft Grecian knot at the top of her head, and tendrils had been allowed to escape to lie on her neck and at her temples.

"You look like Hippolyta," Avon said approvingly. "Very classical."

Emily laughed. "Amazon was one of the names given me in my season, but I don't think it was complimentary in the least. I was tall, of course, and much too boyish, I suppose. Anyway, I was certainly not a success."

"Then you must enjoy being the success you are now," Avon said politely. It was a graceful answer, but he was thinking only of the men who would dance with her tonight. And he felt last night's bitter envy of Arrington's position at her side.

"What would you know of my success or lack of it?" Emily smilingly chided. "You certainly haven't graced the social occasions that I've attended."

"Well," he said quietly, "I have been accused of having very good sources of information."

The comment effectively reminded Emily of the dangers inherent in the duke's chosen avocation. For a moment she could think of nothing else, and he wondered if she were offended by the thought of the clandestine activities he had been involved in for so many years, far different and less noble a method of fighting than that employed by the men she admired. But in spite of what she felt about the rather sordid way he had been injured, she had chosen to stay with him last night. Avon's eyes moved unbidden to the chair she had occupied during those uncomfortable hours.

Following his glance, Emily asked, "Would you like me to sit with you awhile before I have to go?"

The gray eyes came back to her face, and at what, against his will, she saw revealed there, she moved to bring the chair close to his left.

He was aware suddenly that he could reach out and touch the fine material of her gown, and he fought the urge to raise his hand.

"I wanted to thank you for what you did last night," he said instead. "You and your father saved my life, and I find that I've grown attached to it. I am grateful."

Uncomfortable with his thanks, Emily attempted to lighten the mood. "At least you didn't have to deal with again disposing of an inconvenient body in the most fashionable part of London last night. My father was forced to find a solution for that."

"How—" Avon began, but she interrupted.

"I didn't ask. I didn't want to know."

Avon misread the look on her suddenly still face. "Emily," he said softly, "I'm sorry you were the one who had to pull the trigger."

She turned in surprise and shook her head. "Are you imagining that I regret shooting that…" Her vocabulary included the word she sought, but she would never use it before him. So she said very clearly, willing him to believe, "I would gladly shoot him again. My only regret is that I wasn't sooner."

She knew her emotions were too obvious. She rose quickly and looked down at the battered man whose life she had probably saved. In spite of what she had offered in her bargain, she reached down and touched the hand she had kissed last night. She wondered if he felt the almost-physical jolt that moved through her body when she touched him. His fingers caught her hand and he held it a moment. He folded her fingers into her palm and watched his thumb caress the fine kid of her glove.

He looked up and smiled at her, and she knew it must hurt his broken mouth. "You offered me friendship once. And I didn't understand its value. But if you could forgive me for all that's passed between us since that day, I would very much like to be your friend. Do you suppose," he asked softly, "that we could begin again?"

She looked into his eyes and saw that now there was, indeed, only friendship in the clear silver depths. But she remembered what she had seen there last night and slowly shook her head. His fingers involuntarily tightened their hold, and then he released her and let his hand fall back to the bed.

He looked down as if at a loss for how to deal with their situation, and she spoke into the silence.

"I don't want to be your *friend,* Dominic." She placed a gloved hand on either side of his head and, leaning down, kissed him, as she had last night, tenderly on the mouth. For a second she felt his lips part and soften, and then he remained still, not responding to her kiss or raising his hand to touch her or in any way indicating that he desired more now than the relationship he had just offered her.

She finally raised her head, and he smiled at her again, rare and open and without mockery.

"But friendship," he said softly, "is now the only coin with which I have to deal."

Freddy was one of the first people Emily encountered at the reception, and she wondered, in light of her father's comments, if he had been invited. He whisked her onto the dance floor and into a waltz, and she allowed herself to relax and enjoy the sensation of floating in the arms of a very graceful partner. His strong hand guided her easily and he didn't bother her by forcing her to engage in chatter. She realized again how much she enjoyed his undemanding company and hoped that her shrewd father was mistaken in his assessment of Arrington's intentions.

"I believe the lady needed this. I could feel those lovely shoulders all tensed when we began," he commented as the waltz ended and he led her back to her father. He smiled easily down on her and then greeted her father with casual good manners.

Both men watched as Emily was led away by her next partner. "You have a very lovely daughter, sir. I hope to claim another dance later on, but I know that her card is always full."

The general made some reply, wondering if Arrington were finally about to make his intentions clear. Sir William had a better idea of Emily's feelings about their secret guest than his daughter realized, and he understandably felt a mixed reaction to the dangers of any association she might form with Avon. He knew her better than to think he might warn her off, however, and he wondered if in this blond, easygoing young Corinthian was a rival strong enough to break Avon's hold.

He sighed and wished he could get back to his office. At least he wouldn't have Arrington roaming in to check on Emily's plans. He might get some work done. He hadn't forgotten about the papers Devon wanted him to bring home. His son had been like a terrier at a rat hole since his recovery from the surgery.

The general smiled grimly as he realized what an apt analogy that was. Devon devoured material that it took him hours to pore over. He hoped one of them found something soon. Of course, with Avon out of commission for the time being, solving the riddle seemed to rest on Devon's shoulders. He never thought that his hell-for-leather youngest would buckle down to this kind of mental challenge. It seemed that Avon had disrupted his preconceptions about both his children, and the general could not decide if he should be grateful or not.

He sighed again and Arrington looked at him, grinning with quick sympathy. "Bored, sir? I realize that you'd rather

be at your desk than here. Would you like me to escort Lady
Harland home? I'd be very honored, with your permission.''

In accepting Freddy's offer, the general saw the possible
solution to several of his concerns. He wondered if his
daughter would be annoyed, but the thought of the work he
had to do and of the importance of the papers Devon
awaited overcame his scruples.

''Lieutenant, I accept. I'll leave it to you to charm my
daughter into believing this was a good idea.''

Freddy laughed and assured the general that Emily would,
of course, be delighted with his escort. ''I shall take great
pains to ensure that, sir, and I appreciate your confidence.''

The general made his way across the floor and disappeared into the crowd.

Freddy was at Emily's side as the dance ended, and he
took her card, deliberately tore it in two and put the pieces
into his pocket.

''Your father has left me in charge and I refuse to allow
you to dance with any more of those clods. Let's escape. I
know a little room…'' he said, putting his finger to his lips
like a conspirator and drawing her behind him. He carefully
backed Emily behind one of the palms that lined the floor
and then caught her hand and ran with her down a hallway,
tugging her into a small antechamber that was, indeed, deserted.

''My father entrusted me to your care and you drag me
off to some dark corner,'' Emily said, laughing breathlessly.

''At the first opportunity, I assure you.'' He smiled down
into her eyes.

She was not in the least concerned with Freddy's behavior, but knew that their presence together would certainly
cause a ripple in the ton if someone should come in.

''I only need a moment alone with you, Emily.''

He straightened his shoulders like a schoolboy about to

recite a lesson. "Surely you know that I hold you in very great esteem," he began, then allowed his posture to slump slightly. "Or I believe that's the proper line. Besides that, my mother likes you." Freddy laughed. "Not that that weighs heavily on me, but it certainly matters to her. God, Emily, I'm making such a mull of this, but you must be aware of how I feel about you. Of how I've felt for years." He smiled his beautiful smile, and her thoughts flashed back to the swollen, broken mouth she had kissed earlier.

No, Freddy, she found herself thinking, not now. Not this.

Misinterpreting her silence as shock or confusion, he took her hand. "Darling, can you give me any hope? I know you are the only woman I will ever love. I want to make you my wife."

The silence stretched between them. Emily could think of nothing to say, and finally Freddy tried to ease the tension.

"You're supposed to say that my offer is too sudden or that I must speak to your father. You're definitely not supposed to stand there with that stricken look in your eyes. What is it, my love? Surely you knew how I felt."

"Oh, Freddy!" Emily was desperate to make him understand. "Truly I didn't. I thought you were enjoying my company as I have yours. You are so much fun to be with, so undemanding, so understanding."

"Well, that's as unloverlike a description as I've ever heard," he said coldly. "Emily, I apologize for the awkwardness of the position in which I've placed you. I will never subject you to my obviously unwanted attentions again."

Emily knew she had hurt him and sought in the worst possible way to make amends. "I hope we may still be friends," she said softly. "I do love being with you, Freddy, but—"

"But you don't love me," he said bitterly. He attempted

to gather his shattered emotions. "Don't repine, my love," he said, finally relenting. "I expect I'll survive. It's the shock, you see. You know how strongly your heart's engaged, and you just assume the loved one knows what you feel and, you hope, returns your feelings."

In spite of his absorption in his own agony, and perhaps because he really did love her, Freddy caught the flash of pain that clouded her eyes. And with despair, he realized the cause.

"There's someone else, isn't there?" he asked with a sense of deep surprise. "You're in love with someone."

Emily put her hand on his and he saw the tears gather in her eyes. She blinked them back and shook her head helplessly.

"God, what a coil," he said in disgust. "Let me take you home, Emily. Surely you don't want to go back in there."

He guided her unobtrusively across the room and made arrangements for their departure as he tried to imagine who might have captured her heart. She had spent the vast majority of her time with him in the last few weeks, and he had seen no evidence of her interest in any of the throng of admirers who flocked around. She had treated them all with the same casual friendliness. He was often chided with their jealousy of his favored position in her court.

It was not until they were sitting in strained silence in his carriage that the thought hit him—Emily's reaction to Avon's greeting so long ago outside Whitehall. And more telling, the look the duke had given him last night. Freddy had perhaps misinterpreted that look, but if he were the one…

"I saw your iceman last night," he said, and knew by her breathing that he had his answer.

"My iceman?" She controlled her initial reaction very well, but it was too late.

"Avon," Freddy said, feeling the knife of jealousy in his gut. "Limping his crippled way through White's," he added cruelly. "You never did tell me where you met him, Emily. I wouldn't think he'd be a suitable acquaintance for you. There was a dreadful scandal several years ago. He made love to a young girl, ruined her and then refused to marry her. Resulted in her suicide. Of course, in Avon's defense, everyone said she threw herself at his head. He tried to make it clear he didn't want her."

He had hoped to hurt her by the story, but saw by her eyes that it was old news. He wondered that she could love him...crippled, cold, brooding and the subject of endlessly whispered stories. But the stories, too, often concerned his ability to bewitch women with that face. The image of Avon's deformed body touching Emily's sickened Freddy, and he tasted bile at the thought of her preference of that cripple to him.

"He was at school with my brothers," she said quietly. But she had already told him all he had wanted to know.

Moss had been outside for a last smoke when he heard the carriage arrive. In his role as self-appointed bodyguard, he had slipped to the side of the general's house to see who was calling so late. He saw a tall young gentleman jump out lightly and then help Lady Harland down. He watched as the man suddenly pulled Emily into his arms and kissed her very thoroughly. He recognized that Lady Harland's arms did not reach up to caress the man, nor did she respond in any other way. He watched as the embrace finally lessened in intensity and broke.

"Goodbye, Freddy," Emily said at last. "I am so sorry." She turned then and walked into the house.

The man stood a moment watching her and then climbed back into the coach.

Not the kind of threat to the duke I can do anything about, thought Moss, amused with the cleverness of his conclusion.

He could not know what a bitter enemy of the Duke of Avon's he had just watched drive away.

The small room was dark as Moss let himself back in. He had hoped that the duke was asleep, but knew that the pain would be bad tonight, and as his eyes became accustomed to the darkness, he saw that his master was watching from the bed.

"Did you need something, your grace? The general sent laudanum that the surgeon left for his son. I could give you just enough to let you sleep," Moss offered hopefully.

"You know that's not a solution I'm willing to employ," the duke said quietly.

He had never sought release from pain in drugs and there had been occasions in the past when Moss thought a rational man would have made use of the opiates that nature provided. Avon preferred to have all his faculties alert, unhindered by drugs or an excess of alcohol. But he suffered in silence—Moss would grant him that. He always had.

"I heard a carriage," Avon said. It was not phrased as a question, but Moss knew what he was asking. He supposed he had been lying here in the darkness listening for the sound of her return for hours.

"Lady Harland," Moss answered. He provided no more information and hoped that that might satisfy his master. He began to undress in the darkness, folding his clothes carefully and laying them on the chair where Emily had sat and kept watch last night.

"I had thought the general might come in for a while," the duke said. "Did the unlit lamp discourage him?"

"The general wasn't with her," Moss said quietly. He recognized a fishing trip when he saw one.

"Who brought her home?" The duke finally asked the question they both had known would eventually come.

"It was dark. I didn't know him," the valet answered evasively.

"Tall? Blond?" Avon probed, as one does a sore tooth, knowing that it will hurt.

"Handsome. Dashing. Athletic. Yes, all of those. I know why you don't want the laudanum. You enjoy pain," Moss said with disgust. He lay down on his pallet and made as much noise as he could, pulling up the cover, sighing, turning and yawning to signal an end to the conversation.

"And?" the duke asked in the silence that finally fell as Moss ended a convincing display of a tired man going off to a well-earned sleep.

"And what? What the hell do you want to know? I'm no Peeping Tom," Moss said, allowing hurt to creep into his voice.

"Then he did kiss her?" Avon said. "You don't lie worth a damn, Moss, and I'll let you know when my emotions need your protection."

Moss was angry then. "All right. He kissed her. Thoroughly. Seemed to enjoy it a great deal. It lasted a very long time, it seemed to me. Let me think. He put one hand on her lower back and the other arm around her shoulders. I wasn't close enough to hear if there was any conversation. Or any moaning and groaning, for that matter. He had on evening dress, so I guess he'd been to the reception, too. He probably danced with her. They waltzed, no doubt."

He realized he'd gone too far. Nothing was said for a long time and Moss wished that he could take it back, but he knew it was too late. The images had been planted, despite the fact that it was obvious Moss had no way to verify half of what his anger had made him say.

"She didn't kiss him back. She just stood there with her

arms at her side. God's truth, it looked like it was all on his part. I'm not lying about that,'' he ground out, but there was no answer from the darkness. The duke said nothing else in the long hours that followed, but Moss was aware from his breathing that he didn't sleep.

Chapter Twelve

Emily dressed with care the next morning to visit the carriage house. Freddy's practiced kiss last night had merely strengthened her conviction that Avon was the only man she would ever love. She was sorry that she had hurt Freddy and supposed that in his eyes she had led him on by her continued reliance on his unfailing willingness as an escort. But in fairness to herself, she knew that she had never by voice or action encouraged him to believe that she loved him.

She surveyed the sea green muslin morning dress and approved of the new, looser style in which Aimee had piled her curls atop her head. She had laughed at her maid's suggestion that she dampen her petticoat.

"For a casual morning at home, Aimee? I think not."

"A woman should use every weapon at her disposal. And I don't believe you are dressing with such pains to stay at home," the practical Frenchwoman advised.

Aimee had left her former mistress to follow her soldier-lover with the French army into Spain. When he had been wounded, she had stayed behind to nurse him, and the advancing Allies had found her, still cradling her lover's body in the midst of the abandoned French baggage. Emily had taken the heartbroken woman into her capable hands, and a friendship that went beyond the bounds of their positions had been forged.

Today, however, Emily laughingly ignored her too-accurate remarks and hurried down the back stairs and through the French doors into the garden. It was late enough that the gardeners had left, and the small grounds of the town house were deserted. Emily walked, seeming to enjoy the rare sunshine, until she was close enough to slip—undetected, she was sure—behind the carriage house.

Moss opened the door at her soft knock. He was almost sorry to see her, since he had a shrewd idea that the duke's insistence on rising and dressing this morning had its roots in his account of her homecoming last night. He had had his ears scorched with his master's impatience with his own weakness and the pain.

Together they had finally managed to deposit Avon, dressed only in a shirt and trousers, in the chair by the window, but it had been a long and agonizing process. The empty right sleeve had been tucked into the waistband of his trousers and the shirt buttoned over the bound right arm. Moss could only wonder that they hadn't driven one of the ribs through a lung. And he had not been able to watch the pain in the gray eyes. He understood Avon's desire not to appear the invalid, but couldn't approve of the effects on his health that he feared his determination would cause.

The duke had asked for a table and had been supplied with a small gilt one that was patently out of place in that shabby room. The papers Devon had sent him this morning were spread out over it.

Emily's eyes sought the bed first and then, when she realized Avon was sitting upright by the window, she said in exasperation, ''You need a keeper! Have you lost your mind?''

"I find that I prefer to entertain vertically, rather than horizontally," Avon answered coldly, the silver eyes reflecting the ice of his tone.

"How strange," Emily retorted with a laugh. "That's certainly not your reputation. Nor does it fit with..." She stopped at the realization that Moss was avidly listening to every word.

Avon made no reply, and after a moment he dropped his eyes to the charts he had been studying at her arrival.

She glanced at the valet, who rather obviously began to gather up the shaving basin and the breakfast tray. But even when the door had closed behind him, Avon continued his studied disregard of her presence.

So now we're back to the iron control again, my love, she thought as she moved until she stood on the other side of the cluttered table. She smiled slightly at his pretended concentration, and then reached down and took the duke's chin in her hand, turning his head so that she could examine his bruises in the morning light. If possible, they seemed even more colorful than they had the day before, and she grimaced at the sight.

Avon jerked his chin from her clasp and said bitingly, "I realize I look like a gargoyle. My apologies for offending you."

Emily laughed and repeated incredulously, "A gargoyle. My God, Dominic, you couldn't look like a gargoyle if you set out to. And I don't believe you to be vain, either," she said, wondering at the fury in those ice-gray eyes. "What have I done to make you so angry?"

"What makes you think my emotions revolve around your actions?" He deliberately lowered his eyes again to the paper he was holding, unseen, in his hand.

"Well, it's difficult not to when I seem to be bearing the

brunt of them. Shall I leave you, so that you may continue to read whatever that is you're finding so fascinating?''

At his determined silence, Emily's temper finally took fire. "Then I shall bid you good-day, your grace," she said sarcastically, and she curtsied deeply and gracefully.

She stalked to the door, but Avon's voice stopped her before she could turn the handle.

"Did you enjoy yourself last night?"

Emily turned, her anger at him held in check while she examined the new direction of the conversation.

"Yes, I did," she lied. "Very much, in fact. Now that the weather's cooler, many people have returned from the resorts. I saw several old friends that I hadn't seen since coming to London."

"And do you number Arrington among your old friends, Lady Harland?" he asked casually, his eyes still on his dispatches. "I believe you knew him on the Peninsula."

Emily now recognized the emotion that tightened his voice. It seemed the Duke of Avon was jealous, and recognizing the weapon he had placed in her hand, she was elated. She smiled involuntarily at the irony of his throwing Freddy up to her now that she knew she would probably never see him again. She had rather effectively burned her bridges behind her last night. She decided she'd deal with that problem later and would now simply enjoy the sensation of knowing that in spite of his assumed coldness, Avon cared. And apparently more than she could have hoped.

At her silence, Avon raised his eyes, but misinterpreted her slight smile. He felt the knife that was of his own making twist. He had long ago recognized his jealousy of the blond Corinthian, who was so exactly the type of man he believed Emily must favor.

"Freddy is indeed an old and valued friend. He served under my father in Spain and Portugal. I didn't know that you knew him," she said simply, then waited for his next move.

"And did you dance with him last night?" Avon was appalled at the question and dreaded her response. Feelings he had not realized he possessed had apparently been aroused by Moss's description of Arrington kissing Emily and by the thought of him guiding her in graceful circles around the dance floor, something Avon knew he would never do. The images had intruded time and again as he'd attempted to read Devon's detailed charts and graphs. He dropped the papers he was holding in self-disgust.

"Forgive me," he said quietly. "It's no business of mine whom you dance with. Or come home with. I have no claim on you, not even friendship, it seems." He met Emily's eyes and held them for the first time this morning, and she read in them more than he intended.

"Yes, I danced with Freddy. We waltzed. He waltzes divinely. Is that what you wanted to hear? And, yes, he kissed me good-night. Do you want to know how I enjoyed that?"

She paused to gauge the effect of her words, and seeing pain, was pleased. But because she loved him, she relented. "For someone who now professes a desire to be only my friend, you seem to show a remarkable interest in my romantic adventures. He also asked me to marry him, and since I haven't received an offer from the man I love, nor am I likely to, I suppose I shall have to consider Freddy's. I am, you know, quite on the shelf, even for a widow."

She watched the shock in the silver eyes. Your turn, my dear, she thought and moved again to leave.

"The man you love," he repeated softly, seizing on the salient part of her challenge.

She turned back to face him. "For a man supposedly skilled at interpreting data, you seem remarkably slow this morning. I think I've been in love with you since that night in my father's library when you deliberately set out to get rid of me. As you've been trying to do ever since." Emily laughed at herself. "Although I suppose that makes me the one slow at interpreting data. In spite of it all, I persist, clinging to the hope that unlike who knows how many other women who have found themselves in my position through the years, I might be the exception. The one allowed to share more than your body and your bed."

She ran out of breath and emotion at the same time. There was nothing left to say. Since the beginning of her dealings with him, she had made a fool of herself. He might want her physically, but there had been nothing in his words or actions to occasion her practically begging him to marry her. She supposed she deserved what she was feeling. She had done to Freddy what she had put Avon in such a position that he must now do to her. She lowered her head and waited for him to destroy her pride—again, but she knew that this time he would also destroy her heart.

I will not let him see me cry, she thought. Not again.

The room was very quiet after her outburst, and the stillness grew painful as she waited, head bowed, for whatever cutting rejection he would make.

Avon wanted desperately to go to her, to take her in his arms, but he was instead forced to sit and watch that proud head, bent and waiting for his dismissal of what she had confessed, his destruction of that hope. Never in his life had he hated what he was so much as at this moment.

He knew there was nothing he could do that would lessen her pain, but he could give her the truth. He owed her that, at least. It had been an unforgivable error that his pride had not allowed him to explain to Charlotte Stevenson, to make her understand his reasons. An error he had lived with for years. Not Emily, he thought, in sudden fear. God, not Emily.

"My darling," he said softly, allowing finally the endearment he had so long wanted to use, "will you come to me?" and he held out his hand.

She thought she should refuse, to maintain a pretense, at least, of being able to resist doing whatever he asked. But at his tone, she walked straight as an arrow's flight and took his hand. He held her fingers briefly and then pulled her, as Devon sometimes did, to sit at his feet. He seemed to gather his thoughts for a moment and then smiled down at her with the same tenderness he had shown her last night when he had refused the suggestion made with her kiss.

"If I was slow in acknowledging the gift you've offered, it's because I find it hard to believe that you could want what I am." Avon paused, and she could see the deep breath he took before he continued, "And when you know everything, you'll see that what you hope for is impossible."

Ice began to form around her heart. Oh, God, she wondered, what can he mean? What has he done? Even in the images drawn from the fear his words evoked, she could think of nothing that would make her not want him.

He paused and the focus of his eyes seemed to shift to a spot past her shoulder. She dreaded what was to come, but when he finally spoke, it was nothing she had expected.

"When I was born, my father refused ever again to touch my mother. She had stained the line of Avon with something he could never forgive. Nor was he allowed to forget it, for my presence in his home forced him to be forever faced with a son who moved like a broken crab, dragging a twisted and useless leg behind him. He avoided looking at me, turned his head if I walked into his presence. He would have sent me away, except my usually docile mother refused to allow it, and said that if he sent me away from Sandemer, she would follow and make the world aware that he had rejected his own son. Her threat was effective only because my father couldn't stand the thought of the ton seeing the horror their union had produced."

Avon's voice was utterly without emotion, but Emily's shock at what she was hearing was so great that she couldn't speak. She watched the haunted eyes of the man she loved and wondered at the pain of that small boy he had once been.

"My father's doctors assured him the deformity was a hereditary defect that they had traced for several generations in my mother's family, but that his older two sons seemed to have escaped untouched." Here Avon paused again, and Emily leaned her head against his knee, wondering what she could say to counteract such long-festering wounds. He gently, unthinkingly, touched her bright hair with his strong fingers and continued the calm recital.

"My brothers' deaths killed my father. I was suddenly his heir, and he couldn't stand to be in the same room with me. He sent me away to school in the same week they and my mother died, and I never saw him again."

Emily waited for whatever was to come, but when Avon didn't go on, she reached up and laid her hand against his face.

"Dominic?" She shook her head. "I'm so sorry, but I don't understand...."

"Then I'll put it into words for you. Any children I produce will be as I am—as deformed and crippled." He ground out the point of his story as if he couldn't believe Emily had not already realized the barrier between them.

"And so it ends with me. There will be no more like this." He took her hands from his face and put it instead on his knee, as if expecting her to faint in disgust.

Emily's relief was so great, she laughed, and Avon's eyes blazed silver with disbelief.

"Do you find that amusing, madam?" he said with the coldness of tone that must have frozen generations of lackeys who dared to be impertinent.

"'The tainted wether of the flock...' Is that how you see yourself? Oh, God, Dominic, I could kill you for frightening me," Emily said, and her soaring relief led her to tease him for believing his leg could in any way affect her love for him.

"I have a great-aunt who squinted. And another who was quite freckled. Should I not have daughters, for fear they'll throw out spots?" She laughed again. "Dominic, you are far too intelligent to believe that drivel. Whatever your idiot father believed, you must know that many things happen to children in the womb or in childbirth to cause injuries such as yours. Hereditary deformity, indeed," she said angrily, thinking of what he must have endured because of this cruel nonsense he so obviously believed.

"You can't know that, and neither did the doctors who told your father." She had a sudden shrewd insight. "How do you know that's what they said at all? Your father sounds perfectly capable of having made that up to make you or your mother suffer. And he's obviously still succeeding in his plan after all these years."

She laid her palms on either side of his face and spoke clearly, so that he couldn't possibly misunderstand.

"I do not care, my love, if our children limp. I don't believe that they will, but I can see that you truly do. I don't care, Dominic, just as I don't care that your leg isn't straight and that you'll never dance with me as Freddy Arrington did. I do not care," she said very deliberately, and then waited until the gray eyes were focused finally on her face, "but I shall care a great deal if you let your father win in his intended destruction of you, and if you deny me children from your body.''

The image she created hung between them, tantalizing in its sensuousness. But her words evoked the rest of what he had lived with so long, so that he tried again to make her see why what she wanted was so impossible. And why he had tried to protect her from what he had always known they could not share.

''My deformity is such that there is, of necessity, an unnatural stress on the hip when I move.''

She recognized the strain in his measured, dispassionate words and correctly guessed that he had never discussed what he was telling her with anyone except his physicians.

''Eventually,'' he continued doggedly, ''the hip will completely deteriorate. My doctors assure me that in my later years, I shall be unable to walk at all.''

''Then I'll push you in a Bath chair, my darling, and our beautiful, gray-eyed children will follow behind. Oh, Dominic, it doesn't matter. Truly it doesn't. How can you not know that? Nothing matters but that I love you and you love me.''

She stopped, suddenly needing his reassurance.

''You do love me, don't you, Dominic? You do want me?'' she questioned desperately.

He wished that he could lie, but he had promised himself to give her the truth. And this was part of the truth.

''I love you more than my life,'' he said tenderly, ''but I'll never marry you, Emily, and I shall never give you children. It's better that you accept that now and that we close this door forever. It's over before it begins. But before God, I'll love you all my life.''

''Dominic,'' she whispered, and watched the pain move through his beautiful eyes.

''No,'' he said. ''No more. I've known my own feelings

for some time. This decision hasn't been lightly made. Nor is it open to argument. And I want you to understand that in telling you how I feel, I'm asking for your help in dealing wisely with what lies between us.'' His voice was very low now. ''If, as you say, you love me, then help me to do this. And to do it with as little pain for us both as is possible.''

He saw the negative shake of her head and said more strongly, ''There is nothing you can say that will change my mind. It's an old truth. I've lived with it all my life. And always, Emily, this choice is mine.'' As he watched the sudden closing of her eyes, he knew he had cut her to the heart, but he also knew that he was right.

The Duke of Avon looked out the window of the room and spoke again in a voice he might use to her father or his valet. She realized he might never again let her hear the tone he had just employed.

''I'm going to ask you to leave now. Find Moss and tell him to come back. This will be better for us both. I promise that's true, Emily.''

She wanted something more, some token, if only a kiss, but she recognized the implacable nature of his decision. She rose from beside his chair and again placed her hand on his cheek, then left him.

When General Sir William Burke called on his guest that evening, he found him in bed with his papers spread over the sheets. He had questioned Moss quietly at the door as to the state of his injuries and had been told of the abortive morning session at the table. They both feared a setback, but neither expected Avon to alter his determination to return to his hunt as quickly as was physically possible. Nor did Avon admit how much he was feeling the results of his foolhardy attempt to pretend his convalescence was further along than it was.

"How are you, Dominic?" the general asked as he entered the room.

"Hoping that you'd come by," Avon answered. "I can't make heads or tails of Devon's charts. I wish I could talk to him." His frustration at his position threatened to surface.

"So much of what he says he's trying to do seems based on the sheerest speculation—to trace possible leaks based on French movements long after the events, to track when decisions were reached in, or revealed to, various departments in Whitehall, to reconstruct the staff of each office in the whole government at the times that those possible leaks possibly occurred, to find a matching element or elements in that framework. Your son's far too devious for me." He looked down at the papers, then leaned his head back against the pillows and closed his eyes. He looked exhausted. "I can't see how anything can come of this."

"Then tell him to leave it alone," the general recommended.

Avon opened his eyes. "But we have nothing else. You and I have looked. No trail, no mistake on that bastard's part. What galls me most is that the war is winding down—that's obvious from the latest dispatches from the Continent. And that damn butcher in Whitehall, whoever he is, may just get away with it all." The duke ran his left hand through his already disordered hair and sighed. "I don't know what else to do."

"Well, whatever the outcome, you seem to have done enough for today. Put the papers away and start again tomorrow, when you're rested. I don't know that the boy will find our traitor, but I know he has the mind for it. And the heart." The general cleared his throat and looked at the man on the bed. "You can't know what it means to me to see him once more interested in living. I don't mind telling you that there were days I despaired not only for his life, but for his sanity, for his will to live. You've given it back to him, Avon, and for that you will always have my gratitude.''

''I hope for Devon's sake he's the one to find him. I *hope* he's somewhere in these endless lists.'' Avon pushed the papers on his lap with unexpected violence and a few drifted to the floor.

He looked up into the general's eyes and spoke quietly, ''I owe you my life. I recognize the debt and I, too, never forget a service. But I'm afraid that whatever friendship you feel for me now won't withstand what I have to tell you.''

The general didn't speak or move, but only watched the man before him, already anticipating the words to come.

''Your daughter believes herself to be in love with me.'' He stopped, and the general saw by the way he breathed that what was to come was even more difficult than what had been said.

''I have, of course, told her that any furthering of our relationship is impossible. I am afraid that she didn't understand or accept all my reasons. I have asked Moss not to admit her to this room in the time I'm forced to remain here, and I assure you that I shall return to my own home at the earliest possible moment.'' He paused, as if at the end of a long and painfully learned recitation. ''You have my apologies, sir. I never intended to hurt her.''

''You'll find no finer girl, Dominic. She has the same courage as her brothers. Her birth isn't exceptional, but there's no reason for anyone to oppose the match. Or am I mistaken? Are your emotions not engaged?''

Avon shook his head and then, realizing that he owed her father some explanation, said only, ''The fault is not with your daughter.''

The general had to be content with that, recognizing, as Emily had, the look on the other man's face.

After Sir William took his leave, Moss began to prepare

his master for the night. As he put hot poultices on the duke's leg to ease the swelling, he hoped that Avon would allow time for his body to halfway heal before he decided he had to be gone from here. Moss knew his master well enough to know that the only way he would leave would be on his own two feet.

When he had finished, he tried to put the duke into a clean nightshirt, but recognizing the logical argument that they would just have to go through the painful process of taking it off again the next morning, he relented and left him alone.

He put out the lamp, but before he went to his pallet in front of the door, where he insisted on sleeping, he used an old-and-trusted servant's prerogative to have the last word. He spoke into the darkness to the man he could no longer see.

"You're a fool, your grace. I've cared for you man and boy for thirty years, and I've never known you to be stupid before. And you've hurt her to the heart. Don't you go thinking she'll get over it and fall in love with someone else and forget you. She's not that kind. She's the kind that will be there when you're old, and she'll love you then just the same as she does now. You're throwing away something most men only dream about."

As Moss had expected, Avon made no answer and gave no defence of the decision he had made so long ago.

Chapter Thirteen

During the next five days, Emily relived the scene in the carriage house and Avon's refusal hundreds of times. She could see no way to convince him against something that had been ingrained in him since childhood. She dressed and ate and pretended to sleep, while the tortuous circle in which they were caught ran endlessly through her head.

On the morning of the sixth day, she rose early from another seemingly sleepless night and sent word to the stables that she would like her horse brought round. She intended to ride, and ride hard, and if the Londoners who had managed to drag themselves out of bed didn't approve of Lady Harland tearing through Hyde Park at the crack of dawn, they could go to hell.

The morning air was crisp with the feeling of fall and the mist had not burned away entirely. Patches of it obscured the neighboring houses, and it even swirled about her boots as she came down the steps to await her mare. She was standing on the stoop, tapping her crop on her booted foot, when she heard the clatter of hooves on the cobbles. She looked up to find Moss handling the fresh horse with ease.

"Playing at groom this morning, Moss?" she called, and wondered why he was there.

"And why not, my lady? It's where I started. I know as much about being a horse's gentleman as I do about being a gentleman's gentleman, and that's the truth."

She laughed and asked, "Then how did you come to be a duke's valet?"

"Well, you see, my lady, that was more of the old duke's doings. I was a stable boy and he took me straight from there into his son's chambers. An insult, I guess it was. Only, me and the boy, we understood each other from the start."

The mare moved restively, dancing to the side as if frightened by the fog or annoyed by the delay.

"Whoa, girl. Steady down." Moss soothed the mare with practiced ease. "I'll help you up, my lady. She's anxious to start."

He tossed her into the saddle, then reached to adjust her stirrup when they both were aware there was no need. He patted the mare's flank and looked up into Emily's eyes.

"We'll be on our way tomorrow. Going back to Avon House. He says he's as well as he needs to be."

Emily could think of nothing to say as the thought of never seeing him again darkened the morning and all the mornings that would follow. Her hands loosened their control, and sensing her inattention, the mare plunged ahead. Emily pulled her up and around with sure hands and looked down at the waiting valet.

"Thank you, Moss, for telling me."

She wheeled the mare and set off for the park at a smooth canter. Moss doffed his cap and watched her out of sight.

"You're a bloody fool," he said, and even he was not sure which of the three of them he meant.

It was cooler in the small room that night. Moss spent the evening packing the few belongings he had brought from the duke's home. He had not mentioned Emily to Avon since the day he had been told that Lady Harland was under no circumstances to be admitted into the duke's room. He knew that whatever had passed between them was over and done, as far as Avon was concerned. He'd seen that look of bloody determination too many times in the past and had seen the man live up to whatever impossible task he'd set for himself too often to doubt that he would hold the line this time.

When he finished packing, and had straightened the room and laid out the clothes the duke would wear tomorrow, he finally spoke.

"I think I'll sleep in the house tonight. My bones ache in this damp. You know, your grace, I'm not a young man." He stood before Avon as if seeking permission to leave.

"I've told you for days you were a fool to sleep on that floor. I don't know what you thought you were doing. In spite of my rather inept record of late, you must know I'm capable of taking care of myself. I hardly need a body-guard."

Avon was sitting in the chair by the window. He was dressed only in his trousers, and the strapping around his ribs contrasted with the darkness of his skin. He had been sitting there for hours and Moss suspected he looked at the house as often as he looked at the ever-present dispatches.

"Well, I just thought I'd let you know that I'm going up," Moss said.

"Good night, Mother," Avon said mockingly, and Moss laughed and left. He had done all that he could do.

It was well after midnight. With Moss's departure, Avon had given up his pretense of studying the documents spread out on the table. He simply sat and allowed the images to form in his mind and to live there, as he would never give them life anywhere else.

He knew he had made the right, indeed the only, decision, but he knew what that decision condemned him to. And her.

Finally he stood, and taking his cane, went to put out the light on the dressing stand. Halfway there he saw her standing quietly in the shadows by the door. She was dressed only in her nightgown and her hair was loose over her shoulders. He felt the fire from its red, glowing warmth move through his body.

"Why are you here?" His question was the same one he had asked so many weeks ago.

She moved into the light and smiled at him.

"I've come for whatever you'll give, my love," she said softly. "I've discovered that I'm not too proud to beg."

"There is no point—" he began, but she cut him off sharply.

"The point is simple, Dominic. I'm offering you my body. You said I was inexperienced and I am, but I want you so very much. And I love you." She smiled again. "Surely those are coin with which I may deal."

"No," he said, and slowly shook his head. His eyes never moved from her pale face.

"Am I to have nothing?" she asked, and she moved a step closer to him.

"This can only cause pain," he said gently.

"There's already so much pain," she whispered. "Only tonight, only this. I'll never ask you for anything more." She recognized the desperate gamble in that promise. But she had nothing to lose.

"Your father is my friend. I'm a guest in his home."

"But this isn't my father's affair. And tomorrow you'll be gone."

She moved again, and she was so close that he could smell the scent of her, the faint rose, the freshly laundered cotton, even the subtle fragrance of her body.

He tried to control his breathing so that she wouldn't see the effort this was costing him.

She put her hand on his bare chest and moved it slowly, so that her fingers caressed the smooth warmth of his skin. She felt the increase in the measured beat of his heart. "Only tonight," she whispered.

"No," he said again, and moved back so that the space between them widened beyond her arm's reach.

"Oh, God," she said and the emerald eyes flared. "I hate your father. How can you do this? Are we to have nothing?" she repeated. "You say you love me. What do you see when you look down those years that stretch before us? What do you see? How can you bear it?"

"I see a chair or a bed," he said deliberately, and she clearly heard the pain.

"And who will you think of when you lie in that empty bed alone?"

"I'll do what I do now, my dear," he said, unable to stand any more. "I'll pay some beautiful and quite mercenary woman a great deal of money to lie there with me."

"Damn your soul to hell," she said, and she hit him as hard as she was capable across his mouth, uncaring when the half-healed cut split again and began to bleed.

He saw then in her face what he had done to her and said, "No, not like this. Not this way." And he gathered her into his arms like a child.

She cried, and they didn't speak for a long time. Finally, she pulled her head from his chest and looked at his face. With her fingertips she gently wiped away the blood that seeped from the damage she'd caused. It was time to use the only weapon she had ever had against the walls of his determination.

"And shall I do that too, my love? Is that what you want for me?" she said softly. "To ask Freddy Arrington to take your place in my bed?"

She knew by his face that she had done what she had set out to do: she had beaten him. But as she saw in his eyes the horror of the image she had just created, she wanted to say, as he had, "Not this way." Because she was a woman and because she had not, from the first, intended to be denied, she didn't.

She began with trembling fingers to unbutton her gown. Avon's hands closed over hers and gently pulled them away. He smiled at her, his eyes cleared of everything except his love for her. "That's not your place," he said, drawing her to stand beside the bed. He moved to put out the lamp.

"Leave it," she whispered, wanting the visual memories of the hard body that would hold her.

"There's light enough." He doused the lamp and waited for his eyes to adjust to the darkness. She could hear his uneven steps cross the room and then he was there beside her. He lay down and, taking her hand, drew her to lie with him on the narrow bed.

His fingers completed the task she had begun and finally, revealed in the moonlight, her body gleamed under his hands, softly luminescent. His lips moved with some emotion she couldn't read in the dimness, and then they were lowered against her aching breasts and she needed no guide to know what he felt. She closed her eyes against the pleasure of his tongue stroking over and around the tightening nipples and tangled her shaking fingers into the midnight of his hair. He turned his face into her hand and his lips pressed a kiss against her palm. "Don't ever forget, my love," he whispered. "Don't ever forget, through all the years, that you are forever my very soul."

Her heart paused in the frenzy of what his knowing mouth had already begun to create in her body. He was not aware of the tears that welled beneath her closed lids, and then she forgot to cry.

His hands had joined the delicate exploration and were memorizing, by touch, the gentle curve of her waist, the rounding softness of hip and belly, the slender silken length of thigh. She could feel the fine material of his trousers against her skin and wanted instead the sensation of his long legs against hers, flesh molded to flesh. But she forgot to want anything else when his mouth pulled hard, suckling strongly now against the peaking nipples, and her body responded, echoing those sensations, deep within, causing needs she didn't understand.

She knew only that she wanted to touch him. To put her own lips against his skin, against the hard muscles she felt burning into her breasts and stomach, against the long bones. But she was afraid she would reveal how little she knew of what he was showing her.

"Dominic," she whispered against the curling silk of his hair, and felt the reluctant hesitation of his tormenting lips. His mouth moved suddenly up to hers, which opened, welcoming, to accept him, to meet the demanding probing of his tongue. And finally, after a long time, he raised his eyes to watch her face.

"What is it?" he said tenderly. "Don't be afraid. I'm only showing you how much I love you. There's nothing—"

"I'm not afraid." She smiled away the concern in his face. "I could never be afraid of you, but I want to touch you, too."

She saw that she had surprised him. "Then why don't you touch me," he invited softly.

"But I don't know…"

"Wherever you want. As I intend to touch you," he promised.

"Here," she said. She put her fingers against the cut she had opened on his mouth. And lifted her head to tentatively caress the hurt with her tongue.

"And here," she whispered again, kissing the hollow formed by the strong bones of his neck and the discolored shoulder that had been so brutalized.

"No," he said suddenly, "not pity. Anything else you have to give, but not that."

Her lips moved again, and the delicate, frightened touch of her tongue against his own small nipple released his tension in a groan. He lowered his mouth again to the fragrant valley of her breasts and then lower, trailing along the ridges of fragile ribs, circling the depression of her navel, the slight concavity of her stomach, and lower still, until finally she arched against his lips. He listened to the sweet sounds she gasped breathlessly, into the darkness. They were sounds that had haunted his dreams—dreams in which she had moved with him to answer every need, every thrust, every caress.

So many women had moved beneath his body, had learned to please him, uncaring of their own release, wanting only to bind him to them with the strength of desire they tried to create through their performance. In her response there was no artifice, no effort even to bring him pleasure. She was lost in the spell he wove, lost as he had intended, her hands moving unconsciously over his body to answer only her own needs to touch him, to hold, to explore.

And when he finally entered her, moving into the ready warmth that he had so carefully evoked, she said his name again, in wonder at all that he had revealed to her. His mouth moved over hers to catch and hold the sound of it on her lips. And he felt against the long length of his body the shuddering ecstasy that she had never known before move in waves through each nerve and artery and muscle of her frame. He had at least given her this, alms beside the riches he held in reserve for her.

Then, in the spiraling strength of her response, he too was lost, thought and control for once forgotten. Taken by the tide that had risen, demanding, within his body for these months, he was thrown at last to rest on the shores of home.

And he knew and acknowledged that this was home. A home he would never visit again.

In the long years that were to come, Avon intended that the memories of this night would be so strong, so sweet, that no matter who touched her, it would be his hands she would feel on her body, his face that would appear when she closed her eyes.

Their journey began with tenderness and discovery. But before the morning broke, Avon had shown her darker passions and secret places in her own soul that she had not dreamed of, and he had marked her his with the years of his experiences. He deliberately used all that he knew of love to tighten the net of her senses, with his hands, with his tongue and mouth, with his strength and then finally, again, with tenderness, laughter and joy that spoke to her soul as well as her body.

In the morning, when he awoke, she was gone.

The men redoubled their efforts to entrap their prey during the next several weeks. Devon continued to search all correspondence that had been sent from Avon's sources in France and Spain through the network both into Whitehall and, when possible, to trace those that had been sent directly to Wellington at the front. He also charted all outgoing dispatches from the Horse Guards as well.

Avon and the general sent false information, traced the men who came in contact with it and waited for the French to react in some way to the bait.

Devon finally warned them laughingly, "If you go wrong with all that cleverness and the Beau just once gets hold of one of your ingenious plants, he'll kill us all." But they only nodded grimly, quite willing to endure Wellington's displeasure in order to succeed.

The news of Leipzig and Bayonne had given a sense of desperation to their efforts. Avon felt for the first time real despair that in spite of doing their best, they were failing.

He was sitting late one December night in Devon's rooms and had for the last half hour simply been watching the other man work. Devon was marking off names on one of his ever-present lists. Then he would go back to his charts and start whatever process he was involved in all over for another of the names.

Avon had for a while avoided the Burkes' house, but it was necessary, ultimately, that he come to Devon. There was no other possibility for them to work together except there, and he had finally given in. He had found in Devon not only a colleague whose determination matched his own, but a friend whose mind and spirit was compatible. He was also the brother of the woman he loved. He sat now in the small, quiet room and watched the fire, wondering if she were sleeping in the room over his head. If she were aware he was there, below with her brother. If she had thought of him through the long nights of these last weeks as he did of her and of the hours she had spent in his arms.

He was startled from his reverie by Devon's excited exclamation, "By God, there you are, you bastard. And there you've been all along."

"Do you mean you've found him?" Avon questioned unbelievingly.

"Exposed by his own cleverness like a traitor's head on the gate," Devon cried exultantly.

"Can you prove it?" asked Avon, pushing himself to his feet and coming to stand by Devon's chair.

"Do you mean, prove it to you? To your satisfaction? Yes, by God, of course," Devon said with certainty. Then he paused and looked into Avon's eyes, knowing what that which he was about to say would mean, understanding the burden he was laying on Dominic's shoulders.

"But in a court of law, to convict him as a traitor—no, there's no way in hell anyone could ever do that. He's too clever by far. We all underestimated him."

"But you're sure, in your own mind. There must be no mistake, Devon. You must know that this is the man." Avon spoke with great deliberation.

"There's no doubt," Devon said, answering the duke's gravity with his own cold certainty. "Let me show you how I know. There's a trail—in the papers, in the dispatches— that marks him as clearly as if he'd left his footprints." He laughed softly. "And I suppose that's exactly what he did."

He began to arrange his papers to show Dominic the path he had followed through the months to this one man, the man they must now destroy, with as sure and deadly an effort as they had employed to hunt him down.

"Show me his name, Dev," Avon said quietly. "Only his name, for the moment. I want to see our traitor's name."

Devon didn't speak again, and having no way to realize all the implications of what he now handed to Avon, he watched the play of emotions over the face of his friend as he read it.

"What will you do now?" he asked.

Avon straightened the paper his hand had crushed in an

inadvertent response to what had been written there. When he spoke, it was in a voice Devon had never heard him use before. It chilled him to the heart, and he recognized the implacable hatred he believed he had created in Avon for this man.

"I shall destroy him." Avon's eyes focused on Devon's face. "And I'm going to kill this bastard with a great deal of pleasure."

In spite of the coldness of the weather, or perhaps in some way because of it, White's was crowded that night. In the years to come, however, there would be far more men who would claim to have been there than the elegant rooms of the club could have ever held. Men would tell their sons that they had seen the quarrel that led to the duel, but the words that were spoken were too quietly uttered and the implications too subtle for any of them to understand the drama.

Only the two participants fully realized the events that had led them to this point. It was the intention of neither to clarify the malice they held for one another to the audience that hung in delighted anticipation on each soft and deadly word that was spoken that bitter night.

Avon had arrived early so as not to miss his quarry. He had played cards with his usual skill, locking his mind coldly on his purpose and blocking out any image that might cause him to blunder even slightly.

He had listened all evening for the voice he sought and felt the response in his breathing when he finally heard the laughter that marked the presence of his prey. When the group his target was with had had time to settle and begin their own game, Avon languidly excused himself from his table and began to make his slow way across the room.

More than one pair of eyes marked the duke's progress

through the club, but in only one pair of very blue ones did the import of those halting steps, directed so unerringly at his table, register.

To give Freddy Arrington his due, he watched unflinchingly as Avon approached, as deadly as a stalking leopard.

He knew that he had been found out, but he also knew that if Avon had any way to prove what he obviously believed, he would be under arrest. Freddy had worked hard to be where he was today, and he didn't intend to let Avon goad him into the fate the duke had meted out to others so mercilessly in the past.

The duke stopped at his table. His eyes were locked with Arrington's, and he did not acknowledge by so much as a nod the presence of the other young gentlemen gathered there. One of them said later that he literally felt the temperature drop as Avon approached, as if a ghost had entered the room and brought its coldness from the grave to touch the living, and the remark became one of the tales that would forever circulate about the night.

Avon did, however, include them all in his quiet words: "I seem to remember that you and your friends found something amusing in my passage the last time they let you in."

No one moved and certainly, this time, no one laughed. More than one of Arrington's friends felt ice move up his spine.

By God, he's out for blood, thought the Viscount Garrett, who looked in sympathy at Freddy and was glad he was not in his chair.

There was a faint flush across Arrington's cheeks, but he met the cold, gray eyes without any outward show of fear.

"Of course not, your grace. I merely stumbled in my clumsiness," Freddy lied, smiling with ease. Oh, no, you bastard, he thought. You won't get me this way. I won't give you my head on a platter.

He spoke again. "If you misinterpreted the laughter of my friends at my ineptitude, we apologize now. I assure you we meant no offense."

Several heads around the table began to nod, but Avon's eyes never wavered from his target, and he ignored the other young blades.

"So you are too cowardly to admit that my lameness causes you amusement." If possible, the duke's voice had become colder.

The word that was unspeakable between gentlemen had been spoken, and the quarrel was now almost certain to end in a meeting between the two. Considering the duke's reputation, several of Freddy's friends were coming to believe they were witnessing the beginnings of a carefully orchestrated murder. Garrett felt the sweat roll between his shoulder blades and wished he could straighten so that his clammy evening shirt wouldn't cling so to his back, but he was afraid even that small movement would attract those glittering silver eyes to his own face.

Arrington started and then breathed deeply, smiling again into Avon's deadly gaze.

"I am not a coward, but no, your grace, not this way. I won't make it easy for you. Go play your games with someone else. I really don't care what you say. Everyone here is aware you are only attempting to goad me into challenging you. But it won't work—not tonight and not ever." He paused, and again controlled his breathing. "Of course, you can challenge me, but I assure you I shall choose swords. I'm considered to be quite good. How are you, Cripplegate, with rapiers?" Freddy looked with contempt at the cane and then at the duke's twisted leg. "Not so agile, I would imagine."

But Avon was not to be denied. He had waited too long for this moment, and he controlled himself with far less effort than Freddy would have believed possible. The duke knew he had a trump he had not played, a weapon that he believed would strike at the weakest point of his opponent's armor. He would never have used it in this place and before these men, except that he had come here to win, whatever the cost.

"No, not so agile," the duke repeated Arrington's word, echoing the contempt. "I don't ride or dance, Arrington, but my leg doesn't hamper me in more intimate situations. I'm very agile there and, I have been told, very skillful."

He smiled deliberately into Arrington's eyes, and his smile revealed to his opponent his obvious satisfaction with his own performance.

A sick coldness coiled in Freddy's stomach as the implication of those soft words impacted just as Avon had intended.

"You lying devil. You never..." Freddy whispered, with the images newly awakened that he had denied so long ago of Emily's body and this distorted bastard's intertwined.

"Oh, yes," Avon answered softly.

Freddy saw by the glow in the gray eyes that Avon had not lied. He jumped to his feet, and the chair fell behind him with a clatter into the stillness that for the last several minutes filled the whole club. Although Avon had been expecting it, the blow that Freddy delivered backhanded across his mouth rocked him so that he was forced to clutch the back of Garrett's chair for support or fall at his opponent's feet just at his moment of triumph.

Avon put his hand to his mouth and brought it away with his fingers covered in blood. "And I'm getting damned tired of that, too," he grated, but his meaning was lost on them all.

"My second will call on yours," he said, fighting to keep the triumph out of his voice.

"Garrett?" Freddy whispered. He was still standing, with his knuckles resting white against the table and his eyes still seeing the images Avon's words had created.

"Of course," the viscount answered automatically, flinching as Avon nodded to him grimly.

Nothing else was said and the whole room watched in silence as the duke made his way to the door. The doorman already had his hat and cloak, and he helped the duke into them and then ushered him out the door. The silence in the room was unbroken until the door closed behind the implacable, limping figure.

Chapter Fourteen

Devon and the general sat in silence in Devon's sitting room. Their pretense at conversation had ground to a halt more than two hours before and now they simply sat and drank and waited. The general had moved to add a shovel of coal to the fire, but its blaze seemed to be losing the battle with the cold outside, which had frosted even the inside of the windows behind the heavy velvet drapes.

They heard the knocker and the quiet steps of Ashton as he went to open the door to their long-expected guest. They listened in silence to the sounds of the butler's greeting and waited while they visualized his handling of the cloak. Then they heard Avon's voice quite clearly from the cold hall. "Don't bother to announce me, Ashton. I'm expected."

The duke entered and closed the door behind him. He turned, and they knew by the triumph in his eyes that he had succeeded in what he had set out to accomplish.

He limped to the sideboard and poured out a generous portion of the fine old brandy, raising it in salute to the two watchers. It was not until then that the spell was broken.

Devon spoke first. "It's done then?"

"Yes," Avon answered, without elaborating on how it

had been brought about. "I hope, Sir William, that you will serve as my second."

"By God, yes. It will give me the greatest pleasure," the general answered. He had already dealt with his own guilt at letting Arrington run tame in his office. His uncle would have to be informed, of course, but the fewer who knew of the traitor who had worked for so long under their very noses, the better for the morale of the whole Horse Guards.

Devon watched the man who stood leaning casually against the sideboard. "He's an excellent shot, Dominic, and absolutely fearless."

Avon made no answer, but shook his head and smiled at him.

"I should hate to lose so good a friend to that bastard," Devon went on. "I've probably lost more than we shall ever know to him already. I only wish I could serve second to you." He looked down at his useless body and then up quickly, before either of his listeners could be brought to less than euphoria at what they had accomplished this night. "I suppose, though, that you, sir, feel the same desire as I to be a small part of his downfall." And he smiled at his father.

"I'd shoot him in the back myself without compunction," said the general. "It's by far the surest way."

Avon laughed a little bitterly. "I assure you, sir, I shall not miss."

He downed his remaining brandy and crossed the room. He stopped when he reached Devon's chair and put his hand lightly on the younger man's shoulder.

"You've had a greater part than I in bringing this coward to answer for his crimes." He paused, unused to putting into words the feelings Devon had evoked. "I've never had a friend, Devon, and I've always envied the esprit de corp that facing danger together gives those who fight in a different way than the one I've had to choose. What I feel for you is more than I could feel for a brother." He squeezed Devon's shoulder briefly, as it was Emily's habit to do, and the gesture brought her to Devon's mind.

"Someone must tell Emily the truth of this," he said.

No one spoke, until the general asked and then answered his own thought. "Must she be told? But if not, she'll attribute this to something else entirely."

The two Burkes looked at the duke, who met their eyes in turn and said only, "It doesn't matter." He saw that they would question his decision, so he went on before they could speak, "It's over." And then, lying to protect all of them, "No. It never began."

They were wise enough to leave it, and talked then only of the arrangements that would be made. The duke left shortly after that.

Devon's eyes met his father's as the door closed behind him. "She deserves the truth. She will perhaps lose them both."

But the older man shook his head. "There's time enough to decide how best to do it." He realized he had lost all direction in dealing with his daughter. In the weeks that had passed, she had become a quiet stranger who lived with them but was no longer a part of their inner circle. He did not know what was best, and so did nothing, which was, had he only known it, the most hurtful thing of all.

The morning set for the meeting was as cold as the night Avon had succeeded in driving Arrington to challenge him. He and the general arrived first, only shortly after dawn. The horses' breath mingled with the fog and the puddles on the field were as frozen and gray as Avon's eyes.

As they waited for the other carriages, the general looked

at the duke's set face, which he could barely see in the dimness of the coach's interior.

''If—if you fall today…'' he began hesitantly, because he knew it was not the second's place to bring up any possibility that the meeting might result in death to his principal. But he had seen the boy shoot and he knew the chances that they both would fall were very good, so he plunged on with what he had steeled himself to say.

''If you fall today, are there any commissions you should like me to carry out?'' He decided that was too vague and amended clumsily, ''Any messages that should be conveyed?'' He felt like a fool, but he hoped Avon would relent and give him some word that he could take to his daughter, some comfort for the darkness that would come.

But Avon's face was closed and he would not allow his mind to compose any thought of what he wanted to say to her. He shook his head and put his gloved left hand under his armpit to warm it. ''I wish the bastard would come. Let's get on with it,'' he said, his impatience the only trace of emotion he had demonstrated since the general had picked him up.

Too soon, as far as the general was concerned, the duke's wish was granted, and they had climbed out and were meeting the Viscount Garrett, who introduced them to the physician. The viscount's nose and cheeks were red with the cold and he looked very young to Avon, but he carried out his duties with quick efficiency.

The principals did not exchange words nor did their eyes even lock as the formalities were finished and the field was left to them alone. Freddy had recognized in the general's presence that all hope for escaping this was ended. His hopes for Emily were finished as well. All he could do now was to put an end to the coldhearted devil who had taunted him with her treachery.

They began the slow and deadly tableau they were to carry out, and as the count was made, the spectators were forcibly made aware of the differences in the two. Arrington strode with measured grace across the grass and Avon limped, as always, leaning heavily on his stick. The ground was rough and he was careful. He wouldn't fall here, before these men, before the man he had come to bring down.

At the appointed time they turned to fire. The sound of the two shots came almost as one and then a body fell heavily to lie in the hoarfrost.

The Viscount Garrett and the doctor ran to examine the fallen man as the watchers awaited the verdict that at least one of them could have given the second his shot was fired.

Finally the viscount spoke. "He's dead, your grace. Shot through the heart."

Avon nodded once and then put the back of his hand, in which he still held the Manton, to his forehead. The blood was flowing freely, even in the cold, but he knew the wound was minor. The ball had grazed his temple even as he had fired. His shot had been behind Arrington's, but he had taken a dangerous half second longer to be very sure of his aim. He hadn't feared the bullet of the other man as long as he got off his own shot. He had known he wouldn't miss. Not this time. Not this target.

The general rushed to his side and examined the wound. He took out a large white handkerchief, gently wiped away the blood and called for the surgeon.

"No," Avon said. "Let it go. It's nothing."

He gave the pistol to the general and, holding the handkerchief to his forehead, limped slowly toward the body. Seeing the look on his face and knowing that what Avon was doing was against the rigid rules that governed this combat, the viscount stepped between the body of his friend and the duke.

"No, your grace," he said, his shock giving him courage.

The duke looked at him blankly, as if seeing him for the first time, and then, using the hand that still held the bloody handkerchief, the hand that had just fired so surely the deadly shot, he gently pushed the viscount out of his way and advanced to the body.

He looked down on the man he had killed. Arrington's head was turned slightly to the side so that his cheek rested against the icy grass. Even in death his face was beautiful and his body sprawled gracefully. He looked as if he slept— at least until one noticed the large stain that marred the opened shirt and the still-welling hole in the strong young chest. Avon looked for a moment and then, in contempt, he threw the handkerchief he had been holding down onto the face of the man on the ground.

He turned and limped slowly back to the carriage and they all watched as he pulled himself inside. The general followed as quickly as he could, and the watchers on the grass continued to look as the coach made its way to the road and then along it until it was out of sight.

On the morning of the duel, Emily slept late. The last two months had been spent in a dull agony of spirit. The closest experience in her life to what she'd felt after Avon's rejection had been her bitter grief at the deaths of her brothers, but at least then there had been some purpose in the pain, some comfort in the thought that the sacrifice mattered. This was nothing she could rationalize as meaningful, and she fought the bitterness of her loss daily.

She rang for Aimee and rose before the maid arrived. Suddenly she felt unwell, and she sank down on the window seat and pressed her forehead to the coldness of the glass, but it didn't help. She turned her head so that her cheek rested against the icy window, pressed her lips together and swallowed to force the nausea to retreat. "I must be sickening for something," she thought.

She hoped that if she sat very still it would pass. She had long ago agreed to attend a prenuptial entertainment for Dorothea Averly that afternoon, but the thought of the table of exquisitely prepared foods set off the nausea again, and she wondered rather desperately what excuse she could offer today if she were unable to attend. She had used all the best excuses in the weeks past to almost totally remove herself from the social scene.

Aimee found her there when she came in answer to the bell and rushed anxiously to her side. She put her arm around her mistress and turned her head gently to look into her face. She was alarmed by the pale and clammy features, and she asked quickly, "Whatever's wrong, my lady? Do you feel faint?"

Emily shook her head and pulled away, putting her cheek again against the coldness of the glass. "My stomach, Aimee. I think I'm going to cast up my accounts." She tried to laugh at the extremely vulgar expression, but Aimee had no doubt her mistress meant what she said. Luckily, she returned with the basin before Emily did exactly what she had threatened.

When it was over and Aimee had wiped her face and cleaned her mouth, she gathered Emily in her arms and rocked her gently as a mother would a child, but she didn't voice the thought that had come unbidden to her mind. Emily's self-possession in the last weeks had hidden her fragility of spirit from her menfolk, who had been too interested in their own affairs to pry into hers, but Aimee was well aware of her mistress's unhappiness.

There would be time enough to decide how to help this

woman, who seemed not to realize what might be happening to her body. Being French and having been in love, Aimee had no reproaches, but she had already begun to plan the best avenues for dealing with her mistress's concerns.

Emily felt much better after that, and she dressed with care and presented herself at Lady Simonson's door at the appointed hour. She made an effort to respond to the women, several of whom greeted her with real delight and questioned the fact that they had been denied her presence through most of the Little Season. Emily made excuses, lied, and found that she really didn't care whether they believed her or not.

Her appetite had returned, and she ate from the table that had figured so heavily in her morning's illness. Although she didn't listen with any degree of attention to the gossip that floated about her, she felt her heart pause when she heard the name Avon being whispered by the group of women gathered around the Countess of Argyll.

She put down her plate and walked with far-too-obvious determination to join the spellbound group. They paid her not the slightest attention and continued to hang on the countess's every word.

"They met this morning, and Argyll said Arrington died instantly. Shot straight through the heart," she finished with delighted satisfaction, leaning back to watch the shocked looks appear on the well-cared-for faces that surrounded her.

Emily felt her throat close, and the hammer in her chest threatened to prevent her from speaking. "Freddy Arrington?" she rasped, and they all turned to look at her colorless face.

"Oh, my dear," the countess said kindly, and Lady Holland reached to take Emily's cold hand. "I had forgotten that you knew him." The women's thoughts returned to the summer, when Freddy and Emily had danced so gracefully through the rooms of the city's splendid homes. "Oh, my dear," the countess said again, "I am so sorry. I would not have broken this to you in this way for the world!"

"Who did you say he fought?" Emily's voice echoed in her own ears, awaiting the answer her heart already knew.

"Why, Avon, my dear," the countess stammered, and then, fearing the white-faced woman before her had not understood the reference, repeated, "The Duke of Avon."

"And Avon?" Emily breathed, but no one understood the question. She said it too loudly, desperate now to hear the answer. "Was Avon hit?"

A blood-thirsty chit, the countess thought, but there had been quite a bit of speculation that she and Arrington would make a match of it, so she answered as best she could. "A head wound, I think," and she struggled to remember the details of what her husband had been told over luncheon at his club. She need not have bothered, for they watched in dismay as Lady Harland closed her eyes and slid gracefully to the floor.

There was quite a commotion in the room for a long time after that, and although Emily protested, they eventually bundled her into Lady Simonson's spacious coach and sent her home. As she gazed out the window and fought the urge to fly to Avon's side, she realized they were passing the Arrington town house, and she stopped the coachman and explained that she intended to visit here awhile. Although he protested strongly, she finally succeeded in convincing him to return to the Simonsons' and then stood alone in the street before Freddy's home.

A grim-faced butler answered the bell and ventured that his mistress would not see her, but Emily convinced him to ask. She was not surprised when he returned to usher her into the dark room where Freddy's mother was sitting, almost lost in a huge chair.

Emily hurried to her side and fell on her knees before the still figure. Today the face had not been carefully painted in the old style as it had been on the previous occasions when she had visited, and the eyes, surrounded by deep wrinkles, were wide and staring. Emily took Lady Arrington's cold, knotted hand in her own, and finally the old lady looked down at her.

Emily could see the tracks of the tears that had spilled over those sagging cheeks and her heart went out to her. She had learned during these last months that Freddy and his mother shared a deep bond, and that, in spite of her constant bleating about Freddy's ineptitude with finances, she loved him very much. And now she has no one, Emily thought sadly, glad she had come.

"He killed my boy," the old woman whispered, and Emily's heart jumped with dread at what she now must hear. "Freddy never even told me they were to meet. He knew I would have forbidden it."

The thought of this woman forbidding a grown man to fight a duel should have been, but was not the least bit, amusing.

"Why do you suppose, my dear, he picked my son?" and here the voice wavered and then cracked. "My baby." Freddy's mother began to sob. "He always took such care of me. He saw to it that I had everything I needed to make me happy."

Emily soothed and listened to a litany of things Freddy had done to make his mother's life easier and more enjoyable. She hoped she was doing the right thing in letting the old woman talk. She held the frail hand, and since the conversation made no demands on her mind, she felt it wander to the scene as she imagined it had occurred that dawn. Again and again she watched the figures fall and thought about the countess's words, *A head wound.* What did that mean? Emily wondered, and knew from her experiences on the Peninsula that it could mean anything.

Finally, when she could stand her own thoughts no more, she deliberately turned her attention back to the words of the old woman.

"There was a time after my husband's death, I don't mind telling you, my dear, that I feared for my sanity. Tradesmen dunning us for things I'm sure we never had bought. I wanted to have them arrested, but my Freddy laughed and said that I shouldn't worry my head with all that nonsense. He said it was sure to be some mistake, and then he made it all right. We were never bothered again. He moved me to town and disposed of that old pile in Kent and he bought me this house. He loved me so much, you know. He used to say he'd never find a girl to take my place."

The old woman's eyes seemed to focus on Emily's face for the first time in a long while, and she smiled tremulously and said, "But I think he had made up his mind that you were to be the one. I'm surprised he'd not asked you." She looked questioningly at Emily, who only shook her head.

The old woman said as she had earlier, "I wonder why he killed my boy." And Emily couldn't bring herself to answer.

Moss had been frightened at first at the blood. It stained the high collar and white cravat and covered much of the broad shoulder. The look in the gray eyes he had seen before, and it boded no good for anyone in the duke's household. Avon felt himself executioner in these meetings, and the danger he quite willingly faced to accomplish what he believed must be done did not alleviate his awareness of that responsibility. And this time he stood too still by the long windows behind his desk and simply stared out, unseeing, onto the traffic below.

Moss waited as long as he dared, and then he simply brought what he would need and began to lay his materials on the gleaming desk. Finally, the duke turned from his inward contemplation.

"It's done then?" Moss asked quietly.

"Of course," Avon answered after a long pause. Moss knew then that his mind had not been back at the deserted stand of oaks where he had met and defeated his enemy.

"Let me see to your head, your grace," he offered and watched the gray eyes as the duke struggled to remember why he should be concerned. His fingers raised slowly to touch his wound, and Moss saw him wince and then look at the stains on his sleeve as if he had not noticed them before.

"It's nothing," he said as he had before. But Moss reached to remove the perfectly fitted coat, and out of habit, Avon allowed his valet to divest him of it and the other bloodstained garments, then he lowered himself carefully into his chair.

He eventually took the warm cloth with which Moss had begun to dab carefully at the wound, and cleaned the blood from his hair and face. He didn't flinch again when Moss examined the slice the bullet had made through the skin at his temple. With a plaster applied and a clean shirt, he looked almost himself again, and the valet stepped back and watched the long fingers play with the silver letter opener that they had found on the desk.

"You were right, you know," Moss said finally, and watched the eyes come back to the present and meet his.

"I know," Avon said softly, "but still, she didn't understand...." At the look of confusion on his valet's face, he realized that he had answered something that had not been asked.

"About the traitor, you mean?" Avon's disbelief colored

his rich voice. "Of course I was. Do you believe I question the necessity for his death? I think you know me better than that, Moss." He threw down the opener, his twisted smile mocking. His eyes dropped to his long hands, which he forced to lie still on the desk.

Moss waited a long time, doubting the wisdom of voicing what he wanted to say. But because he knew the man so well, he finally said, "I know it's far harder to do what you did this morning than to face the guns in a battle, to charge with comrades beside you. What you do, you do alone. And you always have. And I know you never remember that they have an equal chance to kill you. It could just as well have been you lying dead on the field."

"He had no chance at all, the bloody traitor. Not a chance in hell, Moss, and don't you believe that I regret that. I went there to kill a villain and I succeeded. As I intended to succeed from the first. If ever a man deserved my bullet..." The harsh voice stopped, cut off deliberately, and Avon put his hand to the bandage Moss had put over the wound.

"Thank you, Moss. That will be all for now. I have some correspondence that I need to deal with. Quite enough of the day has been wasted as it is."

The calm voice stopped at the quality of the silence, and he looked up suddenly into the face of the older man. What he saw there made him continue in a far different tone. "It's all right, Moss. I promise you it's all right." And then, "I'm all right."

Moss compelled the gray eyes to hold his a long time, and finally, realizing there was nothing more he could do, he nodded, took the stained clothing and the basin and left him alone.

Chapter Fifteen

By the time Emily left the Arrington town house, the afternoon light was falling and the evening promised to be even colder than the morning had been. She had refused Lady Arrington's butler when he had offered to arrange for the Arringtons' coachman to take her home. Since she did not intend to go home immediately, and since she couldn't explain her destination to this household, she now stood on the frigid, rapidly darkening street and realized that she couldn't walk to where she wanted to go.

She finally stopped a passerby who appeared to be a gentleman and, although he looked at her strangely, he did as she asked and was shortly handing her into a hackney carriage.

When she reached the address she had whispered to the driver, he helped her down, and she paid the fare and found herself again standing alone in the street. She gathered her courage and raised the knocker as she had once before.

"Lady Harland." Hawkins hid his surprise and ushered her in out of the darkness and the cold.

"I should like to see his grace, Hawkins. Would you inform him that I've called?" She watched the struggle in the dignified features, but she could not know of the careful instructions Moss had left. Hawkins personally believed that those instructions would not apply to the composed figure standing before him, whose emerald eyes were now too large for the wan face. He could see the tracks of the tears she had not allowed herself to shed before Freddy's mother. But he had had his instructions, and like Moss, he had seen his master in this mood before.

He cleared his throat carefully and gave her the simple truth. "I'm sorry, my lady, but his grace is not receiving visitors."

With that, Emily's fear was so great that she felt her knees begin to shake and the darkness start to gather around her head as it had at Lady Simonson's. She had spent five years in the worst possible conditions throughout Spain and Portugal and had never fainted, no matter what horrors she'd faced.

And now, she thought, I am about to do it twice in one day.

She must have swayed, for Hawkins' strong arm was suddenly around her waist, and he pulled her down on the sofa that graced the high-ceilinged hall and efficiently pushed her head between her knees. Through the ringing in her ears, she heard him call to someone and then detected the sound of footsteps on the marble floor. Finally Moss's face swam before her eyes, and as she sobbed, he gathered her into his arms just as Aimee had done this morning. He crooned nonsense to her and patted her back, until she finally made him understand her questions.

He looked at her with surprise. "Oh, my lady," he said kindly, glancing at the door to the duke's study, "he's fine. A scratch only, I swear to you."

She looked into his eyes and believed him, and felt her heartbeat begin to slow. Unreasonably, anger then replaced her fear, and like a mother who has just snatched her heedless toddler from the wheels of an oncoming carriage, she now wanted to rant at the very person she had just sobbed out her concern for.

She pushed Moss's arms away, and before either man realized that she was once again in control of her limbs, if not her emotions, she eluded them and was marching through the door of the duke's study.

He was, as she had expected, seated at his desk, and it was obvious by his raised head that he had heard the commotion in the hall and had perhaps even heard her voice. He had had some minutes to prepare himself for the confrontation he was about to face.

She walked to his desk and allowed herself the reassurance of studying the relatively small plaster that marred his forehead. He looked as if he had the headache and as if he had not slept, but she launched into what she had come to say without allowing herself to wonder what he was feeling now.

"Did you kill him because he loved me or because of what I threatened to do that night before I threw myself into your bed?" she asked coldly, forcing herself to remember the lost old woman, Freddy's mother, and not what had passed between them that night.

Avon had learned long ago from his father the futility of defending himself, and besides, somewhere deep inside, he wanted her to believe him innocent of the malice her words suggested as a motive, to believe because she knew what kind of man he was. He made no answer and simply watched impassively as her rage at his continued silence grew. She had dealt with more feelings than he could know that day and her emotional balance was already disturbed by changes neither was aware of.

"Well, Dominic, will you not explain yourself? Or is

there no explanation for your actions but your jealousy?'' she asked haughtily.

The gray eyes didn't flinch before her accusation, and his continued silence seemed in itself a confession that she had rightly read his motive. After all, what other motive could he have?

''Rather dog in the manger, don't you think? You don't want me—you've certainly made that clear in these last weeks,'' she said, admitting the pain she had felt as the hope that he would not fail to come for her after what they had shared had gradually died. ''But you'll allow no one else to have me, either. Is Freddy only the beginning? And you, more than any other man, have reason to know how wanton I am. Do you intend to murder all my suitors one by one? Let me assure you, if that is your intent, I plan to keep you quite busy.'' She smiled at him bitterly, but raised her chin almost in challenge.

His Grace, the Duke of Avon, was angered now himself. She believed him capable of killing a man simply because she had danced with him, had kissed him? She had just called him murderer to his face, this woman who had claimed to love him, just as he was, more than her own life.

With the arrogance that had caused encroaching cubs to quail throughout the years, he allowed his cold eyes to survey her trembling figure up and down, and then he answered with all the disdain he was capable of displaying, ''God, madam, you flatter yourself. Your charms were not quite that spectacular.''

She had hit him once before and had believed he neither would nor could ever again hurt her enough to provoke that kind of anger. But now she used a cruelty calculated to wound far more than her hand could.

''You're as twisted as that pitiful leg you drag around. Twisted and perverted.'' She had to pause to catch her breath, but in spite of what was beginning to show in his eyes, she went on. "You saw in Freddy Arrington what you could never be, and in your jealousy of his strength, his beauty, his grace, you crushed him, knowing that the comparison to what you are," and here she allowed her voice and her eyes to fill with contempt, "could only lead to disgust."

She turned and moved as if in a nightmare away from the look on his face, away from the desk and past Moss, who was standing, shocked and motionless, in the doorway. Only Hawkins had maintained any presence of mind, but then he had not heard the words that had been spoken in that room. He calmly handed her into the care of the Duke of Avon's coachman, who had been waiting, shivering in the cold, for several minutes.

When the coachman who had been dispatched to bring Emily home from Lady Simonson's returned and related to Ashton that Lady Harland had been sent home several hours before, the butler consulted first with her maid. When Aimee heard his story, she sensed that something was very wrong and cursed her reluctance to offer help to her mistress that morning. *If only she's not already done something desperate,* Aimee thought as she sought out Sir William in his study.

The general had not gone into his office for several reasons today, not the least of which was his reluctance to discuss his part in the affair of the morning and at the same time try not to reveal his deep pleasure over Arrington's death. Aimee found the general and Devon in a quiet discussion, and they listened to her tale with less concern than she thought it warranted.

"My daughter is well able to take care of herself, my

dear. I should think you would remember that," the general said, trying to comfort her.

Devon, however, suddenly had an uncomfortable thought. "Do you suppose someone mentioned the duel to her?" he asked.

"Why would a bunch of hens at a bridal party talk of a duel? Shows how little you know of women of this city, Dev. Surely word's not reached the ladies already."

But the seed of doubt had been planted, and since neither could guarantee how Emily would react to Arrington's death, their fear drove them to action. The general donned his greatcoat and called for the carriage. He could imagine how he would be cursed in the stables.

When he learned from Lady Simonson of the incident at the afternoon party, his concern and guilt began to grow. The Simonsons' coachman, when questioned, reported that he had deposited Emily at the Arrington residence. Lady Arrington's butler verified her call, but related her refusal to let him provide transportation home, and the trail ended there. After two fruitless hours, Sir William returned home and told Devon they would simply have to wait and depend on Emily's good sense.

When Avon's coachman deposited Emily on the steps, Devon, who had been watching from his window for the last hour, was relieved. Nothing so terrible would have happened to her if she were with Avon, who was his friend. The general stepped into the hall and called to his daughter.

"Come in here, please, Emily. Devon and I want to talk to you."

"I'm very tired and I haven't felt well all day. Could it wait until morning?" Emily edged toward the stairs and away from another confrontation. She supposed they knew of Avon's duel, but whether they had yet understood the reasons for his actions, she couldn't guess. Devon, especially, had come to admire him so. He had been as betrayed by the quality of the man as she, and she didn't want to face the pain Avon's actions must of necessity cause Devon. Not tonight.

"No, it can't. We've waited too long as it is," her father answered, taking her by the arm and leading her into Devon's sitting room.

Her brother looked up and smiled at her, but at the look in her eyes—a look he had seen in the eyes of troopers who had seen too much carnage, too many friends fall, too many horrors—he began to realize the scope of their mistake.

"What have you done?" he asked her, trying to control his voice.

"I have visited Freddy Arrington's mother," she answered calmly. "Did you ever meet her, Dev? A very difficult woman, I'll grant you, but she loved her son as you loved yours, sir," she said, moving her eyes tranquilly from one face to the other.

"Mothers love their sons even when they are unworthy," Devon answered carefully.

"Unworthy? Of his own mother's love? That's unkind, Devon, and ridiculous. Freddy was reckless and outrageous, but he didn't deserve to die today. No one deserves to be cut down like that. I know you admire Avon, but what he has done today is unforgivable and you must know it," she said.

"Why unforgivable, Emily? It was a duel, an affair of honor. Besides, Freddy challenged Avon," Devon said, continuing his careful probing.

"You know Avon provoked him," she answered, "but what you don't know is why."

"But I do know, Emily. Avon killed Freddy because he

was the traitor we had sought these months. He was the leak in Whitehall," Devon said quietly.

"Freddy? A traitor? Oh, God, is that what Avon told you? You knew Freddy. You fought beside him. Is that the excuse Avon used? And you believed him?" she questioned bitterly. "Yes, I see you did. Well, let me disabuse you of that notion, my dears. Avon killed Arrington because he was jealous of him. Because I taunted him with Arrington's love for me when Avon refused to marry me. And now you know the quality of the man you so admire." She looked defiantly into their eyes and saw not the disbelief, or even the pain she had expected, but something very different.

"Avon didn't discover Freddy's guilt, Emily. I did. And I assure you there was no doubt of it. He had been selling information to the French for almost two years. Very profitably, to judge by the way he was living," Devon said.

"The house in Kent had been mortgaged to the hilt by Freddy's father. The creditors eventually foreclosed, and Freddy, who had no skills except fighting and dancing, suddenly had no way to support his mother. She should have loved her son well. He betrayed his country for her gewgaws," her father said bitterly.

"I don't believe you," Emily answered, but the fear was growing in her chest already. "Freddy would never turn traitor. You knew him, Devon. How can you believe that?"

"Because I traced his guilt through hundreds of dispatches. It could be no one else, Em. There was no doubt."

Emily thought of the elegant house and the care Freddy took of his mother. She remembered Lady Arrington's words this afternoon about the time after her husband's death, and she suddenly knew that what they had told her was true. She couldn't understand it, couldn't fathom money being motive enough for anyone to sell out, but she began to believe simply because of the conviction she saw in the eyes of these two men she loved and respected.

Her father spoke again as he saw the acceptance grow in Emily's eyes. "We could never have proved it in a court of law, and the trial would have damaged the morale of men who didn't deserve to share the guilt for liking Arrington and for trusting him. But he had to be stopped. I wanted to shoot him in the back as the coward he was, but Avon wouldn't hear of murder."

At the word, a flash of pain passed across Emily's face, but her father continued, "Avon knew this was the only way, in spite of the very real risk he took of being killed himself. Arrington was an excellent shot. I went this morning, expecting to bury them both." He shivered as if the image were still too vivid. "Thank God, I didn't have to.

"Who knows what damage his spying did, how many men were lost who would have lived but for Freddy Arrington. How many were injured...." The general's voice faltered and stopped, but his eyes were on his son, and Emily's were drawn there, too. She saw the reality of Freddy's treachery in her crippled brother, and she knew she, too, would have pulled the trigger without a qualm, just as she had shot the man in the alley.

Then he's the one who tried to kill Avon. He's the one who arranged the assassination attempts, she realized suddenly and thought of that terrible beating and its consequences.

"My God, what have I done?" she asked softly.

"What do you mean, Emily?" Devon asked. "You're frightening me. What *have* you done?"

But she couldn't tell them and finally they let her go. She turned at the door and said only, "You should have told me." But there was no answer they could make to excuse their miscalculation, and so they said nothing as she turned the handle carefully and left the room.

The Duke of Avon was extremely drunk. He had begun drinking when Emily walked out of his study. It was now almost three in the morning and he was well into his third bottle. In a society where a man's drinking ability was measured by being a "three-bottle" or a "four-bottle" man, the amount of liquor he had consumed would not be considered out of the ordinary. However, since the duke had never in his life drunk to excess, it represented a monumental deviation from his custom.

He had always valued his control too much to relinquish it to alcohol. And so Avon drank only moderately—until tonight. Tonight he drank in hopes of drowning the pain that Emily had caused. Or if not defeating the pain, at least of blurring the words she had spoken in this very room. They seemed to hang there in the now-glacial air, and as he closed his eyes, he could hear them again...*pitiful leg you drag around* and *the comparison could only cause disgust.* It was amazing how much the truth, a truth he had lived with all his life, could hurt.

Avon put his head on the desk, and the glass he had been holding tilted, then rolled across the surface and onto the floor. At the sound it made, the figure who had been standing quietly for some time in the shadows by the door crossed the room and stood looking down at the man at the desk.

Moss had come once before to try to convince the duke to come upstairs to bed, or failing that, to let him build up the fire in the cold room, but Avon had thrown the first of the empty bottles at his head and told him to get out in a voice the valet had never heard his master use to him before. And so he had gone, angry, to his own bed, but found he couldn't sleep.

He, too, heard Emily's words over and over in his head and knew their power to destroy the one person he had ever loved. Finally he had come again, to tell Avon what she had said first in the hall, of her concern for his life. Perhaps in that telling some of the damage could be mitigated. He knew he could no longer leave Avon alone. He had watched a long time in the frigid room, until he had seen the proud head drop onto the desk.

"Your grace," he said quietly, "let me help you to bed."

Avon stirred and pushed himself upright, and his eyes focused slowly on the man before him.

"Are you still up, Moss? It must be late. Go to bed." And then, knowing why he was there, Avon lied as he had before, "I'm all right."

"It's too cold, your grace. You'll be all stiffened up. Let me help you up and then I'll massage your leg." He knew by the flash of pain in the slightly off-focus gray eyes that he had erred.

"I don't need your help, damn it. I'll come up when I'm ready. I'm not a child and I'm tired of your always hovering over me like a bird with one chick." The words were only the least bit slurred, and the next ones he spoke were crystal clear. "Get out, damn you, and leave me alone."

Not this time, my boy, thought Moss.

Aloud, he said reasonably, "If you're fine, then prove it. Stand up and walk me to the door, and I'll gladly leave you alone. Only a fool would sit here on a night like this with no fire."

"Are you calling me a fool?" asked Avon belligerently.

"You are a fool," said Moss with disgust. "You've let an emotionally distraught woman tear your soul with words. You learned a long time ago that words can't really hurt you. What matters is what you are, what you do." They both knew it was a lesson the duke had learned from Moss, who had repeated it over and over, until that message defeated the hurtful things his father had dinned into his skull.

"But I am what she said," Avon said bitterly. "And she may be right. Maybe I killed him because he wanted her. And now it seems she wanted him, too."

"You killed him because he was a traitor, trash who sold his country for money, and you know it, Dominic. And if she'd wanted *him*—" Moss stressed the pronoun "—he would have obliged her anytime."

"She wanted me, Moss," Avon whispered. "I swear she didn't lie about that. She came to me. I would never have touched her, but she came to me."

"I know, boy. She loves you, but she's confused now. You have to give her time to understand why you did what you did."

"She should know I would never kill a man out of jealousy. She should just know that," Avon argued. Moss heard the pain the brandy allowed him to reveal, and suspected that what he wanted to hear was reassurance that she couldn't be expected to trust him in spite of what it looked like.

Instead Moss said, "Yes, she should know. But people make mistakes, especially people who are in pain or who are upset. She thought when she came here that she'd find you hurt or dying." Here the valet paused to think how to make him understand. "She nearly fainted in the hall. She'd been told you'd received 'a head wound' and nothing else, so she feared the worst."

"But her father knew. He was there," Avon said, not making sense of what Moss was telling him. "He must have told her."

They were quiet as they realized the implications of her lack of knowledge about the nature of his wound.

"It's my fault," Avon said finally. "I told them it didn't

matter whether they explained the reasons for the duel or not. She must have heard from someone else.'' He leaned his head on his hand and said tiredly, ''It doesn't matter. None of it matters. I was right the first time. It was already over.''

There seemed to be nothing to say, and after a while Moss walked to his side and bent to help him rise. Avon struggled to locate his cane, and Moss found it on the floor and put it in his hand.

''Come on, your grace, let's see if we can get you up.'' They both knew, but had never mentioned aloud, that the leg had not been the same since the brutal attack outside White's, the attack Freddy Arrington had arranged. They would never know how much damage had been done that night or how much it might accelerate the ultimate fate they both had dreaded for so long.

Avon gasped as he tried to straighten the leg. ''God, Moss, I don't think I can stand, let alone walk.''

Moss felt the coldness of fear and said more sharply than before, ''I told you it was too bloody cold. You never listen to a thing I say. I swear, I ought to leave you sitting here in the dark.''

He stepped back to think what to do and heard the soft laugh from the man before him. ''Well, if you do, I assure you I'll be here in the morning. You and Hawkins can roll me upstairs.''

''Well, I'm glad you think it's funny,'' Moss declared, and when Avon laughed again, he said in disgust, ''You're too damn drunk to know what you're doing. I'll get Hawkins.''

''No,'' Avon snapped. ''I'll be damned if you'll rouse the whole household. I'll get up. Just give me a minute.''

He leaned his head on his hand again, as if he were too tired to try and needed to gather himself.

"I'm going to Sandemer," he said unexpectedly. "I've been thinking about it all night."

"No," said Moss, shaking his head, "you still have work to do, important work. When Paris is taken, we'll go. Not until. You know that."

Suddenly Avon looked up, and the pain in his eyes almost broke the older man. "I don't know if I can do this anymore. I don't know if I can stand it."

"You'll stand anything you have to stand. You always have," Moss said as he bent again to put his shoulder under Avon's left arm. "That's the cold and the drink talking," he said. And the pain, he thought, all the pain.

Together they succeeded in getting the duke on his feet. The muscles had stiffened and the leg dragged far more than usual, but they made it to the bottom of the stairs, which to them both looked likely to be impossible.

"Oh, hell," said Avon. "Stairs are the bane of my existence. Can't imagine why everyone doesn't just do away with them. Major inconvenience."

But he began the process of navigating them with his left hand on the banister and his right arm now across Moss's shoulders.

"A man who had any sense would have a bedroom on the ground floor." Moss grunted with the effort of the climb.

"'A gentleman does not sleep below stairs.'" Avon quoted his father softly. The man had made his crippled son, even as a small child, climb every night to a room at the very top level of Sandemer. No one had been allowed to carry him or even to help him. "Besides, what you mean is 'a man who has a *pitiful twisted leg* like this and any sense.'"

"Don't," said Moss. "They're only words. They have only the power you give them."

They had no more breath for talking, and in spite of the

cold, they were both sweating when they finally reached the top.

"Just a moment, Moss," Avon gasped as they stood there. "Just give me a minute."

His head hung and the sweat-soaked hair lay damply curled on his forehead. He looked up finally and smiled at his valet. "I told Devon I'd never had a friend. I suppose that was wrong, but I've always thought of you as something else. Wanted you to be something else." He looked down in embarrassment and then, as if the words were forced from him, he looked back up at Moss and said quite clearly, "I always pretended that you, rather than he, were my father."

He began to pull himself along the hall, and Moss, who had been dumbfounded by the words, finally moved to help him. The room they entered was quite warm from the fire Moss had built up before he came downstairs. He led the duke to the soft carpet in front of the hearth, hoping to warm his body, which had now begun to shiver. He began to undress his master, and the words that had been spoken at the top of the stairs reverberated in his head as Emily's had done earlier. He knew that from the pain of tonight, he, at least, had received a gift that he had never expected—had indeed never dreamed of—and one he would treasure all his life.

When he finally got Avon in bed, he began to massage the twisted leg with his strong hands. The distorted muscles of the thigh were tight with cramps, and he knew the hip ached and throbbed from the cold dampness and from the demands that had been made on it. At length the warmth of the room, the brandy and his efforts began to take effect. Before sleep claimed him entirely, Avon opened his eyes and said, "I know I'm drunk, but if I weren't, I suppose I couldn't say this. So for what the maudlin confession of a

drunk is worth, I want you to know that I love you, Moss.''
The remarkable gray eyes dropped closed suddenly like a
doll's, and Moss knew that he slept.

The valet stood for a moment, then gathered up the discarded clothing and straightened the room before he quietly
closed the door and went to his own quarters and lay down,
but as tired as he was, it was a long time before he slept.

Chapter Sixteen

It was very late the next day when someone shook the duke's shoulder. He could tell it was late by the pain the sun caused as he squinted to protect his eyes and, at the same time, bring into focus the face that swam before him.

"Your grace." He now recognized Hawkins's voice. "Your grace, wake up, please."

"What is it, Hawkins?" he managed to croak through the dryness of his throat. "What's wrong?"

"I'm sorry, your grace, but Lady Harland is downstairs. I told her you weren't seeing anyone. I thought, after yesterday, that you wouldn't want to see her, but she said she'd wait, and she's been there for hours. She won't leave. I don't know what to do." Hawkins's agitation could not have been plainer. He obviously had wakened Avon only out of desperation.

Avon couldn't think. He only knew he didn't want to see her, couldn't face her now. "What time is it?" he asked, not because he cared, but because he didn't want to deal with what message Hawkins should take to Emily.

"It's after three, your grace."

"In the afternoon?" Avon asked unbelievingly.

"Yes, your grace. She's been here since dawn, I guess.

She was sitting on the steps holding the reins of her horse when I came upstairs this morning. She's still in her habit. It was so cold this morning that I know she must have been frozen. But I tried to give her tea and she refused. She's refused everything. And she won't go home." Hawkins had reached the end of his tether, torn between his sense of loyalty to the duke and his innate kindness. "Moss won't talk to her and I don't know what to do with her," he finished, despair coloring his voice.

"Where's Moss?" Avon asked, trying to control the pain in his head. He let it fall back on his pillow and closed his eyes. Maybe without the light, he could think.

"He went downstairs to arrange for your bath to be brought up and to check with Francis about your schedule for today. He said you aren't well."

"No," said Avon slowly, "I'm definitely not well."

"Shall I tell Lady Harland that?" Hawkins asked, seeing a way out of his dilemma.

"God, no," said Avon, and his eyes snapped open at the thought of Hawkins painting him again as an invalid. For most of their relationship he'd been either shot or beaten, flat on his back or recovering from injury. What relationship? he mocked himself. She felt sorry for you because you were stupid enough to let Arrington have you beaten half to death.

Even thinking hurt his head. He closed his eyes again and said through the pain, "Get Moss, Hawkins."

The butler left, and with the closing of the door, the duke knew he had at least a few minutes to deal with how best to face Emily. He wished he didn't have to do this today, not the way he felt. He wasn't even sure that his leg would support him. "Pitiful twisted leg!" The refrain beat again in his brain.

He heard the door and looked up carefully, to see Moss

enter the room followed by two footmen with the bathtub
and several buckets of steaming water. The duke let his head
fall back and closed his eyes yet again. Moss waited until
the bath had been fixed to his satisfaction and the footmen
had left, and then approached the bed.

"I know you're awake." He put his arm behind the
duke's shoulders and helped him sit up.

The pain in Avon's head faded as the pain in the hip
began to protest from the strain of sitting. He had no one
to blame but himself for what he was suffering this afternoon, and no one would hear him complain. With Moss's
help he moved slowly across the room and lowered himself
into the water, hoping that the wet heat would have its usual
effect on his leg. Moss began to lather his face, and Avon
realized that his valet had not lectured him yet on what a
fool he had been. That was unlike him, and when he had
been shaved and Moss was putting away the razor, Avon
finally spoke.

"Go ahead. Say it."

"Say what, your grace?" Moss asked calmly.

Avon supposed he must be angry, but he had never before
been too angry to tell him what he thought. Suddenly Avon
wondered if, in his bitterness last night, he might have said
something unforgivable to his valet. He vaguely remembered launching a bottle at his head, but Moss wouldn't let
a little thing like that come between them. No, it must have
been something else. Avon sat in the cooling water and tried
to remember, but the night was a blur and he gave up.

"Whatever I said, I'm sorry. You must know that I would
never deliberately hurt you. I know that I was very drunk."

Moss made no answer, but the look he slanted at the duke
was filled, Avon could have sworn, with quickly disguised
amusement.

"You said nothing, your grace, for which you need apologize. I simply felt that you had enough on your plate today without my adding to it."

And although it somehow didn't ring true, Avon was forced to be satisfied with the explanation.

The bath helped, but dressing was painful enough to remind them both of the days they had spent in the general's carriage house. Those memories brought Avon full circle to today's problem.

"What shall I tell Lady Harland, your grace?" Moss asked as he stepped back to survey the result of their efforts. The dark gray coat fitted the broad shoulders and narrow waist to perfection. The pearl waistcoat and black trousers, the gleaming boots and the spotless, intricately tied cravat were the height of fashion.

"Tell her to go home," Avon answered coldly. He'd be damned if he'd struggle down the stairs in front of her.

"It's been tried, your grace," Moss said quietly. "She says she'll wait until you'll see her."

"Tell her I won't see her, not today, not ever. And see her out," Avon answered coldly.

"You want me to bodily put her out of your house?" Moss asked in disbelief.

"God, no, I don't want you to put her out. What the hell am I paying you and Hawkins for if you can't get one damned woman out of my house?"

"I'll go as soon as I've said what I came to say, Dominic." The quiet voice came from the doorway, and they both looked up in shock to find Emily standing in the open door of the bedroom. "You won't have to have anyone put me out if you only give me five minutes of your time."

It needs only this, thought Avon, and he turned and, leaning heavily on his cane, moved awkwardly to the chair before the fire. After lowering himself carefully into it, he looked up to find both pairs of eyes watching his every

move. He could feel the blood suffuse his face and knew
he was blushing like a schoolboy. The only solution, the
quickest way, was to get it over with, to let her say whatever
she had come to say and then to get her out of his house,
and his life.

He looked at Moss. "I think Lady Harland and I both
could use coffee. Would you have Hawkins send up a tray,
please."

Moss nodded and quietly left them alone.

"Lady Harland," Avon said calmly, "would you like to
sit down?" He indicated the matching wing chair and
watched as she walked quickly and sat, moving as gracefully as she always did. She was dressed in an elegant black
wool riding habit designed like an Hussar's uniform, and
like it, trimmed heavily with silver braid. The contrast with
her red-gold hair and ivory skin was stunning. In the bright
afternoon light from the window he could see faint bluish
circles under her eyes, and he thought briefly that she looked
unwell. Perhaps she had felt as bad as he had last night.
Perhaps, too, sleep had eluded her.

"I won't wait for the coffee. I know that you don't want
me here. I know that I have invaded your privacy again,
and that again, I am unwanted."

For a moment he couldn't understand what she meant,
and then he realized she was referring to the night when she
had come to him, had offered herself and had stayed with
him all night. He couldn't believe that she had thought she
was unwanted and almost told her how mistaken she was,
but he decided that the less he said, the less he was likely
to reveal of what he felt.

"I tried to hurt you last night. There's no excuse for what
I said, but perhaps you may want to at least know what I
was feeling." She looked up for some response, but the
duke's eyes were locked coldly on her face and he simply

waited for her to finish. She wondered in despair why she had come.

"I believed that when I taunted you with the threat of letting Freddy make love to me, I had goaded you into killing him. I know rationally how ridiculous that was. I know you are not a maniac who would kill a man because a woman—" here she paused for the first time, as if struggling to find the right words "—with whom you had…" Her voice faltered and then failed. She licked her lips and began again. "I know now that you didn't, that you wouldn't, kill him for that. I know what he did. And I know that the duel had nothing to do with me." Again she paused and touched her tongue to her lips.

"As for what I said, I know that you can never forgive me for that." She looked down at her hands, which were tightly twined in her lap. "I suppose the worst part of it all is, of course, that what I said is not what I feel."

She looked up again into his eyes, willing him to believe her when it meant so much. "Your leg makes no difference to what I feel for you. It's part of you and it has never disgusted me. I never compared you with Freddy at all." Her words evoked the ghost of the man he had killed, and she knew that she had not helped the situation.

She rose to go and realized that he had said nothing, intended to say nothing. She tried again, using the only weapon she had to breach the cold defenses. It was not a weapon at all, she realized suddenly, but a vow, a pledge.

"I love you, Dominic. I promised you once that I would never ask you for another thing, and I keep my promises. But I hope that some day you'll believe me and perhaps forgive me."

There was no answer and, indeed, she had expected none.

Moss arrived with the tray as she was making her way across the room.

Avon spoke for the first time since the valet had left, and it was to Moss, not to her.

"Would you see Lady Harland to the door, Moss? She's unable to stay."

His voice was not especially cold, but the bored politeness in it hurt Emily more than his anger would have, and she hurried down the stairs ahead of Moss and opened the front door before Hawkins could get to it.

Her horse, of course, was not there. It had been taken to stable this morning, and she looked helplessly at Moss, who turned back to make the arrangements.

Too quickly he returned and took her by the arm.

"He'll get over it. He knows, inside where it matters, that you didn't mean it. It's just hearing you say it that hurts. Knowing that you're capable of putting it into words."

He watched her eyes fill with tears, and because he hadn't really meant to hurt her, he patted her shoulder and said again, "He'll get over it."

"But he'll never forget it," she said with certainty, and Moss could only agree.

The groom's arrival with her horse put an end to further conversation and the valet tossed her up as he had once before.

"I'm going away, Moss. There's nothing to keep me in London. I need to get away from all the people who will try to comfort me for the loss of Freddy. I just wanted to tell you."

"Where are you going?" he asked with concern.

"To stay with my aunt in Scotland." She paused and then asked quietly, "Will you tell him, when you think it's right, that I said goodbye?"

"I'll tell him," he promised, and watched as she rode with her back held straight until she disappeared in the distance.

And then Moss turned and went inside to tell Avon.

* * *

Emily was careful to enter her father's town house from the garden entrance. She wanted to avoid any possibility of facing her father or Devon, although she believed that the general would have returned to his office today. It was so against his character to put off facing anything unpleasant. His work was not completed and, although Freddy Arrington's death had ended the threat of treachery from within, the battle against the enemy without was still very much ongoing.

Devon was really the one she feared encountering. He saw too much and her defenses were far too fragile to evade his sharp intellect. She had never been able to lie successfully to him. She knew that he would eventually have to know it all, but not now, not today. Her spirit was too agonized by what she had done, and she had decisions to make that she alone must plan and then carry out.

Aimee was not in her chamber when Emily arrived. In her tiredness, she simply unfastened the heavy wool jacket of her habit and slipped it off, then lay on her bed. She would call for Aimee later, and undress and bathe and go on living with what she had done. But not now. Now she wanted to close her eyes and not think, not picture his face as she said what she had.

It had been only a few words, but never before had she understood the power of the spoken word. She supposed that that was because she had never deliberately hurt anyone that she loved. She had never before watched her words destroy, burn, bite into someone's soul. She understood very well his coldness today. She wondered how he could stand to be in the same room with her. She who knew better than perhaps anyone else the scars he bore, had transformed them into fresh wounds.

She turned her head and realized that the pillow was wet

with tears. What else could she do? She couldn't go to him and say, "I called you twisted and your disability disgusting. I accused you of murder. Now that I find I am carrying your child, for my father's and my brother's sake I want you to marry me. I came to you and climbed into your bed, and now I, who have hurt you so bitterly—have hurt you in your manhood—demand that you pay the price for what I have done." She saw again his face and knew that she would never ask him. She had no right to seek his help.

There were no solutions. There was only pain for everyone. Soon she would have to tell Devon and her father, and see the pain in their faces as she had seen pain in his. She had gotten what she wanted from Avon. He had made love to her because she had asked so that she should have something of him, and he had given her what she had wanted. That triumph was now ashes in her heart.

All that she had been taught, all the precepts of honor and morality that she had discarded in the face of her desire, came back to haunt her. Her father had already lost so much—two sons and Devon wounded as he was. She had never intended to cause him pain. She wondered if he would feel as if he had to call Avon out. She wondered if Dominic would kill him as he had Freddy.

The door quietly opened in the middle of Emily's painful reflections, and Aimee slipped into the room, to come and sit beside her mistress on the bed.

"Did you see him?" she whispered. "I was worried when you didn't return. What did he say?" She gently removed the damp strand of tangled hair that lay across Emily's face.

"He said nothing," Emily answered truthfully. "He offered me coffee and was polite. He didn't want me there, of course. He would never have seen me, but I went to his room."

Aimee waited for her to go on, and when she said nothing more, she finally asked, "Did you tell him about the child?"

Emily shook her head. "I couldn't. I've already done too much wrong to him to force him into that position. He doesn't want children, and never wanted to marry for that very reason."

Aimee didn't speak for a moment and then she said reasonably, "Men sometimes find that they want children even if they didn't know it before. He is a very powerful man with a very old name. I think, myself, that he will want this baby, perhaps this son, to carry on that name. Men need sons, especially men in his position."

Emily shook her head. "He believes his deformity to be hereditary." She glanced up to see if Aimee's vocabulary extended to that concept. She explained again, "He believes his sons will be crippled as he is."

"He is sensitive to this disability?"

"He feels that it diminishes him." She knew that Aimee would never understand all that stood between them unless she explained. "When I thought he'd killed Freddy because he was jealous, because I had made him jealous…" Emily paused, because she didn't want to admit, even to this closest of friends, what she had done "…I told him that he had done so because he was jealous of Freddy's physical perfection."

"Perhaps he was," Aimee said calmly.

"But that's not why he killed him. I told him other things. I mocked him about his leg." Emily was so ashamed of what she had done even now that she couldn't look at Aimee as she said it.

"If he loves you, he will forgive you," Aimee said, gently wiping the tears from Emily's cheek. "You must make him love you enough, make him know that you don't care about this leg. Or do you?"

"No, of course not," Emily said sharply, "but he'll never believe that now."

"If you marry him and love him very wisely for a very long time, he will believe. Eventually he will believe because it is true. But first you must marry him. Your father will insist. You will have no choice. Your father will tell him about the child if you do not."

Emily knew that Aimee was right and that she must prevent that at all costs.

Aimee recognized the despair that showed quite clearly on Emily's face, and she began to give what comfort she was capable of, to undress and bathe, to comb and plait the long red hair. She brought a tray up later because she knew that her mistress had not eaten, and she even talked Emily into taking a few bites. And she didn't leave her, not through the evening and not into the night.

She knew very well about pain and grief and having no one to turn to. This girl over whom she kept her vigil had pulled her from despair, had offered her a way out, a good and respectable life. She did not intend for her mistress to make the wrong decisions. She intended to guide her as long as Emily needed her.

But a fever began during the night. The exhaustion, the despair, the ride and the wait in the bitter cold probably all contributed to the illness that raged through Emily's body. After the first two days, Aimee became truly frightened. She recognized that her mistress had found oblivion in the illness and its delirium. She no longer had to think and feel; she simply tossed through the night sweats and shivered under the pile of quilts that Aimee tenderly tucked around her body.

The doctor had believed that, as young and strong as she was, she would have a very good chance of fighting off the inflammation. But as the cold, bitter days passed and they watched her almost-physical withdrawal, even he began to fear that they would lose her.

Her father came often to stand by the bed and hold her thin, white hand, but she seemed uncomfortable when he was there, and at first she pulled away and shrank from his touch. Later she didn't respond to him at all, but lay with her eyes closed and listened to his outpourings of love without response.

"Emily," Devon said softly, and reached to brush the fine red strands off his sister's forehead.

Emily was tugged from the peace of the whiteness by the sound of a voice she knew shouldn't be beside her. She hadn't heard it in all the long days of her illness. She struggled to open her eyes, and found Devon's dark blue ones smiling at her. He was indeed sitting by her bed, and her fear for him was so great that she spoke for the first time in three days.

"Devon?" she questioned in a voice that even she didn't recognize. He smiled and touched her face very gently with his fingers. She licked her lips and tried again. "How are you here? Have they moved me downstairs?"

"No, my love, I made them carry me up. I had to see you. Father told me that you're very ill." He paused, trying to choose carefully what he could say to her. "He believes, Em, that you don't want to get well. The doctor believes that, too. But I told them that you're too brave. I know that you would never give up, no matter what. But you must tell me what's wrong."

"You had them carry you up the stairs? Devon, you know how dangerous…" It was difficult to express the thoughts that ran fleetingly through her mind. "Why did Father allow that? You must never do it again."

"I shall do it every day if you don't stop whatever this

is, Em. I swear I will.'' She could hear the fear and the anger running through his quiet words. "I want you to eat and get well. I want you to come and sit and talk with me again in my rooms, but they say that you're not trying." His voice broke suddenly, but he continued, "I can't lose you, too. Father can't lose you. We mean too much to one another."

"Blackmail," she said gently. "You always blackmail me into doing what you want. But please, Devon, not again. Let it go. It will hurt you too much to try to make you understand."

"Nothing can hurt us more than watching you quietly slip away. Nothing can hurt Father more than that," he answered, finally beginning to believe that she had consciously chosen this path. His mind tried to conceive a reason that would cause that choice.

"What's troubling you, my most beloved of sisters?" He smiled at her.

"Your only sister," she answered, with her own trembling smile.

"The only one I shall ever have," he agreed, "who is, I suspect, trying to escape me. Can't you trust me, Emily? I'll never betray you. I'll help you deal with whatever's hurt you. Is it something Avon said to you the night of Freddy's death? Did he hurt you this badly? He doesn't know very well how to be kind, perhaps because of the unkindness his father showed to him."

He stopped when he saw her shake her head weakly. "Can't you tell me?" he asked again and watched the tears begin to brim over her tightly closed lids and run down her temples. He reached to brush at them, but she moved away from his hand.

"What did he say, darling?" Devon asked again, still not understanding.

"Not what he said, Devon, but what I said to him," she answered bitterly.

"And what could you possibly have said that was so awful?" Devon asked, beginning to believe that this was all less than he had feared—a lover's quarrel that, in her illness, Emily had magnified out of proportion.

"I—I told him that he murdered Freddy because he was jealous of his physical perfection. I told him that the comparison between them…that—that his leg was pitiful and disgusting." It came out in gasps, and she cried openly now, in painful sobs that shook her body.

Devon was shocked into silence. He, of all people, realized the damaging nature of the confession he had just heard. He knew what those words would mean to the proud man who was his friend, who he had begun to hope might be more than his friend one day. He had recognized the look in Avon's eyes as he'd watched Emily on the night he'd come to bring the news of San Sebastian's fall. He knew that the attraction he had dreaded was not all on Emily's side. As he had come to know the man fully, he no longer feared the pull between them, but had acknowledged the rightness of it. But this, these words, he knew were enough to destroy whatever Avon had felt, possibly enough to destroy a part of the man himself, especially if he had cared as much as Devon thought he did.

"My dear," he said softly and stopped. Whatever comfort there was for her guilt, he was perhaps the last one to offer it.

"Your eyes look like his did when I said that to him. He'll never forgive me. I went to him as soon as I could, the next morning, and asked for his forgiveness, told him it wasn't what I felt. He never spoke to me, Devon. He never looked at me."

"Perhaps in time…" he began, not knowing how to help.

And because she needed to talk to someone who loved her and because she wanted, now that she had begun, to give up all the pain, she continued with what she had once thought she couldn't say to him. ''You've not heard it all,'' she told him softly.

Devon had been trying not to think of what such words would mean to him if spoken by the woman he loved, and now it seemed there was worse to come. He knew it was worse by her face and her voice.

''I'm carrying his child,'' she said simply.

''My dear,'' he said again and touched her face, at last beginning to understand the situation in all its painful complexity. And then, in a different tone entirely, he added, ''I told him I'd kill him if he touched you again. He said he believed me, but he didn't. And I shall, I swear to you I shall.''

''Is that what you think I want? Is that why you believe I told you—so you can kill one another? Oh, God, I knew that this was how you'd react. And Father? What do you believe he'll do? Why do you think I couldn't tell you? He'll call Avon out and I shall lose them both. I cannot live with that. I will not,'' she said bitterly, and he knew that her illness had offered her a solution that she had grasped.

''I feared that he'd hurt you, but I never believed that he would be capable of this. What kind of man is he to say he's my friend and to make you his whore?'' he said, and his voice was sick with hate.

''I can't believe you can say that to me,'' she said quietly. ''Whatever you imagine passed between us, I was never his whore. He treated me…'' she began, but knew this was not something she could ever tell another soul, that she could never convey what he had shown her, in those hours, of what he felt for her.

She looked at Devon's face and, trying to find some way

to make him understand, asked, "What would you do, Devon—even now, what would you do, if you awoke to find Elizabeth in your bed, in your arms? Would you turn her away? Could you say to her, 'I'm strong enough to refuse what you offer, to refuse you what you want'?" She watched the immediate denial sweep across his features and said quickly, "Think what it would mean, if she asked you, begged you, for only one night, to hold her, to touch her. If no one would ever know. Could you say no?" She saw the answer, the true answer, break his denial and replace it with such longing that she could have wept for him.

The silence between them was prolonged, and when Devon had examined his own feelings as far as his pain would allow, he began to plan for her care, all thoughts of revenge destroyed by his own honesty.

"This isn't the way," he said quietly. "You have a child to think of. A baby, Emily. His child. Have you thought that, in destroying yourself, you are destroying Dominic's child, who will carry his features and his intellect? A baby whom you can love and mold and shape to be the kind of person his father could, perhaps, never be?"

With his words, she began to realize that he was going to help her. And with his help, there might be a way. "I want to go away and have this baby. I won't give it up, Devon. I'll stay away. I won't come back to England, but if you help me, it must be for this child, too."

"I'll help you," he said, "but Father will have to be told eventually. He'll never understand your continued absence. For the present, we'll tell him that the doctor has recommended a warmer climate as soon as you're strong enough to travel, and if this snow ever stops. How long..." He paused, unsure how to ask.

"Perhaps two months more will be safe," she said quietly.

"Then you must start to get well—" he smiled at her "—and hope for an early spring."

Chapter Seventeen

The winter continued to be the hardest in memory. The New Year saw the Thames frozen so solid that the city merchants set up their wares on the river itself. January and February were hidden under drifts of snow that covered the country and prevented travel for all but the hardiest of souls.

Avon's couriers fell into that group. They continued to bring news of the war on the Continent, all of it good. Italy was liberated, Toulouse had been taken and finally the Prussians entered Paris. By April it was over, and with the break in the weather that came with spring, London and all of England rejoiced.

In spite of the pain Emily's words had caused, Avon had eventually resumed his association with General Burke; indeed, it was a professional obligation for them both. But the duke no longer called at his home, and the burden of that decision rested heaviest on Devon. He had found a friend, only to see that friendship destroyed by no conscious act on his part. He couldn't know if Avon felt the loss as deeply.

Avon retreated at last to Sandemer. And it seemed to them all that a chapter of their lives had closed with the death of Freddy Arrington—that in destroying him, they had unknowingly destroyed some vital part of themselves.

It was not until June that Avon returned to town. His arrival in the city coincided with the state visit of Czar Alexander, and the Duke of Avon would have been welcomed at any of the festivities planned for the czar's entertainment. There were men who were now more than ready to acknowledge publicly the very private role he had played in Napoleon's defeat. Avon refused their entreaties, and on his arrival sought out only one home, where he now believed there might never again be welcome for him.

Ashton opened the door to the duke and was so genuinely glad to see him that, in spite of his misgivings about his visit, Avon relaxed slightly and answered the old man's questions about his time out of the city. When he finally asked to see Devon, the butler hastened to assure him that he was sure the colonel would be delighted. Avon wished he could be as certain of his reception, and waited with some trepidation as the old man went to announce him.

When he returned to usher him in, Avon was still unsure what he could say, how he could ask what he had come here to find out. He followed Ashton into the room in which he had spent so many hours through the summer and fall, and which he had not visited since the night Arrington had challenged him at White's.

Nothing had changed, not even the man who waited so quietly for him. The smile and the blue eyes betrayed nothing but friendship.

Devon spoke first and held out his hand. "I had hoped you'd come by when you returned to town. I was afraid..." He stopped himself, aware he was about to reveal more than was allowed, more perhaps than Avon sought.

The man who limped forward to take his outstretched hand quite clearly bore the signs of the last six months. He was thinner and the lines that bracketed his firm lips were deeper. There seemed to be more silver in the coal blackness of his hair, and his eyes were wary.

"Devon," he said simply, gripping the offered hand and fighting the emotion as the thin fingers wrapped tightly around his own. Suddenly they both seemed at a loss as to what they should do next.

Devon smiled and said, "There's brandy, but you'll have to pour."

He watched as the ritual was completed and Avon again sat down in the chair before him. This time he didn't use the footstool, although Devon had seen that the limp was more pronounced.

"How are you, Devon? You're looking well."

"Did you come all this way to make polite conversation, Dominic?" Devon smiled again. "And I had thought we were friends."

"I wasn't sure if that were still true."

"Because of Emily? She told me what she said to you," he stated calmly. "You must know that she spoke out of anger or fear, confusion, emotions that at the time she didn't fully understand, but simply reacted to."

"It doesn't matter," Avon said.

"But I think it does. And I think you have to acknowledge that it mattered very much and then forgive her."

"There's nothing to forgive. She only spoke the truth. What she felt."

"That she compared you to Arrington and found you lacking? You know better than that," Devon said mockingly. "There's no one's truth in that and least of all hers. She spoke out of guilt. She believed that what she had done had driven you to kill a man, a man whose evil she had not been told about."

"Devon, don't. There's nothing you need to explain. I came because—"

"I have something I want to tell you about your truth," Devon interrupted, the force of his personality compelling Avon's silence. The quiet voice continued, "I've hoped these last months that I might have an opportunity to tell you a truth I've learned. I used to be as proud as you are, Dominic. That would be hard for you to believe if you knew what my life is now, if you knew how little I can do for myself. Knew in what small accomplishments I take pride now." Devon smiled at the man before him, and there was no self-pity in his tone. "I also made a choice, a long time ago...and I knew I was right. God, how sure I was about the rightness of that decision. How right and how bloody noble. And I live with it every day. And every night." Devon's voice stopped suddenly.

"Dev..." Avon said softly, not sure what comfort he could offer, or even if any were desired.

"You be very sure, Dominic, about the choices you make. Very sure your pride will be enough through all those long nights." And suddenly, against all expectations, Devon laughed into the painful stillness. "I'd give a lot to have a limp, Dominic."

Avon took a deep breath and said, in answer, "I've just returned from Scotland. The roads are still almost impassable."

Devon said nothing, but finally began to hope.

"She's not with your aunt. She hasn't been there at all. She must have lied to Moss."

Devon still said nothing, only watched with compassion as the man before him finally asked what he had come here to find out.

"Where is she, Devon? Is she here? Is she all right?" Now that it was out, he dropped his eyes and traced with the fingers of his right hand the pattern etched in silver on his cane. "Or perhaps you think I've forfeited any right to ask. I've waited so long...." He took another deep breath and Devon could see the pulse that beat at his temple. "Is she all right?" he asked again, more softly this time.

"She's in Italy. Father arranged for her to stay with a friend—a very trustworthy woman he's known for a long time. She's been there for several months. I believe at one time she intended to go to Scotland, but the snow made that impossible until it was...too difficult."

"Why Italy?" Avon asked. "Surely there were dangers even in the spring."

"She wasn't well this winter." Avon felt a sudden fear move his heart, but the soft voice continued, "The doctors recommended the warmer climate." Devon smiled, "Spain was still a little difficult in March."

"And now? Is she well now?" Avon asked.

Devon waited a long time, until the duke spoke again.

"She's carrying my child," he said, and it wasn't a question. He pushed himself to his feet and stood before Devon's chair. "Will you tell me how to find her? Is there time?"

And Devon smiled and nodded. "Yes, but only if you hurry."

It was late afternoon and the heat from the Italian sun was at its zenith. Emily walked to the window of her bedroom overlooking the courtyard and stretched to ease the cramping muscles of her lower back. There was no trace of a breeze and perspiration beaded her temples. As she lowered her head to brush her hair away from the back of her neck, a drop of sweat rolled slowly down between her breasts. She gathered her hair in her left hand and prepared to knot it atop her head. Maybe that would give her some relief. Unbidden, visions of the night Avon had taught her all there was to know about lovemaking crowded her mind. She felt his hot, moist mouth as it sought and found all the secret woman places she herself had not even been aware of. Deliberately banishing that image and the pain it would lead to, she twisted her hair and turned to the dressing table to find a pin or a comb to fix it in place.

It was then she saw him, standing very still, leaning against the frame of the door. She believed at first she had simply conjured him up in her mind, but then he smiled at her and she knew he was real.

She still had both hands holding her hair in place atop her head, and in the light from the window behind her, the advanced state of her pregnancy was revealed through the thin cotton night robe as if she had been wearing nothing.

He broke the silence that threatened to grow between them. "You will be a Titian madonna." His voice caressed her, trying to tell her he still found her beautiful.

"Well, I'm all van Eyck now," she said crossly, feeling not any of the emotions she had thought she would feel if she ever saw him again. But her fantasies had all involved floating down the stairs of someone's elegant villa, slim, composed, icily beautiful, and surprising a look of raw longing on his face. And in this painful reality all she felt was hot and uncomfortable and at a distinct disadvantage.

She had heard the soft noises that meant something was disturbing the routine of her landlady's well-run establishment, but she had never expected to have to deal with this now.

She saw the allusion puzzle him for a moment and then he laughed, "*Arnolfini and His Wife,* perhaps? As a matter of fact—"

But she didn't want to hear whatever witty phrase he had ready. She wasn't even sure she wanted him now at all. So many months he could have sought her out. "What are you doing here, Dominic? I thought we had said all there was to be said," she interrupted caustically.

He looked down and traced the pattern in the carpet with the ferrule of his cane. "After I stopped trying to drink myself into oblivion and was trying to decide how I was going to get through the next thirty or forty years without seeing you again, it suddenly came to me that a woman doesn't visit a great-aunt in Scotland for over six months unless she's going into a decline—"

Here her well-bred snort interrupted him.

"Or is carrying some bastard's bastard."

There was a pause and then Emily spoke. "My father never told you how to find me," she argued illogically.

"I never asked him. I was afraid he'd kill me before I could get halfway through the question."

"Devon," she said through clenched teeth.

"Devon, of course. I'm beginning to believe he's the only one of your father's children who can be counted on to do the sensible thing."

And then, in a different tone entirely, he said, "Why didn't you come to me, my darling? You must know how much I love you."

His tenderness unknotted the months of pain, so that she said truthfully, "Because I knew how much I had hurt you. I would have done anything, given anything, to have those words unsaid. For months I heard my voice saying them and I saw their impact in your face every time I closed my eyes. I could think of nothing to undo their damage," she whispered. Her eyes searched his face even now to find any reflection of what she had seen before.

He shook his head to deny the pain, but for the first time, he didn't meet her eyes, and she felt despair threaten to engulf her.

"Oh, God, Dominic, you'll never forgive me. How can you?"

His eyes came up then at the raw pain in her voice. "Because I love you and, in spite of those words, you have shown me in so many ways that you love me, too. The only doubts I have concern why you felt I shouldn't know about my child.''

''You'd made it very clear how you felt about marriage—'' she paused and searched his gray eyes ''—and especially about children. What was I to do? Present you a fait accompli to all you had rejected? I seduced you and I'm perfectly prepared to pay the piper.''

He laughed suddenly at the absurd cliche and moved close enough to place his hand on her shoulder. She twisted away and went to stand looking out the window with her back to him. As she began to speak again, he was aware she was crying, and his heart ached for what he had done. Suddenly the sense of her words came through to him.

''...As fat as Prinny. Every time I walk to the market with Signora Lucia I expect to hear Brummell's sally, 'Who's your fat friend?' I have nothing I can wear but my night rail. I haven't seen my feet in months, my shoes won't fit...'' She turned and, like a child, held up the skirt of her nightgown so that he might see her swollen feet ''...and even the wedding ring I had Aimee buy me won't go on.'' She paused and looked at him. ''How could you still want me?'' she asked.

''Because I love you and you are beautiful and you are mine. And because the baby you're carrying is mine, also.'' He breathed deeply and continued, ''And because, in spite of what I've told you, in spite of what I am, you love me. You asked how I could still want you, and I wonder how you could think anything physical, any change, could affect the way I feel about you.'' He paused again, and she watched him swallow and then go on past the emotion that threatened his control. ''And because of the way I feel, I begin to believe that perhaps you can love me enough to look beyond what my father could never forgive.''

Her green eyes darkened with pain as she remembered his comments from so long ago. ''And if this baby's not perfect, Dominic? Will you reject him as your father rejected you? Would you do that to your son?''

He looked at the cane in his hand and deliberately loosened the hold that had whitened his knuckles. ''I could never do that to a child. I'll be the best father I can be.'' He stopped and looked up into her eyes. ''You'll have to help me, Emily. I don't know that I'm sure exactly how it should be done. I had a very poor model.''

He reached out and caressed with his palm, tracing down the swelling curve of her belly, following the slow movement with his eyes. When he looked up from the fullness of her pregnancy to smile at her, she found she couldn't move because of the expression revealed in the gray depths of his eyes. He moved his hand as tenderly as she remembered to cup her breast, which seemed to leap into his palm. His thumb circled the top of the blue-veined globe and he bent his head slowly, deliberately, and trailed his lips gently across it, his touch separated from her heated skin by the thin cloth of her night rail. She raised trembling fingers to undo the tiny buttons of her gown and he watched as she pushed the offending material out of his way. Her eyes met his and he smiled at her again.

Emily's lids closed in anticipation as she saw the dark head begin to lower to bring his mouth in contact with her body. His lips circled and then softly suckled the hardening nipple, and she felt the beginnings of that spiraling heat between her legs. She felt the moisture, too, and knew that there was not, and never would be, another who could make her be what she was with him.

Only when he felt the uncontrolled, shivering response

move through her body did he finally raise his head and pull her to stand trembling in his arms. Her head fit against his shoulder and she felt the strength of his arousal as her stomach pushed into the hard length of his thighs. He groaned and gathered her closer, feeling her body relax in surrender as he kissed the delicate curls on her brow and tangled his fingers in her hair as it spilled across her shoulders.

"There's a priest below," he said softly. "I think it's time to assure that the line of Avon is legitimized, don't you?"

He tried to nuzzle the soft hollow of her throat, but she stepped back in dismay.

"A priest! And did you tell him that neither of us is Catholic?" she asked.

"I told him he should have an extremely large donation for his parish. He seemed very happy with the arrangement. Besides, it's the only marriage recognized in Italy. You've made it difficult for me to make an honest woman of you, my love." Now that he had touched her, he didn't seem to be able to stop, and his hands pulled her again into his arms. His strong fingers massaged the bottom of her spine and she rubbed against him like a cat, the pain subsiding somewhat with his loving attention.

"We'll stop in Paris on the way home and be remarried there. We're bound to find a clergyman in that throng. Half of London's there." His lips caressed her eyelids and continued their assault on her senses. "There's a surgeon, a Dr. Larrey, whom I've heard good things about. I intend to have him come to England and examine Devon. I know that someone, somewhere, can remove that damn shrapnel and I intend to find him."

He felt her tense in his arms and wondered what he had said to cause the sudden rigidness of her body.

"Dominic," she said softly.

She stepped back and removed his hand from her back, although she held on to it rather desperately. Avon felt his heart catch and was afraid she was seeing that terrible image he had tried to create of himself in a chair with a rug lying sedately over his knees as he was wheeled about Bath by his young and lovely wife.

Oh, God, he prayed, don't let her decide she can't face it now.

"Oh, Dominic," she gasped, closing her eyes tightly, and he prepared himself to be told that she couldn't, after all, live with that possibility.

He was suddenly terrified that he might beg.

He watched the emerald eyes open, and what she said was nothing he had expected. "You had better get your priest up here or your son is going to be born without benefit of clergy," she advised as the pain that had ripped her once-slender body finally eased.

After that it seemed to Emily that things happened very quickly. It amazed her that her husband, who didn't speak Italian, was as capable of making all these people rush about to do whatever he wanted as he had been in England.

"All that blue blood," she thought as she rested between pains, gathering her strength. "Nobility must have a universal language."

The Italian doctor who came to the villa could not seem to communicate, however, with the tall, grim-faced nobleman. The doctor was allowed to prepare signora after she had been installed in the finest and most comfortable bedchamber Signora Lucia possessed, but he could not make this strange Englishman realize that the husband did not sit at the bedside of his wife as she struggled to give birth to his child. After the man raked his glittering silver eyes up and down the doctor and said some words that were recognizable in any language, the doctor gave up. Everyone knew that the English were crazy.

The night was the longest in Avon's life. He watched Emily thrash her head on the pillow and let her dig her nails into his palms until she realized what she was doing, and then for a long time she refused to hold his hands and tore at the sheet instead. Finally she cried, "Oh, God, Dominic," and grasped at his strong fingers again. "Hold me, Dominic. It hurts so much."

As her agony went on and on, he began to curse the night he had lost control and made love throughout long dark hours to the woman who lay gasping and panting on the huge bed. He called himself every vile name he could think of for doing this to her because he had been unable to control his rutting body. Finally, Emily reached up and put her cold fingers across his lips.

"Hush, my darling," she whispered. "I would trade my soul for that night. I thought it was all I should ever have of you."

Suddenly, he began to fear that he was going to lose her, and he began to pray instead. He held her and kissed the sweat from her brow and the blood from her bitten lips.

Finally, as dawn was breaking, his son was born and Emily's racked body could rest. He left her then to stand quietly beside the window, which was only faintly outlined with light. The doctor saw to the needs of the infant and then the mother. Finally, he wrapped the baby carefully in the blanket Emily had had prepared and placed him beside his smiling mother.

Avon heard Emily's question in halting Italian and the doctor's startled reply. Then he saw the man look at him and back to Emily. He continued to speak rapidly in Italian, and then Emily thanked him and dismissed him.

"Easy time for first mother," the doctor said in English

to Avon as he passed. The look he received in response had him hurrying out the door.

"Dominic," Emily said with a laugh, "you scared him to death."

When Avon continued to stand by the window, she called to him again. "Come and see your son," she said gently, "whom the doctor assures me is perfect in every way."

Avon moved close to the bed and looked down into the infant's unfocused blue eyes.

"It's all right, Dominic. Take him to the window. I know you must look." Emily reached out and caressed the back of the hand that rested on the silver head of his cane and thought again of how much she loved this difficult man who was now her husband.

She helped place the baby in his left arm and watched him limp slowly to the window, where the growing daylight was beginning to brighten the room. He leaned his right hip on the ledge and propped his cane against the wall. Slowly he unfolded the blanket that swaddled the limbs of his newborn son. When the baby's perfectly formed legs were revealed, he touched the fingers of one of the delicate hands, and when the baby grasped his finger and held on, His Grace, the Duke of Avon, lowered his face and gently kissed the top of his son's head.

Chapter Eighteen

The Duke and Duchess of Avon spent the weeks of her recuperation in Italy and then traveled by easy stages to Paris, where they were married again by an Anglican clergyman. Emily was then instructed by her husband that she should do nothing but rest quietly in the enormous Parisian mansion that he seemed to believe it necessary to lease for their stay of only a few weeks.

His care of her during their marriage was unceasing and devoted. Every comfort was provided for her and the child during the slow journey from Signora Lucia's, and the servants in Paris treated her as if she were a fine piece of porcelain constantly in danger of cracking into a thousand pieces.

When he judged she was well rested from the trip, a succession of modistes was permitted to measure the duchess for the new and elegant wardrobe the duke insisted his wife should have. The fittings were allowed to go on for only a very short time, and at the least sign that Emily was fatigued, Aimee swooped down and threw the chattering swarm out of her grace's chamber, insisting that she rest.

Emily enjoyed a quiet dinner with her husband each evening, during which he shared with her the gossip that swirled through the English colony, members of whom were enjoying the City of Lights after such a long denial. Apparently Avon had once again entered the society of his fellow Englishmen while Emily remained quietly immured at home. Not that she really cared. She delighted in her son, and found that her day revolved around the opportunities to be with him as well as the long afternoon's anticipation of Avon's footsteps in the front hall when he returned from his day's activities.

Each night after dinner he escorted her tenderly to the foot of the stairs and insisted that she retire early so that she might fully recover her strength. The only problem that marred Emily's existence was the fact that her husband never joined her in that very lovely and very lonely chamber to which she retired each evening.

They had been in Paris for over a month now and Emily was so disturbed by Avon's continued avoidance of any intimacy that she was almost at the point of confiding in Aimee and seeking her advice. Perhaps Aimee could tell her what she must do to reawaken Avon's interest in her. She began to fear, in spite of what he had said to her on the night his son was born, that he had not forgiven her.

Yet he treated her with every courtesy and care. His concern was boundless and unceasing. He brought small gifts that he believed would please her. He charmingly entertained her with his dry sense of humor, tempted her appetite with every delicacy available in Paris and listened with his grave smile when she told him of her day and of the baby. He gave every appearance of being a loving husband and father, but the closeness of man and wife was not part of their lives, and each day seemed more frightening to her than the last.

She dressed in the lovely gowns he had insisted she needed, and he complimented her each evening on her ap-

pearance, but his eyes never dwelled on her body as they
had before. Once or twice she thought that she could feel
his gaze and sought his face, only to find that those long,
dark lashes had quickly hidden whatever intensity had attracted her attention.

He arrived home early one dark, wet afternoon and
climbed the long staircase in search of her. The wind and
the storm had driven him from his meeting with Castlereagh
to come home and verify that his family were as well and
tenderly cared for as he intended that they should always
be. Emily was not downstairs as she was each evening. He
suspected that she made sure that she was in the salon when
he arrived so that he wouldn't be forced to struggle with
those endless stairs to find her.

With no one to watch, he rested halfway up. His hip had
given ample warning that the weather was going to be wet,
and a reluctant smile crossed his lips at the thought that at
least he would, as he grew older, be a reliable foreteller of
the weather.

He opened the door of his wife's bedchamber and found
only Aimee, quietly sewing some delicate wisp of cotton
and lace.

"The duchess is in the nursery, your grace," she said,
smiling at him.

"Is she resting enough, Aimee?" he asked quietly.

"I think that she's fully recovered, your grace. I believe
that she's well able to resume her activities," she said sincerely. There was no trace of anything but the proper concern of a servant for a well-beloved mistress in her eyes,
but Avon felt that her words were intended to convey more
than they said.

"Thank you for your care of her. I'll join her in the nursery," the duke said and closed the door.

Emily was feeding the baby, delighting in the feel of his

body in her arms, in the downy softness of his head as it rested against her body. Her serenity was a pleasing contrast to the wind and lightning he could see raging outside the window behind her. She had been whispering nonsense and singing snatches of half-forgotten lullabies to the baby when she suddenly became aware that her husband was standing in the open doorway watching her.

She smiled at him, so glad to see him, in spite of the fact that his absence had been of only a few hours, that her heart contracted with how much she loved him. He was so tall and elegant and so very beautiful. She sometimes found it hard to believe that he could want someone as ordinary as she thought herself to be. And then, unbidden, came the painful thought that apparently he didn't want her. He had made provision for her and his son, but it seemed that he was simply paying the price for having taken her that night she had forced herself into his room, into his bed.

The pain of that admission clouded the welcome that had spontaneously shone in her face. She dropped her eyes to the baby so that Avon wouldn't see the tears she could feel gathering behind her eyelids. She heard his uneven footsteps cross the room and knew that he stood looking down on her and his son.

Suddenly she felt the backs of his fingers trace down the open front of her dress and then across her breast to where the baby nursed. She held her breath, embarrassed in spite of having shared, at least on one night, much deeper intimacies than having him simply touch her breast. She opened her eyes and watched that strong hand caress with one knuckle the darkened areola so close to the baby's mouth. He stopped suddenly, as if aware of what he was doing, and took his hand away. Emily looked up into those silver eyes and surprised such a look of pain that she wanted to cry out, to hold him and demand to know who or what had hurt him.

Before she could speak, Avon stepped back and said in the same kind, impersonal voice he so often used to her now, "I believed that I had instructed Hawkins to engage a wet nurse. Was there some reason for her dismissal? I shall be glad to have Hawkins replace her."

Emily shook her head. "The nurse is still here. You know that Hawkins would never hire anyone who was remotely unsatisfactory," she said quietly.

Avon laughed suddenly. "I seem to remember a certain coachman..." he said in a lighter voice.

Emily waited for him to go on, but seeing her eyes on his face, he simply shook his head and didn't finish the thought.

"Perhaps you'd get your strength back more quickly if the nurse did this. Are you also feeding him at night?" At her reluctant nod, he continued in the same quiet, reasonable voice, "Then you're certainly not getting enough sleep. Are you sure that it wouldn't be better to let someone help you?"

Emily didn't speak for a moment, because she knew that she couldn't make him understand. Her basic honesty compelled her to try, however, and she looked up and said simply, "I enjoy it. It is like nothing I've ever felt before. He needs me and I find that I need him. What would I do with all these long hours if I didn't care for my son?"

Having begun, she didn't seem to be able to stop, and all the pent-up frustrations of the last long weeks rushed to her lips in an anguished torrent. "You're always gone. All day. I only see you at breakfast and at dinner, and then you bundle me off to bed as if you can't stand to be in my presence another minute.

"There are servants to see to every corner of the house.

I'm not even allowed to arrange the flowers or to supervise the menus or to choose my own gowns. I have nothing to do. The servants don't want my interference. You apparently don't want me at all. He's all I have. If I do as you wish, he won't even know I'm his mother. I'll be just another face and another pair of hands that touch him occasionally. I'm sorry if I'm not patrician enough to be your duchess, but I won't give up my son, Dominic. He's all I have.''

"Emily," Avon said quietly into the silence that had fallen between them after her outburst, "I'm most assuredly not asking you to give up your son. I'm naturally delighted that you're such an excellent mother. I simply don't want you to be under any strain." He smiled at her. "I see now that I've tried to wrap you in cotton wool for too long." He reached down to caress her cheek and said comfortingly, "I'm even delighted that you're bored. That must mean that you're much stronger."

The gray eyes considered the pain in the lovely oval face and, although he had dreaded this moment, he knew he must allow Emily the freedom to move back into the society that would welcome her again. "There are several invitations that have arrived in the last few days, some of which might interest you. Would you like to look at them together tonight and choose at which one the Duchess of Avon will take Paris by storm, just as she did London?"

"Will you go with me?" she asked softly, not quite believing that he intended to take her into the *belle monde* of Paris and London on his arm.

"My darling—" he smiled in genuine amusement, seeing the light in her eyes, but misinterpreting its source "—I wouldn't miss it for the world."

In spite of herself, Emily felt a spurt of excitement, not because she had any real desire to be part of the crowd that thronged to the social centers of this capital each evening, but because she thought that perhaps this would be the key to making Avon again care for her. He had certainly reacted to Arrington's attentions with jealousy. Perhaps if he saw that other men still found her attractive, he would again want her to share his bed, to be not only wife but lover.

She wondered for the hundredth time if watching her writhe in childbirth had disgusted him. Or perhaps the new fullness of her figure was not as pleasing to him as her slim, more-girlish body had been. Her eyes dropped to her son, who had now drifted into a relaxed sleep, a milk bubble still moving gently at the corner of his mouth as he breathed in and out. Perhaps this, too, offended Avon. How could she be exciting to him smelling of baby, her breasts so full that they ached and leaked with their burden? His question about the wet nurse had been phrased with concern for her well-being evident, but what if he preferred that she give up this mothering to be his wife?

Oh, God, she thought suddenly, I've been so stupid. Of course, he's repelled. He's a sophisticated man and I've expected him to react to his fatherhood like a Spanish peasant, to coo over the baby and to watch his wife become as common as the wet nurse who sits all day with almost nothing to do. Well, that will certainly change, she thought decisively.

Aloud she said, "You're right, of course, about the nurse. I'll do as you wish at once. I know that this isn't usual for the women of your circle. I'm sorry."

He looked down on her with concern. "Emily, you have no reason to apologize. And as for this idea that you must become 'patrician' enough to be what I want, please know that you are exactly the Duchess of Avon I want. I want you to do and be always only what you are."

But of course, she didn't believe him. She wondered suddenly if he had taken a mistress. Some lovely demimondaine who was as sophisticated as he and far more exciting than Emily thought she could ever be. That would certainly explain why he no longer sought her bed. She wondered desperately how what she had thought in Italy to be so right could now have suddenly gone all wrong. He had offered no explanation of his desire each night to get rid of her or of his daily absences. But since she now believed that she had at least part of the explanation, she resolved to become what she thought he wanted.

"I'll join you downstairs as soon as I've changed," he said, and she watched him limp heavily across the room. She knew that the storm outside would have affected his leg, but she also knew well enough that she couldn't ask him about it. She had forfeited forever by her hateful comments the right to comfort or assuage his pain. She was afraid to even speak about his condition, to express any concern, so that she was forced to pretend that it didn't exist. All she could do was watch him carefully to judge his pain as he entered the room every morning, and trust Moss to care for him.

Avon closed the door quietly behind him so that he wouldn't disturb the sleeping infant. He took a deep breath and leaned against the frame. It was all becoming far more difficult than he had anticipated. He had only wanted to care for Emily and the child. He intended that she should have everything that she could possibly desire to make her happy. He'd watched her suffer for hours giving birth and he had learned from Aimee that she had been very ill during that hard winter with an inflammation of the lungs that had weakened her even more than the prolonged labor. And now it seemed, in spite of his efforts, that she was certainly not happy. He had seen the despair in her eyes and heard it threaded through her voice.

She had complained about the long hours he forced himself to spend away from her, but it was so painful for him to be with her, to want her as he did. At first, of course, she hadn't been well, and his only concern had been to care for her, but now, with the new ripeness of her body such a delicious temptation and her good health obviously restored, he couldn't even watch her walk across the room without wanting to pull her to him wherever they were and make love to her for hours. He wanted to hear again the sounds she'd made in her throat when he touched her body, to feel her hands clutch desperately at his shoulders as he showed her what desire really meant. And he knew that what stood between them now was only his fear, his fear of how she might react to his lovemaking.

If, in Italy when he had first seen her again, he had been able to make love to her in his immediate unthinking response, it might have been all right, as sudden as a fire and as cleansing. But in the long weeks that followed, as he'd sat by her bed and talked to her of the baby and the months of their separation, he had recognized how deeply he loved her and known that if she had in any way meant those words she had spoken in his study, that he couldn't bear it. He knew that if she rejected him again, he couldn't continue this careful charade they were living.

He pushed himself away from the door and limped down the hall to change for dinner. He'd just promised her that they would reenter the social scene, and already he dreaded his response to the admiration he knew she would evoke. He felt like a man on the rack, torn between his fear of her rejection and his growing lack of control over his desires.

When Avon joined Emily in the salon much later that evening, he apologized for making her wait. Moss had spent a long time massaging his leg in an effort to give him some relief, but, of course, he didn't explain that to his wife. She was allowed to see only his habitual mask of courtesy. And although she wondered, she didn't ask. She only took his arm and went into dinner, carefully matching her steps to his own.

After dinner she selected a ball some two weeks distant to be her first foray into Parisian society. They discussed how her gown should be made up and of what materials, and she allowed herself to be guided by Avon's excellent taste. It was quite a bit later than usual when he escorted her to the foot of the stairs and tenderly kissed her hand, but she knew that it was only because of what she had said this afternoon that he had spent this time with her. She was convinced that he had rather be reading his everlasting reports.

"I'm sorry you were distressed today," he said quietly. "Please believe that I only want you to be happy."

"I'm the one who should be sorry. Oh, Dominic, I don't want to be tiresome," she said unhappily.

He pulled her gently into his arms and held her comfortingly, as Devon might have done, and then he kissed her forehead. He smiled into her troubled green eyes and said, "You're not tiresome." His voice deepened with some emotion she couldn't quite read. "I'll never grow tired of you," he said. By the look in his eyes, there was more he wanted to say, but instead he kissed her hand again and placed it on the stair rail and retreated to the salon.

The next night, however, Avon had sent his apologies that he would be unable to join his wife for dinner. Indeed, he and Moss had not returned until quite late, though Emily had not been informed of the hour. But when the duke arrived home the following evening, he brought with him a present, a delicate music box that opened to reveal a golden bird that sang one of the simple melodies he had heard her hum to the baby.

His agent had been very gratified that the duke had been so pleased with the find, but of all the lovely and expensive objects he had laid before the English nobleman that afternoon, this had been the last he would have expected Avon to choose. He had gone away shaking his head and counting the very large commission he had been given.

Hawkins had opened the door for the duke and had informed his master that the duchess begged to be excused from dinner that evening. It seemed that she would have a tray in her room. She was slightly unwell, he continued, but then realized he was talking to himself as he watched the limping figure hurry across the hall and up the stairs.

Avon entered the room without knocking and found Aimee sitting by the bed in the darkened room. The murky light from the rain-washed windows was the only source of illumination, and the duke could barely make out the figure of his wife on the great bed.

"What's wrong?" he asked, and even to his own ears his voice sounded harsh in the quiet room. He felt like an intruder.

"I told Hawkins to tell you it's nothing." It was Emily's voice that answered from the dimness, and realizing that she was awake, he turned to Aimee and with a quick twist of his head indicated that she should leave them. With a regretful glance toward her mistress, the maid quietly opened the door and was gone.

Avon moved to stand beside the bed and to look down at his wife's face. At the concern in his features, she put up her hand and touched his in reassurance.

"I really am all right," she said. "Just a silly woman's complaint. Go eat your dinner and discuss whatever you and Moss discuss in your study late at night."

He took a deep breath in relief and reached down to brush the disordered tendrils of red-gold hair off her forehead, where he felt the heat of fever. "You need a doctor," he said and turned to put that order to his staff into effect immediately.

"Dominic, please," she said desperately. "Wait. I promise it's nothing. I'm not ill. Really I'm not. Please don't do that to me," she pleaded in embarrassment.

"If you're ill, I shall certainly call a doctor. If not, then why are you lying here in the dark?" His concern made his voice sharper than he wished, and he was appalled when he realized that tears had begun to well in those emerald eyes.

"Emily," he said softly, sitting down on the bed beside her and taking her hands in his. They both heard the cane, which he had propped carelessly against the bed, slide to the floor. Emily recognized that as a sign of his distraction. Avon was always careful to handle his stick unobtrusively.

"My darling, what's wrong? Are you still angry with me? I'm sorry about last night. I promise you my absence was unavoidable. You must know there is nowhere I had rather be than here with you," he said, freeing one of his hands to wipe at the tears on her cheeks.

Wordlessly, she shook her head. She was caught in a dilemma of her own making, and she knew that she would have to explain, but she also believed that it would be another mark against her, another wedge between them. She had so wanted to be the kind of lovely and composed woman who should be his wife. Instead, everything she planned seemed to result in failure and embarrassment.

"Then if you're not angry, why are you lying here in the dark crying?" he said gently. The hand that had wiped her tears began to caress her cheek and then moved gently down to her throat to trace the lace around the neck of her nightgown. Almost without volition, it moved to her breast, and then stopped, as what he had found there was not at all what he had expected.

Without saying a word, he pulled his other hand from hers, although, realizing his intent, she tried very hard to hold it. He unbuttoned her gown and quickly pulled back both sides to reveal the tightly bound breasts and the moisture that stained the binding that Aimee had used to try to give her some relief.

She began to sob, and at the quiet desperation of that sound, Avon realized that he had erred again in his treatment of her. He gently touched the soaked binding and she flinched from his hand. He jerked as if he had been burned. He stood up, reached for his cane and realized with something approaching horror that it must have rolled under the bed when it fell.

He stood very still and tried to think what he should do. Finally, he said reluctantly, "Emily, would you ring for Aimee, please."

At the bitterness in his voice, she looked up, afraid of the disgust she would see in his face, and saw something else entirely. "Dominic, what's wrong?"

"I need Aimee," he said without inflection.

"What are you going to do? She only did what she thought would make the pain better. The only other way is to wean the baby away very gradually. Please don't be angry with Aimee. She tried to tell me this would happen."

The distress in her voice intruded on his own, and he looked at her without understanding. "Then why are you doing this? Why are you suffering, if all you must do is let the baby nurse?"

"Because you asked me to," she answered simply. "You wanted the wet nurse—"

He said then the words that she had heard him utter only once before, when they had tried to make him leave her as his son was being born. He reached forward and grasped the tall post of the bed and, using its support instead of his stick, he pulled himself close enough to reach the bell.

Aimee answered the summons almost immediately, and Avon spoke as soon as he heard the door.

"My cane is under the bed. Would you reach it for me, please," he commanded coldly, and when she had knelt and then put it into his outstretched hand, he said in the same brittle tone, "and take that off my wife's breasts."

Both women watched with dismay as he turned and limped out the door, which he slammed behind him. Aimee hurried to do as he had asked, but she hadn't finished when they heard the door open again and realized that he had returned. Emily was sitting up with her nightgown draped around her waist as Aimee removed the last of the bindings. Her long hair drifted about her white shoulders and over her breasts, and Avon thought he had never seen anything more beautiful.

They realized that the duke held his son very gently in the crook of his left arm, and he limped to the chair that Aimee had earlier pulled up beside the bed and sat down. He laid his cane very deliberately on the floor beside him and spoke with no trace of the anger that had colored his voice before.

"Aimee, would you please take Will and give him to my wife. And then leave us."

The French woman smiled at him suddenly and hurried to do what he had asked. When she had left the room, Avon turned to watch his wide-eyed wife and his sleeping son.

Emily sat as erect as she had when Aimee removed the bindings, and she made no effort to hide herself from him. She looked down on the sleeping baby, smiled without any thought of self-consciousness and tenderly moved her nipple over the infant's lips. He stirred and, without waking, began to nurse.

She glanced up then to surprise in her husband's eyes an expression she had not seen since the night in the carriage house when he had so tenderly caused her to conceive this child.

"Would you explain to me, my dear, idiot wife, why you believed that I desired you to suffer?" he asked calmly.

"I know you didn't want me to suffer." She smiled. "I'm not that much an idiot." She looked down at the baby again and finally leaned back to rest her shoulders against the pillows stacked behind her. She wasn't sure what she could say to him in explanation that wouldn't reveal more of her fears and more of her plans for reawaking his interest than she thought he should know.

She continued to watch the baby as she said, "I wanted everything to be as before. I wanted to go to the ball in two weeks as slim as I was before. I wanted to sit down to dinner with you and not worry about milk staining my gown. I wanted to carry about me the aroma of a delicate French perfume instead of *eau de l'enfant*."

She stopped as his laugh relieved the tension between them. "I was afraid that you saw me as an eternal wet nurse instead of a woman."

He knew then that he had hurt her by his fears, and he determined that he would woo his wife, court her with all the charm and courtesies and flattery that she had never had from him. And if she revealed then that she really did find him twisted and perverted, that it disgusted her to compare him with the men she would meet in the coming weeks, he would let her go.

He would provide for her, of course, but they would lead the same kind of married life, a marriage of convenience, that so many of the ton believed to be the only proper relationship between husband and wife. Until then he would do everything in his power to convince this woman that she wanted him as much as he wanted, had always wanted, her.

"I brought you something," he said when the silence grew between them.

"You always bring me something," she replied, smiling. "I feel like the Queen of Sheba in the Bible—is that who I mean? Or did she take gifts to him?"

"Then you don't want it?" he asked lightly.

"Of course, I want it. How could you think any differently? I'm quite spoiled by my husband, who never comes home without bringing something for me." She smiled at him across the distance, and he reached for his cane and stood up to remove the small package from his coat pocket. She watched him lean to lay it beside her on the bed, and she said, before he could sit down, "You'll have to open it for me. I have my hands full of baby again."

He smiled at her, took the package back and quickly untied the cord and paper. Placing it on her night table, he released the tiny catch, and the box opened and the bird began to play its lullaby.

As soon as she recognized the song, Emily realized that he must have heard her singing it to Will. Perhaps he didn't dislike her being a mother so much as she had feared. He seemed not to mind watching her now as she changed the baby to her other breast and tickled his toes to wake him up enough to relieve her here, too.

"It's very beautiful—" She began to thank him for the gift, but he interrupted her.

"Exquisite," he said quietly, and at his tone, she glanced up and knew with pleased certainty that he didn't refer, as she had, to the music box.

She smiled at him and he said in that same quiet voice, "Would you like me to have dinner up here with you?"

She could not know how much he cared about her answer. And when it came, it was all that he might have hoped.

Her smile widened and she said in quick delight, "I would like that above all things, but I'm well able to go down with you if you wish."

"No," he said, "there's no reason for you to dress again. Let me change, and I'll come back when you've finished. I'll tell Hawkins."

He leaned down, kissed her on her cheek and touched the baby gently on the top of his head. He watched them a moment longer and then left the room.

Chapter Nineteen

Emily rang for Aimee when the baby had finished nursing, and after he had been replaced in his crib in the nursery, Aimee returned to bathe her gently and help her dress in a peach negligee that had just arrived from the dressmaker's. She gathered Emily's hair loosely on top of her head and allowed one or two curls to lie on her shoulder in the style of almost a century before. At last Aimee dabbed an expensive perfume in the hollow of her throat and between her breasts.

"At least I won't smell like baby," Emily said, laughing, but when Aimee looked up inquiringly, she only shook her head.

She moved to sit in one of the two chairs that flanked the table where Hawkins would serve their meal, and Aimee straightened, but didn't make, the bed. It looked neat, but lazily inviting, and Emily hoped that tonight Dominic would stay with her, if not here, then in his even larger chamber, which she had never seen.

When her husband returned, he was dressed simply, in a lawn shirt open at the neck and dark trousers. She had expected a dressing gown, but quickly hid her disappointment and smiled at him as he took his place across the table. As soon as he was seated, Hawkins and his staff began to lay the table and then to serve. The presence of the servants destroyed for Emily any pretense that they were alone. Avon truly didn't notice the intrusion, but he was so attuned to Emily that finally he told Hawkins to leave the rest and he would serve them himself. Hawkins was scandalized to picture the Duke of Avon serving his own dinner, until Emily smiled at him, and he realized that she would care for Avon as he would. He bowed, and using only his eyes, ordered the hovering footmen out of her grace's chamber. Finally they were alone.

"Would you care for these?" Avon said, lifting the silver cover from scallops of veal that they had not even touched.

"No, I really am not very hungry. I just ate to keep Hawkins from worrying."

He looked up quickly and knew that she spoke the truth, that it mattered to her if Hawkins believed that the dinner was in some way not pleasing.

He laughed and said, "You'll eventually be very large if you eat to please the servants." He knew by her face that somehow he had erred, and he reached quickly across the table to hold her hand.

"What's wrong? Do you want me to call Hawkins back so you can reassure him?" he teased, trying to restore the lighter atmosphere they had shared earlier.

She smiled and shook her head, turning his hand so that she could caress his fingers.

"I'd rather be alone with you. We spent hours together in Italy and never ran out of things to say. And now it seems I never see you alone." She stopped, not wanting to spoil this night with complaints. "I'm just so glad you're here," she said truthfully.

He kissed her fingers. "And I'm glad I'm here, also. As

soon as the conference begins..." he said, and then halted at the look in her eyes.

"You're going to Vienna? We're not going home? Oh, Dominic, I wanted to take the baby home to show him off to Devon. And my father. I thought maybe..." Her words trailed off and her face revealed her doubts.

"He loves you very much, Emily. If you're worried about his reaction to—" he paused and then continued gracefully "—our marriage, you must know your father well enough to know that the first time Will wraps his fingers about his, he'll be lost. Don't worry, my love. Will will bring your father around. The general will be in his element having another boy to teach to ride and fence and all the things he taught your brothers."

"And are you sure you won't be jealous..." she began to tease, but the quickly concealed pain in his eyes stopped the thoughtless words.

She saw him force a smile and ask in a perfectly normal tone, "Did the baby continue to sleep?" knowing this was a safe subject for them both.

She gratefully grasped the reprieve he offered. "Yes, even his nurse says he's an exceptional baby. Even tempered and always calm. It's rather amazing to think that you and I created someone that placid."

He laughed. "I'll remind you that you said that in about six or seven years."

Emily had a quick mental image of a miniature Dominic racing around, riding, doing all the things that her husband had never done, even as a small child. It would be bittersweet to know that she could lavish on his son all the love and affection he apparently had always been denied.

"And you? Are you all right?" he asked with concern.

Emily shivered to hear the tenderness in the quiet words. Perhaps tonight. Perhaps he would want her tonight. "I'm fine. I'm not uncomfortable at all.'' She was afraid that he would use any excuse she gave him to leave her.

Only, she wasn't sure now how to proceed. She had played the siren only one night, and it had not been like this. Her purpose was the same, but nothing else. Finally she rose and held out her hand to him. He looked up and laughed. ''I've overstayed my welcome and you're about to throw me out so that you can finally rest.''

After the pain he had found her in today, he really believed that to be her motive, and he reached for his cane and stood, prepared to kiss her lightly good-night and then to leave her. He had not come for seduction, but to offer her the security of his continued care and affection.

He began to limp toward the door, drawing her with him by the hand he still held. When she perceived his destination, she stopped suddenly and said sharply, ''No, Dominic.''

He turned back in concern, still not understanding as she stepped closer to him and lifted her hands to his shoulders. As tall as she was, she was forced to stand on tiptoe to reach his lips and to softly brush hers across that hard mouth.

He hesitated still until she whispered, ''Please,'' and then he bent down and his mouth opened to hers. She leaned against his body and willed the kiss to deepen. She moved her hand to the back of his neck and threaded her fingers into the darkness of his hair. Almost tentatively he put his arms around her and then finally pulled her close against his body. Her courage increased when she felt his growing arousal. She stepped back, and taking his hand, began to draw him to her bed.

He followed, watching her face with every step they took. When she felt the edge of the bed against her knees, she sat down and pulled his hand to make him come to her. He laid his cane on the bed and sat down beside her. Almost in that same motion, he leaned them back against the bed, his weight resting on his right elbow and forearm. With his left hand he brushed the long curls away from her neck. She held her breath as he lowered his head to kiss the place where the curls had rested against the ivory of her shoulder.

"So smooth." His voice itself caressed her. "So beautiful," he whispered, and his breath teased against her skin. His lips trailed slow fire across her shoulder to the hollow of her throat, where he paused to kiss the racing pulse beat. The breath she had not even been aware she was holding sighed out in a soft moan. He raised his head at the sound and smiled down at her expression.

Her eyes drifted open to watch as he lowered his mouth again until it covered hers, and he spent a lazy eternity exploring the contours of her lips, until she could wait no longer, and lifting her head, she took his torturing tongue into her mouth. He allowed her to deepen the kiss and then he began a controlled succession of invasions and withdrawals that caused her to whimper his name in protest when his tongue deserted hers.

His left hand moved to slide the silk slowly off her shoulder and then to cup beneath the heavy globe of her breast. She gasped and unconsciously flinched away from the pressure against the soreness, and instantly he raised his body away from hers. She watched as he fought to control his breathing, but there was no recrimination in the gray eyes that smiled down into hers.

"I don't believe that pain is an aphrodisiac, my love," he said gently.

She shook her head and said, "It's nothing." She tried to pull him against her again, but he resisted and remained above her, holding his body away from hers with his right arm. His left hand gently replaced the sleeve of her negligee, and the hard, dark fingers grazed the sensitized surface briefly, seeming to mock her with what she had lost. She caught them and pressed them against her breast, desperate to convince him.

"Don't leave me, Dominic. Stay with me tonight," she said, loving him too much to let him go, to watch him again politely walk away.

He smiled and said, "We have so many nights." He wanted to make it perfect for her, with no discomfort or embarrassment. He had waited so long that he knew he couldn't be gentle, and he wanted her body to be able to answer the hard desire that raged in his.

"But you've given me so much. You're so good to me. And to Will. I've felt your care wrapped around us throughout these weeks and I wanted to give you this. To show you…" She stopped at the look that began to grow in his eyes. It was so nearly like the one she had put there on the night she had taunted him about his leg.

His face closed and his fingers bit into her shoulder as he said savagely, "And in your gratitude you are offering yourself to me…"

"Dominic," she said, frightened by what she saw in his face.

"…As a sacrifice. To pay for what I give you, to bargain for my continued care of you and our son. Well, thank you, Emily, but I don't believe that such a sacrifice is required. You are entitled to my care. You are my wife. I don't have to be paid with your body." He had found his cane and was now standing by her bed. "Please don't feel that it's necessary to barter with your charms. You cheapen what we have."

"And what is that?" she said, her bitterness matching his own. "What do you call what we have now? This mockery of a marriage that we share?"

"It is a marriage. I'm responsible for having given you a child. You are my wife." He paused to try to control the anger that burned so fiercely through his mind and into his heart. He loved her so much and all she apparently felt for him was gratitude. He could taste the bitterness of that revelation. He tried to speak calmly in spite of the pain he felt. He wanted to reassure her that it wasn't necessary to force herself to make love to him. "I will always be responsible for your well-being, and for his."

"Responsible," she hissed. "Responsible. God, I don't want you to feel responsible for me. I knew that your honor demanded that you marry me. You did it for Devon and my father and for your son. But not for me. Not for me."

She pushed herself up from the bed and stood to face him, as angry as he was himself. All her worst fears about his motivations for their marriage had proven true. He had said as much. "Responsible," she said again, with utter contempt.

"No," he said. "That's not true. I didn't marry you out of a sense of responsibility."

"Of course not," she interrupted, hiding her pain in sarcasm. "You found that my inexperienced charms outweighed those of your lovely and so very skillful mistress, and so you came. The attraction was so great that you came, after only six months, to fetch me, trailing your priest and your sense of duty as afterthoughts.

"I'm sure that you married me because you couldn't resist me. I've seen in the last two months how irresistable you find me." Her voice had risen, and she knew their quarrel would be the talk of the servants' quarters tomorrow. She wondered how it had come to this. She had intended to woo him, and instead she was shouting at him, angry and red-faced. No wonder he didn't want her. She was as seductive as a prize fight.

"Emily," he began and did not, for the first time in his memory, know how to deal with another person. He had so mismanaged this encounter. Now she thought that he had married her only to give her the protection of his name. Only the truth would suffice, and so he said, "I married you because I love you so very much."

Again she interrupted to ask, "And if I hadn't been carrying your son? Would you have married me then?" And waited for him to say the right words.

To her it was the only question that mattered. To him it was only a part of the feelings that even now he couldn't evaluate completely given his background, his past. He didn't know if he would have inflicted on her his heritage, his disability, the future his doctors had long predicted, had she not been carrying his child. But that didn't mean that he didn't love her. He loved her more than he had ever loved anyone or anything in his life, and he wanted her even now, knowing that she had probably steeled herself for this night, forced herself to invite him into her bed in spite of what she knew she would see.

"Dominic," she said quietly, her anger replaced by the unhappiness his silence had caused, "would you please leave?"

And because he could not answer her question, and there was nothing left to say, he did. Emily was amazed to find that one could indeed feel a heart break.

Avon returned to his wife's room early the next morning. He came to the end of the bed and watched as she calmly sipped the chocolate Aimee had brought only minutes before. She still wore the peach negligee and his eyes lingered briefly on her throat.

"I think that we can deal together better than this," he said quietly. "I believe that we must."

Emily's anger rekindled at the reasonable tone he had adopted. He sounded as if he were lecturing a petulant child. She knew that sometimes she had acted childishly, but she really preferred that he not treat her to a display of his own calm maturity. As she realized on later reflection, she responded with the most childish thing a wife in her position could say.

"I should like to go home," she said, "to England."

The duke said nothing for a moment, as if evaluating her request, and then he asked as calmly as before, "To Sandemer or to London?"

"To London, to my father's," she said, holding his eyes with her anger.

Again he didn't answer immediately, and when he finally did, he said only, "Then I think you must wait until after the Duchess d'Enghien's ball. We have accepted the invitation. To fail in attendance will cause talk."

"I really don't care. I'm sure there's talk enough already. I would like you to make the arrangements as soon as possible."

He took a deep breath, as if holding to his patience with difficulty. "I think you must wait and we'll attend the ball together. If you don't care personally, I think you should care for Will's sake."

"And what explanation have you put about for our son's birth within hours of our marriage? I'm sure you've handled even that problem with your usual sangfroid."

His lips tightened at her sarcasm, but his tone never changed. His serenity in the face of her anger only served to annoy Emily further.

"You and I were married last October with your father's full consent. Due to the nature of my connection with your father at that time, the marriage was kept secret. We went together in the spring to Sandemer, and you have now joined me here in Paris following your recent confinement. Your father will verify the details if anyone is gauche enough to ask."

"And Freddy's death? What ready explanation do you have for that?"

"I believe that most people who know of the situation will assume that Arrington's death was the result of his continuing and unwanted attentions to my wife."

It was very plausible, but Emily could not resist mocking, "And do you believe that will stop the scandal?"

"The fact that you are now the Duchess of Avon will stop any scandal," he said simply, and she knew that his position was such that it was true. "Our appearance together socially will stop a great deal of the speculation that will necessarily occur. I hope that you'll see fit to accompany me for our son's sake. I'll make the arrangements for your journey for the morning after."

"Thank you," she answered, knowing that what he said was only reasonable and hating him for being so in control.

The remaining days before the ball were spent in the same brittle politeness. They no longer dined together. Indeed, any meeting between them was accidental, and the house was large enough that there were days that she never saw him at all.

Her ball gown was delivered for the final fitting, and her temper was for some reason frayed by the fact that Dominic had known so well what would become her.

Aimee had begun to pack her clothes and the baby's. As the time grew closer for their departure, Emily hoped Avon would make some gesture to indicate that he wished his wife would remain in Paris.

She had very little idea about his plans. He had never answered her question about Vienna, but she knew, because she had broken down and questioned Moss with what she hoped was appropriate nonchalance, that he would not join her in returning to England. It seemed that they would, as did so many couples of their class, maintain separate lives, perhaps even separate residences. He had done what he intended, provided what honor demanded, and now he would simply become a dim figure in the background of their existence.

The day before the Duchesse d'Enghien's ball, Will was sick, an indisposition to which he reacted with uncharacteristic demands for his mother's continual presence. Emily knew from Hawkins that Avon had asked to be kept informed, but he and Moss remained secluded in the study. She hoped rather desperately that he would come, but the hours passed with nothing more than Hawkins's discreet inquiries on his grace's behalf, and finally, late in the evening, Will fell into a tear-stained and hiccuping sleep. Emily returned to her room and probably slept no better than her son, waking frequently and listening to the reassuring silence until she fell back into exhausted slumber.

It was still some hours before dawn when an unidentifiable noise from the hall pulled her again from her troubled dreams, and straining to assess the nature of the disturbance, she heard enough sounds out of place in her well-run household to pull her out of her bed. She hurried into the hall, not even bothering to throw a robe over the sheer cotton of her gown.

The intruder standing guard outside the infant's room was Moss, and he seemed as taken aback by her sudden appearance as she was by his.

"What's wrong with Will?" she flung at him over her shoulder. Her hand was already reaching for the nursery door when it moved away from her fingers and the tall shape of her husband loomed out of the darkness of the opening.

"What's wrong? God, Dominic, what's happened to Will?" she whispered, not able to read the expression in the silver eyes. It was obvious he had not been prepared to find her here.

He moved between her and the doorway to stop her from entering. "He's fine. He's asleep. If you go in like this, you'll wake him."

"But if there's nothing wrong…" she began, and for the first time took in the details of his appearance. He was dressed in the black he had worn the first time she had met him, the night he had been ambushed and had come to her father's home. "Why are you here?" she managed to rasp past the fear that suddenly blocked her throat, and she was no longer seeking information about the baby. "What are you doing?"

She watched his eyes shift quickly to Moss, but she couldn't read whatever silent message passed between these two men who shared a bond far deeper than master and servant.

"Go back to bed, Emily. Will's fine." Avon moved to limp past her, but she quickly stepped in front of him and put her hands against his chest. She felt the deep breath he took, an involuntary reaction against her fingers, and then he stepped back, removing himself, as he had done once before, from her touch. But he didn't attempt again to move past her.

"I'll get the Mantons ready," Moss said from behind her, and she sensed Avon's anger even before he spoke.

"Downstairs," he said to Moss, and she could clearly read the anger in the quiet command. Moss's words had revealed something Avon had not intended she should know.

"What are you doing?" she repeated, and waited for a response. She thought, as the silence lengthened, that he wasn't going to answer her, but he didn't move, and so his stillness held her motionless, waiting for whatever he was willing to tell her.

"I have an appointment," he said finally, his tone devoid now of any emotion.

"Another duel? Oh, God, Dominic, not a duel," she begged, uncaring that her fear might reveal what she felt for him. Uncaring that her careful pretense of these last days was unraveling in her panic.

"No," he said quickly, hearing the rising hysteria. "An appointment. I swear."

"And do you keep all your appointments with your pistols? And dressed like this? Or only the ones from which you are likely to come home with a ball through your shoulder? Or maybe it won't be your shoulder this time. Maybe this time you won't come home at all."

He watched her face, but he didn't answer the accusations. He didn't respond verbally to what she had said at all, but his eyes remained locked on hers as she fought not to cry.

"When will you let it end? It's over. Don't you understand? The war is over and Napoleon is a prisoner. There are no more enemies. What are you doing?"

Again he hesitated. "There are rumors," he said finally.

"Rumors," she repeated incredulously. "Rumors of what?"

"A plot to restore the emperor to the throne," he said quietly.

"My God, Dominic. You can't believe that. It's over. You can't make me believe that you seriously..." She paused to breathe, her fury replacing her fear for him. "And you're going out in the night to chase these rumors? Even if they were true, why you, Dominic? Why now? You have a son and a wife now. Responsibilities. Or have you forgotten that you have a duty to us, too?'' she asked bitingly, her emphasis on the hated word not lost on her husband.

''Have I?'' he said softly. ''Somehow I was under the impression that my wife was leaving me. And taking my son. Or am I wrong? Have your plans changed, Emily? Is that what you're trying to tell me? Have you changed your mind, my dear?'' The sarcasm she had not heard in his voice since their marriage rang clear in the questions.

''And if I stay? Then you won't keep this appointment tonight? Is that what you're trying to tell me?'' She mockingly repeated his question. ''One duty exchanged for another?''

Ask me, her heart pleaded silently. Ask me to stay.

But the silence stretched between them in the darkness again until his voice finally broke it. ''I have to go,'' he said, his tone wiped clean now of both anger and sarcasm. ''I don't have a choice.''

She laughed and in the sound he heard despair. ''Everyone has choices. Except you. And you have only duty. Marry someone you don't love because it's your duty. Spend your life hiding and spying in the darkness because it's your duty. Get yourself killed because it's your duty.'' Her voice rose sharply, ''Damn your duty, Dominic. Who made you responsible for the world? Won't it go on turning if you don't chase down every shadow of danger to crown and country? Don't you care about anything else? Don't you have any other emotion beyond your overdeveloped sense of responsibility?''

He pushed her suddenly against the wall, and the spate of bitterness was cut off sharply with the shock of his body pressed hard against hers. His tone against her ear was harsh and menacing, but his hands, moving knowingly over her body, conveyed a different message.

"A few emotions. A few I've managed to retain. Like this," he said as he lowered his mouth to her throat and then into the dark valley between her breasts. "And this," he whispered more softly a few minutes later, using his hands under her buttocks to pull her up to crush against his hardness. "Do you remember this emotion?" he asked invitingly, and memories of their one night flooded her mind. She knew what he could reduce her to, and he was doing it all over again. In spite of her anger. In spite of all that now lay between them.

"And this?" he whispered as his hand moved tantalizingly to trace over her stomach, and then lower. He took her trembling fingers and placed them to cup his desire, and she could feel him grow into her touch. "A few emotions, Emily, beyond duty," he breathed against her ear, and she felt her body flow into his, content, finally where she had wanted to be. Her hand moved to caress him, and she felt the ragged breath he took against her cheek.

And then Moss's voice spoke from somewhere in the darkness at the top of the stairs. "Your grace—" Avon's body jerked "—it's time."

Emily felt the shiver move through the hard form that held hers prisoner against the wall, and then he stepped back to release her, his head lowered and his hands pressed against the wall on either side of her head. She heard the soft tap of the cane he still held in his right hand when it touched against the paneling behind her as he fought to control his breathing.

"Don't go," she whispered, and reached to touch his cheek. She couldn't see his expression in the shadows, but she felt him turn his face slightly to brush his lips against her fingers.

And then he was gone, and Emily was alone in the dimness of the hallway outside her son's door. Both men had disappeared so suddenly that the entire interlude might have been a dream had the effects of his embrace not been still so throbbingly clear in her body. She put her hand on the wall, moving like an old woman, until she reached the safety of her room. There she sat a long time, waiting for any sound that might signal his return, but she never heard anything, and then it was day.

Chapter Twenty

"And is your life so miserable, your grace, that you've decided to end it? If that was an attempt at suicide, I'm sure there are more certain and less painful ways to go about it." Moss's voice shook with the force of his anger, but Avon recognized the fear that underlay both the sarcasm and the fury.

"Just help me up," he grated, and finally put out his hand for Moss. "Not one of my more successful endeavors, whatever my motives."

The silence of the French countryside was unbroken. There was no longer any sight or sound of the informant they had come here to meet. Only the dust that swirled silently in the moonlight gave testimony that anyone had kept the appointment. And, of course, in the end, he hadn't. Apparently his fear had overcome his greed, and in spite of the large reward he had been promised in exchange for the intelligence he claimed to possess, at the first sounds that signaled the arrival of the duke and his servant, the man had bounded out of his concealment like a hare.

It had taken Moss too long to respond to what was happening, but Avon's immediate realization of the informant's intent and his quick reaction had given him some hope that he might catch up, since the ground was uneven enough to make the man he followed take care with his footing and since the duke himself moved with a total disregard for his own impediment.

The duke's hand had grasped the informant's bridle at the exact instant the man tried to vault into the saddle. Moss could hear Avon's repeated reassurances that they meant him no harm, but his pleas went unanswered. The strange hand on his bit and the sheer terror of his rider were all too much for the informant's poor horse, who panicked at the combined assault. Throughout the resulting frenzy of rearing and turning, Avon kept his death grip, only to be thrown repeatedly against the horse's flank and dragged relentlessly by the plunging, circling animal.

The rider, scarsely less panicked than his mount, fought for control as he tried to attain a firm seat in the saddle and, at the same time, dislodge Avon. To Moss's horrified eyes, it seemed impossible that the duke could escape serious injury, but he realized, as Avon had from the first, that to release his hold on the bridle meant that he would be thrown under the maddened horse and trampled.

The encounter seemed to go on forever, but it was brief enough to be finished before Moss could command his paralyzed limbs to move to his master's aid. A last frenzied lunge by the horse, combined with a vicious kick by his precariously seated rider, finally succeeded in loosening the duke's fingers. Moss's breath congealed in horror as Avon fell beneath the dancing hooves. The duke's long body fluidly rolled into a tight ball, and the horse, realizing its sudden release, gathered and leapt over this last object that lay between itself and freedom. Moss had waited, frozen with terror, until the shape on the ground moved to unfold as the drumming hoofbeats died in the distance.

Moss took the outstretched hand and pulled Avon to his

feet. He heard and ignored the involuntary gasp of pain as the duke was forced to put weight on his leg.

"Why didn't you just let him go? You never had a chance to stop him," he shouted angrily.

"I had a chance until the brute panicked. We came here for whatever information he had. I don't like to be taken for a fool, and I particularly don't enjoy being led on wild-goose chases," Avon replied, his own anger apparent. He moved experimentally, testing his injuries, even as he answered.

"But why would he run?" Moss asked more calmly, now that it seemed Avon would live. He was automatically making his own assessment of damage he knew better than to ask about.

"Fear, obviously," Avon said sarcastically. "Maybe he thought he'd been betrayed. Maybe he just changed his mind. And now we'll never know who he was or why he contacted the network in the first place. I don't even know if he had legitimate information. Maybe Emily's right. It's time to stop chasing shadows. The Allies aren't going to let Bonaparte escape from Elba. Even the diplomats aren't that stupid."

"But the source who sent him to you is reliable. You know that. Your agent didn't believe this was a hoax," Moss said quietly, watching the duke carefully shift his weight off the damaged leg. The battle had not been without cost, a cost that would never be openly acknowledged. As always, Avon would refuse any admission of his limitations until he was forced to by the brutality of the pain he bore. And only Moss was ever allowed to know of or alleviate that pain.

"Then perhaps he'll contact the network again. But there seems to be nothing else we can do here tonight." Avon had begun to limp heavily toward the path that would lead to the coach when Moss's voice stopped him.

"You never answered my question," he said, determination written in every line of his stolid body. He thought the duke might remind him icily of the fate of impertinent servants.

Instead Avon turned, acknowledging his right to ask. "You know me better than that, Moss. I would never seek that solution," he answered softly.

"I know you're unhappy. And I know why. And it makes you take chances you normally wouldn't take. I don't like it when you're reckless. It's dangerous for you and for everyone around you. That need for danger has given you the reputation you bear."

Moss's voice was now deadly quiet. "Your father's gone, boy. It's too late to prove anything to him." He hesitated, and then his love and his fear gave him the courage to finish, "Or has your wife now replaced your father's ghost, Dominic?"

The journey back to Paris was spent in silence, Avon's averted eyes apparently studying, in the growing morning light, the buildings they passed on the outskirts of the city. Moss wondered if he were thinking about their aborted mission or about whatever he had interrupted last night at the top of the stairs. But neither were topics the duke would welcome discussion about and so Moss for once held his tongue.

"You'd better let me look at whatever you've done to that leg," he offered gruffly as they entered the house from the rear.

"I have an appointment with Castlereagh at noon. But you can arrange for a bath," the duke said in concession as he moved up the first steps of the flight that would lead to the safety of his room. In spite of his efforts at concealment, increasing pain etched his face, and Moss watched his knuckles whiten against the rail.

"Then later?"

"If there's time," Avon agreed softly.

"Time?"

"Before the ball," the duke said, and turned finally at the dismay in the concerned voice.

"My God, boy, surely you don't still intend—"

"My wife's leaving for London tomorrow. I have an obligation to escort her tonight. We agreed that this was necessary to put an end to whatever unsavory speculation remains about our marriage."

"But surely…" Moss began again, and saw the negative movement of the dark head.

"This is something I have to do, Moss. She's waited until now only because I asked." The duke stopped and promised softly, "It will all be over tonight. After that, I'll do whatever you think is necessary. But I don't have any choice about this." Even as he said it, he heard the echo of Emily's words of the night before.

"Everybody has choices," she had told him. And if his was to spend the last night he might ever have with her launching her triumphantly into French and English society, guaranteeing her success with the cushion of his name, his position and his wealth, then he would do it right; and he'd deal with the consequences after she was gone. Deal with them alone, as he had always done.

"You're a fool," Moss said bitterly.

"Of course." Avon smiled. "You said my time would come and now it has. I should think you'd be glad to have proof I'm as fallible as everyone else." He waited for some response from the man who watched him, but none was forthcoming, and so he began again the long climb.

"Tell her," Moss urged suddenly, but Avon did not turn.

"No," he said simply. And then, almost as an afterthought, "Nor will you. I want your promise, Moss." He waited without turning, until he heard the whispered, "Aye, your grace," and then he resumed his slow and painful ascent.

It was left to Hawkins to inform Emily concerning the details of their departure for the ball. When she descended the stairs only a few minutes past the prearranged time, her husband was waiting at the bottom. He watched as the lights from the chandelier glinted over the gold spangles that completely covered her straight, low-cut gown.

She had never seen Avon in full evening dress, and although she had always thought him the most handsome man of her acquaintance, the elegance of his appearance tonight caused an explosion of the dread that had gradually been increasing with the growing pile of trunks stacked in her anteroom. She knew that if she were not very careful, she would fall on her knees and beg him to let her stay, beg him to let her remain with him no matter what his reasons for marrying her had been. She had learned that pride was a very cold bedfellow.

She wondered if he would make reference to what had passed between them last night, and she wanted to ask about the outcome of his appointment, but he clearly did not intend to provide that opportunity here before the servants, who beamed paternally as they watched her descent. Avon waited for her to reach the foot of the stairs and then, with his old courtesy, took her hand and, turning it, gently kissed the palm. She felt the familiar sensations in her stomach that his slightest touch always caused and knew that her hand trembled. What she couldn't know was how much that slight tremble reassured him.

"You are more beautiful than I have ever seen you," he

said, smiling at her before he quietly added, "except for one previous occasion."

He turned and signaled for Hawkins to open the door for them, and she was left to wonder, as he had, of course, intended, to what occasion he had referred. Her thoughts went back to the small dark room in the carriage house and then to the afternoon he had brought their son to her chamber. In her confusion, she failed to step forward, and he turned and waited for her as she attempted to pull her thoughts from the few intimate moments of their past.

"Is something wrong?" he asked quietly, and she shook her head. Gathering her courage and pride, she walked before him out of the house and down to the waiting coach. She knew he hated steps, hated to have her walk with him as he negotiated them, and so she moved to the coach with all the grace of her tall, straight carriage and was handed in by the waiting footman. She was pretending to arrange her skirt as Avon awkwardly climbed in to join her.

She had learned on the journey from Italy to avert her eyes from the difficulties his leg caused or she would see the dull flush that marked his anger spread across his cheeks. She had never offered to help him, instinctively knowing that he would hate that above all things. She realized suddenly that this was the first time she had been to any social gathering in his company.

When they arrived at the Hôtel d'Enghien, she didn't watch as he climbed down, but allowed him to hand her carefully out of the coach. The stairs looked to be endless and glazed with the evening's rain. But he smiled at her and held out his left arm, and she lightly rested her hand on it. There was no way to spare him this. The throng seemed to part as they slowly climbed, and she heard the whisper, "Avon," on several lips as they made their slow way up. Once, quite clearly, she heard, "Cripplegate." Avon's face was unperturbed and they entered the brilliantly lighted ballroom and were announced.

Emily felt as if she were on display for the world and was very glad for the steady support of her husband's strong arm. She swallowed and looked up to find that he was watching her with what appeared to be the deepest love and affection in his eyes.

He smiled and said softly for her ears alone, "I'm very proud of you, my darling. They're all thinking that I'm the luckiest man alive to have you on my arm."

She took a deep breath, incredibly comforted by his words, and moved with composure into the *haut monde* of both capitals.

The night was all that she had once hoped it would be. She had been popular in London, and her long absence and secret marriage to one of the most notorious and mysterious men of the ton added excitement to these jaded lives. Her hand was sought for every dance, and Avon graciously answered every request, sending her time and again to the dance floor on the arms of the most handsome and eligible men of the day. When her partners returned her to his side, he answered their compliments on his beautiful wife with every appearance of delight in her popularity.

There was, however, no sign of the jealousy she had hoped to engender. As the night dragged on, she flirted with each partner and, on her return to her husband's side, managed to act as if the departure of each were more painful than the last. She watched him as she danced and saw that the most powerful and influential men sought him out. She had not thought before about his position here, and she began to recognize that he was needed for his expertise and that he probably was unable to simply abandon preparations for the conference to escort his childish wife to her father's.

Suddenly she realized that she was tired of this night. She

only wanted to go home. Perhaps when he finally returned to London, they could begin again. Perhaps the pain would fade and lessen, and there would be a time when he would care about her in a different way. Perhaps tonight had made him see her again as a desirable woman.

When her partner returned her to Avon's side, she looked up into his face to catch his attention and ask if they could go home. Although he smiled down at her approach, she was aware that he was white about the lips and that there was a look in his eyes she had not seen there before.

"Is something wrong?" she asked.

"No, of course not." He smiled at her again. "Only a slightly disturbing piece of news from one of the French ministers. Something one should certainly not discuss with a beautiful woman at her first ball in almost a year."

"Dominic, would you take me home? If you don't mind leaving early?"

"Are you sure you're ready to leave? There must be one or two men here who haven't had the opportunity to dance with the popular Duchess of Avon," he teased gently. "Would you like some champagne to give you strength to dance with every man in Paris?"

"No." She shook her head. "I'd really like to leave."

"Are you tired, my darling?" He raised her chin to look into her face, and mistook the cause of her unhappiness. She saw the sudden tightening of his lips. "I should have taken better care of you. You seemed to be enjoying yourself, and I was so pleased that I allowed myself to forget that you are not so very strong."

"Dominic," she said, laughing suddenly, "you persist in treating me like a delicate flower. I wish you had been in Spain. I'm strong as a horse."

"I wish I had been in Spain, also. I assure you that if I had been there, you should not have been."

"Cotton wool, my dear," she said softly, and they laughed together.

He offered her his arm and they began to make their way to the door. His limp was more pronounced than she had ever seen it, and she suddenly realized that he had stood for several hours on the edge of the floor, waiting for a succession of partners to carry her to and from his side. She had not thought what possible effect standing for so long might have, but she was now painfully aware of the results with each step they took to their destination.

The duke spoke to the people who blocked their way, introducing her with quiet courtesy and apparent pride to those of his acquaintances she had not met. She was in a frenzy of impatience to get him home, to let him rest, but there was nothing she could say or do to speed their progress.

At last they were outside, and the only barrier left between themselves and the carriage was the steps. She wanted desperately to help him, and yet she knew how impossible that was, given their situation. He offered his arm, and she laid her hand on his wrist and they began the descent. They were perhaps halfway down when her dancing slipper slid on the moisture that covered the steps. She felt herself begin to slip and she clutched frantically at Avon's arm. He quickly grasped her elbow, and his strong hand prevented her fall down the treacherous steps.

He had released his cane to catch the balustrade for balance, and she heard the stick fall and roll down the stone steps. Only his quick reaction had prevented an accident that could have resulted in serious injury. Her knees had begun to shake now that it was over, but she moved quickly down the steps and stooped to pick up the heavy cane, which was lying now out of his reach. She watched him straighten carefully away from the railing as she climbed back to him and held out the stick she had never dared touch before. He took it in his left hand and watched her eyes. At whatever he found there, his own eyes dropped and he carefully transferred the cane to his other hand and leaned against it.

"Are you all right?" he asked, his concern clear.

"Yes, just cursed with clumsy feet, I suppose. I'm not hurt at all, thanks to you."

He ignored her gratitude. "Perhaps your feet are only tired from all the dancing." He smiled at her.

"Numb from the number of times my toes were trod upon," she said, laughing shakily, regretting again that she would never know what it was like to move smoothly in his arms across a polished floor.

He held out his left arm and she moved up the stairs to take his wrist, but he suddenly pulled her against his body. He held her tightly against his warm side for a long moment, his chin resting gently against her curls. Finally he kissed the top of her head. She could feel the deep breath he took, and then he released her to stand beside him. He hesitated before offering his arm, and they slowly finished the descent and entered the carriage.

They didn't speak on the ride home. There seemed to be nothing left to say between them. She would leave in the morning unless he asked her to stay. She waited and hoped, but he didn't speak until the carriage had reached the well-lighted entrance to the house and the footmen were waiting to help her down.

"I'm afraid I have a call to make. A rather sensitive problem with the arrangements for the conference has come up. I hope you'll forgive me for not seeing you in," he said, and watched the disbelief in her eyes as she wondered again if he had found a French mistress as charming as his English one was reputed to be.

"Good night, Emily," he said softly, and kissed her hand.

He didn't release it, but held it in his much larger one. And because she was afraid this was the last time she would see him alone, she didn't pull away in spite of what she believed to be his destination. "I'm sorry for all the unhappiness I've caused you. I never intended to make you unhappy."

She shook her head and gazed up into his face, wondering how he could not know what was in her heart.

"But if you believe nothing else of what I've told you, I want you to believe this. No matter what you think, I didn't marry you because I saw you as a duty or a responsibility. I married you because I love you more than I have ever loved anyone in my life."

He lightly touched his lips again to her hand, and she waited, but he said nothing more and finally she turned and climbed out of the coach. He had not asked her to stay. He had not answered her question. It was not all she had wanted, but it was certainly something.

Avon waited until the massive doors had closed behind the straight, proud figure of his wife, and then he spoke to the coachman.

"Drive me to the servants' entrance and then get Moss," he said bitterly.

The duke leaned back against the leather seat and allowed his eyes to close against the pain that had finally grown beyond even his iron control. There was nothing now he could do. He had only to wait for his instructions to be carried out and to think about how, on a night when he had been congratulated again and again for his role in the war, only he knew how miserably he had failed at the one thing that had ever really mattered.

Emily climbed the long staircase, her husband's words echoing through her unhappiness. "If you believe nothing else..." They contrasted sharply with the images she had lived with these last weeks—images of Avon in some elegantly decorated room, alone with a woman whose charm and sophistication matched his own. A woman who knew better than to ask for guarantees and to make demands. A woman who only wanted to please him.

"But that's all I want," she whispered, and knew it for the lie it was. "To be first," her honesty answered. "Before his country. Before the memory of his father's cruelty." And because he couldn't put her there, she had driven him away.

Aimee was waiting to help her out of her gown. As the Frenchwoman undressed her and brushed out the long, red hair until it lay like a silken banner over her shoulders, they didn't speak. They both understood the finality of the night and the fact that he was not here. That he had not, and now would not, ask her to stay.

Finally Emily was alone, except for the memories that moved through the empty places in her heart. She walked across the room to the table beside her bed. With one finger, she touched the music box he had given her and then released the catch, and the golden bird sang its lullaby.

"More beautiful than I have ever seen you...except for one previous occasion."

She closed the lid and stared unseeingly at the box. So many mistakes. So many lost chances. And tomorrow it would all be over. She wondered how it had ever come to this. She couldn't even remember why she was leaving. Because he hadn't answered her question? She realized that she no longer cared about the answer. He had married her. He was her husband. And he would remain so until she chose to end that relationship. As she would do tomorrow.

But she didn't want to leave tomorrow. In spite of the fact that he hadn't come home tonight. With lightning clarity, she realized she could choose not to leave. Avon had never asked her to go. Her pride and her temper had made that decision.

She threw on her emerald velvet robe and hurried down the stairs, to find Hawkins making his dignified way through the lower rooms, readying everything for tomorrow.

"Hawkins, I wish to be informed the moment my husband returns, no matter the hour," she said breathlessly, no longer caring if Hawkins knew she was waiting up for her husband to return from his mistress's.

"But…" Hawkins said, a look of confusion passing briefly over his careful features. His eyes moved to the top of the long stairs and then quickly back to her face.

"Of course, your grace," he said, but he didn't meet her eyes and, her suspicions thoroughly aroused, she, too, looked up the long flight. When her eyes returned to Hawkins, guilt was clear in his features.

"You're really not very good at that," she said angrily, and began to retrace her steps toward the stairs.

"On the contrary—" Hawkins's satisfied voice stopped her "—I always manage to convey the information I intend to give."

Realizing suddenly the implications of that confession, Emily turned and confronted his now-impassive face. "Then…"

"The duke came in only a few minutes after you, your grace," he said softly.

"But why would he tell me…" She stopped, knowing that she couldn't openly reveal Avon's lie. And so she waited.

She could see the regret in Hawkins's eyes as he finally spoke. "I have been his grace's butler for fifteen years. And I wish to remain in his employ."

"Perhaps I should ask him," she suggested defiantly, and hoped for some hint of what she should do.

But there was nothing in his face now but the respectful impassivity of a well-trained servant.

"Thank you, Hawkins." She turned quickly and began to climb the stairs that would lead to his chamber.

Chapter Twenty-One

Emily knew, of course, which room was his, but had never had occasion to enter it, so when she pushed open the heavy door, she didn't know where to look for him. In the dim lighting, her eyes found Moss first. He was standing by a small table that had been pulled near the bed and was wringing out a steaming cloth over a bowl that gave off a sharply medicinal smell. His eyes met hers and then moved quickly to the still figure on the great four-poster.

Emily saw that her husband was lying facedown on the sheets. The pillows had all been thrown off the bed, and Avon lay with his arms stretched up on either side of his head. The long dark body was completely nude, except for a cloth partially covering his right hip and thigh, and contrasted sharply with the snowy whiteness of the bed linens. As she watched, the heavy muscles in his shoulders clenched and unclenched in reaction to whatever Moss was doing. It was obvious that he had not heard the door and was unaware of her presence.

Moss raised his eyes to her shocked, colorless face and asked deliberately, "Any relief yet?"

Avon made no answer and Moss removed the cloth that was draped across the duke's body, replacing it carefully with the steaming one he had just wrung over the basin. He waited a moment and asked, with his eyes still coldly on Emily's face, "And did you stand the entire five hours, your grace?"

Avon moved his head, but again made no spoken response.

"And did your wife not sit with you through even one dance?"

"She danced like a queen with everyone who asked." Avon gasped a little on the words, but Emily heard, and couldn't believe, the trace of amusement in that strained voice. "And I had to listen to each of them tell me how beautiful she was." In his tone there was none of the bitterness that had been evident in Moss's.

Moss wrung another cloth, and his cold eyes looked again at Emily. "If you keep this up, you'll end up in that chair sooner than we feared."

"It doesn't matter," Avon said tiredly. Emily heard the soft gasp as Moss again touched his hip. "Maybe it will even be a relief."

"I'll tell you what will be a relief," Moss said in sudden fury. "When she's gone and you can rest. And stop pretending you're never in pain. That will be the relief."

"She'll be gone soon enough," Avon said quietly.

"And good riddance to bad rubbish," the valet said bitterly.

Avon's hand grasped Moss's wrist almost faster than Emily's startled eyes could follow the movement. She could see the pain on Moss's face and knew that Avon's hold was not light. His voice, when he spoke, was like nothing she had heard before.

"If you ever say anything like that about my wife again, I shall dismiss you, Moss. In spite of everything you have been to me, you'll be gone." He paused and the silence in the room was deadly. "Do you understand?" Avon asked in that same cold voice.

"I understand, your grace. I apologize for what I said."

When Avon released his wrist, Moss removed the cooling cloth and replaced it with a fresh one. Avon flinched slightly when the weight of the cloth was placed against his body, and Emily took an involuntary step into the room. Moss watched her face and said to the man on the bed, "Then you love her still? In spite of it all?"

"You know the answer to that," Avon said as softly as before.

"Then why don't you tell her, show her? You never had trouble making love to a woman before. They've flocked about you like children before a Christmas pudding."

Avon laughed. "She doesn't. She thinks I married her because I felt responsible for our son."

"And did you not?" Moss asked, his eyes on Avon and not Emily now.

"I used that as the excuse, of course—a reason for allowing myself to marry her. In spite of times like this." Again his head turned restlessly as Moss changed the cloth. "But the increasing number of times like this seems to indicate that she'll be better off with only my name."

"If you love her, take her. She won't deny you. If you use half of what I know about your skill, she'll not deny you."

"No, she'll come to my bed out of a sense of obligation—a return, I suppose, offered for my investment." His voice now was as bitter as Moss's. "But I find that I prefer no relationship at all rather than one based on her sense of gratitude and her averted eyes. And I find that I'm tired of this conversation. There are no solutions. Let it go, Moss, as she is going."

Moss looked at Emily again and waited, but she knew

that this was not the time to confront her husband. He was in pain and vulnerable, and for the first time since she had met him, had all his formidable defenses down.

She leaned back against the frame of the door and met Moss's eyes defiantly, as she had Hawkins's. He gazed at her for a long moment and then his attention was diverted by some movement of the duke's body.

"Moss," Avon gasped suddenly, and Emily watched as the valet bent to massage the muscles of the duke's thigh, which she could actually see knotting under his fingers. He worked a long time, kneading deeply, and Emily watched Dominic's fingers grip hard and then loosen until finally the cruel spasm passed and Moss stepped back to rest, flexing his tired fingers.

Moss waited until the duke whispered, "Yes," and then he wrung another cloth and used it to replace the one that he had pushed aside. A sound somewhere between a sigh and a groan was Avon's response, and Emily felt the tears well and begin to slip downward. She pressed her fingers hard against her lips to stifle any sound, but Moss's eyes found her face again. A sharp negative motion of his head warned her and she swallowed the tears building in the back of her throat.

She had made so many errors—out of love or jealousy or insecurity, she supposed, but made them nonetheless. And most of them had rebounded, not on her own stubborn head, but on the dark one twisting in pain on the high bed that should have been their marriage bed. She had forced him into a marriage he obviously didn't want, had ridiculed his disability, and now had hurt him physically by her self-centered determination to be the center of all eyes tonight in order to make him jealous. And all she could do now was to stand and wait through the long hours while Moss tried to relieve the pain she had caused.

The intervals between changing the steaming clothes gradually lengthened, and finally, under Moss's hands, even the terrible cramps eased and then ceased, and at last Avon slept.

Moss trimmed the lamp and then carefully covered the long legs with the counterpane. He moved past her and she followed him into the hall.

"Moss," she began hesitantly.

"Go to bed," he practically growled at her. "You've done enough damage for tonight. Enough damage altogether, don't you think?"

"Moss, believe me, please. I didn't know...I never meant—" she began.

"You never meant," he mocked. "First you rip his soul apart with your words, and then you deny him your body. Is it because he's not as perfect as that fancy boy he shot? Because he limps?"

She desperately broke into the hateful accusations. "No, Moss. Oh, God, no. You're so wrong. I never—"

"You make me sick." He fairly spat the venom engendered by his love of Avon. "You tell him his body disgusts you, and then you set out to prove it. And because he doesn't tell you how he feels, you think he doesn't care, that it doesn't matter. You think because he's the kind of man he is, who he is, that he can bear anything. And he can. He will. But, thank God, after tomorrow I won't have to stand by and watch you hurt him anymore." He looked at her shivering figure, stripped and haunted by his bitterness, and said again, "Good riddance, indeed."

Moss pushed by her and left her alone in the darkness of the hall. She looked at the door of her husband's room, wanting desperately the comfort of his concern and love. On any other night through the long weeks, only her stubborn pride had stood between her and his door. But tonight, out of all the nights of her marriage, she had no right to seek the solace she desired, no right to the consolation of Avon's strength. And so she returned to her room and listened to the golden bird on the music box and remembered.

Emily awoke to the sounds of the well-oiled machinery of Hawkins's staff preparing for her departure. Without waiting for Aimee, she dressed in a simple muslin gown and hurried to the head of the stairs.

She met Hawkins climbing carefully with a tray of coffee.

"I find that I've changed my mind, Hawkins. I apologize to you and your staff, but I don't intend to leave today. I'll wait until my husband can accompany me. Would you please inform your people?"

"I shall be delighted, your grace," he said, but she couldn't tell by his face whether he spoke the truth. Hawkins waited for further instructions, and realizing Emily had nothing else to tell him, bowed slightly and moved sedately down the hall. He knocked once on Avon's door and then entered, leaving her standing again outside the protective circle the household had erected around her husband.

She wondered if it were too late to make amends. If, as Moss thought, Avon would be better off without her presence. Her only comfort came from the words he had spoken to her last night before he'd left her and from what he had told Moss. Surely if he could say that he loved her, even while caught in that terrible pain she had caused, it was not too late.

Emily stopped by the nursery, to gather courage, she supposed. Holding Will in her arms and knowing that Avon, in spite of his determination to remain childless, had loved and welcomed his son from the moment of his arrival, gave her strength. Together they had created this child, whom Avon would never abandon no matter how much his mother abused their relationship. She gently put the sleeping infant back in his crib, and could see the relief in the nurse's eyes that his mother's unannounced visit would not, after all, upset the calm routine of their day.

As she approached the large chamber at the end of the hall, she found that she hated facing once again the loathing in Moss's eyes more than any confrontation with her husband. Moss had always been her friend, her ally in her love for Dominic, and now she had destroyed his goodwill by her unthinking mistreatment of the man they both loved.

As she had earlier, she pushed the heavy door open without knocking and saw with gratitude that Moss was not in the room. The figure of her husband, dressed only in dark trousers, was outlined against a window, through which the morning sun streamed to lie in patterns across the thick oriental rug. He stood with his back to the room, his right hand on the silver head of his cane and his forehead pressed against his left forearm, which was propped high on the glass. The muscles in the broad shoulders and long back clearly delineated the strength she had felt last night when he had saved her from falling and then held her tightly against his side. He didn't turn at the sound of the door and she waited, wondering what she could say against the accusations Moss had made.

"Has she gone?" he asked softly, and finally, as the silence stretched like the fine silk of a spider's web across the room, he turned.

She could see the results of last night in the bruised darkness under his eyes. When he saw her, his mouth moved slightly and then his face was as controlled and composed as marble.

"No," Emily said, "she hasn't gone. She's here, uninvited as always. And perhaps, as always, unwanted."

She saw his lips tighten then, but he didn't speak.

"I made a promise to you once, Dominic, and I'm afraid I've come to break it."

His eyes fell from her face and rested on the back of the hand that held the cane. "I understand," he said, and nothing more.

"What do you understand?" she asked, watching for some clue to help her know how to tell him what she felt.

"This isn't necessary. I never intended to hold you. I know what you want. And, of course, I understand why."

"Do you?" she said, and smiled. "But then you're much quicker than I am. It has taken me a very long time to know…"

She felt the tears of last night threaten, and at the break in her voice, he finally looked up at her face.

"Don't cry," he said tenderly, and then he smiled at her. At the love revealed in that slow movement of his beautiful mouth, she was drawn until she stood before him. She was so close she could feel his warmth, and at the familiar masculine aromas of his body, she closed her eyes, wanting this, at least, to remember.

"Emily," he said again, his voice full of pain, and he watched the emerald eyes open and, glazed with tears, find his face. "My darling," he whispered, "tell me. Or do you want me to say it for you? Do you want a divorce? Is there someone—"

"No," she said sharply. "You're as bad as Moss. Of course I don't want a divorce. How can you think that? How can you believe…"

"Then what promise?" he asked softly. "I don't understand what you're talking about."

"I told you, the night I came to you at the carriage house, that I would never ask anything else of you. That if you would… And I think I have kept my promise. But now…"

"What is it?" he said. "You must know…"

"A chance. Another chance. I know how much that is to ask, but I don't want to leave. If you can ever forgive me, I want to be your wife. Really your wife. If you could still want me. After all I've done to you…" Her voice faded at what was beginning to show in his face.

"All you've done to me?" he said quietly, the disbelief she had just seen in his eyes evident also in his voice. "What have you done that you believe I couldn't forgive?" and she heard for the first time today the familiar, gentle amusement.

She forced herself to begin the catalogue of her sins, without any excuses to lessen their gravity. "Using Freddy, I forced you to make love to me when you clearly didn't want the complication that I did eventually become. I hurt you about your leg, cruelly taunting that you were less than he, when you were instead…" That train of thought was too painful, so she broke and then began again.

"I married you because I wanted you so much, but I knew that you had only come to find me out of your sense of honor, that you didn't really want *me*. I tried to blackmail you by threatening to leave, because my pride was stung that you didn't find me desirable anymore. And then last night—" she breathed deeply in self-hatred "—last night I forced you to stand for hours while I pranced around a crowded dance floor.…"

"Last night?" Avon questioned harshly, reacting to the implications of what she had just said. "What did Moss tell you?" He gripped her shoulders, the cane he still held in his right hand biting into her flesh until her gasp made him realize he was hurting her and he instantly removed his hands.

"I came," she whispered. "To your room. I wanted to tell you…to ask you—but you were… And I had done that to you. I had caused that agony. And I always cause you pain. I always have.''

"Emily," he said hesitantly, not knowing how to answer her quiet desperation, "what you saw last night wasn't your fault. You were right about both the futility and the stupidity of chasing Bonaparte's shadows. Standing didn't cause what you saw, just an additional…'' He paused, and forced himself to smile at her. "So you can put that hair shirt away.''

"What happened?" Emily wasn't fooled by his evasive reply.

"That particular shadow proved to be rather elusive," Avon said finally.

"And?"

"And I—" he determinedly raised his eyes to meet hers, and she could read the self-derision there "—I rather foolishly tried to ignore this." He gestured quickly down to his cane and the ruined leg.

"And you were hurt?" she asked softly, watching his eyes. "After that you took me to the ball. And you stood there all those hours, knowing what would happen?''

"My leg seldom fails to disappoint my expectations of its fallibility," he said, carefully controlling the bitterness.

"But why? You could have told me. I didn't care about the dance. Why would you do that? What possible motive could you have for deliberately causing yourself that agony?" she asked fiercely.

He didn't answer for a long moment, and she knew that he hadn't intended to share his reasons with her. He had only intended to relieve her guilt for this and then ignore it, as he always ignored his limitations.

"I wanted you to dance," he said softly, all trace of the amused self-mockery he had employed earlier erased from his voice. "I hated that it couldn't be with me, but I wanted you to enjoy the night and the popularity I knew you'd find there. And I wanted them all to know you were mine, at least for that one night.''

He paused and his eyes revealed the pain his voice denied. ''I suppose the other reason was pride. I knew I could ask for a chair to be brought at any time. I was willing to send you time and again onto that floor in someone else's arms, but I found that I was damn well not willing to sit there, unable to stand and receive my wife's return on the arm of some handsome and graceful young partner. And so I stood and watched you dance. And at least you always came back to me.''

She knew then how much he cared about her reaction to his disability. He continued to speak in the same controlled voice as he dealt with the guilt she had revealed.

''I also find that my pride infinitely prefers your rather distorted version of our relationship to the one I have been living with.''

''What do you mean?''

He smiled at her gently. ''I'm aware that you've taken all the blame, but if you consider it from my perspective, my darling, you might see that I have had far more to castigate myself for in the mishandling of our affairs than you possibly could.''

''Dominic, you've been kindness itself since you married me. I can't think what you mean.''

''On the night I met you I attacked everything that I knew you cared about. I lied to you about my limp because I found that I preferred even hatred in your eyes to pity. I sent your handkerchief back, knowing well enough that I was trying to provoke some reaction from you, that I wanted desperately to see you again and knowing that, given my situation, I had no right to seek another meeting. I mauled you, sexually browbeat you when you were a guest in my home.'' He stopped with painful suddenness as the confession came to the most damning part, according to his code of ethics.

"I took you into my bed when I was a guest in your father's house, when I owed you both my very life. And then, I deserted you when you were carrying my child to face your father and brother alone. I let my stupid pride leave you to suffer all that while I went to Sandemer to lick my wounds."

She had never stopped to consider how he would feel about the reasons for their marriage. She honestly believed, as she had told Devon, that she had made it impossible for him to refuse her that night. And that she had then driven him away with her words.

"When I found you in Italy, I knew that I'd hurt you immeasurably, and I vowed the night Will was born that I'd never hurt you again. That I'd devote my life to caring for you both. I had hoped that we would have a real marriage. I loved you so much, but I was afraid that, somewhere deep inside, you didn't really want me, someone who could never be like Arrington and all the others.

"And then I saw you begin to avoid looking at me. To turn away from the awkwardness. I didn't know what to do but go on pretending that I wanted a platonic relationship. I wanted you so much. I know that at times you must have known how I felt."

When he stopped speaking, Emily asked with some bitterness, "If that's true, then why did you reject me when I asked you to stay with me? How can you say you want me, love me, when you turned away from my begging?"

"You had said that you wanted to give me something in return for my care of you. I didn't want you to come to me out of gratitude. I didn't want you to force yourself to make love to your crippled husband because he was good to you," he said, and his bitterness matched her own.

"Don't," she whispered, hating the sound of the word, unable to repeat it. "I never think of you that way. God, you're so strong. I've always known that I could depend on your strength. Even when I didn't understand you, I always knew that. Your leg doesn't matter. It never has."

"Of course," he said harshly. "It matters so little that you can't bear to watch when I walk. So little that, like my father, you turn your head…"

He stopped suddenly and she could hear the deep breath he took, finding control. His eyes fell again to the hand that held his cane.

"Forgive me. I'm well aware of how ungracefully I move. I can imagine how distasteful you must find it."

"Distasteful?" she said furiously. "Distasteful? My God, Dominic, it hurts me when I know you hurt. But distasteful? How can you believe that? And don't you dare compare me to your father. If I've learned to turn my head, it's because I know you're angry if I watch or if I dare to offer you my hand. But I'm your wife—"

His eyes returned quickly to her face and she saw surprise there. "Angry?" he said incredulously. "Is that why you turned away? Because you thought it made me angry for you to watch?"

At her quick nod, he said softly, "I don't care anymore what others think. I've had years to learn to block out the comments, the pity or the horror my leg seems to arouse. But I found that I cared very much what you felt as you watched me. And then I became aware that you never watched anymore, that you never walked down steps beside me unless you were forced by the situation, as you were last night. I never realized that you thought I was angry."

"Then what did you think?" Emily asked, and read the answer she expected in the pain of the silver eyes. "Of course! You thought, because I had told you so, that it disgusted me. Of course," she said again. "I am never to be forgiven for that. And it will never be forgotten. I had thought that ignoring your pain was to be the penance for my cruel tongue. I would forfeit my rights as your wife to care about that pain, my right to be able to say to you over the breakfast table, as every other wife has the right to say, 'How did you sleep last night, my dear? Was your leg…'" Her voice broke again, but she gathered her resolution and continued.

"I thought that if I agreed to your charade, you might eventually be able to look past what I had said. I thought those were to be the rules under which we would live. And so I learned to look away," she said.

"But last night as I danced, I thought only about what it would be like to be held in your arms and guided across the floor. Yours were the only arms I wanted to feel, and I knew such a sense of loss when I realized I would never dance with you. My only consolation was the hope that I might still be able to feel your arms around me if only you could forgive me. And so I came to your room last night, hoping that we could begin again."

She waited, still hoping, but he made no response, no longer meeting her eyes. She wondered if he had even listened. She raised her right hand and touched his chest. This time he made no effort to avoid her fingers. Her thumb moved slowly down his breastbone, and then she spread her fingers over the muscle that underlay the small dark nipple. She watched with fascination as it pearled against her touch. She looked up to find Avon's eyes now on her face. She caught the small peak between her fingers and felt his deep inhalation.

On an impulse she would not have believed herself capable of, she moved her hand caressingly over the rise of the muscles and down the ribs, and then to the ridged muscles of the flat stomach. She could feel the texture of the dark hair that centered above the waistband of his trousers. Emboldened by the shiver she felt course through his body, she bent slightly and flicked her tongue over the nipple her fingers had deserted. And then she closed her lips around it.

"Emily," she heard Avon groan, and his hands finally moved to cup her head, to tangle in the red-gold strands and press her mouth closer against his chest. She delicately nibbled, and the shuddering breath he took was all the invitation she needed. She raised her head and her parted lips breathed his name, and then his mouth had covered hers and she was in his arms. Safe, finally safe.

"I love you so much," he whispered hoarsely. "And I've waited so long. I don't think I can be gentle, my love. Forgive me. Forgive me," he said as his hands found the endless buttons down the back of her dress. She could feel his trembling fingers attempting to unfasten them and reached to help him, but he suddenly caught the neck of her thin cotton gown and rent it like paper.

"Forgive me," he whispered again, and bent to touch his warm lips to the low neck of her chemise and to the straining top of her breast, which moved with her breath to meet his mouth. His fingers tangled in the silk ribbon and untied it, and then his hard palm moved inside to cup beneath and free the ivory globe.

He stepped back slightly to smile into her eyes and then to watch the motion of his thumb pull across the sensitive skin.

"And do you want my mouth there?" he asked. "Do you want me to touch you there with my tongue? As you touched me?"

She nodded again, unable to form the words.

"Say it," he commanded. "Say that you want me."

"Yes," she managed to whisper as the sensations she had never forgotten began to curl and smoke through her body. "Yes, Dominic, please touch me."

Her legs were trembling, so she put her hands on his shoulders to steady herself. He smiled at her, and then his eyes closed and that beautiful mouth lowered to meet her breast. She was mindless, beyond thought, totally incapable of responding to the sounds that pulled her husband's head up sharply and made him suddenly move his body to shield hers from the man who had just entered the room.

Chapter Twenty-Two

"**Y**our grace," Moss said, and his shock was as evident to Emily as her own. She began to tremble in reaction to the sudden change in circumstances, and Avon's arms tightened comfortingly around her.

"Not again, damn it," she heard him breathe. He never even turned to the door.

"Get out," the duke said to his valet, the old tone of command replacing the lover's whisper of seconds ago.

"It's Steward. Lord Steward," Moss said, stumbling in his hurry to explain. "Downstairs."

"I don't care if Bonaparte and Wellington are downstairs together. Get out," Avon grated.

"He says he has to see you about—"

Avon interrupted, "I don't care what he says. Whatever he wants, tell him no. And get out."

Moss continued doggedly, "And he has a message for your wife. From her father."

Emily moved in response to that and freed herself from the encircling arms enough to look up into Avon's face.

"General Steward?" she asked softly.

She watched him gather control, using the reins of his

experience to temper his passion. "General Lord Steward," he affirmed resignedly. "Could he have a message from your father?"

"Yes," she nodded, fear now replacing what had gone before. "If it's Devon—"

"No," he promised quietly. "I would have been told. Not Devon."

"And he has business with you, your grace. About the conference. He doesn't want to be seen. He came through the servants' entrance. He's waiting in Hawkins's pantry," Moss said hurriedly, recognizing his opportunity.

She watched Avon thinking. "Then up here. Go down and bring him up yourself. The servant's stairs. And Moss."

"Yes, your grace?" The careful question in the disembodied voice came clearly to Emily's ears.

"Bring the Mantons up with you," Avon said, using the tone she had heard in the alley.

"The Mantons?" Moss sounded shocked. "You surely don't believe that you'll need—"

"Do it," the duke ordered, and turned his head to look at his valet for the first time. "I intend to shoot the next person who opens that door without my express invitation that he should do so. Do you understand?"

Emily could see neither man's face, but she felt the slight relaxation of Dominic's body against hers as Moss's soft laugh broke the long pause.

"Aye, boy," he said familiarly. "I understand."

She listened as the door closed and found the gray eyes smiling down into hers.

"Are you sure…" he began softly.

"Dominic, please. It's the first time my father's communicated with me since I left his house. It's a beginning. I have to know what he said,'' she pleaded.

He reluctantly stepped away from her and attempted to cover her breasts with the remnants of the gown he had ruined. ''I can't believe I did that,'' he said softly, shaking his head. ''I have never...'' Realizing where that would lead, he said formally, ''I apologize. I couldn't wait. There were too many of those damned buttons.''

Emily laughed and reached to kiss him. He pulled her against him again and it was she who finally moved away. ''I have to go if we don't want to be caught by the general in the same rather compromising position Moss found us in.''

He smiled and said, ''Since you are my wife and this is my bedroom, I believe any embarrassment should be on Moss's part. But I don't expect him to feel the proper degree of regret. Knowing Moss, he's probably deciding right now that the reason you're here is somehow due to his brilliant intervention.''

And as she made her rather furtive way back to her own chamber, she wondered suddenly if Moss might not be right.

Aimee helped her change into a dark gold morning dress that Avon had chosen for her when they first came to Paris. Although it seemed to Emily that it took an inordinate time for her toilette, when she was finally dressed, there had been no word from her husband. And so she sat and waited, and tried to imagine what message her father could have sent through even so good a friend as the general.

It was Hawkins who came for her. When Aimee opened the door to him, he cleared his throat and said to Emily, ''His grace requests that you join him downstairs.''

"Downstairs?" Emily questioned sharply. "But I thought—"

"His grace is waiting for you in... That is, he's...he's in the pantry," Hawkins finally managed. Aimee's eyes widened, and she looked to her mistress for explanation.

"The pantry," Emily said simply. "To be sure. If you would, Hawkins, I'm not quite certain..."

"Of course, your grace," Hawkins said, relieved that he wouldn't be called on to explain why His Grace, the Duke of Avon, wanted his wife to join him in the butler's pantry. "If you'll follow me."

And Emily did, down the dim and twisting stairs the servants used. Hawkins moved with all the dignity he would have used to escort an honored guest to the salon. He opened the door to the pantry and announced with aplomb, "Her Grace, the Duchess of Avon," and then backed out gracefully and closed the door, leaving three people together in a room none of them in their lives had ever had occasion to enter.

Emily could read nothing in the two faces now turned to her. Avon was leaning against one of the counters, and she wondered in amusement if he might come away with flour on his dark, straight trousers or on the blue coat that fitted perfectly the broad shoulders she had touched upstairs.

Something of that memory must have been reflected in her eyes, for Avon smiled suddenly and held out his hand to her.

"With your permission, my dear, the general has asked to see you alone. I apologize for the surroundings, but I thought that you could be assured of privacy here," he said softly, and she recognized the invitation to share the amusement he was now able to feel about the constant interruptions of their lovemaking. "I'll wait for you in the dining room. Perhaps you'll join me there for breakfast when you're done."

He turned to Steward and held out his hand, which the general shook awkwardly.

"Are you sure, your grace, that I can't convince you to change your mind?" the older man asked.

Avon's only answer was a slight negative movement of his head.

"Then I can only hope that Lord Castlereagh will be able to convince you," Steward said regretfully.

Avon smiled. "I assure you the Prince of Wales himself couldn't change my mind."

"I hadn't thought of the Regent. Perhaps—"

Avon laughed. "That was intended as a joke, sir."

"A joke? Oh, of course. A joke. For a moment I was hopeful that might make a difference. But if not, then I'll bid you farewell, your grace. I know there will be more formal recognition, but I would like to be the first to render the thanks of this government for all you have done."

"I should think, General Steward, that any gratitude should be reversed. May I thank you for all the years you've devoted to the defeat of the French, and for the sacrifices…" Avon stopped as the general laughingly held up his hand.

"They told me that your sources of information are legendary, but how could you possibly know that gratitude is one portion I can't stomach? I never expect to be thanked for only doing my duty."

"Exactly," Avon said softly, and smiled at the old man.

He turned to his wife and saw the anxiety in her face. "If you need me," he began, but she shook her head, and put out her hand. He took it in his own.

"Whatever the message," he said softly, for her ears only, "remember that you are my soul. And together there is nothing we cannot bear."

She nodded, but could find no words to acknowledge what he had said.

At the expression his whispered words had caused to appear in Emily's eyes, some of the doubts the general had held about her marriage to the notoriously cold and distant Duke of Avon began to fade.

Avon kissed the hand he held and left the room.

"Your grace," the general said, and Emily moved across the small space and held out her hand to him. She was uncomfortable with the sudden formality between them. Although her position had certainly changed, she felt like the same girl he had teased and cosseted all her life. The general had never married, and she had been his pet, the daughter he would never have.

Apparently Steward also disliked the distance Hawkins's announcement had served to emphasize, for all at once he pulled her closer and bent to kiss her cheek in his bluff way, and suddenly she was very hungry to see her family again.

"How are you, sir?" she asked, wondering what he thought about the announcement of her supposedly long-secret marriage and the birth of her son. "It's very good to see you again, and in much more pleasant circumstances. I believe that the last time we met you had just suffered a very painful saber cut."

"I believe you're right, my dear. I often wondered at that time if we should ever bring this off. It's very gratifying to find that all the sacrifices have been worth it, after all."

She knew that he referred to the men he had lost and to her brothers, whom he had also treated like beloved sons and had loudly and frequently chastised for the scapegraces they were.

"I have a message from your father that I think you might like to have."

"I should like that very much, sir," she answered quickly, nevertheless dreading whatever words he had brought.

"He said to tell you that if you had asked him to choose a husband for you, a man who would care for you as he would himself, he could not have chosen better than Avon. He said that he regretted his earlier opposition to your marriage, which he feels has caused an estrangement between you. He hopes that you and your husband will bring his grandson home to England soon."

Steward suddenly laughed. "He also said that he feels very lonely in his old age, and since I'm a good five years older than he, I almost didn't tell you that."

Emily threw her arms around his neck and hugged him tightly. "You can't know how much it means to me to have such a direct message from him. It sounds just like him. I had hoped…" She paused and he smiled at her encouragingly. "I had hoped that he would eventually be pleased."

"Avon's a good man, child. I would have liked to have had him under my command in Spain. Providence, however, was far wiser than any of us. She apparently knew where he was needed the most. I've always believed that God provides the right man for the dirtiest jobs, the jobs no one wants, but that are the most necessary. Had Avon been…" It was his turn to pause, searching for a wording that would not offend.

Emily placed her hand on his. "I know," she said. "If

he had been anything other than what he is, he would not have taken the path he was forced to choose.''

"The very valuable path he chose," the general finished. "And he's waiting for you. Don't leave him any longer, girl. Men don't like to wait while their women talk to old fools."

He kissed her again and asked suddenly, "Do you have any message for your father?"

"Just tell him that I hope we'll be home soon. When Avon finishes in Vienna."

"But…" the general began, and then smiled knowingly. "Of course," he said. "Is there anything else you'd like me to convey?"

"Tell Devon how much I miss him. And thank him for me. He'll understand." And then, knowing that she could trust him not to reveal to the world that this was information her father didn't already know, she added, "And would you tell my father that his grandson is called Will."

When she had seen the general out through the kitchen, she joined her husband in the dining room. Avon rose politely and waited for Hawkins to seat her, and then serve her from the buffet.

Only when they were alone did he ask, "Was Steward's message from your father good news?"

"A beginning," she said simply, and smiled at him. "He hopes that we'll be home soon. I sent word that when the conference has ended, we'll bring Will to see him. Unless you have other plans?"

"As a matter of fact," Avon said and the emerald eyes widened quickly, "I've had a change of plans. And there are arrangements I need to make. Can you possibly forgive me if I attend to business today?"

"Of course." She smiled at him, but wondered how he could think of anything but what had, after so long, almost happened between them this morning. "I know that so many people depend on your advice. I've been selfish in hoping that you could desert those who have counted on you long before I entered your life."

"Emily," Avon said, laughing, "I don't think martyrdom becomes you. Give me today, my darling, and I promise we'll be home in a week."

"But how? You have commitments. I finally understand that, Dominic," she began, a guilty hope stirring that he might mean exactly what he said.

"I told Steward that I'm not going to Vienna, and he'll inform Castlereagh. I've decided that the world will 'keep turning' without my pushing. I'm taking my wife and son home to England. If you'll give me today to make the necessary arrangements for my absence?"

"Of course. But Dominic," she whispered, embarrassed to say what she felt, but knowing that she needed to hear his promise, "you will be home tonight, won't you?"

The day stretched endlessly before her in spite of all the arrangements to be made for the new departure date. Afternoon lengthened to evening and still he didn't come. It was almost ten before she heard the soft knock on her door. She opened it to Hawkins, who presented her a folded note on a silver tray.

"From his grace," the butler said softly and turned away.

"Will you wait, please, Hawkins, for my reply," she said, dread tightening her throat. Had he again decided that what was between them could not be allowed to grow?

Hawkins smiled. "He said you'd bring the answer yourself, your grace, and that I shouldn't wait." And still smiling, he moved away from her door.

When she had unfolded the blank sheet of paper, she smiled as well and closed the door of her room behind her.

Moss was waiting in the corridor outside Avon's room. Afraid that he might try to spoil tonight with his hatred of her, Emily stopped before him and waited. But as always, Moss surprised her.

"What happened last night wasn't your fault. I know that, in spite of what I said. And I apologize, your grace. I was angry at him for taking the chances he does. And at myself, I suppose, because nothing I did seemed to make any difference. I couldn't help him last night, and it just seemed to go on and on." His voice ground to a halt, but not before she heard the pain and the love in it.

"I didn't know he'd been hurt, Moss. He never told me. You must believe that if I had had any idea—"

"I knew well enough that you couldn't know. He'd never tell you. No one's ever allowed to know. That's why he believed he could never marry. His father convinced him that his leg made him unfit for anyone to love. That's a lesson he learned too early. And so you were out of his reach. Until the baby. It was a fair trap he was caught in then." Moss smiled at her suddenly. "His honor and yours on the one hand, and all that imagined unworthiness on the other. And somewhere in hell I hope the old duke knows he failed. I got drunk in celebration the day he took that priest to find you.

"And then, it didn't quite work out like I'd hoped. You were sick, and by the time you'd recovered, he'd convinced himself you couldn't care for him, not if you really knew, if you saw the reality. And so the recklessness came back."

Moss hesitated, sharing things he had never told another soul. "Danger's always been a way to prove his father wrong. He always has to show that he can do anything he sets out to do, in spite of it. But this last..." Moss shook his head at the memory of his fear.

"I never meant to hurt him, Moss. I love him."

"I know, girl," he said, sounding very much like her father. "That's why I had to let you hear and see what he really felt. I betrayed him to you because I knew you were right for him. I've always known. I think I knew he loved you before he admitted it to himself. I've cared for him a long time alone, but I look forward to your help."

"Thank you, Moss. I was afraid I'd lost your friendship. I promise that you'll never regret giving me that chance," she whispered.

"Aye," he said softly, "I knew you'd do. And now, if you'll excuse me, your grace, Hawkins and I have a bottle waiting. A celebration of sorts." One lid dropped in a perfect wink and then, with a dignity to match Hawkins's best, Moss moved past her and down the long staircase.

Avon's room was dimly lit by a single branch of wax candles that were reflected waveringly in the polish of the desk on which they rested. Her husband was propped against the mass of pillows in the great bed, with a sheet covering his lower body. His bare chest was golden in the candlelight, gold against the shadowed cream of the linens.

"Lock it," he said softly, as she closed the door.

"I thought you were simply going to shoot the next person who entered," she answered as she obeyed.

"Disposing of bodies, you know. A very tedious business."

She slanted a quick look at him and answered teasingly, "I suppose that all depends on what you mean by disposing."

Avon said, "Why don't you tell me what you think I mean?"

"No," she said softly, "I have a better idea."

He smiled slowly, watching her, and anticipating her answer. "And what is that, my darling?"

"Why don't you explain why I have been waiting all day and half the night for my husband? Have you finally managed to set the world on a course it can hold until you return to guide it again? Or do you suppose it will be the Regent who calls to remind you of your duty tonight? Are you sure, Dominic, that you can spare me these few hours?" she asked, and watched his smile fade at the unexpected.

"Emily," he said coaxingly, trying desperately to read her tone. He held out his hand, "You know today was necessary—"

She interrupted as if he had not begun to speak. "I don't know why everyone gets so upset about Napoleon. All this running around certainly interferes with any civilized existence I had planned."

She watched the slow smile begin as he recognized her parody of the words he had spoken to her on the night they had met.

She continued to speak as she walked toward the bed and the waiting figure of her husband.

"I'll never understand all this save-the-world business. Give Napoleon back the Continent and let's get on with our affairs." She paused as she struggled with the buttons at the back of her gown. They yielded to her fingers and she slipped out of the dress, dropping it on the carpet to stand before him in her petticoat and chemise. He reached for her, but she sidestepped and continued to quote, "It seems that even such a glory hound as you—" she stopped as he laughed suddenly at the totally inappropriate description "—should get tired of it all."

She untied the strings of her petticoat, and it followed the dress to the floor.

"Oh, granted," she teased softly, "you've managed to bring off the occasional victory," and she slanted a look at him as she untied the ribbons at the front of her chemise. "But the cost, my dear, the cost. You can't imagine the sacrifices."

She moved gracefully to shed the last of her garments and finally stood before him in the candlelight. Its glow highlighted the ivory curves and darkened mysteriously the hollows of her body, and he caught his breath. She saw that he was no longer laughing.

She spoke again, and for the last time for a long while: "The things we have been forced to do without…" She reached out and traced around and then over a dark nipple on his chest and felt it harden, as before, under her fingers. She swallowed suddenly and finished, "You can't imagine the things we've been forced to give up."

Because she could wait no longer, she took the one step that separated them, and he gathered her into his hard arms, lifting her easily to lie beside him under the canopy.

"But, my dear," he said mockingly as his hands began the assault on her senses she had wanted for so long, "all this business never interested me. Far too fatiguing." He lowered his lips to her breast, lazily circled it with his tongue and then pulled delicately with his teeth. He said again reflectively, "I shall probably be forced to go very slowly so that I'm not too tired..." he paused to trail his lips across her stomach and then lower, and she shivered in anticipation of what she knew he intended.

"...to carry out the mission," he said again after a long time.

But she had forgotten already the first of the sentence, and she pulled him down to force his torturing lips back to her body again. "Please don't stop to talk."

And ever the courteous husband, he didn't.

With a single finger the Duchess of Avon traced the corded muscles of her husband's upper arm, which was gilded with the light of dawn. Her nail rimmed the collarbone and then up the strong brown column of his throat, to stop finally at his lips, slightly parted and relaxed in sleep. At that touch, the silver eyes opened and smiled into her own.

"I thought you were going to sleep all day," she whispered, brushing her finger along the sensuously full lower lip.

Avon's eyes moved quickly to the tall window to assess the quality of the light and then returned to laugh into her own as he recognized the earliness of the hour. "And did you have something else in mind to occupy the day?" he asked softly.

"Well," she said consideringly, her eyes now on the broad chest, "unless you're too tired. Or unless you have nothing else to teach me," she offered hopefully.

"Oh, no, my innocent." He smiled, caught her fingers in his hand and brought them back to his mouth to kiss. "There are a few things I vaguely remember from my disreputable past that I haven't shown you."

"Innocent?" she echoed mockingly. "Surely not after last night." And he watched her slow blush at the memories of the responses he had coaxed from her body.

His smile spread at her embarrassment, and watching his face, she said softly, "You are so beautiful. It really isn't fair. How can I ever hope to hold you?"

Avon laughed at that thought and then answered quickly, unthinkingly repeating a comforting refrain from his childhood, from his mother's love. "Compensation," he said softly.

"Compensation?" Emily laughed and then realized what he must mean. Her laughter faded and she watched his eyes.

"My mother always said my face was compensation for...the other. As a child, I thought it very poor compensation, if it were true." Seeing the pain in her face, he lightened his tone and added quickly, "But if this attracts you—" he turned his cheek against her hand "—I'll concede that she was right." She could feel his morning beard move against her palm as he smiled at her.

"Compensation," she said again. "For what your father did to you. For your leg. And do you still need compensation, Dominic?" she whispered. "Are you still afraid that it will affect how I feel?"

He held her eyes a long moment and then offered what she had never expected. "Why don't you look and tell me if it matters? I think that's the only way you'll ever know. And the only way we'll ever move beyond that question."

"My love," she began falteringly, "surely you know that's not necessary—"

"Not to you, perhaps. But for me, Emily, I think it is. For me, my love."

And so she sat up slowly, and schooling her face to show

nothing of what she feared she might feel, she allowed her eyes to follow the line of his long body to where their legs had lain tangled together all night in the center of the massive bed. And what he had hidden from her so long was at last revealed. The muscles of the right thigh were overdeveloped from the effort, she supposed, of moving the wasted lower leg. And the knee itself was slightly distorted inward, like a scene viewed through a swirling fog, with only enough wrong there to give a sense of imperfection.

Its deformity was in vivid contrast to the beauty of the curving muscles and straight bones of the left leg, which appeared to be as strong and finely shaped as Freddy Arrington's. She had not realized the beauty of the left, for Avon, of course, avoided the skintight pantaloons that Freddy had worn to such effect.

"So beautiful," she breathed, and had not realized that she had said the unbidden thought aloud until she heard the soft bitter laugh and turned her eyes to his face. What she saw there made her know he had again misunderstood her.

"Not that," she said, trying to find an explanation of what she had been thinking. "I never realized..." She stopped, knowing she couldn't bring Arrington's name into this room, into his bed.

"It doesn't matter," Avon said. "You needn't explain."

"Damn you, Dominic, you always make me feel so inadequate. I can never think quickly enough of the right words to tell you what I feel. And by the time I have found them, you've already decided that you know what I meant. I know you're supposed to be so blindingly brilliant, but frankly, I'm tired of you telling me what I'm thinking."

"Emily." He began to raise his upper body and she pushed him angrily, so he lay flat on the bed.

"Don't talk. Just listen for a change. I love you. Your leg... Oh, damn you, Dominic..." She watched the coldness settle in his eyes as she stumbled to find the right words. "Damn you," she whispered, and knowing she could never explain, she bent instead and put her lips against the twisted knee. "Damn you," she said again, and with slow, lingering kisses traced the withered muscles down the length of his calf. Her hands moved to caress the hair-roughened skin her lips were touching.

"I love you, Dominic. All of you. This, too. How can you not know that?" she said, and he felt the hot tears splash. Then his hands were on her shoulders and he pulled her up and held her so that she was crushed against his heaving chest.

"Emily," he said softly. "Don't cry. My heart, I know. I know."

He laid her trembling body on the bed and moved his to lie over hers. He kissed her tears, which ceased even as his lips caressed her temples, and then found the curve of her ear. His tongue licked the trace of salt he found there and then moved down the slim line of her neck to her breasts. His mouth feasted on their instant response to his now-familiar touch, while his hands moved lower to ready her body for his entry.

His lips teased, and the pull she felt beneath his mouth was repeated inside her body. But he shifted away, denying a little longer the release she sought. His hand moved between her thighs and the sweetly gasping sound he had waited for slipped breathlessly from her lips.

"Dominic," she whispered, and her hands blindly found his head, tangled in the dark hair and brought his lips back up to her own. She felt the caress of his tongue against hers, echoing now the movement of his fingers.

"Please," she pleaded against his mouth. "Now," she said, and her breath caught with the sudden shift in the intent of his knowing fingers, with their hard invasion. "Now," she begged again, and her body pushed against his.

"Not yet, my sweet, so beautiful wife. Not yet," he whispered, and his lips moved downward to once more nip gently at her breast.

"Dominic. Oh, God, Dominic, please."

"I have something else I want to teach you, my love. Something I think…" He felt with his fingers her body's unconscious response to his words. And suddenly he lifted her so that she was above him. He quickly fitted her shaking knees on either side of his hips and then lowered her, positioning their bodies carefully. He watched her eyes close and her head fall back as she instinctively began the movements that would bring them both what they now so desperately sought. His hands found her breasts and touched them as he watched her face change with this miracle he had given into her control. And then he joined her there, matching his response to hers.

She lay finally against his chest, too relaxed in her fulfillment to do more than move her fingers slowly across the dark, damp skin of his breast. She had felt the heartbeat slow under her palm, then the steady rhythm that had comforted her last night each time she had wakened and wondered if she had dreamed all that had happened between them.

"You are," he said very softly, and she did not raise her head, but listened with interest to the words move through the body beneath her ear, "a remarkably apt pupil."

She waited, wondering, and then she dared to whisper, "And the next lesson…?"

She felt the dark laughter rumble in his chest. "Well," Avon said consideringly, "there is perhaps this." And he moved to show her what he intended, hoping that she never stopped to consider the source of the knowledge he was using to bind her heart deliberately and finally to his own. And then they were again both beyond the ability to think of anything at all.

Epilogue

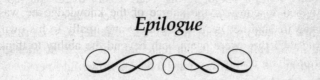

The fact that the Duchess of Avon was wearing an elegant new Parisian walking dress of bronze taffeta didn't help. Nor did the fact that, after hours of frantic preparation, she knew she looked her best help in the least to calm the tumult in her stomach. Her husband's long fingers wrapped tightly about her kid-gloved hand and the baby cradled gently in her other arm were the only things that allowed her to sit serenely in his carriage. She glanced up finally to meet Avon's eyes, aware that he had been watching her since they had begun this short journey from his London town house.

"Dominic, I don't know that I can do this. I'm such a coward. I just left and let Devon try to explain it all to him. He'll never understand. How could he?"

"Because he loves you. And because the blame isn't yours. I wish you'd let me see him first."

"And let you pretend that you're at fault. That you ravished me, I suppose. Took me by force. My father's not that stupid. And he knows me too well. The first time I look at you, he'll know that for the fairy tale it is."

Her heart jumped as she felt the slowing of the coach.

Her hand tightened on his as the door was opened by Ashton, who beamed as he handed her down to stand in front of the house where she knew her brother and father were waiting. Her eyes went immediately to the window of her brother's sitting room, but his chair wasn't there. She supposed he was waiting in the hall with her father.

She looked up just in time to see her father was not waiting in the hall after all, but marching out the front door to stand at the top of the steps and look down into her eyes. She felt Avon's arm move around her shoulder and was incredibly comforted to know that however this visit turned out today, he would always be there.

She turned to smile into his calm gray eyes and felt such a rush of emotion that she had to glance away. She remembered what Avon had said about the baby, and taking a deep breath, she climbed the steps to introduce him to his grandfather. She prayed Avon was right about this. She prayed her father would be as enchanted with Will as Dominic thought. "Please, God," she breathed as she reached the top to look into her father's blue eyes.

"Emily," he said formally, and bent to kiss her cheek. "You're looking well."

"Father," she said. Even to her own ears, her voice sounded thready and terrified. She tried for a stronger tone. "I'd like you to meet your grandson, Will."

He turned back the blanket from the sleeping features and studied the infant for a long time.

"He looks very like his father," he said finally, but nothing else.

"Yes, he does. And Avon adores him. He won't admit it, of course, but he's almost doting."

"Well, his heir. That's to be expected. Why don't you

come in? Devon's waiting to see you both. He has some-thing to show you.''

She turned to find Avon and realized he was beside her. He cupped her elbow with his left hand and his eyes were no longer smiling. They were studying her father's set face. The general's eyes were battlefield hard, but he didn't say another word. He simply turned and moved through the door Ashton had been smilingly holding open for several minutes.

"Oh, God, Dominic, I can't—" she began.

"Devon's waiting for you. If for no other reason, my darling, we are going into the house. We are going to greet your brother, and then your father and I are going to talk. And now," he said in a tone that brooked no argument, "we go in."

"Dominic," she begged.

"I know you're no coward, my love. Show me you're as brave as your brother, who's waiting for you. But first I think you had better let me hold my son."

She wondered what the slight smile meant, but because she trusted him, she obeyed and placed the still-sleeping baby in his arm.

She lifted her chin and moved before him into the hall.

"This way, your grace," Ashton said, indicating the door to her brother's sitting room. She could hear Avon's foot-steps behind her and she moved with only his love and her own pride stiffening her knees.

Devon was standing propped awkwardly on crutches, but there was nothing awkward about his smile.

"I don't do this very well," he said, laughing, "and I certainly don't do it very long, so watch carefully. I wouldn't want either of you to miss a thing."

Emily watched with her heart in her throat as, leaning precariously on the crutches, he took three lurching steps in her direction. And then she was holding him. She felt him rest against her and, unable to release the crutches, he turned his head and kissed her cheek.

"Dev, what are you doing? You'll kill yourself. You know—" she began frantically.

"It's gone, Emily. It's out. It's all over," he breathed against her hair. "It's finally over, love."

She moved back enough so that she could see his face and read the truth in his eyes.

"But how, after all this time? My God, how?"

"Avon's doctor."

"But he said he couldn't. He wouldn't even attempt it."

"Not Pritchett. Larrey. The French surgeon Dominic sent. He didn't tell you, because I asked him not to. Just in case... But Larrey said he could do it. That the danger was minimal and the odds of success very favorable. In the face of his confidence, Father and I talked it over, and we felt that I should take the chance. And it worked." He studied her suddenly colorless face and didn't like what he saw there. "It's all right, Em, I promise. I'm all right."

She took a deep breath and said very softly, "Dev, it's wonderful. I'm so happy for you. If I release you..." She began delicately and he laughed.

"I won't fall down, if that's what you're attempting to find out. I don't move very well, but I can remain upright for at least a minute or two."

"Dev," she gasped, because she had already stepped away from his body, removing her support of his now-swaying figure, before the import of those last words reached her brain.

"I think you've done enough, Devon," her father said, and moved the chair close enough for his son to lower himself gradually into its familiar safety. Devon watched his sister move quickly to her husband and pause before him. He knew her knees were still trembling by the telltale movement of the hem of her gown.

"I can't believe you would send a surgeon here to cut about on my brother when you knew, *you knew*," she repeated vehemently, "what could happen. How could you take that chance? How could you, Dominic? And without talking to me."

"Emily," Devon began, unable to believe that she was reacting in this way to what he had viewed as a miracle.

Avon's eyes simply watched her white face as he spoke. "Pritchett sent all the information about his examination of Devon to Paris, and I took it to Larrey—drawings, diagrams, endless medical details. Larrey told me he could do it and I believed him. He described what he intended to do, and it made sense. He wanted to make an incision two inches to the side and tunnel under the muscle to pull the fragment away from the spine before removing it through the same tunnel. He assured me the danger to Devon was no greater than removing any of the other fragments had been, so I asked him to come here and operate."

"How dare you take a chance like that with my brother's life? How could you, Dominic?"

"That is the correct phrase, my dear. Your brother's life. And his decision. And not one you had any right to make for him. In spite of whatever promises you had managed to extract. Look at him, Emily. You can't want him to go back to what he was."

"Oh, God, of course, I don't," she said, and she turned

to her brother. "Devon, you must know that. You do, don't you? You know how much I've wanted this for you, but when I think... It wasn't fair, Dominic," she whispered, turning back to her husband.

"But it was right. And if the end effect is right, then the methods one uses to achieve that end may be, justifiably, a little wrong. Be happy for Devon. You can get revenge on me later." He smiled suggestively, and she knew she had been foolish. And wrong.

She turned to Devon and her father and said softly, "I'm sorry. A ridiculous reaction, I know. But I was so frightened.... I can always be trusted to react to any real or imagined crisis with a temper tantrum. I'm not even aware of what idiotic things I'm saying at times like these. Devon, you must know how delighted I am."

"You haven't hurt my feelings, Emily. I've lived with your temper all my life. But I'm afraid you owe Avon an apology. He's likely never seen your reaction to being frightened. He probably doesn't know that you're too stubborn to admit it when you're scared to death, so you attack," Devon teased, hoping that his recovery hadn't driven a wedge between his sister and her husband.

"That's not really true, you know," Avon said calmly. "I have seen this maneuver before. When Emily thought I'd been hurt in the duel with Arrington, she came to my home and said a lot of things she didn't mean. Said them because she'd been so badly frightened. She probably didn't tell you about it. I'd forgotten it until now," he finished, revealing the truth he had just recognized with the kindness of that lie.

Emily's eyes locked on her husband's face, and tears began to brim long before he had finished absolving her of a sin she had thought she would do penance for the rest of her life. When his eyes met hers, she knew that he had intentionally and finally freed her from that guilt.

"I love you, Dominic," she said, and was not even aware any longer of their audience.

"And you," he said softly, aware of and unconcerned about those listeners, "you are—"

"I know," she said, and put her fingers against his lips. "I know." She held his eyes a long time. "And now Will and I—" she lifted the baby from her husband's arm "—and my father are going to talk. Across the hall. You can sit down and keep Devon company while I do. You are definitely not invited."

Avon smiled and nodded and moved to his accustomed chair across from Devon's. With Avon arranged as she wished, Emily took her father's arm.

"Sir, I'd like to talk to you. I have a lot to explain. An explanation that's long overdue." Her father studied her face as Avon had and finally nodded, and they went together out of the room.

Devon saw Avon's concern and spoke, not only to distract him from whatever was now happening across the hall. "I haven't thanked you, Dominic. Not because I'm ungrateful, as I'm sure you can imagine, but because I don't know how to thank someone who has given me back my life. You did that once before by offering me something valuable to do with my days, but this—"

"God, Devon, after all I owe you, I certainly don't intend to listen to you talk about gratitude."

"All you owe me? I don't know what you're talking about."

"Well, we might begin with a certain address in Italy."

"With your sources, you would have eventually come up with that," Devon said with a laugh.

"But not in time. Not in time to be there when my son was born."

"A miracle, I suppose," Devon said patiently, expecting to listen to Avon extoll the wonders of fatherhood.

"It was bloody awful," he said instead. "I know now what you meant about watching someone you love suffer. I'd never felt so damned helpless in my entire life."

Devon laughed. "I imagine most husbands feel the same. But I'm sure Emily believes that Will was worth it." He watched Avon shake his head as the scene replayed before him, and decided to change the subject.

"You haven't told me what you think about the success of the surgery. I know it doesn't look like much yet, but Pritchett thinks that eventually I'll recover almost full use of my legs."

"Devon, my friend, I swear it looked to me like the merest limp. So when do you intend to do something about—"

"As soon as it looks like the merest limp to me, too." Devon laughed again.

"I'll send you Moss. He really is very skillful. And he would love to be in charge of your recovery. It will give him something useful to do."

"I doubt Moss would leave you," Devon protested.

Avon laughed in turn. "I think Moss is looking for a new challenge. I've become far too tamed and civilized for his tastes. As much as he chided me about my recklessness, I think he misses the old days of espionage in dark corners far more than I."

"It's hard to picture you removed from that life. Are you

sure Moss is the only one who feels the call to return to that excitement?'' Devon questioned.

''I miss it at times. But I'm finding the mysteries that take place behind the closed doors of Europe's cabinet rooms intriguing enough. And it's what Emily wants. You won't believe what you'll do to make the woman you love happy. And she is, Devon. I promise you that. However this marriage began, whatever mistakes I made, Emily is happy, and I intend to direct all my energies in the future to see she stays that way. You have my word.''

''I never doubted it or I should never have supplied you with that address.''

''And now I only have to convince your father.''

''I think Emily's the best one to do that. He loves her very much. He was hurt that she didn't trust his love enough to come to him. That's a mistake we both made. I've tried to explain Emily's state of mind at the time, but it's like talking to a stone. He just leaves the room.''

''I had thought that Will might be the key to his anger, but he surprised me. And if Emily doesn't succeed—''

The rest of Avon's words were cut off by the opening of the door to the sitting room and the entrance of his wife and father-in-law.

''Dominic,'' Emily began, and Avon stood at her tone. He could see that she had been crying, but he couldn't read her expression. ''My father has something he would like to say to you.''

''And I'm very willing to hear you out, sir,'' Avon said, his eyes still searching his wife's pale features, ''but I think I have some things to say that you should hear first.''

''Dominic—'' Emily began, only to be cut off by Avon's raised hand.

"I need to say this, Emily. I need to tell your father." Avon turned to the man who was standing so militarily straight beside his daughter and wondered how he could possibly find the right words. Wondered if there were any words that could lessen the effects of his actions on this man.

"I know, sir, that I'm not the husband you would have chosen for Emily. For many reasons, all of which, I assure you, I fully understand. And I know there was nothing honorable about the way I made Emily my wife. But having admitted all that and being willing to listen to whatever you wish to say to me about my actions in the past, I want you to understand that I am Emily's husband and Will's father. And there is nothing in my life that has ever meant as much to me as those two things.

"I told Emily that I had no guide to follow in trying to be the father Will deserves. My own father was…" Avon stopped, because that was still too painful a subject, and because he didn't understand the look that was beginning to appear in the general's eyes. "But I've seen you with Devon and Emily. I heard countless stories of your discipline, your lessons, your advice from Ben and Will at school." He hesitated and then admitted, "And I envied them."

"Dominic," Emily said again as the pain of that admission also became evident in the gray eyes. But Avon smiled at her and shook his head, and she was silent.

"I'm afraid that, given my physical limitations, there are many things I want my son to know that I'll be unable to teach him. Perhaps Devon, in time… But until that day, I had hoped that you would undertake to stand in my place. If Will is to become the kind of man that your sons were and are, the kind of man I want him to become, then I need your help. Perhaps I don't deserve it, but I would hate for my mistakes to deny Will his grandfather's love. Whatever you feel about me, at least don't reject my son," Avon said into those blue eyes.

And he waited.

"I don't approve of what was done when my grandson was conceived. I've expressed myself rather strongly to my daughter on that subject. I never intend to speak about it again," the general said finally, and Avon thought again that he had failed, when it mattered so much.

"But whatever Emily did to win you, I find I can almost understand. What I can't understand is how you can believe that I wouldn't want you for my son. Or Will for my grandson. I was afraid that the heir of the Duke of Avon would be held to be above my touch. That you might want him surrounded only by peers whose blood is as blue as his. Only some of my blood flows in those veins also, and if you think I would deny myself the opportunity to have a role in shaping the life of this child, you are not as intelligent as I thought you were, your grace." He watched Avon swallow quickly and begin to breathe again. "I've lost two sons. I can never replace them. But I should be very glad to have you for my son, Dominic. And I hope in time…"

He stopped as Avon began to limp toward him, and was shocked when this man whose reputation for coldheartedness was notorious, and, he had always thought, probably well deserved, moved into his arms, which reached quite naturally to enfold him. The embrace was not long, but it was sincere. And when they stepped apart, there had been unspoken promises made that were apparent to all the occupants of the small room.

"Brandy, I think," said the general gruffly. "Emily, if

you will, and I shall take the opportunity to become better acquainted with my grandson, the future Duke of Avon. That has a nice ring, don't you think, my dear?''

"A very nice ring," Emily agreed as she moved to obey her father's request. "I've always thought so. As long as it's a very long time in the future when he assumes that title."

"And what shall we drink to?" Devon asked when Emily had supplied them all with glasses.

"To your complete recovery," she answered softly.

"And to our family," Avon said, meeting the general's eye again.

"And to my grandson," the general answered. "The future Duke of Avon. I do so like the sound of that."

And he found he also liked the sound of the laughter echoing through the room, a sound he hadn't heard here in far too many years.

* * * * *

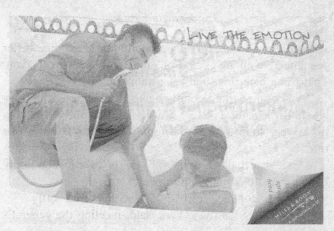

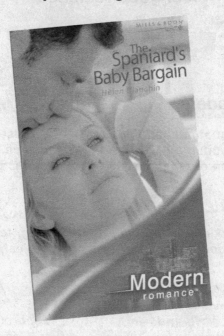

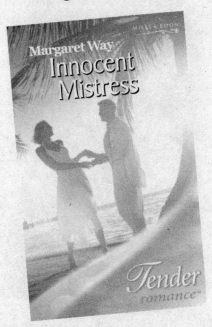